American Triptych

AMERICAN TRIPTYCH
Three 'John Sedges' Novels

{
The Townsman
Voices In The House
The Long Love
}

PEARL S. BUCK

THE JOHN DAY COMPANY · *NEW YORK*

Foreword

Some years ago I woke one morning to find myself strangely oppressed. I felt suddenly that I was no longer a free individual. I had been cast in a mold. I had written so many books about Chinese people that I had become known as a writer only about China. This was natural enough and nobody's fault. When I began to write I knew no people intimately except the Chinese. My entire life had been spent in China and beyond that in Asia. In midstream, however, I had transferred myself to the West and to my own country, the United States. Soon, since any writer writes out of his everyday environment, I began, however tentatively, to write about American people. I became thereby someone else.

This someone else, who now was also I, for the old self, the Asian self, continued to exist and will always continue, was, I repeat, oppressed. The oppression was the result of a determination on the part of my readers, sometimes loving, sometimes critical, to insist that there must be no other me than the one they had always known; that is to say, the Asian me. But here was the new American me, eager to explore and adventure among my own people. To provide freedom for this American me, pseudonymity was the answer. The writer must have a new name. I chose the name of John Sedges, a simple one, and masculine because men have fewer handicaps in our society than women have, in writing as well as in other professions.

My first John Sedges novel was *The Townsman*. It is a long book, a story of the West, Kansas in scene, to which state I had made many quiet visits. I was pleased when Kansans praised its authenticity. Its hero is a modest fellow who refuses to ride wild horses, be a cowboy, shoot pistols into the air, kill his enemies, find gold in any hills, destroy Indians, or even get drunk. He is content merely to become the solid founder of a city. The novel was well received by critics and sold to some tens of thousands of readers. It thus proved itself as a successful first novel by an unknown writer.

Four other novels were published under the name John Sedges, and guesses became rampant as to the author. No secrets in this world are kept forever. Somebody always knows and tells. And my two selves were beginning to merge. I was by now at home in my own country, my roots were digging deep, and I was becoming increasingly familiar with my own people. The protection of John Sedges was neither so necessary nor so effective as it had been. In Europe the John Sedges novels were openly sold as Pearl Buck books. I was moving toward freedom. The shield was no longer useful.

So John Sedges has served his purpose and may now be discarded and laid away in the silver foil of memory. I declare my independence and my determination to write as I please in a free country, choosing my material as I find it. People are people whether in Asia or America, as everybody knows or ought to know, and for me the scene is merely the background for human antics. Readers will still be the critics, of course, but I shall hope and strive to please and to amuse. Why else should books be written?

PEARL S. BUCK

The Townsman

Part One

1

FROM the window of his room in the attic Jonathan Goodliffe could see, if the day were fair, the white sails of ships upon the Irish Sea. The day must be translucently fair, the sky blue and not washed with the pale English mists, so that the sea could be deep blue beneath it, and then the sun could glitter upon the sails. This was his judgment of the day.

The cottage was near enough to the city of Blackpool for him to have walked there to the seacoast if he liked, for he was fifteen years old. His brother Edward, three years older than he, had a job in a ship's chandlery and walked home from there often enough on a Sunday, or even on a weekday in the evening. But he and Jonathan were different. Edward as a boy could put his hoe down any day in the middle of the afternoon and without a word go away. Jonathan could not. He must stay until the work he had allotted for himself was done, and by then it was always evening. He could have gone to Blackpool in the evening, but he had seen how his mother fretted because Edward went too often in the years when he was at home, and now he had not the heart to add to her trouble. So after his supper he helped with the dishes, and then he sat down in the sitting room with her and the younger children. Sometimes he read aloud to her, if his father were not there, and sometimes he played games with the children until they went to bed, and then talked with her, trying to think of what might interest her.

There were four of these children younger than himself. He knew his mother had not wanted the last one, though never had she said one word to him about the children she had. So far as he might have known from her, the child was simply there one day. She was so dainty in her speech, so shy, so small and exquisite in her person, that these great children she bore one after the other seemed to have nothing to do with her. He was glad she did not speak of them. He could pretend they had nothing to do with her, though he was fond of them, too. But so sensitive was he to every look in her delicate face that it seemed to him he could feel the very instant when her being began to divide itself. He could feel her spirit, half-distressed, half-withdrawn, as her body set upon its task again. When this had happened the last time, he had gone quickly upstairs to his room and burst into tears. He had cried silently and deeply for a few moments, without knowing why. While he was crying he heard her step coming slowly up the stairs, and he rushed to draw the wooden bar across his door. She shook the door a little when she found it locked.

"I want to make your bed, Jonathan!" she cried through the crack.

"I'm washin' myself," he called back.

"Whatever for now, after breakfast?" she cried, amazed.

"I scamped it afore," he answered shortly.

He heard her breathe, "Well, I never!"

"Go on," he shouted. "I'll do my own bed today."

She did not answer, and after a moment he heard her go down again. But her coming had startled him out of weeping. He went to the window and stood looking out, and at that moment the last shreds of the morning mist faded, and suddenly he saw the small flecks of white which were the sails of ships upon the Irish Sea. The very sight of them quieted him, as they always did. He was thankful again that, when he and Edward divided the attic, he had chosen this side for himself. It had been accident. No one knew that from this window the ships could be seen. He had been excited when he saw them first, and not for days had he happened to see them. . . .

"Come down out of there, Jonathan!" his father roared at him from the garden patch below. "Whatever are you thinkin' to be idlin' this time of day and all the work waitin'?"

He turned away from the window, sick at the very sight of his father this morning, and rushed downstairs. In the kitchen his mother was moving slowly about the dishes. She looked up when he came in, and he saw she had been crying, too. He longed to hug her, but this he had not done for too long. His father had stopped it.

"Have done with kissin' and huggin' your mother, you great lads," he had ordered his two older sons. "It fair makes me sick to see it."

"Shame on you, Clyde Goodliffe!" his mother had cried, and her fair skin had turned crimson under her yellow hair. But neither Jonathan nor Edward had kissed her from that day.

Less than ever could he kiss her now, though he did not know why. She was always beautiful to him, and now touching as she stood beside the sink, so small in her little blue cotton frock. He was not tall for his age, but already he was taller than she was.

"I'm goin' to plant some of them flowerin' peas for you, Mother," he blurted.

"Those," she said gently, "not them." But she corrected him so gently that he did not mind. He was even glad to be corrected for something. It made her seem more usual to him.

"Those," he repeated obediently. She had been a teacher in a board school before she was married, and she knew about words.

"I'll be glad to have them, son," she said quietly. "They're pretty, if what I hear of them be true."

She smiled, and suddenly he choked.

"Oh, Mother—" he muttered. She turned and looked at him. And she flew to him, and he put his arms around her and was near crying again.

"Let me help you," he muttered. "Let me do the heavy work. You just call me, Mother. I'm goin' to stay around the house more."

"You're my good boy," she whispered.

They hugged each other hard. It was such a comfort to feel her in his arms. But her little shoulder blades were sharp.

"You're thin, aren't you, Mother?" he asked anxiously.

She drew back at this. "Not more than common," she said. She put back a loosened lock of her straight golden hair, and suddenly they were both shy.

"Well, eat your food, Mother, do," he said sternly.

"Aye—yes, I will," she promised. She was back at the sink again, her eyes turned away.

He had gone on to school. But he knew, and she felt his knowledge. All during the long months he had done all he could to lift heavy things and hang the clothes on the line, and every morning he spread his own bed before he came downstairs. And sometimes he was afraid of himself because he hated his father so heartily.

Yet when Maggie was born he was fond of her. He was always fond of them, after they were born. He had been fond of Jamie first because it was a pleasure to have a brother younger than he so that he need not be Edward's only younger brother, and then he was fond of Jamie because he was so full of jokes and laughing. And then Ruth was born, and he was fond of her because she was his first sister. And Arthur was delicate from the day of his birth, and at three was still delicate, so that one could not but grow fond of him because he was so patient and good. And Maggie was soon eight months old, and he was fond of her because she was so hearty and independent and because she was not pretty like Ruth, and so needed his fondness the more.

"A homely woman!" his mother sighed. "She'll have to be made up to somehow, for she'll have a hard row to hoe. God send she's smart!"

Maggie was smart enough for anybody. At four months she had two solid strong white teeth, at five she sat alone, and now at eight months she could walk from chair to table and clamor for bits from Jonathan's plate at mealtimes. He fed her secretly, proud of her ability to eat anything.

"You'll give her the colic, sure!" his mother cried.

But nothing gave her colic. Looking into her round, plain, healthy little face, doomed to freckles, he felt his heart grow hot with the soft warmth which rushed out of it always for his mother and the younger children. He and they were the real family, he sometimes felt. His father and Edward did not seem to belong to them.

And yet neither he nor the younger children possessed the power to disturb his mother that his father did. Years ago he had learned when he came into the house to fear, to pause and listen to whether the house were silent or whether he heard his father shouting, arguing, stamping up and down the bedroom above the small parlor of which his mother was so proud. He could never quite hear what his father was actually saying when he went into his chilly little attic room. But he always went in and stood shivering and listening to the bumbling roar of his father's voice.

He could not hear his mother at all. The walls of the cottage were of stone, old and thick, and plastered again and again by many hands, and the ceiling was close. If the house had been that one in Blackpool which he could only vaguely remember, it would have been easy to hear anything. Yet all he could remember of that house was hearing his mother cry out when Jamie was being born. Perhaps there had never been a quarrel about leaving Blackpool, but he seemed to remember a quarrel between his father and mother about it. His mother had hated the port and the coarse sailors sauntering into the little shop she kept so clean and neat. Wherever they moved she always opened a little shop somehow, in one of the rooms. Her father had kept a draper's shop and was well-to-do in a small way, so that she had gone to school until she was seventeen and then had taught for three years.

It was in her father's shop that she had met Clyde Goodliffe. Then he had been a salesman for dry goods, and old Mr. Layton had wanted him in the shop after they were married, since he had two girls and no son. But it had not lasted. His Aunt Myra could not abide his father, his mother said. There had been a tremendous quarrel, he knew, and then his father had done something else.

His father had done almost everything. They were all used to his beginning one of his lordly tales of a wonderful happening by his smacking his lips and saying, "It was when I was a journeyman once that I saw the most wonderful, fearful sight. . . ." Or he said, "Once when I was in the candle and coal business, a chap thought he'd be smarter than I was . . ."

But for the last ten years they had lived in this house. Clyde Goodliffe had come and gone; had rented this land and that, and given it up in disgust because it was too wet or too dry, too stony or too mucky; had sold one thing and another or nothing; but his mother had kept them all firmly in this low whitewashed cottage that was home. It stood on the side of a hill above the village of Dentwater, and the kitchen garden sloped up the hill in the back, so that Jamie, digging potatoes, tried to roll them into the kitchen door. In the front she had her flowers, and on the other side of their bit of land was the village street. Beyond Dentwater the hill flattened, then went rolling on into the levels around Blackpool.

This home Jonathan loved. It troubled him continually and sometimes in the night frightened him to think he must leave it because he was growing. Plenty of boys left home at fifteen.

"Why for should I be feedin' a lad of fifteen?" his father grumbled.

"Give him another year at school till he's sixteen," his mother begged. "He's as good as a girl in the house and a wonder to help in the shop. And Edward's enough in that filthy Blackpool."

"Money idn't to be found in a hole like Dentwater, though," his father shouted.

"Money idn't to be found anywhere, Clyde," his mother replied with a gentle firmness. "It's got to be made."

All his heart moved to his mother. But between these two who were his parents, Jonathan Goodliffe had long since learned to keep silence, because he knew, somehow, that in spite of all their quarreling, they loved each other, and this love shut him out from between them. However much his mother loved him, she loved his father more. The consciousness of it kept Jonathan humbled and quiet, and whatever he did for his mother was never quite enough.

On the thirteenth of January in the year 1866, at half past four in the afternoon, he was coming home from the village school cold and hungry for tea. If his father were not home, he and his mother and the small ones would have their tea about the kitchen hearth. All day long in the damp chill of the schoolroom he had been imagining that hour before the fire, his knees hot, his face burning, his hands and feet warm at last, and he drinking hot tea. If his father were home, tea would be set out on the table, and he would have to take his place there and listen to his father's boisterous talk.

He plodded steadily down the cobbled street, holding an umbrella against the windy drizzle. It was already dark, and the twenty-odd cottages of Dentwater were lit as though night had fallen. One by one the four older pupils of the school had stopped at these cottages until only Archie Bainter, a boy a little younger than he, was with him. Then Archie stopped, too.

"Well, here I be, Jonathan," Archie said as a light grew out of the mist.

"So you be," Jonathan answered. "I'll be seein' you tomorrow, Archie."

"Well, maybe you will and maybe you won't," Archie said solemnly.

"Where'll you be goin'?" Jonathan asked, amazed. He paused under the umbrella to stare into the vagueness of Archie's face.

"I'm sick of school," Archie said.

"We're all that, I reckon," Jonathan said soberly.

"Yes, but I'm goin' to rid myself of it," Archie said.

"Runnin' away to America?" Jonathan teased him. He laughed when he spoke. It was the word for ridicule in Dentwater. "Oh, run away to Ameriky!" people roared at each other, meaning the utmost folly.

"I dunno," Archie said sullenly. "But I'm agoin'."

"I'm goin', too—but home," Jonathan rejoined. "I've a good tea waitin', and I'm froze."

He went on, forgetting Archie's childishness. Archie Bainter was always in trouble at the school. "For shame to you, Archie Bainter!" the master had cried at him only this afternoon. "A great lad that ought to be a sign and sample to the younger ones! If it wasn't that they are dismissed earlier than you, I'd feel called to punish you before them to teach them what happens to lads in school that don't study their lessons and read wicked yellow-covered books inside their geographies!"

He had held up between his thumb and forefinger the yellow book. "American trash!" he had snorted.

But there were no younger children after three o'clock, only the four of them being coached for the examinations. If Jonathan passed the examinations, he could go on to be a teacher. That was his private hope. He wanted to go on, maybe even to London University, and be some day headmaster of a school. His mother knew—no one else.

"*Hic—haec—hoc—huius—huius—huius—*" he muttered. He should have begun Latin long ago, but they did not teach it in the village school. Mr. Hopkins, the master, was teaching him every day betweentimes, as he could. He should have told Mr. Hopkins long ago he was going to be a teacher. But it had seemed presumptuous, and he had not done it. Some day when Mr. Hopkins was old he maybe would have this very school— or a better one. And he would live with his mother at home. By that time he'd have done all she wanted done, like a bit of porch put on the south, glassed in, where she could keep her flowers in winter.

He turned in at the little gate, and from the low-set windows candlelight gleamed softly through the fringing mist. Now, if only his father were not at home, he'd tell his mother what Mr. Hopkins said today about his Latin, how he said, "You learn so uncommonly fast, young man, it's a downright shame I have to spend hours on a lot of numbskulls and let a lad like you have the minutes. But 'tis the educational system we labor under."

And then he gave up every hope. He heard his father's voice resounding through the room as he opened the door.

"I say to Ameriky I'm goin', and so I be agoin'!"

He shut the door quietly. Nobody noticed him. They were all staring at his father, who was standing in the middle of the kitchen. He had a loaf of bread against his chest and was cutting a great slab from it. Edward was there, too, leaning against the small wooden mantel behind the stove, his hands in his pockets, his mouth pursed under his young moustache. The children were at the table, eating buttered bread and drinking their mugs of milk and water. But Jonathan looked at his mother. She was sitting at the table with the baby Maggie at her breast; and her face, turned toward his father, was white and woeful.

"Oh, Clyde!" she whispered. "You'd never go off to America!"

"Why not?" Clyde Goodliffe retorted. "I been hearin' of it. It's the on'y place now on God's earth a man can hope to get land for himself. Here in this danged England you've to be born with land under your feet, else you go tiddlin' along the rest of your days. I'm sick of puttin' my back and my blood into land for another man."

"A lot you put into it!" she cried, goaded. "A great big lazy chap, allays at Blackpool where you've no reason to be, and the land waitin' to be tended!"

"Ah-ha, but 'twas at Blackpool I heard of this!" he said triumphantly. He put down the loaf now and smeared butter upon the slice he had sawed. "Listen, Mary, you get on a boat—"

"Not free, I'll lay," she broke in, but he scorned to notice this.

"And you sail away to New York, see, and then you go part by train—well, maybe all the way by train—to Kansas. Kansas is the country for us. The soil's that thick and black there's no plumbin' it—and it's free—or all but. They want enterprisers there—chaps with large minds that'll build the country big. England's a tiddlin' place."

"England'll treat you fair if you treat it fair," his wife broke in.

Clyde Goodliffe banged the flat of his hand on the table so hard that the thick dishes jumped.

"I'm goin' to Ameriky," he said sternly. "I've signed papers to go. And you're all goin' with me. The man asks me, 'Have you help?' and I sayed, 'I have—three on 'em.' And he sayed, 'Good—it's a country where the more sons a man has, the better!' "

"I'm not goin'," Edward said in his hard voice. He was a square young man called handsome by his fellows because he was fair-haired and his skin ruddy.

"You'll go if I say it," his father shouted, turning on him.

"Not I, Father," Edward said. "I'm doin' well in my job, and Millie Turner and I are engaged. I was goin' to tell you tonight, Mother."

"You and Millie— Well, I never, Eddie!" his mother cried. She was diverted by this news, and her look on Edward was surprised and full of simple admiration.

Nothing else, Jonathan knew, could have staved off his father except this news. Old Mr. Turner owned the best ships' chandler's shop in Blackpool and the one in which Edward worked.

"I knew you were doin' wonderful well, Ed," his father said, amazed, "but not so well as that."

Edward grinned complacently. "Look to the top while you're lookin', says I," he replied. "So I popped the question last night, and she took me."

"Well, may God bless me," Clyde Goodliffe roared. "Why, bring 'er along, lad, and we'll start a ships' chandlery in Kansas!"

"But it ain't by the sea, is it, Father?" Jonathan put in.

His father stopped drinking and looked struck. "Dang it," he said, "it's in the middle of Ameriky!"

"So a man would be a fool to go if he was me," Edward said triumphantly.

"He would be a fool if he was anyone," his mother retorted. "And you, too, Clyde, if you leave the land you've lost money on five years runnin' and this year the first, after all the manurin' and tillin', that it has brought us in a bit."

"Rented land!" Clyde Goodliffe muttered. He was pulling at the loaf of bread again, tearing off great snags of the crust and wiping them in the butter before he put them in his mouth.

"Land's worth what you get off it," his wife replied. "And what about my shop and the cottage and the garden— Oh, Clyde!" She broke down into weeping; and Maggie, solemnly watching all this, began to roar. Jonathan, leaning with his back against the door, came forward and took her from his mother's knees.

"There now, lass," he soothed her. "Come to Jonnie. Here, Ruthie, give 'er a sup of your milk and water."

He put Ruth's half-empty mug to the baby's lips and silenced her.

But there was no way of silencing his mother's weeping. They were used to it, and yet they would never grow used to it. The children hung their heads miserably and tried to go on eating and drinking. Ruth held a lump of bread and butter in her cheek and could not swallow it, and tears came welling into her large hazel-brown eyes. Pale little Arthur shrank smaller in his chair, and only Jamie seemed unmoved. He kept his eyes down and went on chewing steadily.

His wife's tears always made Clyde sweat with rage. The dampness sprang out now on his forehead, and he leaped up and threw the loaf on the floor.

"Dang the last lot of you!" he shouted. "You're allays holdin' a man down with your bits of shops and your talk of a man ought to do this and do that until I'm fair crazy, like a boat tied to a rock. Stay with your tiddlin' shops! I'm goin' to Ameriky if I live a lone man the rest of my days!"

He kicked the loaf across the kitchen and stalked out of the door and slammed it so that lime flew from the whitewashed walls around it.

Behind him they sat exactly as they were, except that the mother stopped weeping. She turned her head away from them and wiped her eyes on her apron. Then after a few seconds she went and picked up the loaf and dusted it with her hands and put it on the table. No one spoke. She stroked back her hair, her hands trembling. Then she sat down again and put out her arms.

"Give me the baby, Jonathan," she said.

He set Maggie upon her knees and, bending over her, saw that the cup upon the table beside her was unused.

"Shall I pour your tea now, Mother?" he asked.

"Yes, please, Jonathan," she replied in a quivering voice.

He poured her cup and then his own, and they sat, a sober little group, in the quiet kitchen. The kettle on the stove began suddenly to sing, and the yellow cat, asleep underneath the oven, came out stretching itself and yawning.

"When will you be countin' on marryin' Millie, Edward?" his mother asked.

"I dunno, Mother," he replied. "I said, 'Name the day, Millie,' but she says, 'Oh, it's early for that, Eddie.' But I count on summer, maybe."

"There's no use in waitin' when the girl's as much a prize as Millie is," his mother agreed.

She was almost herself again, and the children began to come out from their shadow. Arthur drank his milk, and Jamie spread jam upon a fresh slice of bread, and Ruth jumped from her seat and ran over to her mother and squeezed the baby heartily.

"Oh, you're a sweet tiddlin' thing!" she cried, and skipped away to a corner where she kept her dolls.

"Where'll you be livin', Edward?" his mother inquired.

"I'll move into old Turner's house," Edward said solemnly.

"You'll never!" his mother cried.

"He wants it and so does the old lady," Edward replied. "Millie bein' their only, they won't hear to aught else."

"It's a handsome place," Jonathan said respectfully.

"You're wise not to give in to your father," his mother said.

"Don't you give in to him neither, Mother," Edward told her. He rose as he spoke. "Must be goin', I reckon," he said. "Millie's waitin'." He began putting on his reefer coat. Outside, the twilight had thickened into night. "Hope you don't think I was too rough, Mother. But you see how silly 'twould be for me with my chances to go off to Ameriky."

"I do see it, Edward," his mother answered. She was sopping bits of dry bread in her milky tea and feeding the baby.

Edward bent and kissed her on the cheek and then kissed the baby.

"Well, good-by, all of you," he said. He stood, his hand on the door. "Shall you be givin' in to 'im, Mother?" he asked.

His mother lifted tragic eyes. "How do I know what to do with him?" she replied. "I only know when I think of leavin' England I feel myself sick inside. 'Twould be bad enough to leave Dentwater and this bit of a place I've held together for home for all of you. But to leave England!"

She bit her lip and shook her head, and tears gathered again in her blue eyes as she went back to feeding Maggie.

And Jonathan, watching her, for the first time saw the full meaning of what might come. To be leaving England! He had never thought of such horror. To leave England was to leave all that was life and home and place in the world.

"I'd advise you stay by your own mind, Mother," Edward said.

"There's more to things than that," his mother said sadly.

"I reckon there is," he admitted. He hesitated awkwardly. "Well, good-by all—till next time," he said and went out.

Left behind with his mother, Jonathan resolved to ask her nothing. How could she know what to do? How could any of them know what to do? He wiped Arthur's mouth and untied his bib, and the child slipped down. Jamie was already playing behind the stove with his ship.

Suddenly his mother looked up. "Draw back the curtains, son," she said. "Your father will be comin' home after his rage. He always does, though he'll be late, maybe. And set the candle on the sill."

He drew back the brown homespun curtains as far as he could, and then, after an instant, he set the lighted candle upon the deep stone sill.

2

THEY were going to America. Jonathan knew when he came down to breakfast in the morning that they were going. Night had done it again. There was some strange power in the night. He had seen it work before to change his father from anger into good temper and his mother from rebellion into acquiescence. When he had gone upstairs last night, the candle still burning in the window, he had been troubled. If only night were not ahead! His mother had seemed quite calm all evening, though his father had not come back. The children were in bed, and she sat stitching on a shirt. He had wanted to sit with her and read aloud to her after he had finished his lessons. She was fond of having him read to her, but tonight she put him off.

"Better go to bed, Jonathan," she said. "It's late."

"It's late for you, too," he objected.

"Aye, but it's my duty to sit up for 'im," she replied.

He looked at her. Her small, fine-featured face looked composed and firm again. He leaned and kissed her cheek and went up the narrow stair, hung like a ladder against the wall. He might have been tempted to trust her if there had not been night ahead, he thought, and sighed, being bewildered by what he did not understand.

He always gets around her by somehow I don't know, he thought sadly, and lay awake a long time after that, the bedcovers drawn decently up to his chin, and the close ceiling near enough above his head to reach if he put his hand up to touch it.

And then in the morning he did not need to hear his father's loud and cheerful voice to know the night had worked once more as he had feared. He had overslept himself a little, so that when he hastened down the stove was already hot, and the kettle on, and his mother setting the breakfast table. Near the stove his father was shaving himself before a milky mirror and talking as he shaved, and around the room the children were dressing themselves. Only Maggie sat upon a rag mat on the floor, still as she had been lifted from bed, sucking a crust and watching them all with sharp bright eyes.

"Hey there, Jonnie!" his father called to him. He stretched his jaw as he scraped at it. "Lend a hand to Artie's boots, will ye, lad? He's been hollerin' against the laces. I can't abide lacin' their boots—there's no end to 'em on such a lot as I have. Well, when we get to Ameriky they can all go barefoot. The sun's that warm over there, they tell me."

So he knew. He stooped and laced Arthur's small patched boots, and Ruth stood waiting to have her pinafore buttoned.

"Wash them a bit before they eat, Jonathan," his mother bade him. "The kettle water's hot."

"Yes, Mother," he said.

He waited until his father had finished with the pottery basin and then emptied it outside the door. It was still dark outside, and the air was raw. He shut the door quickly and, filling the basin, washed one face after another of the row before him. They were all good children except Jamie.

"I'm washed," Jamie said briefly.

"You're not," Jonathan said sternly.

"I am, too—I washed in Father's water," Jamie said doggedly.

Jonathan seized him firmly, his head under his arm, and scrubbed his face.

"Then you'd best be washed once more," he said.

"Gently, Jonathan," his mother called.

"Kick him, Jamie!" his father cried, and roared when Jamie let out his foot and kicked at Jonathan's shins.

"For shame, Clyde!" his mother said. "Jamie, you should thank your brother. Come and sit down to your porridge, all of you."

It was like every other morning and yet like none other. He finished his breakfast and washed his bowl and spoon and set it away on the shelf as he always did and put on his coat and cap and his brown knit muffler and took up his books. He had said nothing to anyone, though all through the meal his father had been gabbling about what he would do. Through the wall he put up by long habit against his father, he heard only fragments of the boasting, windy voice.

"A thousand acres. . . . You don't manure, you just toss in your seed. . . . A handful of folk to a land ten times the size of England. . . . I s'all build you a house, lass, that's a dook's castle to this 'un. . . . The Indians are driven off, I tell you—it's not like it was—the land belongs to English folk now, like us. . . ."

"I'm off now, Mother," Jonathan said at the door, and waited for her answering look.

"Good-by, son," she said.

But her mind was not on him this morning, and he saw it and went lonely away, trudging through the gray streets into the chill lantern-lit schoolroom. Mr. Hopkins was there already, setting a problem in square white figures upon the black-painted wall.

"Good morning, Jonathan Goodliffe," he said briskly. "You're here fine and early. There'll be time for the fifth declension before the rest of them come in."

Jonathan put his books down upon his desk.

"I doubt there's any good in my goin' on with Latin, sir," he said.

Mr. Hopkins turned upon him, astonished, the round lump of chalk in his hand.

"What's that?" he asked sharply.

"We're goin' to America," Jonathan told him.

"America!" Mr. Hopkins repeated. "Whatever for?"

Jonathan shook his head. "I don't know, sir," he said.

Mr. Hopkins took off his glasses with one hand. "Why, I never heard of anybody goin' from these parts!" he said earnestly. "From Cornwall, yes, they're poor enough to go anywhere, and the Scotch and Irish—why shouldn't they go to get away from what they've got? But here—it's folly! You poor lad, Jonathan Goodliffe! No, you're right. What'll the savages over there be wanting with Latin?"

Jonathan felt his throat swell. He could not speak.

"Well, I never!" Mr. Hopkins said slowly and, putting on his glasses, stared at Jonathan so severely that he felt weak and sat down and began studying furiously.

The morning dragged its length along to noon, and he went home to dinner. But there he found his father not at home and his mother unexpectedly cheerful.

"We don't have to go for a year, Jonathan," she told him the moment he came in the door. "That is, you and me and the children don't. Your father's goin' first. If he likes it when the year's up, we'll come along to him. If he don't, he can come back to us. I stuck out for that," she added triumphantly.

They looked at each other.

"Mother!" he cried, and suddenly she began to laugh, and he laughed with her.

"A year!" she said mischievously. "When did he ever like anything as long as a year?"

It was reprieve and all but final pardon from a sentence.

"Then I'll go back to Latin," he said joyously. "Mr. Hopkins said as how savages wouldn't need it."

"And I shall go on with the garden," she said. "I was countin' on a new rosebush or two this year. Last night I thought 'twas no use. But today when he said he'd leave us behind a year, I said, 'Then I'll get the rosebushes from the vicar's wife, after all.'"

She looked years younger than she had at breakfast. She was a small, cheerful, chirping little creature upon whom sadness always sat foolishly. But joy became her. Her blue eyes shone, and her cheeks were pink, and she ran about the kitchen putting the meal on the table.

"Mother!" Jonathan cried at her again, and when she looked at him in astonishment as childlike as Maggie's, he rushed to her and threw his arms about her and could not speak.

A year, he was thinking, a whole year, he and she and the children!

"There!" she said, pushing him away. "Let be, Jonathan. Sit and eat your meat."

Her practical, reasonable voice, clear and soft, seemed on the instant to set the world secure again and drive away the huge dark continent of the unknown, and he sat down and ate heartily.

The new year began the day his father left them. Clyde Goodliffe could not do quickly enough whatever he had decided upon. He had the furious determination of the impatient and variable man. Within twelve days he was ready to sail for America. The only stumbling block had been the twenty acres of land he rented from three different men. He wanted to give it up, leaving the winter wheat in which much of it stood in lieu of rent.

"'Tidn't as if I was goin' to be here to harvest it," he said.

But Jonathan had seen his mother's wish to keep the land. "Land is easy to be rid of and hard to get back again," she had said.

"I'll never be wantin' them bits of acres back again," Clyde shouted back with contempt. "Why, twenty acres don't make a kitchen garden in Kansas!"

"What you'll do with more I don't know," she retorted, "seein' that twenty's been too much for you here."

"Tiddlin' English land," he sneered, "allays awantin' manure and lime and stuff put in it!"

"I'll take care of it," Jonathan said. He had never done all the work alone before, but now he felt he could. With his father gone, he would work twice as hard for them all, and what he did not know he could ask of his neighbors.

"I want to be rid of the rent," his father said shortly.

"I'll make the shop pay for it," his mother broke in. "It does seem right down folly for us to give up what was just beginnin' to pay. Stands to reason there'll be good crops this year after the bad ones."

"It's been a good winter with snow and all," Jonathan said earnestly.

"Have it your own way, then, so long as my money don't go for it," Clyde retorted. "I got to put by enough to bring over the lot of you by next year's spring."

His dark eyes grew mischievously tender. " 'Twould be a wonderful good chance for a man to free himself from a burden of worry and trouble and start out new. What'd you do, lass, if I let old England have you and said good-by for good 'n' all?"

"I'd be glad enough to be rid of you," his wife retorted, "if that's the way you feel."

He threw back his head until they could see his hairy throat, and gave his bellow of laughter.

"Danged if I'm not fond of you and all your brats," he shouted, and tumbled her head in his two hands like a ball until she cried, laughing and protesting, "Clyde—Clyde—let me be—I'm all dizzy!"

Jonathan slipped out into the yard. He was suddenly sick. He could not bear the sight of his mother's smooth blond head rolling between his father's big hairy hands.

He's so cruel rough with her! he thought passionately. His chest heaved and he wanted to weep. Why don't she stop him? he thought furiously. He needed to do something hard and immediate and driving, and he stooped and began pushing and pulling at the big square stone that made the upper of the two steps down from door to path.

The door opened, and his father stood ready to come out.

"What're you doin', you daft boy?" he demanded.

Jonathan, on his knees in the mud, looked up at him.

"I'm makin' these steps straight," he said sullenly. "They've been crooked this long while."

"I haven't seen 'em crooked," his father said gaily. He stepped down and went to the gate. "Allays settin' somethin' right, you be!" He went down the street, whistling.

He's goin' to the public house again, Jonathan thought bitterly, and then was no happier for knowing he was unjust. His father was not a drunkard and did not spend much time with drinking men. That was the trouble with him, Jonathan thought. There was nothing you could lay a finger on. He had no real wickedness. It would have been easier if he had. He longed for his father to be a downright plain bad man like Archie's father, who drank and when he was drunk beat his wife.

If I saw my dad lay a hand on my mother to hurt her! Jonathan thought savagely. But, no, his father kicked the furniture, and he could throw a loaf of bread or a plate across a room; but he beat not even one of the children. And on the same day when he was lowering and quarrelsome and angry about one thing after another, he could stop everything to pour a saucer of milk for the cat and set it under the stove. A mixed-up, trying sort of man, Jonathan thought with frequent gloom. Today as he watched his father go toward Blackpool, he added, "Allays thinkin' too big about what isn't there, and never seein' what's under his nose to be done!"

If it weren't for him, her son, what would become of his mother with a man like that?

And yet on the day when his two older sons went to Blackpool to bid Clyde Goodliffe good-by, it was a sorrowful day for them all in its strange way. He had found a berth to work his way on a freight ship sailing from Liverpool to New York.

"Never tell me it don't pay to hang about the town a bit, lass," he said to his wife. "That is, if you're a clever chap, like me."

From Blackpool he was going on a coal ship free because the captain was a man he knew. At the cottage his wife had cried quietly now and then while she packed his bag, until he looked at her with impatience in his eyes.

"Give over, Mary—do! S'all I carry the memory of you weepin' and wailin' all the months I'm to be away? You'll be safe from me for a year. Think about that and dry up, lass. Ain't that a comfort? For a year you can sleep safe in your bed and not wake up to worry whether you're goin' to have a baby or not!"

"Oh, Clyde!" She was so shocked that she stopped crying.

"You've thought of it, I lay," he said, his eyes dancing. He seized her and rubbed her cheek with his. "Own up to yourself, now, lass."

"I will not!" she cried.

"Then ye have," he said, laughing.

"If I have, it's not to say I won't long for you," she said. "Oh, Clyde, dear lad!"

She threw down the coat she held in her hand and curled against him in the sweet way she had. She did not do it often now. But when she did, it caught hold of him just as it always had.

"Don't look at another woman, Clyde!" she begged him in a tight little whisper.

"Never fear, Mary!" he whispered to her.

"You'll come back if you don't like it, won't ye, Clyde?" she begged. "You wouldn't be proud and stick to America just to be stubborn, would you? And make us all give up England if America isn't what you think it is?"

"If it ain't better than I think it is, even, I'll come back," he told her. And then he had kissed her hard twice and then again, and she picked up the coat and put it in the bag. They went downstairs, and he kissed the younger children and pulled Jamie's nose, "for extra," he said, because Jamie was his pet, and they stood watching him go with the two big ones, Edward on one side of him and Jonathan on the other, carrying his bags.

"Here, you lummoxes," he had said, "it'll be the last time for many a month."

They picked up the bags, Edward the smaller one, and Jonathan, always silent, the heavy sack. Down the street before the road went over the hill Clyde stopped, turned, and waved both arms to the little group in the door; and Mary's apron waved like a flag in reply. Then he went on again, his thick boots clumping the cobbled street. What he was thinking his sons did not know. But when they were down the shallow hill and out of sight of Dentwater, and there was only the low-lying Blackpool ahead, he began to talk, not of them, but of America.

"I'm free inside for the first time in my life," he said in his harsh, loud voice. "Smothered I've been in this little bit of an old country. There's been no room here for a hundred year, I'll lay. A new country is the country for men and lads." He remembered then that Edward was not coming. "Don't you shut yourself to coming, Edward," he said to his oldest son. "Soon's I find everything goin' big, I'll let you know, and you can set up one way or 'nother, you and Millie, and whatever children are yours. I aim to begin big. That's the secret in Ameriky, they tells me. Everybody begins big. The little 'uns are lost."

He took off his cap, and the wind lifted his rough black hair from his forehead that was low and square. His high cheekbones were red, and his full lips pressed together with unusual firmness. None of his sons had the largeness of his build. The fineness of their mother had tempered his share in them. Edward was as near his father's height as he would ever be, and he was three inches shorter.

"Jamie'll beat me, and the only one to do it," Clyde always said. But Jamie was only a small freckle-faced boy now.

"It's a wunnerful good thing I'm doin' for you all," he went on. The road was muddy, but he went tramping through it. "You'll live to thank the day I was bold enough to see it and make up my mind to do the big thing."

They were going over the long flats now, and Blackpool lay ahead, dark against a windy gray sea. It was February, and they had not seen the sun in a month. There was no sun today, but the air was not cold as they walked. A carter came by. His cart was empty, and it was drawn by two great sluggish gray horses. He pulled up.

"Want a ride?" he inquired. He peered down at them from under a rusty felt hat, and his face was narrow and askew.

"We do," Clyde said gladly. He was beginning to feel embarrassed by the long walk with his sons. He was not used to being with them alone. They climbed in, bags and all.

"Leavin' for somewhere?" the carter inquired affably. Seen now face to face, it was apparent that his jaw had once been dislocated and never set properly. But one saw such faces in Blackpool.

"Goin' to Ameriky," Clyde answered proudly.

The carter whistled. "A long way," he said. He looked at Edward. "You goin'?" he asked.

"No," Edward said coldly. He sat on the side of the cart carefully to save his clothing from coal dust.

"You?" the carter asked Jonathan.

"I—don't know," Jonathan faltered and glanced at his father.

The carter grinned. "Looks like you're the gay chap, old 'un," he told Clyde Goodliffe. "Ameriky, hey? There's a lot of talk about Ameriky now."

"It's the only place for a man as is a man," Clyde said.

"I'll hold my end up in England, for all of Ameriky," the carter said and spat over the side of the cart.

"Do," said Clyde. "Ameriky's on'y for them as wants room."

And yet not until they had climbed down from the cart and gone to the wharf did his sons feel that he was going. All the time it had seemed only another one of his big windy schemes. But on the coal-stained wharf it suddenly came true. There the ship lay that was to take him to Liverpool, a small freighter bobbing against its ropes. They went aboard and put down the bags on the deck, and then came the moment of good-by. They had never told him good-by before. For all his arguing and fuming, he had never left them. He became for the moment at once pitiable and heroic. He was going so far. There was the ocean and the unknown continent ahead of his solitary figure. How could he manage alone when he fuddled the least thing at home? And yet he was calm and full of courage.

"Good-by, lads," he said heartily. "Edward, I ask you not to let Millie take up your whole mind. Go to see your mother."

"I will, Father," Edward said solemnly.

"And, Jonathan," his father continued, "when I send for you all, help her to see it's right and for the best. She's that fond of you that if you want to come, she'll be more'n half ready to do it."

Jonathan felt still more softened. "Yes, Father," he said solemnly.

He grasped their hands and shook each of them hard.

"Now get along with you. I'll have no standin' about," he ended.

They obeyed him and walked slowly away from the ship. They turned once as by common accord. He was still there, and he motioned them sharply to go on—go on! They went on then until they reached the corner where Turner's chandlery stood, and here Edward stopped.

"Reckon I'll go in and finish my day's work," he said.

"I'll go on back, then," Jonathan answered.

They lingered a moment.

"Will you be home soon, Edward?" Jonathan asked.

"Yes, I will, and I plan to bring Millie as soon as it's announced," Edward said.

"That'll be nice for Mother," Jonathan replied.

They had nothing more to say to each other.

"Good-by, then, Jonnie," Edward said at last.

"Good-by, Ed," Jonathan replied.

They parted, each thinking of the solitary figure starting alone that night to cross the sea; and Jonathan, plodding home in the afternoon twilight, wondered at himself that he could feel so dreary because his father was gone.

Reckon there's something about him, after all, he thought. Ahead of him the severe horizon was black against a neutral sky.

3

HE MUST make his mother happy. He had always felt this necessity upon him, but now it became a passion. He alone could make her happy. Edward had Millie, but his mother had only him. He rose in the morning and lit the kitchen stove and had the porridge steaming before she came down. He stayed after breakfast to clear the table and rushed back at noon to help her with the children. And every Monday morning he got up at five o'clock to help her with the wash. That was the one thing his father had used to do. On Mondays his father got up and set the tubs for her and doused the clothes in them and wrung the sheets. He would not hang them on the line, but he carried the baskets out for her.

As long as Jonathan could remember, he knew Monday morning before he even came out of sleep, because of the soapy hot reek of soiled clothes rising from kitchen to roof. It filled his corner of the attic like a miasma, and he woke stifled, his nostrils acrid. The reek was the reek of poverty to him, dreary and sodden; and he got up weighted with the plight of his parents, who must work so hard. He felt apologetic for his existence when his father, blowing and blustering, sat down to breakfast. "Mind how you lads use your breeches and shirts, in God's name," he shouted. "I've about wore myself out on 'em today. If I had the doin' of it, I'd let you run naked, I would, and you'd wash your own skins when you dirtied 'em."

But now he liked being up early and alone with his mother. She had a routine—the white things first in the clean suds and then the colored ones, and then the rinsings in the small tin tub which they used for baths on Saturday nights. The smell of the soap was sharp and clean when he plunged it into clean water.

"Let me wash my own shirt, now, Mother," he commanded. "And them breeches with the mud on the knees I'll do."

"Those," she corrected him gently. "Take care, Jonathan, how you speak. Grammar's sign and seal on a man. 'Tidn't his clothes—he can put them on himself as fine as he likes, but how his words come out of him tells you all he is."

She handed him his garments, and then she went on a little diffidently, "If you'll copy your father's downright good heart and speak after me, I'll be pleased."

"I'll take after you in everything if I have my way," he told her.

"Mother's boy you always were," she said smoothly.

He felt a dear strong happiness warm in his belly as though it were something hot he had drunk.

"I hope you're happy, Mother," he said dizzily. "I hope you don't miss him too much."

He had never come out with it like that before. But he had to know whether or no she was happy alone with him and the children. Suppose his father never came back—would she be happy?

"I do miss him," she said quietly. "But that has nothing to do with you."

Her soft voice saying these words seemed to shut him out. He felt his happiness throb and stop, wounded.

"You're bein' happy has a lot to do with me, Mother," he replied hotly. "When you—aren't happy, I feel it so."

"How do you?" she asked. She looked at him curiously from her tub.

"It's like cloud over sun," he answered.

She smiled ruefully. "I have to be gay whether my heart is or not?"

"No, you don't," he answered, and then could not go on. When he tried to tell her something he felt about her he was always stopped by the tight thickness of his breast. He was bound in by it. There was nothing to do until he had freed himself by moving away from her. It was sweet and yet intolerable to be so close to her. When she was gay he was happiest, for then he felt she was all right, and it did not matter whether he was there or not. When she was sorrowful he was suffocated in her sorrow. He must make her happy so he could be free.

"I'm glad you like Millie so well, Mother," he said, to talk about something else. Edward had brought Millie yesterday afternoon.

"I do like her," his mother replied.

He tossed the wet, curled-up sheets to her as he finished them, and she rinsed them.

"She isn't a bit like you," he went on, making talk.

"That's nothing against her," she replied, smiling a little.

" 'Tis for me," he said stoutly. "When I marry, it'll only be when I find a girl like you, Mother."

"Oh, there're lots like me," she said. "You'll have a hard time pickin'."

"Likely I'll be a bacheldore," he returned politely.

She laughed, and he was pleased with himself and smiled and winked his eye at her.

"You're the girl for me," he repeated.

He thought of Millie Turner. She was a large, loosely built girl, big-boned and yet with a turn to fat. Her pale brown eyes, a little popped, under scattered brows, were anxiously kind, and her dark hair was scanty and straight. But she had tried very hard to do her share of getting tea, and not to seem a guest.

"Now let me cut the bread and butter it, do, Mother," she said, when Edward brought her to tea.

"It was 'Mother' here and 'Mother' there," Mary Goodliffe said to Jonathan when they were gone. Her eyes twinkled, and she laughed softly. "It makes me feel downright queer to have a great hulkin' woman callin' me 'Mother.' She's three years older than Edward and looks it. . . . Not but what the girl means well," she added, "and she'll be good in the chandlery and anxious to please her husband. That'll suit Edward." She had twinkled again. "Or any man—"

. . . "Go on, Jonathan Goodliffe," she retorted.

"As you say," he laughed, and picked up the basket of wrung clothes and carried it out. His father would never hang them because the neighbors might laugh at a man doing such work, but he did not mind. He lifted the sheets and shook them out and felt their wetness flapping against him as he reached for the line.

She's happier than she ever was, he thought gladly. She's better with him away.

Very often during the day he thought she was happier. Together they planned the planting of the rented acres, and when he was able to get it ploughed she came out and seeded it to oats and corn and a little of the new maize that his father sent them in a tin box from America. Maize they had never planted before, but they had heard of it, and here were the big yellow grains. Part of it they had planted in furrows before the letter came, and then they found it must be put in hills, a few grains together.

"S'all we dig it all up again to do it right?" he asked his mother anxiously.

"No, indeed not," she replied stoutly. "They're planted in good English ground, and they'll come up however."

And so they did, big strong spears of bright green and of a shape they had never seen before.

"A savage, wild-lookin' grass, I'd say, if I didn't know," his mother said, staring at it. It grew faster than a reed as soon as summer came.

He had never worked so hard as he did that summer, and he found out once for all his life that he was no farmer. He hated the labor of the land, the back-break of weeding and the reluctance of proper growth.

Danged silly weak things, crops are, he thought, sweating in muggy

July days. Now that school was out he attacked the land early and late. Weeds have all the strength. It's evil that's strong, after all.

He hated above all being dependent upon weather. To know that all his labor and thought brought to bear upon fruitage from seeds he had planted were nothing if there was no rain or if there was too much, forced him to desperation. And yet anxiety and revolt were useless. There the skies were, impervious as stone or turning suddenly to soft, endless rain.

It's the feeling that my brains are no use that I can't abide, he thought. A man may as well be a dolt as not if he's a farmer—thinkin' will do him no good.

But he was careful to hide this hatred from his mother. The land was precious to her.

Yet he was only sixteen, and he could not keep from shirking a little sometimes the endless routine of the land, nor from coaxing and bribing Jamie and sometimes sternly forcing him to help in cultivating. The maize when it was ripe they did not like. It tasted green, though they boiled it, as his father had written them to do, and when they dried it and ground it into meal it had a strange musty taste.

"It tastes like mice smells," Jamie said bluntly and, though they made it into porridge and poured milk on it and mixed sugar in it, none of them liked it. Even Maggie spat it out solemnly, aghast at its strangeness upon her tongue.

"There's a whole acre gone for nothing," Jonathan groaned. "And a million weeds hoed off it."

"We tried it, though," his mother said practically, "and we know we don't like it. That's something to know."

They did very well that autumn. They used almost none of the money his father sent now and again.

"Save it against your comin', if you don't spend it," he wrote them. So his mother saved it in a tin biscuit box she kept in her room.

The little shop did well, too. It was a good year in England. Crops were fair, and people had extra money to spend and gave their children pennies for sweeties.

"If I was sure your father was comin' back," his mother told Jonathan, "I'd put piece goods into the shop. But—" She shook her head.

"You still think we'll go, Mother?" he asked. He searched her face for all she might not say in answer.

"You wouldn't want me to leave my husband," she replied.

He turned away. None of his labor had any fruit if while he labored her mind was not there in her body.

He still dreaded the night. For then, when the younger children were in bed and only he and she sat there, he with a book and she sewing or knitting, the moment came when her eyes were far away, and he knew what she was thinking. In the summer when the twilight was long he could push the moment away. Sometimes, even, if they worked over her rose bed, the moment never came at all. Or it only came so much as this, that her face grew wistful and she said, "I just couldn't bear to leave this bit of a garden. I couldn't make a garden on other ground. Nought would grow for me when my heart wasn't there to make it grow."

Then he knew that England was working for him against his father. England was still holding her fast, and all that England was—the long reaches of soft green, the shallow hill where Dentwater lay, the old church and the trees stooped from the sea winds, and the cottage. When Mr. Hopkins came back to open school and asked, "Are ye going to America, Jonathan?" he answered with precious doubt, "It's far from sure, Mr. Hopkins."

"Good," Mr. Hopkins said. "Then you're still for Latin?"

"If you please, Mr. Hopkins," he answered gratefully.

"And your father?" Mr. Hopkins asked.

"He's workin' for a farmer there same as here," Jonathan answered with a grin.

And so indeed Clyde Goodliffe was, but always with the hope of land. Other chaps, he wrote, had come ahead of him. Kansas was not so open any more. He was not sure where they would stay when he got them there. He was not buying any land yet—only getting enough money together to bring them over. Then they would see. But still it was wonderful to have a country so big all around that, let a man look anywhere, he could know a thousand miles waited for him. His letters were like him—full of big things, all not done.

The letters were what Jonathan feared in the darkening autumn evenings that grew longer with the hurrying on of winter. For the first time a year was short to him. Until now in his life a month had been nearly endless, and a year eternity; but his father's letters cut time to pieces. Once a month they came, and it was too quick for peace.

For in the long dark evenings, when she had worked a while, his mother grew restless. First she would hear the wind, and then she would murmur, "Anyway, he's not on the sea. It's better to have him in America than a sailor."

Then she would put her work down and mend the fire and see if the cat were fed. And then she settled to nothing again. Sometimes she counted over their money, and sometimes she stirred up a batch of bread, or she went to the window and stared out. And Jonathan, his books spread on the kitchen table, waited until she went to the chest of drawers and pulled out the top one and found the letters. When she did this she was lost to him; for she sat down with them in her lap and read them over one by one, and pondered over them and over the last one the longest. And all he had of her were the bits she threw at him from her thoughts.

"For all he sayed, I can't see the place, can you, Jonathan?"

"No, Mother," he said miserably.

"All flat, as far as eye can see," she went on.

"Sounds terrible dull, Mother."

"I don't know—there's trees, he says, and the flowers growin' wild like nothin' we have here."

Clyde had put Kansas wildflowers into his letter, but their colors were gone when they reached England. Only their strange shapes were left, and even these soon crumbled to dust.

" 'Rare colors,' he sayed," she repeated, looking at their dust.

Jonathan did not answer. He was beginning to learn that, out of the struggle within herself, if he agreed with her when she spoke against his father, she hastened to defense, either direct or by defending the country she had never seen.

And worst of all was the letter his father wrote when he had been ill. Malaria, he said, but none of them knew the word until he said chills and fever. Then she was nearly wild. She wrote him a long letter, sitting up half the night to do it, pleading with him to come home.

"What if your father should die out there alone among the savages?" she whispered to Jonathan. But her letter on the sea crossed his saying he was better again with the cold weather, and he told her about the colors on the autumn trees and how never had he seen such colors in England where the damp kept everything down to green and gray. A wonderful country, he said over and over, and violently beautiful. That letter reached them on a cold November day when the gray sea fog seeped up over Dentwater and shut them out of the world. The children had colds; and Maggie, staggering about, fell against the stove and burned her arm and shoulder. Jonathan saw tears come into his mother's eyes as she smeared lard over the screaming child. Neither he nor she had slept that night until nearly dawn because Maggie kept crying. Long after midnight Jonathan heard his mother murmur in her distress, "Dear God, can a lone woman stand this?" He wanted to cry out, "But I'm here, Mother!" and could not, being too humble for it. If she did not think of it herself, what good would it do him to remind her?

Even Edward's wedding, postponed until January, scarcely lifted the darkness of the damp winter. They all went to it, for Edward sent a wagon from Blackpool for them. They dressed in their best, and Jonathan yearned over his mother's sweet looks in her brown dress with its full skirt and cape and the little brown bonnet with pink ribbon quilted under the brim. She had the gift of putting her clothes on well and looking far better even than the vicar's wife, who was dressed always in black silk. His mother looked better than anyone at the wedding. Millie could not be pretty even as a bride. Her dress of heavy white satin only made her thicker, and her round red face never lost its anxiety for a moment under her veil of coarse lace. It was a solemn wedding until the eating and drinking began; and then, women with women and men with men, they began to talk, and Jonathan saw his mother always the center of a little cluster, listening to her tell of Clyde Goodliffe. She looked pretty and faintly important while she told them deprecatingly what he had written.

"A fearful country, so big and all, but the flowers wonderful and plenty of land and such a wide sky as you never see elsewhere unless in the middle of the ocean and big trees and plenty of black rich soil—deep as you can dig—"

"Has he bought land yet?" This was Millie's father, edging over to the woman, a thick man with a flat voice.

"Not until he's sure of the spot," his mother answered.

"You'll not be leavin' England, though, Mrs. Goodliffe?" Mrs. Turner, the bride's mother, said. She was a small wrinkled woman with a pursed mouth and a wide waist.

And then, though Jonathan strained to hear what his mother answered, he did not hear, for a fresh, sharp voice said beside him, "Are you Jonathan Goodliffe?"

He turned and saw a brown-faced girl beside him in a red woolen frock with a white lace collar. Her black hair was straight, and her eyes blue and strange-looking in her dark face.

"Yes, I am," he said. He was not exactly shy, because he was too self-reliant for that, but he had scarcely ever talked with a girl in his life.

"Constance Favor—Connie, I'm called—and in a manner we're related. At least now that my cousin Millie is married to your older brother, what does that make us?"

She spoke with a sort of laziness, her full, rather pale lips scarcely moving, and he felt at once that she must be older than he. But she was not quite as tall as he was, and he liked her clear blue eyes instantly.

"I don't know, but something surely," he said, and smiled.

"And are you goin' to America, or do you stay with your brother?" she asked. Her hands, smoothing her collar, were as brown as her face.

"It depends on my mother," he said soberly. He turned his head back to his mother, but whatever she had said was said. He had missed it. She was talking now to Mr. Turner about Edward.

"You'll find him a bit stubborn at times, Mr. Turner—that's his father— but he's steady once he begins—that's me in him. And I don't believe your Millie will rue this day."

"Hope not," Mr. Turner replied.

Mrs. Goodliffe bristled a little under her pink quilted ribbon. "No, I hope not, too, and I hope Edward won't, either," she returned.

"Hope not," Mr. Turner said more mildly. "It's a little late for that after the knot's been tied." He paused and stroked his thick red moustache. "Anyways, as I see it, a marriage idn't just thinking of each other. It's the shop and gettin' on and the children and all that. Folks do best to remember that."

"Surely," Mary Goodliffe agreed.

The fresh clear voice was at Jonathan's ear again.

"If I were you, I'd go to America. It's stupid here. I'd go quick as a wink."

"Why?" Jonathan asked.

"Oh, I don't know," she answered.

"Connie—Connie!" Mrs. Turner called. "Come here, child!"

"Oh, dear!" the girl said. "Just when we was gettin' acquainted! Do you dance, Jonathan? There's to be dancin'!"

"I never did before," he answered.

"Then I'll show you," she said. "I'm a rare good dancer," she added, with a mischief in her eyes which suddenly lit her face.

Her going left him alone again in the crowd, and he sauntered over to his mother. She was sitting now with Maggie asleep on her lap and Arthur leaning against her, rubbing his eyes.

"Jonathan, help to put these children to nap," she told him. "They'll be underfoot, once they start dancin'."

He lifted the fat, inert child from his mother's lap, and they went into a dark bedroom, and he found a spot upon a bed where two children were already asleep and laid Maggie down. She did not stir.

"Lie here, my little lad, on this nice mat on the floor," his mother said to Arthur, and the little boy curled upon a wool mat by the bed, and she covered him. Music burst out in the other room.

"Where's Jamie and Ruth?" he whispered to his mother.

"Jamie's out in the chandlery," his mother replied, "watching the ship's sailors come and go. He asked if he could, and I said yes. And Ruth's gone to play with a little girl next door."

He was quite free, then. If Connie wanted to teach him to dance, there was no reason why he shouldn't learn, except that he was suddenly shy before his mother to be dancing with a girl.

"Mother," he said, "do you mind if I dance a bit?"

Her eyes were round. "I didn't know you could dance," she cried.

"Constance Favor said she'd teach me a bit," he said.

He felt his chest grow hot, and the heat spread upward into his cheeks. His mother looked at him with a mingled touch of doubt and surprise.

"Well, I reckon it won't matter," she said, and doubt grew uppermost in her face as he walked away from her.

They were already dancing when he came into the big room, a jiggy reel that made voices hum and sing as people danced. At the end of the line of dancers he saw the bride and groom, Edward more carefully casual than ever in his position as bridegroom, and Millie still anxious. She held up her skirts in both hands, her foot tapping and her head nodding, fearful lest she miss the movement. Even so, she lost it by a fraction. "Here, girl!" Edward cried.

"Oh, Ed!" she screamed.

But Edward swung out, and she rushed to meet him, while everyone laughed and clapped. And Jonathan, hesitating, felt his hand seized in Connie's firm grasp.

"Come along," she said. "I was looking for you. Now, mind you follow!"

There was no time to think about anything. He was swept into the dance and forced to take thought lest he disturb its pattern through his ignorance.

He thought sometimes that, if it had not been for that dance, all his life might have been different. But how could he know it then?

"A silly fool you looked," his mother said to him in sharp disgust, "leaning to hear all her gabble, and her dress so low you must have seen her stummick."

Here at home again in the kitchen he was drenched with shame.

"I didn't," he muttered. No, but he had seen a bosom, divided into its two full circles. He hadn't wanted to see anything, but he had looked again and again.

"I don't care for her nor any girl," he said angrily to his mother.

"It's a queer way to hate them, then," his mother retorted. On his shoulder Maggie began to whimper. The other children were already unlacing their shoes, silent, their faces white with the fatigue of pleasure. "Talkin' to her and dancin' with nobody else!"

"There was nobody else, Mother—except old women," he answered.

"She's too old for you, too, if that's what you mean," she cried. "One Turner's enough, I'll thank you to remember! Millie Turner's all right for Edward. She idn't bold like Connie. This girl's got foreign blood in her. Her father was a sailor, and he brought her home with him, a baby. The mother was dead—he said."

"Mother—Mother!" he begged her. "Don't talk so—as if I was thinkin' of marriage—when I've only seen her tonight!"

"She was thinkin' of it—the likes of her always is," his mother retorted. "Here, give that child to me. Anything in breeches, that sort always looks at. Oh, Jonathan, you're to be a teacher, remember, and go up in the world! Edward won't be a candle to you if you go on without gettin' mixed up."

"I won't get mixed up, Mother," he muttered.

He gave Maggie to her and bent and in blind confusion began to unbutton Arthur's little shirt.

"Sleep in your drawers tonight, eh, Artie?" he said. "It's so late and you're that tired."

He drew Arthur's thin little body into the curve of his shoulder and went upstairs with him and laid him in the bed and covered him. Jamie was already asleep in the same bed. He had gone to bed dressed, and Jonathan began carefully to untie his shoes and then slipped them off without waking him. There was comfort in taking care of these small and helpless creatures.

I didn't do anything, he thought sorely, 'tidn't as if I went anywhere with the girl.

And then Ruth came stealing upstairs in her long flannel nightgown, and he tucked her into the cot in the same room.

"Kiss me good night, Jonnie," she begged him.

He bent and kissed her cheek and smelled the straw-sweet odor of her hair. She smelled different, even though she was only his sister Ruth, because she was a girl. Neither Jamie nor even Arthur would have begged him for a kiss or thrown arms about his neck when he gave it. Girls were different. He was a man. There was that in it which he did not understand. He went downstairs, feeling there was something between himself and his mother now that separated them until eternity. He would never be near her again. He did not know how to get near her any more. He had done nothing, and yet he had done everything.

He went miserably downstairs to find that she had apparently forgotten him. She was sitting by the fire still in her good brown dress. But she had put Maggie to bed and taken off her own bonnet and cape.

"I dunno," she said sadly. "I dunno but what we'll have to go to America, after all. He's not comin' back, Jonathan. I can tell it."

They looked at each other.

"Wait, Mother," he begged. Somehow now more than ever he did not want to leave England. "Wait till the spring comes."

His mother turned her head away from him. "Spring'll only make me want him more," she whispered. "I'm daft for him, Jonathan."

He could not answer. All that he did not know forced itself upon his consciousness. Night and his father and his mother, music and dancing with Connie's supple, plump body in his arms, and the circles of her bosom when he looked down and the smell of Ruth's hair and all the pull between human beings which he felt and could not understand. Millie and Edward on their wedding night! He thought of them and turned his mind away in self-disgust, and saw them still and loathed the sight.

"Whatever you say, Mother," he said in a low voice.

"You wouldn't mind, would you, Jonathan?" she said.

"Why should I be the one to say, Mother?" he replied.

"Lads usually like adventure and all," she said, beseeching him.

He thought of the sea with hatred. He had never liked the sea, even the bit of it he saw at Blackpool. And beyond it were thousands of acres of land. Twenty acres had been too much. Twenty acres of land had taught him he wanted to teach school.

"Everybody says I'm lucky to have so many sons to put on the land," his father had written. . . .

"It's likely be fun for you," his mother said.

He looked away from her. He felt somehow that he had made her suddenly want to go, he and Connie, though he had done nothing.

"Maybe," he said bleakly.

There were in Dentwater countless small things he had not noticed until now that he must leave them, and each became precious. If he had been asked what he hated most to leave, he would have wavered between the hours he spent at his desk by a window in the schoolroom, and those in the kitchen of the cottage, especially the hours in the evenings when the curtains were drawn, or in the rare mornings when, because he could see the ships on the Irish Sea, he knew when he went downstairs the sun would be shining across the brick floor. From the window in the schoolroom there was very little view—a few old graves in a corner of the churchyard and then the gray wall of the church. But even this bit of view seemed dear when he knew that soon he would not see it again. He had never cared greatly for church because he did not like the vicar's wife. He knew his mother was shy because of this elderly woman and did not like to go to church when she had nothing to put in the collection box.

"Mrs. Clemony looks at me that sharp!" she said. "I daresay she thinks I ought to be a better manager. But I manage the best I can. 'Tidn't as if I had anything regular coming in like she does."

He had therefore a strong dislike for Mrs. Clemony, a tall skeleton of a woman always in black silk. Of the vicar he never thought unkindly and not much at all, because no one did. He was a vague sort of a man who never came out of the mists except to climb into his pulpit. Usually he mumbled over the sermons he wrote out on half-sheets of paper, but sometimes he was upset about something, and then he had no paper but preached out of his head, and then everybody listened to him, though no one could imagine why he was so excited. Why, for instance, should an old man whose white hair floated like a fog about his bald crown shout and wave his sticks of arms in the pulpit and groan that God would punish England because of what Englishmen were doing to the blacks in India? It was not as if anybody in Dentwater had anything to do with such things. Jonathan, hearing the talk after church, felt ashamed because he had been secretly moved by what the vicar had said.

"Suppose them blacks do feel things the same as us?" he had once asked his mother when he went home to dinner.

"Those," she corrected, and forgot to answer the rest of it.

On their last Sunday Mr. Clemony had come into the pulpit, and the moment he lifted his head after invocation they knew he was in one of his rare fits. But this time he began talking about the wildest thing he had ever talked about—"disarmament," he called it, everybody agreeing together not to make guns—and then he ended by praying for Lord Clarendon. Who was Lord Clarendon?

After church the men gathered in the churchyard in the weak sunshine of a mild day in late February to talk about it.

"Fair crazy, I calls it," Mr. Haynes, the butcher, said. He plucked a bit of dried grass from a forgotten grave and chewed it. ". . . when Proosia is thinkin' how to cut us up proper. If so be this Lord Clarendon's thinkin' like that, why, England's goin' to the dogs, I say." He spat and looked as gloomy as his round red face allowed.

Jonathan, hanging about with the other older boys on the outskirts of the men, listened to this not so much for what it meant as for sorrow that on another Sunday he would not be here but on the sea. It was like thinking of how it would be if he were to die. Everything would go on exactly as it now did, only he would not be there.

At the dinner table he said out of his thoughts, "I'm glad the vicar had one of his days today, Mother. I like to remember him the way he was this mornin', his hair stickin' out and his eyes like lights."

"Queer how he looks two men," his mother agreed, "so shadowy when he doesn't care what he says and today like a lighted torch."

So now, though he did not mind never seeing Mrs. Clemony again, he did mind not seeing the old vicar any more. By the time he ever could come back to England, such a frail old gentleman would be gone, and he'd never hear him get excited and preach a real sermon again maybe.

It all became a melancholy death of many moments which Jonathan scarcely knew he had loved until now. Mr. Hopkins, who could be so sharp when he missed the ending of an irregular Latin verb, seemed now always to be gentle, and his furrowed, too-early-aging face less irritable than ever it had been. His very desk seemed impossible to leave behind, and the big inkstain upon it dear and familiar. Archie Bainter he had in his private heart considered a poor sort of chap, always talking of running away and never doing it; and yet in those days he became intimate even with him and found that Archie was a troubled soul who was afraid of himself because he had such dark thoughts of his father so that he wanted to kill him and was afraid he would. He confessed this to Jonathan, his pallid face twitching and his hands trembling.

"I've wanted to tell somebody this long time, Jonnie, and didn't dare. Do you think I'm the same as a murderer according to the Bible?"

"No," Jonathan said quickly, "no, I don't." He hesitated and then felt it dishonest to accept this confession from Archie and say nothing himself. "Fact is," he said in a low voice, "I reckon I've been glad all winter that my dad's in America."

"Ah, but he don't drink," Archie said.

"No, he don't do that," Jonathan admitted.

He wanted to go on and say what he felt about his father's rough ways and his big talk, and yet these seemed unimportant when he remembered Mrs. Bainter, sometimes with a black eye, sometimes with a bandaged head.

"He's wrenched her wrist now," Archie muttered.

"I wouldn't stand it!" Jonathan said angrily. What he saw was not that untidy, gawky Mrs. Bainter, but his own mother, pretty and fragile and always neat in her little print dresses, her head hanging limp. He could hear her voice, "Oh, Clyde, you hurt me!"

"Fact is," he said to Archie, swallowing as he spoke, "I'm agoin' to America just for my mother, to see that my dad is good to her. Else I'd stay behind and let 'em go."

And as soon as he said it he knew that this really was why he was going, although until now it had not been clear to him. Of course he must go to America, so that she would have someone to defend her and take care of her. Quietly, as he thought of it, this became his duty. He had not seen Constance Favor since the night of the wedding. Now he resolutely forgot her.

4

WHAT his mother would have done had he not seen his duty clear, he did not think of asking himself. No sea had ever been so vile as this one, and there was not time to think about anything except the next immediate demand upon him from the three who were ill—his mother, Ruth, and Arthur. This left him Maggie, who, once she became established to the change, wanted nothing except to be on her feet. She had learned to run anywhere before they left Dentwater and would now run, though the ship heaved and threw her against the long lines of trunks in the steerage. Then she fell and wept, her din mercifully lost in the crash of the rough seas and the creaking of timbers. Whenever he could, Jonathan held her, though against her will, to save her bruises and cuts. But there was not much time even for this, except when he fed her upon his knee while he himself ate at the rough board tables where twice a day they dipped into the tin bowls of soup or stew or porridge which the sailors put down for the steerage. The rest of the time, his eye upon Maggie, he went from one to the other of the ones ill, or he ran to mitigate some damage Jamie had done.

"Dang you, Jamie," he cried one day when a steward came to tell him that Jamie had been caught upstairs in the saloon. He was goaded by weariness and worn by the foolish, incessant motion of the ship and by Jamie's impudence, which sea air had only sharpened. "I wish you was good and sick like the others is! Can you not stay where you're told and not go peekin' and peerin' into the first class where you don't belong?"

"I'm as good as the folk there," Jamie said, his freckles lost in a red flush.

" 'Tidn't whether you're as good as them or not," Jonathan answered, "it's whether you can pay."

Jamie, his flush drenching away, flung out at his older brother, "You

don't care what people thinks of us! You're just like a—a servant or somethin'—takin' things and never answerin'!"

"I don't take that from you, anyways!" Jonathan gave him a clip over
the head, and then, at Jamie's hurt astonishment, hated himself. "There,
give over, will you, Jamie? I don't want to be angered with you. On'y
you do allays say the thing that makes me so."

"I wish I was with my father!" Jamie cried, and choked and bit his lip.

"There you go again," Jonathan said. "You want to be with him because
he spoils you and leaves you to your own way."

This was interrupted by a weak cry from Artie. "Jonathan! Jonathan!"

"See to Maggie a minute, Jamie," Jonathan ordered the sulky boy. "She
went around the bend there."

And he hastened to the berth where Arthur lay at one end and Ruth
at the other. Ruth was sleeping, though it was midmorning, but the little
boy sat up, ghastly and white and retching. When he had vomited he lay
back, trembling and spent.

"I be so sick," he whispered faintly.

"You'll be better sure," Jonathan answered heartily, though he was
afraid to see the child's weakness. An hour ago he had persuaded him
to eat, but since they came aboard he had been able to keep nothing down.

"Shall I die?" he whispered again, turning up his great pale blue eyes
to see Jonathan's answer.

"Mercy on us, no!" Jonathan cried. He leaned over and took the small
bone-thin boy in his arms.

"I don't want to be put in a box and thrown in the water," the child
whispered, his eyes filling so that the tears overflowed them.

"Now, wherever did such notions come into your knowledge?" Jonathan
cried angrily. He was so miserable that he wanted to weep, and his only
refuge was anger.

"Jamie told me," Arthur answered.

"That Jamie!" Jonathan scolded. "Wait till I see him! I'll clip him harder
nor I did a minute ago. Lie down, Artie. I must go and find Maggie. Lie
still, or you'll wake Ruthie, and then she'll be sick, too. 'Tidn't but ten days
more. Today noon we're half gone. Then every hour brings us nearer the
good land."

"We don't have to go back no more, neither," Arthur said, faintly
cheered.

"No, never," Jonathan agreed, against his heart. To himself he said
steadily, "But I'll go back to England one day, when they're all growed
up and Mother's safe somewhere. Maybe she'll go back with me—just her
and me." He'd make her old age beautiful and full of peace if that happened. They wouldn't even go back to Dentwater. He'd find a good school,
say in Devonshire, and a cottage nicer than the one they had left, although
how dear it had seemed when they left it that morning, empty of them
and all their life! It was so mad a thing to do—to walk out of a door he

loved and lock it, knowing he would never enter it again! He peered into the upper berth where his mother lay. She was awake, the gray ship's blanket tucked under her chin.

"Is Maggie takin' her food?" she asked when her eyes met his.

"Like she was at home," he replied. "I don't give her the meat, though, Mother, even if she wants it."

"Give her a bit," she said apathetically. "She's a great one for meat— she'll eat it raw if you let her."

He longed to say something to comfort her and could think of nothing. "Don't you worry," was all he could imagine to say.

"I cannot," she replied simply. "I've not the strength for it."

Outside, the sea thundered and beat upon the sides of the ship so that it trembled in every joist and joint.

"Dear God!" his mother murmured and closed her eyes. Upon her forehead sweat broke out, and she pressed her lips together hard.

He had no time, and yet day and night were endless. There were many others in the crowded steerage who were going to America, but he had no time to talk with them or find out why they went. Most of them were families absorbed in themselves, but there were young men who were apparently alone. One of these slept in the berth next to Jonathan's, and that was the first face he saw every morning when he woke in the murky foul air. It was a blond English face, high-colored and big-nosed, handsome if one took it all into account, as belonging to a huge man. They struck up a sidewise sort of friendship, the man amused at Jonathan's troubles, and Jonathan struggling to pretend he was not nurse to three sick and all but father to Jamie and mother to Maggie.

"Has your hands full, hasn't you, young chap?" the young man asked good-humoredly. "Here, give us the little tyke."

The "little tyke" was Maggie, at that moment howling for food. He carried her off with him to the breakfast table and did not bring her back for an hour.

"Eats anything, don't she?" he said admiringly when he brought her back, smiling and full of food. "Ate my porridge with me after she'd done her own, drank my coffee, and would ha' smoked my pipe if I'd let her. She's my sort, she is—hearty-like."

He came back every now and again to ask for her and carry her off, and when on the last day they stood watching the harbor of New York come into view, he handed Jonathan a bit of paper whereupon he had written in a large round writing, "George Tenney, Screw Falls, Arkansas."

"Got an uncle there, with a sheep farm," he said. "Write to me, will you, boy? I'd like to keep up with that red-headed little tyke. I'm fond of her. Makes me laugh, she does."

Jonathan folded the paper and put it in his breast pocket and went down with Maggie in his arms. Now nothing seemed of importance except getting all the children together and ready to put their feet on land. His mother and Ruth were dressed and lying in their berths, waiting, and he put Maggie beside his mother. Jamie he had sequestered in a spot between two life boats, on a strict promise that he stay there until he was fetched.

His mother was piteously thin, but she had been able to dress herself behind the blanket Jonathan had strung around their corner. And Ruth had grown well enough to eat a little the last two days and keep it down. But Arthur's delicate system could not right itself. He lay, his shrunken face anxious with fear lest he be forgotten.

"Jonnie, you wouldn't go away and leave me, would you?" he begged in his little weak voice when Jonathan came to tell them New York lay on the edge of the sea.

"I shall hold you in my arms until we find Father," Jonathan promised, and he sat down on the berth beside the child.

He had told no one, but the great secret fear he had was that his father might not be there on the dock. They had had almost no money left after they paid for their tickets and cleared away the bits of bills they had at the butcher's and the baker's in Dentwater. The shop they had sold, good will and all, to a young couple just married in Dentwater, who were to come to live in the cottage after their honeymoon. Otherwise there would not have been enough for the bills.

He lifted Arthur up and wrapped him in a shawl and felt his heart thick with fear at the child's lightness and the looseness of his bones. Nothing seemed to hold them together.

"Put your arms about my neck, there's a good boy," he said, and felt Arthur's little arm creep about his neck and lie there as feebly as a shadow and scarcely more warm.

"Where's home, Jonnie?" Arthur inquired.

Jonathan stared down at him. "Danged if I know," he answered. "Anyways, somewhere in America."

If his father were not there to meet the ship, what would they do? I'll have to find work, he thought, as soon as ever I can.

He sat on the edge of the berth with the thin, clinging little boy in his arms. He was a grave youth of middle size and middling looks, neither dark nor fair, nor anything that one would remember. People were passing him quickly now, hurrying to the deck to see the approaching city. Still he sat there, dreading to see the new shores of America, until at last even they must go upstairs and be ready to leave the ship.

But Clyde was in the crowd, straining his eyes like all the rest for a glimpse of them. Jamie saw him first.

"I can see my dad!" he screamed joyfully.

"Where?" Mary cried.

She had been watching the dock, her lips tight and her eyes narrowed. She would not for any cause have told her children how fearful this new shore looked to her, a bare terrain, with none of the soft, fulsome green of England. She knew Blackpool was not beautiful, but, receding from them, it had seemed beautiful, set and surrounded with the new green of spring. But there were no trees here, nothing to hide a flat city scattering itself to the water's edge. It looked, for all its houses, somehow still wild and unsettled, as though the buildings had been thrown up in haste, to endure no more than a day. And this, Clyde had told her, was the biggest city in America! Then all else must be wilderness indeed. Around her people were laughing and shrieking with excitment. But she felt only a huge mounting certainty within her.

I shall never see England again, she was thinking. And then she heard Jamie's scream and cried out and followed with her eyes the line of his small forefinger and saw Clyde.

The certainty turned less dark without leaving her. "Yes, that's him," she answered, and said nothing when Jamie tore himself loose from her hand and burrowed his way through the crowd like a mole underground and climbed the rail and, holding onto a post, screeched at his father, "Hello there, Dad! Dad—Dad!"

"Go and hold him by the legs, Ruthie," she said.

Now that she could see Clyde's face coming slowly clear, the certainty seemed less crushing by the moment. She lifted Maggie, clinging to her knees, and held her up, her arms still weak from her seasickness.

"See your daddy, Maggie!" she said.

She could see him now quite plainly. He wore the same suit in which he had left England. But it had been a good rough brown tweed, bought to last. His face was redder than it had been. That would be the sun and winds. He had spoken of the unending dry winds, but she could not imagine them. He was heavier than she remembered him, thicker and more solid. Maybe the hard work had done him good. She felt a shy, unwilling joy steal over her as she looked at him. A woman had to follow her man. She had done what was right. It would not have been well if she had refused to leave England, or had made him stay. He would have blamed her for every failure after. Now she was always in the stronger position, having done what he wanted her to do. It would not be her fault, whatever happened. She felt lightened and suddenly easier than she had felt in many months. That was the way a woman ought to feel when she could lean upon the man.

Then she was aware of something fastened upon her face, a heat and a pull, and she turned without will and found herself caught in the gaze of Jonathan's eyes, fixed upon her face. She could not understand this look, but instantly she was uncomfortable under it, and he felt her discomfort and looked away.

"Anyway, he's here!" she said defiantly, though why should she need to be defiant to her son about his father?

"Yes, he's here," Jonathan agreed, and voice and eyes and expression became as colorless as a mist. Behind that hiding mist he was not so much thinking as feeling, with a sick disgust that still was of heat and not of cold, that when these two who were his parents came together it would be the same thing all over again. His mother would always yield to his father. She had yielded even in being here. In his arms Arthur cried, astonished, "Why are you shakin', Jonnie?"

" 'Cause you're a mortal heavy load," Jonathan said gravely, and set him down abruptly.

Now that he had them all here, Clyde Goodliffe could not do enough for them. He was a different man; they all felt it at once and saw it in the look of his face, in the freedom of his movements. In England he had gone sullen and slouching, and when he spoke he was either reckless or surly. The recklessness had become a loud gaiety, and the surliness was gone. He had pushed his way onto the ship almost before the ropes were thrown out to hold her to the pier. He was there, and he lifted his wife off her feet and kissed her while she clung to him. Maggie was frightened and then angry and burst into weeping, and Arthur clung for a little moment to Jonathan because his father seemed a strange man. But Ruth and Jamie fell upon him and seized his legs, and then he was hugging them all, even Jonathan; and Jonathan, feeling the warm, strong clasp about his shoulders, let his doubts die a little. Maybe America had done his father good, and maybe they would all be happier.

"Dang me, if this idn't the happiest day of our lives, Mary!" Clyde shouted. "Better even than our wedding day for me! Everything is wunnerful, lass! Drought's broke out there. We've come just right. Wheat's headin' out, and it don't matter now if dryness does come back a while. We're sure. Hunnerds of acres, Mary, all stannin' even in wheat—hard red wheat like England never saw!"

"Thought you said it was corn, Clyde," she said.

"Corn's wheat here," he explained, "and maize is corn."

"Is it, now!" she cried, laughing. "Whatever made 'em get that mixed!"

They all laughed, and Maggie stopped crying.

"Now then, to the hotel," Clyde said. "I got two rooms for us there."

"But we're not stoppin' here, are we, Clyde?" Mary asked.

"To see the New York sights, we are," he replied. "We'll not be back East in a long time, Mary, and I've planned three days' good time before we take the train. Come, Magsie, to your dad."

He stooped to pick up Maggie, but she would not have him. Instead she clung to Jonathan's leg. They saw then the first glimpse of the old Clyde.

"Dang the brat!" he said with strong irritation. "She's not glad to see me!"

"She's wee, yet—that's all," his wife said quickly.

"Silly, I call it," he said carelessly, and turned away from her. "Come, Jamie," he said, "you and me against 'em all!"

The three of them went off, Jamie between his parents; and Maggie, seeing her mother go with this man, looked up at Jonathan and puckered her face and opened her mouth to cry.

"Don't cry," he said briefly. "I'll carry you." Stooping, he took her up in his arms and followed behind the family, Ruth clinging to one side of his coat and Arthur to her hand.

Long before three days were gone Maggie had forgotten that she was ever afraid of her father. They had all forgotten everything that had ever been unhappy, and they all believed in him. For the first time in his life Clyde Goodliffe felt himself head of his own family. Every day he decided what they would do and what they would see, and they followed him in a sort of joyful dream.

"Now you listen to me," he proclaimed. "I been plannin' this all winter long, how it'd be. I've it all fixed."

"But it oughn't to cost too much, Clyde," his wife cried.

"Shut up, Mary!" he cried back at her, but with laughter. "It's me has made the money—it's my money from now on. There's more where this came from. Besides, just lookin' don't cost money, do it?"

In the three days it was the looking that she liked best. All of the children except Jamie were held back a little by her secret fear of cost, increased for them by Jonathan's silence when he felt her fear. Once this made Clyde angry. They had been walking the streets and had paused in front of a great hotel.

"Look at it!" he cried, as though he had made it. "Six stories high, it is, not counting the fresco around the top and chimneys!"

They stood in front of it, staring upward. Jamie began counting.

"One—two—three—four—five—yes, it's six, Father!"

"Carlton House." Mary Goodliffe read aloud the name over the door.

A man in a bright blue uniform with many brass buttons looked at them kindly.

"English, ain't you?" he asked through his nose.

"They're just from there," Clyde said, and added quickly, "but I'm from Kansas."

"I reckon you don't see anything like that out in Kansas, though," the man said, nodding at the building.

"Not yet," Clyde admitted, "but it'll come some day."

The man looked doubtful and changed the subject. "I reckon you've heard of Charles Dickens?" he inquired.

"We have," Mary replied. "It would be queer English folk not to know him."

The man kept an important silence, then spat before he spoke. "Once when I was a young feller just come to this job, he et here," he declared.

"No, never!" Jonathan exclaimed. He gazed up at the building.

"Such a crowd as we've never had since," the man said. "All the big fellows and their ladies. He was a little fellow himself, but he had big black eyes, and a way of lookin' as though he was ready to bust out laffin!"

"Jonathan!" his mother breathed. "Think of that!"

"He come back two years ago," the man went on, enjoying the effect upon her. "But he was sick then. People said he was yellow and wrinkled and not the same man. Nobody saw him oncet."

Mary Goodliffe was not listening. She turned to Jonathan.

"It makes me feel we aren't so far from England," she said dreamily.

"It does," he agreed.

Time after time he had read aloud to her out of the paper pieces of stories Mr. Dickens had written. They were never able to buy them all so there were large parts they skipped. But Jonathan saved anything he found with them in, and Mr. Hopkins had sometimes given him papers he had bought.

"We s'all have dinner here ourselves, then," Clyde Goodliffe announced. "What does it cost, my chap?"

"Too much, with all them kids," the man said. "That is, if you're thinkin' of the big dinin' room where he et. The coffee shop, of course, wouldn't be so bad—"

"Oh, no, Clyde, please!" Mary begged. "Don't let's—we aren't fit to go in such a place."

"This ain't England," he retorted. "We're as good as anybody here."

"That's right," the man put in, grinning. "It's only if you can pay for it. That's all we ask."

"I can pay for it, right enough—" Clyde began.

But Mary interrupted him. "Clyde, you talk like a rightdown fool. We're plain people, and you know it—and I know it. This idn't for us. If you want to eat there, go on and eat alone. The children and I'll find a public house or a little inn. Come, Jonathan—bring the little ones. Your father's out of his head."

And she marched down the street, her head up, one hand leading Maggie and the other Arthur, and Jamie and Ruth longing and uncertain.

For once Jonathan was sorry for his father. "Reckon we'll have to go," he said, apologizing for his mother.

But Clyde caught up with her in three strides and began his furious argument with her, an argument which began that day and was to go on to the day she died.

"You don't unnerstand how it is in Americky, Mary!"

"I understand what's right and fittin' to my station in life that I'm content with because I was born in it!"

"There ain't no high and low here!"

"Who's talkin' about high and low? It's folly and sense I'm talkin' about. And it'd be folly for us to push ourselves into that big fine place—us eatin' in there!"

"But we're as good as anybody!"

"Don't be a born fool, Clyde Goodliffe! My father was a shopkeeper and yours was a hired shepherd!"

"It don't matter here."

"It matters everywhere, so long as the world stands, and no shame to us or anybody."

"You're the same as you allays was—full of gloom and darkness and pullin' a man down where he was again when he gets himself up a little!"

"Wisest, if he gets where he don't belong!"

Even the sharp bright sunshine of New York, such sunshine as they had never seen before, was dimmed by the ferocity of this argument, until Mary Goodliffe, looking by chance at the shadowed young faces of her children, ceased it abruptly.

"Here's a place says beef stew for ten cents, and I could eat it fine," she announced.

And a moment later they were sitting around a clean, unpainted table in a room half underground, and a fat woman in a checked blue and white apron was saying kindly, "Sure, you can take one portion for the two little ones, and they kin have all the milk they want for nothin'. The boy looks pindlin'. You must eat plenty, little feller, and catch up with the rest of 'em."

She smiled at Arthur and planked thick white dishes upon the table.

"Here's where we belong," Mary said firmly, "and all of America won't make me believe different."

No one answered her, and so she relented, and in a few minutes it seemed all over, and she was feeding Maggie bread dipped in stew gravy.

Within herself she was thinking with inevitable remorse: I'm too hard on him—he meant to please me; and her eyes, soft with this remorse, looked at her husband.

"Would you like to treat us to a bit of that queer cold pudding?" she asked.

"Do you have ice cream?" Clyde asked the woman.

"Sure we do," she answered.

"Then ice cream for everybody," he ordered.

Then in showing off how he liked the frozen stuff which they ate so gingerly and with such astonishment, he forgot to be sullen any more, and when they came out and he hailed a passing horse car and they all climbed in, Mary held her peace and let him pay for everybody except for the two little ones. But even this she did in a whisper.

"You take Arthur, Jonathan, and I'll take Maggie. There's no use in payin' for them."

"Where are we going, Clyde?" she asked aloud when the car began its jolting way.

"To the Battery, to see the Aquarium," he said proudly.

"Well, if that's what you say," she agreed, and sat looking as peaceful and yielding as though she had never told her husband he could be wrong.

Jonathan, always watching her, caught her eye. She leaned over to him. "We'll just let your father enjoy himself," she whispered.

Her eyes, looking into his, were bright with tender laughter. He felt drawn to her, close to her, moved by their secret mutual understanding of this huge child of a man who must be humored and circumvented without his knowing it. And in this partnership for the moment he was happy again.

5

THE TRAIN rocked and jumped beneath them, swerving and bending and swaying. None of them had ever been on a train before.

"It does seem to me it doesn't need to go so mortal fast," Mary murmured. She was sitting upon the dust-filled, plush-covered seat, with Arthur's head in her lap. He was feverish, and his lips were black with parch.

"You'll find everything's fast in Ameriky," Clyde boasted. He was as restless as Jamie, who now was occupying himself by swinging up and down the car between the seats. The car was full of people—all, it seemed, with children, so none could mind another's child. "You sud be thankful you've a train to go on," he went on, folding and unfolding his legs. " 'Tidn't so many years since folks went West in covered wagons—do yet in some parts."

"No part I'd go to," Mary retorted.

" 'Tidn't too bad, Mary," he argued. "It's like a big picnic, the old folks say. They camp together every night and spread theirselves in a circle against the Indians, and inside they make a big fire and cook their food, and everybody is chummy-like."

Jamie, swinging past, caught the word "Indians."

"Shan't we never see Indians, Dad?" he inquired sadly.

"There's always talk of 'em," Clyde said. "But such few Indians as I see in Kansas don't look more excitable than ones that have been well beat. It's past me how folks was ever skeered of 'em."

He had told them they were going to a town called Median. It was a fine place, new and small as yet, but full of promise.

"You'd not be gettin' me there with all this family if they were still wild," his wife replied. She glanced at Jonathan. "Jonnie, fetch me a bit of water again, there's a dear good boy."

Jonathan rose from the seat where he sat beside his father and walked unsteadily down the aisle, thrown from side to side as he went. At the end was the water cooler, now nearly empty of its tepid supply. He filled the tin cup half-full, and then the slow stream ran dry. But it was late afternoon, and before sunset they would stop somewhere on this wild flat plain and draw water from a reservoir set like a sentinel tower in a desert. He guarded the cup, trying to catch the movement of the train and save its spilling.

"Here's all until we stop to fill up," he said to his mother.

"Then I'll dip a clean handkerchief in it and wet Artie's lips while he sleeps," she replied.

In the morning the bustle of people getting washed and fed and ready for the day made the car tolerable, but as evening came on and they were at the threshold of another night of discomfort, gloom fell upon them all.

"See what's left in the basket for Maggie, Jonathan," she said. "Best feed 'em all, maybe, before it's dark."

Jonathan opened the big wicker basket they had bought in New York and filled with bread and salt meat and cheese and fruit and preserved foods. Everything fresh was gone in these four days they had been on the train. But by now Maggie had proved her ability to digest anything. She took a wedge of bread and ham from Jonathan and sat down in the middle of the aisle to eat it, unconcerned by the procession of legs that stepped over and around her.

Jamie took his and gnawed it, his face pressed against the dirty windowpane. But when Jonathan gave some to Ruth, she shook her head. She was sitting quietly, her hand against her cheek.

"What's wrong?" he asked.

"Toothache," she whispered.

"Is that why you're so still, sittin' there with your back to us?" he exclaimed.

She nodded, and at his look and voice of sympathy, her eyes swam in tears.

"It's hurt me the day long," she said in the same whisper.

"And you didn't tell," he exclaimed.

"I didn't want to bother," she confessed. "Not when Artie's so fevered."

"But you could have told me," he reproached her. "It would have eased you, and maybe I could think of something."

Her lips trembled, and she wiped her eyes and did not answer.

"Wait a minute," he said.

He remembered that during the day he had several times seen a hard-faced man four seats away drink from a whisky bottle he took from his pocket. He had expected to see the man grow fuddled, but nothing of the sort had happened. He had gone on playing cards with three other men, hour after hour, in fierce concentration. He was still playing now as Jonathan drew near.

"I ask your pardon," he said sturdily. He hated talking to strangers, but he could do it if he had it to do. He touched the man on the arm, and for an instant the man looked up at him out of hard blue eyes.

"Whatcha want, boy?" he asked in a drawling nasal voice.

"My little sister has the toothache," Jonathan answered. "Could you let her have a drop of that whisky to hold in her mouth against it?"

"Sure it's your sister has the toothache?" the man inquired.

The other three men, bearded dirty fellows, laughed.

"It's her, right enough," Jonathan said calmly.

"I never refuse a lady," the man replied. He drew out his bottle and handed it to Jonathan and went back to his cards. And Jonathan, tipping Ruth's chin, poured a little of the hot raw stuff into her mouth. She gave a small scream of pain, but he encouraged her.

"Bear it, Ruthie—bear it a moment only and 'twill help. I've done it myself. It's bad, but if you bear it, the ache grows numb, and then it's wunnerful easy for a while."

He corked the bottle and wiped her quivering face with her skirt and then carried the bottle back. The man paused one moment to glance at it.

"Looks like the truth," he said carelessly, and thrust it into his pocket again.

Now the smoky oil lamps were lit, and instantly darkness snatched the landscape away, and another night was upon them. One seat Clyde Goodliffe took for himself, his legs hanging into the aisle. Maggie slept on a rug put down on the floor between two seats. Mary sat immovable with the sick boy's head on her knees, and upon another seat Jamie lay against Ruth. The whisky had made her tooth numb, as Jonathan said it would, and she was sleepy with relief, and her head drooped against Jamie's. Jonathan sat opposite them, half-asleep, too, but waking every little while to look across at his mother.

So the hours dragged over them. Once he rose to go over to his mother. "Shan't I take Artie on my lap so you can stretch out?" he asked.

But she shook her head, looking down at the little boy in her arms. "I don't like this long sleep," she said. "It's more as if he was unconscious-like."

Their eyes met in mutual anxiety.

"We'll get the doctor to him the minute we get to Median," Jonathan promised her.

"Aye, but is there a doctor?" she retorted.

"There must be in such a town," he said.

He lingered a moment and then went back to his place. People were sleeping everywhere in foolish helplessness. They looked like creatures in a nightmare, he thought. Once in Mr. Hopkins's room when he had stopped for tea he had seen a book of pictures of people in hell. They had looked like these people, sprawling in the convulsions of uncomforting sleep. He sat wide awake while the train bolted them all through darkness to their unknown end.

The train did not go to Median. They must get off at Fort Thomas, and drive from there all day in what Clyde called a hack.

"A wagon-like with a top," he explained to them.

The long journey was over, and they were sitting, as tidy as they could make themselves, ready to get off, all except Arthur, who lay in his lassitude, his head on his mother's lap. He was no better, and yet no worse. Today indeed, and now, he seemed even a little better. He had asked for an egg.

"There idn't an egg here, my love," his mother replied. "But surely there'll be one when we get there. Your dad'll find you one, won't he?"

"Surely will," Clyde replied heartily. "An' a few days of sun and wind'll cure 'im. Never was such a country for sun and wind."

"That I believe," his wife replied. All the days had been full of hard bright sunshine. Her head indeed ached with the light.

"The sky is surely bigger here than it was at home," she said now, gazing out of the window.

" 'Tis only there's nothing between us and it," Clyde said.

No hill, no tree, no rise of any sort, indeed, cut off the sky from this earth. The earth lay flat and pressed down around its circular edge by the weight of the sky, heavy and metal-blue by day, and star-sprinkled steel by night. The sky was infinitely more important here than the earth. For the earth was unchanging. Nothing stopped the eye for mile upon mile of even green grass. The handful of houses that made a town were meaningless and passing. The sky was the pageant. The eye went to it again and again. Stars were of enormous size and shining color, and the moon by night was a spectacle. Sunrise and sunset were hidden by nothing and flung out their color like the flags of armies in the sky. There must be noise somehow to such color, Jonathan thought, staring half-fearfully night and morning at the skies. But when the train stopped, the silence was profound. At midday there was nothing between sky and earth. They shivered with cold in the night and morning, and at noon were at the mercy of the merciless sun; and women and children grew sick with heat. There had been no rain since they landed.

But now it was all over. As the time drew near for them to reach Fort Thomas, other passengers came up to bid them good-by. Half of them had already got off in one place or another, and as they left had given away what remained of food to those going farther. Now Mary also divided bread and meat among those who went still farther, keeping only what they might need before nightfall when they would have supper in Median.

It was early morning. Clyde Goodliffe pointed to a few dots ahead and to the right of them.

"It's there," he said. "That's the Fort."

"Why is it a fort, Dad?" Jamie asked.

"They had 'em against the Indians once," his father explained. "There's forts all the way to California—regular hand-over-fist string of 'em. 'Course they're not wanted now."

"It idn't much of a place," Jonathan said doubtfully.

The train was galloping along, and he could see a scattering of un-painted wooden shacks. If Median looked like this, what would he do? He realized that in his mind Median had come to be something like a new Dentwater, a neat little village with a church and a school and a post office, maybe, and the houses tidy-looking with their gardens held behind painted fences.

" 'Tidn't any reason why a fort should be big in these days," Clyde retorted. He picked Arthur up in his arms. The train was slowing down. "After me, now, all of you," he ordered.

Jonathan took Maggie on one arm and the big basket on the other, and all together they stood, holding their belongings. Kindly people helped them, and the man who had given the whisky for Ruth came up, hitching his pants over his hips.

"Toothache still gone, sister?" he shouted, and when she nodded, too shy to do more, he laughed. "Whisky's good for 'most anything in these parts," he said. He was on his way to Oregon. Kansas, he said, was too civilized for him. He had come lounging by to talk to them sometimes.

"Well, I'm plain glad to hear 'tis civilized," Mary Goodliffe said. "I don't desire to live in savagery."

"Kansas don't suit me, though, ma'am," he said. "Too many people."

He spat upon the floor a great blob of brown spittle, and she looked away and whispered fiercely to Jonathan, "Don't let the children step in it—oh, the dirty beast!" She pressed her lips together and gazed resolutely out of the window, and Jonathan could see she was determined not to be sick.

"Clyde Goodliffe," she said in a low fierce voice, "if you ever take to chewing that stuff, we'll not live in the same house longer!"

Clyde had burst out laughing. "I've tried it, though, lass. But I don't like it, luckily, if to chew would make me a grass widower."

"Filthy, nasty, hateful!" she cried.

"Well—well," he said, pacifying her, "but good men do it, you'll find, Mary."

"I don't believe it," she retorted.

But the tall chap was very good to them now. He helped Ruth to the wooden platform and went back for their bundles and boxes until every-thing was piled around them, and swung himself on the train just in time, yelling to Jamie as the train carried him away, "When you're growed up, come West, boy!" A likable chap, Jonathan thought, though upon the plat-form he had left behind him his blobs of spittle, too, so that they had to heed them.

"Now wait here at the station till I see if Harvey Blake's got the hack ready," Clyde told them. "I ordered it before I went, but there's no tellin' what's happened between then and now."

"Give me Artie," Mary said. She sat down on a bundle and put out her arms for him.

Around the dusty platform had been standing six or seven men and three women. At every station there had been such people coming out of the unpainted wooden houses to stand in slack silence and stare at the train. They all looked the same, colored an even hue by weather, their flesh seasoned and dried by it. They were not Indians, and yet Jonathan was surprised when now one of the women came forward and said in a soft voice, "Is the little feller sick?" A foreign tongue would not have surprised him.

"Thank you kindly," his mother answered. "It was the sea upset him. He was that seasick he hasn't got over it."

"Where you goin'?" the woman asked again.

"To Median."

"Would it please you to come and lay the little feller on my bed? That's my shack there."

"No, thank you," Mary said, half-alarmed. "We must be getting on."

"Are you from around here?" the woman asked with a sort of gentle hunger in her voice as though it were pleasant to her merely to talk. She was looking at Mary's garments as she spoke.

"We're from England," Mary said primly.

Jonathan could feel her deciding against this woman with the withered, haggard face and sweet voice. After all, he could feel her thinking, this was a stranger. The woman felt it, too.

"Well, I'll be going," she said vaguely. "I'm real sorry about the little boy."

She drifted back toward one of the houses, and one by one the little group followed her until they were alone again.

"Are we home where we're going?" Arthur asked, and opened his eyes to inquire.

"Not yet, lovey," she answered.

She drew an edge of her shawl over his face to shield him from the sun. But mercifully at this moment great masses of billowing silver-edged cloud had come up and were floating between them and the sun, the first clouds they had seen for days. Between them the heat was dry and searing. They watched for the next cloud, and when its edge touched the sun it was like something cool and wet upon their flesh.

"I wish them huge big ones stuck there would come up," Jamie cried.

He pointed with his finger to the horizon, where a massy base of dark-gray cloud, silvery-white, piled up and up into rounded peaks and turrets. But they seemed immovable, so huge were they and so secure.

"They look stormy, or would in England," Mary said. "But the clouds have such space here I can't tell their meaning. They're merciful now, though."

They sat gratefully under the shade of a cloud as it passed across the sun, and then, before it was gone, Clyde was there with the hack. He was driving its two horses himself.

"There's a chap in Median wants to come back tomorrow," he explained. "So I'm to take it over, and he'll bring it back. Harvey don't want to take the time. Thinks a storm is brewin' and wants his hay in."

He paused and looked at the sky with strange anxiety. "If it wasn't for Artie, I'd say wait and see what the storm is," he said.

Mary Goodliffe looked up in surprise. "A summer storm won't kill us," she said.

"Storms here are bigger than what you're used to," he answered.

"I'll take the chance of storm rather than this child another night with no doctoring," she said decidedly.

"Well, I reckon it's best," Clyde admitted.

He got down and packed in their bundles and bags and the small trunk, and then they all got in and the horses began moving steadily across the flat green country—a green which the two dusty ruts that made the road scarcely broke, for between them the same grass grew.

The stillness was intense, except for the soft clip-clop of the horses' feet in the deep dust, a stillness felt and heard. It was more than absence of sound. It had weight and pressure, and nothing moved except them as they went across the endless green.

"There idn't a solitary tree," Jonathan said after a long while. And it was an effort to lift his voice against the silence.

No one spoke. He saw then that they were all half-asleep. Even his father, nodding, held the reins slack in his hands. But the horses seemed used to this and went steadily on. There was, indeed, no choice for them, since there was only the one road and no other crossed it. The pure air, the warmth, the slow rhythm of the wagon's movement had calmed them into sleep. But Jonathan had never felt farther from sleep. He felt oppressed and strange and half-afraid. Everything was too big here. In England one knew the sea held the land together, so there was an end to it. It was a fence around a field, and all within the fence belonged to you. But here the land went on and on. No one could possess it. Even if you cut off a piece of it, there would be all the rest.

He sat holding Maggie, now sleeping, and felt afraid to be the only one awake. For to his horror the great shining mass of cloud which had looked so immovable upon the horizon began now to swell and grow and spread out into brighter edges and higher peaks and more glittering towers. And the land which had lain so quiescent began to break into movement, or it seemed movement, though he knew it was only the quickly moving light and shade upon the green. But how could green look so dangerous and livid when there was no sun upon it? While he stared, the grass began to shiver and ripple as though the earth quaked beneath it. Was it the earth that rumbled? He heard a deep soft roar.

"Father!" he screamed. At the sound of his scream Maggie woke with loud crying and they were all awake.

"Hey!" Clyde shouted. He wiped his hand across his mouth. One of the horses tossed its head and whinnied.

"Father, look!" Jonathan cried. He pointed at the sky.

"Oh, it's goin' to come, after all," Clyde said, peering out. "Harvey said it would. I'd better get out the curtains and be ready."

They stopped, and from under a seat he brought out oilcloth curtains. "Help me, lads," he ordered.

Jonathan put Maggie, still crying, upon Ruth's knee, and he and Jamie fumbled at the curtains.

"Like this, butterfingers," Clyde commanded.

In a moment Jonathan had the way of it and was fastening them more quickly than his father did. He was compelled by terror. He had never in his life been so terrified. By seconds the sky had blackened, all except the horrible scarified edge of silver to the black clouds, all except such lightning as he had never seen in his life. The lightning in English skies was soft torchlight compared to the great furious rents which this lightning tore in the sky, and the thunder muffled drums compared to this crash heaped upon crash. He felt his sweat pouring down him, his tongue dry, his eyeballs tight in their sockets. Self-respect, pride, everything left him except terror. He wanted to run as fast as he could, anywhere. But his legs were lifeless, and he could not breathe. He felt his head swim. He barely heard his father's voice crying down the roar, "Now in with us all —here's the rain!"

He could barely crawl into the last curtain left open. His mother screamed at the sight of him.

"What's wrong with you, Jonathan?"

He could not answer. All his being was caught and held in a spasm.

"Clyde—Clyde—Jonathan's gone daft!"

He saw them turn to stare at him. But he could not speak, not while about him this crash and roar went on. And now here were the wind and the rain, a waterfall of rain, rain that dripped and ran through every crack. The horses were standing still, no more able to keep on their way.

He felt a sharp, strong slap on his cheek, and to his shame and agony, he burst into weeping. His father had struck him.

"Come to!" he ordered.

"Clyde Goodliffe!" Mary cried.

"Shut up, Mary," he said. "It's the thing to do—the lad's about to go out of himself with fright. He'll cry a minute and be himself."

But he was not himself. He kept shivering and crying, though he tried to hold himself back. Every time the lightning sprang at him and the thunder beat upon him, his being dissolved, and he lost himself. He could see even his mother only dimly. She was distressed for him and frightened herself, but he could do nothing for her because his being was dissolved. Only at last, when the thunder grew less and the rain went on like a dark wave, could he begin to gather himself together again.

They let him mercifully alone. He had frightened the children, and they sat staring at him. His father took off the curtains without speaking to him, and his mother found a towel and handed it to him.

"Wipe your face and head, Jonathan, love," she said tenderly. "You're wet with your sweat, and the air's cool. A terrible, terrible storm," she added kindly. "We were all scared of it."

He did not answer out of the depths of his shame. The horses, wet and shining, took up their way again, and the clouds retreated once more. He did not know what had happened to him. He sat, helpless in his exhaustion. After a long time his mother turned to him.

"Are you better?" she asked gently.

He nodded, and then he wanted to speak, but did not know how to explain anything.

"I was struck-like," he said.

"Not by lightning, or you'd not be able to say it," his father put in.

"No," Jonathan replied.

Then after a moment he admitted his enemy, a new enemy in this land.

"I reckon I was plain down scared," he said in a low voice.

"I reckon," his father said dryly.

"We must find a doctor for Artie at once, Clyde," Mary said an hour later. She swayed as she spoke, trying to take up in her own body the unevenness of the muddy road.

"Oh, he'll right himself in this air," Clyde said heartily. "Wunnerful air it is. There's hardly no doctors can do business in it."

He did not want to tell her that there was not a doctor near Median. Time enough for everything, now that she was here. Besides, it was true that people were healthy. The lad would pick up now that he was off the sea. He turned his mind to his plans—big plans they were, and he was glad to see Jonathan had grown to be a man and could help him. It was queer, though, the scare he took in the storm. He glanced at his son as he sat beside him. A little on the small side, he thought. Jonathan would never be as big as his dad.

"Want to take the horses a bit?" he inquired.

"No, thanks, Father," Jonathan said. "I've not driven 'em like this before."

"Take 'em," Clyde said shortly and threw him the reins.

Jonathan bit his lip, but he took them; and the horses, seeming to feel the change in the grip, tossed their heads and tried to quicken their pace. It was impossible. The mud dragged at the wheels. But Jonathan, not yet knowing that mud, sat erect and silent, his heart beating against his father.

Clyde watched him. A pale dinky man Jonathan would make, he was thinking. Mary had put her smallness upon him. Edward was the better of the two.

"Did Edward say he'd be comin'?" he asked abruptly.

"Not a word," Jonathan replied, without turning his head.

"Edward's fixed well," Mary put in. "Some day maybe we'll be thankful there's one lad at home with a good shop."

"This is home now," Clyde retorted.

A strange wide place for a home, then, Jonathan thought. The heavy leather reins pulled at his hands. He threw a quick glance to the right and to the left. Ahead or aside, everything looked the same. The country was flat under the long waving grass. The road was two muddy ruts dividing north from south. Ahead of them the sun poured through a crack in the clouds a clear yellow light over the wet grass.

"Can't we see Median yet?" he asked.

"You can see it if you look at it," Clyde retorted. He nodded, and they all looked ahead. Against the yellow sky a low rectangular roof rose a few feet above the horizon, and another and another, until there were perhaps half a dozen.

"Them!" Jonathan said in a low voice.

"That's never Median!" his mother cried.

"Median it is," Clyde said half-sullenly. In the surrounding silence he defended himself. Let 'em think what they want, it's me has borne the brunt of it, he thought. He had worked a hard year with no home and no woman, and he had paid their way over the sea. Let 'em look at Median, because there's going to be time ahead when Median'll seem wunnerful and a place to remember, he thought.

"It's goin' to be a big place, Median is," he said aloud. "They're goin' to make it the county seat, and there'll be streets and houses and banks and a school, even."

"There's no school now, then," Jonathan said.

"There's no need for it," Clyde retorted.

"There'll be need for it when we get there," Jonathan said. But in this one moment he had given up all hope for his own learning. Who could teach him Latin here?

"Not for you," Clyde said.

"There're the little ones after him," Mary told him.

"Readin' and writin' and a little arithmetic is all a man needs here," Clyde answered. "It's one of the beauties of America," he said in a loud voice. "A man can get ahead with his hands and his own brains, and he don't need to sit with his nose in a book."

No one answered him. He lifted his eyes up and caught a look at that moment passing between Jonathan and his mother, and, leaning over, he seized the reins from Jonathan's hands and slapped the horses' backs.

"Get along, there!" he shouted at them. It was good to speak to beasts who could not jaw back at him.

But Jonathan, after the communication in that long look from his mother, took comfort. Ever since he had come to this country he had felt a wandering wretchedness in his mind. His mother had been so glad to see his father again that he felt he was no longer necessary to her. He had remembered mournfully the year in Dentwater when she had turned to him as the man in her house, a year full of a sweetness pathetic because now it was over. His father's presence had thrust him back to being young again and not much good. What he had done always for the younger children when his father was away was by his father's presence nothing but woman's work. And he had been made miserable by his mother's fondness for this man. In the New York streets she had hung upon his arm with both her hands, and he had looked away when he saw it.

Now in her long look she called him back to her. She needed him still, and in the warmth of this need he leaned over and took Maggie from where she sat half-asleep against Ruth.

"Give me the tiddlin' thing," he said gently. "She's all in a heap." He lifted the fat little lump in his arms and held her tenderly in the silent dusk.

6

MEDIAN was mud. They looked over the side of the wagon at the scarcely moving wheels and saw the black stuff clinging to the spokes and halfway to the hubs, a smooth, shining substance as thick as gum. The horses stopped and snorted.

"Dang 'em, I s'all have to get out and lead 'em," Clyde muttered.

"Can't you pull over to the side of the street and let's walk?" Mary asked.

"Walk where?" Clyde retorted. He crawled along a horse's back and leaped down and sank halfway to his knees. "Come on here, you beasties," he said, and seized the bit.

The wagon moved slowly again, a few inches at a time. They could hear the sucking sound of Clyde's boots as he forced his way. It was dark now, and the faint waves of light which the wagon lantern sent out showed them not even the side of the road, nothing but the thick surface of the mud, smooth until it curled heavily about moving feet and wheels.

"Is Kansas all mud, then, Clyde?" Mary called.

He did not hear her. He was pushing the reluctant horses along, urging them with the whip when they stopped. A quarter of a mile, and then they saw faint lights on either side of the wide mud. The wagon swerved and drew over and stopped.

"Here we be," Clyde panted. He threw the reins over the backs of the sweating horses and came to the side of the wagon and put out his arms to his wife. "I'll carry you both in," he said, and lifted her with Arthur in her arms. "Hi there, Drear!" he shouted.

A door opened, and in the light streaming out of the house stood a tall, thick figure.

"Hi there, yourself!" a deep voice roared.

Clyde staggered the four or five feet between wagon and door and set his wife upon the threshold.

"There's more to come," he cried. He went back. "Now you, Ruthie, and Jamie, the two of you." He lifted them, one on each arm, and stopped to look at Jonathan. But Jonathan was already taking off his shoes and socks.

"I'll roll up my trousers, Father," he said.

A moment later he slipped down into the dark mud. In the tidy, meager life of Dentwater he had not since he was a little boy felt his feet upon the ground. But this was nothing like the smooth wet cobblestones or the sandy soil of Dentwater. The mud sucked in his feet and his legs and dragged him down until he was afraid. He clung to the wagon and lowered himself by one hand, Maggie upon his right arm.

"Put your arms about my neck, Maggie," he told her. She did so, and he cautiously put down his other foot. He felt the mud bottomless until he was all but ready to pull himself up again. But it was more difficult to pull up than to sink down. He let himself go, desperately knowing the bottom must be there, and then felt it beneath him, the solid subsoil of the land. He walked upon it somehow, pushing himself through the mud until he stood at the inn door. He hesitated to step upon the floor, and then saw that he need not. Muddy feet had come and gone upon the rough planks until there was an inch of mud upon them like a carpet. His first thought was for his mother's skirt as she stood, still with Arthur in her arms, looking about her. She was dazed, he could see. And Maggie suddenly began to cry in a loud wail.

"Well, here we be, Drear," Clyde said. "A lot of us, when we're all together."

"We'll feed you," the man said heartily, "and bed you, if you don't mind where you sleep." He turned his head and bawled, "Wife!"

"What?" a shrill voice called back.

"Goodliffes is here!" he shouted.

"Well, I never!" she screamed.

But she came running in, a tall, broad woman of middle age, with a sharp face and dry sandy hair combed into a braided knot on top of her head.

"Well, God save us," she said, staring at them. "I didn't expect you till tomorrow, but come on."

"I said maybe today," Clyde told her.

"Today's usually tomorrow with you," she retorted, though not unkindly.

But Mary, seeing another woman, came to herself. "Could I get a doctor for my little lad?" she asked. "He's very ill."

"A doctor!" the woman repeated, astonished. "Why, I haven't seen a doctor in these parts for nearly a year. There was one last summer goin' to the coast." She turned to her husband. "Henry, when did you hear tell of a doctor?"

He shook his head. "Don't know," he said. They both came over to look at the child. "Is he asleep?" the woman asked.

"He just lies so," Mary replied. Her lip quivered, and tears came into her eyes. "Clyde, if I'd ha' known there wouldn't be a doctor in Median, I wouldn't ha' come," she said fiercely.

"Oh, now, Mrs. Goodliffe!" the woman cried. "You're tired. Why, it's a wonderful country. He'll get well. I'll give him a little mush and milk. Lucky we've got a cow. Lay him in here on my bed." She moved to a doorway and put aside the blanket that was its curtain. Jonathan put Maggie down and, stepping forward, took Artie from his mother.

"I'll carry him," he said. He went into the room behind Mrs. Drear and laid the little boy down, while his mother followed. Beneath even Artie's lightness the straw of the mattress rustled. But it was a bed, covered with blankets and a woven counterpane of blue and white. Artie did not stir. Mrs. Drear leaned over him and felt his forehead.

"I've seen 'em come back from the very jaws of death," she said solemnly. "It's the air. I'll fetch some hot milk." She bustled away, and while Jonathan and his mother stood beside the bed his father came in.

"Drear's the right sort," Clyde said. "He says we can stay in this room for the night. Seems their other three rooms are full of a party going West. The rain's upset everything. They couldn't go on like they expected. Drear and Mrs. will sleep in the kitchen."

"But however—" Mary began, and stopped. Mrs. Drear came in again, a bowl and a spoon in her hand.

"Now then, folks," she commanded them, "Jennet—that's my daughter —is ready to feed you. Get along and leave this little feller to me."

She sat down and began with a sort of clumsy gentleness to put the milk between Artie's lips. Without opening his eyes he swallowed.

"He's all right," Clyde exclaimed. "Come along."

"You all go," Mary said. "I shan't leave Artie."

"I'll come back quick then, Mother," Jonathan said.

He followed his father into the other room. Ruth was still standing in the middle of the muddy floor, holding Maggie's hand, and Jamie beside them, his hands in his pockets, staring at everything about him.

"Come along," Jonathan said and lifted Maggie up. They sat down beside a long unpainted table. A red-headed young girl with a dirty blue apron came in with a wooden bowl of mush and a jug of milk. She set them down and went away and came back with bread and slices of thick bacon. The rain had begun again in a long droning roar upon the roof.

"Lucky we made it," Clyde said. "Lucky I got the horses put away even."

Jonathan took Maggie on his lap and made ready to feed her, and as he did so a thin stream of water began to patter on the table from the roof. Drops flew into his face. He moved and the girl Jennet, seeing it, went out and brought in a pan and set it under the leak as though she were used to it. Jonathan watched her.

"Does the roof always leak like this?" he asked.

She looked at him with a sudden glint in her large greenish eyes. "No," she replied impudently, "only when it rains."

She went away in the midst of loud laughter from Clyde and Mr. Drear, her face straight but her eyes glittering with laughter she would not allow to escape.

Jonathan hated the laughter. There was nothing to laugh at that he could see. He hung his head and made an ado about feeding Maggie, refusing her bacon and insisting upon the mush and milk so sternly that she was unexpectedly cowed in this strange place and swallowed the spoonfuls that he ladled into her open mouth. He ate between whiles, loathing the food and yet too hungry to refuse it. His mother was a dainty cook, and he was accustomed to goodness in her simple dishes. But he ate, and when he was fed lifted Maggie and took her to bed in the other room. Mrs. Drear had gone, and his mother was alone.

"Where'll we all sleep?" she said when he came in. She was dazed, he could see, and dismayed.

"There'll be pallets," he said. "I'll just lay Maggie here by Artie."

Artie had not wakened. She watched him while he put Maggie down. She was so silent that he was startled and looked at her. Her eyes were full of fear.

"Your father's brought us to a terrible country," she said. He could not deny it. But he cried out to her what he had always cried.

"Don't you mind, Mother. I'll think of something!"

What he was thinking of was how to get her back to England. He would find work, and he would save and put together enough to take her back again. And even while he thought, his father came tramping cheerfully into the room, loosening his belt as he came.

"I'm full and sleepy, lass," he cried. "Mrs. Drear will put down the pallets for the young ones, and you and me'll sleep in the bed, eh, Mary?"

"Mother hasn't eaten yet," Jonathan said angrily. "Go on, Mother, and I'll sit here in your place."

"Go on yourself," Clyde said in good humor. "I'm going to take off my clothes as soon as Mrs. Drear's out."

She was coming in as he spoke, her arms full of quilts. "Don't stop for me," she shouted. "I've seen a plenty in my time. How many pallets, Mr. Goodliffe? Your young man—"

"I shan't sleep in here, if you please," Jonathan broke in.

"Oh, Godamercy," Mrs. Drear said laughing, "sleep in the other room then. Jennet takes a corner, but you needn't take the same!"

"Haw!" Clyde burst out, but Mary turned suddenly as lofty and cool as a lady. She put her hand on Jonathan's arm.

"We'll go out now. Do you see to Artie, Clyde," she said. Jonathan felt her small hand strong upon his arm, and as they went out, "A downright coarse woman—as if you'd look at a serving wench, Jonathan!" she murmured as he lifted the blanket curtain.

He could see in the morning the name of the tavern. A long, broad shingle was nailed across the door, and upon it was painted in white the letters "American House." Above it upon a square board was a stiff-looking gilt fowl meant to be an eagle. The rain continued to fall. The house was full of people, for at breakfast seven men came down a ladder from the attic. To wash they held a tin basin under the streaming eaves and brought it in. Jonathan, after a few questions which always brought laughter, asked no more, but watched to see what others did. Thus he waited, and in his turn caught rain water and washed Maggie's face and hands and caught again and took the basin in to his mother. She, he perceived the moment he saw her, was in a mood of black despair.

Mary had spoken to Mrs. Drear about a house, and Mrs. Drear had laughed.

"Lord love you, dear," she said. "Houses don't grow here—they have to be made."

"You mean there isn't a house to be had in the town?" Mary asked.

"There ain't but six houses besides ours," Mrs. Drear said. "Some day we're goin' to be a big town, but everything's got to begin, I guess."

Mary did not answer. She had got up early and had dressed herself neatly and had seen to the children. Artie was a little better. But she had gone into the kitchen for hot milk and what she saw had sickened her. A tumbled dirty pallet was still on the floor, and the girl Jennet was sauntering about her business of breakfast, her face unwashed and her red hair uncombed.

"I shan't eat until I'm in my own house," she told Clyde when she was back.

He was sitting on the edge of the bed dressing himself. "Don't be so choice, Mary," he said. "They've fed me when I hadn't food."

"Clyde, how much money have you?" she demanded.

"None—or as good as none," he said frankly. "But I've got the promise of work. Drear's puttin' up a chicken coop and says I'm to do it."

"You!" she cried. "You never drew a saw in your life."

"I can try it," he retorted. "It don't take brains to draw a saw. Besides, Jonathan s'all help me."

She did not answer. Jonathan must help indeed until they were started.

"I must get a house," she said, half to herself. "But how?"

"We'll build one of sod," he replied.

"Sod!" she repeated.

"Sod," he said firmly.

It was at this moment that Jonathan came in, bringing the tin basin of rain water.

"Jonathan," she said, turning to him piteously, "there's only sod for houses here—"

He had not the least idea of what a sod house was, but he cried out with all his heart to comfort her.

"Never you mind, Mother! It'll be the best sod house there is!"

They lived eleven days and a half at American House. On the second day the rain cleared, but they were still imprisoned by mud. The door of the inn looked out upon an empty square, and from this square the grass was worn away by wagons and the feet of horses and oxen, so that now it was a field of thick dark mud. Once or twice, sometimes as much as four times a day, a wagon straggled up the road, painted with mud. The beasts that pulled it were caked to the eyes, and sometimes the man leading them had fallen and was an image of mud from which his eyes looked out whitely like a ghost's. The inn grew unbearably crowded. Quarreling and laughter and the crying of children crowded the air with noise. Jennet was silent with endless work until Jonathan took to carrying in the bowls of food for her and setting them down on the table. In a moment the food was gone. He could not see how it was that these men ate so quickly. The only silence of the day was while they ate, throwing bread into their mouths, gulping down great mugs of coffee, between dishes of meat and potatoes. They took the hunks of salt pork with their hands to chew off huge bites, and he was sick at the sight. Seeing Jamie imitating them, he cuffed him sharply over the left ear.

His father saw it. "What're you beatin' Jamie for?" he cried at Jonathan.

"I wasn't doin' anything," Jamie muttered sourly.

"You know what you were doin'," Jonathan said. "You know what Mother don't like!"

"And I say if there's beatin' to be done, I'll do it," his father retorted.

For answer Jonathan took his plate beside Ruth and ate slowly and fastidiously, cutting his meat before he ate and drinking his coffee quietly. He longed for a cup of tea, but there was none. Everybody drank mugs full of bitter black coffee sweetened with molasses. It made him gag unless he sipped it slowly.

In these few days he had completely forgotten school and books. He had first to find the means of living at all—somehow the shelter of a home and privacy and quiet. Artie was still in bed, a little better, or so he seemed. Ruth stayed with her mother, away from the roughness of men coming and going. But Jamie was excited and happy. He hung about the men listening to them and copied their swagger and their ways. And no one could stop Maggie from running about meddling everywhere. In these few days she had grown pert and willful because they all laughed at her and Jennet spoiled her with food and made her bold to disobey Jonathan so that one day when he told her to come and be cleaned she cried, "No—no!" and ran to Jennet, and Jennet laughed. He went glowering to find his mother.

"If we don't get away from here," he said, "Jamie and Maggie will be out of hand forever."

His mother sighed. "I wish I'd never come," she said.

"But if Dad was set on America?" Jonathan asked.

"I'd have let him have it without me," she replied. "Almost," she added, seeing his look.

By the seventh day the mud was drying and shrinking in cracks. Underneath the thick skin of its surface was still softness, but the skin held. By noon of that day the travelers were gone, and there were a few hours before night brought three more men, cattle drivers from Texas who had driven cattle up the trail to the Northeast.

In the afternoon's silence Jonathan sat down on a bench by a window in the big room and took a small book from his pocket. For the moment there was nothing to do, and in the emptiness he was aware of a yearning to read and to think. He had brought a few books with him, and this one was Virgil. He had not opened a book since he left Dentwater. He had scarcely opened this one when Jennet came in. She had taken off her kitchen apron and had brushed her red curly hair and washed her face. She sat down at the long trestle table, yawned, and laid her head upon her arms.

"I could sleep till my hair turns white," she said.

She had not spoken to him since the first night. He saw her swinging pots on and off the stove, mopping the tables with sweeps of her long arm and a dirty rag in her hand.

"You have to work hard," Jonathan said politely.

"Dog hard," she agreed carelessly. Then she sat up. "Want to know what I'm goin' to do?"

"What?" Jonathan answered, seeing that she expected it.

"I want to go West, clear to Californy," she said. "Everybody's goin' West."

"But what would you do?" he inquired, astonished.

For answer she lifted her head and looked at him from under her drooped eyelids. Her pale eyes, as clear and pale a green as liquid shadows of trees upon water, gleamed out at him.

"You'd like to know, would you!" she said. "Well, I won't tell you!"

She got up and sauntered to the door and stood there leaning against the jamb, looking out. And he, bending his head over his book, wondered what she meant and did not dare to ask.

Mary, before dawn, urged Clyde in his bed, "It's a fair mornin', Clyde. Hadn't you better get up and have the start on the day?"

He was an incurably late sleeper, one of those who, slow to sleep at night, seem to find their midnight when others are rising for work.

"Let me be," he grunted without moving.

She lay a few moments longer until every muscle in her body ached to be up and at work. She could endure it no more, and she rose. The moment she stepped out of bed Ruth sat up, and Maggie rolled from the same pallet to the floor and picked herself up, and fell again, tangled in her long nightgown. Jamie was already up and outdoors somewhere. Arthur stirred and called out faintly, "S'all I have a drink, Mother?"

"You shall, this minute," Mary replied. He was better these last two days, but how weak! She longed to give him an egg, but there was not a fowl to be found in Median. She could not believe it, but so it was.

"I always aimed to get some hens," Mrs. Drear had said, "but I ain't got around to it."

Mary, hearing such a confession of shiftlessness, determined the moment she had her own roof to find a few hens somehow.

"Clyde!" she called sharply. The sun was streaming in the small window. "It'll be noon!"

Two days of full time, Clyde had said, and they could get up a sod house; that was, provided she did not have her notions. A sod house could be laid up rough or smooth, he said, sixteen feet wide and twenty feet long.

"I want it smooth," she said without waiting to find out what "smooth" was, "and there must be four rooms to it, Clyde, for decency."

This was what he called "notions." "Dang you, Mary," he said, "you can't be finer nor everybody else in America. It makes 'em mad. Why, nobody's got four rooms in a sod house in Median."

She had finally agreed that, for the present, if he would do it quickly, she would manage on the two rooms. Jonathan will help me, she thought privately.

She watched Clyde scramble out of bed and into his clothes. He could be so active and quick when he was awake, but half-asleep he moved as though he were drunk. She hurried out to see to his breakfast.

In the other room Jonathan was ready and dressed in his oldest clothes. "The horses are ready, Mother," he said. "Where's Dad? I've hitched 'em to the plow."

"He'll be along as quick as I can make him," she replied. "Where's Jamie? He's to help."

"So I told him," Jonathan said. She went on into the kitchen, and he let her go without telling her that half an hour earlier he had pulled Jamie out of a wagon going West. The boy had hidden under the big cover and had been found at the last minute by the owner, a tall New Englander. He had not let Jamie know himself discovered. Instead, grinning slightly, he had gone to find Jonathan.

"Reckon I've got some of your property by mistake," he said.

Jonathan, following him, saw Jamie crouching behind a small bureau among mattresses, pots, a clock, and bundles of clothes. He reached in and with an arm suddenly strong pulled the boy out and clapped him hard over the head.

"What are you in there for?" he asked severely.

"I don't want to stay here," Jamie said. His round face was red. "I want to go West to where the gold is."

"Gold!" Jonathan said scornfully. He held Jamie firmly by the collar and slid him back to the inn and sat him down on the doorstep.

"Think of our mother!" he said, and met Jamie's rebellious stare with a gaze so stern that Jamie's eyes fell.

"Get over to the barn," Jonathan went on, "and see if the horses are fed. Mr. Drear says we can borrow them and his plow today." He did not take his eyes from Jamie until he disappeared into the sod-house barn where the Drears had once lived. To think of Jamie, wanting to go West, like that girl Jennet! As if we wasn't at the ends of earth already! he thought, before his mother came back, and went outside to wait in the sunshine.

7

CLYDE, driving the horses, pushed the plow deep into the sod and then looked behind him.

"Dang the beasts," he said to Jonathan. "They're cuttin' the furrows everyhow." He stopped and wiped his forehead.

"Give me a try," Jonathan said. He had hardly been able to endure the wavering of the furrows. Drear had told him the furrows must be even deep and even wide, or the house would be crazy. He handed his spade to his father and gave a sharp look to Jamie, who was piling the sod squares up on the float. In a little while there would be more help. Henry Drear had promised to come as soon as his chores were done, and three more men he could bring later in the day.

"I'll take spade, then," Clyde said. " 'Twill be easier to trust my own brains instead of beasties."

Jonathan took the reins and held them tightly, forcing the horses to slowness. They were young, and the morning air and sunshine made them gay, and there was grass green beneath their feet. He held them mercilessly to work.

His mother, when they left her at the door, had said to him quietly so only he could hear, "Keep them to work, son, else we'll never get the house done."

"I will, Mother," he had promised.

In his mind he understood the process of this building with the earth. He had talked it over with the Drears, asking a question now and then, and he had gone out to the old sod-house barn and studied it, and walked a mile down the quaking surface of the drying road to look at a sod house. A woman was hanging out clothes and stared at him.

"Do you mind if I look at the house?" he asked politely. "My dad's building, we're newcomers, and I want to see how they're done."

She was ready and eager for talk and led him in. He had been sickened with what he saw in the squalid windowless hole, but he said nothing. No reason why there shouldn't be windows in a sod house, he thought, nor why filth should lie on the floor. It's these folks.

Nevertheless, he determined as he took pains to drive his furrows deep and straight that they would have four windows somehow.

"Don't never build against the river hill," the woman had chattered. "The rattlesnakes come out. My ol' man built us a dugout on the river bank so's it would be handy to fetch water, and soon as we lit a fire the snakes came out. We moved quick, I kin tell you!" She laughed and showed her snaggy teeth.

"It's not to be by the river," he said briefly, and wondered if by a river she meant the sluggish little brook that crept south of Median under some small reedy trees.

The first day it did not rain his mother had stood looking over the endless grassy plain in which Median stood.

"Where are all the trees?" she had asked, bewildered by their lack.

"Why, there's the cottonwoods," Mrs. Drear had said, and made them sound like a forest.

"We'll plant trees, Mother," he had said.

"It's grass country, you'll find," Mrs. Drear replied.

But he was going to plant trees somehow about his mother's house.

"Does your floor always puddle?" he asked the slatternly woman.

"Only in spring thaws or so be it rains hard in a summer shower," she replied carelessly.

"Well, good-by," he said at last, and went away thinking he had learned more from her what he did not want than what he did. And with his father he chose a site on Henry Drear's land, two acres whose rent was to be paid in such labor as Drear might ask. Clyde was very lordly about it.

"If I be horse tradin', as I s'all be come good weather," he said largely, "Jonathan'll fill the obligations."

The site was a little far from the road, but it stood high enough, though not a hill, to run off water and have no puddled floors. A little far, but Henry Drear said certainly, "Another year or two like Median's growing, and it'll be the middle of the town."

The sun beat down by nine o'clock, and Clyde sat down to rest, groaning and grunting.

"Seems a lively long time afore the men come," he said.

Jonathan did not answer. He had never loved the earth, and even in England plowing the small fields had been toil. Here a field stretched to the sky, and he liked a limit to everything. Yet to plow these furrows and cut them into squares and lift them in flat, solid mats of substance was good work. It was the air, perhaps. This air cleared the brain and fed the blood like food. It was clean and swept by the wind. He could even see the wind here. It began far away in a ripple of light on the long even grass and came rushing on like waves upon the sea, fresh and full of power, wave after wave.

"Is there always wind here, Dad?" he asked, watching it.

"Always," Clyde replied. "And wait till it ties itself into knots in a cyclone! A whirligig of a thing a cyclone is, grabbin' the earth and pullin' at the sky and movin' both." He took out his pipe as he talked. "A big large thing the wind is here," he said, "like everything else in America."

Jonathan did not answer. Across the grass he saw Henry Drear and three men coming, and he was ashamed to have them see his father sit smoking so early in the day's labor.

"Take the horses again, Dad," he said abruptly. "I'll lend a hand with Jamie."

But to his anger a few moments later Jamie was gone. He had taken the chance of the men's coming to slip away from Jonathan's eyes and run through the grass toward the town. Jonathan saw him and shouted, but Jamie did not pause.

"I'll go after him," he said firmly.

"No, you won't," Clyde said. "Leave him—he's too small for such work anyway."

The men were there. One of them was leading a team of mules, and Jonathan saw that which put everything else out of his mind. One of the men was black.

"Samuel Hasty, miller—come last year from Vermont," Henry Drear was saying, "and Lew Merridy, storekeeper and his mules, and this here's Stephen Parry."

"Pleased to meet you," Samuel Hasty said. He was a small man with a long nose on a long face.

"Glad to see you," Lew Merridy said heartily, putting out his hand to Clyde and then to Jonathan.

But the black man did not step forward or put out his hand. "Howdy, suh," he said in a soft bass voice and at once began to work, lifting the three-foot strips of sod to the float.

"Well, dang it, how the town grows!" Clyde said.

"Median grows," Henry Drear agreed. He spat into the grass. "She doubles her population every year or two. Ten years ago when I put up

American House at the crossroads I was the only white man in a hundred miles, I reckon. Now they's a hundred people here, ain't there, Hasty?"

"A hundred and three," Samuel Hasty said.

"Twins was born last night in my house," Lew said shyly.

"A hundred and five, by God!" Drear roared. "Damn it, Lew, you're a good citizen!"

None of them were working except the black man, who said not a word; and Jonathan, feeling young and unnoticed, began to help him. He could not keep from looking at Stephen Parry. He had never been close to a black man before. When his father had written to them in England of Negroes and Indians, his mother had sighed, "The country's full of savages." But they had seen very few Negroes and as yet no Indians. Now he watched secretly the strangeness of black skin upon a human frame. But there was nothing savage in this man, he thought. His skin was not coal black, either. There was a light in it. He was the color of chocolate, and his head was handsome. His hands were most strange, so dark-fleshed, but the palms a pale, dead pink. Jonathan was shy of him and tried not to be.

"It's good of you to come and help us," he said stiffly.

"Folks has been kind to me, too," the man said in his soft deep voice. "Folks is mighty kind around hyeah."

"Have you been here long?" Jonathan asked.

The man hesitated, then answered, "The endurin' time of the big war I was hyeah." He hesitated again and saw the men were not listening to him, only this slight, gentle-faced young man. "I run away, suh, in de early days of de wah. I was a slave, suh."

Jonathan looked at him, revulsion in his bosom. A slave!

"I am glad you ran away," he said indignantly.

"We all free now," the man replied quietly.

"Float's full!" Henry Drear shouted, and Merridy began to hitch his horses to the sledlike frame. He smiled at Jonathan, a kind, comprehending smile.

"Want to come along and help unload?" he said.

"Certainly, sir," Jonathan replied.

He walked beside the float as it slid over the long grass.

"Think you're goin' to like the country?" Lew Merridy asked.

"I don't know," Jonathan replied.

Merridy looked surprised and then laughed. "Sure you will," he said. "It's a great country for a young fellow like you—greatest country in the world."

Jonathan did not answer. He was not used yet to the talkativeness of the Americans, nor to their shameless boasting. England was a great country, too, he told himself, but he would not say so. It makes things common-like to talk about 'em, he thought, and worked in steady silence until Lew Merridy gave up talk and whistled instead, a whistle as loud and clear as a wild bird's.

That night the house was drawn to its shape and guided by the North Star. They had worked all day plowing, cutting, and carrying the strips of sod to where the house was to be. Then, when the North Star appeared in the darkening sky, Henry Drear drew a line direct from its point and paced off twenty feet and drove in the stakes.

"There," he said, "the house sets right. It's straight to the Northern Star."

They went back to the inn, tired and hungry.

"Come in and have a drink," Clyde said at the door to the men who had helped him. "It's ill luck to a house not to drink when the foundation's decided."

Only Stephen Parry shook his head to refuse coming in. "Thank you, suh, but I'll be gettin' along," he said. He touched his old straw hat to them all and went away.

"Good man, Steve," Henry Drear said as they entered the inn. "He's as good as anybody and he knows it, but he don't press it. Kansas is a free state and all that, but a nigger's got no business settin' down by a white man anywheres."

"Turns the stomach," Samuel Hasty agreed.

They sat down and from somewhere in his pockets Clyde brought out a coin. Drear shouted and Jennet came in, her hands white with flour.

"Rye," her father said without looking up.

"How can I git it in the middle of the bread?" she demanded.

"I'll get it for you," Jonathan said and rose.

"All right, then," she said.

He went after her and saw that her red hair, which he had never seen otherwise than tumbled upon her head, was brushed and braided in a long braid down her back to her knees.

"What wonderful long hair you have," he said surprised. He had indeed never seen such long gleaming stuff. "It looks fine."

"I had time today to clean myself," she said shortly, but her face was not angry. She thrust out her chin at a low door. "In there," she said, "rye's in a keg. You can dip it out into a jug that stands on top."

She went back to her bread, and he went to the lean-to and dipped up the whisky. It smelled so strong it was fire in his nostrils, but when he took it to the tables, the men drank it like tea.

"Taste it," Clyde ordered him.

He poured out a glass, and Jonathan put it to his lips and felt his mouth go raw. He swallowed hastily, and his stomach curled. His eyes were full of tears, and he longed to rush for water, but they were laughing at him.

"What's the matter, boy?" his father roared.

"You'll have to learn to take rye down," Drear said, "else what'll you do when you get fever and snakebites?"

Samuel Hasty said nothing, but he laughed a silent mean laughter that was hateful. But Lew Merridy got up and fetched a dipperful of water and handed it to Jonathan.

"Drink it," he said, "and don't mind laughin'. Folks have to laugh at somethin' or other here."

Jonathan drank the water and cooled himself.

"Now take another," Clyde ordered him.

But Jonathan stood up. "No, I won't, thanks, Father," he said, and without waiting walked away into the other room to find his mother.

She was sitting by the bed where Arthur lay, and she was mending a torn garment. She looked up when he came in.

"How did it go?" she asked.

"Fair," he said. "Tomorrow we'll begin the walls." He frowned. "Did Jamie come back?" he asked.

"He did, and I let him go out with a man shooting hares," she said. "Jack rabbits, they call 'em here," she added.

"He gave me the slip," Jonathan said.

Mary smiled. "He's only a child," she replied.

"He's twelve," Jonathan said doggedly, "and at twelve I knew better."

"Oh, don't be so preaching," Mary said suddenly.

He was very tired, and he felt hurt to the core of his being. This was the one thing in her that he could never understand, that in the midst of his doing all for her, she could defend Jamie or his father for the very lack of what he was for her. It made him feel forever unsure of her and insecure in his being. He was angry now, but the fear made him mild. He was silent for a minute, then he searched for something to say to please her and found it.

"I'll tell you something pretty, Mother," he said. "It was dark and we set the house by the North Star."

She looked up, her face quickened and lightened with perception of poetry. "Oh, very pretty, Jonathan!" she cried warmly, and in her pleasure drew him near again.

By dawn they were working. Now the house was begun. The foundation was dug, not deep, for earth would join to earth by rain and snow. Into the foundation the first sod bricks were laid and others laid upon them three deep, except where the door was to face the south.

"Now put the cracks full of earth, and then two more layers of sod," Henry Drear ordered them. They all worked fast and hard today, and there was very little talk. Stephen Parry stood at one corner and another, keeping them true, and shifting a sod if it did not perfectly break a joint.

"Three layers and then crosswise," Drear said sharply to Clyde, about to lay a fourth the wrong way. "Allow the window when you put up two more," he said.

Jonathan spoke. "There's to be four windows, please."

Every man stopped, astounded.

"Four windows!" Drear repeated, stupefied. "Why, boy, four windows will gather in the wind until the roof'll blow away."

Jonathan felt his face burn with shy blood. "My mother likes sun and light," he said stubbornly.

They looked at Clyde, and he spat on his hands. "It's folly," he declared. "I say build it as is best and let her lump it."

"She shan't, Father," Jonathan declared. "A sod house is bad enough, but it'll be a cave if there's not but one single solitary window."

"Why, a sod house is nothing wrong," Merridy said. "Cool in summer and warm in winter! I was born and raised in a sod house, and if you prop up the roof so it don't fall in with water and snow, it's a good house. But Drear's right about wind. Two windows is plenty—one to a room."

They made two windows and, building until night, had the house ready for its roof. Jonathan lingered by it after his father and the men were gone. The place looked solitary and without hope in the evening light. It would be hard to say whether it was new and had sheltered no one yet, or whether it was roofless from desertion. He walked about it sadly. It would have wooden window frames tomorrow, and there would be rafters to hold up the weight of the sod roof. Stephen Parry was to make the woodwork, and Samuel Hasty had lent the lumber, to be paid for half in cash when his father had it and half in labor at the busiest time at the mill. "And as soon as I have a penny of my own," Jonathan planned, "I'll put in a wooden floor."

The stone cottage in Dentwater had seemed poor enough when they were in it and knew themselves the poorest people in the village. But it was a rich man's house to this earthen heap, and yet here they would be as well off as most of Median, where only the inn, the store, and the mill were even of wood. But he was not yet an American. It gave him no cheer that most of them were like himself. Instead he felt it a doleful thing to think that this was true. It shut a door to somewhere better.

He went tramping back to the inn full of this dole. The ground was solid enough under his feet now, baked by the sun. He walked down the road which was Median's only street to where it ran around the empty barren square which was the center of whatever Median was.

If I must stay here, he thought, I'll put trees there, too.

8

THE QUESTION of whether he must stay became his inner being, but he never revealed it. Stay he must now because there was no way to go. There was no money to return to England, and of what use would it be to set out across the endless prairies? Median must be his life.

Somewhere in his mother he comprehended, by that delicate inexplicable communication which he had with her, that her own inner being was in despair as wild as his own. But if it was, she said not a word of it. She set herself to the house as soon as the roof was on and before glass was in the windows. Glass they would have as soon as Lew Merridy could get it fetched, but half of Median had no glass. Their windows were curtained with buffalo skins or old blankets.

"Leave the grass on the floor until we get wood," she told Clyde. "It'll be cleaner than mud."

Wood and glass she would have, and if she had to live in a sod house she would show everybody how to do it. The children would be brought up properly, too, and with their manners, and not rough the way Clyde had got to be. Jonathan'll help me, she thought.

Thus she made in a very few days a sort of home out of the earth. Mrs. Drear gave her an old bed from the inn, and one by one women she had not seen came over the quarter of a mile of grass and brought her a pot, a plate of food, a mended blanket, a wooden stool. From Merridy's General Store she had six wooden boxes. The store was the one place in Median where for an hour she could forget the limitless plains and sky which frightened her whenever she looked at them. She was amazed at the store. Even in Dentwater there was not a better collection of goods— all thrown together, it was true.

"If I could put my hands to it," she told Jonathan, "I could make a place you could find something. People drive for miles, Merridy says, to buy of him, and wagons stop for food and clothing and blankets, and everybody has to wait till he sorts out what they want."

"There's an idea, Mother," Jonathan said. "I'll hire myself to him if he'll have me."

"You can't," Clyde said. "You're promised to Drear to pay the rent of land and his horses to plow up a garden."

"I thought you were to work out for Drear," his wife retorted.

"Me?" Clyde cried. "When the chicken coop's done I'm workin' now, and it won't be but a matter of five days or six for that, I s'all go and homestead somewheres. Land we must get while it's free and before all the greedy ones has got it. It's late now. Ten years earlier would have been better, and by now I might ha' been a rich landowner with my cattle and my horses. I s'all—"

"Oh, you!" Mary cried bitterly. "Shut up, do, Clyde!"

He went off in one of his sudden huffs, and Mary sewed hard for a moment on a curtain she was making out of a flour bag. Mrs. Drear had given her a heap, washed and bleached and ready to use.

"Go to see Mr. Merridy tomorrow, son," she told Jonathan. He was putting up a shelf above the deep sod fireplace. A ticklish job it was, too, for he had to drive two short, stout blocks of wood into the thick sod wall to hold it. But he was learning how to hold and use tools he had not needed in England; and Stephen Parry, whose home was a dugout on the side of the river bank below Median, had lent him a hammer and a saw and given him some nails. Thus he had nailed together boxes to make a closet for their clothes and upon boxes had nailed three boards for a table, and with a broken scythe from Drear's barn he had smoothed the inner walls of the house.

Labor was all he had to exchange for all else they needed, and he worked until he fell upon his straw mattress at night. Mindful of his need for a place of his own, his mother had hung a blanket across a corner and put his mattress upon boards behind it, and above it he had driven in wooden blocks for a shelf for his books and some pegs to hold his clothes. It was almost as dark by day as it was by night, unless he lit a candle. Sometimes he remembered that he used to see from his window the Irish Sea and the sails of ships white in the sunshine.

But on that next day there was no doubt that he must hire himself wherever he could for best pay. It was halfway between morning and noon when Mary, hanging the curtains she had made, saw out of the window a wagon coming near. It was Henry Drear's wagon. She knew its red body, and in a moment she would see the yellow letters painted on its side, "American House." When it came near enough for that, she saw something else. It was Clyde, propped up on the seat and looking as if he were dead.

"Whatever now!" she muttered and put down her curtain and went hurrying out.

There he was, fainted sure enough, but not dead. Henry Drear was holding him up, and the horses stopped before the house.

"He's cut his leg," Henry Drear said impatiently. "A more orkward feller never was born, I told my wife yestiddy, watchin' him handle the ax."

"He's never chopped his own leg!" she cried, and knew he had, for his thick woolen trouser leg was soaked with blood, and blood was trickling out of his boot.

"Nigh off, I reckon," Drear said. "Is Jonathan about?"

"No, he's gone over to Merridy's this morning," Mary said; "and Jamie, of course, is never where he's wanted. Ruth!" she called.

Ruth came out. "What, Mother?" She clapped her hands to her mouth. "Dad!" she cried and stood still.

"Come here and help me, silly," Mary said. "Now, Mr. Drear, we'll hold him if you'll let him down."

Together she and Ruth took Clyde's dead weight until Drear could step down. Then he hoisted Clyde across his great shoulders.

"I'll carry him in," he said, "and I'd advise you to find Stephen Parry's wife. Some say she's a witch, but there's times you want a witch. Anyway, she sewed a man's head on again, they say, after he'd been to the gallows."

Clyde's blood was spurting, soaking into the drying grass on the floor, soaking into the straw of the mattress where Arthur lay, his blue eyes enormous. He had not said a word.

"Oh, that Jamie!" Mary cried in misery. "He's not here to send."

"I'll go for her myself," Drear said gravely. "Damn the man for a cussed baby, with an ax, but he don't look good. Tie his leg tight under the knee, Mrs. Goodliffe."

"Yes, yes," Mary moaned and tore off her apron and wrenched off the strings. "Help me, Ruth."

Henry Drear strode away, and Mary in terror wrapped the strings about Clyde's leg and cried to Ruth to hold the knot. Upon the threshold Maggie, wandering unheeded, saw a pool of bright red. She stooped carefully, being fat and unsteady, and dipped her finger in it, stared at her red finger, and then tasted it. It was not good, and she made a sickish face. But the color was irresistible, and now she dabbled in it.

Arthur called out faintly, "Mother, Maggie's playin' in father's blood!"

"For shame, Maggie!" Mary screamed and flew to Maggie. "Wicked— wicked—wicked!" She shook the child with every word. "A wicked, unfeeling, naughty thing!" she cried and burst into angry sobs. Oh, Clyde would cut himself and maybe die and leave them helpless in the wilderness!

She sat down and for the first time since she had left England she cried aloud, and the children, seeing her, began to cry, too, Maggie loudly, Ruth in soft sobs, and Arthur in a sort of silent misery. But she paid no heed to them and cried on and on helplessly because, having once begun, she could not stop.

"Well, what's all dis to-do?" a soft voice said at the door. They looked up. Ruth stopped crying. It was the witch woman! Maggie, sitting on the floor, looked at her, astonished; but Mary saw only another woman.

"Oh, come in, if you please," she said, catching her breath. She was suddenly ashamed of herself for crying like a great baby. "My husband's cut his leg sorely, and Mr. Drear tells me you can mend anything."

"I can mend some things," Stephen Parry's wife said. She stepped in and around Maggie, smiled at her, and went to the bed and began unlacing Clyde's boot.

"Is the little feller sick, too?" she asked.

"I can't get him up," Mary said. "I don't know what's wrong with him."

The big brown woman did not answer. But Artie felt her glance upon him, warm, piercing him kindly so that he was not afraid. He stopped crying and lay still, waiting.

Steadily, quietly drawing off Clyde's boot and his woolen sock, she uncovered his wound. He had gashed himself to the bone, and the great lips of flesh hung quivering and raw. She shook her head.

"It'll be many a day befo' dis man walks," she said, "and it may be he'll never walk straight again, at dat."

She laid his leg down and took the kettle from the fire and, opening a small package of brown paper, shook something into the tin basin which stood on a box, and poured water over it. Then, opening a closed cotton ball she had in her bundle, she took out the raw cotton and dipped it in the brew and washed the wound. Clyde muttered and groaned.

"Dang," he began, opened his eyes, and fainted again.

"I'd just as soon he didn't come to," the woman said. She took a needle and thread from a spool in her bundle and dipped them in the water; and then, as though she were sewing a rent in cloth, she drew together the lips of his wound.

They watched her silently, and then Ruth cried, "Is this how you sewed the man's head on, too?"

The woman smiled. "Honey, I didn't sew anybody's head on. They was a po' niggah down South once got slashed in the neck by some mad white folks, and he got away and hid in a swamp, and I fixed him up so he was whole again. Dat was befo' de wah."

"Oh," Ruth whispered. Her eyes were bright with questions, but she did not ask them. And when her sewing was done, the woman took some clean white strips out of her bundle and bound Clyde's leg carefully and tightly.

"Don' let him stir 'at leg," she told Mary. "He's just got to lie there. If he gets a fever, I'll come again. If he don't get a fever, he's all right." She tied up her bundle as she spoke and was ready to go.

"I do thank you, Mrs. Parry," Mary said, "and when I can, I will repay you."

"Nothin' to pay," the big woman said. "Nobody pays me for this kind of he'p. And nobody calls me Mrs. Parry. I'm just Sue." She gave them her slow, deep, peaceful smile and went away.

Jonathan walked across Median from Merridy's store and down the path toward the house. Some day this'll be a street, he thought. He felt in better spirits than he had since he left Dentwater. This morning, his shyness hidden under his usual sturdy stolidity, he had gone to Mr. Merridy and offered himself as a clerk. He came at a good moment for himself. Mr. Merridy was distracted by his wife's absence and by the prospect that for months to come the twins would take her time away from the store.

"I certainly do need somebody real bad," he said mournfully, looking about the disordered dusty room. It was being further disordered by farmers and their wives who had come in for Saturday buying and, impatient of being waited upon, were turning over garments and taking down goods from the shelves.

"Hi there, how much is them, Lew?" one after another shouted.

"Comin'!" he roared back and went on talking to Jonathan. "Even Katie —that's my oldest, and only thirteen—she's tied hand and foot to the babies till my wife gets around again. I tell you, you wouldn't realize the difference between twins and a solitary child. You ain't ready for it—it's a shock."

"Yes, sir," Jonathan said.

A thin, dark-haired little girl in a dress of faded red-and-green cotton plaid came to the inner door and said primly, "Papa, Mamma wants you."

"All right, Katie," Mr. Merridy said. He turned back to Jonathan. "There, that's the way it is. Kin you begin now?"

"Yes, sir," Jonathan said.

The little girl at the door waited. "Papa, are you coming?" she called. But she was looking at Jonathan from quiet, shrewd hazel eyes. She was not at all pretty, he thought, and forgot her.

"What can I do for you, sir?" he began at once to a stooped old man who stood without moving beside a barrel of crackers.

"Two pounds of them," he said, "and a side of salt pork and some beans and black molasses."

Between customers he tried to tidy the counters and sort the tumbled dry goods. It was noon before he knew it.

"You're welcome to a bite here," Merridy said.

"I'll just go back and tell my mother about the job, thanks," he replied. "I'll be back in an hour."

So he had struck over the path to the sod house which he could not yet call home. And yet, as he drew near, he imagined that he could see the touch of his mother even upon that rough earthen mass. Stephen Parry had put in the glass as soon as it came, and it shone in the two windows, and there was an edge of white curtain. From behind the house he caught the flutter of garments hanging on the line, and was surprised because his mother did not usually wash on Saturday. But he could not see what the garments were. She would never hang her wash near the road. "Family wash tells everything," she always said. "How many you have, how poor you are, and if you're good at your mending or not. I don't want strangers knowing all about us."

When he walked into the house she was on her hands and knees, chipping at the sod on the ground.

"Why, Mother!" he cried.

"Your father's bled all over," she said. "He's cut himself terrible, and there's nothing for it but to get rid of this grass."

"However did he cut himself?" Jonathan asked, stupefied.

"With the ax, chopping at Drear's, of course," his mother replied shortly. She kept on hacking at the sod.

"Don't, Mother," Jonathan said. He took the stump of a scythe away from her and down on his knees hacked out the stains of his father's blood.

On the bed he saw his father lying, but he did not speak to him at once. His father would cut himself and be past work, he thought bitterly. That was all he needed to do now when his work was all he had to give them.

"Well, Jonathan," Clyde said feebly, "there you be."

"Hello, Father," Jonathan said.

"I'm hurt terrible," Clyde said.

"Sorry for that, Father," Jonathan replied. He was ashamed of his coldness and went over to his father's side and stood looking down on him.

" 'Twas the ax," his father groaned. He looked sunken-eyed and white from loss of blood. "A long-handled, unhandy thing, flingin' itself everyway in your hands. I had just drove in a post for the corner, and the dang thing turned on me like a beast bitin', and first thing I know I was spoutin' blood. I couldn't no more'n get to Drear's door and stand there roarin', when I dropped."

"Too bad, Father," Jonathan said. He must not show disgust, for this was his father. But silence for once was hard. He leaned over and gathered Arthur's little body and lifted him.

"Come and sit on my knee a bit, Artie," he said. "Your wee bones must be tired layin'."

"Lying," Mary said abruptly from the stove.

"It don't matter here, I think, Mother," Jonathan said. "There's nobody to know the difference between right and wrong ways of talkin'."

"All the more reason to be right," she said sharply. Then she softened. "Jamie's getting clever at catching hares," she said. "Until I get fowl it's a help, too."

"Where is he?" Jonathan asked.

"He can't stay away from the wagons going West," she said. "Likely he's up there by the road, watchin' 'em. That's one thing about Median—he can't come to much evil."

Clyde interrupted them. "Jonathan, I reckon you'll have to finish the coop for me."

Jonathan cuddled Arthur in his arms. "I can't, Father, unless on Sundays. I have a job at Merridy's."

"No, Jonathan, never!" Mary turned a bright face toward him.

"Yes, steady, Mother. Wage we haven't talked yet, but I shall stick up for what's right and then do my best."

"Oh, good son, Jonathan!" his mother cried softly, and to his astonishment she came to him and kissed the top of his head as he sat. Then, because she was embarrassed, she bent and kissed Arthur and said, "Now, my own, you shall have something to make you better. Jonathan will bring it you."

And Maggie, seeing all this as she played on the sod, bawled out, "Kiss—kiss!"

"Oh, you," Mary said, laughing. "You must always have everything, too!" She lifted the heavy child and kissed her on the cheeks and set her down again and turned back to Jonathan. "Oh, Jonathan, it's a terrible helplessness for a woman to know nothing's to come in at the end of the week."

He could scarcely bear in these days his mother's dashes of bravery and her moments of trembling. This was trembling, and something trembled in him, too. He said quickly, "We can take it in goods or cash as we need." And then, softened because he could do something for her, he said to his father, "I never made a fowl coop in my life, but I'll try, come Sunday, Dad; and this afternoon I'll tell Mr. Drear so. And now, Artie boy, I must eat and get back to work." He laid Arthur down tenderly beside his father and went to the table and sat down on a box that served for a chair.

Work was a good word to have upon the tongue, and he savored it with his food as he ate.

The store stood opposite the hotel and across the empty square. It was a frame building, made of planks nailed on a wooden skeleton and then covered outside with unpainted shingles and on the inside with thin lath and plaster, whitewashed. To Jonathan the shape of the building was like the dragon he had once seen in a picture of St. George and the Dragon at the vicarage in Dentwater. It had been a dragon with a great scaly ruff that stood up around the head but its body had been small. From the front the dragon had looked a terror, but behind it was nothing. He thought of this often with dry, secret amusement as he approached the store from the side each day. A great false front the store had, a high structure of painted boards, single thick, and across it painted in big letters "Merridy's General Store," and under that, in letters almost as big, "Median." From the front, with the two show windows for eyes and the door, always open, for a mouth, the store looked something stupendous. But behind this painted front was the boxlike building, an oblong for the store, cut off in the back to make three rooms for Lew Merridy's family. At almost any moment in the day customers could hear coming from those rooms a thin wailing duet. It prompted the kind to ask, "How's the twins, Lew?"

"Fine," he said. "Savin' their always wantin' more nourishment than their mother can give. What they need is a nanny goat."

From these rooms Katie came and went, a sharp, efficient child, quick to notice if Jonathan put a thing down where he had not taken it up. And yet he got on with her well enough in a curious meager way, with little speech and some dry joking. She was quick to see what he meant to do and to help him when she saw. The windows were his bane. Lew Merridy used them for dumps and leftovers, and this was an offense to Jonathan. He began on his fourth morning to carry out a plan he had been making in his mind from the first moment. It was midweek, and not many farmers came in, nor women; and he drew back the soiled gray half-curtains that separated the windows from the shop.

"What you at, Jonathan?" Mr. Merridy inquired. He sat on a keg of whisky reading a two-weeks-old newspaper that had reached him this morning by mail.

"Shall you mind, sir, if I clean a bit?" Jonathan answered.

"Naw," Merridy answered, his eyes on the paper, "though you'll find, Jonathan, it ain't no use to put time and stren'th in it. Kansas blows right thoo anything."

He forgot Jonathan and read the fine print, frowning. "Nigger population in Kansas is goin' up somethin' terrible," he said. "It's this talk of 'forty acres and a mule' is doin' it. Exodusters, they're called."

Jonathan, his head wreathed in dust, thought of Stephen Parry and his wife. I could do with more of them, he thought, and was about to say so when he sneezed violently, and when he came to himself Merridy had gone on. He began sorting everything into piles as neatly as he could— tobacco, lamp wicks, chipped dishes, candles, old copper, buttons, nails of all sizes, yards of sheeting yellowed with rain from a leak, a heap of small mothy skins of rabbits and moles and badger brought in for barter. He whistled under his breath as he worked to keep himself from speaking out what he thought. All this refuse!

"They's a feller named Buffalo Bill," Mr. Merridy announced, "he's hired to shoot buffalo meat for the railroad out West, and he's killed four thousand and more buffalo—a regular David and Goliath!"

Jonathan looked up. "Shall we get a railroad in Median, Mr. Merridy?"

"Shore wish we would," Merridy replied. "I would git my stock in easy, and the town would boom. Why, some towns around hyere when the railroad skips 'em just pick up and move the whole shebang to where the railroad is, they're so anxious not to miss it—put the town on wheels and go—"

"Well, I never!" Jonathan said simply. He was sweeping the window floor, and now Mr. Merridy himself sneezed and looked stern.

"I swear it ain't healthy to stir up all that old dirt," he said.

"I'll sprinkle it," Jonathan said. He took up a pail and went to the pump outside. Katie was there pumping, her thin arms flailing up and down.

"Here, I'll do it," he said good-naturedly and pumped her pail full first. "Wouldn't have a bit of rag to scrub with, would you?" he asked.

"Scrub what?" she demanded.

"Windows," he replied.

"Ma was goin' to clean them windows," she said, "if she hadn't had twins."

"Those windows," Jonathan said gently. But she did not understand, and he laughed and went back. A queer sharp female thing, he thought, brown like a scrawny hen. But a moment later she came, a rag in her hand.

"It's hard to find a rag since the twins came," she said. "We've used everything up for diapers."

She stood, watching while he sprinkled the dusty boards and swept. Then she dipped the rag into the water. "I'll scrub it up," she said.

He watched her, amused by her body moving in little quick hops as she worked. Like a grasshopper, he thought.

"They's some talk here of Median bein' a county seat," Mr. Merridy said. "Well, why not? We got a river that don't go dry, and we're at a crossroads. We're bound to grow—growin' all the time. Why, we've trebled in the last two years! Drear was the first, then I built my store, and look at the way folks are beginnin' to pile up!"

Jonathan doused the windowpanes.

"I wouldn't bother about them panes," Mr. Merridy said. "The first little shower will dirty 'em again."

"I'll rub them again, then," Jonathan answered peaceably.

"Katie!" Mrs. Merridy's voice rose above an outburst of dual wailing. Katie got up from her knees. "I'll have to go," she said quickly.

"Yes, sir," Mr. Merridy mused, "Median's goin' to be a great big town."

9

MEDIAN was the small heart of a vast body. There were days when the heart scarcely beat, and then Median seemed to Jonathan as remote from all the other parts of the earth as though it were alone upon a star. On such days few customers came in. Jennet ran in from the inn to buy saleratus, or Mrs. Drear came in for dried apples to make a pie, and perhaps through the day a straggling one or two of the other women came in for spool thread or a package of needles or a pound of coffee. His mother could not leave the sod house so long as his father could hobble no farther than the door. His leg healed, but in a wealed scar so that, as long as Clyde lived, he would limp.

Jonathan welcomed all except Jennet, but her he disliked, or thought he disliked. But it was only when she was there that he disliked her. When she stood by the counter, her face, soft and bold together, somehow shocked him. She was not bad-looking, but he hated the green glass color of her eyes, and he distrusted the way in which she spoke to him, as though she had known him all her life when they had only talked a few times.

"Hello, Jonathan, boy!" she always said carelessly.

"How do you do, Miss Jennet," he always replied in his best clerkly manner. "What can I do for you today?"

"Well, say, you can stop talking like that," she said.

He waited stiffly. He would talk as he pleased.

"Oh, heck, what do I care how you talk?" she cried discontentedly. "Give me a yard and a half of red ribbon."

"Not for yourself, I hope," he said.

"Why not for myself?" she demanded.

"Not with that red hair," he said, without knowing why, for it was none of his business.

"It's my red hair," she retorted.

"There's enough of it without red ribbons," he said.

She snatched the ribbon from his hand and tied it about her hair and made a bow over her ear. "There," she said.

He would not say it was handsome, but it was, though everybody knows a red-haired woman should never wear red.

"Anything else?" he asked coolly.

"Red calico," she said, "for a red dress. That! Eight yards."

He measured off eight yards of striped red-and-white calico, folded it, and in intense silence handed it to her. Lucky she had queer pale skin and did not freckle as most redheads did! But he would not tell her so.

"I'll come and show you the dress when I've made it," she said insolently.

He did not reply. He disliked her presence, and yet when she was gone he could not forget her. She was one of those girls whose every movement one remembered. She made him think of Constance, who had taught him to dance. But Constance was fluttery, as though she knew all the time that perhaps she was not quite nice. Jennet would not even know what niceness was. He looked thoughtfully out of the windows he kept so clean, and his eyes wandered on and on over the prairies, and he put Jennet out of his mind. The skies changed but the prairies never, except when they borrowed light and shadow from the sky. One would say not a soul lived upon that flat, endless plain.

Yet the more he looked at the prairie, the more he perceived that it was not flat at all. It rose, smooth and even, on a long, slow, steady pull westward. Walking over it day by day, he felt the earth was flat under his feet; but if he could have made steps a mile long, he would have felt the earth swirl upward. Sometimes, if the sky was cloudless at the horizon, especially at the moment of clearest twilight between sunset and night, he saw the slant of the earth against the sky, and then Median was in the middle of it. That long, level, rising plain was Median's body, and the people who came out of it were lifeblood flowing through Median. There were two kinds of people: those who came only once on their way to the West, and those who stayed and came again and again; and Lew Merridy and Jonathan were never agreed as to who should be served first if they came together.

For there were days when the store was full of clamoring, impatient people, anxious to get their wagons stocked and on the trail again, and others as anxious to get food and salt and goods to take to their homes. There was rivalry and sometimes even dislike between the two kinds of people. Those who were going on were sure that all who did not go with them were stolid fools, losing all for the sake of supposed prudence; and those who stayed and built sod houses and cleared land for farms and grew cattle and pigs and fowl and sowed crops and planted fruit trees scorned the great windy dreams of those who were going West.

"Hey, Jonathan!" Mr. Merridy roared, "git them folks waited on! They're goin' to Nebrasky and got to git started!"

"Just a minute," Jonathan called back, and went on filling the careful order of a farmer who lived ten miles across the long grass. "Two pounds of brown sugar—yes, sir—a small keg of black molasses, and a pound of bacon, and some nails—yes, sir—" This man would come again and again with the same needs. "Nice day," Jonathan said as he added the figures.

"A mite windy," the farmer replied. His eyebrows and hair were full of dust, and dust lay in the wrinkles of his face. "You don't get the wind here in town the way we do. Reckon I'll take a stick of that there peppermint for my little fellow. He's laid up today with a stone bruise and couldn't come."

Jonathan put in two sticks.

"Thanks," the farmer said. A look passed between the two, and Jonathan smiled. This was the sort of man he liked, a steady chap, working his bit of the prairie. He wrapped the order carefully and cut the string extra long. String was handy in a house. Then he went over to a huge hairy man with a big hat who was waiting for him and pulling at his beard furiously.

"Damned if I wasn't about ready to pull out of here," the man shouted. "I would have if the next store wasn't three days away. Now you just hustle yourself, young feller, and get me corn meal—a sack of it—and a side of bacon and plenty of beans, dried apples, a keg of black molasses, and sugar and salt and coffee—a kettle, for we busted ours last night—"

Jonathan put things together in silence. This man would go on and never be seen again. At the end of the day in the quiet of closing Mr. Merridy would say gravely, "It's like this, Jonathan. The steadies will come again and again. You can let 'em wait. But you got to wait on the others quick and git what you can out of 'em."

"But the store is built on the steadies, Mr. Merridy," Jonathan said. "I should think it's them you ought to consider first."

"Well, not necessarily," Mr. Merridy said, "not at all necessarily so, Jonathan. Their money ain't so sure, when you let 'em run bills the way I have to do, and then again I git run over with the stuff they bring in instead of cash. But the others have got to pay cash, 'cause we won't see 'em again and can say so."

"In the long run—" Jonathan began.

"You don't need to think about the long run in a country like this," Mr. Merridy interrupted. "All you need to take care of is right here and now."

"I don't agree with you, Mr. Merridy," Jonathan replied.

Mr. Merridy stared at him over his pipe. "Well, don't then!" he said. "But you're kind of young to say so like that."

"Yes, sir," Jonathan said respectfully. But walking home across that long slant of land under Median, he thought stubbornly, I'm right, and Merridy's wrong, for all that. It's the steadies that come first, anywhere.

"Jonathan's got to go in my place."

Behind his blanket curtain he heard his father say this sullenly in the night. He had taught his ears to be dull once he slipped into his own corner of the sod house, but now they picked these words out of the darkness, and he heard them. He had been aware of a low conversation between his parents, just as in the evening when he came home earlier than usual he had been aware of controversy in the atmosphere. But his young manhood demanded some sort of privacy; and, since there was none except what he and his mother made, he ignored his father's restlessness and busied himself about an improvement.

"I don't need to sleep on the floor any more, Mother," he said cheerfully. "Somebody told me something today, quite accidental-like. Seems folk make bedsteads just with slats driven into the walls and a post. I'm going to the river to cut cottonwood."

"Well, I never," Mary said without attention. Clyde must not say before Jonathan what he had been thinking and talking all day.

Jonathan took his father's ax and put it over his shoulder. Jamie, at home because he was hungry, started after him.

"Reckon I'll come and see if there's mushrats," he said.

"Muskrats it is, Jamie," Jonathan said kindly.

"Mushrats they call it here, though," Jamie retorted.

"You don't want to get talking like them, though," Jonathan said. "Most of them never had the chance for school."

It had not occurred to him for a long time to think about school. There had been no time since they had come to Median when anything could be thought of except shelter and food and the store.

"I don't need school here," Jamie said. "There's no books to read. And if I go with you, like Dad says I'm to, I'll never need school."

"What's Dad say?" Jonathan asked quickly.

"Him and Mother," Jamie replied. "They've been jawin' all day, every time I came in they were at it. Dad says you're to homestead for him over in the West. He says he can't make it this spring if he don't start, and he can't start with his sore leg, and so you're to go and me with you."

Plains and sky lengthened before Jonathan's eyes. "And who'll feed them while I'm gone?" he inquired bitterly. "That's like Father, saying what I'm to do and giving no thought to Mother and the little ones."

"He says he'll tend 'em," Jamie replied.

"And what did Mother say?" Jonathan asked.

"She says if you go, she goes," Jamie replied. He had been a step behind his brother, but he ran and caught up with him and cried, "And oh, Jon, don't say you won't go! Let's go! I hate this little bit of a place. Everybody says it's better out West."

Jonathan looked down into Jamie's pleading face. It looked suddenly strange to him, vivid and handsome as Jamie would look when he was a young man.

"You've got freckles," he said. "You didn't have them in England."

"There's more sun here than in England, that's why," Jamie said. "It idn't fog and rain all the time."

"Rained mud when we came," Jonathan said shortly.

"I know, but when it rains it rains, and then it's done with rain, and the sun comes out hot. It in't betwixt rain and sun all the time like it was in Dentwater."

"You like it here?" Jonathan asked.

"Lots more than England," Jamie replied. "Do you?"

"No," Jonathan said.

They were at the river now. It flowed before them almost as straight as a ditch because there were no rocks to turn the current, and the dark soil was smooth and free from obstruction, and the cottonwoods grew in clumps near the muddy water. They slid down the side of the gully, and Jonathan began his search for a tree.

"You'll go, won't you, Jonathan?" Jamie clamored.

"It'll take thinkin' of," Jonathan replied sternly. But it did not. He would not go. He would not leave his mother and the children to his father. He would not leave the small certainty of his job. He wanted to build another room to the house. And what was the use of pulling up their new roots they had scarcely put down to go to another place? "Lucky there's the Pacific Ocean to stop folks," he said sarcastically, "else they'd be goin' round and round the globe like cats chasin' their own tails."

Jamie looked up from a hole he was prodding with a stick. "There's gold out West," he said.

"If you like digging," Jonathan retorted. He began to chop at a small strong tree until in a few strokes he had it down. Henry Drear had taught him the Sunday he had finished the fowl coop how to swing an ax clear of his legs. By the time the coop was finished, the ax felt comfortable in his hands. Now he stripped the branches off quickly and chopped off two lengths and a shorter one.

"I'm done," he said.

"I'll wait a little," Jamie said. "The feller's hidin' in here." He lay on his stomach peering into the hole and did not offer to help Jonathan pull the poles to the top of the gully, and Jonathan did not ask it.

Jamie's the only one of us like Dad, he thought, and struggled up alone and home again.

They were still quarreling. He knew because talk ceased so abruptly when he entered the house. But he would notice silence no more than talk, he had made up his mind by now. If his mother could win without putting her battle on him against his father, let her. Once he began that quarrel, there would be no end to it.

"Come and help me, Ruth," he commanded his sister. She was curling Maggie's hair.

"Wish I could help you, Jonathan," Arthur said. He was sitting by the fire in their only chair, a quilt folded behind him for a pillow.

"So you shall one of these days," Jonathan said. He went behind his curtain. "Now then, you see, Ruth, the post goes here, and then I jam one pole into this wall and the long pole the other way and notch 'em into the post. Now, what you're to do for me is to sew up those sacks I brought from the store, and we'll slip the poles through before I nail 'em firm, and I'll have myself a good bed off the floor."

"Oh, Jonathan, it's clever!" Ruth cried. "Whoever told you?"

"A chap told me at the store when he came in wantin' bags," Jonathan said.

His mother came to see, and Maggie trotted in and out while they worked; and to Jonathan the house seemed for the first time a home. The outdoor air was warm, but there was a fire in the sod fireplace for cooking their supper. They were more lucky than most, for Jonathan could bring home from the store boxes of wood too thin to use for planks, and these made the green cottonwood burn. There were still some women who used buffalo chips, but Mary hated the dung in the house. She had scraped the walls very smooth, and in the deep earthen window sills had set jars of prairie flowers. Since the flowers had bloomed she had been happier, though they were flowers strange to her and to everybody, so that most of them had no names. Jonathan had made two benches and stools, and had brought home red-and-white checked oilcloth for the table. Now when the oil lamp was lit the light upon white cotton curtains, the flowers, the fire, and the smell of cornbread baking made home.

Jamie came in late with three fish on a string.

"I'll clean 'em if you'll cook 'em, Ruth," he said.

And they sat down to their meal of cornbread and fish and a dish of beans, and dandelions that Ruth had picked and washed.

They ate, but Clyde was silent and Mary talked too much, as though she were trying to keep him silent. But Jonathan noticed a change in her. The last week her talk had been all of a garden if she could get the sod peeled off, and he had promised her now that the coop was done for Mr. Drear that he would chop out the sod tomorrow, which was his first Sunday, and she could scarcely wait. She had gathered seeds from here and there, but most from Stephen Parry's wife.

Tonight she said nothing of gardens. It was all of how glad she was to get his mattress off the ground and how good he was to think to hear about such a thing, and how Arthur had eaten well today with no coaxing, and how Maggie ran away twice and the second time came running back because there was what she called "a big long thing."

"A snake, of course," Mary said swiftly, "and I was in terror. It might have been a rattler or a copperhead, even. Naughty Maggie!"

"Naughty Maggie," Maggie repeated with pleasure. "Oh, oh, Maggie!"

Then, in the middle of the night in the unusual softness of his bed hung in sacking instead of spread upon the sod, he heard his father say, "Jonathan's got to go in my place," and knew what it meant.

He got up solemnly and put on his trousers and coat and went out into the space where the other children slept. His parents slept in the space beyond, and under the blanket hung in the doorway he saw a light. He went to it and called softly, "Mother!"

She was not in bed. But he saw when she came to put the curtain aside that she had been in bed and had got up, perhaps because she was angry, for she had her shawl wrapped about her. From under it her unbleached cotton nightgown flowed like a skirt.

"Mother, I couldn't help hearing," he said.

"Then come in," she replied. "You may as well hear everything."

He went in with her. A small oil lamp made out of a tin can and a wick lit the dark walls in flickers of light and shadow. He sat down on a box.

"I heard what you said, Father," he repeated. "So I got up to see what it was all for."

Clyde sat up in bed. He had not shaved since he cut his leg, and his black beard shadowed his smooth, eternally youthful face. "I'm glad you did hear me," he said. "Your mother's been ahushin' me until I'm fit to bust. Wants to down me, she does, without your hearin' the yes and no of it. It's this way, Jonathan. Land's to be had cheap in the West, and 'tidn't goin' to last forever the way folks is goin'. Jamie says fourteen wagons come through yestiddy. Stands to reason it won't last, for the land is wunnerful. I herded sheep on it last summer for a chap. Grass is short but full of richness for stock. But I don't want to herd sheep. The land's too good for it. It's not black gummy stuff like this mud under our feet. It's sandy light, and wheat's the thing."

Mary broke in, her voice dry with scorn. "Seeing how you couldn't grow a bit of corn in England, I don't see how calling it wheat over here will teach you."

Clyde paid no heed. He was talking to his son now as man to man. "You can't do with a tiddlin' bit of land out there, neither. It ain't a matter of a horse and a cow and a couple of pigs and a little bit of this and that to harvest whenever it likes to grow ready. Out there a man must work in a big large way, and if he does, then he's rich."

Mary groaned, "Oh, I've heard everything big and large ever since the day I first saw you in Blackpool, lounging on a street corner, talking about how you'd caught a whale!"

"And you stopped to listen," Clyde said.

"Yes, and it was the devil I didn't see hanging on my skirts made me," Mary retorted, "for I was in good circumstances teaching school, and my pay like clockwork every week, and never was again after I married you."

Clyde laughed. "Wait till I get my section of land, Mary, and a big frame house built for you in the middle of it!"

"It'll have to have trees before I like it," Mary said moodily. "I'm sick of this naked country."

"Trees I s'all plant when the foundation's set," Clyde said largely.

"Oh, we're fools," Mary cried. "There's no house and no land, and we're talking about trees!"

"There'll be everything if you do as I say, Jonathan," Clyde said earnestly. "Here's the plan. You get a seat on a wagon and go out there and pick a place for us. Sooner the better, for maybe the best is gone a'ready. The law is you must put up a sign of habitation. Well, a bit of a sod house will do it, a shelter-like, and you can get help by tradin' your own help. That's easy. Then when my leg lets me—"

Jonathan sat watching his father's full red lips moving in his black beard.

Mary cried out, "I won't have Jonathan going there by himself. 'Tisn't fair, Clyde, the way you put your work on him."

"As if I weren't givin' him the better job!" Clyde roared. "Why, here I be, alayin' in a place as dull as a ditch, and everythin' waitin'!"

"Everywhere you are is always a ditch to you," she said, "and what's ahead is always everything. You've dragged us out of England here, and now it's not six months and this is a ditch—though I'm not against saying for once you're right."

The look Jonathan and his mother both knew came over Clyde's dark face. If he could have walked he would have walked out of the house. But he could not.

"Put up or shut up," he muttered.

And all the time they were quarreling Jonathan was making up his own mind. He was not deciding an answer so much as allowing his natural being to gather into a great negation.

"Father," he said, "I won't go."

"Now, Jonathan—" his father began.

"I don't mean to go," Jonathan said. "Why, I couldn't put in words. I didn't want to leave England, but I left it. Now I'm here, and I won't pull up again."

"Of all the danged silly talk for a young chap to make, that's the worst," Clyde shouted. "Where'd the world be if folk were like you, Jonathan? Why, the world wouldn't ha' been discovered at all, and we'd all be stayin' in the same little hole some'ere killin' each other and fightin' for the same bits of bread, and not knowin' that out beyond was plenty and richness."

"I'm not sayin' everybody ought to be like me, Father," Jonathan said mildly. "I'm only sayin' how I am. The way I look at it, there's two kinds of folk in the world, just like there's two kinds of life in a seed. Something sends one kind up to hunt its food in the light and air, and sends the other kind down into the earth to make the roots. Well, the root is me."

He was aware of his mother sitting on the side of the bed listening to all he said, her braid of yellow hair over her shoulders, her arms wrapped in her shawl; and he used his figure for her ears, though he spoke to his father, and his father answered in a snort.

" 'Tis only sense even in a root to find the best place."

"Root begins where seed falls," Jonathan said calmly, "and here I stay."

"And I'll stay with you, son," Mary said.

Clyde flung out his arms and shut his eyes and ground his jaws together in a groan. Then he slid down into the bed and drew the patchwork quilt about him.

"Oh, dang the two of you together!" he muttered.

"All right, Father," Jonathan replied, and went back to his bed. To his mother he said nothing, but there passed between them a deep look, and it was enough.

The next morning when Jonathan came out his father was sitting at the table dipping cornbread into a cup of tea and biting it off. Jamie sat beside him.

"Well, Father," Jonathan said and sat down away from him. Ruth moved quickly and silently across from the stove and set tea before him. He nodded at her. "Where's Mother?" he asked.

"She's a headick, and I told her to stop abed and I'd do," Ruth said.

"Right," Jonathan replied. A good girl Ruth was getting to be, he thought, quiet and good. He must go in and see his mother before he left.

"You're up," he said to his father.

"Have to be," Clyde said bitterly. "My leg's no good to me yet, but I s'all have to do with it and Jamie—eh, Jamie?"

"Yes, Dad," Jamie said. He eyed Jonathan warily over a slab of cornbread spread with molasses.

"Jamie and me is goin' West," Clyde said loudly. "I'm goin' to get over to Drear's today and see to it."

This was why his mother had a headache, then! He was about to exclaim in answer to his father and saw that his father expected it and so he did not. But would she let him go and take Jamie with him?

"Jamie s'all help his old Dad," Clyde was saying in heavy self-pity. "Jamie's the only one in the family that feels like I do. We'll have a rare good time together, eh, Jamie? We'll see lots of sights. There's buffalo runnin' out there yet and wild horses, and you can snare quails and wild fowl, and at night we'll camp around a big fire. There's Indians, too, nice ones, not cruel, and they'll bring you maize with the husks off and show you how to catch fish by ticklin' them under their chins."

All the time his father talked to Jamie, Jonathan felt himself used as a channel through which to wound his mother. His father was striking at her. He tried by silence, by eating his food, by calling for Maggie to come and have a cup of tea, to close the channel, but Clyde kept talking.

"We'll ride over the mountains, and we'll find us a good place, Jamie and me together, and we'll build a fine house, and then when you all come we'll be stannin' at the front door sayin' we told 'em so, eh, Jamie?"

Jamie was disconcerted, feeling something beyond himself in all this. "All right, Father," he said.

"An' then we'll see about roots movin'," Clyde said in a loud voice.

Jonathan could bear no more. He rose. "Shall you be goin' today, Father?" he asked coldly. Maggie had his teacup tipped tight against her face, waiting for the molasses at the bottom of it to run into her mouth.

"As soon as I can find a wagon with a place empty," Clyde replied. "Happen today, happen tomorrow. I can't waste my time no more if I'm to get ahead of others."

"I'll hear news later, then," Jonathan said. And, holding his slender shoulders square, he went in to his mother. She was lying curled up very small on the spot where he had seen his father stretched last night.

"Are you feeling bad, Mother?" he asked.

"My head's fearful," she said faintly and did not open her eyes.

He stood there longing to comfort her, longing to say to her, "Don't mind him, Mother. Let him go. You and I'll manage." But his intuition told him that the balance of her soul at this moment was very delicate, and a little could change it away from him if he spoke against his father. So he put away what he longed to say and thought of something else.

"Mother, I'm going to Stephen Parry's this noon and ask him to lay the floor down. I can manage it now that I'm working Saturdays too."

She opened her eyes at this. "That'll be just fine, Jonathan," she said, and he saw the pleasure in her eyes.

"Good," he said and kissed her forehead, and as he stooped she put up her hand and touched his cheek, and he knew he had kept the balance of her soul.

Six days later Clyde left Median. The wound in his leg was not healed yet, but it was closing healthily from the bottom, and he was not as lame as he was to be later when the muscles made a knot under the scar. Still, his leg could not bear his weight, and he had a stick in one hand and with the other he leaned upon Jamie's shoulder.

Jonathan ran out of the store in midmorning to see the wagons start. What sort of a farewell there had been between his parents he had not been there to see, and he was glad of it. It was as well for his mother to have a few hours before he came in at noon.

"Good-by, Father," he said sedately.

Clyde did not hear him. He was full of joy, and his black eyes were snapping with laughter and light. Just now he chanced to look at Jennet, who came running out of the tavern door, her arms full of loaves of bread.

"Here—I baked 'em last night," she cried. A tall young man took them from her, and she did not hear Clyde calling her name. "I wish I was going," she said to the young man boldly.

"Come along," he replied as boldly. He was tall and blond, and he drawled as he spoke. "I'll take you," he said.

"But will I take you?" Jennet said, laughing.

"It's for you to say," the young man replied. He pulled his belt and knotted a red handkerchief around his neck and tilted a big straw hat he wore.

"Ask me again," Jennet said.

"When?" he asked.

"Oh, in a year or two," she said, pretending to be careless. But she did not move her green eyes from his face.

"Too long," he said. "You'll be too old. A month from today if a wagon comes along, hop on it, and ride till you come to a river that crosses the trail once and doubles on itself in a mile. Somewhere in that mile I'll be watching for you. What'll you be wearin', so I can see you far off?"

She caught sight of Jonathan. "A red dress," she said.

"That'll be topping," he said. He leaped up on the wagon beside Clyde.

"That's the kind of lass I admire," Clyde said heartily, "always ready."

The tall fair young man looked at him. "You old goat!" he said softly.

Jonathan went close to the wagon and touched his father's knee. "Good-by, Father," he said clearly.

Clyde jumped at the touch and looked down. "Good-by, Jonathan, I was lookin' for you."

"I was here all the time," Jonathan said dryly. "Good-by, Jamie, mind you take care of Father and don't run ahead of him."

"You needn't tell me," Jamie replied. His cheeks were red, and he sat squeezed against the side of the wagon beside his father, a bundle on his knees.

The wagon started, and the young man whipped his horses until they galloped away in whirls of black dust, in rushes of grinding wheels and squeaking axles. Jonathan watched them until the noise was lost in the distance and upon the wideness of the prairie the dust was no bigger than what a man might gather in his hand and let fall again.

Who, he wondered, was that tall young chap, and was he joking with Jennet or not? It was not easy always to know whether men on the prairie were joking or serious. They told of large happenings in cool, careless voices, and there was no line clear between truth and lying, either in their minds or out. He could only discover the truth of anything by chance and by his own common sense.

But when he turned his head Jennet had gone, and it was none of his business to follow her to find out what she meant. He had his work to do, and he went back to it. He went home at noon, dreading but dogged and determined to be usual. He was never sure of his mother's mood. If the farewell with his father had been hard, then she would find something to blame him for, and he prepared himself for this.

But he found her quiet and cheerful and full of some sort of relief that he could not understand. They had an hour at table that was gay as they had not been gay since they left Dentwater. He was so relieved that he could not but let her know. Alone with her a moment as she followed him out of the door, he said, "Mother, I was frightened to come home because you might be sorrowful."

"I am sorrowful," she said quickly. "A woman's always sorrowful when her man is away. Everything is tasteless, like salt left out."

He felt crestfallen, but did not speak because he saw she wanted to say more. It was something hard, for her smooth small face grew shell-pink.

"It's time I said something to you as a man, Jonathan," she said, "because some day you'll have a wife. I've asked your dad to speak to you and Edward, but he always dangs himself and won't, he says, for shame. But I think of your wife, and I thought of Millie, and on Edward's wedding day I screwed myself up and said to him, 'Let Millie have the say-so, between you.' That's been the one thing wrong 'twixt your father and me, Jonathan. He's always had the say-so, and however I was afraid of a child coming when I hadn't the strength for it, his was the say-so. I did cry when he went this morning because I do miss him sorely, and still I was glad to be shut of fear for a while. I don't want more children, Jonathan, though I love you all so dear."

She had grown more confident as she spoke and yet not less shy, and she spoke to him with a sort of tender, delicate dignity. As for him, he was repelled and drawn and a little sickened, too—not by her, but by the opening of a door he wanted closed between them. All other doors he wanted open, but not this one. For through it he saw her apart from him; he saw her not his mother, but a woman having secret problems in her womanhood which he could never understand, until perhaps he himself was married to a woman. He withdrew from the thought of this woman to come, wanting no confusion, indeed, no connection between her and this one now before him.

"I think I understand, Mother," he said, his mouth very dry. He looked out over the prairie, searching for something to see and mention. But there was nothing. The long grass waved for miles in the unfailing wind, and the sky was its endless blue. He looked down to the earth at his feet, and then he thought of something.

"I shall start your garden when I come home tonight, Mother. Evenings are long now."

"Do, son," she said quietly and, in comprehension, they parted.

10

As THEY had clung to the cottage in Dentwater after Clyde left it, so now they clung to the sod house in Median. But the cottage had not seemed so much an island as the sod house. There had been a score of connections with life in Dentwater, but here a line thrown out could never reach the other side of anything. Median was a steppingstone, a wayside stop. Even those who stayed had no life of their own. They spent their days in serving those who were going on somewhere. The inn was made for these, and the store prospered on travelers, and Stephen Parry put a blacksmith forge in his carpenter shop that he might shoe horses that passed by.

He came to Jonathan one day with a smooth white pine board. "Please, sir, Mr. Goodliffe," he said respectfully, "will you write me some letters on this yere boa'd?"

"I will, of course," Jonathan said. He was a little startled at being called Mr. Goodliffe. No one had ever given him that name before. He was shy and pleased. "But what letters?"

"I don' know the name of any letter," Stephen Parry confessed sadly.

"What do you want said?" Jonathan asked.

"I'd like my name put," the man answered, "and that I can do carpenterin' and blacksmith's work and I don' cha'ge no more'n fair."

Jonathan drew a sheet of paper toward him and printed, "Stephen Parry, Carpenter and Blacksmith. Prices Moderate."

He looked up to see Parry's eyes full of wonder and wistfulness upon his pencil.

"Sho' do wish I could read," he said. "A man's like in prison when he don't read."

"Would you like me to teach you?" Jonathan asked.

Stephen Parry hesitated. "I'd shore like my children to learn," he said. "Wish they was a school for them." He looked at Jonathan with sudden earnestness. "Mr. Goodliffe, why don' you open a school?"

"No one has asked me," Jonathan said diffidently.

"Wish somebody would, then," Stephen Parry said.

"How many children have you?" Jonathan asked. He had seen small dark creatures coming out of the dugout in which Stephen lived.

"Six," the man replied, "but only four old enough to learn."

"Tell you what I'll do, Mr. Parry," Jonathan said. "If you'll lay a board floor in our house, I'll teach them Saturday afternoons and evenings."

"I'll do it gladly," Stephen Parry said. He stood turning his hat round and round. "I don't know if you noticed my son Beaumont, Mr. Goodliffe. My wife and me, we think he's real smart. We'd like him to have a chance, not jest because he's ours, but because we figger that now us colored folk got our freedom, next thing is to show what we can do with it. My wife and me, we figger we can't do much 'cept give our younguns a chance to do what we cain't. Beaumont's the one, or so we think."

"Beaumont," Jonathan repeated. "A queer name."

"My wife belonged to Beaumonts befo' we married," the man said. "I was always a Parry, though, and my father befo' me. Well, I'll be gettin' along, Mr. Goodliffe. It'll be good news to my fambly. And I'll git the lumber together right away for the floor." He walked away with his peculiar long, loping step. As a boy he had run beside his master's coach, and his muscles had grown to it.

Thus it came about that Jonathan taught his first school to four black children. They appeared early in the evening of that same day. Stephen Parry came with them.

"Here they are, suh," he said, when Jonathan came to the door from the supper table. "This yere's Beaumont. How old you, Beaumont?"

"Thirteen," the tall dark boy said quickly.

"He's the on'y one we had befo' de war," his father said. "The res' is all bohn free. This yere's Melissa, and this one is Gemmie—name's Gem from that hymn about 'gems in His crown'—and this one's Paul. Kin I come in, suh, and take measure of the floor?"

"Come in," Jonathan said. He felt a little shy before the four children, all eager and very clean. But he pulled aside the buffalo skin that hung as a wind curtain against the door, and they came in, standing in a tight small circle. His mother looked up as she cleaned the table of dishes and food.

"Sit down, children," she commanded them. They did give one a turn, she thought, looking at them, but God had made them, though why black it would be hard to tell. They sat down at once, the girls' starched dresses crackling. Mary laughed. "I haven't seen starch since I left England."

"Ma makes it out of 'taters," Melissa said in a small voice and coughed for shyness behind a dark little hand.

"I'll have to get the receipt," Mary said.

"She soaks 'em real good," Gem spoke up, not shy at all. "Somepin white comes out and lays in the bottom of de pan. It's starch."

They were all spellbound by the row of black children, lips so red, eyes so large and black and white. Now Maggie burst out of the spell with a loud bellow of fright, and Ruth caught her up and took her into the other room.

"For shame, Maggie!" Mary called, and to make amends cut four slices of bread and spread them with molasses. "Now eat before you begin to study," she said. "Reading is very hard. I know, for once I taught school myself in England."

Stephen Parry looked up from the ground he was measuring. "Did you, ma'am? That's how your son is so smart, I reckon."

"Jonathan's always been very hard-working," Mary said calmly.

And Jonathan, to rid himself of their talk about him, lifted Arthur to the chair at the end of the table. "This chap knows how to read as well as anybody," he said playfully. "You can help me, eh, Artie boy?"

He arranged the small boy carefully in a quilt and tucked it firmly about him to strengthen the bones that never seemed strong enough to uphold even the thin body.

Stephen watched him. "Ailin'?" he inquired gently.

"He's much better," Mary said.

"My wife mought be able to fix him some yarbs," he said. "She's good on declines. She can tell in a look whether a body's goin' to get well or not."

"There's no doubt about Artie's gettin' well," Mary said quickly, and as quickly hurried on, "Now, Artie, lad, you shall tell the first letter. Draw it big, with chalk on the table."

She handed him the piece of crude chalk which Jonathan had brought home from the store, and carefully Arthur drew the two long triangular lines and the cross. Everyone watched. Mary watched the pale face. I don't want anybody looking at him to see death in him, she was thinking. The four black children leaned with passionate eagerness to watch.

"That's A," Arthur said, very gravely and clearly, looking up.

"A," all the black children said, loud and quick.

Jonathan felt something pull at him. He looked up involuntarily and saw Stephen Parry, staring at his children as though he had been struck. He raised his eyes to Jonathan, and suddenly they were full of tears that brimmed over his cheeks. He dabbed them away with his big black hand and laughed.

"Nobody in my fambly's ever been able to read a letter befo'," he said, "but I don' know why I have to cry about it now that they're gonna learn."

Two days later in the afternoon Jennet came into the store. He saw her as soon as she stood in the door. She was wearing her red dress and a small red bonnet that she had made of the same calico. Everyone in the store saw her. There were no women there. The rush of the day's business was over, and the seven or eight men were talking as they lingered over small purchases of snuff and a dipperful of whisky or a handful of sugar in a twist of brown paper.

The men around the cracker barrel drew aside to let her pass, and she went to Lew Merridy, who was dipping whisky out of a tub for an old man whose feet were tied up in rags.

"Any mail in today, Lew?" Her voice, carelessly clear, floated above their heads.

"No, the bag ain't come in yet today," Merridy replied. "You expectin' a letter?"

"Yes, I am," she said. She stood, her full red skirt swaying slightly. "What whisky is that?" she asked.

"Stuff I made myself outa corn," he replied. "Wanta taste it?"

"Don't care if I do," she said, and put out her hand for the tin cup. She drank it as easily as water and tipped her head, and the eyes of every man were upon that white throat. She drank the last drop and handed the cup back.

"It's good," she said.

"Don't burn, eh?" Merridy replied.

"Nothin' burns me," she said. And then, her green eyes shining, she sauntered over to Jonathan, and he could smell her breath, sweet and strong.

"Folks tell me you're teachin' school, Jonathan," she said.

He looked at her and quickly looked away again. "Mr. Parry's making us a floor, and I'm teaching his children for pay," he said, and went on folding up calico that the morning's business had disarranged and piling it up.

"Don't know any Mr. Parry," she said. "I never heard of anybody but ol' Steve Parry. He's a nigger."

Jonathan did not answer. The men were recovering themselves now as they sat about the store. It was the quiet end of the day. No one was buying, only talking. He heard the bits of their talk, the news told and retold from mouth to mouth, the scraps of opinion, the forecasts, prophecies, reminiscences which were forming without his being aware of it a background of knowledge better than books or newspapers could have given.

"There's more'n twelve hundred miles of railroad in the state now, they say."

"Did ye hear that meat's bein' shipped clear to New York now, in them newfangled icebox cars? Looks like we all better take to cattle."

"Capital buildin's finished in Topeka—yep, I saw it last month myself. A mighty fine sight."

Thus he knew that telegraph lines ran across Kansas, that there were colleges begun, that railroads were taking out cattle by the thousand and bringing back money to be thrown away by wild cowboys in Abilene and Dodge City, that fortunes were to be made even out of buffalo bones picked up from the prairies and shipped east for fertilizer. But none of this had anything to do with Median nor with himself, when days for him were as evenly alike as though he had stayed in an ancient English village.

"Like my dress?" Jennet demanded.

"I haven't seen it," he said prudently from behind a pile of calico.

"Well, look at it," she retorted.

He waited a moment before he threw a glance at it.

"Very nice," he said, purposefully colorless. He was startled at heart to see how she wore red. The violent scarlet subdued her to real beauty. It dominated her red curls and made them gold and tawny, it deepened the whiteness of her skin. Only the green of her eyes remained sharpened for contrast. These eyes were now terrifying to him in their power. He knew as he knew his own name that he could love a girl and lose everything he was in loving her. He felt his body tremble and turned his back on her abruptly, pretending to search a shelf.

"I can wear red because I love it," she said. "A woman can always wear what she loves."

He tried to whistle softly as he ran his hands over the stuffs and could not because his lips were too dry.

Danged if I will love her, he thought, and suddenly felt sick enough to retch. He turned about to face her. "Time for me to go," he said.

"Time for school?" she teased him. "If I weren't older'n you, Jonathan, I'd come and be your pupil. As it is, what could you teach me?"

"Nothing, it's true," he said against his longing will. Too tight across the bosom her dress was, he thought, looking at it. He moved to the door and out into the square, and she followed him and caught up to his side. He was ashamed to have her there in her loud red dress, and, as conscious of all her beauty as though he had her in his arms, he walked sturdily on, not looking at her and enduring all the whirling of his blood.

She stopped him in the middle of the square. "Jonathan, I'm going away."

"Are you?" he said stupidly.

"Do you care?" She looked from under her red bonnet to his eyes, exactly level with hers.

"No," he said, and went white with the effort of the lie.

"You lie," she said.

He did not answer this, having no answer.

Then she asked him one more question. "Are you going to stay in this hole of a Median all your life, Jonathan?"

"Yes," he replied.

"Oh, well," she said, and parted from him abruptly, carelessly, moving through the clear summer light like fire springing along out of prairie grass. He looked away from her and went on. Fire, that was what she was. He could not play with her, for she would go on alive, but he would be ashes. Let her go into the West and burn it up if she would.

He heard the next day that she was gone. She had run away by the earliest wagon to leave the inn that morning. Who the man was that drove it no one could remember, once she was missed.

"It was that feller from Pennsylvania, that Dunkard or somethin' with a long beard," Henry Drear moaned.

"No, it wasn't," his wife snapped at him. She was shrill with anger. "It was one of them Rooshians from land knows where."

They thought by the end of the day it was neither of them, but an Englishman, the landless younger son of some nobleman, come to America to found an estate. He had come to Median two days earlier, very elegant in a waistcoat and high boots, his trousers tailored in London, and his blue coat tight across his shoulders. Jonathan had seen him and waited on him and had listened in silence to his frequent and impatient cry, "Good God, you don't have that, either?"

He had grown tired of it finally and had said quietly, "We carry all that the people here seem to want."

The young Englishman had been astonished at his impudence and looked stern for a moment.

"I say, you're never English!"

"I was," Jonathan said.

"Then you still are," the Englishman retorted.

"No, I'm not," Jonathan said firmly. He had not thought of such a controversy until this moment, and would not have dreamed of denying England until now. "I'm American," he said.

"The devil you are," the young man replied. "Well, certainly this isn't England," he added.

"No, it isn't," Jonathan said, and resisted and conquered the instinct to add "sir."

"A blasted proud feller if she's taken him," the opinion in the store said. "That sort of feller makes you glad we won the war in '76."

Jonathan at his post said nothing. If Jennet had gone with the Englishman, it would be for a purpose of her own. He thought of the directions the tall fair young man had given her three weeks ago, the day his father went away to homestead. Beyond the prairie, farther than the sight of his eyes would ever reach, a river doubled on itself and made a rich green valley. Somewhere in that valley she would stay, at least for a day, at least for a night. He felt a great wrench in his vitals and endured it and went on about his business.

That evening when he went home he stepped inside the door and felt beneath his feet a floor of clean white board. His mother hurried to meet him, and he saw her small face bright as it had not been since they left England.

"Oh, Jonathan, the floor's done!" she cried.

"Like it?" he asked. He pretended to test it, to examine it, as he walked about stamping on it here and there.

"It's just wonderful," she said, "it makes me feel at home again to have my feet on a floor."

"That's good, Mother," he said.

The wintry spring in which Clyde had gone gave way to a summer so different from any they had ever known that the very sun seemed another than the one which had shone upon England. Summer in Dentwater had been mornings of sun-shot mists rolling away at noon over miles of soft green spreading to blue water in the distances. That green even on clear days was shadowy with trees and valleys; and under the trees, centuries old, cattle and men could lie at noon and always be cool.

But in Median there were no trees. The sun flattened the earth with light and heat which none could escape. Cattle went to the drying river and stood fetlock deep in the shallow water and moved as the thin shadows of the cottonwoods moved and shrank and stretched again at evening. The store became a trap of heat, and if the windows were opened the dusty winds tore at every floating end of paper and scrap and string and rattled and cracked until the place was full of restless noise intolerable to hear.

Then the sod house seemed as quiet and cool as a cave. Jonathan left it reluctantly in the morning and at noon entered its dimness gladly. His mother kept the windows closed and the door shut and sprinkled water upon the walls, and the fresh smell of damp earth added to its coolness. She had continued somehow week by week to make a place of comfort out of what had begun as a hovel. The floor had been a cheerful thing to her, and after it was finished she braided rugs for it out of ends of goods Jonathan brought her. Remnants he had always. It was one of Merridy's complaints against women that they would not pay a penny more for a few inches which were useless to him. For the women of Median had not yet taken to making rugs and quilts and cushions and all those signs of staying that women have. They were not sure of Median yet, and if someday a man shouted, "We're moving on!" then all their work would become useless stuff in a wagon too small for necessities.

But Mary in Median had all the desperate certainty of one stranded upon an island in midocean, to which no ship sails. There was no hope of return for her, and she would go no farther; and so bit by bit she created about herself a little England. Thus, out of all the helter-skelter homes in Median, sod houses, dugouts, a few of frame, some of frame and earth together, only hers was like a home when one stepped into it. She had made a pair of chairs out of two barrels and cushioned them with brown-and-white calico, and they stood beside the fireplace. Her floor was clean, even though water was as dear as silver and had to be carried from the tavern well; and upon shelves made of boards resting on pegs driven in the wall her plates and tin cups were shining bright. When the spring flowers were gone she picked grasses and put them, merely for greenness, in the bottles and cans she had made into vases.

Until evening she did not stir beyond her door. The garden which Jonathan had planted rushed into fruitage, but now it was dying in the summer sun. There was too little water, and rain came in storm and deluge and in a few hours was gone.

"Everything in this country is crazed," she told Jonathan one Sunday while the sky above them sprang with light and roared and crackled and dropped down upon them in a fall of water. "Nothing is moderate and thoughtful-like." She was darting about as she spoke, putting pans and earthen crocks under familiar leaks. Now that the floor was done, the roof was their sorrow. Jonathan had talked with Stephen Parry about it.

"It'll have to be took off," Stephen had said, "and proper rafters and a real roof put on. But it'll never be so cool no more."

"Wait until autumn, then," Jonathan had said. Let the roof shelter them from sun, at least. It was a queer-looking roof, for the sod had grown long grass, and the wild sunflowers had seeded in it, and it was like a garden. But it let the rain through in streams and grew sodden with the weight of water, until Jonathan, frightened at its sag, put posts and planks under it lest it fall upon them in their sleep and the sod house be their tomb.

"Crazy it is," Jonathan agreed with his mother.

He was glad it was Sunday when this storm came and that he was in this low earthen home that clung to the ground, instead of in the flimsy store building where the lightning seemed to dart through from window to window. He was ashamed to show fear after he had once seen Mrs. Merridy afraid. He scarcely ever saw her, for she seldom left the back rooms where she lived; but if the sky darkened to storm, she came into the store, a thin, nervous, silent woman, carrying on either arm a twin. She set them down in empty boxes and then, herself on a stool between them, she waited, her arms locked across her breast, until the storm was over. No cheerfulness could touch her. Between the cracks of thunder she said doleful things to her husband.

"It was a storm like this that struck Hasty's Mill last summer, Lew."

"Didn't do much hurt," Merridy said, twiddling his fingers at his baby sons sitting placidly in the packing boxes, sucking at hardtack.

"If they hadn't caught it, the whole place would have been burned up," she reminded him.

"Yep, but it wasn't," he said. "You never seem to remember that. Besides, couldn't nothing burn in a rain like this." The rain was pounding upon the tin roof.

Jonathan, working hard over books, trying not to see the flashes of greenish light, trying not to hear the falling of the heavens in thunder, felt the sweat stream under his clothes until he seemed to stand in water in his shoes. It occurred to him once to wonder where Katie was in storms. She darted in and out of the store daily to cry out, "Ma wants some crackers, Pop!" or "We're clear out of salt," or to bring the empty molasses jug. But in a storm he never saw her. He asked her once, "What do you do with yourself in a storm, Katie? I should think you'd come in where we are."

She threw her skimpy brown braid away from her shoulders.

"I ain't afeared like Ma is," she said, and after a moment went on, "Lightnin' only hits you if you're feared of it."

He thought of this saying of hers thereafter in any storm, and he thought of it now, under the dripping ceiling of the sod-house roof. If it were true, one day he would die by this prairie lightning.

But summer was made of storms and drought and dry blue sunshine. They were wrenched from one extreme to the other until they were physically weary of it, except Maggie, who thrived and grew. Against the violence of weather, each maintained himself as he was able. Ruth that summer began to study Latin. She begged it out of Jonathan at meals and while he hoed the garden in the morning, trying to coax dew into rain by his mulching. Arthur took to his bed again and lay long hours with his eyes closed, holding his life in him by silence and stillness. And Jonathan maintained himself by marking off the hours of his days into exact routine of one kind of work and another.

The one marvel which the days held was Beaumont, the black boy. For in this child of a strange race there was an intelligence the like of which Jonathan had never seen, and he knew humbly that it was far beyond his own. The other three children learned well enough, stammering through their primers by the end of summer; but Beaumont was reading not so much by letters and words in sentences as by the ideas he discovered. He was the tawniest of these dark children, in the brownness of his skin a dark gold, and in the blackness of one of his eyes was a strange blue fleck. His hair, too, was thicker than that of the others and less like wool.

"What'll I do with you, lad?" Jonathan asked half in play, but in alarm, too. "My learning won't last like this."

"I don't know," Beaumont said simply, "and my mother, she don't know. She's always askin' me that."

They looked at each other in mutual wondering gravity. This boy, Jonathan told himself, must not be wasted; and yet was he not doomed to waste?

The summer ended sharply on a day that Clyde came home. Twice he had written, vague windy letters full of matters of which they could not discern whether they were plans or things already done. The land was filling fast, he wrote. It was lucky he had not delayed. People were coming in from all over the world, from England and Russia and Germany and Sweden. There was even an English duke's son, people said, with plenty of money. How would she like to be neighbors with a duke's son? But everybody was the same here and a duke's son no better than anybody else.

"Oh, the big zany!" Mary cried, when she had made this out of Clyde's wandering handwriting and fanciful spelling. "As if a duke's son could ever be a neighbor to us! Jonathan, you mark my words, some day there'll be trouble out of all this equality, for all of Clyde's talk don't make him equal to anybody if he isn't born so."

"That's sense, Mother," Jonathan agreed.

They put Clyde's letter away, both decently disturbed at the idea of a nobleman for a neighbor.

"What'll happen next?" Mary said severely.

On a September day, early and suddenly cool, Clyde came limping in, his leg healed but a stick still in his hand.

"Mary!" he shouted at the door. There was no one in sight, and they might have been dead if it were not that there were squashes yellow in the garden and the home so clean, and a painted green tin of autumn flowers on the table, which made him know that Mary was alive.

"Clyde!" she screamed and came running in from behind the curtain. "Oh, Clyde!"

She flung herself upon him, and he held her with one arm and laughed.

"You've wanted me!" he cried triumphantly. "You've missed me, eh, wife?"

"Terrible," she said, forgetting everything.

Nobody was in the house to hear her, except Arthur in bed—luckily Jonathan was not home yet and Ruth had gone out with Maggie to keep her safe from the snakes in the long grass.

"Oh, it's been sore without you," she sighed. "They do their best, the children, and Jonathan always a dear lad; but they're another generation from us, Clyde."

"Ah," he agreed. Now that he was sure of her, he suddenly felt hungry and tired. "Let me alone, dear heart, for a minute. My leg's hurtin'."

"Oh, is your leg still bad?" she cried. "Let me see, Clyde."

He sat down and stretched it out, and she pulled up his trouser leg and looked at the deep angry scar of twisted muscle in the side of his calf.

"It'll never be right," she mourned, touching it gently. His flesh was sweet to her again.

"I can manage," he replied. "I've managed wonderful."

"Where's Jamie?" she cried suddenly. "Why, I'm a wicked mother, forgetting my son. Where's the boy, Clyde?"

"I left him out there, Mary," Clyde said.

"Clyde!" she screamed. "Not alone in all that wild country!"

"There's neighbors in the next section hut," he said. "And you can't leave a foot of homesteadin' now, Mary. Somebody'll steal it while you're gone."

"Oh, but, Clyde, a little boy!"

"He's growed wonderful this summer," Clyde said. "And thirteen ain't a little boy. He was thirteen last month."

She was on her feet now, very angry. "All the same, you had no right to leave him, Clyde. But then, you never had proper feelings for a father. It's always what your children could do for you, never what's your duty to them."

"Of all the rambunctious silly notions!" Clyde cried. "If I hadn't begot 'em, where'd they be? I gave 'em life!"

"And dragged 'em here to live it!" she retorted. She sat down, sighing, and wrapped her arms together. "What's he living in?" she demanded. "Has the child a shelter?"

"Now, Mary," Clyde said. "Listen to me before you're all slathery and frettin'. He ain't goin' to be there long. I'm goin' back—with you and the children is my prayer, without you if so be I must. I've decided you're right about Jonathan. Seventeen is a man, and let him have his own mind. But I've a home and three hundred and twenty acres of the best land—"

"What kind of a house?" she interrupted him.

"Mary, I won't say it's anything but a good sod house, but frame's to come," he replied. "I'll promise you—"

Upon them at this moment Jonathan returned, for it was noon.

"Well, Father," he said.

"Well, lad," his father replied.

"Jonathan, your father's left Jamie behind," his mother cried.

"Only for a matter of a few weeks," Clyde said to him. "You wouldn't know Jamie. He's growed like a man—inches higher he is, and he rides a horse like a cowboy. There's wild horses out there, and he's corralled two of them and gentled one of them. Wonderful clever, he is, and born for the life. It's a big life and calls for big men."

Within himself, at that familiar loudness of his father's voice, Jonathan felt stubbornness solidify in his being.

"I daresay," he replied and, coming in, he poured a little water into the tin basin and washed himself before food. "Got to get back," he said. "Mr. Merridy's busy this afternoon with autumn stock." He threw his water carefully upon the squash plants outside the door.

His mother rose and began to set the table. In the distance over the rising slant of the land Ruth was following behind Maggie racing ahead of her.

"Median's growed, I see," Clyde said to his son.

"Twelve families," Jonathan replied.

"Too thick for me," Clyde remarked. "Now, out there you can look as far as eye can reach and see only your own land."

"And Jamie there without a living soul!" Mary cried. She could not forgive him.

"Oh, shut up, do!" Clyde shouted.

They're off again, Jonathan thought hopelessly. But somehow he felt himself no longer in the quarrel. He had no more to do with it. It lay deep between them, man and woman of whom now he was no longer a part.

He sat eating while they wrangled. When Maggie came in he lifted her to his knee and wiped the dusty sweat from her face and fed her from his plate. Then he left them still wrangling.

What might have been the end of that quarrel who could have known? It was ended by Arthur, that feeblest of all their house.

The quarrel had come to her saying over and over, "Anyhow, I will not take Artie so far, Clyde."

"You'll be no furder from doctors there nor here," he retorted. "And the air's better there—fine upland air it is, and it goes straight up till it hits the Rockies, folks say."

"We've kept him alive somehow by staying put," Mary said. "He'll never stand moving."

They discussed this, looking down at the pallid little boy upon the bed, and he looked up at them as though it were hard to draw his feeble breath between them.

"But would you come back, Mother?" he asked in his small weak voice.

"I'm not going, duckie," she replied.

"You could leave him with Jonathan until he grows stronger," Clyde said.

"I will not," Mary retorted. It was now taken for granted that Jonathan would not go. Neither of them saw the terror in the sick child's eyes.

Jonathan, that night, gathering up the little armful of bones to rest them, felt them feverish.

"You're hot, Artie," he said.

"Jonathan," the little skeleton whispered, "is my dad stronger than my mother?"

"He is, I reckon," Jonathan replied, "but what of it, my whippet?"

"Then I'm afraid of him," the child replied.

"Nonsense," Jonathan said cheerfully. "He's fond of you like all of us." He felt Arthur's forehead and was alarmed. "Mother!" he shouted. "This boy's burning!"

She came hurrying in and felt of Arthur's hands and head and feet. "He's cold and hot in different parts," she said. "Oh, Jonathan, put him down and go for that black woman!"

He ran through the autumn twilight for Stephen Parry's wife. But with a strange slowness she did not come at once. He left her promising to come, and they waited for her through a night of fitful sleeping wherein he sat for hours holding Arthur in his arms.

She came in the early morning when another clear autumn day poured out its sun, and in that strong light she looked carefully at the sick child, beside his thistledown so large and brown and strong that none of them doubted her for a moment. Then she went into the other room and stood among them.

"I kin bring him some yarbs," she said in her deep voice, "and I kin bring down his fever. But when it's brung down, he won't have nothin' strong enough to live in him. The fever'll draw his life all out when it goes." She looked at Mary. "I didn' wan' to tell you, ma'am, but the firs' time I saw him I knew his end."

She stood there as though she herself were beyond the life and death she seemed to understand so well. "I'm mighty sorry for you, ma'am," she said to Mary. "But not for him. It's a hard time to live now except for them that's strong. He'll be spared what would have been beyond his strength. You remember that."

She went away, and in the silence left behind her there was no more quarreling. Mary went to Clyde and crept into his arms, and he held her before them all, and Jonathan rose and went into the other room and, kneeling beside the bed where Arthur slept, he buried his face in the quilt and silently wept. In a moment he felt someone there and, looking up, saw it was Ruth. He need not be ashamed before her, but he rose and together they stood hand in hand, their eyes solemnly upon their brother.

Only Maggie knew nothing. She was outdoors, running after the big brown woman. But she could not keep up with that long, tireless stride, and after a few minutes she sat down in the middle of the road and happily sifted its dust in her hands.

The house was intolerable in the waiting hours. Strangely, it was Clyde whom they all comforted, for he was the one the least able to bear it. He sat with his stiff leg outstretched before him, blaming himself for everything until for sheer necessity of relief they comforted him.

"I'm the one that's killed him," he said again and again. "It's me that's wicked and wouldn't see how my poor little lad was."

"Hush. What could we have done?" Mary said.

"I could have took him back to the East," Clyde moaned. "I'd have took him to England afore this."

"He'd have died upon the sea, Father," Jonathan said.

"At least he'll be buried on proper land," Mary said. She had not wept nor for a moment left Arthur, except to come as she had now to fetch something for his need. Clyde rose to follow her, but she stopped him.

"Stay away from him, do," she said. "Let's let him sleep himself away in peace."

It was a heavy peace in which Arthur died. Stephen Parry, when his wife came home and told him that the child was set for death, had made a small coffin from green cottonwood.

"Shall I black it, Sue?" he asked her. "I got about enough lampblack to do it."

"He's so little," she replied. "Let's use whitewash."

He made the small casket as white as snow with lime inside and out and brought it on the day when it was needed, and lifted the little body in and laid it down.

Arthur was dressed in the suit he had worn when he left England. He had been proud of it that day because it had a tie, and Mary remembered. There was no cemetery in Median, but in an acre to the south of the town some lay buried, nearly all of them those who had been on their way westward and overtaken by age or illness had been delayed forever. Beside a newborn child whose mother had gone on, Arthur's grave was dug.

This day was the first in which Jonathan saw, all together, Median's people. They had come one by one to bring food and fuel and water and offers of help in those last days, but now they were all here. Samuel Hasty and his wife and two boys, Henry Drear and Mrs. Drear, and he remembered for a second Jennet and put her out of his mind again. He saw Stephen Parry and his family standing a little apart, and a man married to an Indian squaw and his five half-breed children, all whom he knew well or less well. They made a blur of people, poorly dressed, sunburned and windblown. They were strangers until Lew Merridy, because there was no minister among them, began to read aloud a psalm.

"For the days of our life are as grass that perishes," he read.

Around them the long prairie grass waved in the autumn sunlight. But in the midst of it stood this handful of people gathered about something of their own now to be buried here. Jonathan saw their faces kind and full of sorrow. Some, to whom this hour brought memory, were weeping, and suddenly he felt them friends.

That night in the house that seemed empty because something out of its life was gone, he was not surprised when his mother said, "Jonathan, I'm going with your father, after all."

"I know, Mother," he answered.

"There's Jamie to think of," she said.

"I know," he said again.

Once she had set her mind, she could not quickly enough do what she had decided, and Clyde hurried her because he said they must not waste the autumn weather. Winter would fall soon that year, everybody said. The prairie beasts were already digging deeper holes, and the grass was dying early.

In sad haste to be gone, Mary packed into a wagon that Clyde had bought the things that she must have—a mattress, quilts and her English blankets, their winter clothing and other heavier clothing from Merridy's store, dried food and seeds of all kinds, and she sliced the best of her squashes into strips as the Indian woman who lived in Median had showed her how to do and dried them in the sun and wind.

But all she truly valued she left behind with Jonathan. There was the family Bible which she had brought from England, into which at her bidding he now wrote in his most careful hand, "Arthur John Goodliffe, born in Dentwater, England, November 10, 1862. Died September 3, 1871, in Median, Kansas, in the United States of America." There were the pictures of her mother and father and of herself and Clyde on their wedding day. There were her few linen sheets and her two pair of pillowcases edged with crocheted lace she had made, and her half-dozen china plates and teacups, and a silver necklace with an agate set in a locket, and a brooch with her mother's hair, and the picture of Edward and Millie on their wedding day, and the picture, only newly come, of their first child, a boy, Tim, named after Millie's father.

And with all she put into the wagon she took care to leave the house looking as it had for Jonathan's sake. In the midst of her daze of sorrow and unwillingness she had her moments of thinking of how he would manage and even of whether she ought not to leave Ruth to take care of the house for him.

"Though how to do with that Maggie without Ruth I don't know," she sighed. "Sometimes it seems as if Maggie took all after Clyde. She's on the run from dawn till dark, and what with the deathly snakes and holes in the ground and now out there wolves maybe and Indians and I don't know what, I haven't the strength for her. Jamie was the same, only it's worse when a girl's like that."

"You keep Ruth, Mother," he said. "I'll manage."

And to Ruth he said privately, "Mind you think and spare her all you can, and some day I'll make it up to you and give you whatever it is you want most."

"Oh, I will without that," she said.

He noticed her shadowy sweet eyes when she spoke, and thought to himself that somehow none of them noticed Ruth enough. She was one of those easily forgotten, whatever they do. It would have been pleasant to have her here, but he could let his mother go more easily if Ruth went with her.

"Do you think you could manage a letter to me sometimes to tell me how Mother is?" he asked.

"I never wrote a letter, as you know, Jonathan," she said seriously, "but I can try, and the words I don't know I can ask Mother."

"It's you I should have been helping instead of those black children," he said in quick remorse. "But it's too late now."

"I had always to get Maggie to sleep and see to things at night," she said patiently.

They left in seven days from the day it was decided, and Jonathan stayed away from work that morning to help them off. There was agitation and excitement, and Clyde kept shouting things forgotten and promises of what was ahead. He hustled them into the wagon at the door of the sod house. Two mules he had not paid for pulled it, but Jonathan had signed the note that promised payment if his father failed to do it.

"Get in, get in, woman!" he shouted to his wife. "A late start is bad luck all the way."

But he delayed them after all. They were in the wagon, and the wheels all but turning when Mary said, "Have you the homestead papers, Clyde?"

"Of course, of all things," he retorted. But he felt in his pockets, and the papers were not there. Then began the tumbling of goods and the searching and Clyde's cursing and swearing, until Ruth, looking up at the family Bible on the shelf, saw papers sticking out and pulled at them, and there they were. Clyde had put them there.

"Dang it, the Bible's the place for safekeeping things, and I never dreamed you wouldn't put it in," he cried to Mary.

"The Bible's to stay here with Jonathan," she said.

"What, and we have no Bible?" he roared.

"I want it with Jonathan," she said stubbornly. "Then I'll know it's safe."

He yielded at last, and they were off in such confusion that there was only a moment left to Jonathan in which to say good-by to anyone. He gave it all to his mother.

"Oh, Jonathan," she cried, weeping, "take care of everything."

"You take care of yourself, Mother," he said. He held her in his arms, and for the first time knew how big he had grown because she felt so small to him. "Good-by, my dearest dear," he muttered, and let her go.

Part Two

11

WHETHER he had stood looking after them or whether he had turned blindly back into the house, he never knew. He saw their faces, each stark clear for an instant—his father's full of haste and absorption, Ruth's frightened, Maggie's round with wonder, and then his mother's, yearning and weeping as she looked at him. Her gaze reached for him. He felt a tangle of pain in his breast, and his eyes smarted. He must have rushed back into the house, because when he was clear again he was working in a fury at the dishes to be washed and floors to be swept.

"I hate to leave such a mess for you, Jonathan," his mother had said in her last look about the rooms.

"I'll clean up in a jiffy," he had answered.

But it was not a jiffy. He lingered over everything, exhausted now that there was no more need for him to be strong. And now that his mother was gone, there seemed no reason why he should not have gone with her. The house and the garden, which had been impossible to leave when she was in it, was nothing when she had left it; and his job, that had been an anchor when it brought into the house the only sure sum of money each week, seemed worthless. He did not like shopkeeping, he thought moodily to himself as he went about the house. Shopkeeping ancestry and his mother's belief in the soundness of trade made him good enough at it, but it did not satisfy his own hungers.

He had had no time in these months to think of his hungers, but now they rose up in him. He paid them heed as he worked through the afternoon. His mother had said, "When we're gone, Jonathan, make the house comfortable for yourself. Take the inside room for sleeping, and then you can live in this one with the fireplace, and it'll be more convenient."

He had asked Merridy for the day free and had been given it, and he moved his belongings and took down the curtains from his corner. The sod house seemed big and full of room now when only he was in it; and, as the hours moved on, the quiet and the space enlarged, and with them his loneliness and his unsatisfied longings. He felt himself grown and a man. But a man's life must have more substance than he had in Median. In Dentwater there had been sources to which he could go—Mr. Hopkins and school and colleges and books and learning; the vicar and those good days when he had tinder in him; the sea and the ships at Blackpool and Edward's business in the chandlery, which, buying and selling only common things, yet touched every port in the world. He thought of his own room in the stone cottage when upon a fair day he could see white sails upon the Irish Sea, and he went to the door of the sod house and stood looking out. He saw nothing except the long, unchanging slope of the prairie. There were no sources for him here.

But as he watched he saw coming across that space, so nearly level, four small black figures. They were his pupils, Stephen Parry's children. He wished that he had told them not to come because he was tired and because he wanted to go on with his mood of dreaming melancholy. He had forgotten to tell them anything, and so they were here as usual.

He watched them drawing nearer. The two youngest loitered behind, and Gem walked quietly along alone. But Beaumont, when he saw Jonathan, broke into a loping run and reached him far ahead of the others.

"Hullo, Mr. Goodliffe," he panted.

"Hullo, Beaumont," Jonathan replied. The boy's dark face was in an ecstasy. "What's happened?" he asked.

"Say, Mr. Goodliffe, I finished that whole book you gave me yesterday. I couldn't stop—I kept on reading, and my father let me have the candle last night until I was finished."

The book was *Robinson Crusoe*. Jonathan had won it once as a school prize in Dentwater. What he saw was himself, now in Beaumont, mustering his courage once, long ago, to walk bravely to Mr. Hopkins and to say to him, out of deep excitement, "I finished the whole of that book, sir—I couldn't put it down."

His book had been a translation of the *Odyssey*, but that did not matter. What mattered was the eagerness and even the adoration with which he had looked upon the schoolmaster as the source in which he could find knowledge and wisdom. Now he saw in this boy's eyes the same adoration and the same eagerness, and it was he who was the source.

"Good," he said shortly.

He was too touched and too alarmed to say anything more. But at the head of the table he taught twice his usual length of time and with a new and stern exactness.

The next morning he rose early and made and ate his breakfast. Then he crossed the square to the store. The door was open and he went in, but nobody was there except Mr. Merridy, picking his teeth and looking at the last newspaper to reach Median.

"Good morning, Mr. Merridy," Jonathan said.

"Hello there," Lew replied without looking up.

"Mr. Merridy, I want to give you my resignation. I hope you won't mind," Jonathan said.

"What's the matter?" Merridy demanded.

"I'm going to start a school," Jonathan replied.

Mr. Merridy put down his paper and looked up. "We don't need a school here, Jonathan," he said. "There ain't enough children to support it."

"There're sixteen children that I know, sir," Jonathan replied.

"No, there ain't," Mr. Merridy replied. "Hasty's have only two young boys, and that fambly down in that dugout on top of the river bank has four. That's only six. And the newcomers ain't settled yet whether they're stayin' or not. Median's a town that's bound to grow, but there'll be a lot of comin' and goin' before the final shakedown, and folks that's on the move can't bother with schools."

"There're four Parry children," Jonathan said gently, "and Bill White has six."

"You ain't goin' to have a school for niggers and half-breed Indians!" Mr. Merridy cried. "Why, it'll ruin 'em if we begin educatin' them. Besides, what'll we do with them when they're educated? They'll be fit for nothin', I tell you, Jonathan. I been meanin' to speak to you a long time about your teachin' those children. You're doin' them no real good, nor the town."

"Beaumont's a very bright boy," Jonathan said. "He's much brighter than I am, Mr. Merridy, and I know it."

"Then there's all the more reason why he shouldn't be educated, for the day he knows it will be a sad day for you and for all of us," Mr. Merridy said. His voice grew severe. "I tell you, Jonathan, it was a terrible thing to bring black slaves to this white man's country, but it was more terrible to set 'em free. No man knows what'll come of it for any of us. And when you teach 'em to read and write and figger, you're puttin' the white man's weapons into their hands, and they'll use 'em on you and on me."

They looked at each other steadily.

"I can take that risk better than I can the risk of saying I won't teach Beaumont," Jonathan said, and after a moment he said again, "Not to free the mind after you've freed the body doesn't seem to me fair."

Lew Merridy grunted, picked up the paper, shook it, and pretended to read.

"Besides," Jonathan went on, "there's Katie, sir. I should think you'd want her to go to school."

"No, I don't," Merridy replied. "I don't believe in educatin' females. She's learned to read from her mother, and I've taught her how to count up figgers to help me. I can't see any mortal use for her to know more."

He rattled the paper, looked grim, smoothed his uncut moustaches and coughed.

"Will you take my resignation, sir?" Jonathan inquired.

Mr. Merridy threw down the paper once more. "Why, you son-of-a-gun, are you still resignin'?" he shouted.

"Yes, sir."

"Well, go on and git out of here!"

"I will," Jonathan replied, and he put on his hat and walked out, his knees trembling. Merridy owed him nothing. He had drawn the last of his wages to give to his mother two days before. And he had nothing except the small stores of food in the sod house. If he was to have a school, he must have it at once—that he might live as well as work.

But there was only himself to feed. For the first time he saw good in his loneliness. If they had not gone away and left him, he would not have dared to do what he was doing. He would not have recognized himself in Beaumont's eyes or waked in the night to discover that what he wanted to do was to teach school and not to stand behind a counter.

He suddenly ceased to miss even his mother. The front room he would make into the schoolroom, and the fireplace would heat it in winter. The other would be all he needed for himself. If each pupil brought his own stool, he could put up long planks on posts for desks, two rows of them with an aisle between. He had only his own few books, but there was the big Bible, and in every house which he entered he would ask for books. A blackboard he could make easily enough, and there were lumps of chalk in the store. He had enough wherewith to do his work.

It was a fine day, he now noticed, a fine day for his family moving somewhere over the edges of that horizon between earth and sky. But it was a fine day for him, too. The autumn sky was blue, there were no clouds, and the long grass was turning a deep red-brown. It moved in the ceaseless waves of the wind, but the wind was no enemy today. It blew the clean cool air across the prairies, and he breathed it in and was strengthened and excited. This was a good country, and maybe all the better because there was everything to do in it. In England he would have been struggling to get a job ahead of hundreds of other chaps wanting schools. Here he was the only one between east and west, north and south, as far as his eyes could see, who wanted to teach a school; and suddenly in loneliness he recognized adventure.

Ah, here was the biggest adventure under the sky right here in Median! Why did folk go traipsing West? Tramping along he began to whistle loudly an old song his mother sang, "Oh, you'll tak' the high road, and I'll tak' the low road, and I'll be in Scotland afore ye!" and, still whistling, he knocked on the door of an old, usually empty sod house. A new family was stopping there for a few days. He knew their name was Cobb, and that they were moving on. But they might not go on if there was to be a school in Median. He had seen boys and girls running about.

A small plain-looking woman came to the door. "What do you want?" she asked.

"How do you do, ma'am?" Jonathan said gently, taking off his cap. "I'm about to start a school here, and wanted to know if you'd be interested."

"Come in," she replied. "Come right in."

He stooped as he went in, for the door was too low even for his medium height.

"Sit down," she commanded him. "Now then, tell me about the school. What's your own abilities, young man?"

Her sharp gray eyes picked out of him what she liked, and he submitted to them.

"I've been taught in England," he said. "I was to have gone up for the college exams if I'd stayed. The man who taught me was Cambridge, and he thought well of me. My mother was a teacher, too."

"Why ain't you goin' West like everybody else?" she demanded.

He did not want to open his soul to her. "This seems far enough to me," he replied.

"So 'tis," she agreed. "More'n far enough for me, too. Ohio was what we started for, but as long as there's any West left, my husband seems bound to get at it. I tell him he'll keep on till he hits the Pacific and then go on wadin' until he's drowned. It's a disease, that's what it is."

A boy and a girl of nine and twelve came in softly on their bare feet and stood behind her, staring at Jonathan.

"If we could get some kind of job to tide us along, maybe I could persuade Adam to spend the winter here and give 'em six months of school, anyways," she said.

"He could ask for my job at the store," Jonathan said. "I've just quit it."

"Say," she cried, "that's an idea!"

She jumped up, a dry little figure of energy. "I'm goin' to put it through —what's your name, young fellow?"

"Jonathan Goodliffe."

"That's a mouthful," she said, laughing. "Well, Mr. Goodliffe, this is Martha and this is Matthew, and they'll be there—if we can pay the tuition, that is."

"The fee'll depend on how many I can get," Jonathan replied. He had only this moment thought of it. "Maybe a dollar a month apiece wouldn't be too much?"

"If we get the job, we can manage somehow," she said. "The oxen we won't need if we stay, and we can maybe sell 'em. Yes, sir, put down Martha and Matthew Cobb."

"Oh, Maw!" Matthew wailed. "Ain't we goin' West?"

"Not this winter if I have the say-so," she said firmly. "It'll be your last chance at books."

"But you always have the say-so!" he cried.

"So I do," she agreed.

"Well, good-by, Mrs. Cobb," Jonathan said. Matthew and Martha—he gave them a quick look. Martha had said not a word. She stood motionless, a sandy-haired, drab child in a sacklike dress of buff calico.

"Good-by," he said, putting out his hand to her.

She was still speechless, but he felt her rough little hand in his.

"Good-by, Matthew," he said. "I think you'll like school, maybe."

"No, I won't," the boy said. "I don't see any use in books."

"I'll remember that," Jonathan replied with mildness. This was a queer grim-looking lad, his mouth narrow and tight and his eyes already sharp.

He went away and walked across the square and down the road a quarter of a mile to the mill on the edge of the river. He knew it very well, because he had taken grain there which farmers brought to the store to exchange for goods, and now he went to the mill door instead of to the house. Samuel Hasty was there in the midst of a dimness as white as mist with flour.

"Hello, Mr. Hasty!" Jonathan shouted above the racket of wooden machinery.

The little miller saw him and came out, as white as a moth, from behind a bin. "Hello," he said. "What you want, Jonathan?"

"I'm going to start a school, Mr. Hasty."

He went on, and the miller, chewing tobacco steadily, listened. That black hole of a mouth was startling in the dusty whiteness which covered him from head to foot, so that even his pale blue eyes were lost in it. He spat a blob of black saliva that rolled into a ball in the floury dust at his feet.

"I dunno," he said. "Schools are awful dear, and boys get such notions at 'em. I don't know about the whole idea. Afore we know it we'll be havin' an aristocracy in this country with all this education."

"But I plan to have everybody send their children," Jonathan said. "Stephen Parry and Bill White—"

"I dunno's I want my sons goin' to school with truck like that, though," the miller objected.

Jonathan did not answer for a moment. Then he began gently, "A school's a civilizing thing, Mr. Hasty. We can scarcely call this country equal to England if we don't build schools."

Mr. Hasty looked away. "I can't pay your costs," he said.

"Pay me what you like," Jonathan replied, "in meal or in flour or in hay bundles. Fuel will be my problem. I won't have time to gather grass."

"Well, it'll take thinkin'," the miller said.

"Think about it, then, sir, and send me Abram and Sam if you think well of it," Jonathan replied.

He tipped his hat and went on. By the end of the day out of Median's thirteen houses and out of four farmhouses within walking distance he had the promise of seventeen pupils. And then in the late afternoon, being well content, he turned toward Stephen Parry's carpentry and forge.

It was empty when he stepped into it, but there was a fragrance of cooked and seasoned meat and of corn pone. He grew ravenously hungry as he smelled it and, picking up a horseshoe, he struck a slab of iron which stood against the wall. Beaumont came running out, a piece of pone in his hand. He put it behind him when he saw Jonathan.

"Pa'll come right out," he said.

"No, I'll come in, Beau," Jonathan said gaily. "I'm hungry, and you can give me a bite, maybe."

He did not see Beaumont's look because he was already across the room, and then because he clapped the boy's shoulder and walked along beside him through the door.

The family were at supper, but everyone sprang up.

"Don't get up!" Jonathan cried. "I just thought maybe you'd give me a bite, Mrs. Parry. I want to talk to your husband about school desks. I'm going to have a school. Will you give me a bite?"

"Yes, suh," Sue Parry said in her soft big voice. "I'll set you a place in the shop, Mr. Jonathan."

"No, you won't," Jonathan said. "I'll sit right here between Beau and Gem. Then we can talk."

He was already sitting down when Stephen stopped him. None of them had sat down.

"Mr. Goodliffe, suh, we take it as an honoh. But it won't do you no good, suh. They's goin' to be trouble enough without it, anyways. It's hyere a'ready, suh."

"What trouble?" Jonathan demanded. He stood up, compelled by their refusal to sit down with him.

"The town's split clean in two just today already," Stephen Parry said. "Right on your trail Mr. Sam'l Hasty has been follerin', and it looks like I oughtn't to send my children at all, on account of the trouble it'll make, suh. I got my livin' to make."

This, Jonathan perceived, was what Hasty had meant by "thinking."

"You mean you're not going to send your children to me?"

Stephen looked down. "Ain't no use educatin' 'em if I cain't feed 'em," he said simply.

"Mrs. Parry," Jonathan began, but she stopped him.

"Mr. Goodliffe, you're newcomer, suh, of co'se, and I know that you means kindness. But it would be better if you jes' said Steve and Sue, like everybody does. We's black and we knows it."

"Beaumont," Jonathan began again but she took it away from him. "Beaumont is black, too," she said firmly.

"Why, there was a war about this!" Jonathan said.

"War ain't changed no feelin's," Sue said.

She was so large, so sure, so wise, so sad, and all of them were so silent, that he felt overpowered. Then he saw Beaumont. All his life he had hated his father's petulant profanity, and out of this hatred he had never once used it. Now suddenly he needed it, and it burst out of him.

"Of all the dangety-dang, dod-blasted, goddamned injustice!" he shouted. "I won't give in to it!"

"Beau ain't my son," Stephen said quietly, and Jonathan stopped as suddenly as though a sword had been put to his neck.

"His father's a Beaumont," Stephen said, "young Pierre Beaumont."

"I hadn't no choice," Sue said, sadly. "I wasn't but fifteen when he was bawn, and I belonged to the Beaumonts."

"When ol' Mrs. Beaumont found out," Stephen went on, "she wanted to marry Sue away, and I heard about it, and I had seen her, and so ol' Mr. Stephen Parry, mah massa, spoke for me. Beaumont knows how it all happened, don't you, son?"

"Yes," Beaumont said, "I know."

That purely shaped golden-brown face did not quiver, but Jonathan looked away from it.

"I shan't give up," he said stubbornly.

All of his blood was troubled and sickened and stirred by what Stephen had said, but he was determined in spite of it. Somehow in the end he would have them all sitting together in his school.

"You're mighty kind," Stephen Parry said.

"No, I'm not," Jonathan said. He frowned. "What I really came for, Mr. Parry, was to see if you would make some long desks—planks set on posts will do."

"Yes, suh, I'll be glad to," Stephen said.

"All right," Jonathan hesitated. They were all looking at him except Sue. She stood with her head drooped and her hands hanging by her sides. Upon her soft, full face there was a look as still and as curtaining as a cloud.

"Well, good night, Mrs. Parry," he said sharply.

"Good night, suh," she replied, without lifting her eyes.

He went out, walking very quickly and loudly, and turned toward the sod house. He was not hungry any more, but when he got there he would boil some milk and stir a little corn meal into it and feed himself.

This he did, and all the time angry and confused and torn between caution and impetuous wish to go out and demand justice from everyone for the black children. Why had Stephen told him that story? He could make nothing out of it for a reason. It was not white blood that had put any genius into that dark body. Plenty of white blood was stuff as dull as skim milk. No, it was Beaumont seed in Sue Parry's fertile flesh.

He felt an excitement so strong that he was abashed by it, and he got up and began to pull at the furniture he wanted to arrange. Yet it was not an excitement of the flesh, nor had it anything to do with anyone he had ever seen, nor even with himself. It was as vague and as powerful as the pull of the earth beneath his feet and as the light of the moon and the stars now above his head, and its excitement lay in the mind. For suddenly his mind perceived that, when two bodies lay together, male and female, anything might come of it, and it all depended on the two. For the first time he thought definitely of his own marriage and of the sort of woman he wanted and would have.

No middling sort, he thought, but someone big and glorious, like what I've never seen. Except maybe, a little like Jennet outside, if inside she could be like his mother. He meditated upon this magic until his head was swirling and his face was hot, and the floor scrubbed so clean that he could not bear to step on it himself.

The school opened on the first day of October, and he was tolerably content because before that day he went to every house and argued out, whenever it was necessary, the matter of the Parry children. To some it meant nothing. Bill White, drowsing in the autumn sunshine, woke up to laugh.

"Hell, I don't care," he said. "Some likes 'em black, some likes 'em white. Myself, I like 'em brown. My squaw satifies me. It don't worry me none when she has a papoose what it'll be. I figure in a country like this, give 'em time, we'll all be mixed anyway. There's yeller men from China over at the Gold Coast, they tell me. Hey, there!" he yelled at the Indian woman who was cutting pumpkins into long strips, "you don't care what color your ol' man is, do ye?"

She shook her head and laughed and showed big white teeth.

"Naw, she don't care," he grunted.

So three half-Indian children sat in school as erect as statues and stared at Jonathan as he wrote the alphabet upon the blackboard. For days they would say nothing, and never was he to know how much was silence and how much ignorance. But they were the ones who brought him prairie fruits he had never eaten before, wild plums and grapes and hazelnuts and pecans and black walnuts of trees so distant he did not know they existed. They brought strings of diced dried pumpkin and dried blackberries and raspberries and rhubarb and pickled buffalo peas and, before frost came, sheep sorrel that Katie stayed after school one day to make into a pie, still sourish even though she poured in molasses. And they brought him freshly killed rabbit and quail and prairie chickens. He had half his living from the Indian children, and never a dollar in cash.

But not all were so easy. Lew Merridy held out against the school until Katie herself settled it. "Sure I'm coming to your school, Jonathan," she said. She had come into the store one day when she heard his voice.

"Oh, you are, hey?" Merridy said. "And how about your ma and the twins?"

"Ma's got 'em about weaned now," Katie said in her practical little voice.

Merridy stared at her, scratched his head, and laughed. "Well, if she says she's goin', she's goin'," he said. "But it don't alter anything I said, Jonathan. I don't believe in educatin' colored people, Indians, and females. They don't need it, and it only makes trouble for the rest of us."

A farmer and his wife came to the door, and Mr. Merridy shouted at his new clerk.

"Hi there, Cobb!"

A long-legged man unfolded himself from behind the counter and Merridy watched him.

"Says he's goin' on in the spring," he turned his head to tell Jonathan, "but I ain't so sure. Looks like the missus wears the pants there, however long his be!"

"Wouldn't it be better to educate females, then?" Jonathan asked, smiling.

But Merridy shook his head. "Naw! Naw, sir! They'd all be wearin' pants then!"

So out of the bustling little handful of individuals that made up Median Jonathan gathered together the children and started his school.

In late autumn he had his first letter from his mother. He read it over and over again, trying to lift the curtain of the stiffness which fell upon her whenever she took up a pen. But the years in school had shaped her beyond change. He had seen her when she wrote, her preparations, her gravity, her solemn summoning of pious phrases.

"My dear son Jonathan!"

He could see her small pursed mouth and straight figure, and the pen held elegantly upon her little third finger.

"I take my pen in hand to say that we have with God's help reached our destination and, while our circumstances are not the best, we can endure them for the winter. Your father plans in the spring to stake out still another claim in the hope and expectation that by large-scale farming of cattle . . ."

"Oh, my little soul, but how are you?" Jonathan muttered. There was no finding out. If he had not had his school, he would have set forth to find her. But he had these children, for another family of his spirit, and he could not leave them. To teach them satisfied him in ways he could not himself understand or indeed perceive. He only knew that he was happier than he had ever been, even in Dentwater; and, though he often missed his mother sorely and in other ways missed Ruth and even the lively mischievous presence of Maggie, he had other things. He had that profound fulfillment of putting into hungry minds something which fed them. Not that all minds were hungry! Even in these children of all ages and several bloods, there were as many minds as he could imagine. But he learned to know them one by one—which wanted food and which must be fed even against its will; and which, like Katie, knew positively what it wanted and would have no more.

He laughed at Katie a good deal. She had suddenly begun to grow, and her spare little body took on the curves of a meager adolescence. This seemed ridiculous to him. The first time he observed the slight swelling of her new breasts under an outgrown cotton dress, he thought them as absurd as pinfeathers on a bristling pullet. When she began to put on grown-up airs he teased her and pretended to defer to her. But she was always equal to him.

"Jonathan, you should lay up hay bundles for winter, else you'll get caught by the snows," she told him one day after school.

"If I must I will," he said good-humoredly.

"And you must ask one of the big boys to tend fire for you," she said. "Better ask the biggest Indian. And the water bucket isn't filled often enough, and I saw that biggest Cobb boy pour back the water out of his dipper today."

"I'll attend to everything, Madame," he said.

She was such an ugly little thing, he thought, looking at her out of laughter; so completely commonplace except for that aggressiveness of her nature which burst out of her stiff pigtails and her sharp hazel eyes and out of every movement of her quick, thin little body. He could not imagine her growing up into a real woman.

"Jonathan, there's a preacher coming through on Sunday," she said.

"A preacher!" he repeated. "Well, I never, Katie! There's never been a preacher in Median before, has there?"

"Yes, sometimes he comes once a year or maybe twice," she said. "And I want you should go to the meeting, Jonathan."

"Why?" he asked, amused.

" 'Cause folks say you ain't hardly religious enough to be the teacher of a school," she said. "They say you don't read the Bible and pray before school like you ought."

"Oh, that's what they say now, is it?" Jonathan retorted.

He thought about this a moment. He did not doubt for a moment that it was true. Katie brought him everything she heard said in the store.

"Well, it won't hurt me to go to church once a year," he said. Then to tease her he added, "Will you be there, Katie?"

"Of course," she replied solemnly. "I'm a baptized Christian."

For some reason he could not understand, he went into loud laughter, and when she plainly thought him mad, only laughed the more.

"Oh, dear," he cried at last. "Oh, Katie!"

"Are you laughing at me?" she inquired.

He nodded and began to laugh again.

"Don't you like me?" she inquired again, and he saw she was hurt.

"Of course I do," he said and stopped at once, and on an impulse reached over and took her little claw of a hand and patted it. Then to his horror he saw her thin child's face change and turn crimson.

"I like you—something terrible," she whispered.

"That's nice," he stammered, and dropped her hand as though it burned him.

12

JUDY SPENDER, waiting for her father to announce the hymn, sat holding upon her knees the big old accordion she had played for him ever since her mother died. He was at least six minutes away from the hymn, and so she looked idly upon the faces of the people gathered in the main room of the tavern this Sunday morning to worship God. She knew American House very well. Off and on they had come here, she and her mother and father, almost as long as she could remember clearly, which, since she was seventeen, was now almost a dozen years. At first there was only the tavern at the crossroads, east and west, north and south, and people drove to it for meetings. Then year after year a few houses began to collect in this place called Median, until now it was a prairie town like so many she knew. Her mother used to think that her father would be a great preacher some day, maybe in a city church, and then they would settle down. But long before she died she had stopped talking about it, and they all knew this hard traveling from one small town to another was what had been and would be, as long as Joel Spender lived. "A bearer of good tidings," Joel called himself.

"What's to become of you, Judy?" her mother had fretted. Her fretting kept her alive long after she wanted to die. "I could go in peace if I knew what was going to happen to Judy," she moaned to her husband.

"The Lord'll look after His own," Joel said positively.

"There's never been any sign of Judy's being the Lord's," Mrs. Spender retorted with a faint revival of old rebellion.

"Well, she can come along with me, and certainly I am the Lord's," Joel said.

His wife groaned. But there was nothing she could do about anything; and one day, when Judy was not quite twelve, Mrs. Spender gave up to the tumor that had enlarged her thin figure into obscene shapes. Years before she had wanted an operation for this tumor, in the days when it was still manageable; but Joel would not hear to it.

"I would hold it to be a lack of faith," he said. "You know I'm a faith healer, Mitty, and I'm not goin' to yield to temptation."

He prayed faithfully at certain hours every day that God would heal his wife and believed each day that she was better, and then, as the tumor grew in size and power, he lengthened his hours of prayer and increased the strength of his pleas.

"O God!" They could hear his voice booming heavenward through thin boardinghouse walls in towns and under trees beside inns and out of the shadeless prairies. "Hear Thy servant and heal Thy servant's wife! Thy servant don't ask for anything beyond Thy will, O God, but I do ask that it is Thy will to heal Mitty!"

When she spoke again of operation, he was sterner than ever. "No, Mitty, there ain't goin' to be any operations. This here's come to be a tussle between me and God, and I'm goin' to win."

Mrs. Spender said no more. She had hoped in God for a good many years, but now it became plain to her that the trouble all along had been that there was no way of discovering what God's will was until it was too late to do anything about it. And it began to be clear to her before long that in her case God would triumph over Joel. She did not tell him so, but she made her own preparations. One of these was to talk as plainly as she could to Judy, who was the only child she had left out of seven. The other six had died young, and sometimes when she lay helplessly supporting the parasite that fed upon her, she remembered them, and she wished she had not given them Bible names. Only Judy had not died, and Judy she had named after a woman on a boat who had helped her when the child was born. "Judy" the woman had been named, and that was all Mrs. Spender knew about her. Later she had found the name Judith in the Bible, and then she told Judy, "Your name is just Judy, not short for anything else."

Or maybe the child had lived because she was born on the Missouri. People said it was good luck to be born on water. Anyway, she had always been a strong, healthy little creature with red cheeks and bright dark eyes and yellow curls. Joel was dark, too, but he had never been healthy because of his weak digestion, nor ever smart enough to account for Judy's forwardness. It was terrible to die when Judy was just beginning to need her mother's care. But God's will was the one unchangeable thing in the world, and there was no use in asking for mercy if God had made up His mind. She called Judy to her one day and said, "Judy, I'm going to die."

Judy opened her brown eyes enormously. "How do you know, Mama?"

"It's God's will, so there is no use in talking about it. What I want to talk about is you, and what you're to do after I'm gone. You listen to me now, Judy."

"Yes, Mama," Judy replied. Her mother was so matter-of-fact that it was like being left behind at a boardinghouse the time she had whooping cough.

"You go on with your father and play the accordion for him like I do, and lead the hymns real good and loud. And don't ever let a man put his hands on you—never! Not for nothing! But if a plain hard-working man with a job in a steady place asks you to marry him, you leave the work right away and let your father fend for himself, and stay with your husband as long as you live."

"All right, Mama," Judy said.

"That's all, but don't you forget it."

"No, Mama."

At the bottom of her heart she never had forgotten it. She kept it there as a secret with her mother from her father. When her mother was alive they had often had secrets together, such as the keeping back of pennies from the collection to save for a dress for Judy.

"It's all right to have secrets from Father, if God knows," her mother said.

"Did you tell God?" she once asked her mother.

"God knows everything anyway," her mother had answered.

If God knew about this secret, He gave no sign of it, though sometimes she was sure He did know and purposely kept anybody with a steady job from asking her to marry him. Now in the tavern at Median she yawned, and remembered that her mother had told her to put up her hand whenever she did. Then in the middle of her yawn she caught a pair of blue eyes looking at her with secret laughter, and she closed her mouth abruptly. The eyes belonged to a young man of medium height whom she had never seen before. He did not look like anybody else in the room. He wore a neat suit of brownish cloth and a stock and collar, and his brown hair was smoothly brushed. His face, she noticed in the quick, all-seeing glance she gave him, was pale, a little thin, and, while it was neither ugly nor handsome, it was pleasant.

Her attention was snatched by her father.

"Judy!" he said sternly. "I've called the hymn—it's 'Beulah Land.'"

She started into the tune and pumped her accordion back and forth as hard as she could. Then she lifted her voice, loud and clear.

Watching her, Jonathan thought to himself that he had never looked at so pretty a girl. He had seen her almost at once when he entered the room. Coming out of the brilliant sunshine of late autumn, for a moment everyone had looked pallid to him and shadowy, everybody except a fair-haired, brown-eyed girl in a dark red dress who sat with an old accordion across her knee. She did not see him, for her eyes kept wandering, but he watched her while the people gathered to sit on stools and benches and on kegs and boxes set in ragged rows in front of the bar. The shelves behind it were decently draped with Indian blankets to hide the bottles, and the bar was made into a pulpit with a white sheet. Mrs. Drear had put a salt jar full of goldenrod on it, and behind it a tall dark man stood to preach and pray.

Jonathan, his ears too sensitive, could not listen to him. The preacher's fervor was poured into sentences every one of which had words pronounced awry and mistaken in grammar. So he kept looking instead at the young girl, a beautiful, pouting thing, sitting so carelessly beside the pulpit that, if one brown hand had not held the accordion firmly, it would have slid from her knees. She had sat smiling and brooding and certainly not listening and then suddenly lifted her head for a great yawn, and in the middle of it she had seen him laughing at her.

He was a little alarmed by the suddenness with which she shut her jaw and by the look she gave him. Then he decided doggedly not be afraid of her, and to give her look for look. He kept on looking at her when the preacher called to her, and she began to play furiously with all her strength upon the accordion. When she sang in a clear loud voice he found himself singing, too, although he hated singing in church. The vicar in Dentwater had not encouraged the congregation to sing, and it seemed indecent so to expose oneself.

But he excused it now because here was, after all, only the tavern, which was always full of noise and roistering, and he could not believe this ranting evangelist was a minister like the vicar, and this was no proper hymn tune, either. The girl was playing it like a dance, swaying as she played it, exaggerating its rhythm and letting her voice soar—a glorious voice, but not for hymns. In Dentwater he would have been shocked by it, but here it made him want to sing too.

"A pleasant true voice, our Jonathan has, but not good enough for the church choir," was what his mother had said once long ago. He cleared his throat and let his voice out a little louder.

And after the meeting was over he went up, not to the preacher, but to her. He had always to forget his own shyness, and he fought it now.

"I am Jonathan Goodliffe," he said. "Excuse me if I introduce myself."

She put out her brown hand, and he felt it soft and plump. "I am Judy Spender," she said.

"The minister's daughter?"

"Yes."

He could not restrain himself. "Then you'll be going on, won't you?" he asked.

"It depends," she said. "Sometimes we stay, if folks want a protracted meeting."

"Then I hope they will," he said earnestly, "in fact— That is, I'm very sure they will."

She laughed with a hearty parting of the reddest lips he had ever seen. "I hope so," she said. "I'd like to stay somewhere for a few days, anyway, just to get a chance to wash our clothes."

"You must stay," he said. Under his calm face his heart echoed, "You must—you must," and then he felt her hand pulling softly out of his and realized, to his horror, that he had been holding it all this while.

He went away so confused that he did not think of anything else until the middle of the Sunday dinner which he was eating with the Merridys. How it had come about that this was his weekly habit he could not have said himself, but so it had become. Katie had begun it by demanding one day what he had to eat in the house because, she declared, he was looking thin, and then had answered herself by looking into his crocks and opening all the boxes and bags. The next day she said firmly, "Maw says you're to have Sunday dinner with us reg'lar, and if you're too proud you can take it off my tuition."

That was at least the beginning of his going each week into the three rooms back of the store and playing with the twins while Katie and her mother worked. Mrs. Merridy, thin and pallid and corded with stringy muscles, was a born cook. Her rabbit pies, her saleratus biscuits, her corn dodgers with pork cracklings, her spoon breads and sour-cream cakes, her greens and pickles and preserves and corn-meal puddings were concocted for strength and delight; and in spite of himself once a week Jonathan ate to the full and spent Sunday afternoon in a pleasant stupor with the family. He was aware at such times of a great deal of comfort in these three rooms. With the resources of the store at her command, Mrs. Merridy had muslin curtains looped back from the windows, braided rag rugs on her wooden floors, a big circular stove in winter, and rocking chairs and cushions padded with cotton. She had somehow found plants to pot for her windows, red geraniums and swollen begonias and a hearty Boston fern. Upon the walls were texts and mottos worked in wool, and two large crayon portraits of her parents framed in gilded wood.

In the midst of all this comfort Jonathan was aware, without noticing it, of Katie's narrow, bustling figure, arranging and rearranging, setting the table, lifting the cat out of a chair, keeping the twins quiet with sharp little slaps and sudden scoldings, and insisting upon some whim of her own for his greater comfort. She darted at him from time to time. "Jonathan, don't sit there. The brown rocker's better . . . Jonathan, put your feet on this stool."

He always submitted to the pushing and pulling of her determined little hands, because it was easier to submit to her than not. She was capable of endless argument until she had her way.

Today in the midst of dinner she said sharply, "Jonathan, you ain't eatin' a mite."

"Yes, I am, Katie." He was embarrassed by her notice, for it was true he had no appetite. He could neither eat nor think because of Judy.

"Leave him be, Katie," Mrs. Merridy said dolefully. "I know how it is when you've been to meetin'. It takes your appetite sure enough to get thinkin' again on eternal things, and then it don't hardly seem worth while to feed the body. I declare, Mr. Merridy, I think we ought to ask Brother Spender to hold a week's meetin' before the winter sets in. 'Twould give us somethin' to think about in the long evenin's, and maybe save some souls from goin' to hell if anybody should die, as they're bound to do."

Lew gave a grunting chuckle and swallowed a great mouthful of roast pork. A farmer had brought him a side of freshly killed pig in payment of the season's bill, and he loved it.

"Well, you know what I always say, Lula—they's more souls made than saved at these here protracted meetin's."

"And I always say for shame, Lew Merridy, for such talk, especially before young folks, to put such notions into words."

"Godamighty, Lula, Jonathan's a grown man—"

"Well, you'd oughta begin to think about your own daughter," Mrs. Merridy said.

Mr. Merridy gasped. "Why, Katie—she ain't but a little girl."

"I'm almost fifteen, Paw," Katie said severely.

He looked at her, pretending to be astonished. "Why, so you are, you little pullet!"

"And I know what you mean," Katie said virtuously, "and I don't think you ought to talk about it."

Lew, about to pick up his great mug of coffee, set it down again and burst into big laughter and clapped Jonathan on the back.

"You and me'll have to go eat in the kitchen, Jonathan," he bellowed. "We ain't decent."

Jonathan smiled and glanced at Katie with a faint disgust he did not understand, except to know that he did not like to think that her mind comprehended such things as—as the making of souls. But, though he did not know it, this disgust, too, was because of Judy. Ever since he came walking in a daze and a glory into these rooms he had been thinking of Judy and of how to go about getting a protracted meeting. He was too honest to pretend to a religious need. Such vague need as he had was satisfied by the chapter of the Bible he read occasionally at night before he slept, and by the prayers he said night and morning, simple ritual prayers that his mother had taught each of her children when they began to talk. Such variations as he had privately added to them had never come to anything. When he had prayed the last one it had been that his brother Arthur might not die, and when Arthur died, his first thought had been, "I'll never ask God for anything again." There was no rebellion in this decision, but the simple giving up of hope that his destiny could be altered by any plea of his. God's mind, whatever it was, was always made up beforehand, and it seemed more dignified in a man not to go whining and begging with his own prayers. He could not honorably persuade his neighbors to have a week's meetings of prayer and preaching when he himself considered such prayers futile and wanted only to see a beautiful young girl every day for as long as he could.

He listened when Mrs. Merridy began scoldingly, "Now, Lew, stop acting like a behemoth and give me some help. There's a lot of unconverted people come into Median over the summer, and if we could get 'em converted we'd all have a better winter. You know you say yourself meetin's do a lot of good—folks pay their bills and men buy things for their families."

"Oh, I ain't objectin'," Lew said. "Howsomever, it's a little late for folks to sit outside, and I don't believe Drear could let 'em have the tavern every day right now when folks are humpin' through to get West before winter."

An inspiration fell upon Jonathan. He lifted his head and said quickly, "They could use my schoolroom, if the parents were willing for school to let out a week."

Lew was struck. "So they could," he said. "That's a real idee, Jonathan, and parents won't mind. They're always glad to get their children converted young—it saves a lot of switchin' sometimes. I ain't switched you since you was babtized, have I, Katie?"

"No, Paw," Katie replied.

"Don't know but what it's a good idee all round," Merridy said. "Folks can drive in and get their winter stores and get some soul food, too. You gotta have religion in a community, or folks get to killin' each other, especially in the winter when they're all shut up together. Don't know but what I'll mosey around myself this afternoon and see Brother Spender and the Median folks. I'm a religious man at bottom, Jonathan." He laughed somewhere down in his belly. "That is, if you can find bottom!"

Jonathan pushed his plate away. Food dried and swelled in his mouth, and he could not swallow.

"I don't feel quite well, after all," he said. "Please excuse me, Mrs. Merridy." He leaped to his feet and went out of the room. He was so excited that he could not sit still nor listen nor speak. He must get away by himself to think and to try if he could to see what to do with himself. He was going to fall into love with Judy Spender!

In those days of the protracted meeting, because of a peculiar inarticulate honesty, he gave up his own private prayers. His house was full of praying, but he felt embarrassed to pray his little childish prayer. He rose early every morning and swept out the rooms and wiped off the benches and tables and the blackboard, and went outdoors and picked purple autumn flowers and put them on his table that was Joel Spender's pulpit. Then he ate his breakfast and waited. But he had only to wait a little while. For Joel came early to have him write upon the blackboard his text for the day, and with him came Judy. In his neat, square, very clear script Jonathan wrote great violent thundering curses, while Joel stood roaring them out.

"Thou shalt be brought down to Hell, to the sides of the Pit, They that see thee shall look upon thee saying, 'Is this the man that made the Earth to tremble, that did shake Kingdoms . . .' Thou art cast out of thy Grave, as a carcass trodden under foot, for the End of Evildoers shall never be renowned."

"Howl, O gate! Cry, O city!"

"The cry is gone round about the borders of Moab, the howling thereof unto Eglaim, for the waters of Dimon shall be full of blood."

"Father's practicin' on you, Jonathan," Judy said mischievously. She stood by the door, pulling whispers of fragmentary music out of her accordion, beginnings of tunes she did not finish, the catch of a gospel chorus, the lilt of a tune she had heard in a river boat somewhere, a deep chord or two unfulfilled. She looked sometimes at Jonathan, but more often out of the door at the sky and the prairie.

"I ain't," Joel said. But he could not go on rolling out his words. He was pricked and angered. "You're a real thorn in the flesh, Judy, like your ma was to me," he said indignantly. "I prayed God like Paul for years to pluck it out, and when your ma died, I thought He had. But He shore left a stinger behind in you."

She did not answer, and Jonathan, turning his head quickly, saw her profile, smiling, and he turned away again, frightened at the vehemence of his first love.

Then, that men and women and even children might be quickened to hear God's word, there came over the prairies that week such long golden days as he had never seen. People from Median came walking in the quiet sunshine and along the path the school children's feet had beaten every day to the sod-house door, and through the long grass a few wagons came in, bringing men and women and children. They looked alike, their garments faded to drab, and their skins burned red and brown. But when they talked they changed, and their eyes kindled differently, blue eyes though most of them were. They lingered outside to talk, starved for talk, and Joel had to call to Judy to start music before one by one they came into the shadowy room.

"My squaw says it's the Indians' summer," Bill White said. He sat in the sun, drowsing upon a bench at the door from where he could look away from Joel's dark face out to the smooth tawny red of the grass, quiet for once under a windless sky. When he looked long enough for peace he would listen to Joel's demands. "I will confess before men that God is good," he drawled.

"Are you saved, Brother White?" Joel yelled.

"I been saved a long time," Bill White said.

"Anybody else been saved? Anybody else want to be saved?" Joel cried and raked them with his red-hot eyes.

If nobody answered, he shouted at Judy, "Play something, girl! Play something to waken 'em outen their death-sleep!"

And Judy, her beautiful face unmoved, played "Just As I Am Without One Plea" with such passion, such pleading that they stirred upon their seats, and a few rose miserable and sweating to mumble out their sins. But Jonathan could not move. He was not for one instant deceived. When Judy played he knew he thought, not about God, but about her.

As day went into another day, his thinking ceased to be thought and became mere longing; until one afternoon, unable to endure, he rose and went into his bedroom and sat there upon a stool waiting for them all to be gone. When they were gone she came in, pushing back her hair from her face.

"Oh, I'm tired," she sighed and, seeming to belong here as she belonged anywhere, she threw herself upon his bed.

He was shocked and yet he trembled and looked at her and saw every turn of her bosom and her thigh. And she opened her eyes which she had closed and saw him.

"Come here, Jonathan," she said.

He rose, unwilling and yet compelled, and went over to her and sat upon the very edge of the bed.

"Is this your home, Jonathan?"

"Yes," he said.

"And shall you live here always?" she asked.

"I daresay."

"Oh!" She sighed and flung out her arms. "Think of waking up in the same place every day!"

He did not answer this, being too busy with his own feelings. "Oh, my lovely," he was crying to her inside himself. "Oh, my lovely, lovely dear!"

"Jonathan, lie beside me!" she said suddenly.

"No," he said grimly.

She opened her eyes at him. "Didn't you ever hear of bundling?" she demanded.

"No," he said.

"Well, it's nothing wicked," she said, and laughed at him. "Why, you just lie down together, all dressed, like this, and talk, an' that's all."

"How could it be all?" he muttered. And, terrified because he was rushing headlong down into the pit he saw ahead of him, he leaped to his feet and strode into the other room. It was empty. Even Joel had gone, forgetting Judy, as he often did. And when Jonathan saw the emptiness, he went straight out of the door and on to Median.

I'm terrible wicked, he thought. Wicked he was if it meant what he wanted to do and would have done if he had stayed a moment more beside her. He went into the tavern. Henry Drear was behind the bar.

"Give me a mug of whisky," he ordered.

"Never knew you to want that," Drear said, grinning. He dipped up the liquor from a tubful that stood on the floor behind the counter.

"Never wanted it before," Jonathan replied. He stood drinking the hot stuff morosely and waiting the subsidence of another heat in himself.

"Guess it's religion," Henry Drear said affably. "A lot more folks stop in here for a drink when meetin's are goin' on."

"They do, eh?" Jonathan said.

He hung about the tavern silently all evening while men came and went. Once he went into the kitchen where Mrs. Drear was cooking over the red-hot iron range.

"I sure do miss Jennet," Mrs. Drear said, mourning. "I wish I could get a letter from her. But I reckon she can't find nobody to write it, and she never would learn her letters to write herself."

He had not thought of Jennet in weeks, but it seemed to him now that Jennet had begun the love of Judy in him. He went home at last and listened half-fearfully as he lit the candle. If Judy were here, he was lost. But she was gone. He lifted the curtain between the two rooms and saw his bed tumbled where she had lain on it, perhaps to sleep. He went and stood looking at that impress, and love came creeping into him again. She was innocent, an innocent untaught child. Was she not innocent? His heart cried out that she was; and then his mind, remembering her flung upon his bed, put forth its cold little doubt. Could she be innocent?

The strange heat of delaying summer steeped the prairies in warmth and in silence. Day after day of the seven days even the wind was still, and in the sod house Joel Spender changed the manner of his preaching. He left the prophets and turned to the Song of Solomon. He showed them a God no longer angry, but pleading and longing to win their hearts by love. He stood before them in his old black suit, a shabby man until one forgot him in the dark fire of his eyes and in the power of his sonorous, pliant voice. If this was the voice of God, then these were the words of love, and hearts of flesh were moved to answer love with vague love. They stood up, ashamed, shy, muttering something of what they felt without understanding what it was, their faces red or pale, but always disturbed and always ashamed as though they were miserable. Only Beaumont was joyful and without shame in his confession.

"I do praise Gawd!" he cried gladly, and leaped to his feet.

"Praise Gawd!" Sue murmured from the corner where they sat apart.

But they forgot their shame when Judy played her accordion in great surges of sound. They were at her mercy when she played, and she played as she willed, and they followed her. Sometimes she made them gay, and once the little black children even began to clap to her rhythm.

She played more quickly, and suddenly Sue's high voice seized the melody and led it along to ecstasy, and they were all singing:

"Jesus! Thy very name I love,
Thy sweetness fills my breast."

Jonathan, his eyes upon Judy, felt his heart smolder in his bosom. For she, drawing her accordion to and fro, swaying to its measure, turned to him and looked at him directly as he sat in his corner far from the door. They had not spoken together again, and tomorrow would be the last day. He had not prayed, nor had he risen when Joel had cried out for them to speak and to declare what God had done for them. He had sat through all exhortations, disliking them and feeling shamed by them. Yet he was converted and he was changed, though not, he knew, by God.

Lew Merridy, sitting next to him, nudged him suddenly. "The devil's goin' to make the most of this, Jonathan!" he whispered. "You cain't take the lid off folks without somethin' happens!"

Jonathan did not answer. He must speak once more to Judy. What he would say he did not know, for he did not know what he wanted of her. But he could not let her go without tying between them some sort of bond. Not a promise, for he was not ready to promise and too prudent to do it unless he was ready. Only he must know at least that she was coming back.

At the end of that day when the people, weary with exhortation, were straggling across the ragged square into their homes, into the tavern, some of them harnessing horses to wagons to go to their farms, Judy delayed at his door. Joel had gone ahead and did not look back to see whether or not she followed him.

"Well," she said, "it's almost over."

"Yes, it is," he agreed. He spoke with the mild preciseness that was natural to him and that hid so completely his turmoil.

"Has it been like you thought it would be?" she asked.

"You mean—the meetings?" he asked.

"I mean—any of it."

"I don't think I thought how it would be," he replied.

How would he ask her anything when he did not know what he wanted to ask her? How seek an assurance when he did not know what he wanted assured?

"I hope we'll meet again," he said.

"I reckon I'll be back in the spring," she said carelessly. She was looking away over the prairies as she spoke; she was always looking over the prairies. "We usually come to Median about twice a year, and I don't see any change ahead. We're heading south now because Father can't preach up here in winter. Folks don't get out once the blizzards begin."

She seemed so careless, as though it did not matter to her where they went, that he was terrified. He wanted to pull her gaze back to himself.

"I hope you'll come back in the spring," he said earnestly. "If you do, I'll look forward to it all winter."

"You want me to promise?"

Her black-lashed eyes flashed to him, and their gaze upon him was so warm that he was moved out of all prudence.

"Yes, I do," he said.

"All right, I promise," she said. She smiled, then suddenly she put out her hand and touched him on the cheek with the palm of her hand, a touch too light for a caress, and immediately she went away into the twilight.

And he stood there, by the touch upon his cheek her slave, and she knew it. From what wisdom she had known that this young man would be repelled by passion shown too soon she had not stopped to think. But instinctively she had chosen the one right spell to put upon him, a touch of flesh to flesh, sweet, fleeting, and not to be repeated, because she was going away. She liked this young man, so different in all ways from her father, whom she half-despised, and different, too, from the unshaven rough men she saw every day.

He looks clean, as if he bathed every day, she thought. She knew he did not, of course, bathe every day. Nobody could do that on the prairie where water was more precious than whisky. Something about Jonathan made her think of her mother. If he asks me to marry him next spring, I maybe will, she thought and, thus thinking, entered the tavern, gave a peculiarly brilliant smile to three strange men standing at the bar, and went into the kitchen.

"Shan't I help peel potatoes?" she inquired of Mrs. Drear.

" 'Twould be a mighty help," Mrs. Drear said fervently. Judy tied an apron about her waist and peeled in long nimble curls of skin.

"Your paw satisfied enough to come back in the spring?" Mrs. Drear asked. She was mixing corn meal furiously with milk.

"I reckon," Judy said dreamily.

His cheek had been as smooth as her own, she thought. She could feel it still on the palm of her hand. There was no reason why a man's cheek should not be smooth.

And yet the next day they did not once speak to each other, not so much avoiding each other as knowing there was no more to be said. Winter must come before spring.

Jonathan's school was restored, and once more he began to teach. But it had become a task. The taste for it had gone out of his mouth. He looked at the children with deep doubt. A dirty ragged lot, he thought gloomily. The Brewitt children from the river dugout wore sacks with holes cut out for sleeves. What they had on beside was little, and already they shivered. All of the children were barefoot, but then so was most of Median. But hair was not combed and faces were not clean. Among them only Martha and Matthew Cobb looked tended and washed.

"Everybody with a dirty face can take time off to wash," he ordered suddenly. "That's all of you Whites, and Sam and Abram Hasty and all of Brewitts and Mary Anson and Jim Anson—the lot of you except the two Cobbs. Cobbs and Parrys are clean."

He watched their astonishment with some shame. He had never lost his temper before with any of them, and it was not their fault if they were dirty.

"Reckon we'll have to git water then from Drear's well," Sam Hasty said.

"I ain't goin' to wash," Abram said. He was a tall strong boy with black hair to his shoulders. At fourteen he was unwillingly beginning his letters.

"You will, Abram," Jonathan said. He wished that he had let them be dirty, for after all it had nothing to do with their brains, and he had seen their dirt to mind it so much only because he was full of his own gloom. Judy was gone. He had not told her good-by. He had simply let her walk away on the last night without a word.

"Eight dollars," Joel had said sadly after he had counted collection. "I reckon we'll have to preach our way south, Judy. God didn't prosper me much in Median, Mr. Goodliffe."

She had spoken for him quickly. "It depends on whether you're countin' souls or dollars, Mr. Goodliffe will be thinkin', Pa."

"That's a cruel sharp thought of your own, Judy," Joel retorted. "The Lord knows He's responsible for feedin' His own. Who's goin' to feed me if He don't?"

She did not answer this, but she went away and as she went she gave Jonathan a look, full of pleading for his mercy. And he gave her mercy quick with comprehension. It was their only good-by.

She's not like her father, he thought. She's good and delicate—she *is* innocent!

He had watched her walk away, her head bare and her bonnet in her hand, and now winter stretched between them, an eternity.

"Sam, you and Abram take the two buckets and fill them," he said sharply.

Sam got on his feet and hesitated, glancing at his older brother.

"Sam ain't goin'," Abram said, and Sam sat down.

"Yes, he is," Jonathan said, "inside of three minutes."

What he would do in three minutes with this great boy he did not know, and he had only three minutes. He had never been a fighter, nor had he ever struck a pupil. He had been criticized for this. "No learnin' without the rod," Mrs. Cobb had said to him one day.

"Folks say you're too mild to be a teacher, Jonathan," Lew Merridy said to him at a Sunday dinner table.

"Everybody's feared of Jonathan's light-colored eyes, though," Katie had said.

"Afraid of my eyes!" Jonathan had repeated.

"They say you've got a queer eye," she said.

"Why?"

"I dunno," she answered. "It's the way you drill into a body when you look at 'em."

He remembered this now, and he rose and slowly and steadily went toward the big boy. Abram watched him sullenly out of his hair, like an angry dog, until he stood near him.

"Abram," Jonathan said, "I could fight you, but I won't, because I can do something else that'll be easier for me. You're going to fetch that water." He paused, then slowly began to recite the opening lines of Virgil, which he had once learned by heart because of their music.

"Arma virumque cano—"

He chanted them slowly and clearly, his eyes never moving from that dark face, until suddenly Abram howled and jumped up and leaped for the door, and Sam after him. They snatched the two buckets as they went, and Jonathan walked to the blackboard and put down twenty words.

"Study these until they come back," he said sternly. There was no sound of stir or whisper in the room. He waited a moment and then sat down by his table and opened the big Bible. It fell by magic to that Song of Solomon, and he read it, his heart aching for love.

> "Let thy breasts be as clusters of the vine
> And the smell of thy breath like apples,
> And thy mouth like the best wine
> That goeth down smoothly for my beloved,
> Gliding through the lips of those that are asleep."

God, speaking to His blessed bride, the Church, Joel had said when he read aloud those words. But Jonathan knew better. They were the words of a man to a woman. He shut the book.

13

THE END of the autumn was come. The grass was red and then brown. The wind stayed, and there was no cloud large enough to hold in it the hope of rain. Day went into day until the tenth day after Judy had gone. It was night, and Beaumont was there. He stored up in himself questions and thoughts and wonders which he poured upon Jonathan at night; and Jonathan, struggling to keep his wits clear in the swirl of Beaumont's mind, was stimulated and strengthened and always at last exhausted because he knew he was not enough for this boy.

Beaumont had grown fast in the last few months. He was taller than Jonathan and much heavier, though without fat. He carried his weight in the size of his skeleton, and yet his bones were well shaped and even graceful.

"I wish you could go away to school," Jonathan said. "In England you'd be thinking of going up to a university."

"Would they let me, in England?" Beaumont, suddenly alert, lifted his head.

"I reckon," Jonathan said. "At least I never heard them say there they let a man's skin decide his brains."

They went outdoors as they talked. Whatever Beaumont would have said next was not said. His head up, he sniffed the darkness.

"I smell something," Beaumont said.

They stood still together, smelling the darkness.

"I can only smell the dusty dry grass," Jonathan said after a moment.

But Beaumont's nostrils quivered in and out like a dog's. "I smell fire," he said.

And yet there was no fire to be seen. If it were over the horizon, there would be a glow against the sky. But there was no glow. The sky was close down upon them, deep and soft and black.

"Nothing," said Jonathan.

"Fire," Beaumont repeated.

Then, while they waited, there was a quiver of wind out of the west. It was scarcely more than a night breeze rearing out of the grass, except that it carried the mild faint fragrance of smoke. It was no breeze, but the first thrust of a very distant wind.

"Smoke!" Jonathan exclaimed.

The moment he said "smoke," it seemed to him he could smell it. He had heard of fire upon the prairies; men talked of fire as they talked of the wind and lightning and snow and all those forces which were their enemies. He had listened to their stories when he clerked in the store. Men sat upon barrels and leaned against the counters, spat and rubbed their noses and scratched their heads, and laughed ruefully.

"We-ll, I declare, when I saw them flames r'arin' round me I knowed that I had to run like the gophers and the coyotes, and I loped along, kickin' 'em outa my way. On'y thing that kep' ahead of me was the wild horses, but soon I was areachin' for their tails—"

He had listened, not knowing how much was truth and how much the enormous lying which the prairies taught men to do. But there had been the storm and the wind, larger than even they were able to lie; and he knew inevitably that sometime he would have to fight fire, too—the fire that began no one knew how and ended none knew where.

"Gotta tell folks," Beaumont said. He began to run with long leaping steps toward the tavern. Jonathan moved to run after him and then halted. All he had was here in the sod house. It was his home and the one refuge he had for his mother and the children. He thought a moment, remembering what men had said they did against fire. The river people were safe. But the sod house stood a mile away from the river. He had no beast to help him haul water, and no water here except what he carried for his own use from Drear's well or collected in a barrel when it rained. But it had not rained for many days. Once, they said, a woman had poured upon her roof the milk she had saved to churn butter. But he had not even tasted milk for months. All he had wherewith to fight fire was more fire, and even as he thought of what men had said about this he saw other fires lighting out of the darkness about the scattered houses of Median. Men were setting the prairie on fire, and he went in and brought a stick of fire out of the fireplace. The wind was growing moment by moment, and he stood a second to catch its direction, that it might carry the flames away from the house. And as he stood he saw his garden full of yellow pumpkins. He had left them to ripen continually one day after another, daring frost. In the corner of the sod house he had piled those already ripe.

"Soon's I get ours dried, I'll dry them for you, Jonathan," Katie had once said. "And I'll make them Indians help."

"Those," Jonathan had said gently, but she had paid no attention to him.

While the grass burned he would gather the rest of the pumpkins and throw them inside the door. He stooped and, sheltering his face with his hands, lit a blade of grass. It caught instantly, as dry as any dust, and then blade lit blade as the wind hurried it. He stepped back, full of solemn fear. It was a grave thing he had done—to set fire to the prairie. He looked across Median for courage and saw the other fires already. They were blazing in circles about homes. Men were beating them back when they came too close. He ran and lit one blaze after another in a huge circle about the sod house, and then ran to his pumpkins and snatched them from the vines and rolled them into the door. His patch of corn he had plucked a week before, and there was nothing but the stalks left, and yet he bitterly regretted them because they were to have been part of his winter fuel. But he must let them go, for the fire he had started farthest from the house was already too close. He rushed at it to stamp it out and flail it out with an old broom. In a few minutes it was beyond him, and he was terrified. Better to have let the wild fire burn him than the fire he had set with his own hands, he thought. He leaped from one quickening flame to another, but the fire seemed turned into a liquid to creep along under the grass, red as blood until it burst out into flames, small but eluding him everywhere. He began to sweat with heat and with fright, and then suddenly he heard his name roared at him.

"Jonathan!"

It was Henry Drear, carrying two great pails of water and around his neck some old buffalo hides.

"Jonathan, wet these and hang 'em over the windows and doors. Then give over fighting this bit of fire. It can't damage the sod house. We got to get out and do some burnin'. Real fire's comin'—look at that sky!"

Drear was already dipping the robes and packing them into the window frames. "Got no time to waste, Jonathan," he said. "Any minute we'll see fire blazin' there at the edge of the sky."

Jonathan hung a long dripping hide into the open crack of the door and closed it hard. Then he followed Drear, running with him toward the west. Far out from Median fires were beginning to blaze. Everybody was out lighting a huge circle of fire. He could see men on foot, on horseback, bright for a moment against the blaze.

"Git as far as we can," Drear panted. "The wind's blowin' against us."

They ran toward the burning sky until they saw the black horizon line break into points of flame.

"All right!" Drear shouted. "We dassent go furder!"

They stooped and lighted the grass and with handfuls of blazing grass for torches lit other grass, parting and running in opposite directions until in the broken darkness and light Jonathan was lost. But he went on blindly lighting fire after fire until suddenly he was in the midst of a roar of flames, and choked with smoke. He stood up, and a jack rabbit ran between his legs and nearly knocked him down. He caught himself and then he saw the big fire was upon him, and he turned and ran from it. He ran for the only shelter he knew, the sod house. The sky was as bright as though a bloody sun were lighting it, and in that hideous light he saw he was only one of many animals. He did not stop, but he saw beside him a deer and a fox; and ahead of him a small squat animal he did not know humped itself along upon its short legs; and prairie chickens half-ran, half-flew upon the blackening grass; and birds rushed through the smoky air. But he stopped for none of them. He was a fair runner, steady though not swift, and his wind was good. He had need of good wind, for the air was hot with smoke, and by the time he reached the sod house and jerked the door open and closed it again he was gasping.

The air in the sod house was still good and cool, and he flung himself on the floor to breathe for a moment. But not for more. In a very little while the fire would be around him, and he must save the air he had. He leaped to his feet again and looked for rugs, for paper, for anything to stuff in the crevices of the windows and door. All he had was not enough, and he seized upon a few sheets of paper he had given the children. Paper was precious, and only when a composition was perfect could he allow them to have a sheet of paper to write it upon. Now he snatched them up, crumpled them in his hand, and then saw that one of them was Beaumont's. The boy had written the story of a pet he had kept in a cage and had freed at last because it became torture to him to hold it in a cage. It was a strange little tale, half-childish and half-passionate. He stopped and took out this paper from the others and put it back upon the table.

Then for half the night he sat waiting for the fire to end. At first he could not sit. He was compelled to move, to walk about, to do anything except sit and wait. He had to fight continually a stupid compelling desire to open the door and run. But he controlled this by cold reason. Run—with all the animals? The river was too shallow to hide him. Even if it were not, would he drown or burn? No, the walls of the sod house were thick, and earth could withstand fire, so he made himself calm. He lay down upon his bed and thought how well it was that his mother was not here nor the children, and how doomed by terror they would have been. And Judy—he was glad now that she was gone. He thought of her as he had seen her most, in the long hours when Joel was preaching. She never listened, so upon what did she brood in that deep musing out of which she roused herself only to play the throbbing rhythms she put into hymns?

He was afraid even to think of her, lest he never see her again. He sat up, stifled with heat, and lit the candle on the box beside his bed which served as a table, and took up his Virgil and began to read. Yet all the time he read with only a part of his mind. If he lived would he ever be able to cope with this huge willful country? Was it not too vast for a man such as he, who loved his world small and clear and sure? If he lived to walk out of this house, should he not turn away from it forever and go back to England and, by hook or crook, work his way to what he knew?

He felt the air of the room grow hotter and heavier with smoke. A huge deep roar was growing about him, a dry crackling growl that was the voice of fire. He got up, not able to breathe, and dipped a towel into his pail of drinking water and bound it about his face and breathed through it. But his lungs were stretched tight and ached. He stripped off his shirt and sat half-naked, and the sweat streamed down his flesh, black with smoke. He would die, he thought grimly. This would be his end, the sod house about him like an oven.

When he was at the point of fainting with the heat and the smoke was forcing its way into the house, suddenly he felt the fire pass over his head and sweep on. He waited a few minutes. The air grew cooler. The hideous growling roar was quieting. He made himself wait. When he could wait no more and it seemed sure he would die without air, carefully he opened the door. There was no light. He looked out into a pit of blackness. Sky and earth were black. But the air was cooler and the silence was good. He stood breathing. Only to breathe was enough. It was acrid air full of ash, but it was air, and cool, and he took it into himself like drink and grew strong. When he went back into the candlelight he was black. His hands and his face were covered with grass soot. But he did not care. He left the door open and threw himself upon his bed and slept.

None came to wake him in the morning. Median slept—men, women, and children—unwashed, unfed, but safe.

When it was late afternoon he waked and sat up in his bed. Everything in the house was black. Bed, table, chairs, floor were covered with ash. Upon the walls, upon every slight ledge, were layers of black ash. But the air was clear and cold, and his lungs felt clean and sound again. He leaped up and went to the door. The sky was blue, and the unshadowed sunshine poured down upon a strange blackened land. As far as his eyes could reach there was not a sign of life in all the dark desert. The sod house, upon the roof of which grass and weeds had grown, stood as black as an oven; and Median was a few scattered black lumps. Over the tavern door the sign had been burned away, and it hung down, a charred board or two. The wooden ell to the store was gone. He saw no signs of any human being. Yet if he was alive there would be others.

He had planned to go to the tavern first, but as he came to the store, there at the door was Katie, her head in a cloth and her face a smudge. She was sweeping furiously.

"Jonathan!" she screamed and waved her broom.

He stopped and she cried, "Soon as I finish here, I'll come and clean you up, Jonathan!"

"What are you cleaning with?" he asked.

She was sweeping out piles of blackness.

"Dirt," she said cheerfully. "Dirt cures dirt. Water's no good against this soot. You want to sprinkle everything good with dry dirt so's nothing can fly and sweep it all out together."

She looked so cheerful that he laughed.

"What's the matter?" she inquired. She never saw any cause for laughter.

"Oh, you," he replied.

"Why, what's the matter with me?"

"Nothing," he said.

She was so ugly, and so careless of her ugliness, that he felt an affection for her and, reaching for her ear, he pulled it.

"You're a good girl," he said and went on to the tavern, marveling that the world could contain two female creatures so different as Katie and Judy.

Katie was bawling something after him and he stopped to hear her.

"It'll be winter now," she was saying. "That fire burned up the fall!"

14

THE WICKEDNESS of the fire was that it had taken all the fuel for winter. There was nothing more to burn upon the prairies.

In the schoolroom the children sat bundled in all their own garments and old coats and skirts of their parents. The Indian children were the most comfortable, for they were wrapped in blankets; and the Negro children were the most miserable, and they looked gray with cold.

The winter grew deep. It became the occupation of Jonathan's life to find fuel for his school. On days when there was no school he borrowed Henry Drear's wagon and horses and drove for miles beyond the barrenness the fire had left. When he found long grass again, he pulled it up and pressed it into the wagon. He walked along the river and caught at branches and roots which the water had torn out of soft banks. In the evenings when he sat alone he took the grass he had cut in the daytime and twisted it into cats and stacked them against the end walls. In the tavern there was a hay-burning stove; and, after seeing it, Jonathan bought a tin washtub at the store and took it to Stephen Parry.

"Cut me a top to this, if you please, Mr. Parry, and set in a stovepipe at the side."

"You fixin' a hay burner?" Stephen inquired.

"That's so," Jonathan replied.

Stephen Parry brought it the next day and set it up in one side of the big sod fireplace. When it was full of the hay cats, it could burn for an hour.

But before Christmas Jonathan saw that there must be help if he were to keep the children warm. He spent a Sunday going from house to house to tell the parents.

"I can't teach and keep them warm together," he said over and over again. "It takes a man's time to fetch fuel and keep the fire going. Since the school's a public concern, in a way, I thought you might help."

"Surely we will," one man said and another.

Before Christmas Day, Jonathan had half his bedroom stacked with fuel, with hay cats and cornstalks and bundled weeds and sunflower stalks, carted from beyond the fire area. He even accepted the cow chips which the Indians brought by the basketload.

"Sun and wind has cleaned 'em good," Bill White said.

"I'm glad even for dung," Jonathan said.

He thought of his mother when he spoke and, as he always did, suffered for an instant a pinch of dulled pain. Since winter had begun and the movement West was stopped, he felt as cut off from her as though by an ocean. But if she were alive, she would send him something for Christmas.

And he did not need her as much as he once had. Other lesser securities were growing up in him. Thus the store of fuel in his room was a small security, not merely for its own sake, but because the people of Median had come to his help and put it there. He felt them united about him in a friendliness—not intimate, yet solid. Lying in his bed sometimes in the straight, still way which was his, he thought of them, one by one. Cottonwood was from the Bentley's down in the river dugout, and Cobbs brought hay cats, and from somewhere Parrys had brought cornstalks. Stephen must have traded them for labor somehow. And Hastys had brought straw twists from the mill refuse. Poor Abram Hasty would never get beyond the second reader, however long he stayed, and perhaps it was only fair to tell his father. Then he remembered something. Last night Beaumont had said he wanted to be a surgeon.

"A surgeon!" Jonathan had exclaimed. He looked at Beaumont's hands, olive-skinned, the fingers long and square at the tips. "I never thought of you wanting to be that," he said. "Where did you ever hear of surgeons?"

"My grandfather Beaumont's a surgeon," the boy answered, and in the proud look he gave Jonathan he was suddenly as alien to Sue as though her blood had forsaken him. For the moment all his white blood took command.

"That gives me a notion," Jonathan said, thinking. "You say your grandfather's living?"

"He's a very old man," Beaumont replied. "But I know he's alive. My mother has ways of knowing. If he was to die she says she would know."

"Where does he live?" Jonathan asked.

"In New Orleans," Beaumont said. "Pierre Beaumont's his name, and Pierre is my first name, too. I took it for myself, when I found out who I was."

Excitement sounded in his voice and shone in his eyes, and Jonathan, feeling it, retreated to prudence. The boy was always too eager.

"Well, I don't know," he said. "I'll have to think a while."

"Yes, sir." Beaumont's face shadowed quickly. He was hurt, and yet what could Jonathan promise? The boy was sensitively ready to hope at a straw, and as quick to retreat if the hope were delayed an instant. Without another word he went off into the winter twilight.

Thinking it over now slowly and carefully, Jonathan came to a determination to write to Pierre Beaumont in New Orleans without saying anything to Sue or Stephen Parry. Something must be done with this glorious boy, and what was there in Median?

This morning was the Sunday before Christmas, and when Jonathan had washed himself and eaten, he put on his stock and coat and sat down close by a small fire to write the letter to Pierre Beaumont.

"Honored Sir," he wrote in his clear colorless handwriting, "I take up my pen to address you upon a matter Personal to yourself. I am a Schoolmaster, and in my School I have as a pupil a youth whose name is Pierre Beaumont."

He wrote carefully and baldly in the literal plain way that was natural to him and made his request.

"It seems to me, therefore, Sir, that the Instincts of Nature and Virtue will move you to educate this unusual Youth in whose Veins is your own Blood and who bears your Name."

He signed his name and after it wrote "Schoolmaster." Folding the sheet, he sealed it with wax and superscribed it "Doctor Pierre Beaumont, New Orleans, State of Louisiana, in the United States of America"; and took the letter with him to Lew Merridy's when he went to dinner. The mail went once a week from the store, on Monday or Tuesday, except in storm.

On this day, as he walked across the black, frozen ground, he felt a new and vicious bitterness in the wind. Lew came to open the door for him.

"Takes a man to hold the door against this wind," Lew said. "Come in, Jonathan. I don't know as you'll get back today. It's fixin' to come a blizzard."

They walked together across the store, unheated because it was Sunday. "It's early for blizzards," Lew said. "Mostly we get 'em after Christmas."

The wind forcing itself under the door caught at their ankles. But when they went into the back rooms they were full of comfort. Lew had old boxes and kegs to burn, and sometimes farmers brought him hay cats and corncobs instead of cash for goods. Katie was throwing cobs into the stove now, and the room was roaring warm.

"Well, Jonathan," she said. She never called him by his name in school, but outside of school hours she maintained an equality with him. "Sit here," she commanded him, "and put up your feet to the fire." She pulled a stool to a chair.

He sat down obediently. Now that he was in the warmth, he knew he had been very cold in the sod house. But it seemed not right to use for himself the fuel parents had brought for their children. He drew out his letter from his breast pocket.

"See that this letter gets stamped when the mail comes by, will you, Katie?" he asked.

She took it and spelled out the name. "Who's this Pierre Beaumont?" she demanded.

"Oh, I'll tell you one of these days," he said to tease her, knowing he would never tell her. "Mind you mail it, Katie."

"Katie'll mail it," Lew said, spitting carefully into a tin can full of ashes near the stove. "She tends mail now reg'lar and takes a hand in the store Satidays. She's gettin' so she earns her salt."

"Store work's easy," Katie said. She threw a look at Jonathan as she spoke, and he smiled, aware of her longing for praise and touched by it. He smiled at her, and then he thought of Judy and looked away from her.

By midafternoon, when they had finished dinner and the dishes were washed, it was evident that the blizzard was come.

"You'll stay with us, Jonathan," Lew said.

"But there's school tomorrow," Jonathan demurred.

"There'll be no school this side of Christmas, with a wind like this," Lew said.

In an hour he saw that Lew was right again. The wind had risen, and the house shook in its blasts, and the sky was already dark with snow. By three o'clock Jonathan, peering out of a window, saw only his own face staring back at him into the lamplight. He ought to be at home, he thought.

"Reckon I ought to get back, though," he told Lew.

"Why?" Lew retorted. "You ain't got a beast or a human there waitin' for you."

It was true, he had not. There was no reason why he should go back to the sod house, except that in some vague way it had become home, since he had no other, and he wanted to be at home.

"You'd never find your way there, Jonathan," Lew said. "Why, in a blizzard a man can get lost and froze to death between his house and his barn. Stay here with us. We'd admire to have you."

"Reckon I must then, thanks," Jonathan said after a moment, still unwillingly—though, when he thought of it, he could not tell why he should be unwilling. There was indeed no living creature waiting for him anywhere. He was struck with sudden loneliness, and he turned away from the window to the warm room and the light and fire and to the sight of Katie, tying bibs around the necks of two small boys sitting in little high chairs Lew had built out of barrels.

"Stop your racket, you two," she said loudly, and then kissed them. She looked practical, sure of herself, sound in all her habits. He said, "You're a rare good girl, Katie."

She looked up at him with a shyness so strange upon her sallow plain features that he was moved by it.

"I mean it," he said.

For once she had nothing to say. She hesitated a moment, her cheeks reddening, and then suddenly she turned and ran out of the room.

In the roar of the storm that night he and Lew sat alone by the stove. Mrs. Merridy had gone to bed early.

"I might as well sleep if you're settin' up, Lew," she said. "You can let me know if the house blows away."

"I'll tell ye," he replied dryly.

Then Katie got up.

"You goin' too?" Lew inquired.

She nodded.

"You're mighty quiet," he said. "Ain't sick, be you?"

"No, Pa," she replied.

"Never knowed you to be quiet before," he said.

"A body can be quiet sometimes," she said.

"Oh, shore, if it's natural," he said, staring at her with doubt.

And then in the stillness of the warm room, in the midst of the shrieking wind, he lit his pipe and smoked. "A man takes thought out in these here prairies, Jonathan, when he's settin' in the middle of a storm," he said after a while.

"Ah, he does," Jonathan agreed.

"He takes thought for them as he's brought into the world," Lew said mournfully.

Jonathan did not answer, having no idea of what was in Lew's mind. But it was his habit to wait.

"A man," Lew said, raising his voice, "says to himself, how will he pervide for his children, especially the females? A female has a sorry chance in this life, Jonathan. Bound to be dependent on some man or other, and it's all luck what she gets. She has to take her pick of what's before her at best, and a girl like Katie has to take her pick of what wants her."

Still Jonathan did not see what was behind Lew's graying moustache and bushy eyebrows. But he became aware of embarrassment in Lew's look.

"I daresay," he said, wondering.

"Katie'll make a wonderful wife," Lew said, "but it'll have to be for a man wise enough to see behind her face."

Jonathan did not speak. Prudence began to stir in him.

"Hell," Lew said suddenly and smacked his knee, "it'd be a Godamighty relief to me, Jonathan, if you was that wise man."

Jonathan felt his body grow stiff as he sat. He could not have spoken if he had known how to speak what he knew. He was fond of this big slatternly man, fond, too, of Mrs. Merridy with all her acid, and fond of this home where he was always welcomed. But he knew he could not marry Katie.

"She's like a good fierce faithful bitch dog," Lew said. He did not look at Jonathan. He filled his pipe, picked a coal out of the ashes under the stove and lit it. "She'll stick to a man as fierce and faithful, and she'll have younguns and keep 'em clean, and teach 'em to fight fair and tell no lies, and she's a good cook and savin'. A man'll be lucky if he can see what Katie is."

Jonathan cleared his throat. "I'm sure that's all true, Mr. Merridy," he said. His voice sounded thin. The roar of the blood in his ears was stronger than the wind wrenching at the windows. Lew waited, but Jonathan could not say more, and this penetrated into Lew's mind at last. He drew a few long breaths of smoke and then knocked the ash from his pipe.

"Don't you mind my sayin' it, Jonathan," he said.

"I do mind, though," Jonathan replied. "I mind it terrible, for I'm— I'm fond of you, sir—"

"Call me Lew, like anybody else," Lew broke in.

"Yes, sir," Jonathan said, sweating. "I will, thank you—and I'm fond of Katie, but I am not free—in a manner, that is—" He stopped.

"Why, I never see you lookin' at nobody!" Lew exclaimed.

"But I'm—in love," Jonathan confessed.

Lew stared at him, and his blue eyes grew solemn.

"Then I'm sorry I spoke," he said. "I shouldn't have spoke if I'd dreamed it. But I didn't. And Katie's fond of you. She's terrible fond of you. It's seein' that put it in my mind to speak. She can't coax and tease and drawr a man like some girls can. She can't p'int to herself—somebuddy has to do it for her, and since you and me is good friends, why, I says to myself, I can speak for my own child. It's goin' to be hard on her."

"Does she know you were going to speak?" Jonathan asked.

"No, but I gotta tell her, Jonathan, that she mustn't think about you."

Jonathan's head began to hum. "She's just a child," he murmured.

"Fifteen ain't a child for a girl here," Lew said. "A girl hereabouts marries any time after she's sixteen."

He got up and took the lamp and went to the window. In the light the furious snow seemed stabbing at them with darts.

"I feel I oughtn't to stay here," Jonathan said miserably. "I feel I ought to get right out of your house."

"You can't," Lew said. "Besides, I wouldn't let you. What I've said is to be fergot. I'll be downright mad with you if you don't fergit it. Now let's go to bed. Think you can sleep on that sofy?"

"Yes, of course," Jonathan said. He stood up involuntarily as Lew went to the door.

"Well, so long till mornin', and we have to dig ourselves out," Lew said over his shoulder. "You'll fix the fire?"

"I will," Jonathan replied.

Alone, he tended the fire and banked it with ash, and then he lay down on the narrow sofa and drew a buffalo hide over him. Katie had brought it in and left it there for him. He lay under it warm and comfortable if he did not turn, but he could not sleep. He was thinking of Katie while all his being steadily refused her.

I couldn't have spoken other than I did, he thought solemnly, with sorrow for his own ingratitude. How willful was love that it denied itself to one who deserved it and poured itself out upon another who did nothing except to look as Judy looked, to walk and smile and talk as she did! He was sorry that it was so, but there was no cure for it. And in the same mood of destiny and fate he thought, I've engaged myself to Judy tonight, though she doesn't know it. I'm promised to her.

He lay awake and trembling in the midst of the clatter of the storm and did not notice it, until long after midnight he perceived it had ended. He rose and lit the lamp and saw that the silence was because the snow was deeper than the windows, and so the wind was no longer to be heard. He was buried in this house.

15

IN THE small dugout which Clyde had made against a hill in the middle of his acres, Mary, lying back upon her pillow wrapped in a bit of old gray blanket, looked at her child just born. Then she looked at Ruth, who stood hesitating beside the bed. It was indecent that Ruth, her own daughter and still a child herself, had had to help her. But the baby had come too soon. Clyde was away, and there had been no one else. She was only grateful that Jamie was hired to a man for herding sheep on the foothills. She looked at Ruth with miserable and apologetic eyes.

"I'm sorry to the heart," she said weakly. "I've done you a wrong, Ruthie."

"Oh, no, Mother," Ruth said quickly. But she would never forget, never; and Mary saw it in her sick averted eyes.

"Don't let it turn you," she said pleadingly. "After all, it's natural—a thing women must endure in one way or another; only not you, pray God, like this."

Ruth did not answer. She could not, for she was ashamed that her mother had seen what she was thinking.

"Shan't I fetch you some tea, Mother?" she asked.

"I'd be grateful," her mother said faintly. The tiny creature on her arm was barely alive. She looked again at its little curled shape. "Oh, my poor wee!" she muttered, and closed her eyes.

But Ruth said nothing. When she had brought in the cup of tea and had lifted her mother's head with her hand so that she could sip it, she went out to loose the rope with which she had tied Maggie to a scrub tree to keep her from running away while she tended her mother. Maggie had cried in great roars and then wailed herself to sleep. She lay now in the short brown upland grass, her face muddy and her sunburned red hair full of bits of grass and earth.

Ruth stooped and lifted her, but the stout child was heavy for her in her sleep, and so she sat down on the ground and cradled her head on her knees. It was too cold to stay long, though the day was Indian summer.

She shook Maggie gently. "Maggie, wake up!" she said. "It's gettin' cold." She rose and dragged the little girl to her feet, and they went into the house.

"Ruth!" Her mother's voice from the bed was suddenly alert.

"Yes, Mother?"

"Don't tell Jonathan anything. Have you written him?"

"Not yet."

"Then leave it to me to tell. He'll be disgusted-like with your father."

"All right, Mother."

She went on cleaning Maggie and picking the bits out of her hair, and then she fed her with corn-meal mush and put her to bed.

But Mary did not write to Jonathan even when she got up. She could not. How could a middle-aged woman explain to a young man, sensitive and fastidious and her son, why she went on bearing children against her will? So she told herself she was too tired.

She scarcely put the little thing out of her arms. Everything else was neglected. She let Ruth manage as she could, and day and night she lay upon the bed or sat up against a pillow holding the scrap of a child to her body to keep it warm. Clyde grew impatient.

"You act like it was all you had," he grumbled.

She did not answer. She ignored him unless at night she felt him press against her. Then she whispered fiercely, "You keep to yourself, Clyde! I've enough on my conscience with this wee sorrowful child."

"Oh, you're always thinkin' of one dinged thing when I come around," he retorted. "And it's the last thing I want of you when you're like this."

"Stay away, then," she said. "Children are wickedness in a hole like this."

She kept her voice to a whisper because of the indecency of all their life having to go on in this one room.

They were living like beasts in a den. She had no furniture. Her bed was a mattress on posts driven into the ground and crossed with slats. The children slept on pallets spread on dried grass. And the last beastliness was to give birth to a child in this hole—she, a decent Englishwoman! She remembered the cottage in Dentwater and how nice her kitchen had been and how shining were her bits of copper and brass and what a good window it had for a plant or two.

I don't have anything good to write to Jonathan, so I'll not write, she thought.

Her strength did not come back, and at last she did not rise from the bed. The child grew weaker with her weakness, and on Christmas Day it died in her arms. Upon the bed she turned to Ruth.

"The little thing's gone," she said. She had told herself ever since its birth that it would be better if this little creature did not live, and yet she had thought of nothing except how to make it live. Scarcely mine it seemed all the time it was livin', she thought. But now it's dead, I know it was mine.

"Oh, Mother, and we didn't even name it!" Ruth cried and burst into weeping.

"We'll call her after me," Mary said.

She covered her dead child and waited until evening when Maggie was asleep, and then with Ruth's help she washed it carefully and put on the little christening robe she had saved and brought with her from Dentwater because all the children had worn it. And then, because there would be nothing better, she told Ruth to bring one of the goods boxes they used for stools, and she laid the gray blanket in it and then the child. All the time Ruth wept silently.

"Don't weep, my dear," her mother said sadly. "How could we want her back into this place? But I wish she could have been christened, somehow. It's like the animals, else."

"Oh, Mother, don't!" Ruth wailed.

She flung herself upon the bed, and Clyde came in and found them so.

"What's the to-do?" he began, and then saw the little figure in the box like a doll in its long white dress, and he stood still, and his face altered. "Why, when did it happen like this?" he said.

"This afternoon," Mary answered. Her face quivered. "Oh, Clyde, it was bound to come!"

"I reckon it was," he said slowly.

He stood a moment, then asked, timidly, humbly, "What'll I do, Mary?"

"Take it over to that little hollow, Clyde—you know, the one I always called the Fold. And, oh, Clyde, put a stone on top—against the coyotes."

"Sure—I would have—" he said.

He searched and found some planks and was about to nail them down when he paused.

"What is it?" Mary whispered.

"This bit of gray blanket, Mary—she don't need it and we will."

Mary's eyes burned at him. "Clyde, you leave that on her!"

"But, Mary—"

"It's all she has—that miserable bit of stuff—no proper coffin, no burial—"

"All right, Mary! Godamighty, I just was thinkin' of the livin' instead of the dead!"

"I know—" She began to cry, and he came over to her and sat down beside her.

"Mary, my dear—"

She could not stop crying, and after a while he sighed and gave her up and went to the door, the box under his arm. Then she called to him and he stopped. "What is it, Mary?"

"Clyde, don't put her away without saying something."

"I'll say the Lord's Prayer," he said in a low voice.

When he was gone, she lay quiet on the bed. At last she could rest, if this feeling of weakness and loss could be rest. She had no strength. The child's birth had taken what she had left. An unwanted birth was a deadly thing for a woman to endure. It tore the strength out of body and will. She lay, too tired to weep, now that Clyde was gone.

And then in the stillness, with only Ruth sobbing softly, she thought of Jonathan. She had not written and she would not write. There was no use in telling him anything at all.

'Twould only be to his distress. At least I can be spared that, she thought.

Thus Christmas had brought no letter from Jonathan's mother or Ruth. For three days Jonathan had stayed in Lew's house. Lew had taken advantage of a moment alone with Jonathan to say, "I ain't goin' to hint nothin' to Katie till you kin go home."

"I feel that badly I don't know how to express myself," Jonathan said sorrowfully.

"You needn't," Lew said. "You cain't help it. I know how 'tis. I picked my own wife without knowin' why. Lotsa prettier girls, lotsa girls more fun; but I had to have only her. Craziest thing! I sit an' think about it sometimes."

On Christmas Eve they tunneled through to the main road and there found a great patch of bare black ground. The blizzard had freakishly heaped up snow in drifts twenty feet deep, but to do it the wind had scooped an acre bare. Over barren ground Jonathan walked to wallow again through shallow drifts and dig through deep ones until he stood once more in the sod house. Everything was as he had left it. The air was damp and icy cold, but he was glad to be there. He was home again. He was even glad he had refused Lew's invitation to stay to Christmas dinner. He had brought food along, crackers and corn meal and dried peaches, and he would rather eat here alone. In Lew's home he had felt ashamed even to think of Judy. Here he could summon her as he would, sit at his table and remember her, lie on his bed and dream of her, read his few books and see her in every line of poetry and every picturing word. He had written to her three times, but she had not answered. He suspected, half-tenderly, that she could not write, and she would be too delicate to give another her thoughts of him. Ah, well, I'm a master at waiting, he thought.

But he was not alone on Christmas Day after all. Henry Drear came roaring through the snow to the sod-house door and beat upon it so hard that the top of the tunnel caved in upon him. When Jonathan opened the door, in fell man and snow until it seemed the room was half-full of both.

"Of all the darned ways to treat a man on Christmas morning!" Henry shouted. "And me come to ask you to drink my hot buttered rum!"

Jonathan grinned. "You've made a fair mess here," he said in his calm voice and reached for the shovel and began to ladle out the snow.

"It's your snow," Henry returned, "and all I did was to bring it in with me. Well, Jonathan, come along at noon or so and drink with Median folks at American House."

"Thanks, I will," Jonathan replied, "though I'm no great drinker, as you know."

"Oh, well, you're schoolmaster and folks'll want you there."

"And I want it, too," Jonathan said.

"Good," Henry shouted. To shout was his only voice, and everything he said was a bellow. He clapped Jonathan's shoulder. "Come along out and help clear the roads—we're all at it."

"I will," Jonathan said.

He spent Christmas morning shoveling snow as dry and crystalline as salt. But he enjoyed it. He saw men he had not seen since Joel's meeting, and in the brilliant sunshine they stopped to talk and compare this blizzard with blizzards of other years. It was easy, neighborly talk, and full of the boasting to which he was now used, though he could never take part in it.

"This-here blizzard," Bill White said, spitting a great stain upon the snow, "ain't nothing like the blizzards we used to have when I first come to the prairie. Them was blizzards! First the snow would all come down. Then the wind would toss it all up and stir it round until it made you dizzy did you look out of the window. And if you opened the door you never got it shut again. I've knowed folks whose doors busted open and they froze solid in their beds and was excavated in the spring!"

"This is enough of a blizzard for me, though, Mr. White," Jonathan said mildly.

"You have to get used to big things out here," Bill said.

They spent Christmas afternoon at the tavern. Everybody in Median was there except the Parrys. Now that he saw them all merrymaking, it occurred to him how youthful Median was. There were few white heads. Mrs. Cobb's mother was there and an old man he had not seen before, but most of Median was young. There was singing and dancing, and he saw Katie dancing again and again. There were no other young girls in Median since Jennet went away, and Katie shone in a solitary glory which, if it could not be splendid because of her plain face and dun-colored hair, was nevertheless real. She was young, less than a woman but more than a child, and men danced with her half-teasingly, half-provocatively, and she went from one to the other with a sedate industrious energy. She did not once look at Jonathan.

Ah, she knows! he thought and was at once relieved and foolishly hurt. He was fond of Katie. Sometime when he could he must tell her how a chap could be fond of one girl even when he was in love with another. But he did not go near her. He danced a little with Mrs. Drear, who told him she had heard from Jennet. She was in San Francisco and hoping to be married to a rich man. There were plenty of rich men there.

"Have you heard from your folks?" she asked.

"No, but I'll hear as soon as the roads open," he replied.

"Sure you will," she said and laughed. "There, Jonathan, leave me be. I'm breathless and too old for a young feller."

He let her go and stood watching the crowd. Tired of dancing, they had suddenly begun to sing, and when they sang they were most themselves. Each dropped unaware into what he was. And Jonathan, who had only once yielded to one of Joel's hymns, was suddenly moved, and he lifted his voice shyly and began to sing, too. But he would never be able to sing himself out in Henry Drear's rollicking roar, and he could only sip his hot buttered rum instead of swallowing it down in big gulps. The scum of butter was too rich for him, and after a moment he put his mug down.

Yet all was good, and he liked being there. They liked him, and he felt this. He was deeply pleased when Mrs. Cobb came up to him and said in her plain way, "I want to tell you, Mr. Goodliffe, that it's been real worth while stoppin' in Median. The children both read wonderful."

"I'm glad of that, Mrs. Cobb," he said earnestly.

"And I'm just as pleased that Martha's a mite smarter than Matthew," she said. "I tell her, too. I aim to have my girls hold their heads as high as any man."

"Why not?" he agreed, though privately he did not. A woman ought not to be quite as smart as a man. Even with all his feelings against his father, he would have loved his mother less if she had not been subject to him. "Though I have a very high opinion of Matthew," he said. "He is very able in mathematics."

Mrs. Cobb looked proud. "So he ought to be, for he has the skinflintest grandfather in the state of Massachusetts. Old Mr. Cobb's a real rich man, but it don't do anybody any good, because he hoards it all. That's why we left the store and come West."

"Is it now!" Jonathan said politely.

What touched him most that Christmas Day was to go home at dusk and find upon his table a small bundle tied in newspaper dyed red with something and secured with string made of woven grass. "Merry Christmas from Parrys" was written upon a piece of paper in Beaumont's best hand, and a branch of berries was thrust under the string. Inside the package were molasses candy and dried wild raspberries and some black walnut meats in a little wooden box made very light and thin and polished until it was like porcelain to his touch.

He lit a small fire and sat near it and ate some of the candy and nuts and thought of his mother and the children and Judy. Then, to his own amazement, he thought a little of Katie. He discovered that he was hurt because she had let this day go by without a mention of something he knew she had long been making for him. He suspected it was a shirt because more than a month before this she had brought a piece of string to school and measured his arm and the breadth of his shoulder and chest.

"Don't you ast me nothin', Jonathan," she had said importantly. "You'll know sometime—Christmas, maybe."

But this was the end of Christmas, and she had not spoken to him. He felt foolishly irritated with himself that he cared. I'm an unreasonable chap, he thought, after some pondering, and was much surprised at himself.

16

ON THE ragged northern fringe of the city of New Orleans, Judy stood in a crowd and watched its behavior. It was a crowd mostly of men, but this did not trouble her. Crowds were usually made up of men because most women stayed at home. If she had a home, maybe she would stay in it. When she thought of this she thought vaguely of Jonathan without deciding anything. Her wandering life had made her able to live only in the moment.

Around the jail between two and three hundred men stood stolidly waiting for something. She knew what it was, because she had asked. She had come out of the boardinghouse where she and Joel had rooms, and with a basket on her arm she was going to the market to buy food. Across the street down which she went every day, she found the dense mass of men, and she paused.

"What are you here for?" she asked a young man in a drab brown suit and a tall hat.

"Lem Beaumont's to be taken from jail to court today," he replied.

When she heard that, she gave up the marketing. She could do that any time, but she could not see any time this big Negro who had killed old Pierre Beaumont's son, Pierre. She had heard all about it because everybody was talking about it. Nobody cared whether young Pierre died or not. He was the worthless son of a good father. But he was a white man, and Lem was the son of a black mother, a mulatto who had once been a Beaumont slave. People said young Pierre was his father, but Lem's real sin was not patricide. It was that a black man had killed a white man—and, more than that, a white man to whom he would have belonged legally if the war had not turned the wrong way.

The crowd was quiet. Had they been noisy she would not have been afraid of them. She was used to men in excitement, and it did not matter much what the excitement was. But these men were perfectly still, their faces turned attentively to the door of the jail. A man spat, another tore a bite from a plug of tobacco and put the plug back into his pocket. But these slight movements scarcely broke the rigidity of the mass.

A fat elderly man in a dirty linen suit stared at Judy. When she looked up, her eyes drawn unconsciously by his, he said, "You'd better go on where you were goin'. What's about to happen is for us men to see—"

"I don't mind," Judy replied. She gave him a look from her eyes, so purposely pure and fearless that he was disconcerted and moved away from her.

Under the quietness something waited. It stirred when the door opened and the sheriff came out. He was a tall, lazy-looking man, and he surveyed the crowd with tolerant eyes. When he spoke it was with a sort of slow and genial power.

"Lookahyeah, you-all oughtn't to act like this. The co'se of justice is proceedin'. They ain't a mite of doubt Lem's gonna be hung. I'm willin' to give my pehsonal wuhd of honah."

The men stared back at him in silence and stillness. He spat and, taking off his broad-brimmed hat, scratched his head.

"Well, I ain't responsible," he muttered, and he turned and went back into the jail.

Now little movements were to be felt rather than seen. Men shuffled their feet in the dust, men tightened their belts, men drew their hands across their mouths and pulled down their hats over their eyes and waited.

The door opened, and the sheriff came out again. Behind him were two guards and between the guards was a big Negro with mud-colored wool and slaty eyes.

The crowd, like an animal long crouched and waiting, leaped forward. Judy, behind them, saw them spring, fasten upon their prey, and move away with him. The silence was broken with moans and mutterings, and then suddenly with the Negro's yelps. She stood motionless, watching them go. Across the emptiness between her and the doorway to the jail she saw the sheriff and the guards. They did not look at her, but she heard their voices clearly through the sunshine.

"Reckon old Doc Beaumont'll be mighty mad with me," the sheriff said.

"He shorely will," a guard agreed.

"Seems like they just couldn't stand it when they heard old Doc didn' want the State to prosecute. It made 'em mad."

"It shore ain't healthy in this here town not to prosecute a niggra to the full extent of his crime," the guard agreed.

The sheriff turned to spit and, seeing Judy, paused to smile; and she, at the familiar sight of that sort of smile on a man's lazy, handsome face, recalled her errand and went on her way thoughtfully.

Beaumont! There was a handsome boy in Jonathan's school called Beaumont. When spring came, if they went back to Median, if it happened that she and Jonathan met again, she would tell him about this morning. She felt sobered by what must now be happening to that gray-skinned Negro with his wrong-colored eyes, but she was not shocked. Such things had to happen. Even the sheriff could not stop them. There was something like the will of God in them. Everything was God's will, and there was nothing to do about it. If she got back to Median, if she married Jonathan and obeyed her mother, that would be God's will. But if she did not, that would be God's will, too.

She bought beans and corn and some greens and a piece of cow's meat and stared at some bright red fruit.

"What's those?" she asked the slatternly white woman who served her.

"Them's love apples," the woman said.

"Are they good to eat?" Judy asked.

"Some folks says they're pison, and some folks eats 'em," the woman replied. "I dunno, I've always stayed on the safe side, myself."

"I'll take two," Judy said.

On the way home she paused under a magnolia tree and, putting her hand into her basket, picked up one of the brilliant fruits and bit into it. It was full of juice, and the red juice ran down her chin. It had a strange bland taste at first, but after she had eaten it her mouth was acid. She wiped her chin and went on, waiting for anything.

If it's poison, it'll be God's will, she thought, and if it isn't poison, that's God's will, too.

She walked on, meditating, and reached the shabby boardinghouse and went into the two rooms on the ground floor where she and her father were stopping. He was not there, and she put away her vegetables, all except the love apple, which she put on the mantelpiece above the iron grate.

I feel perfectly all right, she thought calmly, looking at it. And then it seemed to her that she had discovered the only way to know God's will. It was to do as she liked and wait for God to do something to her—or nothing, if He did not mind. She laughed, yawned, and threw herself on her bed. She could sleep at any time of day, and now, after a moment, she fell into sleep, her head turned a little to one side, her red lips closed and smiling.

In his library old Dr. Pierre Beaumont sat motionless while he listened to the sheriff.

"Sit down, Harry," he said suddenly.

"No, suh, I'd rawtha stand," the sheriff replied. "Anyway, I've said all I kin say, jes' as I did all I could. They was plumb determined, Doc. Nothin' I could say, nothin' I could do, would hold 'em back. Seems like they was druv by somethin' inside 'em."

Dr. Beaumont did not answer. The room was dark with the shadows of vines from the windows, vine shadows upon oak panels. But he would not have anything in the garden cut because years ago his young wife Lavinia had planned that garden. "My garden," she had called it.

She had died under the knife when their son Pierre was not quite four years old. She had had a strange internal inflammation, and in a few hours was in such fever and agony that he had insisted upon an operation. Young Mallory Bain had done it, a brilliant surgeon, and he had stood by. Thousands of times he had recalled that hour and had examined it second by second. He could not have operated. To have cut into that sweet romantic flesh would have been beyond his power. His hand would have trembled. Love could not take up a knife even to save. It needed Bain's cold youth. There was nothing he could say was done wrong. And yet if he had forced himself to operate, with all his experience, could he not have saved the few minutes too much for her heart? And yet, if she had died under his hand, could he have lived for Pierre? Much of his life had been spent in this pondering. He pondered it more and more as Pierre grew up into a worthless youth, and then into an idle and worthless man.

Eleven days ago when he was killed by a slate-colored Negro boy, the son of one of the Beaumont slaves, the question was answered finally. He ought to have operated and tried to save Lavinia because the boy was not worth saving.

"I reckon you did do all you could, Harry," he said now. He was a very old man, eighty-one his next birthday. He felt tired and wanted the room to himself, and this big, sweat-smelling man filled it and used up the air. "I reckon if the boy was doomed to die, it was just as well to get it over with. But I hate to have my family mixed up in lynching. I believe in a fair trial for a nigger, even if he has killed my only son."

"Yes, suh," the sheriff replied. "Ev'ybody knows how you love justice, Doc."

"Yes," said the old man slowly. "I love justice."

He was reminded by this of the letter he had received from a young man in Kansas which he had not answered. It was in regard to a lad named Beaumont—Pierre Beaumont. A false claim, he would have said, except that there was the name Sue. He remembered Sue very well, a beautiful mulatto child that had belonged to Lavinia's Bettina. Bettina had come with Lavinia and had brought with her a six-months-old baby. He had asked Lavinia once about it, and Lavinia had shaken her head.

"Don't ask me, Pierre. We don't know. Bettina's half-white, and the baby is more than that. I've never asked Bettina. We don't want to know. Anyway, the white blood doesn't count—the black blood decides." Lavinia, so soft and exquisite a creature, could sometimes be crystal hard.

"Good-by, Harry," he said faintly.

"Good-by, Doc. Sho' do regret it happened like it did."

He backed away out of the door, and outside in the hall came upon an old Negro man, straightening up from the keyhole.

"Hey, you," he said. "What you doin', Joe?"

"Nuthin'," Joe answered.

The sheriff stared at him. "Don't look like nothin'," he remarked. "It looks doggone funny when a man bends hisself over to look in a keyhole."

"I wan't lookin', I was listenin'," Joe said. "I wanted to know somepin'."

"What?" the sheriff asked.

"Did I unastan' you to say, suh, 'at dey got Lem?"

"They did," the sheriff replied.

Joe's wrinkled face quivered. "'At's all I wanted to know, suh," he said.

"What's it to you?" the sheriff demanded.

"Lem was my boy," the old Negro replied. "Least, he was my wife's boy. She guv 'im birth eighteen years ago when she was chambermaid hyeah and Doc Beaumont tol' me to mah'y her, because somebody oughta do it quick. I did it to oblige him, and then Lem was bawn. But she was all right. She was a good wife 'cept she always loved Lem bes' of all de chillen. Reckon I gotta go tell her Lem is daid."

He shambled away. The sheriff stared after him, shrugged, and put on his wide hat.

Everythin's all mixed up, he thought. How you goin' to get justice that-a-way? He let himself out of the house and ran down the marble steps to the lawn.

In the library old Dr. Beaumont sighed and stirred himself. Justice must be done, he thought wearily. He found his quill pen and sharpened it, and with long pains and many small waverings and unnecessary movements he sat down at his big table of English oak to answer Jonathan Goodliffe's letter.

DEAR SIR:

In view of your letter of the twenty-first December I beg to say that if the Young Man in question has Merit and Ability I shall be pleased to extend to him the Sum of Five Hundred Dollars a Year until his medical Education is completed, provided it is understood he makes no Claim upon me otherwise.

I remain, sir, yours faithfully,

PIERRE DUBOIS BEAUMONT, M.D.

Then he sat down again and watched the long hanging shadows upon the dark oak. . . . How could a little blond boy with Lavinia's eyes grow up to be a tall laughing stranger, an idler, a wastrel? When had the change begun, and how had he not seen it until it was finished and too late? He had failed in everything—a brilliant surgeon, but not able to save his own wife; a father, but not able to save his own son. Justice! It was a great cold word, but it was all that remained to a solitary old man.

I must put it in my will, he thought.

17

WINTER ended and spring was come, and Median was beleaguered in mud. Each year Jonathan forgot the mud, and it was worse each spring. To be snowbound was one thing, but to be mudbound was another. A blizzard, a roaring tigerish wind, snow banked to the roof—these could be large noble enemies. Men boasted of them and compared their labors against them. But mud was a disgusting slime, ensnaring the feet. It was enraging to look into a sky as softly blue as a field of English forget-me-nots, with clouds as innocent and white as lambs upon it, and to have the feet held and made filthy in a spreading of mire.

"There'll be no wagons until the worst of this is over," Henry Drear said dolefully in his empty inn.

Jonathan gave up cleaning his floor because the children came muddied to the knees. He was a harder teacher than he had ever been because he was so impatient with the mud. There was no good in spring as long as there was this mud. Judy would not be coming, for he suspected Joel's comfort and the will of God would be closely allied. It was misery to sit at his desk with the door open and feel the sweet warm air and know that if he stepped beyond the threshold he would sink into black mud. He loathed it with a personal fury because he hated to be unclean. He could not go about all day as the rest of Median did with a casing of mud upon his legs, halfway to his thighs. It put him into a fret.

"I'll begin roads," he said one day in the store where he had gone for food.

"You'll be beginnin' somethin' if you do," Lew said dryly. "Where'll they begin and where'll they go to in a country like this that spreads itself out over everything?"

"They'll begin at Median," Jonathan said firmly, "and they'll go as far as Median folk need to go."

He did indeed begin his work on roads that spring by himself digging from the sod house toward the square the path of a straight narrow walk.

"What you goin' to put in it?" Bill White asked, having heard of it. "There ain't a stone in a hundred miles."

"I'm going to put in posts and boards," Jonathan replied.

"It'll be like layin' a floor to the square," Bill said, astonished.

"It'll do until someday we'll have roads like a Christian country," Jonathan retorted.

That was the beginning of boardwalks in Median. When Jonathan could walk out of the sod house and around a side of the square to the store in eleven minutes Lew said, "Reckon I can add on as far as Drear's, and Drear can finish out to the corner if he feels good."

Drear did, after great objections. And then Jonathan, looking into the drying mud of the square, thought of something else.

" 'Twould be pretty to plant trees and grass there," he said, " 'twould improve the town wonderfully. Why shouldn't the school do it?"

He impressed his pupils, though it was against the will of some. Abram Hasty saw no good in it, but Beaumont was ardent to help and, to Jonathan's surprise, so was Matthew Cobb.

"Where we come from in Massachusetts there was trees and grass along the streets," Matthew said.

"When are you folks going West?" Jonathan asked.

"Don't look hardly like we're goin'," Matthew said despondently. "Maw's made up her mind she won't go no farther now that Paw's got a good store job. She likes it here."

"And you don't, I take it, from your looks," Jonathan said.

"There's nothin' to do in Median," Matthew said.

"Nothing to do!" Jonathan said.

"Well, anyways, no Indians to fight or gold to dig out of the ground, and no cowboys."

"We won't hold school tomorrow," Jonathan said. "We'll plant trees instead."

He saw Katie, tying her books with a string, look severe at this. "I can't get my feet wet," she said.

"You don't have to get your feet wet," Jonathan retorted. Katie had come regularly to school since Christmas, but now she never stayed to sweep up or straighten as once she had. She came and did her lessons moderately and went home with the others. And he had broken abruptly his habit of Sunday dinner by saying frankly to Lew, "I'll feel better not to come Sundays, Lew, if you'll forgive me."

"Sure," Lew said casually.

Now he glanced at Katie with private disgust. He perceived her meaning. She looked important and remote and her bristling little pigtails she had tied up in loops around her head. He felt suddenly angry with her for growing up into a woman.

The next morning he took the boys to the river. They found small cottonwoods and dried them and put them onto a mud sledge and, with a team loaned by a boy's father who was a farmer near Median, they dragged them to the square and planted them. Katie did not appear, and he was glad of it. With the others he worked hard, and by the end of the third day they had planted fifty young cottonwoods. People stopped to look at them with curiosity and pleasure.

"Don't know why nobody thought of plantin' trees before," Henry Drear said.

"Makes a body feel the town's here to stay," Abram Cobb said from the door of the store.

"It's a good job," Jonathan said heartily to the muddy children. "School on Monday'll be more fun after it. And you, Abram"—he turned to the great gawky boy—"you were good at it. I saw you heaving the trees."

Abram was abashed and spat before he spoke. " 'Twa'n't nothin' to me," he said.

"It goes to show books aren't everything for some jobs," Jonathan said pleasantly.

Abram, dazed by this perception in his teacher, could look only confused.

"Good night, all, until Monday," Jonathan said tranquilly.

Sundays were his good days. He portioned them out carefully into what he had to do. First there was his shaving and washing, then he ate breakfast, and then he cleaned house. That took most of his morning.

He was in the midst of this the next day when, looking up from sweeping the floor, he saw Sue upon the threshold. She carried a live chicken in her hand by the legs.

"Come in, Mrs. Parry," he said surprised. He saw Stephen often, but not Sue.

"I'll only take a minute, Mr. Goodliffe," she said.

"Sit down," Jonathan said, putting down his broom.

But she could not sit easily in his presence. She sat on the corner of a chair, and the chicken began to flutter and squawk.

"I brought this-hyeah fowl," she said, "thinkin' you might like to start chickens. She's full of eggs and will set, I'm sure."

"Thank you, I'll be glad of it," he said.

She stooped and tore a bit of the hem from her petticoat and tied the bird's legs and took it outside. Then she came back and sat down edgewise again and looked at him out of sad and solemnly dark eyes.

"Mr. Goodliffe, did you evah git an answer to dat letter Beaumont tol' me you wrote for him?"

"I never did," Jonathan said. "I was about to write another as soon as the mud clears. The mail's delayed by mud."

"I been waitin'," Sue said, " 'cause I know somepin."

"What?" Jonathan asked.

"A Beaumont is daid," she replied gravely.

"Have you had a letter?" he asked. There was something strange about her.

"No," she replied. She wore round gold earrings in her ears set with small grayish pearls. "But I know. I began to know a while back. But I wa'n't sure. Now I am."

"How?" he asked. He wanted to be amused and somehow was not.

She turned her strong profile to him, first one side and then the other. "See, Mr. Goodliffe? Them earrings was soldered on my ears by my Beaumont master. He said I wasn't never to take 'em off until he died. He said they was full of spell, and as long as he was alive the pearls would shine. But when they turned dark I could know he was daid. Then I could take 'em off."

He saw them gray against her fine dark skin.

"I can't believe that, Mrs. Parry," he said firmly. "I believe he said it, of course, but not that it can be true."

"No, suh, I wouldn't expect you to believe it," she said quietly. "But of co'se I knows what I knows, suh. All I wanted to know was if you heard anything."

"No, I haven't," he said. "But I'll let you know if I do, and if I don't I'll write again."

She went away, and he went on sweeping. He did not believe in that sort of thing.

But the first mail brought him a letter folded and sealed with wax, and when he opened it he found it was from a lawyer's firm. Old Dr. Pierre Beaumont, the letter said, was dead. His last act, apparently, for he died alone in his library, was to write a letter granting five hundred dollars a year to a young man named Pierre Beaumont. Could information be sent concerning this individual?

Jonathan was so astonished that he forgot that five minutes before he had been sore with disappointment because this was his only letter, and that still there was no word from Judy or his mother. He took the letter at once to Sue Parry. She was washing clothes outdoors under a cottonwood tree, and Jonathan hastened to her.

"You were right," he said. "A Beaumont is dead. And it looks as though he has left enough money to your boy to make him free."

She lifted her dark hands out of the suds and raised them upward. "Thank You, God," she said to the sky. Her hands dropped and she cried out for Beaumont. He came running barefoot out of the house. "Boy, you is free," she said solemnly.

Beaumont's red lips parted. He looked at Jonathan, speechless, and Jonathan said quickly, "I think it's all right—I'm going to write back to the lawyers and tell them who you are."

He gave the letter to Beaumont. The boy took it and read it carefully, and handed it back.

"Thank you, Mr. Goodliffe," he said, and stood still for an instant and then raced away over the plains, and Jonathan and Sue looked at each other and smiled.

The mud dried, and the caravans of spring came upon Median. Jonathan, happening one day to be at the tavern to fetch his loaf of bread, found the house lively with people he had never seen before.

"Folks are on the move," Henry roared at him. "Two wagonloads today, and looks like there was another comin'."

Jonathan turned involuntarily to the door. Over the soft, deepening green of the new grass he could indeed see not one wagon but three, hurrying, doubtless, to make the haven of American House by night.

"When I see the first wagon, I know winter's over," Henry said. A young woman came out of the kitchen with a bowl of mush and disappeared into the inner room. Henry watched her, then he spat into the tin spittoon inside the bar. "Awful nice folks," he said. "Seems like every spring we get nicer folks. Don't know what the East'll do with all the up-and-comin' ones gone. She's from around Philadelphy, she and her husband and two little boys. Little feller's got a upset stomach, so they're layin' over a day. Then they're goin' straight on West."

"Why do they all want to keep going West?" he asked curiously.

A tall, long-faced young man came in. "Howdy," he said and passed by them into the inner room.

"That's her husband—name's Blume," Henry said. "Hell, I don't know," he went on. "It's maybe because the world whirls that way. 'Least, that's how I figger it. We don't know we feel it, but somehow'r other, we do feel it aturnin' and th'owin' us west. Look at Columbus—what made him come this-a-way? And I bet you the Pacific Ocean won't stop us, neither. Come the land is full up to the shore line, we'll just keep goin' on across to Chiny."

"It's senseless," Jonathan said. "At that rate, we'll just keep goin' forever, round and round." He got up and went into the kitchen and took from a board table one of the freshly baked loaves there. Mrs. Drear, her face purple with the heat of the hot range, looked up at him.

"Jennet's not goin' to marry that feller after all," she said abruptly.

"No?" Jonathan said. "Why not?"

"She don't say why," Mrs. Drear said irritably. She wiped sweat from her eye with her thick hand. "It's a curse to have a pretty girl in these-hyere parts, Jonathan. There's too many men to pick and choose from. A girl tosses 'em up like dice to see which one'll give her most. I wish Jennet'd come home, but she won't. Now she's talkin' about Oregon. What's a troupe, Jonathan?"

"Why, it's actresses," he said, astonished.

"She's in a troupe," Mrs. Drear said gloomily and clattered the oven door.

Jonathan went out. The wagons were driving up now, and he could see the faces of people in the brightness of the late afternoon. But he went on toward home. Under his arm the loaf of bread smelled deliciously fresh, and he pulled off a bit of crust and ate it. . . . Why should people go on and on restlessly when all they needed for happiness was in four walls under a roof upon a bit of ground? If wagons were coming, Judy was coming.

By the door Beaumont was spading up his garden. Jonathan, remembering his own first hungers, had told the boy he would give him a dollar if he would do the first spading, and with the dollar buy him some writing paper and a pen of his own or, if he preferred, a book.

"I'll wait to decide till I feel the money in my hand," Beaumont said. "Whichever makes it feel lightest, I'll spend it for that."

When he saw Jonathan come, he straightened and leaned on his spade.

"Did you hyeah from them lawyers in N'Orleans yet, Mr. Goodliffe?"

"No, I haven't, Beau," Jonathan replied. "If I don't hear soon, I'm going to write again."

"And if you don't hyeah again, suh?"

"Maybe I'll have to go and see them," Jonathan said. "But I don't want to go just now."

"No, suh," Beaumont said.

Jonathan went into the house. He did not want to leave here just now when Judy might be coming any day.

Beaumont's handsome head thrust itself in at the door.

"Mr. Goodliffe, did you tell 'em I wasn't white?"

"No, I didn't," Jonathan said sharply. "It wasn't their business, I considered. But I did think I ought to tell them you were a natural son. That's their legal right to know. Want some bread and treacle, Beau?"

"I do indeed, suh, thank you. I'm hongry all the time," Beaumont smiled, shamefaced. "Last night we trapped somepin like a groundhog, only it wasn't that exactly, Paw said, and Maw made a stew an' I kep' on eatin' after evybody was full, but today I'm empty again. It's real discouragin'."

He put out a big delicately shaped earth-soiled hand. Jonathan looked at it as he always did. He knew Beaumont's hand better than his own.

There was nothing of any interest to him in his own, indeed, with its broad palm and rather short fingers. He did not like his own hand better for being like his father's.

He cut two slices of the loaf, gently because it was so fresh, and spread it with molasses, and they stood at the door eating it. Then Jonathan put his hand in his pocket and took out a silver dollar.

"Here's your money, Beau," he said. "What's its weight?"

Beaumont, smiling, held it a moment. "It weighs lightest when I think of a book," he said.

"What book?" Jonathan asked.

"An anatomy book, please, suh," Beaumont said. "I'm mighty curious about people's insides."

"Very well, Beau," Jonathan said. He had long ago cut from newspapers the advertisements of bookshops in the East and had bought, during the course of the year, four books, though always with a sense of guilt because his mother might suddenly need all the money he could muster. He had at times a serious sense of disaster overwhelming her, because still she did not write.

"Thank you, Mr. Goodliffe," Beaumont said. "I'll be goin' home, then."

"Good night, Beau," Jonathan answered.

He stood a moment, as he often did now, looking out over the smooth green prairie, so joyful after the sodden black of the burned ground. If he did not look toward Median he could imagine that no human being was upon the earth and under the sky except himself. Then, against the afterglow in the eastern sky, he saw the cocked black shape of a wagon top. There was still another wagon coming. If he did not get some word from his mother, soon he would have to get a seat in one of them and go to see how she was, he thought; and then remembered that he might have to go to New Orleans. He would have to go if there was any trouble about the legacy for Beaumont.

At the barest thought of going anywhere, this foothold of his upon the prairie was suddenly precious. I shan't go before Judy comes, he thought. Upon this great prairie two people, after waiting all winter, might miss each other in the spring, if one did not stay steadily where he was.

18

HE WOULD have said that the day of Judy's coming must be different from any other, or at least that he would wake with a sense of her approach. Every day now brought more wagons, and Median was full of restlessness. In the store Lew was so busy that Katie stopped coming to school. Jonathan saw her one afternoon cleaning her bit of the shelf underneath the long table at which they all sat. He paid no heed to her because she often cleaned and rearranged her small belongings. Today she tied everything together with string, and he saw this and knew what was about to happen. But he said nothing. He seldom said anything to her nowadays. It was she who spoke to him.

"Jonathan, I'm not coming to school any more. Pop needs me in the store."

"Well, Katie!" he said. She stood before him, an angular young girl, slight but without any grace except goodness. But because she was so good, his heart pricked him.

"Good-by," she said.

"Why do you say good-by?" he answered. "I'll see you whenever I come to the store, and maybe you'll be coming this way sometimes to tell me how badly I keep house, and maybe even clean a bit for me—eh, Katie? Like old times, eh?"

He had the impulse to put out his hand and did not yield to it, knowing that he did not really want to touch her hand. She was watching him closely.

"I'm goin' to be busy," she said sullenly.

But he understood that sullenness of hers and forgave it.

"Then I'll come sometimes and help you," he said. "Good-by then, Katie."

He went back to his work of setting a lesson on the board for the next day, and so he let her go, though somehow he felt, even though his back was turned to her, a faint pull of the heart, or perhaps only of the conscience, as she went. But he let her go and did not turn his head until he knew she was gone, and then she was trudging along the boardwalk. And what he saw then was that her long feet turned out too much as she walked.

Nevertheless, this faint regret, this compunction or whatever it was, clouded his being slightly. Otherwise how was it that he did not perceive Judy's coming the next day?

It was a Saturday and a holiday. But his school tasks were shortened now anyway because the older boys had work to do on farms. Only the Hasty boys were still able to stay because the mill would have little work to do until a harvest came. And Jonathan, some weeks before, turning over in his mind, ways of earning something more, had found that on Saturdays and Sundays he could work at the tavern for Henry Drear for his food and half a dollar a day. Thus it happened that in the midst of Saturday morning's stir he saw a wagon come in, and out of it unfolded Joel's long stiff shape, and then he saw Judy, poised with her skirts in her hands, waiting an instant before she jumped to the ground. He saw her from the tavern door, a beautiful girl in a full green dress and a green bonnet, her golden-brown curls on either side of her rosy face. He saw her great black eyes glancing everywhere and thought with a lift of the heart that they searched for him.

He went out, wanting to run; but, compelled by the habit of his shyness, he walked sedately toward her.

"Hello, Judy," he said in so offhand a voice that he was disgusted with himself. But he could not speak differently or make his voice warmer, because his heart beat so strongly that he had to hide it. Then he perceived that people were looking at her, men and women, as they came and went from store to tavern from their wagons, and he hated her to stand there before them.

"I'll help you down," he said.

"I can get down myself," she said quickly and jumped before he could help her. He felt her fall against him for a second and he put out his arm. But she righted herself.

"How are you, Jonathan?" she asked.

"I'm well enough," he replied. "And you?"

"I'm well," she said.

This was stupid talk and like nothing he had planned. He was angry with it, and yet he could do nothing. Whenever he had dreamed of their meeting, it was always alone.

Joel came hurrying up, full of his business. "Good day, Goodliffe." He put out his long, thin, always-dirty hand. "Nice to see you. Judy, we aren't stopping. There's a wagon pulling out this afternoon for California. It is against my principles, of course, to travel on the Lord's Day, but I've just prayed and God tells me to go ahead, since it's hard to find a wagon that can take two people straight to California without stop. But God has prepared this way. The brother's wife died and one of the older girls, and so there's plenty of room. Well, Mr. Goodliffe, I've long felt the call to California, and now it looks like I'm goin' to get there, a land flowing with milk and honey. So, Judy, just get out and rest a little, and after we've eaten we'll start. Excuse me, Mr. Goodliffe. I have some details to attend to."

He nodded, his dark eyes glittering, the wind under his broad hat lifting his long, straight black hair from his shoulders, and hurried off. But what he had said drove away Jonathan's shyness.

"Oh, Judy," he gasped, "you can't go—not when we've had no chance —Judy, you didn't even write to me!"

"I was going to write," she said in that slow, pleasant, rich voice of hers, "but somehow the time just escaped me."

She could write, then! He was suddenly very angry.

"Judy, you knew how I'd be hoping and hoping—and all my letters to you!"

"I kept them, Jonathan," she said.

He was comforted a little and grew gentler. "Judy, that's sweet. But think of me, without a letter from you to keep!"

"I surely ought to have written," she said sadly, turning her big eyes to him. When she looked at him full he saw again how extraordinary were her eyes. The irises were unusually large, the whites so clear, and the lashes long and thick.

"Oh, Judy," he muttered, "where shall we go?"

"Let's go to your house," she said.

His head swam, and he struggled for reason. "You oughtn't maybe to come to a bachelor's home alone," he said. "We're not children any more, Judy." Certainly no child could feel as he did, he thought solemnly.

She laughed. "Well, you go along yourself, and then I'll just walk that way," she said.

He caught at her words and smiled back at her, and, feeling more reckless than he ever had in his life, he strode to the sod house.

Judy, looking after him and seeing everything, seemed to have forgotten him. She tugged at a small cherrywood box in the back of the wagon. Two men from different directions who were apparently in great haste on their own business stopped.

"Let me help you," the elder one said.

But the younger one was there first. "Let me," he said, and lifted down the small box.

"Oh, thank you," she said to them both, with her lovely smile for each.

"Where shall I take it, Miss—?" the young man asked and hesitated, hopefully, for her name.

But she did not give it. She took the box from him gently. "I can take it now, thank you," she said and let him for reward just touch her fingers. She understood men so well and allowed them these small harmless rewards. She took the box and went into the tavern, pausing at the kitchen door to speak to Mrs. Drear.

"Well, mercy me," Mrs. Drear said, "are you and Joel here, too, Judy? Every room's full, my dear. Seems like the whole East is movin' at once this spring."

"We're not stopping, thank you, Mrs. Drear," Judy said. "May I just brush my hair in your bedroom?"

"Do, child," Mrs. Drear said in absent distraction. How to feed thirty people at once was a puzzle, she thought. And Judy, perceiving she was forgotten, smiled and sauntered toward the bedroom. It was in morning confusion, the bed still not made and Henry's clothes on the floor. Not from any compulsion but merely out of half-lazy kindness, she made the bed and hung up the clothes on a nail on the wall. Then she poured water from a pitcher into a china basin on the washstand and washed her face and hands. Opening the cherrywood box, she took out a small round mirror and her comb and brush and brushed her hair into ringlets and brushed her eyebrows with a feather, and powdered her nose from a little bag of cornstarch. She put on her hat and closed the box. Looking as fresh as though she had not been weeks traveling, she went quietly down the walk toward the sod house, avoiding her father without seeming to do so. He was arguing with Lew Merridy outside the door of the general store. Lew, she noticed calmly, was sweating, and that meant her father had God on his side.

As for herself, she had not the least idea what God's will was going to be for her in the next hour.

"Jonathan?" she called softly but very clearly at the door of the sod house. He came out instantly from his bedroom. She saw that he had changed his shirt and smoothed his brown hair, and she smiled at him.

"Judy, come in—sit down. I made some tea, without even knowing if you like tea, but my mother always wants a cup of tea. Sit down here in this chair. Oh, Judy!"

She sat down, and he stood looking at her.

"Judy," he said solemnly, "I've seen you here again and again—all through this long winter."

She smiled, quite understanding how he felt. "Where's your mother?" she asked.

"She's out in the West with my father and the children. Judy, let's not talk except about you and me—Judy, did you think of me?"

He longed to kneel beside her and was too shy to do it, at least until she gave him a sign. She was taking off her hat and smoothing her curls, and he watched every movement of her white hands in that bright hair.

"I did think of you, Jonathan, often."

How, she was wondering, would she know God's will? Maybe if she could make up her own mind it would be easier.

"Did you, dear?" he cried. "And did you long to see me as I longed to see you?" Now he could kneel and he did and was surprised to find that he was scarcely shy at all.

"I did want to see you," she said gravely. Her eyes upon his face were so honest and pure that he could not put out his arms. He was awed before this lovely goodness.

"Oh, Judy, you can't go, when you've just come!" he cried. "I can't bear it. We haven't met for so long, we love each other—don't we, dearest? —but we scarcely know each other. Can't you persuade your father to let you stay behind?"

"Where would I stay?" she asked innocently.

He longed with all his heart to cry out, "Stay with me—marry me—" But his native prudence forbade it. A man ought not to marry a woman he did not know, even if he loved her. It was not prudent, and in his heart he knew that he was compelled above all else by love of wisdom.

And she, waiting, thought, If he asks me to marry him, maybe I'll let that be God's will.

"You could stay with Mrs. Drear until—until we know each other better," he faltered and cursed himself, and then thought irrelevantly of his father and how if he had been his father's son he would have Judy in his arms and be telling her quickly all he longed to tell her. But he was not thus his father's son.

Judy's voice broke, sweet and troubled. "Suppose you didn't like me so well when you knew me, Jonathan, and then I'd be all alone here."

This at least he could deny. "Oh, my dearie dear," he cried, "I'd only love you more."

She looked at him, her eyes very large and full of question.

"What is it, Judy?" he urged her.

"Nothing, Jonathan," she said in a small voice. But what she was think-ing was that if he would only love her more, then why did he not ask her now to marry him and so let God's will be done? She would have said this except it was not fair, perhaps, to force God's hand.

"Judy, it's something—I can tell by your eyes."

"No, it isn't," she insisted, and then, to deny this, she allowed two large clear tears to well up in her eyes as she gazed at him. Jonathan was dis-tracted. He put out his arms without knowing that he did, and she came into them gracefully, with a little sob, and put her head upon his shoulder, and he felt her sweet weight.

"Oh," he groaned, and held her to him breast to breast, cheek to cheek. The breath went out of his body. She was so clinging, her flesh so yielding and warm. Only once had he ever held a girl in his arms, and that had been when he danced with Constance Favor in Dentwater. But her body, stiff with stays, had been nothing like Judy's here in his arms. Beneath her gown he felt her sweet, unrestrained shape, slender and soft. He moved his hand to hold her more closely and touched under her bodice her lovely breast. He was stupefied with the wonder of this, and then he drew his hand away again quickly, knowing by an instinct that he must stay master of himself, for she could not help him.

"Oh, my little dear," he said tenderly, and smoothed her hair from her face so that he could see her closed eyes.

This, she thought, is just the same as if he asked me to marry him. We'll be engaged now, and if I like being engaged to him, we'll be married.

And he was thinking, in the core of the whirling of blood and brain, that when he told his mother she'd be asking him a hundred questions about Judy that he could not answer. Was she a clever girl and did she like books, to match him, and could she sew and cook and make a sod house into a home, and did she like children and was she brave to stay alone with little children when the man must be away, and did she lie abed late in the morning, and was she saving and sweet-tempered in pov-erty and wise in riches—only he'd never be rich!—in this beautiful body had she wisdom—had she wisdom—

Judy lifted her head suddenly. "I couldn't just stay behind and give my father no excuse," she said.

He stared at her. "No, you couldn't," he agreed. He felt a strange little pushing force come from her to him, as though she were compelling him to a point he was not able quite to reach himself.

She waited, and after a moment said in her gentlest voice, "So I reckon I had better go on, Jonathan."

"But you'll come back!" he whispered. "You will come back, Judy? See, dear, we'll write letters—we'll get to know each other very well in letters, and then we'll know what we ought to do."

She did not move her eyes from his face. He felt their warm, unmoving gaze flicker once to his lips and then back to his eyes again.

"Judy, you do love me?" he demanded.

The beautiful clear eyes did not fall. "How do I know, Jonathan?" Judy said. "I don't know you well enough."

That night after she was gone, in the midst of the most acute suffering he had ever had he discovered this speech of hers left like a small dagger thrust secretly into the tenderest part of his being. She had risen soon after the thrust, saying so amiably that he was wholly deceived, "I must go back now, Jonathan—it'll be time to go."

"But you will write, dearest?"

"Every week, Jonathan, if you will."

"I will—I promise, without one fail!"

"Good-by, Jonathan." She lifted her face and kissed him on the cheek so sweetly that his knees trembled.

"Oh, Judy, I can't—" he gasped.

But she moved away from him with a gentle quickness toward the door, paused to smile and give him a look. He made to run after her and then stayed himself. He could never hide from that teasing, hearty, eager crowd what he was feeling. If he stood there to see her go, all his habits of restraint would burst and leave him what he was, a wretched suffering man, in love with a woman and yet determined to keep his own soul.

He let her go and spent the hours after she was gone working fiercely upon his garden. Work, work— But the sun went down and he was hungry and must eat and then it was night and he lay down to sleep, and then he discovered the dagger she had left in him. Somehow or other she had taken his wise and right decision and twisted it and sharpened it and thrust it back into him. How did she know she loved him, she had inquired of him calmly, when she did not know him well enough?

This was only his own wisdom. He recognized it, thus returned to him, and then the wound bled. He could have had her; she would have stayed.

"But I know I was right," he said doggedly. "I was right, and she'll have to love me that way or I'll have to go without—"

But the wound bled steadily on, for all that, and for him the spring was over.

19

"WHAT good's land to a man who'll never know how to farm it?" Mary said bitterly. In the hot summer wind that blew endlessly across the short, stiff grass, she put back a lock of her dry hair. She was talking to Clyde, but they all heard her, because they were at the table. She knew she was violating her deepest instinct of decency when thus she accused Clyde before his children; for if a woman destroyed a man in the eyes of his children, the center of the home was gone. All through the years she had insisted that the children respect their father. Even from Jonathan she had refused to hear complaint against him. But now she could no longer hold back her own bitterness.

"If you couldn't make harvest from a rich bit of earth in England, how can you do it here in this wild place, full of savages?"

"It ain't full of savages, Mother," Jamie said. He was home for a Sunday, a tall, brown-faced, blue-eyed boy with curly black hair burned by the sun. He was in the swiftest of his growth, and he ate corn and beans and the fish he himself had caught, and many of the scones Mary had made for a treat spread with black molasses. "Just because an Indian stopped by yesterday and scared you doesn't mean the country's full of savages!"

"I don't like them and I'll never like them," Mary said bitterly. She was not less bitter because she could not tell them the real fear that still darkened her. In usual circumstances she could have let it pass that she was frightened badly by an Indian, though she had never seen one close before. She had not even thought of them, knowing that they had been taken away from Kansas and put into a reservation to the south. And then yesterday, in the middle of the afternoon when she was alone in the house, with Clyde away buying sheep and Ruth out in the fields with Maggie to guard her from snakes, an Indian had come straight into the house.

"Without knocking or so much as a cry to know if anybody was in, or a by your leave," Mary had said angrily, telling them about it over and over in the evening. "I was standing there mixing my dough for bread, and I felt a hard hand on my shoulder, and I looked up and there was a big ragged Indian, his wicked dark face right by mine. I dropped the crock and screamed and dough all over to clean up, and then he pointed into his mouth. He was hungry, if you please! And I had to go and fetch him bread and good meat before he would go."

She told none of them, not even Clyde, the reason for her remaining terror. It was that, at the moment of her fright, when she looked up into that wild face, she felt the first quickening of the child in her womb. What good could come of a child thus awakened to life? She kept brooding over this, and because she was afraid she could bear nothing.

"Besides, Mother," Jamie said, "sheep's the thing here, and sheep're easy. Mr. Banks says he'll easy clear three thousand on the herds, and that's not to count the cattle, neither."

"If your father gets sheep, they'll all die of something or other," she said.

"Give over, Mary, do, there's a good girl," Clyde said, restraining himself. She was angry, he thought sullenly, because she was going to have another child. Women were danged creatures at best. They wanted husbands, and when they'd got them they were everlastingly complaining because they were men. And Mary, he thought resentfully, would be the first to be angry if he looked sidewise and cross cuts at any other woman. He'd found that out when he was only ordinary to Jennet Drear. It had not been in his mind to think about Jennet Drear that time she came West in the same lot of wagons as theirs, except to mind how nice it was to see a girl laugh again. Women turned solemn so soon. And then Mary had said to him, "I'm coming all this way to see you go hanging your tongue out at a loud young girl, Clyde Goodliffe."

"Oh, you be danged!" he had shouted.

"You just remember," she had said so gravely that he was roaring mad and had flung away. Still, he had remembered, and he had turned his back when Jennet laughed, next time. He had enough trouble with the homestead and his family on his hands without Mary angry at him. She was so small and at times so amiable that only fearful experience had taught him what she could be when she was angry with him.

"There's no luck in you, Clyde, and there never will be," Mary said sadly. But she did give over, not because of Clyde or Jamie, who always defended his father, but because she saw Ruth's eyes suddenly fill with tears that she turned to hide as she cut Maggie's meat. Ruth was adolescent and so filled with sensitive feeling that everything hurt her, and most of all quarreling in the house.

"I want more meat," Maggie said loudly.

"Here 'tis, poppet," Clyde said at once. He laughed at the child's hearty red face. "Pity she's a girl, eh, Mary? She'd have made a rare boy an' we could do with another boy. A man can't have too many boys on a homestead."

"That's easy to say, seeing a man don't have to bear them," Mary said.

Clyde gave up. He pushed back his chair furiously. "Reckon I'll get along," he said furiously. "It's pleasanter anywhere than here."

"I'm sure it is," Mary cried after him, "yet here is where I've got to stay!"

"Oh, Mother, don't!" Ruth pleaded.

Mary sighed and wiped her face. "You're right," she said, "for what's the good? Nothing'll change a man from the moment he's born."

"You're at him so, Mother," Jamie said. "It makes my teeth on edge, too."

Mary looked from one to the other of her children. "Take his side, do," she said sharply. "It's always that way—a mother has to bear the children and teach 'em decency and how to behave, and a man pays 'em no heed, and so they love him best after all."

"No, we don't, Mother," Ruth began, her eyes filling again. "We love you best, but it isn't that—what Jamie means—"

Mary gathered the scattered bits of her dignity together and rose to her feet. Everything about her she loathed—the earth-dark walls of the dugout, the earth floor, the table made of boards, the few miserable dishes, the old ragged clothes they wore, the food that she could not make worth eating. The garden she had begun in the spring had come to nothing. She had longed for the taste of fresh green in her mouth and had nagged at Clyde until he had plowed up a patch of the tough, short grass. But one plowing had not been enough to kill those tenacious roots. They had come to life again, crowding down her tender seedlings, and then had come the dry summer winds and long weeks with no rain, and there was no shade anywhere, and she had given up the garden, and the prairie had seized it. She could scarcely tell that the grass had ever been disturbed.

And now with all her being she rebelled against her pregnancy. Yet what was one to do when she had to live with a man who turned sullen and tempestuous if she refused him her body? It seemed incredible to her now that once Clyde's kiss had been magic and his flesh her deepest excitement. Something was wrong between men and women forever if usage could so dim a glory. But she knew of nothing to do to save it, though its loss had become the tragic atmosphere of her being in a way that she could not understand and only dimly felt. Sometimes she longed to recall the old glory and yet when she let Clyde see her longing in some slight look or appealing word it had always the same end in this which had somehow become meaningless except as a thing to fear.

"I'm going to lie down a bit," she said. And then her quick heart was touched by these three, her children—Ruth so troubled and Jamie sullen, and even Maggie not knowing what to say. "Don't heed me," she said. "Poor things, you'll never remember me as I really am—not a tired, cross old woman—"

In their silence she went away and saw through the open door the distant road. It was only a trail across the grass, the beginning of which was far to the east and the end at the edge of the Pacific Ocean. She could see tiny moving spots in the heat shimmering above the summer-burned grass, spots shining white in the sun. They were wagons.

"Go on," she muttered, "keep on going, as if there was any sense to it!"

Jonathan wrote to his mother: "Now that the summer season is full, I will not be idle. I have many plans in my head and even transcribed in part upon paper for the improvement of Median. The town is well located as to water and crossroads, but it is being allowed to grow up haphazardly and presents a careless appearance. When you return, it will present a very different face, I hope."

The letter lengthened into the fullness of his plans, and upon the back of the sheet he drew like a map what he hoped Median might become. It was a picture as neat as a draughtsman could have made it of streets crossing each other evenly. He had taken the present few houses of Median and the square and had drawn them into the plan so skillfully that one would have said they had been placed purposely as they were instead of anyhow and by chance.

No one in Median knew of this plan. He would have been abashed to show it to anyone because he well knew it was presumptuous for a young man and a newcomer to plan the town. Yet only to himself was Jonathan a newcomer. He was used to the long life of father and son and grandsons in a place such as Dentwater. But to the people in Median Jonathan seemed, in spite of his youth, one of the settled citizens, because upon the prairie to stay a day was usual and men delayed longer in a place only if there were illness or an impediment of some sort, and beyond that only if it was a destination. And for most of them there seemed no cause to make Median a destination. It was not better than any other little village in the middle of the prairie, and there was no reason to stay in it when the uplands lay covered with rich grass for cattle, and beyond were mountains where gold could be washed from the sands of the streams. Median was a place only to pause for a night.

But to Jonathan it was a place as good as any other. He had come here by chance, like a seed dropped by winds or a flying bird; and, like the seed, having found here earth and sky and water, he could put down his roots and send up his leaf.

For if it was not in him to dream the big dreams of his father and to imagine the best always beyond, so it was not in him either to mope and sit idle where he was. He was more restless after Judy went than he had ever been in his life. Food was tasteless in his mouth and the school a drudgery until it was over in the summer. Nothing he started could be finished, and ill luck seemed to follow him in small ways. Thus his garden, like all others that year, grew lushly in June but in July was set upon by grasshoppers. There were not many, not more indeed than could be caught by careful picking two or three times a day; but Jonathan hated the feel in his hands of their soft bodies and crackling dry wings as he picked them off into a bucket with a few inches of coal oil in the bottom to catch them.

He heard nothing from the lawyers concerning Beaumont's legacy, and when he had begged his mother to write to him she wrote one of her stiff, short letters beginning, "I take my pen in hand—" He read it many times, unable to tell anything from it. "The weather is very fine," he read. "But are you, Mother?" he muttered, striving to see behind the neat writing. "The wind blows tiresome, but I try not to complain."— Ah, but did she have something much to complain of? "Your father has bought two hundred head of sheep to be paid for when he sells. Jamie is fretting to go West to hunt gold. He is not fond of farming. But he must help his father. Ruth is my comfort, but Maggie is a trial, so willful and naughty and her voice very loud, and I have little time to teach her manners. Dear Son, I long to see you and pray God we will meet somehow. Your loving Mother."

She did not complain, and yet, breathing through the bare words, he felt the atmosphere of a secret despair. But it might only be his imagination, always too quick to feel trouble in her. When he was even a little boy he used sometimes to go to her when he saw her grave and say sorrowfully, "Mother, why don't you smile?" And sometimes she kissed him, but sometimes she was impatient and said, "A body can't be always laughing, Jonathan. There's serious things, too, and one has to think of them."

So now, to comfort himself, he wrote of what he was planning and drew the map of Median for her with the streets all neatly locked together and where a church would stand some day and a bank and a schoolhouse and a post office and a town hall such as Blackpool had and where new shops would go—stores, they would call them—and maybe some day a little factory for spinning wool from the sheep that men in the western parts raised. But he told her nothing at all of Judy, and his letters to Judy were not about Median. They were about himself and her.

And Judy, in California, found the letters waiting for her at the post office in San Francisco, where he had told her he would write. She had written him almost every week, but not letters like his. She had not written of herself because she spent little time thinking of herself or of what was ahead. She had learned to let what was about her be her life. Thus she wrote to Jonathan that on such a day they had made twenty-six miles, and at a certain town they had come to a railroad and for a day had ridden on the train, which was very filthy with dust and had frightened them all because it went so fast, and the road was so rough they could scarcely keep their seats and the bell on the engine rang continuously because of the jar, and once the conductor's gun went off by accident. Nobody was hurt, but they were all frightened, thinking that Indians had attacked. And at another place when they came down from the train they had to wait a week before they could find a wagon to cross the mountains.

As he read these gently flowing letters over and over alone in his house, Jonathan felt that he had her and yet that she escaped him, that telling him everything she yet told him nothing.

"Write me what you think and feel, my dearest dear," he wrote her, "though I want to know everything else, too, and it's sweet to read everything that happens to you, but I want most of all to know what you are thinking and feeling about everything, but most about you and me."

Judy sat in a small, gray-walled shabby bedroom in a cheap hotel in

San Francisco, his letters in her lap, looking down into the vivid, ugly street below. She tried to think and to feel so that she could write to Jonathan, but she could not keep her mind on it. The street was a wonderful sight. It was full of ragged gold miners from the hills and well-to-do farmers and their wives in wagons full of vegetables and fruits and ladies driving in carriages and gentlemen in tall hats and bright waistcoats and carrying canes. It looked mixed and gay and as though everybody was friendly, except she noticed shrewdly that the ladies and gentlemen only spoke to each other. But there were quite a lot of them and some of them were very handsome. She wondered if the ladies bought their dresses here and if indeed such dresses could be bought in San Francisco.

She had honestly planned when she had read all of Jonathan's letters to write him a long letter full of her thoughts and feelings. Instead, after a while she got up in her slow, graceful fashion and laid the letters away in a drawer; and, putting on her best straw bonnet that she had herself lined with rows and rows of narrow ruffled lace, she went out into the sunny street.

I can think and feel while Papa is preaching and I'll write him afterward, she thought. And to a tall young gentleman who happened then to be passing she said, her eyes upturned with their purest, most innocent look, "Excuse me, sir, but will you tell me how to find the best shops for ladies? I am a stranger in this city."

He lifted his high silk hat. "I shall be charmed," he said, and his voice was delightful.

20

ON THAT day Jonathan was actually farther away from Judy than he had planned. He sat in the law offices of Bartlatt and Bayne, in the city of New Orleans. He had come here so unexpectedly that he could scarcely believe he was here. He had been at work one morning upon whitewashing the inner earth walls of the sod house. It had occurred to him thus to lighten the schoolroom for the new session. He was to have seven new pupils this year, and he was hard put to it to find the space. He had been thinking of the new schoolhouse he had put down in his plan for Median and wished he might have it now. It was put opposite the church on the square. At any moment, night or day, he could see that schoolhouse clearly in his mind. It was to have two rooms and many windows. While he was whitewashing the sod house, Beaumont had come in.

"I've brought you a letter, suh," he said. "I was in the sto' and Mr.

Merridy said mail had just come in and I said I'd take yours to you. It's from N'Orleans, suh."

At the word "letter" Jonathan's heart had turned over, because there was always the possibility of a letter from Judy. Then it ordered itself again and he put out his hand.

"Let me see, Beau."

It was from New Orleans, a curt legal letter from the firm of lawyers in whose offices he now sat. The letter asked for proofs of the alleged Pierre Beaumont's birth, and it desired to know whether or not the alleged son was born of a white mother.

"In case the mother was not white," the letter concluded, "the whole case must be reconsidered."

"I'll have to go and talk to them," Jonathan said when he had read the last sentence.

But first he had gone that night to the Parrys' dugout home and had stayed for hours probing Sue gently. They sat out in the moonlight under a cottonwood tree, out of hearing of the children in bed. Beaumont had slipped away into the darkness, knowing that his mother could speak more freely if he were not there, and they let him go.

"Anything you can tell me will be of use, Mrs. Parry," Jonathan said gravely.

"Maybe I better go, too," Stephen said.

"No!" Sue cried. "What for need you go, Stephen? I've tol' you ev'ything, many a time."

But still he sat apart from her a little, upon a stump and in the shadow of the tree. In the river not far away the frogs croaked. Beneath their feet the grassless bit of earth was as hard and dry as a floor. Stephen worked under this tree by day, and the family ate here, and here the children played.

And then after a silence Sue began.

"What'll I say? I wasn't a fiel' hand, Mr. Jonathan. My motheh was Bettina, and own maid to Miss Lavinia, who was Pierre's motheh. I'm more'n half-white—my fawtheh was Miss Lavinia's brotheh, suh. My motheh grew up in a great house just like I did. We hadn't anything to do with otheh niggras, even hardly in the house, 'ceptin' to eat with 'em. But my motheh didn' even eat with 'em. We just pieced along wherever we were, so's we needn't."

"Then Beaumont is nearly white," Jonathan said.

"It's the black bit that counts, though," Sue said bitterly. "Don't mattah that his brains is white or that his skin is light and his hair brown. Why, Beaumont could pass for white if he went away fum us."

"He must go away with this money," Jonathan said.

Stephen's voice came deep and melancholy out of the darkness under the tree. "Honey, don't let him try to pass. It's like a man gets out of jail.

Some'eres dey'll fin' him and put him back again, and then he cain't stan'
it sho'."

"What was the wah for?" Sue asked.

There was silence and the soft full throatiness of the frogs, and the
moonlight as white as a mild sunshine; and then Jonathan said, trying to
be natural, "If you could tell me the circumstances of—of your relationship
with Beaumont's father, it might help me later. That is—if force was used
—if you were cruelly treated—"

"No, suh," Sue said sadly. "There wasn't any force, I guess—unless you
could say a slave would always feel sort of forced by her young master
if he tol' her to—to—let him come into her room."

In the shadows the darkness that was Stephen stirred a little, but he did
not speak.

"My motheh brung me up wrong," Sue said suddenly. "She used to tell
me, 'Ef a white man wants you, you go to him. Any kind of a white man
is bettah than a niggra. A bad white man is bettah than a good niggra,' she
said. 'Don' eveh let a niggra touch you, you hyeah, Sue? But when a white
man wants you, you say, "I'm comin'." ' "

"You nevah tole me dat, Sue," Stephen moaned out of the shadow.

"I know it," she said. "I didn't tell you 'cause it ain't so, that's why. I
know it ain't so. Any kin' of a niggra is bettah than a white man that wants
a niggra girl. That's what I found out for myse'f. My motheh was wrong.
She said, 'The on'y way we can git out of bein' niggras, is by changin' our
blood. Ev'y niggra woman with a white man's chile in her is steppin' up
and up and gettin' away to freedom.' But that was befo' the wah showed
us different. It showed us that liberty don't make us free. We're always put
back where we was—black blood to black blood."

"Oh, Lawd God!" Stephen moaned out of the shadows.

Sue said, "I thought Pierre loved me—he tol' me he loved me. Once he
said he'd even maybe marry me and go no'th, and we could say I was
Spanish. And I was sixteen and believed him ev'y word he tol' me. He was
eighteen—maybe he believed himself—I don' know. But when Beaumont
was bawn Pierre was th'oo with me just like that." In the moonlight Sue's
hand was raised and her thumb and finger snapped and her hand fell
again. "And Ol' Marster come and said to my motheh that she must marry
me off to a good niggra, and he gave her money and two new dresses, and
when she tol' me I said, 'I want the blackest niggra man in God's worl'.' "

"That's me," Stephen moaned.

"That's you, I thank the Lawd," Sue said. She got up and went over to
him and stood by him and he clasped his arms about her strong waist.

Jonathan turned away delicately. "Now I know. Good night, and I
thank you both."

And so he had gone away from them, leaving them there together in
the shadows.

Now in this office he sat and waited. He would have said he could wait easily enough for anything if needful, but this waiting made him angry. Twice he had come here in the last two days, only to be put off until today, and he had during the days seen a good deal that he did not like. This city was beautiful and ugly. The Negroes and poverty made the ugliness, and white gentlemen and ladies and their luxury made the beauty. Negroes stood in the presence of the white, and they stepped quickly aside out of a white man's path. An old man had so stepped out of his own way yesterday and when he said as he would to anyone, "I ask your pardon," the aged black man had only looked frightened, as though he had been spoken to by a lunatic. A beautiful city with mansions and gardens and flowers growing among moss-hung trees, but he smelled the air foul as he sat stiffly in the office, dressed in his best brown suit, waiting, though the room was empty.

At last a young Negro manservant came in, his hands full of letters.

"Mr. Bayne's ready for you now, suh," he said, holding the door open.

Jonathan rose quickly and went into an office where everything, it seemed to him, was covered with a snowdrift of open letters, documents, and newspaper. At the table sat a tall, black-haired young man with his coat off and his feet on the table. He was so handsome that Jonathan's anger changed instantly into shyness.

"Morning," the young man said in a gay voice, but without getting up. "Come in. I hope you don't mind seeing the junior partner. I'm Evan Bayne. Mr. Bartlatt's pleading a case."

"I'm glad to see anyone," Jonathan said.

The young man laughed as if he would laugh at any possible excuse. "Lawyers always keep clients waiting," he said. "We're taught that in law school."

The impudence of this made Jonathan speechless. He sat down and for a moment looked stern. Evan Bayne did not notice it. He was lighting a long thin brown cigar.

"Have one?" he asked.

Jonathan shook his head. "I don't smoke," he said, "and if you please, Mr. Bayne, I should like to proceed to my business. I am a schoolmaster and my duties begin on a date which compels my early return."

Evan Bayne brought his long legs down from the table nimbly.

"Sorry, sir," he said, and with quickly moving, supple hands found by some miracle a letter upon which Jonathan saw his own handwriting. Evan Bayne studied it, his dark straight eyebrows drawn down. He looked serious for a moment. Then his mobile face changed. His black eyes sparkled, and his right eyebrow flew up.

"You're from Kansas! I've always thought I'd like to go there. Say, what's it like?"

"I only know what Median's like," Jonathan said carefully.

"Well, what's Median like?" Evan Bayne demanded.

He put his feet on the desk again, and Jonathan felt his gaze like a warm light upon him.

"It's not much now," he said. "In fact, it's not a town you'd pick to go to. I'm there because my father brought us all over from England. They've all gone to the West, but I'm the staying sort. It doesn't seem any good to me just to keep on going somewhere."

"You'd find it hard to get many people to believe that," Evan Bayne laughed at him.

"Median's not too bad," Jonathan said. "It's at a crossroads north and south, east and west, and there's a river—small, but it never dries up. The wagons all come through."

"They do?" Evan Bayne took his feet from the desk again and sat up.

"I've made a sort of plan in my mind for Median," Jonathan went on, "not that it's anything of my business, but I like planning for something to grow, and Median can grow, I think."

"Does the railroad go there?" Evan asked. His eyes were brilliant, warm, sharp, and shining.

"Not yet," Jonathan said.

"Any reason why it shouldn't?" Evan demanded. "There's another road projected through to the coast, south of the Union Pacific to Denver."

"No, reckon not," Jonathan said slowly.

They had both forgotten altogether why he was here.

"Go on," Evan Bayne said. "What's your plan?"

Jonathan pulled his chair to the table and drew a pencil and envelope out of his pocket. In the envelope was Judy's last letter, but he did not notice this. He turned it over and began to draw.

"See, here's the square," he said, "a fair big square, and my pupils planted it full of trees this year. Over here's the general store, and here's the inn. There's empty land to the west and east. Down here toward the south is my house—schoolhouse, too—and here's four or five other houses. Down here's Parry's, carpenter he is, and whatnot—and over here near the river is the mill."

"Farmers come in from a long way?" Bayne asked.

"Thirty and forty miles, and sometimes more," Jonathan said. "Now this spring we put in boardwalk around the square—mud's fearful in the spring. That'll come out one day and macadam go down, if macadam's as good as I hear on Kansas bottom. The square we'll keep as a park, but put the town hall in the middle, and the post office here, and the new schoolhouse here. Then off from the square will run the streets, like this—"

He drew a Median he felt he knew as well as the one that stood there now, and Evan Bayne watched him.

"Say," he demanded, "how do you know all this is going to happen?"

Jonathan, looking up to meet doubt, felt a flare of defense for his town. "There's enough folks there now to make it happen," he said. "The land around is rich, and there's no town for miles for farmers to go to for spending their money; and, besides, there's the wagons. Why, all spring and summer there's been a dozen and two dozen wagons a day around the inn."

"Any lawyer there?" Bayne asked.

"No lawyer, no doctor, no church," Jonathan said, "and need for all."

Bayne laughed. "You're persuading me," he said.

"No, I'm not," Jonathan said quickly. "If I am, it's not meant. I know very well how Median looks to a stranger. When I first saw it it seemed to me a mudhole in the prairie and the prairie nothing but a green desert."

"But you don't feel so now?" Bayne said.

"And I can't tell you why I don't," Jonathan said frankly, "for it was as muddy as ever this spring, and winter was long and bitter, and a fire swept away the autumn grass so fuel was scarce and dearer than gold, and for five months nobody came near the place. But the prairie doesn't seem a desert any more. I've grown to like plenty of sky overhead. And though I live in nothing but a sod house, I teach school in it, and there's no other school in two hundred miles for those children to go to. I keep thinking there's no reason why Median shouldn't grow."

"I am persuaded," Evan Bayne said with gaiety.

"Never say I persuaded you," Jonathan retorted.

"No, I won't. The truth is, I was three-fourths persuaded before you came. I'm sick of this office. It was my father's. He's dead but his old partner isn't, and I have to jog along with him. I want to get out on my own. But I can't do it here—too many old family associations."

They sat for a moment in silence and in that silence Jonathan found to his surprise that he liked this young man exceedingly. He had never seen a man in his life that he liked so quickly and so well. There was something about him that was frank and open, tempestuous, humorous and unaffected and swift. It occurred to Jonathan that he had not a single man near his own age with whom he could be friends. It would enrich Median for him to have such a young man as this there, a man educated and able to argue with him about everything and able to be his companion as no one in Median was able.

"I daresay Median would grow faster if you were in it," he said with a glint of a smile.

Evan Bayne burst into his loud musical laugh. "It would grow or bust," he cried. He leaped to his feet and put out his hand. "I'm coming," he declared. "At least, I think I'm coming. When are you going back?"

"As soon as my business is done," Jonathan said, smiling now very broadly.

Up shot that fluent right eyebrow on the handsome face before him. "God, that's right—what was it? Never mind, consider it done!"

"No, not until you know at least what it is," Jonathan said, and by his gravity compelled the young man to his seat again. Then he told Bayne all that Sue had told him and what Beaumont was and how he had written to old Dr. Beaumont, and what the letter from Bartlatt had said.

Evan Bayne sat turning a quill pen over and over in his hands, his eyes downward, listening. "Everybody knows that young Pierre Beaumont was rotten," he said. "I call him young but he wasn't young. He was forty when he was killed last winter, but he'd never done anything but live off the old man. The old gentleman was good—a wealthy man who needn't have done a day's work, but he was a great surgeon because he wanted to be. The son was nothing."

"Killed?" Jonathan inquired.

"Murdered," Bayne said shortly, "by a niggra. It was patricide."

"No!" Jonathan cried.

"Yes," Bayne repeated, and then told him how Lem had died. "I heard that the crowd was gathering at the prison-house gate, and I went to see the sheriff. Old Dr. Beaumont was our client. Bartlatt always had him, but I knew all about the case, of course. Dr. Beaumont wouldn't prosecute. He had a long talk with Lem in jail, and when he came out he looked sick. 'My son's dead,' he said, 'but I make no charge.'

"Well, the state had to prosecute, of course. But the people took things in their own hands. I was there in the crowd, and I saw it was going to begin. The crowd was too quiet. If they sing and yell you can hope to do something with a crowd, but not when they're quiet. They hanged Lem."

"But why—if the state was prosecuting?" Jonathan demanded.

"A black man can't kill a white man here and be sure of living to be tried," Evan Bayne said simply.

"I shall never tell Beaumont," Jonathan said in a low voice, "no, nor his mother either."

He rose and stood looking down at this man he liked. "You see how it is —this lad of mine's three-fourths white. He's no darker than a Spaniard— nothing so dark as an Indian. And his lips are thin and his hair barely curly. And there's genius in him. If we could get him somewhere to a place where in a crowd he could mingle—if I could get him to England, say—he'd grow to be a great man. You can feel it. If I could get him to England I'd write a man there I know—my old teacher, he is—and he'd see to him and get him on."

"But he'll always be a niggra if he comes back here," Evan Bayne reminded him.

"Maybe by the time he's ready to come back, things'll be different here, too," Jonathan said.

"Don't build on that hope," Bayne returned. "Black will be black, and so will black and white be black, as long as memory lasts in this country."

"I will hope, nevertheless," Jonathan replied steadfastly. "And if I am wrong, then he can stay abroad. There are other countries."

They looked at each other, doubt meeting hope until doubt gave in. Bayne smiled.

"I like you," he said without shyness. "I've never liked anybody as

much at first meeting—who wasn't a woman, that is," he added mischievously.

And Jonathan, though he felt himself blushing and knew his face was so
crimson he was ashamed of it, forced himself against his shyness and answered, "I like you in the same way."

"My name's Evan."

"And mine's Jonathan."

"I'm coming to Kansas with you."

"I'm glad of that."

They clasped hands warmly and firmly and Evan stood up. "When are
you going?" he asked.

"As soon as my business is done," said Jonathan, twinkling at him.

"Oh, God, again!" Evan cried.

They laughed together, and Evan said, "See here, I'll manage it for you.
I'll tell old Bartlatt he has to give in—not a legal leg to stand on. I'll tell him
the boy's pure white."

"No, that you must not," Jonathan said instantly. "You must tell him
the truth."

Bayne was laughing again. "What—and I a lawyer?"

Then he had Jonathan in confusion and not knowing how to put aside
this joke. So he gave over.

"I won't tell that particular lie," he said. "Now go on and be content. I
won't tell you how I'll do it, but I'll do it for you. When do you start?"

"Tomorrow?" Jonathan asked.

"Day after," Evan said. "I have to make it right with my mother and
my sisters."

"Very well," said Jonathan.

"And dine with us tonight, so they can see you and trust me in your
company," said Evan, with that quick laughter brimming up again. He
scrawled a name and a place on a bit of paper as he spoke.

"I will, thanks," Jonathan said, taking it.

They shook hands again and parted, each content with the other and
secretly astonished at the speed of their friendship.

At half past six Jonathan stood before a big cream-painted door in an
old brick house and struck the brass knocker. He had walked from his
small hotel through streets of shops into streets of houses, and at last into
this quiet wide street where large old houses of brick or painted white
wood stood, set in vine-draped, moss-hung trees. Every home had its flower
garden, and he walked along a path lined with flowers to this door. It was
opened by a black manservant who said gently, "Come in, suh, if you
please," and took his hat.

The door opened into a hall out of which a wide staircase swept up.
And then Evan came hurrying out of an open door, looking very handsome
in fresh garments. He should have changed his own clothing, Jonathan

thought ruefully, but he had only these, and he had put on his last clean shirt this morning.

"Come in, come in!" Evan cried. "I knew you'd be on time, so I was, too. I could see you'd be the sort of fellow who was always where he said he'd be at the time he said he'd be." He clapped Jonathan on the back and whispered, "Your business is done!"

"How did you—" Jonathan began.

"Hush!" Evan said. "Didn't I tell you not to ask? Come in—my mother's here and the girls are all titivated at the idea of a new young man. You're English, now remember, Jonathan—not a Yankee. You'd never get in this house if you were a Yankee!"

This he poured out upon Jonathan in his bantering musical voice, his eyes mischievous and his mouth playful and the right eyebrow dancing. One hand had Jonathan's coat lapel and the other was punching him gently in the ribs.

"Evan!" a clear voice called.

"Coming, Mother!" he cried.

His arm through Jonathan's, Evan marched into a big oval drawing room where a small red-haired lady sat on a green tapestried chair, her feet crossed on a stool before her. Behind her was a tall pretty girl who looked like Evan, and a smaller younger girl, not yet out of her childhood, who looked like her mother.

"This is Mr. Jonathan Goodliffe, Mother," Evan said.

Mrs. Bayne put out a little hand so abruptly that it seemed a thrust. "You're welcome, Mr. Goodliffe. This is my elder daughter Laura, and this is Louisa."

The two girls bowed, the tall one gently and the small one slightly. Mrs. Bayne withdrew her hand as quickly as she had put it out. For the moment it had touched Jonathan's it had lain in his palm like a dried leaf.

"Sit down," she said. "My son tells me you are English. Do you live in London? I know London very well. My husband's father was a famous barrister there, and I went to visit in his house as a bride on our honeymoon."

Her voice, so clear and all the consonants soft and the vowels lengthened, was nevertheless imperious, just as her tiny feet in black satin slippers, though crossed upon the stool, seemed not resting there but merely waiting to run.

"I don't know London, ma'am," Jonathan said, seating himself on a gray satin sofa. "My home was in a village near Blackpool, a small village it was, and we came here to better my father's conditions."

"I hope they are bettered for being in Kansas, but I doubt it," Mrs. Bayne said with soft sharpness.

Evan laughed. "That's for me, Jonathan. She thinks me a fool."

"I don't, because you're my son," Mrs. Bayne retorted. "But I think going to Kansas is silly, no matter who does it."

Evan laughed at her and bent to kiss her, but she pushed him away with her hand.

"No, you're not to kiss me. You think you can do as you like and then come and kiss me, and I'll forgive you. But I won't forgive you!"

She spoke playfully, and yet there was something in her that was not playful, and Jonathan felt it. But if the girls felt it they said nothing, and if Evan felt it he was still gay.

"Let's say I'm only going on a visit, Mother, or a trip or whatever it is that young men do when they finish their education."

"If your father hadn't died, you'd have taken the grand tour like a gentleman," she said.

"Being an excellent and patriotic American, I'll go West instead," he replied.

"It's not the same," she retorted.

All during this gay battle that was not altogether gay, the two girls stood, Louisa smiling a little and Laura not smiling at all. She was, indeed, looking at her mother furiously, and at last her mother seemed to feel this look and she turned her head.

"Laura, go and tell Jeems to have dinner," she commanded.

"I'll go," Evan sprang to his feet.

"No, I!" Laura said eagerly.

They met at the door behind their mother's chair, and Jonathan saw that meeting, merry enough, but meaningful, for Laura put her arms about her brother's waist and gave him a great squeeze and Evan pulled one of her short red curls. And Louisa, behind her mother's chair, smiled at them.

"Sit down, Louisa—you make me nervous standing behind me like that," Mrs. Bayne said, and Louisa sat down on a seat by the window.

All through the evening Jonathan felt those three pulling at Evan, each in her own way. Talk was gentle, there was plenty of laughter, and Evan was constantly teasing one and the other of the three; but underneath there was the pull of love too sharp and diverse for ease. Jonathan, saying little and listening much, saw how Evan, without knowing he did it, continually watched the three women. When one was silent, he turned to her, and somehow one after the other and together he seemed to be talking to each and to all. It made Jonathan think of a juggler he had once seen on the green in Blackpool on a holiday, who kept three plates whirling in the air at once so skillfully that none struck another and none fell to the ground. And yet throughout the meal, anyone would have said here was a home of plenty and ease where all was well with the people in it. The light fell softly from a chandelier above the table, and long windows were open from ceiling to floor, and a small night wind cooled the air. The food was well served and more delicious than he had ever eaten in his life—a turtle soup, very thick and smooth, young chicken fried brown with a creamy gravy, biscuits, and new peas and a lettuce salad and an orange pudding. And yet with everything there was the underplay of love pulling this way and that between the three against one, though it was strongest between Louisa and her mother, and Laura took the smallest part in it. So it went on until Mrs. Bayne rose and the girls followed her and left him and Evan together, and the black manservant put wine and nuts on the table. Then the strain went away with them, and Evan sat silent for a moment and he looked tired.

"I miss my father," he said.

"It is inevitable," Jonathan replied, merely to make an answer.

"I never knew how we all leaned on him until he died," Evan said. And then he looked at Jonathan with all his gaiety gone. "Do you think I should stay with my mother and my sisters?"

Jonathan was taken back. "How can I tell?" he replied. "Is there another man in the family anywhere, and do they need your support in money?"

"Louisa is engaged," Evan said, "and will be married in June to an old friend of mine, and live next door, almost. And we have two uncles here and their families—hundreds of cousins, more or less. And my mother doesn't need money. And my God, but I need—freedom!"

He whispered the word. Jonathan nodded.

"I know how it is," he said soberly. "I love my own mother and grieved when she went away, and yet I'm happier. There's not something deep inside pulling at a man all the time if he's alone."

"Exactly," Evan said. He poured out wine for them both. He lifted his glass. "Here's to you and me and Kansas," he said, and drank. Gaiety came back again, and Jonathan drank and knew that another part of his life was begun.

21

THE JOURNEY back was more of a jaunt for Jonathan than anything he had ever had. Evan made it so by his very presence. To have a young man only two years older than himself his companion, and such a companion, so seeing and full of talk about all he saw, so amiable in his quick eagerness to share every good, so courteous even in the narrowness of their cabin upon the river steamer in which much of their journey was made, was to make every moment pleasurable.

Whatever Evan's parting with his mother and sisters had been, he told Jonathan nothing of it. They met at the quay, Jonathan there early with his one carpetbag, and Evan leaping out of his carriage at the last moment with two Negro boys carrying four bags and two boxes of books and a carryall.

Evan glanced about in mock fear. "I won't be easy until I'm sure old Bartlatt's not here to grab me," he said. "I never knew I was so indispensable to the firm! I thought I was an office boy, dirt under the old fellow's spats, or a nurse, a niggra, anything but an indispensable junior partner. But I was wrong."

He took off his tall hat and wiped his forehead with a white handkerchief. The boat whistled and a mulatto roustabout rattled the gangway. Jonathan had been standing with his hand on the rope watching for Evan.

"Cast off there!" a loud voice shouted.

They hurried aboard, the two Negroes pushing and pulling Evan's bags and boxes. " 'By, Marse Evan—'by, suh! We sho' hopes we don' like Kansas!"

Evan flung some money to them. "Goddamn you, Pete and Solon, of course I'm goin' to like Kansas! Get along home and mind you take good care of things!"

"Yas, suh!"

They ran off. The gangway was lifted and that good journey began— good, because every day the two young men liked each other better and talked more freely of all their lives. Jonathan listened more than he talked, while Evan told him of the travels he had made, the girls he had loved, always gaily and lightly and never very long. And yet there was a sweetness in this young man which drew out of Jonathan, too, his own story. But he did not speak once of Judy. He kept her for himself.

As they came to the end of the journey and Median was only two days away, Jonathan found himself uneasy lest he had made Median better than the truth. It was hard for him not to see Median as in thought it would be some day. When they left the train and began the drive across the prairie he found himself still more anxious. Evan was staring across the prairie.

"My God," he said, "does it simply go on and on like this?"

"It does," Jonathan said.

"Not a hill nor a rock," Evan said.

"Never," Jonathan answered, "at least not until you go far westward. The land slopes upward, but you don't see it unless you see the long horizon of it."

"Good land, though, if it grows this grass," Evan said.

"It's said to be," Jonathan said cautiously.

Evan glanced at his profile. "You don't care whether I like it or not," he said.

"I do care," Jonathan replied, "but I will not persuade. You see what it is for yourself."

So at last they came to Median. The sky was gold in the west, and even the east was lit with that western light. Median was so set that, coming into the town from the east, they saw between the few houses across the empty square to the west; and, since there were not yet any houses except north and south of the square, Median was like a gate to the west at sunset.

It looked well tonight. Mrs. Drear had washed the flag that flew from a pole on American House, and it fluttered, red and white and blue, and the store had new cloth in the windows, and Katie had picked a great bunch of grasses and put them in the middle in a big green bottle. Around the doorways of the dozen or so houses late sunflowers grew, and Mrs. Cobb had asters from seed she had brought from her home in New England. There had been recent rain, for the young trees in the square were green and so was the grass growing under them.

Evan pulled at the reins in Jonathan's hands. "Stop," he said, "let me look at it." He gazed ahead. "Not much of a town," he said. "But what a West beyond!"

"Ah," Jonathan said, "you're like all the rest."

He picked up the reins and drove across the grass to the sod house. He was depressed by the thought that Evan might not want to stay in Median after all, but he determined not to show it. Let him stay or go, he would manage for himself, and in Median.

In the twilight the sod house looked as small as a hut, and the garden in front less than nothing in the long wild grass all around. Jonathan opened the door in silence, remembering the house from which Evan had come.

"It will seem a poor place to you," he said. "But here is where I live and work."

They stood together a moment, and while Evan looked about Jonathan looked at Evan.

"It looks comfortable," Evan said.

"I've found it so," Jonathan replied.

He lit the oil lamp. It was one of his luxuries, because it had enabled him to read at night with more ease than he would have had with a flickering candle. In the yellow light he seemed to see for the first time how his home, grown as familiar to him as his mother's face, might look to a stranger. He saw small things he had not noticed—the scars his pupils had made on the unpainted table, Abram Hasty's initials cut there in one end, the unevenness of the board floor, the leaks from the roof which had washed streaks in the whitewash, holes burned about the fireplace, the meagerness of his chairs and his garments hung upon pegs on the wall.

"I shall have to go to the store for some food," he said. "Will you come or stay?"

"Stay and wash off some of this dust," Evan replied.

"I'll have to fetch water first," Jonathan said.

"Then I'll help," Evan replied. Still in his long brown frock coat and tall hat, he took up one of two buckets and Jonathan the other, and they went to Drear's well.

In the door of the store Katie stood with the two little boys and watched them.

"How are you, Katie?" Jonathan called.

"Fine," Katie replied, still staring.

"That's one of my former pupils," Jonathan said, pulling the windlass rope.

"I trust she's no fair sample of Median girls," Evan replied in a low voice.

"There aren't any girls here," Jonathan said.

"Now that you should have told me," Evan said teasingly. "That's important."

"You should—" Jonathan began, and stopped. What he was about to say was "You should see Judy," and he changed his mind. There was no reason why Evan should see Judy.

Two and the school was too much for the sod house, Evan said. Seven days had passed, and each day Jonathan felt Evan as uncertain in Median as a bird in passage. He himself had spent the rarest week of his life until now, and he knew it. Not even Judy had given him what Evan gave him— the constant gay resourceful companionship of a mind more varied than his own. If Evan felt lack of ease and comfort, he never spoke of it or indeed seemed to notice it. He ate salt meat and river fish and boiled potatoes and corn meal in bread and mush as though it were what he would have chosen to eat, and when Jonathan picked fresh beans from the garden Evan made them a treat.

In the week Evan had come to know all of Median, always gay and seemingly careless and always able at night to talk shrewdly with Jonathan about each one he had met.

"Drear's a man to tie to," he said, "and so is Merridy. Hasty is an ignorant low fellow, and Cobb is from stock run thin. He's left New England too late. But his wife's different stuff, and she's put good strong blood into the children, though the weak will come out sometime or other."

But what won Jonathan was that Evan joined altogether in what he thought of Beaumont. Beaumont came to see him the first morning, diffident and yet hot with eagerness to know what his fate was. He arrived at the door when the two young men were eating breakfast and waited. Jonathan saw him there when he came out for water to wash dishes.

"Come in, Beaumont," he said. "I have good news."

And to Evan he said, "This is Pierre Beaumont."

The boy bowed, and Evan, his hands full of dishes, did not need to greet him except by a nod and a smile. "Hello," he said.

"Good morning, suh," Beaumont replied.

"This gentleman, Beau," Jonathan said, looking with affection at Evan, "is the one you must thank. He is the one who, in some way or other which he will not tell me, settled your case for you."

"I thank you, suh," Beaumont said. He was light enough to flush, Evan saw. In France he could pass as a Frenchman.

"You must go to Paris, you know," he said lightly. "I can see you there, growing very French, and all that—not England, Jonnie, after all, but Paris!"

"I don't know anybody in Paris," Jonathan said with doubt.

"You're not the only man in the world," Evan retorted. "Let me remind you of myself. I happen to know some Beaumonts in Paris—second cousins of the old gentleman. He had me look them up once when I was there with Mother after my father died. We took her abroad."

"I've never heard of any solid folk in Paris," Jonathan said.

"They run a nation, somehow," Evan replied, laughing.

"I've never seen a Frenchman, though. How do I know what Beau might grow into there? Besides, they might not be good to him."

"They'd love him," Evan declared. "A bar sinister is their joy."

Thus they argued until Jonathan saw the boy's dark eyes look afraid. Then he stopped it.

"Oh, well, we can decide later," he said. "The thing is, you've your legacy, Beau, and Mr. Bayne got it for you, and you're going to be a surgeon."

Beaumont listened and took this into his mind, opened his mouth, closed it again, and shook his head.

"I thank both you gentlemen," he gasped and rushed out of the room. They went to the door and saw him running and leaping through the grass, not homeward, but out toward the open prairie.

Evan laughed aloud. "Precious little niggra there, certainly."

But Jonathan did not laugh. He perfectly understood that Beaumont was crying as he ran. He would run crying until he was exhausted, and then he would curl down into the grass and sleep. And after he had slept he would come back, and then they could plan.

"Paris is right, you know, Jon," Evan said, looking after that leaping, flying figure.

"Perhaps," Jonathan said. At this moment he too could not imagine Beaumont in London. "Well, we'll see what we must," he added reluctantly.

"Paris is a good town, you know, Jon," Evan said, smiling.

"Is it?" Jonathan retorted without believing him.

Evan burst out laughing. "Oh, Jon, I swear I love you! Do you mind my calling you Jon?"

Jonathan felt himself red from head to foot and answered therefore with utmost calm, "You can call me that," he said, "though until now I've never let anyone call me out of my name."

Once, dreaming of Judy, he had thought she might want to call him Jon, later, when they were married, perhaps. But let Evan have the name if he wanted it. In a day or two Evan had made it seem more natural than any other. Jon—when he heard it Jonathan felt quickened and brightened, a gayer fellow and more able to put down his conscience.

So now when Evan said, "Two and a school is too much for a sod house," Jonathan was frightened.

"You're leaving Median," he said slowly. "I knew you would—it's not big enough for you."

"I'm not leaving," Evan replied. "I'm only deciding to build myself an office. It'll be an office, but I'll live in it, too, and you and I'll see what we can do. Why shouldn't Median be the county seat? Drear says they're going to split this county into two. A county seat, and then we'll get the railroad to come this way, and no reason why Median shouldn't grow to be a city as big as Chicago some day. I believe in planning big."

"Ah," Jonathan said, "that makes you sound like my dad. But you've got more wisdom than him. He's always talking bigness, but he never does anything to bring it about. But I don't know as I want Median to be like Chicago."

"You won't be able to stop it once I get started," Evan said.

He began it by moving into American House on the day that Jonathan opened school. Next door to the inn he bought a square piece of land from Henry Drear and contracted with Stephen Parry to put up a two-story frame building, one room on top of the other, the one below to be his office and the one above his home, the whole to be finished in two months.

Meanwhile, he paid Henry Drear ten dollars a month for his storeroom cleaned out except for a table and two chairs, and under the new eagle which Drear had put up after the fire had burned the old sign, Evan nailed a neat block he had drawn and painted himself, "Evan Bayne, Lawyer."

To this sign, as sinners approaching heaven, came all those who were discontented with their neighbors, and those who had been cheated in land claims and mortgages and by cattle thieves, and many so troubled. But Evan seemed never to be busy with what he did. All day long he sat in his office, his feet on the table, listening, laughing, shouting to someone passing the always-open door.

Everyone in Median liked him. If Jonathan had been able to be jealous, he might have been now, for everyone went to Evan and claimed him for a friend. But Jonathan could not be jealous. Besides, sooner or later each night Evan would stroll down the boardwalk to the sod house and come in and help Jonathan at whatever he was doing. Sometimes it was midnight before he went away again.

Those were good hours. In them they planned for Beaumont, and they sent him away one day, dressed in Evan's own suit of drab broadcloth. It was a little tight on Beaumont's broader frame, but their height was equal enough, and Beaumont, with his hair cut close, looked a gentleman.

"Never say you are a niggra," Evan told him. "From now on, forget anything except that you are returning to the land of your ancestors. And learn French until it is your mind's language."

The boy took everything into his heart and went away, his purse full of money and his few clothes in Evan's best bag. No one else in Median except Stephen and his mother knew where he was going, or indeed that he was gone. To have said "Paris" as a destination would have seemed madness, and Evan and Jonathan agreed not to let it be said.

These two young men, sitting in the moonlit darkness of the door open to the prairie through the mild evenings of early autumn and by the fire when autumn deepened, shaped their world to their imagination. They were made to work together, Jonathan often thought.

"Now what we need—" Evan would begin, and Jonathan listened.

When his turn came he would begin, "The first step we must take is—"

And in argument and argument and argument again before they parted, Jonathan forgot for hours together what distressed him when he was alone —that Judy did not keep her promise to write him every week. If Evan thought of his mother and his two sisters, he never spoke of them to Jonathan.

Stephen Parry, working overtime on Evan Bayne's house, had most of it to do himself, for labor was hard to find. No one wanted to stop to lend a hand at a house on the prairie when land was to be had farther west, and the eastern markets were opening for all the cattle the West could muster. He had a week's help from a Pennsylvanian whose wife gave birth to a child at American House before they went on. Mrs. Drear took time to be midwife and start another lusty boy westward. "That's the ninety-sixth," she said proudly. Stephen had a few more days from a man who had lost his wife in childbirth; then they, too, went on. The Hasty boys did crude labor when their father could spare them, but the best help was from Matthew Cobb. Matthew was growing into a tall thin boy whose squeaking, broken voice made a joke of him, but he was able to put his brains to what he did and fit a joint and nail a beam as well as a real carpenter. For the first time he found something to make him content with Median.

"I like wood," he told Stephen. "It's clean and dry, and there's no muck when you work in it." Even after the sod-house school began, Matthew spent his other hours at carpentering for Stephen. It was now accepted that the Cobb family was to be a part of Median. Mrs. Cobb was planning the making of a new house near the store.

Judy had only once written to Jonathan every week for three weeks together. Of his letters she had one for every week and one other which he wrote in the overflow of his heart at Thanksgiving. After he had taken a great deal of thought, he put down what the year had brought him for which he thanked God. These two gifts, he told Judy, would be always the two best parts of his life whatever else was to come. The first was Judy herself— "My dear, my love," Jonathan wrote, "whose least little look I have as my treasure, and every touch of your hand my precious memory." After Judy came Evan, "my friend," he wrote Judy, "a clever, honorable, gay man. In him are the best qualities a man can have, such gaiety as my own father has, but not in Evan joined to rashness and heedlessness; such honor that he will do anything for a friend, as indeed he has for me; clever, because he has come to Median and in a few weeks he has won a name that makes anyone whom he takes sure of winning the case. His office, only newly opened in his new house, is already full, and he talks of enlarging it. He can persuade anyone to anything."

Jonathan sat alone as he wrote, for Evan was giving a great dance at American House that Thanksgiving night. Jonathan was only waiting until the hour to go to it; and, feeling thankful and buoyant and full of sure hope for the future, he put down in words the warmth of his heart. Evan had made him less prudent than it was his nature to be, and he had come twice as quickly to writing these words as he would have had he never met Evan.

"My dear darling," he wrote to Judy when he had written the two causes for his deepest Thanksgiving, "now I am ready to ask you, will you be my own wife? I have missed you so fearfully these months. Darling Judy, I do not reproach you for writing me such a few letters that in all these weeks I have only eleven. When Sunday comes and there is no new letter from you, I sit down and read the old ones again. But we must have it so that we are always together and then there need be no blame if letters are not written."

When he had written this he stayed for a while feeling very solemn. Much must be done if Judy was to come into this house as bride and wife. The school, for one thing, must be moved. He would talk it over with Evan and see if by issuing bonds there could be collected enough money to put up the schoolhouse he had planned on the side of the square nearest the church that was not yet there.

He rose and walked back and forth once or twice; and then, happening to glance at the face of the school clock hanging on the wall above the fireplace, he saw that if he did not make haste he would be late for what Evan had called his "shindig." He hastened across the moonlit square to the tavern. It was bright at every window. Though the night promised frost, the door was open, and from it came the sound of voices and laughter and dancing feet. He went to the door and stood looking in. Everyone was there who could drive a farm wagon to come. Small children not yet asleep ran about or clung to their mothers' skirts. When sleep overcame them they would be laid on a mattress somewhere. Every face was gay. A childlike lovable folk, Jonathan thought, and loved them. Yet he wondered, curious at himself, that he could not ever cast prudence aside and be as childlike. Was it only the childlike, perhaps, who left hearth and home somewhere as these had and went westward without knowing where they went?

Evan swung past him in the dancing. He was dancing with Katie, and he saw Jonathan and paused for a moment, his arm still about her. "Well, Jon! I was about to send somebody for you!" he shouted.

He was so handsome, his dark eyes so clear, that Jonathan took fresh pride in him. Even Katie, in the effulgence of Evan's beauty, height, and health, was nearly pretty. She wore a pink dress he had never seen before. Her shoulders were bare, and the skirt ruffled to the floor.

"Why, Katie!" he said.

"Isn't she fine?" Evan cried.

"Change your partners!" Bill White's voice rang out. Bill White, long ago too fat to dance, played a banjo and called the dances.

Evan made a large gesture. "Here, Jon—I've been keeping her for you, the youngest and prettiest girl in Median!"

He bowed deeply and handed Katie to Jonathan and went away. Jonathan saw him a few minutes later not dancing but leaning over the bar talking to a strange man; a cattleman, he guessed, by the man's leather trousers and open collar. There was an increasing number of cattlemen now coming through Median, rough noisy men who drank too much and swaggered about the store and the tavern.

Then he looked down at Katie. She was dancing sedately to the new tune Bill was plucking, her thin little face quite grave. In his hand Jonathan felt hers lying passive and without pressure.

"I don't dance as well as Evan, I fear," he said ruefully. Evan had taken away with him the small glow she had seemed to have.

"You dance all right, though," she replied quickly. But she did not look at him nor smile, and though he knew she had no coquetry in her, it occurred to him that perhaps Lew had been wrong. Perhaps she had never cared for him. They were too much alike, two somewhat grave young people, too ready to think of work instead of play. What more right than that she should rather love Evan when it came time? He examined her face just beneath his own—a plain, regular little face, each feature well enough, but the combination somehow lacking the magic for beauty. He thought of Judy with sudden and enormous desire and knew that, for him, she alone was beauty and there could be none other.

The music stopped, and he and Katie stood for a moment uncertain. "Thank you, Katie," he said and let her go.

He and Evan returned to the sod house when the night was near to dawn. Houses were darkening as they walked back and wagons rumbling out of the town homeward, sleepy children crying. Again and again Evan had shouted, "Good night—good night all! Mighty glad you came, mighty glad!" Each time, Jonathan thought, listening, his voice was as joyous to one as to another.

"Grand folks," Evan said, sitting down at last in Jonathan's most comfortable chair. "Mend your fire, boy—your house is as cold as a cave. I shall be staying the night with you, Jon. I'm as full of talk as an egg of meat. Don't hope for sleep, for you shan't get it."

"Well, tomorrow's a holiday, luckily," Jonathan replied. He reached for the bellows as he spoke and blew the embers red and built corncobs above them skillfully and the flame burst out. Evan sat sprawling in the chair, his feet to the blaze and his hands locked behind his head.

"Jon," he said suddenly, "I'm going to make Median a cattle town."

Jonathan, on his knees, held the bellows. "Evan, you didn't tell that chap— I mistrusted he was a Texas rancher!"

"I did," Evan said. "Why not? Why shouldn't Median have their money? American House would profit, the store would profit, it would bring all sorts of business in."

"But the trail's end is too far north," Jonathan said slowly.

"Median would bring it two days nearer the railroad—we're going to have a railroad, Jon."

Jonathan put three pieces of wood on the fire, sparely and so that the fire would catch them all. Then he rose, dusted himself, and sat down on a wooden stool.

"And where would Median be?" he demanded.

"What do you mean?" Evan retorted. "There'd be more Median than ever!"

"There'd be lunch wagons and dance halls, and American House would be a saloon, and there'd be brothels and fightings and killings—there wouldn't be any room for Median."

"Why, you son of a gun," Evan said, laughing. "Median would boom! There'd be thousands of men paid off here if this was the shipping point, and the men would leave their money here."

"Yes, and what else? Tick fever for every cow around and bad diseases for our own folk, and sicknesses worse than that for us all. No, Evan!"

Evan brought his chair down with a crash and his hands from behind his head. "Jonathan, you're not serious!"

"I am," Jonathan said.

"Why, it's the law of growth, man! You can't stop the sources and expect Median to grow!"

"Maybe you and I don't see Median the same," Jonathan said.

"Maybe we don't," Evan said. "Maybe you don't see Median a prosperous city, bigger every year, drawing money into her banks, business into her stores, sending goods out all over the West, an exchange between the two halves of the country. No reason why not, when we are geographically almost the exact center of the nation! And you and I, Jon, could be anything we liked—governor, senator—anyway, rich men."

"I don't want to be rich," Jonathan said shortly.

"You certainly don't want to live in a sod house all your life, Jonathan! You don't want to live miles from a railroad and use candles and oil lamps all your life and draw water out of a well like—like Abraham did!"

"I want a good town," Jonathan said stubbornly. "I want a town with a schoolhouse in it and a proper church. Business, of course, but not the brawling, cursing, fighting sort of business cattlemen bring in."

"What's going to bring in business, though, Jonathan? You can't just sit and expect it to come! You must hold out some promise!"

"Median's in the middle of a lot of good land," Jonathan said soberly.

"Stands to reason solid farm folk have to buy and sell somewhere and put their children in school and have fairs and meetings. They'll move to town, when they've done well enough on the land and get old, and they have money to spend, too, as well as cattlemen, and better money."

"But we'll be gray-headed before Median gets anywhere!" Evan cried.

"It'll be solid when she gets there and good going the whole way," Jonathan declared. "The sort of town a man would want to settle in and bring up his family," he added.

The two young men looked at each other, their faces clear in the firelight. Evan laughed.

"You're in love, Jonathan!" he said, not suspecting he had hit truth.

"Yes, I am, I own it," Jonathan said simply, "and I speak out of all my thoughts about what's most valuable to me."

"Why, who could it be, Jon? There's nobody here—it's not little Katie Merridy!"

"No, it isn't," Jonathan said, growing red. "It's nobody you know, Evan, though I've been going to tell you a long time. It's a young lady I've known a year now and fell in love with as soon as I saw her. Her father's an evangelist and she's in California, and I wrote her today asking her to marry me and posted the letter tonight."

"And have you reason to hope she will have you?" Evan asked, his eyes merry and full of affection at the same time. How impossible not to love this Jonathan, he thought with tenderness and impatience!

"Yes, I have reason to hope," Jonathan replied.

He sat there with his hands on his knees, looking so innocent in his determination that Evan grew quizzical.

"And so all of Median is to be shaped to you, is it?"

"Not to me," Jonathan replied, "but to the thing that's best."

"And suppose I don't agree?" Evan asked.

"Then I reckon we'll have to see who of us can win," Jonathan said calmly.

"Well, I'm damned," Evan said.

22

IN A TALL narrow house in Paris, Beaumont was feeling his way. He was like a blind man. Nothing he had seen before helped him here, beyond the ordinary objects in a room. That is, a chair was to sit upon, a bed was to sleep in, the stairs were to climb up and down from the room he shared with Georges, his second cousin. He had not yet dared to call Georges cousin, though Georges introduced him proudly at school as "my cousin, Pierre, from America." Once in an excess of honesty when the two of them lay awake in their cots after Marie the maid had put out the lamp, Beaumont said, "I ought to tell you, I reckon, Georges. My mother—was a slave."

What he had wanted to say was, "My mother is a Negro." But he could not. It was easier to say "slave."

To this Georges answered in surprise. "But what is it? All slaves are now freed in America. My father says it is so."

Pierre did not reply at once. Then he said, his temples beating, "She is—not white, you know, Georges."

"And what of it?" Georges asked. "I once saw a black man in a great carriage on the Champs Élysées. There were ten carriages following him, and he was dressed in red and gold, and he wore on his head a gold turban with a white cockade with diamonds as big as apricots. He was an African prince, and he was also French." Georges yawned. "Pierre," he said with sudden interest, "did you see that fat boy who pushed me today purposely as we came from gymnastics? Tomorrow I shall push him twice as hard, and with all my strength. He is a German sausage, that boy!" Georges, two years younger than Beaumont, ground his teeth together in the dark.

Beaumont laughed and then fell silent. Between Georges and him were years never to be shared. He could never share entirely with anyone what it was to come here where no one cared what his race was. At first he felt Georges' parents must be pretending when they said he was to call them uncle and aunt. "Though we are only your cousins, dear Pierre," Georges' mother said kindly, "it is more suitable, since we are so much older, that you say 'mon oncle' and 'ma tante.' It is fortunate, dear Pierre, that you have come to us, since we have only our Georges, and sometimes he is lonely with only elderly parents. We married too late, and now it only remains that you learn to speak our language quickly, so that we may be a happy family. English we cannot."

He was learning to speak French very quickly. He was glad to change even his language. He wanted to change everything. Perhaps his very skin was changed now that people did not call him a Negro. But he was not sure of his complete change until nearly a year later when he met Michelle DuBois. This meeting was stiffly polite, in the narrow gold and white drawing room. Madame DuBois was Georges' aunt on his mother's side, a widow who lived in the DuBois house in the country. Once a year, at New Year's, she came, with Michelle, to spend the holiday in the city with her sister. Georges had talked, a little and carelessly, of Michelle, as a brother might speak of a sister.

"She's a nice girl—rather pretty, but a girl!"

But Beaumont, coming forward to bow as Madame Beaumont had taught him, saw a young angel, whose fair curling hair, cut in bangs over a white forehead, was a cloud of gold about the heaven blue of her eyes. When he touched her hand his heart spilled out of his bosom and lay at her feet.

Two days later they had declared their love secretly to each other.

"But I am so dark, Michelle!"

"But you are so handsome, *mon* Beau!"

From that day on he was Beau to his beloved.

Across the mountains in San Francisco Judy read Jonathan's love letter, put it down on the bureau, and went on brushing her long, softly waving bright hair. She sat before the bureau in her full white petticoat and camisole and watched herself thoughtfully in the splotched mirror. The room in which she had been living for several months was neat and even pretty, because she always succeeded in making her rooms so. Thus, over the blistery top of the bureau she had spread a clean hand towel and upon the bed a crocheted spread of her own making. Joel's room next door, with exactly the same rough furniture, had none of the same air.

When she had brushed her hair to a flying mass of electric life, she subdued it with her comb and curled it about her fingers. Then she pinned the curls carefully to the back of her head in a waterfall and, rising, slipped under the full skirt of her gown hanging from a hook on the door. A smooth slide, a graceful undulation of her body, and her head came through the low neck, the curls undamaged. The gown was a yellow muslin, a fall of ruffles from her bosom to the floor, with a ribbon sash at the waist. She had made it herself, hemming the ruffles with fine stitches. It had been the work of her whole summer, but she considered it worth all the hours she had spent upon it. She dampened a scrap of turkey-red cotton cloth in the jug on the washstand and touched it to her cheeks and lips, and then she dusted her face and neck and arms with cornstarch. The gown had a small reticule of muslin. Into it she put her cornstarch bag, her handkerchief, and then Jonathan's letter.

Thus frocked, she tidied her bureau, touched her ears and bosom with perfume, and knocked on her father's door.

"Come in!" Joel shouted.

She went in and found him at the window frowning out over the bay.

"I'm ready now, Father," she said. "Capt'n Lusty will be coming for me any minute."

"You made up your mind?" Joel asked sharply.

"No, I haven't," she replied quietly.

Behind him his room was in its usual disorder. Almost as though she were unaware of what she did, she began to straighten it.

"The truth is, Father," she said, hanging up Joel's snuff-brown coat tidily, "the Capt'n hasn't spoke of marriage."

"He will," Joel declared. "If you manage right, Judy, so he'll know he ain't goin' to get what he wants by any sinful means and he'll be compelled to righteousness. That's the way God works."

"Yes, Father," Judy replied. She was sorting Joel's shirts, clean from soiled. "And what'll you do, Father, if he doesn't give in to God?"

"It'll be kind of hard to know," Joel replied. He sat down and put the fingers of his long, thin, never-clean hands together. "I reckon I'll just have to search the Scriptures."

There was a loud thump on the door, and a boy's voice shouted, "Capt'n Lusty's downstairs!"

"Good-by, Father," she said, as nearly in haste as she ever spoke.

"Good-by," Joel said, without looking at her or without changing his frown.

Judy, moving smoothly down the narrow corridor of the rooming house, went down the stairs with the same gliding steps, holding up her skirts on either side. She knew how she looked to the tall man waiting for her in the hall below and was content without caring enough to be vain.

"Well, my beautiful," he said in a hearty voice when she had reached the last step.

"Good evening, Capt'n Lusty," she said, putting out her right hand. Her middle finger was rough with stitching, and he felt it as he put her hand to his lips.

"Why, what's this?" he asked, examining it.

"I always stitch my finger when I hem ruffles," she said, and smiled so innocently that he felt a swirl in his head. There was no one else in the hall, and he slipped his hand around her shoulders. His fingers were in the soft warm pit under her left arm. They sent shattering messages to his brain, and he was lost.

"I'm going to kiss you," he muttered.

She did not speak, but she swayed to him gently and closed her eyes. Upon her full warm mouth she felt his kiss without returning it. It was, she reflected, pleasant enough—too moist, perhaps, but men's kisses were usually so. She allowed him to continue it for a second more and then opened her black eyes wide. The sight of those eyes, so close to his and so direct in their gaze, spoiled the kiss for Captain Lusty. He was not able to go on, and he straightened himself and laughed unsteadily, still conscious of his fingers in their warm nest.

"You've about got me," he remarked.

She moved a little without any appearance of repulse, and he found his arms empty.

"Shan't we go?" she asked.

"You want to go?" he countered.

"Well, I want to see the ship," she said. "I've never been on a real sea ship. They're not like river boats, are they?"

"They are not," he retorted scornfully.

She put her hand in his arm and by an imperceptible pressure guided him to the door.

"I know," she said with a fresh, urging eagerness. "That's what I say—I want to see how a real ship is, and how folks live on it."

Outside the door a cab waited. Captain Lusty handed her into it, leaped in, and then thrust his head out of the window.

"Ahoy there!" he shouted to the driver. "Get along back to the docks where I picked you up and stop alongside the *Virgin Queen*."

The cabman grunted and they set off. Captain Lusty sat back. While he dressed himself for the evening in his cabin he had thought persistently of the possibilities of this half-hour, alone in the cab with a beautiful, childishly innocent girl. But now he was aware only of her dark eyes and of how queer they had looked just under his—eyes too big and too black. She was chattering along, sitting gracefully erect as the cab lurched over the rough street.

"Oh, I'd admire to see the Sandwich Islands," she was saying earnestly. "Seems as if I never hear enough when you talk about them!"

Captain Lusty took her hand and fondled it. "You'll come with me maybe, eh, Lady, some day?"

She let him have her hand, she even smiled. But when she spoke it was with simple gravity. "If it's God's will, Capt'n Lusty," she said.

He put her hand down. "You've a real discomforting way of talkin', sometimes," he said.

"Do I?" Judy asked, surprised. "But I couldn't do what wasn't God's will—you wouldn't want me to, would you, Capt'n Lusty?"

Captain Lusty swore to himself in a mutter.

"What's that, Capt'n Lusty?" Judy asked.

"I said, Goddamn," he replied.

She laughed, and in the flickering street lights he saw her lovely face suddenly quiver and grow warm with amusement. She was laughing at him! All these months when he had been wanting her she had perhaps been laughing at him. Plying back and forth between Honolulu and California, he had thought of nothing but her ever since one day on the street she had asked him where to find a store. He had gone with her that day, thinking her easy in her virtue. He still thought her easy. When he was away from her he was sure of it. And yet, though she had allowed him to kiss her sometimes, she had allowed no more—not, he felt wrathfully, from refusal so much as lack of interest in lovemaking. And yet he could not be mistaken in a woman who had mouth and eyes like hers.

He sat up, full of sudden dignity, and made no effort to touch her. After all, he was the captain of a good vessel, and a well-to-do and successful man, and what was she but the daughter of a crazy traveling preacher? He had said carelessly, "Come and preach in Honolulu, man—there's lots of sin there," and Joel had lit as though a fire had been kindled in him.

"Maybe that's what God means, always leading me westward," he had exclaimed. . . .

"Here's my ship," Captain Lusty said suddenly.

There she was, her well-known lines trim and sharp against the still-bright sky. The cab stopped. He got out and paid the fare, then, taking Judy's hand with ceremony, he led her to the gangway. A sailor standing on the deck saluted and stared at her.

"All well?" the captain inquired.

"All's well, sir," the sailor replied, "and the others are waiting."

There were others, for Judy had refused to come alone, and he had been compelled to invite his mate and bid him bring his wife. "But clear out, you hear," he had said carelessly. "Aye, sir," the mate had replied, thinking of the gold piece that was his when he obeyed his captain.

And Judy, following the captain and caring nothing for the stares to which she was so accustomed, was full of pure pleasure at everything she saw. In the saloon she dimpled sweetly when she bowed to a gray-haired woman with a hearty red face and a man whom the captain introduced as "my mate, Mr. Briggs, and Mrs. Briggs—my thanks to you, Mrs. Briggs," he added.

"My pleasure, Capt'n," Mrs. Briggs said demurely, without looking at Judy.

It was all pleasant, Judy thought. The dinner was delicious—guinea hen, which she had never eaten before, and wine, which she tasted and did not drink. They laughed and the others told stories at which she laughed and it was all delight until suddenly the Briggses were sent for because their little boy was taken ill.

They went so quickly that she scarcely knew them gone, and then she was alone with Captain Lusty. And yet not really alone, she told herself, for there were the sailors and the steward.

"Take the coffee and dessert to the cabin," Captain Lusty ordered that steward, and he rose and put Judy's hand in his arm.

"We won't part for dessert, since there's only the two of us," he said, and she went with him doubtfully, and yet saying to herself that she must go on if only to discover what God's will was. Besides, there was so much she had not yet seen about the ship.

The moment she entered the cabin she knew it was wrong. The devil, not God, had led her here. Behind her the Captain shut the door. His handsome face was red, and his hand trembled as he took up the coffeepot. Judy's eyes, flying about the small luxurious room, fell upon a photograph standing on a shelf below the mirror. It was the picture of a woman, a delicate fair face, with sad eyes and a small sad mouth.

"Who is that?" she asked.

"That's my wife," Captain Lusty replied.

And then she knew that indeed she should not be here.

"You never told me you were a married man," she said.

"You never asked me," he retorted. He put down the pot he was holding and turned on her. "You never asked me anything, my dear."

"Because I took you for an honorable good man with right intentions," she said in a whisper of horror. It occurred to her how narrow was the path to salvation for her—only, indeed, that bit of a plank between her and the shore.

"Dear God, save me," she said aloud in simplest tones.

"It's a little late for God," the Captain replied, smiling. He went up to her and put his hands on her warm bare shoulders. "A little late," he repeated, and slowly moved his hands down her arms and back again and into the two pits under her shoulders, and then he lifted her sharply.

And she, in solid horror, hung limp as a doll. She felt herself go cold, and she suffered without an answering movement his kiss.

And he in the midst of that hot kiss saw those great wide black eyes that had so disconcerted him before. They stared into his eyes so blank, so empty of all feeling, that to save himself he drew back. Was the girl crazy like her father? He shook her. It was like shaking a sack.

"What's ailing you?" he shouted.

"None of this is God's will," Judy whispered. "None of it, I say!"

"You're mad," he said, and let her go.

She sank down upon the seat, and panted, and felt in her little yellow muslin bag. Yes, there was Jonathan's letter.

"I'm engaged," she said. "I'm engaged to a solid good young man that's asked me to marry him, and I never dreamed you were so wicked."

"You don't act innocent, so you must be a fool," was all he said. He rang a bell and when the steward came he said, "See that this lady gets safe ashore, Tom."

"Aye, aye, sir," the steward said. He was astonished, but he did not show it. He waited while Judy rose and passed through the door and then led her to the gangway. It was there safely leading to the shore, and she trod it as joyfully as any sinner ever looked toward heaven.

But her face was as innocent again when she entered Joel's room.

"I came to say good night, Father," she said.

Joel turned on her with eyes of solemn fire.

"Judy, I've been on my knees since you went. God has bade me go westward to the islands of the sea."

She looked at him without moving. "Has He, Father? Then you and I must part."

"But J-Judy——" Joel's astonishment broke against the calmness of her eyes.

"I'm going to marry Jonathan Goodliffe," she said.

23

In the sod house Jonathan read the words again and again.

"For my mind is set, dear Jonathan, and it is to marry you."

Judy's letter was short. Why should she write much when she was starting at once for Median? The roads would soon be closed for winter, and if she delayed it must be for months. And there was nothing more to delay her. Captain Lusty she had swept from her mind as a woman sweeps dust from a room before she closes the door upon it, clean and empty. Judy had the gift for finality which was finality itself, so that she saw no irony in Joel's sailing for Hawaii in the *Virgin Queen*. None of it now had anything to do with her. She had set about her own journey with composure, and with growing pleasure.

I shall have something to call mine, anyway, she had thought after she had written the letter, as she folded ruffled skirts carefully into a small round-backed trunk. The trunk had been her mother's, and of her mother she now thought with pensiveness as she made quick, exact movements that in so short a time left the room in which she had lived for months emptied of her presence.

I must go and see Mrs. Drear, Jonathan thought. Judy'll have to stay there a bit. His pale face reddened as he thought of Judy. She would be here before Christmas. They would be married at once. What could he do with his school? He pondered the possibility of persuading Henry Drear to let him hold it in American House. It was impossible to have it here if he and Judy were married. He wanted the house to himself, alone with her. And Evan—Evan must be told, first of all. He leaped to his feet. Lucky it was a Saturday, he thought, so he was not tied to his work. If he had everything ready, he could wait better for her coming.

He found Evan, as he was always to be found these days, in his office and surrounded by men. In the midst of them Evan sat smoking his pipe, his feet on the desk, listening, laughing. It was hard to know whether the men had business or were only there to talk. To Evan everything was business. A man who came to talk might stay to tell him a grievance against a neighbor that would develop into a lawsuit. Evan's dark, warm eyes, his easy laughter, his endless patience for listening, drew men to him. Lew complained of it openly, with grumbling good nature.

"Doggone you, Evan, you're takin' away my trade. Fellers used to come into my store to talk—then they'd buy somepin to take home to their younguns. Now they stop at your door before they ever get here, and when you're through with them they can't afford to buy a salt cracker offen me."

"Then I'll bring them," Evan said. He did bring them, sometimes a dozen at once, to buy a dipperful of Lew's homemade whisky. Just often enough to keep Henry Drear content, he took them to the bar at American House, though there he went most often with one or two men, not farmers, but men from railroads and in the cattle business in other states. Together they talked long in low voices, sitting at the corner end of the table.

But to Jonathan Evan was always the same. He said now as Jonathan entered, "It's only fair to tell you, Jon, that we stand a mighty good chance of being a cattle town!" He smiled his beautiful lazy smile at the men sitting about his office, where there were always plenty of chairs and spittoons.

Jonathan did not reply. Judy's name was not to be mentioned here. He came in and sat down. Evan introduced him casually. "This is my best friend and warmest enemy, fellows. He agrees with me on everything except how to make Median a big town."

"Hell, nothin'll do it quicker'n cattle," the man cried.

"That's what I tell him," Evan said. His brown eyes upon Jonathan were full of affection. "But he's a stubborn son of an Englishman. He doesn't want you here, fellows," he said. "I do. Want to bet on which of us is goin' to win?"

"Bet on you, Evan," a man shouted. "Yeah, ten to one," another growled, and spat his brown juice to the far side of the nearest spittoon. Evan, who did not chew, had covered his floor with sawdust. Once a week Sue Parry swept it all out and Stephen put it down new.

"These fellows are from 'way down in Texas," Evan said amiably to Jonathan. "The railroad's certainly going to run south, Jon—I had their promise for that when I was in Topeka last week. It'll come through Median if plans go right. It'll sure come through if we make Median a big cattle center. Sit down, Jon."

"English, hey?" a man said to him, wondering. "Say, what's it like over there?"

"It's another country," Jonathan said dryly.

"Goin' back?" another asked idly.

"No," Jonathan replied.

He caught out of the air in the room, out of the slightly excited triumph he could perceive in Evan, a feeling of immediacy. Before he did anything else he must measure the speed of whatever Evan was about, and to do that he must wait here and listen. But Evan was quick to discern him as well. Between these two was something so close that neither could hide himself wholly from the other. It made Evan want now to be away from Jonathan's eyes. He was not ready yet to tell Jonathan everything. When he had finished what he was determined to do and had made it irretrievable, he would tell him. He rose from his chair.

"Come on over to Lew's, you fellows," he said lazily after a moment. "I'll buy you a drink."

He let them all pass through the door and then he turned to Jonathan. "Anything you want of me, Jon?"

"Only to tell you I'm to be married," Jonathan said. His voice was quiet but weighted with his feeling, and to his own astonishment tears came into his eyes. "I couldn't speak before strangers," he added.

And suddenly Evan was all he wanted him to be. He came back into the room and threw his arm about Jonathan's shoulder and hugged him, and his joyfulness was real.

"Jon! Is it Judy?" he cried.

"It could be no other," Jonathan said solemnly.

"Oh, Jupiter, but I'm glad!" Evan was squeezing him and patting him and now with his right hand he seized Jonathan's hand. "Now I'll see her and I shall tell her if she doesn't make you a good wife, it's I who'll take a hickory switch to her. You'd never beat your wife, Jon—you're so soft-hearted! But she's got to make you happy—I swear she's got to!"

There was an edge of breaking in Evan's voice. He laughed to avoid it. "Gosh, I—I—love you, too, you know!" he said.

Jonathan, dreading the edge, grew calm. "Thanks, Evan—and it's only fair to warn you, I s'all do all I can against Median's being a cattle town, now more than ever."

"What? Oh, all right!" Evan laughed. He clapped Jonathan's shoulder. "Go on, man. Don't forget the odds are ten to one against you, though!" He ran out of the door and after the men now sauntering down the board-walk toward the general store.

And Jonathan, looking after him, thought to himself that his work lay ahead of him. He must see every man in Median before Evan could reach him and tell him what it would mean if Median were a cattle town. Henry Drear would be for it, because American House would prosper. But Drear had no sons, and Jennet was gone. He would not waste time on Drear. He would begin with family men like Cobb and White and the Irvings, who had just come from Illinois, and the Bennetts from New York State. They all had big families. He went out into the cool sunlit noon and turned his steps toward White's house. Judy would have to wait while he made a home for her.

Evan said, "We'll put it to the town."

There was not the smallest seeming difference in his manner toward Jonathan. The last few days might have been, for all he showed otherwise, a game between them. A grim game, though, Jonathan thought as he looked at Evan with his quiet blue eyes. It had come to be a race between them as day went into day, to see who was to be first at the scattered farms. A few times they had arrived together at a lonely dugout or sod house. Then each had been scrupulously fair. Turn and turn about each had stood to let the other one go in first. Neither inquired of the other what had been said. But Jonathan came to know fairly well which would be Evan's men and which his. What he called "solid folk" were on his side, men who came determined to farm and to stay, who wanted to send their children to school. Jonathan found that to these it was best indeed to begin by talking about the school. If Median were to be the proper town he wanted it to be, the sooner he got a schoolhouse built, the better it would be. Bonds were the thing for it, he thought. He had first thought of bonds from hearing Evan talk about issuing railroad bonds. If men paid for railroads in such ways, why not a schoolhouse?

Thereafter when he went into a farmhouse he put the matter first of all thus: "I'm the schoolteacher in Median. I see you have school-age children here. Would you want to send them to school?"

It was more often the woman than the man who spoke, "Sure we want 'em to git schoolin'."

"I dunno," the man said. "I can't get along 'thout the boys' help."

"You can get along as good as I can 'thout the girls," the woman cried. "Anyway, we can manage. How much would it cost, mister?"

"Well, it depends," Jonathan said in his slow, plain manner which always made what he said seem the voice of truth. "A dollar a month is the regular, but I'm thinking of a schoolhouse. We need it. My little sod house can hardly hold another pupil. Anyway, Median ought to have a schoolhouse. Would you feel to put something in it? I'd be willing to take half my price and put the rest into the building, if so be you could add to it."

"I ain't got cash," the man would say more often than not, "but I could put in labor." Or he might say corncobs or hay cats for fuel, or a team for hauling, or rarely, if he lived along a stream, a few trees for wood. Most often of all were notes on next year's harvest. "If it's a fair harvest, I could let you have maybe fifty or even a hundred dollars." After that it was easy to talk about the sort of town Median ought to be. Jonathan at the end of two weeks and a day had his pockets full of such promises, written upon pieces of paper.

"I'm willing to put it to the town," he said to Evan. "That's fair enough. And I'll tell them about the schoolhouse at the same time."

"Will you want your school in a cattle town?" Evan's mischievous eyebrows flew up at Jonathan.

"It isn't going to be a cattle town," Jonathan said calmly, and smiled when Evan laughed.

The first town meeting of Median was held in American House. Evan had been quick to say, "Your schoolroom is too small."

"So's your office," Jonathan had replied.

Each refusing the other the advantage of his own ground, they had agreed upon the big room in the tavern. Drear, all for Evan in the matter, was hearty and willing.

"I'll stand to treat everybody twice around free," he declared. "Though if I'd known what a crowd there'd be," he declared the day of the meeting, "I'd have thunk twice."

Jonathan himself was secretly surprised to see the number of people who came in to Median that cool December day. It was a day such as early winter may give on the prairies, a day mild and without wind at morning and evening. At night anything might happen. The wind might rise and bring winter in by the next day, or a sodden rain set in and turn the earth to its old bottomless mud, and this would freeze until spring. As though they knew it might be their last fair day, every family within horse distance and return came in, their food in baskets, and women with babies in their arms.

Evan and Jonathan had discussed together how they should begin.

"We must have an order of talk," Jonathan said. "There ought to be some sort of head to the meeting."

They had looked at each other.

"You'd be better than me, and I know it," Jonathan said. "But all the same, I shan't yield you the advantage unless I can see reason."

"Don't blame you," Evan had said carelessly. "How about lots?"

Jonathan stooped and picked two leaves from a scrubby bush and put them in his hat.

"Red leaf'll begin, yellow leaf'll wait," he said. "Fair?"

"Fair," Evan agreed.

He turned his head away and put his hand into Jonathan's hat and drew the red leaf.

"Fair?" he had asked Jonathan.

"Fair enough," Jonathan had said steadily.

When the people gathered in the tavern on this day long before noon, Evan stood up first and Jonathan sat waiting and watchful.

"Ladies and gentlemen," Evan began, "friends all—" He went on. The natural friendliness of his brown eyes grew warm. Faces turned toward him, and he let his eyes grow warmer. "Jonathan Goodliffe and I have taken a mighty big responsibility on ourselves in asking you to come, some of you a mighty long way. But he and I have two propositions to put before you, and since it concerns everybody the only fair thing seems to be to put it to all of you folks and let you decide. We drew by lots who should talk first, and that's why I'm doing it."

He let his eyes pass from face to face, lingering upon each long enough to catch response. Then he went on.

"We each of us maybe see Median in a different way. Jonathan, here, sees one kind of a town. I see another. Folks, here's my town. It's more than a town—it's a growing, busy, prosperous city. It's a railroad city—trains come here from the East, taking cattle and grain from all over the

Southwest. These trains will come back again to bring us manufactured goods of all kinds. There won't be sod houses and dugouts in my town. There'll be fine houses and schools and churches, and big stores and hotels. We'll be a great center, we can be, because we're on a thoroughfare east and west, north and south. We're the center of the great country west of the Mississippi. Now, folks, a city doesn't just come because you whistle for it. You've got to make it come this way. Money must be spent here, business attracted. And our great chance is the cattle business. All the cattle regions can head up here. That means thousands upon thousands of dollars spent here in Median. Men will get paid off here, they'll have money to spend."

Jonathan, watching the faces before him, saw hard, fearless eyes, firm mouths, hands rough and misshapen with work. There was scarcely a soft face even among the women.

"What about saloons?" a white-haired woman spoke from the end of a bench. She had refused the drink Henry Drear had offered her. Evan turned to her at once, his face full of sympathy.

"Madam, I know what you mean, but we can do what we want to do about that," he said. "Nobody can make us do what we don't want to do, not in this free country. We can put the cattle concession away off at the end of the town, if we like, far enough off so that the cattlemen will disturb nobody." Evan's face grew solemn. "Madam, we can do more than that. We can make Median an ideal cattle town, a place where men will grow better rather than worse. We can refuse to license—"

Henry Drear broke in. "Hell, Evan, if you won't sell licenses, where's your money goin' to come from?"

"That's right, Henry," Samuel Hasty's high voice cackled.

A dozen voices began at once. Evan let them talk and stood at ease, listening to one, catching a few words from another, somehow making each feel he was heard. From the confusion his ear sorted any aid to himself. When he found it he raised his voice.

"Here's a man with a good idea. Stand up, mister, and tell everybody—"

A man would shout out, "What I say is, why should we let some other place get the business? What I say is, get the business, and then let's talk about how to run it when we've got it—it's too good a chance to miss!"

After an hour Jonathan could endure no more of it. He and Evan had agreed to talk an hour each. Evan had talked less, but by the skillfullest trickery—"for trickery it is," Jonathan said to himself wrathfully—Evan was repeating what he wished to repeat from what was being said among voices shouting and crying down each other. He was making it seem that what they wanted was the cattle business. Upon some faces dismay was growing. Men and women cried out, "We don't want 'em!" but others were talking, and Evan did not hear them. In the confusion of the room Henry Drear had long since forgotten that he was treating only two drinks to a person.

Jonathan rose. His was never a conspicuous figure, and nobody now saw the neat young man of middle height as he stood in the back of the tavern. Jonathan waited a moment to catch Evan's eye; and then, since it was not to be caught, he walked across the room toward the bar against which Evan leaned as he stood, smiling, listening, talking.

"Your hour is up, Evan," Jonathan said clearly.

Evan looked surprised and took his gold watch from his pocket.

"So it is," he said. "I thought it only about half gone. But, Jon, you won't hold me to it? I thought it only fair to let people speak for themselves. I haven't half said—"

"I shall stick by our bargain," Jonathan said.

"A pound of flesh, eh, Shylock?" Evan's eyes, still smiling, sparkled too brightly.

"If you like," Jonathan said doggedly, meeting those eyes full.

They looked at each other, and in the moment the room fell silent. Everyone was staring at these two young men. Evan gave up gracefully.

"Oh, all right, Jon," he said. "Folks, this is my friend the schoolmaster. He's on the other side of the debate and wants to keep Median the way it is!"

A roar of laughter provided for Evan the opportunity to bow and stand aside. He did not sit down. Jonathan waited, but still he did not sit down. He continued to stand gracefully aside, his face humorous, his eyes affectionate.

"Go on, Jon," he said cheerfully.

He was going to stand there, as a guide to people's opinion. They would look at him and see him taller than Jonathan, far handsomer, quick to laugh, to look tolerant and scornful, as a man of business looks at a schoolmaster.

This Jonathan perceived. Then he put it aside. He stood without leaning, and with his hands in his pockets he began to speak in the quiet rather colorless voice of his usual conversation. He addressed them by no name, but he looked from one face to the other as he spoke. Some he knew, some he did not.

" 'Tisn't that I want to keep Median as it is," he said. "In fact, I don't, as Evan very well knows if he stops joking. It's just that I see Median a different kind of a town from a cattleman's town. That's natural, because I think of my pupils—and all of them are your children, too. It's no use hiding from ourselves or each other what the money's spent on in a cattleman's town. Those men spend their cash on drink, gambling, and women. They eat as little as they can, and they need little in garments. If we want their money, we've got to let brothels come in and saloons and gambling halls. The choice is a plain good town with a library and school and a church and homes and shops, or a cattleman's town. Theirs'll be the town—it always is. Our boys'll grow up thinking it's wonderful to ride horses and gallop up and down drunk and shooting off their guns, and our girls'll have to stay indoors. And what's the use of money to us if we have to live in that way to get it?"

Jonathan's quiet passionless voice in the heated room was like cool water.

"Amen!" a woman's voice cried.

"Amen—amen—" women's voices echoed.

"The ladies commend you, Jon," Evan said, his voice full of laughter.

Behind his bar Henry Drear looked alarmed. "See here, fellows," he cried, "this hyere's a man's country!"

Lew rose lumbering to his feet. But upon the tails of his coat two women laid their hands. One was his wife, but the other was Katie, and Jonathan's quick eye saw it.

"What do you say, Lew?" he inquired.

But the two hands held Lew fast. He stood for a moment stubborn, and then the eyes of everyone were fastened upon him in his predicament. He was a florid man at all times, burned crimson with prairie wind and sun. Now his face grew purple as he saw the faces about him grinning at him.

"Nothin'," he muttered and sat down abruptly.

Around him the room bellowed with laughter. And on the surge of this laughter Jonathan won his town.

"I hope you don't let it come between us, Evan," he said apologetically. He had asked Evan home with him to eat bacon and mush. Evan had hesitated, struggling against a wish not to go. Then he had yielded and come. Now they were walking side by side along the boardwalk to Jonathan's house.

"Of course I don't," he said quickly. His dark eyes glinted. "What really hurts me, Jon, is that it was the women who helped you win against me. I had the men easy enough. There isn't a man who won't groan in his heart this night at the good chance lost. But the women were for you, and I'm hurt. I always thought I could win a woman, Jon!"

Jonathan smiled. This was the sort of banter he never could answer or share in, but it showed him Evan was unchanged. He felt his admiration of Evan quicken. A big man, Evan was, and beyond any little grudging envy. He could lose without loss of his own good nature.

"I never was so successful like that before," Jonathan said, trying to answer Evan in kind.

"I don't know why you say that," Evan retorted. "On your own word you're engaged to the prettiest girl you've ever seen. Of course I haven't seen her, but—"

"You'll say so too when you see her," Jonathan said with gravity. "Not that beauty's the best of Judy, as you'll find, Evan. She's a solid good girl, too—a minister's daughter."

"Oh, I'm sure you're right," Evan said teasingly. "But my point is, how do you win them all, Jon? You're a nice-looking fellow, but—"

"Give over, do," Jonathan said. He was always miserable under such teasing. "You're ten times as much as me for looks, Evan, and well you know it and so do I."

"Not ten," Evan said with mock judicial accuracy, "but maybe two times —yes, I'll go that far with you."

Then he saw he was tormenting Jonathan and gave it up with a great laugh and a nudge of his elbow in Jonathan's ribs. "Oh, Jonnie," he cried, "I wouldn't trade you off for all the girls in Kansas! If your Judy takes you away from me, I'll hate her. Promise me a wife won't come between us!"

"Judy'll like you as well as I do, Evan—I know that," Jonathan promised him. In his grave young heart he made his promise deeper. Never as long as he lived would he forget that Evan was his friend.

Near the end of a gray day Judy stepped down from a wagon. The cold had only deepened her pallor. Even the tip of her straight small nose was not red. She accepted pleasantly the help the two men in the wagon gave her with her bag and box, not seeming to notice that the other woman struggled alone with her goods. The wagon held no family but only the few persons who at this time of year had wanted to come eastward. Judy had tried to talk to the hard-faced elderly woman, but had given it up. It was always easier to converse with men, she thought.

American House stood solid and welcoming as she stepped down the dry bare earth of the roadway and up a step to the boardwalk. Jonathan's trees in the square were beginning to look big. She saw everything sharply because now everything in Median would be a part of her life. Then she stepped into the tavern.

Mrs. Drear, bustling out of the kitchen, embraced her with floury arms.

"Goodness gracious, it's Judy!" she cried. "Now I must send someone straight off and tell Jonathan."

There were men at the tavern bar, as there always were, and one of them came forward instantly.

"Let me go, Mrs. Drear," he said.

In the quick habit of her eye, Judy saw a handsome man, tall and young, whose eyes were dark.

"I'd admire to be the one to go, Miss Judy. I'm Jon's best friend—Evan Bayne. He's expecting you."

He put out his hand, and she put hers in it an instant. Then she withdrew it.

"Wait just a bit of a while," she begged him. "I'm hungry and tired and real cold."

"Sure," Mrs. Drear chuckled, "she wants her young man to see her at her prettiest. Wait till she's fed, Evan, I've got supper ready. Will you have it in the kitchen, Judy, or right here?"

"Right here," Judy sighed.

Without seeming to see anyone she sank to the bench beside the table and drew off her gloves and took off her brown felt hat with velvet bows. Warmth brought back to her cheeks their usual soft color, and her lips were growing red again.

"Had a hard trip, Judy?" Henry Drear called from behind the bar.

"The cars were dirty, and then the wind was cold, that's all," she replied.

"Want a nip?" he inquired.

"A little hard cider, please," she said. She smiled up at him as he set a small tin cup before her.

He inquired, "Where's your paw?"

"He's had a call to be a missionary in the Sandwich Isles," she said.

Henry grinned. "Still goin' west?"

She nodded, her cup at her lips.

"He'll be comin' in here from the east one of these days if he keeps on goin'," Henry chuckled, and Judy smiled again.

She sat sipping her cider, seeming to see none of them, her head bent, her eyelids demure; but they were all watching her, helpless not to watch her. Even Mrs. Drear stood in the kitchen door watching her, though she was thinking of Jennet. She had not heard from Jennet in many months. The girl had become lost in that West which changed and grew so fast that in that growth it threw human beings from one chance to another.

"You didn't hear tell of Jennet anywhere out there, did you, Judy?"

Judy lifted her great innocent eyes. "No, I didn't, Mrs. Drear, and I'm sorry."

Mrs. Drear sighed. "Well, I didn't expect it—it would be a needle in a haystack if you did." She went back to her kitchen.

Evan did not move as he watched her. He would wait, he thought, filled with fury, until this girl had finished her supper to the last mouthful before he went to find Jonathan. He hated her already, a selfish, cold woman, thinking of herself instead of Jonathan. He thought of Jonathan with a passion of protection. Jonathan had been engrossed in this business of getting the school out of his house so that this woman might have a home. It was folly, and everybody told him so, to get the schoolhouse built before winter. Ice froze already except in the middle hours of the day, and at any moment there might be a blizzard. The winter winds made work on a house beyond endurance of frozen hands and cheeks. But for Jonathan's sake Stephen Parry was trying to do it.

"Your only hope is a temporary sod house, Jon," Evan had said.

But Jonathan had shaken his head. "I shan't put the bit of money I have into something to be torn down in the spring. It's not fair to the people who've given it."

What does this girl care? Evan thought gloomily, staring at Judy's beautiful face. She doesn't even hurry herself over her food.

It was true. Judy, always dainty at table, was daintier tonight than ever. It was her only response to the eyes upon her. Evan made a deep bow when at last she put down her spoon.

"Now, Madam, may I go and tell my friend that his fiancée has arrived?"

His voice was weighted with sarcasm, but Judy only lifted her eyelashes at him.

"If you please," she said gently. Her eyes rested on him reflectively, and Evan turned away and strode out of the door into the deep cold dusk. It only made things worse for Jonathan, he thought, to have her so pretty. It would be very hard for a man to forget so pretty a woman. He walked fast, thinking with melancholy how this was the sort of woman who would demand every service of a man so that his life was consumed in trivialities. And he wouldn't even know it, he thought in a strange sort of terror.

He gave a great thump to Jonathan's door and walked in. Jonathan sat by his fire with a book in his hand.

"Well, Evan!" he cried.

"Judy's come," Evan said.

Jonathan dropped his book and leaped for his greatcoat. "I had a pre-monition, not ten minutes ago," he cried. He blew out the lamp and took the lantern from Evan's hand. "Here, I'll carry this."

"What sort of a premonition?" Evan set his stride to match Jonathan's.

"A queer soft feeling, as though something good had happened, though what I couldn't think, for it's been a day like any other. How is she? Does she look well?"

"She looks well enough," Evan replied, so coldly that Jonathan was amazed.

"Evan, what's up!"

"Nothing."

"You're not telling me something, Evan!"

"There's nothing to tell," Evan retorted.

"Then why—"

Evan stood still. "I don't like her, and that's a fact," he said. They were talking in the darkness.

Jonathan lifted the lantern and saw Evan's stern face in the light of it. "You don't know her," he said.

Evan saw Jonathan—too young, too good, he thought. What he wanted to say was, "I knew her the minute I saw her."

"Maybe I don't," he said instead, and they went on.

But he did not enter the tavern again.

"Come in," Jonathan said to him.

"No, I've got a brief to write yet tonight," he replied, and then he added, "You don't want me and you know it."

Jonathan smiled at that and let him go. He could wait for no one, not with Judy in there waiting.

At the sound of his voice at the door, Mrs. Drear motioned Judy into the kitchen with her beckoning finger and came out and shut the door.

"She's in there waiting for you," she told Jonathan. Her red face was suffused with vicarious tenderness, and when Jonathan went in she sighed.

"Let 'em have it," she told the men. "It'll never seem so good again."

"Hey, ol' lady!" her husband roared at her. He sat on a high stool behind his bar, stirring a spoon in a tin cup.

"No, it won't, Henry Drear," she said and, seizing a towel from the wall behind his head, she fell to mopping the bar.

Behind the closed door Jonathan and Judy stood for the least part of a moment. Then Judy put out her hands and lifted her head.

"Dear Jonathan!" she said softly.

And at the sound of her voice he stepped toward her and took her in his arms. "Judy—Judy!" he muttered. His lips were on her hair, her temple, on the smooth firmness of her cheek and then her full throat, and with every kiss his arms hardened about her.

"Why, Jonathan," she cried. She was a little frightened.

But the passion, deep and slow in his being, was stirring and waking, rising to the surface of his eyes and lips, new passion that had never stirred before. He crushed her head against his shoulder and held it there, his palm against her cheek, and then he kissed her lips and then again and yet again.

And yet in the end it was he who let her go, not she who withdrew herself. He loosed her, and he turned his head away and tried to laugh.

"What am I doing, Judy girl? But we're to be husband and wife, eh, Judy?"

"Yes," she whispered. She had been so surprised that she had not moved. Jonathan was just like other men, after all, she was thinking. Somehow she had not imagined he would be because he looked so calm and gentle and pale. But inside maybe they were all the same. . . . She drew away a very little and began to straighten herself in small secret ways, by a touch at her hair, at the lace fichu about her neck, the lace about her wrists. By means of these movements, so swift and slight that Jonathan scarcely saw them, she set herself right.

"Are you glad to be here, sweet?" he asked.

"I'm real glad," she said. Her eyes, lifted to his, were now full of a lovely soft timidity. It seemed to him the essence of all that was exquisite in a woman. He felt ashamed of his passion. He did not want to be a man like his father, God knows! He wanted only to be a strong, protecting, able man to meet this clinging, needful woman whose body was complete beauty. He took her hand.

"My very dear," he said, "my dearest dear!"

He drew her toward him gently, and when she was near was horrified to discern in the brown depth of her eyes a thing like fear, and in her hand a small reluctance.

"You aren't afraid of me, Judy!" he cried. "Why, nobody's afraid of me, my dear!"

"I'm not afraid, exactly," she said.

"What, then?" he asked. He had her very near again now, but passion was held back by this look and this reluctance.

"It's only—oughtn't we to go out now? They're waiting for us out there."

"I've waited a long time, too, Judy," he said.

"I know." She came of her own accord the last space between them and kissed him. He felt her kiss, soft as a snowflake on his cheek, and he said abruptly, "Reckon you're right, Judy. Let's go out."

With her hand in his arm he threw open the door into the tavern, and at the same moment noise broke like bedlam. The room was full. All of Median was there—no, not the Parrys, but everybody else—and not a soul without a tin pan or a horn or a cowbell to make a noise, and to noise everyone added yells. Judy hid her face against his shoulder, and he put his arm about her and stood in the doorway smiling as long as the noise blared. Then Evan leaped on the bar, beating Mrs. Drear's tin washtub, turned over like a drum. When he caught Jonathan's look he beat the louder.

"Let's see the bride!" Evan yelled.

"Look up, lady!" a man's voice shouted.

"Give us a look, Judy!" Henry Drear roared.

"Look around for a minute, Judy," Jonathan whispered. "They mean the best."

And Judy, after a moment's coaxing, pushed back the curls from her face and lifted her head and every man in the room saw her. But Jonathan, gazing at her too, saw the direction of her eyes. They were fixed upward in soft appeal, and Jonathan followed as he might follow the path of a moonbeam and he found the end. She gazed at Evan, and Evan gazed at her.

24

STEPHEN PARRY put down his tools. He was working against deep winter on the schoolhouse, but winter would win, and now he knew it. The day had begun with a bitter wind, and by midmorning snow was glowing. From the north a smooth, even gray spread over the sky. The wind heightened, and he had to be careful lest he slip on the new-fallen snow. By noon he gave up. He clambered down the shell of the house and found the lunch Sue had wrapped for him. He ate it, standing in a corner under the roof. The bread and pork was as hard as stone, and in the thick pottery jug the coffee was ice cold.

When he had eaten and drunk he plodded through the now driving snow to Jonathan's sod house and knocked at the door. A child opened it, and as he opened it the noise and talk and laughter of children at noon recess came out in an uproar. Jonathan stood mending the fire, and he looked up at Stephen, the tongs in his hand.

"Come in, Steve," he shouted. "That is, if you can. Shut the door, Melissa. Most of them brought their dinners with them today, and that's why all this hubbub. You see why I want to get them out of my house, Steve."

"Sure," Stephen replied. He hated to tell Jonathan, but it must be done. "Mr. Goodliffe," he said gently, "I sure do hate to tell you, but I ain't gonneh get that schoolhouse done before spring. I jest cain't."

He held up his hands. "I got frostbit today as it was, and if my hands are gone, I got nothin' to earn my livin' with."

The noise of the children stopped. It was not much to them whether the new schoolhouse was finished or not. Jonathan's house was comfortable, and it had become their own.

Jonathan's face tightened at the mouth. "I don't want you to freeze your hands, certainly," he said. He put down the tongs. "And I reckon you've tried to get help."

"Yessir, everywhere. But nobody wants to work in the open this weather. I'm fixin' to snatch any warm days they is and git the roof finished so's there'll be cover. But plaster would freeze before I could git it mixed. 'Tain't only jest labor."

"Well," Jonathan said, "I reckon it's not to be helped." He paused for a moment and then went on, his face with only its usual careful expression. "You'll make it the first job in the spring?"

"I will," Stephen said, backing toward the door. "I'm terrible sorry." Jonathan inclined his head slightly and wet his lips.

"Well, good day, Steve," Jonathan said. "It's time for school to take up for the afternoon."

"Good-by, suh." Steve let himself out of the door and closed it.

"Pupils, attention please," Jonathan said calmly. The school shuffled back into its place, and Jonathan took up his pointing stick and went to the blackboard.

"The square of the hypothenuse of a right triangle," he said, "is equal to the sum of the squares of the other two sides, thus—" He began to draw his usual beautifully neat figures upon the board.

I shall have to compel Judy, he was thinking.

"I shan't give you a choice, Judy, sweet," he was saying to her. They were in her room at American House. She had made it comfortable and somehow pretty. She had curtained the bed off with Indian blankets so that the rest of the room was her own sitting room. There was a tin stove in it and a heap of split wood beside it. On the table was an oil lamp. He sat in the rocking chair by the fire but not rocking, because she sat on a hassock with her head against his knees. Every evening they spent together in this room.

She did not move her head from under his caressing hand. He loved her hair. It was not soft, as his mother's hair was. It was full of spring and curl, and no smoothing could make it smooth. He loved to feel it catch and curl about his fingers.

"You're marrying the schoolteacher," he said playfully, "and so you'll have to put up with my school."

"But where'll I sit all day?" she asked. "There's only the bit of bedroom. And winter's still here."

He had only thought of their evenings when, he had told himself, he would move the desks and stools into one half of the room. He had not thought of all the hours when she would be alone. Now he remembered, too, how cold the bedroom was.

"You can come and sit by the school fire," he said.

She smiled without answering. Her face was rosy and placid, but under it she was thinking of what she wanted for herself. But she did not speak.

"We want to get married quickly, don't we, dear?" Jonathan asked, his hands tender under the curls upon her white neck. "You and me together'll make the winter short. When spring comes the school will move out, and we'll have a fair house then all to ourselves."

She rubbed her head like a cat against his fondling hand. "I don't seem to care whether we're married or not so long as we're together," she murmured.

Jonathan laughed. "I believe you're too lazy to get married," he said. Her sweet softness of movement, her pretty dallying over anything she did, her long drowsy silences when they sat together, she like this or on his knees, he loved to call her laziness, but it was sweet to him because under his own calm he was so full of restless and nervous energy. He had never known rest, he often thought, until she came. But rest would not be complete until they had slept together, night after night. But he could not tell her that. She smiled up at him without answer. She had known since she was born that if she smiled she need not speak. She was a little irritated therefore when a moment later Jonathan pressed her.

"Shall we marry at once, Judy? Why not? Tomorrow. There's a preacher here now." An itinerant preacher had come to Median and, because of an infected hand, which Mrs. Drear was poulticing, he was delaying.

"No, not tomorrow," Judy said.

"Next week then," he urged. "Why not, dear heart?" He took her chin and looked down at her. "Judy, do you love me?"

"Of course." Her lips framed the words silently.

"Of course what?" he demanded.

"I love you—"

"Then it'll be next week—eh, Judy? On Saturday."

He held her chin so hard that it was uncomfortable and she could not escape.

"All right, Jonathan, but only if you'll make it two weeks."

"Why?" he persisted.

"I'm—not ready—next week," she said.

He felt himself flush. He knew enough about women to know there were times. He had plagued his mother with questions once because she had looked so pale, until she had said impatiently, "Give over, Jonathan—it's only my woman's curse."

"What's that, Mother?"

"Eve's curse, I reckon. Once a month a woman's got to be ill a bit, and you may as well know, for you'll be marrying a woman one day, and she'll thank you to leave her alone then."

Now instantly delicate, he agreed. "Two weeks, surely, Judy—if I have to bribe the preacher." He let her go and lifted her to his knee. "That's my own wife," he said comfortably.

They sat together in the chair, the room warm and still. Around the house the prairie wind howled, and in the tavern there was the clatter of pewter and tin cups and plates and men's voices. In the inner silence Jonathan heard the door bang and there was a roar of laughter.

"That'll be Evan," he said immediately.

He questioned, scarcely aware that he did, the sweet weight of Judy's body relaxed in his arms. In all these days he had not discovered what Judy thought of Evan or Evan of Judy. Neither mentioned the other to him. But there was not now the quiver of a nerve in Judy's flesh. She did not stir or move the direction of her eyes as she gazed into the open door of the stove.

"Everybody likes Evan," Jonathan said. He could hear men still laughing. Evan could always set laughter afire in any place he chose.

"I don't," Judy said lazily. "I hate him." She spoke without a flicker of intensity in the soft slow way in which she said everything.

"Why?" Jonathan asked. He was greatly astonished.

"I don't know," Judy said pleasantly. "I just naturally hate him."

Jonathan laughed with his delight in her. She was so lovely and so unreasonable, so adorable in all her foolishness.

"You mustn't say that, my Judy," he scolded with tenderness. "Why, Evan's my best friend, a wonderful chap and loyal as made. He'd stick to me through anything, and to you, too, for my sake."

"I don't like his eyes," she murmured.

"Why, he's thought to have uncommon fine eyes, so dark and flashing-like."

"He's conceited," she said.

"No, now, that he's not," Jonathan protested. "It's his great abilities—a natural-born orator, Judy, so that it's a treat to hear him argue a case. I've not seen him in court, but sometimes he's rehearsed a case with me for practice. His voice can be heard anywhere. It was in the paper once in Topeka that his voice could be heard all through the courthouse when he was arguing a case for the railroad company."

"He thinks all he needs to do is to raise his right eyebrow at a woman," Judy said. In his arms she did not move.

"No, now, he lifts his eyebrow like that whenever he's about to crack a joke," Jonathan cried.

She sat up. "You like him better than anybody—better'n me."

He was deeply shocked. "Judy, shut up, my dear. Such things can't be said. He's my friend, but you're my wife."

But he thought to himself here was the seat of the coldness between Evan and Judy. They were jealous of each other with him. Only the other day it had occurred to him that he and Evan had scarcely met for days. It was his own fault. Every free moment he spent with Judy, and Evan in delicacy had not pressed himself.

"When we're married you'll see that Evan is your friend just the same as he's mine," he told Judy. He pressed her head back into the hollow of his shoulder. "Lie back, my sweet," he said.

Long after he was gone she sat without moving by the stove, her elbows on her knees and her hands soft fists against her cheeks. There were still voices in the tavern, and she was listening to them. Besides, what use was there in going to bed when she could not sleep?

It was nearly midnight when silence fell. Jonathan had gone at half past nine, tender of her good name. Now she rose in this first silence and went to the door and threw it open. Evan sat there alone at a table, a mug of beer in his hand.

"I hoped you'd gone, too," she said. "I want to sleep."

"I'm going," he said shortly.

She came in and stood by the table. "I'm marrying Jonathan on Saturday, two weeks," she said.

"Goddamn you," he answered, staring at her.

Mrs. Drear came in, her eyes bleary with sleep. "It's closing time, folks," she said. The words were easy, but her voice was sharp.

"I was just telling Evan that Jonathan and I have set the day," Judy said without moving. The purity of her face grew more pure, as it always did when she felt anyone was angry with her. "It's a week from next Saturday. The schoolhouse can't get finished, he says, so we may as well."

"I'm glad to hear it," Mrs. Drear said. She swept up an armful of dirty mugs.

Evan got up. "So'm I," he said heartily. "Jon's waited long enough for you, Judy."

"He shore has," Mrs. Drear agreed.

"I think so, too," Judy said. Her voice was tender with sweetness. "Shall I help you with the dishes, Mrs. Drear?"

"I don't care if you do," Mrs. Drear answered. Nobody could put a finger on Judy, she thought. The girl was always kind and willing. Then why did she feel queer about her sometimes? Jennet had been bad enough.

Though Jennet was Henry's own daughter, there was no use pretending she had not taken more after her slut of a mother than she had after Henry. But Jennet was as open as a book. Mrs. Drear yawned over the dishpan and then sighed. Yes, Judy was good about helping. It couldn't be denied she was a real helpful girl. You would say she was a good girl if somehow you could be sure she was.

Jonathan in his bed lay awake with desire. He recognized it and was ashamed of it. Love and desire were two different things, and he meant to keep them so. I shan't be like my father, he thought. I shan't have my Judy growing into what my poor mother is.

He knew by now that his mother had had another child and lost it. Ruth had written him secretly one of her printed letters. Without wanting to be a murderer, he was glad the child was dead. Things were hard enough. Maybe he ought to have gone West himself to see how things were. But he had had letters, scanty as usual, from his mother. It was natural enough that she had not told him of the child. She never spoke of childbirth to him. The life was hard there, she said, but maybe it would be better, she always said. And he couldn't go now.

But desire for Judy ebbed out of him as he thought about his mother. He was going to make up everything to Judy. She shouldn't have babies unless she wanted them. And never, never would he persuade her against her will, and never make her afraid of his ill-temper if she did not want him. He lay thinking of his father with deep unyielding anger. He would be to Judy all that his father had not been to his mother. And then, strangely, having begun thus to think about his mother, he could think of no one else. She seemed to possess him. He had not for weeks given over his mind to her like this. He tried to recall Judy, but there was only his mother. He grew restless and at last sat up in his bed. If I believed in anything of the kind, I'd be wondering if aught was wrong with her, he thought.

He was not superstitious, but he sat listening and feeling through the darkness toward his mother. Coyotes were crying in the night. The wind had abated, and he could hear the wailing agony of their crying. But it was a sound common enough to the night, and he gave it no heed. He pushed his mind beyond through the darkness like a quivering, searching probe. Something was wrong, maybe, or for sure.

It was nearly an hour before he could lie down again. He'd write tomorrow. Once more he tried to think of Judy and could not. He fell asleep thinking only of his mother.

25

IN THE poor sod house in the midst of the western plains, Mary gave
up her struggle. Beside her Clyde lay sleeping a hard snoring sleep. The
harsh labor of his days had coarsened every part of him. His body, nerving
itself to the day's work, indulged itself in food eaten quickly and roughly,
in loud noise and quick temper, in a passion often savage in its demands,
and then sprawling sleep. Mary, lying awake on the edge of the bed, away
from his unwashed body, was crying quietly.

I s'all give up, she thought. It's no use. I can't die here with nobody but
Ruth. It's too hard on her. Oh, Jonathan!

Such a yearning burst out of her for her son that she felt her head grow
giddy. "Jonathan!" The name broke from her again in a low groan, involuntary, as though something had wrenched it out of her. Clyde woke.

"Eh!" he grunted.

"Clyde!" she whispered in the darkness.

"What?" He had no mind to wake.

"I'm going back to Median," she said.

That waked him. "What for?"

"I daren't stay the winter here again, with a new baby."

"But we're all right."

"I'm not. If I hadn't got caught again 'twould be different. But things
aren't as they should be in me. I can tell."

"You're allays nervous when your time's near," he said sullenly.

"This isn't only that," she said. "I've had enough babies to know."

He flounced himself. "How can I go when I've got the sheep and the
cows to care for? And it's the worst time of year for me to take such a
journey. If there's a blizzard, who'll tend the beasts while I'm gone? Jamie
can't manage alone."

"But Jamie can drive Ruth and Maggie and me," she said. "And you
can stay with your beasts."

If she could only get to Median where Jonathan was, it would be almost
like going home. And Mrs. Drear could help her when her time came.

"I'm going, Clyde, so it's no good your talking."

America had made her mean-tempered, but she could not help it. Everything was against a woman here. She had to fight for her life.

"Then I won't talk, if it's no good," Clyde said. He turned his back and
jerked the covers. She knew he was full of fury and could not care. Plenty
of times she had said to herself that he had it hard, too. He wasn't lazy,
at least the way he used to be in England. In his way he worked hard,

but he had no luck. The cattle strayed and were lost, however he branded them. And the cowmen in the next homestead were thieves, as everybody knew, but how to prove it? You couldn't expect a common chap like Clyde to have his word taken against an educated Englishman's, and he owned the ranch. Besides, there was Jennet.

Jennet had come and gone twice, and now she was back again. Ruth had told her that Jamie had seen her.

"I don't want to know about it," she had told Ruth.

She tightened her lips in the darkness. When she got back to Median she did not want to have to tell Mrs. Drear that Jennet had lived with the Englishman twice, once for three months and again for a month, and now she was back again.

She felt suddenly faint with nausea. But it was not the usual nausea of pregnancy. The sickness was mingled with pain in her lower belly, not sharp pain but one so vast and deep that it was as though it grasped some center of her vitality.

It's a wicked kind of pain, she thought anxiously and retched as sweat burst out of her. This, she thought in terror, was life or death. I'll set out tomorrow, she thought wildly, or it'll be too late.

Two days before his wedding Jonathan was shaving himself at twilight. For a fair man he had a rough, quickly growing beard, and he shaved evenings instead of mornings because he wanted his cheek smooth against Judy's. He was whistling and full of happiness. Everything was going right for him except one thing, and that maybe would, after all. Evan was not sure he could stand up with him at the wedding. He had spent half the afternoon today after school arguing it in Evan's office.

"Put the wedding off a few days and I'll come," Evan said in his off-hand way.

Jonathan was deeply shocked. "A man doesn't put off his wedding."

Evan laughed. "Of course not, and I was only teasing you. What I say is, go on and I'll be here if I can, boy. It's bad luck this case had to be called right now in Topeka. Wait till I get Median the county seat. Will you let me do that, Jon, if you won't have it a cattle town?"

He had forgiven Jonathan, but he used their disagreement for teasing. Jonathan smiled without answer. Evan went on, "No, son, I've got to go. After all, I'm the corporation lawyer for the Santa Fe in these parts, and the claims for cattle killed on the tracks have got to be settled. It's getting to be the way a lot of unsuccessful cattlemen are growing fat. They drive their cows on the tracks—"

Evan's rich voice rolling along was befuddling in its ease. Jonathan stopped it.

"I won't have anyone else," he said. "If you don't come, I'll stand up alone."

"If it's humanly possible I'll be at your side," Evan retorted, "even if I don't approve the match." He made no bones about Judy.

"Is that the real reason why you don't want to come?" Jonathan asked.

"I don't like the woman, Jon, and you may as well know it," he said.

"But why, Evan?" Jonathan demanded.

"Too pretty," Evan said promptly. "A woman as pretty as that is thinking only of herself. You deserve someone who'll think only of you."

"You mustn't say such things, Evan."

"I must and I will if I'm to stay your friend."

Jonathan let it pass. He knew them both, he thought tenderly, and some day, when Judy was his wife, Evan would come to see her for what she was, and Judy would learn to appreciate his friend. He would wait.

"Well, I don't give up hope," he said with his wry smile.

"That's right," Evan said heartily.

When he had stopped a moment to tell Judy, she had looked strange, he thought.

"I'm glad he's not coming," she said. "He always makes me feel I've put my clothes on wrong, somehow."

Jonathan had laughed. "Oh, you two," he had said. He kissed her very lightly. "I'll kiss you hard later after I've shaved," he told her half-playfully. He was so happy these days that all his slight instincts toward mirthfulness were awake in him. And so he had turned homeward to make himself ready for her. He did not like to wear his work clothes when he went to her at any time. But these last two nights before their marriage were very precious. He wanted no slightest withdrawal in Judy from him.

He heard something. Razor in hand, he stopped to listen. The early dark beyond the windows was like midnight and the door was closed against the early cold. But a wagon had drawn up and stopped. He put down the razor on the shelf under the small mirror, and wiped the soap from his cheek. Then he threw the door open.

The light from the house streamed upon a sad-looking group of people. For a moment he could not believe his eyes. A tall boy and a girl were clambering out of the wagon.

"Jonathan!" a voice called faintly. He leaped forward.

"Mother, it's never you! Ruth—Jamie—why, what in heaven's name! Maggie, too! Where's Dad? Oh, Mother, whatever's wrong with you?"

Mary had raised herself out of the end of the old covered wagon, and he saw her sick face. He lifted her out, and then he saw what was the matter and he ground his teeth.

"Come in," he said, "come in quick and lie down in the bed. My God, Ruthie, to let her come like this!"

"She would come," Ruth said. Her old timidity had grown deeper in the long months upon the plains, and was as wild as a hare's now. She blinked in the light of the room and clutched Maggie's hand fast.

"Get me down, quick," Mary groaned. "Quick, and call Mrs. Drear,

Jonathan. I mistrust it's my time. Dear God, how I've prayed to get home first! Well, for once He's let me have my hope."

She was sighing with pain, and she sat down on the bed and tried to pull off her shoes.

"Take 'em off for her, you, Jamie—or Ruth," Jonathan shouted. "I'll go for Mrs. Drear."

He rushed out into the darkness and ran over the clattering dry boards to the tavern. Mrs. Drear was sitting alone at the kitchen table eating her supper before she served up the food to others. He ran in upon her.

"Mother's come," he gasped. "And, Mrs. Drear, will you—she's going to—to—to—she needs a woman, fast."

"My soul and body," Mrs. Drear shrieked. She jumped to her feet and lifted a kettle of boiling water from the stove. "Henry, you'll have to dish up," she shouted as she passed the bar, and then she was gone.

Far into the night Jonathan worked at her side. He forgot Judy or where he was to have been. He and Ruth and Mrs. Drear fought together for his mother's life. He had never seen a child born before, and he was terrified at what he saw. Did every birth so devastate another's being? He was drenched with sweat and groaned aloud without knowing until Mrs. Drear bade him be silent. He rushed out for a moment and wept heartily before Jamie's awe-stricken face, and then rushed back again for fear she might die in the moment he was away.

The child was born at midnight, a girl, small and thin, but living, and less than an hour later, Mary died.

He had a strange feeling as he sat before the fire with the little newborn creature in his arms that somehow he had been widowed before ever he was married. The blanket curtain was drawn between the two rooms. The two rooms were very still. Jamie had gone to ask Stephen Parry to make the coffin. Ruth was moving about the room, tidying it, and crying quietly. No pupils came to school, for he had announced a week's holiday for his wedding. Mrs. Drear had stayed to make Mary neat for burial and then had gone home, taking Maggie with her.

"This one's too lively for you to have around now, I reckon," she had said. She hesitated, Maggie's hand in hers. "Jonathan, I'll tell Judy. It'll mean puttin' off tomorrow, 'course."

He had actually forgotten that tomorrow was to be his wedding day. Now he remembered and nodded.

"What to do with that mite—" Mrs. Drear's mournful brown eyes turned toward the hearth where in a wooden box the baby lay asleep.

"I don't know," Jonathan said. "I'll have to think about everything. I do thank you, Mrs. Drear."

"Don't mention it," she sighed.

So she had gone. The little baby began suddenly to wail and Jonathan picked it up and, wrapping his old coat about it, he sat down for the first time he had sat all night and held it. Some soothing quality in him flowed into the child, and it slept again.

It seemed to him that somehow it was his own child whose mother was dead. He was bereft of something beyond his own mother. He was responsible for more than a son's duty.

"We can't wait till Dad knows, can we?" Ruth's half-whispered question startled him.

"No," he said shortly. "How could we? I s'all just have to do what ought to be done." He controlled a strong trembling in his throat. "However did you not bring her home long before?" he demanded. He was thinking of his mother's body. After the baby was born it seemed to shrink into a wisp. She was such a small little thing even at her best, and now there was left of her only a handful of bones. A woman murdered, if ever there was murder, he thought somberly, and was glad that his father was not in this house.

"How could I?" Ruth asked timidly. "Besides, she always said as how things would be better maybe, and how could she leave Dad?"

"He didn't see, I suppose, that he might have brought her?"

"No, he didn't," Ruth said simply.

Jonathan looked at her sternly over the sleeping child. "Tell me the truth—was it terrible for all the time?"

Ruth nodded. "Yes, it was. She was always afeared. There was the snakes and she always would think Maggie would get bit one day—a mortal lot of snakes, there was, Jonathan, and they'd crawl in between the sod in the walls. And there was one on her bed, and she dreamed about it all the time after. And the water was bitter and hard. And Jamie swears something terrible now, and she minds his growin' up rough and ignorant-like. And Maggie never minds nobody and, oh, the wind, blowin' and blowin' night and day, used to drive her daft-like. Once she went outside and screamed and screamed, and I thought she was daft for sure, but then she began to cry, and after she cried a while she was herself again."

"Did Dad see nothing?"

"He's away all day and lots of nights, too."

"And were there no neighbors?"

"No, unless—no, you couldn't say there was neighbors. The Englishman wasn't a neighbor, and Mother never even wanted to hear tell of Jennet."

"Jennet?" Jonathan cried.

"She was there at his ranch sometimes. She was there when we left."

He sat with this news, thinking of it. "I thought she was in Frisco," he said.

"So she was—she's only sometimes at the ranch," Ruth replied.

"Don't tell Drears," he said shortly after a while.

"I wouldn't nohow," she said.

"Anyhow," he corrected her. If he did not correct her now, there was no one to do it.

"Anyhow," she repeated humbly.

The baby began to wail again, and he wondered if it were hungry. There was no immediate need for food, he knew, but this one was such a wee thin thing maybe it would want food earlier than the others had. He hushed it and at last rocked it in his arms, but the child cried on.

"What'll we do?" he asked Ruth.

"Could I mix a bit of flour and water?" she suggested.

"That can't hurt, can it?"

"I reckon not," she replied.

But while they hesitated the door opened, and Sue and Stephen came in. Sue had a shawl over her head and a man's coat tied over her shoulders like a cape. She threw both off with one sweep of her arms.

"Give her to me," she said. She took the baby from Jonathan and hesitated a moment. Then she went firmly on. "Mr. Goodliffe, suh, do you min' if I give it mah breas'? My baby is six mont's, but I think it'll be fresh still, and I sho have plenty."

He stared at Sue for one startled moment and with her abnormal sensitivity she seemed suddenly to grow in stature before his eyes.

"If you don't want me," she said proudly.

His reason controlled him instantly. "I thank you very much," he said. "It may save the child's life."

But he left the room at the same moment and went into the other with Stephen and stood there while Stephen in sad silence measured the sleeping figure on the bed.

"Cottonwood timber's all I've got on hand jest now, suh," he said when he had finished. "But I can use pitch to make it tight."

Jonathan nodded.

"Sue's got some white cotton to line it," Stephen said gently.

Jonathan nodded again.

"I'll have it done tonight—will you want it tomorrow?"

"Yes," Jonathan said, and then remembered that tomorrow was to have been his wedding day.

26

"AIN'T you goin' right over there to Jonathan's?" Mrs. Drear demanded of Judy. "He shore needs a woman to help out."

She felt exhausted this morning, and the sight of Judy, very pretty in a red wool dress with a red velvet collar and cuffs, somehow added to her exhaustion. She poured more milk into Maggie's cup.

"I'll go the minute I've had my breakfast," Judy said gently. She moved gracefully about the tavern kitchen, pouring herself a cup of coffee from the big granite pot on the range, and cutting herself bread and buttering it without giving a glance at the round-faced, red-haired little girl at the table in the middle of the kitchen. Mrs. Drear had waked her half an hour before to pour out the story of the night. She had sat up in bed, listening, her shining hair curling over her shoulders. Mrs. Drear, looking at her without liking her better, had nevertheless felt sorry for Jonathan because the girl was so pretty in her nightgown.

"'Course you can't have the wedding tomorrow."

"No, of course not," Judy had agreed. That was all she said. But she had climbed out of bed and poured water into the porcelain basin on the washstand. Mrs. Drear had gone away then.

Whether she cares or whether she don't—she had been thinking the half-hour since as she fried salt pork and slabs of mush.

When Judy came in, in her red dress, her curls neatly pinned on her head, there was still no telling. Red, Mrs. Drear thought, wasn't suitable, either. But probably the girl hadn't thought. She sat there by the window eating her bread cut in little narrow strips. Mrs. Drear, glancing at her, saw Jamie go by the window with Stephen and Sue, and she ran to pound on the pane.

"Jamie!" she screamed, and when he turned clawed at him to come in. A moment later he was there at the door, a tall black-haired boy, his face cheerful in spite of what had happened.

"Come in and eat," Mrs. Drear ordered him. "There'll be trouble enough at your house without fixing breakfast for you. This hyere's Judy, your sister-in-law to be. You can take her along after you've et."

"Pleased to meet you," Jamie said. "Hello, Mags."

He felt embarrassed in Mrs. Drear's presence because he had seen Jennet a few days before he left his father's ranch. She had been riding with the Englishman, loping along at his side upon a chestnut horse, riding astride, too, wearing corduroy pants and high boots and a big cowboy hat. He had been herding sheep, and she pulled up when she saw him and stared at him, and when she recognized him she flicked his nose with the end of her whip.

"You don't know who I am," she had declared.

"I do, too," he had said so sullenly that she laughed.

"Then don't tell me," she had said, "for I don't want to know."

The Englishman came cantering up then, a long lazy sort of chap.

"Who's this, Jenny?" he asked.

"A boy I used to know," she answered mischievously.

Jamie had stared straight back at the Englishman's pale blue eyes.

"Ah," the Englishman had said at last, "then don't know him any more, will you?"

They had gone galloping off together then, and he had watched them go, until the prairie swallowed them into a mirage. But he had felt queer because Jennet looked so different from the way she had used to look in this kitchen—older, and not so pretty, and yet he had wanted to look at her.

He lifted his eyes secretly to Judy, met hers, and looked hastily away again.

"There." Mrs. Drear handed him a plate of fried mush. "Sit down across from Judy."

"Thanks." He took the plate and sat at the opposite end of the table. Her soft voice made him lift his eyes again.

"I'm ever so sorry—about last night."

He nodded and suddenly found his throat choked so that he could not swallow.

"Will you all stay here now?" Judy's gentle voice was at him again.

He forced himself to swallow. "I reckon I'll have to get right back to help Dad. One man can't hardly handle the sheep and cows, too. Don't know even as we ought to try both."

"Then the others will stay with Jonathan?"

"Reckon they'll have to," he said. "We couldn't hardly handle a baby out there."

She did not speak again. She sat sipping her coffee and eating her bread and butter daintily and slowly, and when she was finished she rose and smiled. "I'll put on my bonnet and go."

"Oh, Judy!"

Jonathan leaped to his feet and took her in his arms and put his face down upon her shoulder.

"I knew you'd come. It's been a dreadful night."

She put her hand to his cheek. "I knew it," she said. "So I came."

She saw a young dark-haired girl, and over Jonathan's shoulder smiled at her.

All these people, she was thinking, all to live in this house! Of course I can't be married now.

She drew herself gently out of Jonathan's arms, but she kept his hand. "Is that the poor little baby?" she asked. She went toward the box where the baby now lay asleep since Sue had left it fed. "It's very small," Judy said. "What's her name, Jonathan?" She gazed down at the child but did not touch it.

"I haven't—we haven't thought about that," Jonathan said sadly.

"Why not Mary?" Judy asked, "after your mother?"

Jonathan's eyes met Ruth's. "Why not?" he agreed. "You see, Ruthie, how Judy knows the right thing at once. Mary it is—she'd like that."

"But we named the baby that died Mary," Ruth said.

"All the more reason why this living one should take the name," Jonathan said.

He had not wept at all, but now with Judy's hand softly in his he wanted to weep, to tell her—

"Run outdoors a bit, Ruthie, there's a good girl," he said.

And when she had gone he put his head down on Judy's shoulder and let the tears well up into his eyes. He gave one sob.

"Can you marry a chap like me, Judy sweet—with all these here in the house?"

"Don't let's talk about it now, Jonathan," she said in her gentlest voice. So gentle was her voice that it could not tell him anything. "Only we mustn't put Ruth out," she said. "It's cold today, and she's no coat on." She gave him a little squeeze and went to the door, "Come in, Ruth," she said. "It's too cold outside."

So there was no time for him to weep, after all.

She stayed nearly all day in the sod house. With Jonathan she went into that inner room and stood beside his dead mother, lying in the bed that tomorrow was to have been hers. If she thought of this she said nothing. And when at noon, as she was helping Ruth to prepare the meal, Sue came in to nurse the child again, she let no surprise escape her.

"I didn't know what ever to do, and Sue offered," Jonathan said, half-defensively and ashamed of his defense.

"It's good of her," Judy said peaceably.

In the afternoon she sat down to mend a rent in Jonathan's coat and looked so quiet and so beautiful that his sore heart took rest. He drew a three-legged stool to her side.

"Maybe we could manage after all," he said.

She smiled. "And put Ruth and the children out when we wanted to be alone?"

"Maybe we could all live at American House."

"And leave no room for travelers, besides the cost?" She shook her head and stitched steadily. She seemed so remote that he was frightened.

"Will you wait, Judy?"

She lifted her beautiful black eyes. "What do you think?" she asked.

He thought she would, but he did not speak. He took the pretty thimbled hand, the skin so smooth and white, and kissed the palm passionately.

"Dear heart!" he murmured.

She drew it back again to use. And after a moment she said, "Won't Evan be surprised when he comes back!"

He had not thought of Evan, or only to remember that he was in Topeka.

"What made you think of Evan?" he demanded.

"Only because he'll be pleased," Judy replied, "because he doesn't want you to marry me."

The composure of her face did not break. He sat watching her quick hands, his heart clinging to her in his sadness. Not for a moment had he forgotten all day the quiet body lying upon his bed. And even now he could not forget. At sunset, Stephen said, he would bring the coffin.

"It's getting late," Judy said suddenly, glancing at the sky. "I must be going, Jonathan, if there's nothing else I can do. Ruth's so handy." She smiled across the room at Ruth, who sat holding the baby, her back turned carefully toward them.

And he thought, I must let her go. There's no reason why she should be here when Stephen comes. It'll be too hard on her.

So he let her go, wrapping her cape about her and tying her brown hood under her chin. He walked a few steps with her into the biting wind, and then he saw Stephen and ahead of him Sue.

"Good night, my true love," he murmured and tipped her head to find her lips.

"Good night, Jonathan," she said. Her face had never looked more sweetly pure than now, in the pale evening light, and her lips were softer than a child's.

Mary was buried the day before the great blizzard. The wind as they stood about the open grave was bitter beyond any Jonathan had ever felt. Maggie had cried with cold, and Mrs. Drear had taken her back to the sod house to stay with Sue and the baby. Ruth was trembling against him with cold so that at last he whispered to Jamie, "Stand on the other side of Ruth."

Over the grave a traveling preacher was reading the Twenty-third Psalm, but the wind tore his big voice to echoes and left of the psalm only shreds. Judy, Jonathan had seen in a moment, was not here. He had postponed the funeral a few minutes waiting for her. Then Henry had shouted through the wind, "We'll all get frostbite, Jonathan."

"Where's Judy?" he had muttered.

"She was dressed to come, but we hadn't oughta wait," Henry had bawled against the wind. He looked up at the sky lowering over their heads. "It might break any minute."

So they had gone on with the sad little ceremony. Stephen Parry had dug the grave through a crust of earth already frozen. It was in the corner of the two acres that was to be the graveyard about the church that was not yet built in the town that would one day be Median. Jonathan and Evan together had planned it so.

" 'I shall not want!' " the preacher's voice roared like a trumpet in a second's abatement of the wind and was lost again.

But Jonathan had not dreamed that his mother would lie here first. And she had wanted everything in her short life. He made up his mind now that in the spring he would move little Artie from the hollow to here beside her.

" '. . . the valley of the shadow . . .' " the preacher's voice cried out, and the wind snatched the words away and flung them over the plains where there was neither hill nor valley.

Evan was not here, and Judy was not here. But everyone else was.

They stood, a handful of drab-colored human beings in the midst of the wide emptiness about them. They were dwarfed to the size and shape of insects by the land and the sky. A few rods away was the flimsy shelter of Median. He looked at them all in a sudden terror because he too was one of them.

It's too big for us here, he thought, and longed with a sudden sickening longing for the smallness of England to be tight about him again. Now I'll never be able to take Mother back to England, he thought. The old age he had planned to give her when they left Dentwater he could never give her, for she would have no old age. There's nothing to go back for, he thought. And he would miss her in England if he were alone there without her. England and his mother were one.

No, he was committed now to this new country. Judy— Where was she? He searched the roadway toward the hotel, but she was not there. And then, his gaze returning sadly, he met by accident another pair of eyes. They were Katie's. He had scarcely seen her for months. She had been away all the summer visiting her aunt in Topeka, Lew said. When she had come back he had not thought to ask. But here she was, a tall, somewhat gaunt-looking young girl, who had grown so much in the few months that now it seemed only her hazel eyes were exactly as they had been. They were as round and honest as ever in her plain face, and now red with weeping.

He felt grateful to her for weeping. She had scarcely known his mother; she was weeping, he knew, for him. And across the open grave he smiled at her, a small, sad smile.

" 'And I will dwell in the house of the Lord *forever!*' " The preacher's voice triumphed over the wind at last, and he clapped the Bible shut with a bang.

. . . Judy, in good time for the funeral, had tied her brown fur-trimmed cape under her chin and then tied on the small fur bonnet that went with it. She smoothed the ribbons of the bow and glanced at the big clock as she passed through the empty tavern. It was exactly the hour at which she should have been marrying Jonathan, and in this very room, if his mother had not come home. Even if she had died out there in the West, the wedding would have been going on now because they would not have known it. But the children would have come home to Jonathan, and then it would have been too late for her to do anything to save herself. Now she was saved. Something always *saves* me, she thought solemnly. It must be God.

She stood for a moment looking out of the panes of the tavern door. The wind was whirling in great coils of dust and snow.

I wish something would save me now from having to go out, she thought. The tavern was warm and sheltering. She hated winter as Joel did, and every winter of her life they had gone south for his preaching. "There's souls to save where the climate's good, too," he had always said.

If she had gone with him, she thought, she might have been now in the

Sandwich Isles, a lovely spot, Joel wrote her, where only man was vile. If she had gone, probably she could have married there, too, and settled down.

She lingered on at the risk of being late. Everyone else had gone, and she was alone. If she said afterwards that she had been taken suddenly faint so that she dared not go out, nobody was here now to say she was not. But she waited a moment more for some salvation not of her own making.

And then it came again. The door of Evan's office next door opened, and he hurried out, wrapped in his great cape, his head bent to the wind so that he had to hold on his hat. Then he had only just come back from Topeka, she thought, for less than an hour ago Mrs. Drear had said as she went out of the door with Maggie, "This is going to hit Evan real hard. He's that fond of Jonathan."

And no one has told him, Judy thought, watching him. So he will come here because he will think it's still the wedding. She instantly forgot the Sandwich Isles in the excitement of this present salvation.

She sat down quickly beside the big tavern table and buried her face on her arms and waited. When she heard the door open, when she felt the bluster of the wind against her, she did not move. She waited for his voice.

"*Judy!*" he whispered.

Then she lifted her head. Her lips were red and trembling and her eye-lashes were wet. She had never looked so beautiful and so piteous.

"What on earth—why, what's—"

"There's no wedding," she faltered. "I'm not being married, after all. It's a funeral instead. Jonathan's mother came home and she died. There's a baby."

She turned her quivering face up to him, seeming not to think of him or to care who he was, but only to be full of her own trouble. "I was just—going to the funeral. And then it came over me that this was the very moment when if things had gone right, we'd have been standing up together—so I couldn't go—"

Evan was dazed. "Why, I rushed back—for Jonathan's sake—" He breathed out the words. He glanced about the empty room. "Where's— I suppose everybody's at the—the funeral."

She nodded and drew a little lace handkerchief from her muff and put it to her lips. Evan sat down on the long bench but not quite near her.

"But—you'll be married very soon, Judy."

"How?" she asked. "There's nowhere to live. The house is full of the children—and there's the baby. I don't know how to take care of new babies. Besides, Jonathan—he can't marry anybody. He oughtn't to—he hasn't a home to offer."

"You mean—you wouldn't marry him anyway now?" he was breathing in great sighs. "Is that what you mean, Judy?"

"How can I?" she replied in the gentlest voice. "There is no place for me."

"That—could be remedied." His lips were suddenly too stiff to speak. "If you—"

"Evan—oh, don't think me wicked," she said quickly, "but how did I know? The last few days have shown me—I don't love him. I couldn't have married him. God saved me, Evan. I might have gone on and been so unhappy. Now I'm saved."

He was leaning toward her, searching her face, drinking up her words. His black eyes were terrible in their burning blaze upon her, but she did not shrink from them. She wanted to throw herself into that blaze, to be taken with it, to be consumed. She flung back her head and stood up. And he leaped to his feet and snatched her into his arms and kissed her upon the lips again and again, and she who had so often turned cool under men's kisses was warm now. He's loved me all the time he was hating me, she thought with triumph. Never had a man been rude to her as Evan had been, nor flouted her so openly, and it was because he loved her like this. And yet as he kissed her he was groaning and frowning and she could see his face dark above hers, and she could hear him muttering, but not to her.

And all the time he kept kissing her, and she clung to him until at last she was exhausted and faint truly enough now, so that he had to hold her to keep her from falling at his feet.

"We can't help it," he groaned. "But who'll tell him?"

He put her down on the seat and wiped his lips again and again with his handkerchief, and she leaned her head against his thighs, as he stood beside her, and she shivered with chill and ecstasy and fear. Who would tell Jonathan, indeed? Who could save them now, save her and Evan together? She looked at him in real fright.

"Let's run away," she whispered.

"In this storm?"

"Is it too bad? You came through it."

"Yes, but—because I had to see you once more before you were—lost to me."

"Is that why you came?"

"Yes."

"Evan, have you loved me always?"

"Yes, ever since I first saw you."

"I loved you, too," she said simply.

It seemed to her now that she had so loved him. At least she had looked at him that day and had known that he was a man she could love. She divided all men into those she could love and those she could never love, and now she knew that Jonathan belonged to those she could not. Oh, she had been saved again! She felt suddenly strong and happy and good, and she stood up.

"Let's go. I'm not afraid. Evan, we could go now, and no one would ever know you had come back. They will just find me gone. And I'll write

Jonathan from Topeka that I've changed my mind. And then later, we can just—tell him we're married. You see, you wouldn't even lose him, that way. He couldn't blame you if, after I changed my mind, I married you."

She was so pretty, wooing him with her eyes and her voice, with her fingers on his cheeks and his eyelids and lips, and he was sure that she should not marry Jonathan. That, at least, he had always been sure of—

"You'd make him miserable," he muttered.

"I know I would," she said with her smile most gay, most coaxing. "You've really saved him from me."

He laughed grimly. "At my own cost, probably!"

"Ah, but I'll make you terribly happy!"

His head swam, and his blood burned. She was the sort he wanted, the opposite of his mother and his sisters, this earthy, passionate, sooty-eyed woman, with her cool ways and her skin as pale as cream, and her lovely soft voice, and that promise of heat within her which showed in the very way she walked across a room and in the most casual look from her eyes.

"And if Jonathan ever knows," she said in that sweet deep voice, "he's so good, he'd understand."

Yes, he could see Jonathan, could hear him almost. "Of course if he ever knew, he'd want this," he agreed. "But as you say, he needn't know."

"Never!" she whispered.

And without more words, his arms about her, they hurried out of the tavern, and she waited while he harnessed his horses to face the storm again.

27

MRS. DREAR went back with Jonathan to make sure that the baby was all right. Sue was nursing it and she had a slight start at the sight of that small pale child at the dark breast. But she controlled herself. All sorts of things happened, and one took them. But Sue, feeling that surprise upon the quick of her flesh, threw an end of her shawl over her breast.

" 'Twon't be long I has to do this," she said, her speech always the mixture of slave and master pronunciation. "I'm weanin' her a'ready on cornstarch and water and cow's milk. She's right smart at suckin' on a rag out of a bottle. I got one of them flat whisky bottles and washed it clean."

"You're doin' a good job, I can see," Mrs. Drear said politely.

Jonathan had gone straight into the bedroom, and now he came back in his old clothes, Maggie clinging to his hand.

For all the world like a widower, Mrs. Drear thought, pitying him. She thought of Judy, and her big nose itched as it always did when she was irritated, and she rubbed it. The minute she got home she would get after Judy hard.

"Do you have enough vittles, Jonathan?" she asked.

"Yes, thanks," Jonathan said. He could not mention Judy's name, so deep was his hurt that she had not come to see his mother buried. But as soon as the children were fed he would go to the hotel.

"I'll bring you a loaf of bread tomorrow," Mrs. Drear said.

"Thank you," Jonathan replied.

She looked around on the family. Ruth was taking off her coat. It was her mother's old one, and she bit her lips and turned away to hide her tears. Jamie stood by the fire, warming his hands.

"Nothin' else?" Mrs. Drear asked.

"I reckon we can manage," Jonathan replied. He tried to smile and found it too difficult. "I may be up along a little later," he said.

"Do," Mrs. Drear answered heartily. "It'll be good for you."

She left them then and plodded her way through the heightening wind and snow. A smaller woman might have been swept from the boardwalk, but she had fought her way through too many blizzards to feed beasts and to care for sick human beings. She knew how to draw her shawl across her face and make a shelter for breathing and how not to shrink from the wind but to breast it. Nevertheless the hot liquorish smell of the warm hotel had never seemed more welcoming than now as she stepped into it.

"Pour me out a mug, Henry," she gasped. Her head swam with the warmth after the biting cold. A few men of Median were in the room—Lew and Adam Cobb, Bill White and Samuel Hasty, and two newcomers this year who, though not in Median properly, had the nearest farms. She knew them all and paid no attention to them.

"Where's Judy?" she asked truculently.

"Ain't seen her, hide nor hair," Henry replied.

Mrs. Drear marched toward Judy's room. "I'm goin' to tell 'er what I think of her for not comin' to the funeral," she cried loudly. Let her hear, she thought. She threw open the door of Judy's little room and glanced about it. Somehow Judy had managed to make it the only pretty room in the house. All her small belongings were there, the lace-edged bureau cover, the embroidered cloth on the table, cushions in the one old rocking chair, pillow covers and a spread over the bed, and ruffled curtains across the windows. They were the things she carried with her everywhere to transform, as far as she was able, the dreariness she found inevitably about her.

"Where's the girl hidin' herself?" Mrs. Drear shouted. Her black bonnet fell away as she hurried to look in the wardrobe. There hung Judy's scant store of dresses, all clean, all neat. "She ain't took nothin', so she must be around," she muttered. She turned to the men gaping at the door. "You reckon she could ha' got lost just goin' to the funeral?" she asked aghast.

"Looks that-a-way," Lew said slowly.

"Then git out, every man alive of you," she shouted. "This hyere'll about finish Jonathan." She paused. "But I reckon he'll have to be told. Henry, you go and do the tellin'," she said.

The search for Judy upon the plains Jonathan led with such fierce vigor that never afterward did the people of Median think of him as a medium-sized fellow with quiet ways and a gentle voice. He was a flame scorching them with his anger, a general driving them beyond their duty, a giant of endurance and anger.

"No, we'll not rest," he shouted at midnight when they staggered back to the hotel. His eyes burned at the bottom of their sockets, his lips were cracked and his face gray with cold. His pale hair was stiff with a fringe of ice under his cap. He drank off a cupful of whisky neat. "Shame on us, great men, if we can't stand the blizzard a delicate girl is lost in!"

Jamie, who had been about to speak, did not. He had taken his full part with the men and could go on again as soon as he was warm, though it seemed waste to keep looking. Mrs. Drear in her purple flannel wrapper and her braid screwed on her head brewed them coffee in grim silence and watched them go out again. Then she crawled between the gray blankets of her bed and lay waiting.

I can't think that Judy is in any real hardship, she thought. I can't think she'd get to any place of sufferin' without savin' herself before she reached it.

She half-expected Judy to walk in, her garments arranged as neatly as ever. But she did not. Long after the dull sunrise the men came back exhausted. She woke from a doze and climbed out of her bed, screwing her braid up again, and pinned an old black skirt over her nightgown.

"Any luck?" she asked Henry.

"Nope."

"I'll bet she ain't dead," she retorted.

He gave her a slow wink with a half-frozen eyelid. "I ain't bettin' against you," he said. The little icicles in his long moustache clinked in minute music.

"But Jonathan'll take it like sure death," Mrs. Drear groaned.

"He does a'ready," Henry replied.

In the sod house it was so still, so warm, that for a wild moment Jonathan thought, She's here! She had come, perhaps, and made this warmth for him. There was the smell of bacon frying and of boiling coffee.

"Sit down, Jamie," he ordered his brother. "You're beat out."

"No, I ain't," Jamie gasped. But he sat down. He'd have said he was stronger than Jonathan any day, but Jonathan had stood the night better than any of them. Thin-lipped, white-faced, he still moved with energy, and his pale eyes burned.

"I'll eat and go out again," he said.

"You're foolish," Jamie retorted. "It's comin' on heavier."

It was, and Jonathan knew it. But nothing could have kept him here while he thought of Judy, struggling through the storm. She must have been blown out of her way like a little ship at sea, he thought, groaning to himself. Great men were sometimes blown across the prairie miles out of their way.

"You ain't goin' out again, Jonathan Goodliffe!"

He jumped at the unexpected voice. Someone came out of the bedroom. It was Katie, the baby in her arms, and he faltered in his surprise.

"Katie! Why, it's—it's terrible good of you to be here."

"No, it ain't," she said in the prim childish voice with which she had so often contradicted him though now it came oddly from her new height. "I thought to myself that I brung the twins through when they was newborn and I cud be of use here, helpin' Ruth. Ma can spare me now, ours are so big."

She handled the child with brisk certainty which gave it content. It lay with its small face against her flat young breast, and looked at her and yawned. Jonathan had scarcely seen this child.

"How is she?" he asked.

"She's as good as gold," Katie said heartily. Her plain brown face grew soft. "She sucks the sugar rag wonderful. You needn't worry a mite."

"I don't," he said bluntly. "I can't."

She did not answer this. But when Ruth came in at this moment with Maggie washed and dressed and her red hair in round tight curls, she gave her the baby and busied herself with breakfast. Jonathan ate, not wanting to talk further. Food choked him, and yet he knew he must have it. He tried not to hear the wind rising in howls about the house or to see the darkness growing blacker against the windows. The sun had risen but the day was not lighter for it. He would go, but he would not ask it of Jamie. When he had eaten the food Katie had set before him, he rose and put his hand on the block that barred the door. Only then did Katie speak. She called to him sharply from the stove.

"If you don't come back, what's to be done with the children?"

He had never thought of not coming back. If she had begged him not to go he would have pushed her aside, insisting on his sure return. But when she put the question thus baldly to his responsibility he stopped short. He might not come back, and then what would happen to these children, to Ruth and Maggie and little newborn Mary?

He flung open the door to test the storm before he answered and was blown across the room. They rushed together, he and Jamie and Katie, through a sheet of icy snow and forced it shut again and pushed the bar. And this he knew was the answer. He went headlong into the bedroom and flung himself upon the bed, and to the bitterest of death he gave up Judy.

Judy, in a little sod house less than twenty miles from Topeka, was sitting at breakfast with Evan and the owner of the house. She had slept fairly well upon a hay mattress in the bunk while Evan and Joe slept in blankets on the floor. The horses were in shelter on the leeward side of the house.

"Travelin' to Topeka, be ya?" Joe inquired.

"We are," Evan said.

He glanced at Judy's left hand. From somewhere, to his wonder, she had produced a plain gold wedding ring, and it was now upon her hand. Did she keep wedding rings ready for such need? He asked himself the question sarcastically and saw with unwilling eyes and a sullenly stirring heart how fresh she looked, and how neat, though she had slept in her clothes. He had been sleepless. Once when the fire flared after fresh fuel, he had gone to look at her in the bunk. She was sleeping in such sweet silence as he had never seen upon a human being. It was impossible to believe ill of her, his love told his reason.

"You live in Topeka?" Joe asked. He was hungry for talk but he had to screw talk out of these two, he thought.

"Yes," Judy said. She had cooked the breakfast and made saleratus biscuit. Joe took his fifth.

"Shore is good to have home cookin' again," he said. "I don't wish you folks bad luck about the storm, but let 'er rip, says I!" He smiled through a snap of teeth at Judy, and she smiled back.

"I'll make an Indian pudden for dinner," she said sweetly.

"It's pyore luck the storm blew you my way, ma'am," Joe said.

But she was not quite saved, she thought. Everything depended on how she held Evan in this storm. If her sure instinct failed, if she could not conquer his remorse—no, fight it at its very root—he could leave her yet for Jonathan's sake. His love for Jonathan was stronger at bottom than what he felt for her. She saw it this morning in the coolness of his hand and the aversion of his eyes, and she accepted it without jealousy, though with wonder. What had Jonathan in him to make a man like Evan love him so well?

She busied herself in small slight ways all day in the wretched sod house, always shy and quiet, saying almost nothing to Evan, but looking at him often with large eyes that weighed him, he thought, feeling them upon him, in some secret judgment of her own. His pride was pricked.

"Not sorry, are you?" he asked when in the afternoon Joe fell asleep.

She gave him her wordless lovely smile and crept against his breast and waited. When she felt his heart begin to beat harder under her cheek, she took courage. She was going to be all right.

"I have no one in the world," she murmured. "I am all alone, except for you."

"No going back?" he asked.

"I can't," she whispered. She tightened her arms about him and lifted her face. "Even if you should die, or if you should leave me—I'd never go back."

"Why?"

"'Twould be wrong. I know it now."

He bent to lay his cheek upon her soft bright hair, and she put her hand to his lips. It was then he felt the ring.

"Where did you get that ring just when we needed it most?"

"It is my mother's. I wear it on a ribbon about my neck, ever since she died."

She was so right in all her ways, things came about so rightly for her that the belief in the inevitability of their love overwhelmed every other feeling in him again today as it had yesterday.

"You're sweet," he murmured, "you're perfect."

She smiled and swept her lashes downward and felt upon her lips his hot, strong kiss.

Now this will last, she thought. Anyway, until we're there.

28

IN HER own wry way, Jonathan thought heavily, Katie was perfect. At the end of the second day he knew he could not have lived out the storm without her. If he had been shut up in the sod house with Jamie, reminding him at every movement and word of Clyde, he would have come to quarrels with him. Maggie's incessant chatter, her meddling fingers and bustling ways, would have tried him sorely, for Ruth could do nothing with her, and besides Ruth was absorbed now in little Mary. And what would have made him most weary and angry together would have been the single sorrow of this family of his for their mother, a sorrow subdued in him to his loss of Judy. For that she was lost he was now convinced. Unless she happened upon the shelter of a farmhouse, she could never have outlived the storm. But he had visited every farmhouse near Median when they had searched for her, and beyond that she must have perished. True, other men hearing of her loss had pushed out beyond that, and there was the frailest of hope that when the storm had quieted, word would come in that she was found. But his native melancholy did not allow him to build upon this hope.

Through all his suffering and silence Katie moved serenely, managing everything well. She knew his trouble, but she did not once speak of it. It would have been intolerable had she spoken. But she spoke to him very little, and only of something she wanted done.

"Can you fetch in more chips, Jonathan? We mustn't let the fire down."

He felt his way around the corner of the house, grateful for the buffalo chips the half-breed children had piled there as pay for their winter's schooling. He disliked their ammoniac odor as they burned, and he seldom used them, but they burned and gave out warmth now, and he was glad he had not refused them as he had nearly done when the children brought them first. He had wanted to spare their feelings of being even poorer than the others. But Katie put the chips into the stove neatly with a bit of paper between her thumb and finger.

"They make a good heat for bakin'," she said.

Somehow she created order in the home and order in their sorrow, too. Her intensity in small activities, her very energy in cleaning and washing and cooking subdued the possibility of emotion; and Jonathan, engulfed in his tragedy, clung to this sharp and practical presence. Life had to go on, Katie made him feel. Eating and sleeping and washing and cooking and caring for children—they went on, though all else were lost. Slowly he began to take his share in the work while he waited for the storm to pass. And at last he was able to eat a little and to sleep fitfully and to plan in the night as he lay on a pallet before the fire that he would go out the first day that Henry Drear would let him have a horse and ask at every house upon the plains for news of Judy. And yet, he thought, perplexed, they would brings news in to Median, and would he miss it if he went? He might wait two days, he decided at last. That would give them time.

He steadied himself against that decision, and when the storm cleared he stuck to it though every bone in him ached for action. Then before the next day was over the first mail came in from Topeka. Jamie, gone to the hotel to ask for transportation westward, brought back a letter for him. Jonathan took it and saw upon it Judy's writing.

He stared at it and looked about for privacy. There was none anywhere in his house, and he went outside into the silent sunlit snow and, standing with his back against the wall, he tore open the envelope.

"Dear Jonathan:" The thin paper crackled in his trembling hands. "It is best to tell you straight out that I went away because I could not marry you. It came over me like that when I was ready to come to the funeral. So I took seat in a wagon that happened then to be going to Topeka. I will find some work here. Forgive me if you can, but whether or not you can, I know I am right, and it is kindest in the end to both. So I give you no address because I don't wish to be found. Judy."

He crushed the letter and held it in his hand and stood staring out over the endless snow. The sky was brilliantly blue, and the whiteness stabbed his eyes, but he felt nothing. He was beyond pain any more, having suffered to what he could endure. This was beyond.

She doesn't say why, he thought stupidly. But Judy never said why she did anything. And when in any letter she had ever written him had she told him anything? His mouth went dry, and he felt suddenly sick, as though his being must empty itself of everything. In the wrenching of his flesh he groaned and leaned his head against the house. Oh, if he need never enter that house again! If he could but walk on and on across that endlessness before him and in its final emptiness be lost!

But the door of his house opened, and Katie's voice flew out, "Jonathan! Dinner!" She thrust out her head and saw him. "What's the matter with you?" she cried. And he who had not wanted to mention his trouble to her, now felt that someone must know because he could not endure his loneliness otherwise. He put out his hand with the letter crushed into the palm, and she took it. He heard the faint crackling as he stared on into that blind white space, and there was silence while she read. Then he heard the sharp sound of paper torn to bits and felt his hand seized by her rough hand.

"You come right in and get your food while it's hot," she said.

Between Jonathan and Katie there was now this secret of his broken love. Neither spoke of it, but it was in each of them, though not by any jot of change in Katie could Jonathan discern it in her. Every change was in himself. He was so bottomlessly lost in the emptiness in himself that all he did was useless, and he never stopped working from his waking at daylight to his sleep when sick fatigue compelled him to it. He brimmed every moment, grateful to school children; grateful to little Mary, who must be fed and cleaned and put to sleep; grateful to Maggie, meddling everywhere at once. He managed somehow all this life under one roof, though how he would have managed it if Katie had not come morning and night to keep all straight was a thing he thought about. For Ruth was not good at doing several things together. With the tenderest heart and the softest ways and a will always sweet and ready to lend itself to another's, she seemed never to have anything finished. Work as she did, she would still by noon have not one full task ended—the dinner stewing, but half the morning dishes not washed; the floor swept but a bed not made; Maggie fed, but her red mane of curls not brushed and her face unwashed. Yet Katie in an hour of energy could have the home docile and all of them cleaned and fed.

It was injustice to her goodness that, with knowledge of all she did, no one was grateful to her. But she could at the same time do a kindness with her hands and snatch it away with her tongue. A strange thing in women, Jonathan thought sorrowfully, that Judy who did nothing for anybody and who had wounded him for life he would love and long for because of her lovely looks and her sweet voice and her gentle ways. And though Katie was better than Judy, he was on certain days in agony until she was gone, though she was so kind always to him. He felt every edge in her voice and saw every abruptness of her thin sharply shaped frame.

"Ruth, why don't you do like I told you and save the scraps of fat for soap? Waste not, want not."

"Maggie, you're a bad girl. Don't poke the baby's eye."

"Jamie, there's plenty to do around here for everybody without you sittin' waitin' to go West. Hurry yourself and go out and hunt chips if nothin' else. I do despise laziness!"

When at last the roads opened enough for a horse to go through, she made no pretense at not being thankful to have Jamie gone. She disliked his carelessness and hearty appetite and the dirty feet he always forgot to wipe.

And yet she could not leave Jonathan alone either. If she stayed to share the midday meal she often cooked, she was at Jonathan to eat when he could scarcely swallow. His wish for food had left him, and yet she made him eat.

"Now, Jonathan, you ain't goin' to sit there spurnin' good food. You eat that good boiled meat. Take a real slice of it. Here, I'll fix your plate for you."

His stomach, always too delicate for food when his mind was desponding, turned against the great plate she set before him, the slabs of yellow corn bread, the heaped potatoes and salt pork. He said once, "I could eat some of Mother's scones if she was here to make them," and Katie said, meaning only kindness, "Well, she ain't, and I'm sorry to say it but you'll just have to eat what you got!"

He must eat what he had. The words took on a sad symbolism in these days when he made symbols out of everything as he tried to know what he should do.

Should he not go to Topeka and look for Judy? But how, except to search from house to house? And who would teach school and who tend this house? And then he thought how Judy herself had cut him off.

Days passed and Evan did not come back to Median. Another blizzard came and went, bringing six days when he had no school and two days when Katie even could not come and he fed the baby on thinned gruel for milk. It was a bitter winter for blizzards, and Jonathan blamed them when Evan delayed. At first he was glad that Evan was not there to prove himself right about Judy. Then he came to longing for Evan's comfort and his friendship and his talk. He could always forget everything in the talk he and Evan had together, and there was not another in Median who had such thoughts as he and Evan had. If Evan came I'd tell him everything and feel better, he thought.

But Evan did not come. February ended with a handful of mild days before March burst in, and then something began to trickle back to Median about Evan and Judy. A distant farmer, George Lacey, had gone to the city to set right a boundary to his land that the railroad had cut off, and the lawyer for the railroad was Evan. He went in the company offices but found it was late and the lawyer wasn't there, so he got his address and went to his house. "It was a good brick house, square, and set back from the street, and his wife opened it, a soft-spoken woman she was, all dressed up like a lady," George said, around the stove at the store.

"Why, Evan ain't married!" Lew roared.

"He shore is," George Lacey said.

"Why, why in heck didn't he tell us?"

"Don't know," George Lacey said. "I didn't know him well—just saw him here maybe once or twice."

"Did you hear her name?" Lew asked. He was weighing a slice of store cheese, and his eyes were on the scales.

"He called her Judy or Julie, or suthin'," George Lacey said. The cheese was his, and he picked off a piece and ate it.

"Judy!" Lew whispered. "Did she have big black eyes?"

"Yep—I noticed 'em. Why, you know her?"

"Mebbe." Lew's mouth shut into a downward line between his flat, unshaven cheeks.

He took the news in to dinner with him. Katie was home that day. Though she could not have let Jonathan know it, he had hurt her in the morning by a chance gruffness. She had said, "Don't let them school children traipse in here with their feet all mud, Jonathan. There's no sense to it. I've tied some straw together for 'em to rub their shoes on."

And he, who seldom spoke at all, had answered quickly, "I have enough to teach their heads without bothering about their feet."

"You don't scrub after 'em—" she began, but he had not let her go on.

"Give over, Katie, do. There's things I care more for than scrubbin' and cleanin'."

So she had untied her apron and gone home then and there and, though he had shouted after her to come back, she had not come back.

"I've heard somethin' damned queer," Lew said slowly to his wife at dinner, staring at nothing while he chewed.

"Mr. Merridy, I wish you wouldn't swear before the children," Mrs. Merridy said.

"This is just plain cussedness I can't help swearin' about," Lew said. He looked at his wife solemnly. "Evan and Judy're married."

Mrs. Merridy choked on her tea. "They're never, Lew Merridy!"

"Shore as I'm born they are," Lew said. "And if Evan ever shows his face in Median again, I'll take a shotgun to him."

Katie said not a word. Into her freckled face there crept a deep color. She stopped eating and put her hands tightly clasped in her lap.

"Who's gonna tell Jonathan?" she asked.

"I dunno," Lew said. "It's plumb awful, that's what it is. Why'nt you tell him, Katie? You're there most every day."

"I couldn't—" Katie said, her throat tight.

"I'll go and see Drear," Lew said.

He lumbered over to the tavern after his dinner, and in an hour all Median knew except Jonathan and nobody wanted to tell him, and then

Jonathan himself came in, as he often did on a late Saturday afternoon, merely to see men's faces and sit and drink a little with them, and he made the excuse of a loaf of Mrs. Drear's salt-rising bread.

When he came into the room tonight silence fell upon the half-dozen men as though he were a stranger. Then they were too quick to greet him and their voices too hearty. And then Mrs. Drear put her head out of the kitchen to see who it was. Her face grew stern.

"You, Jonathan, come here," she said.

He went into the kitchen, and she shut the door. "Sit down," she said. "Now listen. You've got to know somethin'. It's terrible—"

"Nothing's happened to Jamie, has it?"

"No, it's what's happened to you. Judy's married Evan."

Her face before his eyes swam and receded, was lost and appeared again.

"Evan!" he whispered.

"Here—you drink this." She put her own cup of beer before him. But he did not see it.

"But—but—Evan—hated her," he gasped. "At least, no one could hate her but—but—"

"That's it, I guess he didn't," she said. "Now, Jonathan, you take it like a man. There's other girls as good and much better. It's a pity you had to see Judy first. Every man's got to see one woman first, and he thinks that's all there is. And they all see somebody like Judy. Look at my Henry. What does he do but fall in love with a low-down girl from the East on her way to Californy and she stays here and swears Jennet was his, and then runs off and leaves him with a month-old baby. Where'd he be if I hadn't took pity on him and answered his advertisement for a good cook and took care of the motherless child and married him and give him a home?" Her face quivered. "But do you think he's forgotten how that slut looked? No, he'll say, 'Jennet's pretty, like her maw.' He'll say it till he dies."

Jonathan listened and heard nothing. Nothing that had ever happened had anything to do with him. He rose to his feet, his eyes on the ground.

"Thanks," he said vaguely, and then walked to the door, and through the silence in the other room he went outside. He stood hesitating, longing to be gone anywhere into the world so that he was not here. But ahead of him and around him the prairie lay purple under a purple sky. In the west there was still a glow, but so dull that it did not dim the sharp stars. There was nowhere to go. The prairie cut him off like an ocean. He had only his house, and after a moment he buttoned his coat and pulled down his hat and went the road he knew the best.

At the door of his house he met Katie. When she saw him enter the hotel, she had put her mother's old red shawl over her head and run down the boardwalk to his house. She did not want to meet him, nor have him see her; but she could make sure, while he was gone, that everything was right in the house and his supper cooked. As she ran through the store she took up a tin can of fruit, peaches from the East, and planned how she would open them into a bowl for a dessert. She worked in furious silence to tidy the rooms for his coming and fed the baby and put her into her box and then washed Maggie after her supper and put her to bed, and last she mended the fire and took a moment to whisper furiously to Ruth, "You do like I said about them peaches—don't tell 'im I brung them, but say they're from my pop."

"All right, Katie," Ruth said, bewildered.

All this had made her late, and so she met Jonathan at the door when she opened it. He looked down at her face, shadowy under the red shawl. In the twilight he could scarcely see her features. But he could feel her sturdy presence, and he knew her goodness.

"You've been in to clear me up again, eh, Katie?" he said somberly. His hands were in his pockets and his collar turned up, but the wind blew bitter over the plains.

"Nothin' much," she said, her lips dry.

"Yes, it is much," he said suddenly. "It's very much. It's more than anyone in the world would do for me." He took his hands out of his pockets and put them on her thin, sloping shoulders. "So I ask you, Katie —will you be my wife?"

She stood under his hands for one brief moment, her breath so tight it caught in her lungs. Then she gasped and ducked and went running up the walk in the darkness and left him with neither yes nor no. And he stood looking after her.

Why not? he thought heavily. It doesn't matter now.

He went into his house and ate his food and knew where the peaches came from without asking. He was very gentle to Ruth and wiped the dishes for her, and then he said, "Would you mind if I left you a bit, Ruth?"

"No, not if it's not long," she said.

"It won't be long," he said gravely.

He lit his lantern and through the darkness plodded back to Lew's store and opened the door. It was Saturday night, and Median men were still there. Lew was behind the counter near the cracker barrel, but he came out and Jonathan drew him outside the door.

"Is Katie at home?" he asked.

"She's gone to bed," Lew said. "Came in a while back and said she felt bad."

"Then I won't disturb her, Lew. I must tell you—I asked her to be my wife."

"Katie?" Lew's thick jaw dropped. "See here, Jonathan, don't you go on a *re*bound. It'll shore be a mistake—"

"No—no," Jonathan broke in, "it's not that. You tell her, Lew, that I told you, and tell her I'll come tomorrow for her answer, and I hope with—with—all my heart, tell her, that she'll have me."

He bolted into the darkness and left Lew standing there. He was glad he had not seen her. It would give him time. There was all night ahead.

He spent a long evening with Ruth. It was unexpectedly quiet and good, in spite of the pain in his breast. That pain was for something over and ended. Pain might never end, but he was going on with life, whatever it was.

He mended the fire and drew the curtains his mother had made. No one drew curtains in Median, but tonight he wanted to shut out the prairie and shut himself in with these three of his own flesh and blood. He put fresh fuel into the tin stove and sat down in a rocking chair which Katie had brought one day for them to sit in and rock the baby. Though many houses in Median had rocking chairs, he had felt them foolish furniture.

"I can't sit swinging my legs like I was on a fence," he had always said.

This chair had a woven reed bottom, and Katie had put an old blue gingham cushion on it, and now it felt easy under him. He sat in it, swinging gently, and after a while he talked with Ruth as he had not talked since their mother died, asking her questions of those months when his mother had been away from him and piecing together the bits of her life that Ruth thought to tell. When he had gone to bed, for the first time in nights past he felt he could sleep. He had reached some sort of bottom to suffering. Nothing worse can happen to me, he thought. From now on it must be up.

He thought quietly of Katie and of how he would speak to her tomorrow, and then he was too drowsy to plan. It'll come natural between us, somehow, he thought without excitement.

After long sleep he woke, and after a moment's wild agony he remembered. He rose and washed himself and put on his second-best suit and then, happening to put his hand to his cheek, stayed to shave himself. My cheek'll feel as rough to Katie, he thought.

Without hurrying he ate and tidied up after himself, for Maggie had Ruth up long before; and then he put on his hat and walked slowly up the boardwalk. It was a forward day for March, and more like April. The air was clear with sun, though under the boards the mud was bottomless with melting snow. But he kept himself clean of it and went straight into the store and knocked on the door of Lew's house behind it.

Lew himself opened the door. He looked solemn. "Come in, Jonathan," he said and coughed behind his hand. "Lula, here's Jonathan."

Mrs. Merridy was sitting on the sofa in her best black dress. "Howdy, Jonathan, come in," she said.

They shook hands with him as though he were a stranger, and he felt strange and put an end to it.

"Is Katie here?" he asked simply.

"She's in the parlor," Lew said gently.

He went into the parlor, where he had never sat down in his life. It was the only parlor in Median, and there had been no occasion since his coming grand enough for its use. But Katie was sitting there now on the horsehair sofa, her hands clasped in the lap of her brown poplin dress. She looked at him wretchedly, two bright red spots in her cheeks; and, though she had brushed her brown hair smoothly into the coil upon her head and put a narrow collar of white lace at her throat, she looked as she always had. She was one of those women who, no matter what they wear, always look the same. The thought grazed his mind, and he let it pass. It did not matter. He sat down beside her and took one of her hands. It felt stiff and unwilling, but her fingers quivered when they touched his.

"Have you made up your mind, Katie?" he asked.

She nodded, and he saw that her face was white.

"I hope it's yes," he said.

She nodded again, her mouth too dry for speech.

He hesitated and in his bosom felt his heart give one last turn of agony. But that was all. In the deepest silence he leaned and kissed her cheek, and they sat a moment hand in hand. Then he said gently, "Shall we go and tell your folks?"

She rose at once and with her hand still in his he led her out.

"It's settled," he said to Lew and Mrs. Merridy.

They stood up and put out their hands to him, and he shook them, one after the other, and then they all sat down and Lew cleared his throat.

"Now that's over," he said, "and I—"

But Mrs. Merridy broke in sharply, "Katie, go and see what's burning. I declare, if I forgot to add water to the stew—"

Katie suddenly looked herself. "Oh, *Maw!*" she cried, and rushed out of the room.

But in the night, that second night, he woke to scarify himself. What had he done so quickly? He had rushed to his own crucifixion, without waiting to find even if it were necessary. He should have gone to Topeka and seen for himself whether the thing were true or not. He had not even asked Lew how the news had come. He should have found Evan and asked him if Judy was his wife. He lay writhing at what he had done to himself. It was too late. Was it not too late? If Judy was still free, if he could prevail upon her and bring her back to him—in the still night any madness seemed possible. But he could never bring her to Median. Median would stand by the Merridys and spew him out.

He thought on, sleep far from him. And the more he thought, the more inevitable it seemed to him that Evan and Judy were together. Their seeming hate was clear to him. They were trying not to call it love, he thought. In a small way, but the same, he had once hated Jennet like that.

Anyway, I'll write, he thought grimly. He sent a letter to Evan that day.

"Evan, where is Judy? Jonathan."

This was all he wanted of Evan.

In the time it took any letter to come and go, Evan's letter came back, many lines, written and crossed, in that fluent and familiar script.

"You must know, dear old Jon, that I did not take her until she had decided that she had made a mistake. I found her ready to run away— she insists that had she never seen me the results would have been the same so far as you are concerned— Believe me always unchanged—and eager to give you any help. Would you like a position in the high school here at a good salary? I might be able to secure it for you—"

He read the letter and put it in the stove and went out to find Stephen Parry.

"When are you going to finish my schoolhouse?" he demanded. "Winter's nearly over, and I want to begin everything new this spring."

"I'll git mahself right to work," Stephen promised.

29

JUDY was in her new home. It was a handsome house, spread to look its best in a lawn unusually wide, though not much deeper than the house as it stood back from the street. Four cottonwoods and two elms gave shade and dignity, and there was a carriage block. In the afternoons the colored man she had hired drove the carriage up to this block, and she stepped in, her small ruffled parasol open over her head, and drove down the street to Evan's office to wait for him at the curb. She had not usually to wait long. He came out briskly, very debonair in a frock coat, tall hat, and a striped gray waistcoat and trousers, and took his place beside her. Together they drove up the street, which was not yet paved, though it had sidewalks and small new elm trees.

At such times Judy's eyes were dewy with happiness. She was lovelier than ever to look at, lovely to be in love with, Evan thought to himself. He could not possibly have married a plain woman. Most—indeed, very nearly all—of the time he was delighted with Judy, proud of her beauty and prouder even of her quick instinct for rightness in any company. In a public place she was easily the prettiest woman, but she was more. She was the most quiet, and the other women were not usually quiet, and she was the most graceful among women who were framed to angles or heaviness.

When they were alone together in their new home, the fine details of which had cost him more than he cared to think about, she was no less lovely, no less perfect. Night or day she was amiable, passionate when he demanded passion and delicate when he did not.

He planned his first visit to his mother's home with no terrors. Judy, who could abandon her body to him without scruple, could in the presence of other women be as virgin as a young girl. He took her to New Orleans in May and bought her summer dresses that billowed about her little waist and great drooping hats under which her eyes were like dark pansies.

"Very nice," Mrs. Bayne said, surveying her. "I didn't think they could do as well in Kansas, Evan. Judy, your skin is good as Laura's."

Judy laughed her fresh low laughter. "I wasn't raised in Kansas," she said.

"Where?" Mrs. Bayne demanded.

"Nowhere in particular," she said demurely. She made no pretense of her family, although she never spoke now of Joel. Had he not left her?

And Evan never admired her with more reason than he did in his mother's home. If she was not a lady, she played herself one so well that to the world there was no difference. There was mirth mingled with his admiration when he drew her behind the big cape jessamine bush in his mother's front yard, and when he kissed her there was still excitement in it. It was as exciting as though he stole the kisses when he placed the flowers between her round breasts.

But sometimes, in the night, in their own house, when she joined so cheerfully in his passion, he remembered how coolly she had put Jonathan away, how easily come to him. He loved her body and would have loved her wholly as well, if he could have forgotten altogether that she had betrayed his friend. But he could not always forget, and under their life together there stayed alive the thin and secret nerve that quivered with distrust of her.

But of this Judy knew nothing. She lay in his arms in the pleasant emptiness which was her happiness. Ahead of her the days stretched full of delight. Small changes in her furniture, flowers to be arranged in a new vase, lace to sew into her wine-red taffeta dress, the direction of the black woman Evan had hired for the housework—all were things to be done with joy and without responsibility.

"I wish Mama could see me now," she said suddenly to Evan.

"Not quite now!" he said teasingly. He tousled her curling hair loose upon his pillow, and when she laughed he gathered her into his arms in fierce delight. She had the trick of making herself so soft, so yielding when he did this, that even her bones melted. He felt only softness and clinging, and he smelled her faint perfume. Oh, she was good enough for him, he thought, or very nearly, having already asked himself the question and in one way and another answered it.

He found Jonathan's letter on his desk at the offices of the Santa Fe railroad company the next day. He had made the desk a permanent part of those offices because of his brilliant defense of the railroad's right to cross a man's land. "Progress, the right of the nation over the privilege of an individual." These were words he had dwelt upon ardently. Besides, was not the whole West open? A man could always move on if he was dissatisfied.

He walked gaily through the sunshine of the morning, twirling his cane and thinking of how Judy had looked in a cream-colored lace peignoir as she sat behind the silver coffee service that had been his mother's wedding present. In such a mood he had not been disturbed by Jonathan's letter for more than the moment it took him to read it. And the moment after he was thinking, half-pityingly and with not too much remorse to bear, of what he could do for him—a job, perhaps in the city school, and cash for pay instead of corn meal and buffalo chips and potatoes and black molasses. If Jonathan were here, he could help him in other ways, not to make amends, but to show him that a woman was not cause for change in friendship between men. There might be spice, even, he thought gaily, as years went by, in the memory that his best friend had once desperately loved his wife.

When Jonathan's reply came he shrugged and felt he had done all a man could do and had been refused.

Jonathan began the building of a new life that spring with zeal determined by his mind. What the heart had not, the head could supply. He told Katie, "We shan't be married until everything's the way we want it."

He told Lew, "I shall have everything for Katie the way I once planned it—for the other."

Lew, picking his teeth at the threshold of the store, threw him a look from under the bushy eyebrows that met over his big nose.

"That's only right, I reckon, and still I take it to be good of you."

"Katie deserves it more," Jonathan said.

"I reckon," Lew said peaceably. He ruminated a moment and then went on, "You don't have to say nothin' to me. You and Katie kin run your own show. A man's own marriage is all a man can tend to, and mine ain't done yet."

The Sunday dinners were begun again, and Jonathan and Katie sat in the parlor for a while, or if the day were fair they took a walk along the river. He talked a great deal at these times, his arm about her shoulder or her hand in his. He was always conscious until he fought it out of him of the difference between Katie's hand and Judy's. Judy's hand had curled into his with the angelic softness of a baby's hand, but Katie's was always stiff. He looked at it one day. "A good working hand," he said gently. "A useful, kind hand, always busy." He thought loyally that there was something here more firm than the pink and cream of that hand which he had once so passionately put to his lips. He never kissed Katie's hand and never would, perhaps.

But he talked to her as he had never talked to Judy. Judy had always put everything out of his head. With difficulty even had he thought of his school. He could only see how Judy's hair curled about her ears and how smoothly her throat shaped into her lovely bosom. But when he was with Katie, his mind built his plans and she, who always fell silent and shy at any hint of tenderness, replied quickly enough with good sense to all he planned.

The schoolhouse grew, paid for by bonds the townsfolk put out. There was not enough to pay for one of the newfangled basement stoves he had read of in a school magazine to which he subscribed. He wanted it sorely, for how would they keep a great two-story house warm otherwise? He had a little money in the Farmer's Bank in Topeka, saved to bring his mother home. But Katie would not let him use it.

"Once you begin usin' our money for the school, there'll be no end," she said, so definitely that he dared not disobey her.

He swallowed his pride and wrote to Evan, asking for a loan to buy the stove, he being willing to offer his own note for security. Evan replied at once with all his old gaiety. He was glad Jonathan had turned to him, though he had no money to lend. His own new house had cost him dear, and he had wanted Judy to have all she liked. But he could arrange a loan with the city bank, and he himself would give security.

Secretly he was glad to do this. He was in Jonathan's debt, and this put him out of it. "I want to help you in any way I can," he wrote Jonathan, and Jonathan wrote to thank him, making no mention either of Judy or of Katie. Thus the two were friends again, though very distantly.

By midsummer the school building stood finished, a square frame building on a brick foundation, two-storied and roofed with tin. Inside it were rooms with good windows, four rooms downstairs and four up. Jonathan kept the smallest near the door for his office. He had advertised for teachers in an eastern newspaper. A dozen letters reached him, and out of them he chose two, one a man and one a woman.

Without planning to delay his marriage, he did delay even when the schoolhouse was done. The sod house, he told Katie one Sunday, was too small and dark.

"When I come back out of my new office now, the sod house is like a cave," he said. "Besides, how will it hold us all, Katie? Ruth's a young woman nearly, and she and Maggie and little Mary should have a room for themselves. And we should have a sitting room anyway and a kitchen."

There was never any talk of not having the three children with them. Neither he nor Katie thought of living alone. The end of it was that he took out of the Farmer's Bank in Topeka the money he had there—and Katie was willing for this—and they bought from the township of Median a lot next to his school big enough for a small one-story frame house. He and Katie planned three bedrooms, a sitting room, a small kitchen, and a front porch.

"I'd like one of those newfangled rooms for bathing," he said. People in the East were beginning to have bathrooms, and in the catalogues that he had ordered for the school building he had seen pictures of heavy wooden bathtubs lined with metal and painted white.

"Whoever heard of such a thing!" Katie cried. "A whole room to wash in, when there's the kitchen, too? It's waste."

So he let it go for the present, having indeed all he could do to build the house. He helped to build it himself to save cost, and young Matthew Cobb worked with him and Stephen through long summer days and evenings. Matthew was nearly fifteen now, and as tall as he would ever be. He had settled into a plain-faced boy approaching young manhood, and he talked quietly of buying a farm somewhere not too far west when his earnings were enough. The boy's eye was true, and he could see a window frame into a wall without a slant. His fault was that all he did was done too carefully, so that in no day did he ever do all that he had set himself, and the knowledge that each day's work dragged upon the next made him always sober and anxious and pressed in mind; but that was scarcely a fault in a young man, Jonathan thought.

He came to know Matthew very well that summer while they put up the slender framework of the house and nailed the clapboards under the tin roof and lathed and plastered the inner walls. Lew told Katie to choose her wallpapers from his stock and, though what she chose were all too flowery for Jonathan's plain taste, he kept silence. He had a constant sense of some debt he owed her, as though he had done her an injustice, and more and more he let her have her way. Yet when he searched himself to find out what he did that was unjust, he could find nothing reasonable. He knew that no other man had asked to marry her. He knew that with him she was safe and that his kindness would not fail, and that her father and mother were grateful to him. It was on his wedding day, the last Monday in October before school opened, that he discovered why forever he would be in Katie's debt.

When he had dreamed of that other marriage, it was with impatience to have it done and over quickly and all guests gone and he and Judy alone forever. But now it was not that marriage, and he let Median have his wedding for its holiday. There was great talk about where it should be.

Mrs. Merridy cried out, "It's nothin' but proper that a girl should be married from her home."

But the parlor was small, and Jonathan insisted doggedly that all his pupils and their parents should come to his wedding. This, with what was left of Median, made the parlor a mere closet. His own little new home was no better. Besides, Katie would not have it there.

"I don't want to have a housecleanin' on my hands the first day after," she declared sensibly.

There remained the hotel, but it was crowded at this season with travelers westward and, besides, there were too many things to be remembered —his mother standing at the door with Artie in her arms, Jennet sitting at the table, her head upon her arms, and Judy the night she stood in the hollow of his arms—gazing at Evan, as he remembered now with the deep inward wrench that made him know pain was still alive.

Then he found the place himself, stepping into the empty sunlit schoolhouse one day in early September. Why not here? he thought, here, where my work is? There were no shadows in this house, no sadness. It was waiting for its life to begin. Let it begin, then, with him. The benches Stephen had made of pine boards shipped from the East smelled fresh and clean. By opening the doors between, the rooms were big enough. And they could make a pulpit where the desk stood. If it were too late in the year for traveling preachers, he would hire a minister from Topeka to come for that day.

He worked quietly at his desk until noon and then went home and on the way passed by to see what Katie thought. He found her in her mother's kitchen stirring cucumbers in boiling vinegar and sugar on the stove.

"We'll be married in the schoolhouse, eh, Katie?" he said.

She had on a gray gingham apron that covered her neck to floor, and her face was red with the stove's heat. She did not stop her stirring when he came in, nor when he spoke.

"That's a real good idea," she said.

Out of the passing flocks of travelers, Median caught twelve new families that year.

"It's the schoolhouse gets 'em," Henry said. "A woman with kids sees a school, and then heaven and hell and all her menfolk can't drawr her past."

He was cheerful because of a full house and the two teachers to board all winter, and for a long time had ceased to blame Jonathan that Median was not a cattle town. His hopes now were in the new railroad coming westward.

"Though we might find gas or oil like some of these-hyere places do," he rumbled through his beard. "A town's got to have somethin' besides a schoolhouse, Jonathan."

"Find it—find it," Jonathan said cheerfully. "School's my share to Median, and I'll stick to it."

There were already days when, ignoring moods, he thought his life solid and good. He grew anxious now to have his wedding over. When it was, a certain door would have closed behind him, and there would be no opening it. On the other side of it he and Katie would make their life. She loved work and so did he, and of work there was plenty.

He did little himself toward that wedding day. Women of Median went out into the prairies and gathered goldenrod and grasses, and Sue devised a silver-papered bell to hang over the desk made into a pulpit, and Katie baked her own wedding cake and cut and sewed a wedding gown, not of white, "for what else could I wear a white dress at?" she said. She chose a bright blue silk that Lew had in stock.

And Jonathan kept his eye out for traveling preachers and picked up by chance a small humpbacked man one day in the early fall, tramping westward with his clothes tied in a bundle. He was dressed in dusty black, and on his head was a wide black hat, and when he spoke he had a twist to his tongue that made Jonathan jump, it was so familiar.

"You're English!" he shouted to the man's good morning.

"Eh, what if I am?" the man had retorted.

He had been nailing a board to one of the trees in the square; and Jonathan, seeing it from his desk, had rushed out to stop him. The trees were growing, and he was touchy about them. He begged water for them in summer and shielded them in winter with brush he had the big boys cut from the river banks.

"What are you about?" he had shouted from the schoolhouse door.

"My Father's business," the little man cried back, and Jonathan saw the board. It was smoothed and clean and on it were painted in bold black letters, "Ye must be born again."

"Did you come all the way from England for this?" he asked, smiling.

"I did," the man said. He had a strange, grim little weazened face. "God sent me," he said.

"We're not heathen here," Jonathan said.

"Not only heathens are sinners," the man said.

"Are you a regular minister?" Jonathan inquired.

"Methodist, by God's grace," the man said fervently.   .

Jonathan laid hold of his crooked left arm. "Then I reckon God did send you," he said. "Will you stay and marry me to my young woman?"

"If it's God's will," the man said calmly. With no ado, he dropped to his knees before Jonathan's legs and, screwing up his eyes and moving his lips, he prayed silently for a minute or two and then rose and dusted off his knees. "God says, do as you like this time, Paul Higgins. So I'll stay and get rested up a bit. I'm fagged with walking. 'Tain't every day I get a ride, and I've mostly walked from Indiana."

"Paul Higgins, eh?" Jonathan said. He was quietly astonished at this small gnarled man who now chattered freely as though God had given him permission.

"Christened Saul by my parents in England, but I was converted ten years ago and changed to Paul. Ten years I been nailing God's words to trees all over this country. 'Twas on a tree Christ died, I figger, and to trees men must look for their salvation. Though here I travel days on end and never see a tree. Today I saw these trees stickin' up miles off, and so I made for 'em. 'Ye must be born again' 's my favorite, but I have others too."

He drew out of a sack other texts and laid them on the ground. " 'God so loved,' of course, and 'Where will you spend eternity' and 'Many are called but few are chosen'—"

"I like 'Ye must be born again' the best," Jonathan said, not knowing whether to laugh or be grave.

"Eh, well, it's suitable to all occasions," the little preacher said. "There's no one so good he can't be made better, is how I figger it out. Where'll I put up, mister? Will they be easy on me in Median, seein' I'm poor and a minister of the gospel and has only what God moves folks' hearts to give me and there's plenty of hearts beyond even Him, I can tell you?"

"I daresay," Jonathan said dryly. "Come with me."

He led him to the hotel and found Henry Drear in his woodshed making corn whisky for the winter.

"Here's our preacher," he told him.

Henry stared and clapped the hunched shoulders halfway between his own waist and shoulders.

"Well, suds!" he cried. "How'd you come by him?"

"God driven," the little man said simply.

Henry's jaw dropped. "Well, I seen 'em all kinds," he said, and added his usual greeting to anyone who passed. "Come in and eat."

The strange little man married them expertly enough. He had a book in a torn cloth cover, but he did not read from it. Under the big silver bell he was grotesque.

"I learned the burial service and the marriage and birth by heart," he told Jonathan as he stood waiting for the ceremony to begin. "I was ready then, I figgered, for anything people wanted."

"Dearly beloved, we are gathered together—" He had a sweet and plaintive voice, as reedy and clear as a wild bird's.

Jonathan watched him, listened to him, and made his responses and heard Katie's. Her voice squeaked with earnestness when she said, "I do," and she put up her right hand and coughed behind it the polite two-syllabled cough that women make for apology.

He was being married, for better, for worse, as long as he lived, never to part from Katie until death parted them. But they were young, and life was long ahead. There was no use in thinking about death now except that it was the far end to any life.

"I pronounce you man and wife."

He turned with Katie's hand heavy on his arm. The rooms were bright with autumn flowers, and October sunshine poured into the uncurtained windows. It fell upon these patient people of Median, hard-working and good, and not one of them beautiful. He went silently and carefully down the aisle toward the door. He was one of them now. He had married himself into them, flesh to flesh and spirit to spirit.

At the door they stood and waited. Bill White fiddled the wedding march madly, and the people rose and came forward to pour out good wishes and shouts and congratulations and cheers.

"Eats is ready upstairs!" Lew bellowed, and upstairs they went, Jonathan and Katie leading the way, and behind them Ruth and Maggie, and Sue with Mary, her eyes enormous, clinging to her. That small creature, growing slowly and painfully through her first year, could always be quieted if Sue held her.

Laughter and loud good-natured talk and the chatter of children filled the rooms and streamed out upon the silent prairie. Jonathan went here and there seeing that all had food, pressing sandwiches and cake upon everyone. Ice cream was Lew's share, and he was not content until every saucer had been filled twice. There was no haste for any to be gone. The evenings were long and the hour set purposely early. And Jonathan and Katie were going nowhere except to step into the new house next door. He had no wish to travel with school so near its opening, and Katie was eager for the house.

"If we went anywhere I'd be thinkin' about the things waitin' to be done here," she had told Jonathan.

So he loitered at his own wedding and listened, smiling, to Lew and Henry telling stories to each other for the benefit of the newcomers.

" 'Member that young feller walked in one day with his scalp pulled down over his eyes?" Lew asked Henry. "Got away from Indians. Well, Bill White took a string off his fiddle and sewed it back again and feller got well again, 'cept he stayed crazy. Had to ship him back East to his folks."

"Indians was bad them days," Henry said gravely.

Samuel Hasty, always on the outskirts of any group of men, lifted his thin voice. "When I come here in sixty-five—"

"In sixty-three"—Henry's roar took the words and drowned him with them—"I was in Lawrence, and by Jiminy I slid out the night before with a bunch of wild horses I was drivin' east and next day Quantrill and his gang bust on the town—left hundreds of people dead in the streets."

Jonathan found his pupils one by one and spoke a word to them and had his reward in Mrs. Drear's good-by.

"Seems as if the whole of Median got married and not just you and Katie," she said, leaning her head to his ear.

They lingered. There were so few times for merrymaking that when one came they held it as long as they could. There was no haste in Jonathan, either, only stillness. He stood listening, joining in the talk and forgetting a good deal that Katie was his wife and this their wedding day. Once, having forgotten, he saw her stiff young figure without thinking until he happened to see upon her finger the new wedding ring he had put there. He had chosen it from a dozen or so that Lew kept in stock for travelers west who met and married on the way.

My wife? he thought.

It would take time.

When they were gone at last and only he and Katie left, they closed the windows and went downstairs. Katie looked around the disordered rooms.

"This'll take a lot of cleaning," she said soberly.

"Don't think of it now," he said. "There'll be time tomorrow."

Tomorrow! There was the night between. But this was only Katie. She stood waiting for him, and he put her hand on his arm. She kept it there inert, and he thought again of that strange lack of relation between the quick energy of her body and her large, heavy hand. But he put his own hand over hers loyally, and together they walked across the little space to their house.

The sun had set with all the colors of the autumn in the sky. The prairie was dark and smooth, deep strokes of purple and black until gold edged the horizon. In the new house the shades were up, and Ruth had lit every light. She was watching for them and opened the door as they came. Mary was in her arms and Maggie at her side. "Welcome home," she said shyly. She had spent much thought about this moment and feared it. It's only natural they'd like to be coming home alone, she had thought. If it had been only herself, she could have gone back with Jamie. But there were the two small ones.

If there was any wish that they were not there, neither Katie nor Jonathan showed it. "Thanks, Ruthie," Jonathan said, and took Mary into his arms as he did every evening when he came home, and Maggie clasped his leg and laughed when he scuffled her along as he walked.

Katie came in briskly and shut the door. "It's cold," she said. "I wouldn't be surprised if there's frost tonight."

It was like any other evening, except that they were in the new house and everything was being done in a first-time sort of way. It was more like a house moving than a marriage night. After supper in the new kitchen he went to the door of the second bedroom and saw Maggie and Mary tucked into bed, Mary in her crib that he had painted a nice blue, and Maggie on a pallet.

"I shall get a bed for Maggie soon," he said, bending to kiss her good night.

"A big high bed," Maggie cried.

"For you to fall out of?" Katie said. "No, a little low bed."

"Maggie's a big girl," Jonathan said gently, seeing Maggie's full lips pout.

He kept Ruth with them without knowing he was doing so, talking of their mother and Clyde.

"We must write Dad about the new house," he said. He kept thinking about his mother and father and how once he had hated the night and how he had distrusted it because night took his mother away into a world he did not know.

Night lay ahead of him now. There was no postponing it. Ruth slipped away from them, and he and Katie were alone. Without looking at her, he wound the clock and put the ashes over the fire. She rose, and then he did look at her and saw what he had never seen before, fear cold in her eyes. Instantly pity made him calm.

"You mustn't be afraid of me, Katie," he said. "Nothing is changed, I'm what you've always known, my—my dear."

She could not speak, and he took her shoulders and turned her toward the door.

"You go in," he said. "I'll stay here for a bit."

He sat down then alone and thought to himself that he wished he smoked a pipe, though he had never felt the need of such a thing before. The house was very quiet—his home, of which he was now the head, and Katie was his wife. And then he was terrified. There was no stir in him of passion. Now he knew why he was in Katie's debt and would be as long as he lived.

I've done a fearful thing to her, he thought heavily. I've married her without loving her. A mist of tenderness rose in his heart, and pity strengthened him again. He rose and blew out the coal-oil lamp and went resolutely toward the room where she waited. At least he could behave so she would never know, and at least she need never be afraid that he would be cruel to her because of love too strong.

She was in bed when he came in, her pale brown hair braided in two braids as she used to wear it. She looked exactly as she always had, and for a moment he felt the night impossible. But he undressed doggedly and put out the light and climbed into the big bed that had been her parents' wedding present. They lay awake, talking in fragments of one thing and another, each afraid of what they could not say.

"Jonathan, did you lock the door?"

"Yes."

And he, "Hush—is that the wind rising?"

And she, "If it is, there won't be frost."

But sometime in the night, he could not have told the hour, his virgin body woke to hers of its own accord and separate from himself, and so the thing he feared was done.

Out of that involuntary union his marriage took its shape. It was a wordless marriage. The fountain of his spirit was sealed. He marveled sometimes, remembering how in his love for Judy words had poured out of him, unconscious, as poetry. When he had Judy in his arms he had not been able to keep from murmuring as he caressed her. It was as though she had unstopped all his sources and his whole soul ran fluid in her presence, like silver made molten.

But there was only silence between him and Katie except when they spoke of his work and of their daily living. She could be voluble enough over a weasel in the henhouse or a snake under the porch, and she could talk endlessly, he thought sometimes when he was tired, over a rag of gossip in the town. But when they were alone together, when in the night the involuntary union took its place and became spare habit, she was silent and he. Their life together was scarcely different, he thought as time went on, from what it had been before they were married, except that Katie never went away from his house.

They were three years childless and then Katie conceived her first child. She kept her silence, in the reticent way of all prairie women, until she could not keep it any longer. Then, blushing her furious spots of red upon her cheekbones and her neck, she told him.

"Maw says I'm in the family way, Jonathan."

She blurted it out one night in spring when he sat figuring his school accounts and she sat mending. He looked up, not comprehending at first.

"What—Katie, you mean—" he stammered, and then he too began to blush. He felt the hot blood pour up from his body and drench the very roots of his hair. "Well," he said, and put down his pencil.

The silence fell on them again. He felt as though he had been given a blow, and familiar tenderness came creeping into his heart. It seemed piteous that a woman should bear a child to a man who did not love her, and at this moment his debt to Katie began to pile into a mountain before his eyes.

"My dear," he said gently, but not rising and not going to her, "I'd rather have a child than anything on earth."

She looked at him in her awkward shyness, and he thought he saw tears in her eyes. She put down her mending on her lap. "I pray it'll be a boy," she said in a low voice.

"Boy or girl is welcome," Jonathan said. He could figure no more that night, and he put the books away and sat watching her while she finished her mending, and then he saw his watching made her ill at ease and so he rose and wound the clock and set the house ready for the night.

The days went on, and their silence did not break. When the first deep snow fell in December, Katie laid herself down in her bed early one evening and before midnight his son was born. He did not go in until Sue Parry called him.

"The little child is bawn," Sue said softly. "It's a boy, suh." He had not gone in because he knew that Katie would have been shy before him. But now he rose and in dignity Sue stood and waited for him to pass her into the bedroom.

There in Katie's arm he saw a small form, a round black head, and he bent over it. For the moment he forgot her. He was so absorbed in this new being, his, as no other being in the world could be his, he thought with a rush of painful joy. He had his own at last.

Then he saw Katie's face, turned to look at him, and the heart in his breast gave a great and separate heave. One other could have been more his own—his child and Judy's. Had her flesh and his mingled, his fruit would have been perfected. He knew one instant of pure agony. He waited for it to pass, then he touched his boy's head.

"Thank you, Katie," he said.

He was surprised to see her little hazel eyes fill with tears. "You're tired, my dear," he said gently.

But she shook her head. "It's not that," she whispered.

"Then what?" he urged her. Her hand lay loosely on her breast, and he made himself take it and hold it. "What, my dear?" he asked again.

But she shook her head a little. "I don't know," she faltered. "It's me ought to thank you, Jonathan."

When his daughter was born two years later, he told himself that he would have no more children. His son he had named Jonathan, and Katie named their daughter Lula after her own mother. But he did not tell Katie that he would have no more children. The silence between them was never broken.

Part Three

30

"Ruth, there's a tramp coming in the gate."

Maggie, a plump, pink-faced girl of fifteen, put down the dish she was drying and tiptoed to the window of the kitchen, her red braids bobbing up and down her back, and peeped out from behind the curtain. "He's got a big black beard," she whispered.

"Oh, dear," Ruth cried under her breath.

There were many tramps in this year of 1881. It had not rained well for two years, and from the western half of the state there trickled through Median a stream of ruined men. Those with families went on; but solitary men lingered until the town's patience was gone.

"Median ain't no Chicago," Lew Merridy grumbled. "We've got to scratch our livin' off the country, too, rain or no rain."

"I wish Katie wasn't over at the store," Ruth said. All her old timidity of the plains trembled in her. She thought of the two children upstairs whom Katie had left to her care while she went to help in the store. Lew had had a stroke last year, and Katie spent many of her afternoons there.

"Anyways, I wish she'd taken little Jonnie and Lula," she said.

"He's coming right to the door," Maggie cried.

Ruth's ready fear mastered her. "Run over to the schoolhouse by the front door and tell Jonathan to come right over," she whispered. "I'll lock the door quiet-like."

She gave Maggie a push and slipped to the door and noiselessly turned the key. Then she stood with her back to the door. If the tramp looked in at the window he could not see her, and the kitchen would be empty. She stood there, and between her shoulder blades she felt the thump upon the wooden door of a powerful hand. Thus she was standing, dishcloth in hand, when Jonathan hurried in.

"Whatever—" he began.

"It's a tramp, a big one!" she whispered.

"Well, he can't eat you," Jonathan said shortly. "Move away from the door, there's a good girl."

He could never be impatient with Ruth's terrors because they had their beginnings in the years she had shared too young with their mother. Ruth's fears were his mother's fears, and sometimes it seemed to him he could see his mother over again in this girl's too-gentle face. But Ruth had not the final power of desperation that had made Mary strong. When no help came, Ruth was helpless against her own fears. Why else did she hesitate so long over marrying good young Matthew Cobb! She was afraid of marriage because she had seen marriage too close in that dugout on the western plains. It was one of his problems, and he thought of it every time he saw her, because it had somehow to be settled. Matthew was continually at him.

He pulled at the door. "Why, whatever—"

"I locked it," she said breathlessly.

He turned the key. "Really, Ruthie, it's very inconvenient for me. My history class is sitting there—" He threw the door open in spite of himself with impatience. There was no need to be afraid of these men wandering into Median and out again. If it would ever rain they would go back to being good farmers. "Good day," he said in a firm voice.

A burly bearded man stood there in dust-colored garments, his feet wrapped in rags and a bundle under his arm.

"Hello, Jonathan," he said. "You haven't forgot your dad, I reckon."

Jonathan stared at him. Clyde had grown heavier, hairier, browner. But his lips were as red as ever in his dark beard. "No, I haven't forgot," Jonathan said, "though I didn't think to see you like this."

But he had thought of it, as he had seen the stragglers tramping through Median. His father and Jamie, to whom he never wrote any more because they never answered his letters, he had asked himself, where were they in these evil times?

"Come in," he said. "Where's Jamie?"

"He's with an outfit as catches wild horses and breaks 'em in and sends 'em East," Clyde said, shuffling into the kitchen. "It's all right for a young chap, but I'm beyond it, though hearty enough for anything, nearly. Hey, that'll never be you, Ruth!"

He stared at Ruth and then clapped her on the shoulder blades. "Give us a kiss, girl! Eh, you're like somebody I miss sore to this day!"

He put his face close to hers, and Ruth felt the wetness of his full lips in the bristling cushion of his beard and shrank back. But Clyde did not notice it.

"Make me a bit of dinner, there's a good girl. I'm famished." He sat down and put his bundle under the chair and began unwrapping his feet. "I lost the last bit of leather from my soles a while back," he said.

"Couldn't you get a ride?" Jonathan asked. He was still standing. What would he do with this man? The house was too full already. If the times had been better he would have added a room to the house for his two children, but the times were bad and no sign of better unless rain came. Summer had passed and it was midautumn, and still no rain came.

"Folk don't give rides for nothin'," Clyde said. His feet were bare, and he sat up and looked about the kitchen. On the table Ruth was putting a cup and a plate, fork and spoon, bread and butter and sugar. He got up and went over to it and picked up the loaf and pulled at its end.

Instantly all the memory of his childhood rushed over Jonathan. The kitchen at Dentwater the day he came back to find Clyde set on America, pulling the end from an English loaf—here he was, a beggar still!

"You're very fine here, Jonathan," Clyde said. "A little bit of all right this is, I'd say." He stared around the room. "A coal cooking stove, too— and a pump in the kitchen—eh, Mary'd like that. What's the water, spring or deep well?"

"A well," Jonathan said shortly. He hesitated. Could he leave Ruth now or not? "My history class is waiting, Dad," he said, looking at Ruth. She nodded slightly, but he was not sure. "I'll send Maggie for Katie, and she'll be back in a jiffy, while you're eating your food."

"Where's Maggie?" Clyde demanded. "I'd like to see the little tyke."

"She's not little any more," Jonathan said, "and likely she's gone back to afternoon session now."

Clyde sat down at the table. "You go on to your job," he said, loud and cheerful before food. "I'll clean myself a bit after I've et, and be more civilized-like when your missus comes in."

"Very well," Jonathan said. "Make yourself at home," he added.

"I s'all," Clyde retorted. "You don't have to tell me that. Coffee, Ruth. Tea seems wishy-washy stuff to me now."

He was not changed, Jonathan thought grimly. He went out and then looked at his watch. It was too late to go back to his class. The hour was over. He would go for Katie himself. She would be what she always called "put out," but that must be got over with Katie when anything new happened, and once over, she knew what she wanted to do.

He walked quickly the six blocks to his father-in-law's store. They were proper blocks now. The old rotten boardwalk was gone, thanks to his own insistence two winters ago, and the square was bordered with a hard-surfaced stuff a fellow named McAdam had invented. It made good streets except for being sticky sometimes under the summer sun. But he always suspected they had not mixed it just right, though he himself had read the directions out loud while the Hasty boys put the stuff together. Abram Hasty took up the road-building business after that and went everywhere in the state. But it was a good thing he had forced the road through Median before this drought set in. He glanced at the cottonwoods in the square as he did every time he passed them. Big as they now were, they would not last much longer. He had tried to persuade people living about them to throw their waste water to save them, but they wanted it all for the parched vegetable gardens at their kitchen doors.

If they die, I shall plant elms and maples and black walnuts, he thought. They're permanent.

He had reached the store now. It was not changed since the first time he saw it, even by a coat of paint. Inside Mr. Cobb was measuring striped calico for a solitary woman customer whom Jonathan did not know. That was how big Median was, he thought, so big there were now people here whom he did not know.

"Where's Katie?" he asked.

Mr. Cobb moved the tobacco cud in his cheek and wiped his chin with the end of his cotton tie. "Inside," he said. "Lew don't feel so good today."

He went on and, opening the door, saw Lew, now enormously fat, lying stretched on the couch, an old crocheted afghan across his stomach. Mrs. Merridy sat rocking sadly at his side, her thin hands clutched across her waist.

"Well," Jonathan said to them both. "Sorry you're not so well, Lew."

"My belly don't give me no rest." There was a rumble under the afghan. "Hear that? It's goin' again—clamorin' for food. And if I put anything like a square meal down, it sets up such a to-do I'm all wore out. I et canned corn for dinner, and this hyere's my result."

"You used to could eat canned corn like a hawg," Mrs. Merridy said sorrowfully.

"Well, I am sorry," Jonathan said. "Where's Katie?"

"In the kitchen, bilin' up some pep'mint," Lew said faintly. "She thinks it'll help."

He went into the kitchen and found Katie scrubbing furiously at dish towels while she waited for water to boil. She looked up as Jonathan came in.

"I declare Maw's eyesight is gettin' so poor she can't see whether a thing is clean or not," she said.

It never occurred to her to come out of her world into his. He had always to wait until she had spoken herself out before he began.

"I'm sorry you have to do that much extra," he said gently.

"Well, I do," Katie retorted, "and there'll be more. The store's goin' to ruin. That Cobb's no good except to hand out something over the counter when it's ast for. I declare, if he was all that Matthew was made outen, I'd say Ruth'd be sensible to say no."

He stood a minute, dreading to put anything more upon her.

"Anything wrong at home?" she asked. The tone of her voice made the question a dart.

"Well, yes, I suppose you'd call it that. My father's come, Katie."

"Your father!" she echoed. She paused, her hands in the scanty suds. "Why, what for?"

"He looks badly off," Jonathan said apologetically.

"You mean he's come to stay?"

"I don't know—of course he can't live with us, Katie, but—"

"As if there wasn't enough," she cried. She fell to fresh scrubbing. Flecks of soapsuds flew out and spattered his coat, and he wiped them off. "Is he sick?" she demanded.

"No, no, he looks fine," he said quickly. "He hardly looks any older, even. It's surprising."

She did not speak while she rinsed the cloths, emptied the dishpan, and piled them into it. "I'll hang 'em out and be right along."

"I'll help you," he said.

"No, you won't," she retorted. "I don't want people sayin' you've got to help me hang out my folks' clothes. You go on—I'll ketch up."

Long ago he had learned to yield to her on this pride of hers concerning him. She was bitterly independent. His position as principal of the school she made into a fetish, and only second to it was her determination to do her own work without help except what Ruth and Maggie could give her. "The men," as she called Jonathan and little Jonnie, were not to do women's work.

"All right, but let me carry the pan for you." He took it, and they went out of the kitchen door into the back yard, and then she seized it. He hesitated, as he so often did when he was with her, feeling incompleteness between them. "I'm sorry about my dad," he said.

"It can't be helped," she said. It was all she would say, it was what she always said, and he let it pass as he always did and went homeward. It had taken him a long time to realize that the phrase was neither bitter nor unkind, but merely a sign that Katie, after being "put out," was ready to make the best of a situation. He walked quickly through the dry October sunshine, deciding whether he could go back to his work or had better see how his father did. Then it occurred to him that the children might awake and be frightened, as he himself had used to be frightened when he was a little boy and his father rubbed his hairy face into his neck.

"I won't have that," he said sternly, thinking of his little son. He hastened into his house and then heard Clyde's laughter roaring out of the kitchen and went in. Lula was on his knees and Jonathan standing a little off, sucking his thumb!

"And then I says to the old bear, 'It's me as s'all have the honey, my lord, not you.' An' so in I dashes with my stick, an' the bear sees my beard, and thinks, 'Ah, that's a bigger bear nor I be, and mebbe I better go home.' An' that's how I had honey on my buckwheats next day's breakfast."

At the sink Ruth, washing Clyde's dishes, was smiling. No one saw Jonathan, and he tiptoed away. Never in his life could he remember sitting on his father's knee. But he remembered that in his way Clyde had been fond of Artie and Jamie, and that he had fondled Maggie roughly when he felt like play. Maybe he's changed, he thought.

He entered the schoolhouse, wondering for the first time in his life if his mother had made him unjust. Marriage belonged to women, and men had not much part in it, perhaps. He sighed and straightened his shoulders and, sitting down at his desk, he took up the paper he had put down when he left for his class. It was the copy of a bill newly passed by the state legislature making the selling of liquor illegal in the state of Kansas, and it was signed by Evan Bayne, the speaker of the legislature. He never saw that name without the old stir within his breast, and he saw it often now. All these years he had not been face to face with Evan, though they wrote when there was some matter to write about—he when Median had paid off the debt on the schoolhouse, Evan to congratulate him, and he again to urge Evan for his help in putting the branch railroad through Median southwest, and Evan to tell him it was done, and he again to ask Evan's advice about the new post-office building, and Evan to tell him what forms to send for and sign and what more to do; and now the post office stood on the other side of the schoolhouse, a small handsome one-story building of brick. And then last year Evan wrote to him begging him to fight this very prohibition bill he held in his hands now, and he had written to say he would not, though he hated as much as any man to put in government's hands the right to say whether a man could drink or not.

But there were six saloons in Median now, and the hotel was little better than a saloon, and he had his boys in high school to think of, the sons of farmers who came in to Median in wintertime to go to school. If they had been in their own homes, he would not have cared, but they lived where they could to come to his school, and he could not forget that woman who strode into his office last year and flung words at him like fire because in Median her son had learned to drink. He had taken it coldly until at last her anger was put out by her own tears, and she sobbed, "What's the good of learnin' out of books if he's to be a drunkard? And everybody talks so good about you I thought you'd be lookin' after him!"

He had looked after his boys ever since, and he had fought for this bill against Drear, stumping the county to do it all through the summer.

"I believe in man's independence, but I speak for those who are not yet able to be men," his speeches always began. When he and Henry met, he maintained his good humor against Henry's violence.

"Your own nose is too red, Henry," he said gently, "but that's all right with me. It's your nose. What I'm talking against is young Will Healey, tumbling out of your door at sixteen. He's one of my senior pupils."

"If we're goin' to run Median for babies," Henry bellowed, "I'll move out. Why, I can't make money on a hotel without a bar, and you know it, you blasted son of an Englishman! Yes, an' I wish your own father could see you. He liked his liquor as well as anybody."

"So do I—so do I," Jonathan said impatiently, "but tell me how to keep my boys out of your bar!"

The end of it was victory, made a little less sweet than it might have been for Jonathan, because Katie was so heartily for it. He was ashamed of himself, but it was true that he could fight more zealously for a thing if Katie were not on his side. She could not remain friendly with an enemy as he could, nor would she forget. It embarrassed him that still she would not speak to the Drears. He found in himself a perversity he wished to ignore when her very interest pressed her to question him.

"What'd you tell Drear when he said that?"

"I merely said that boys of sixteen were not babies exactly, and that they were important to the future of the town."

"If it had been me, I'd have told him a thing or two. He runs a gamblin' place in that hotel of his."

"Oh, I don't think so, Katie."

"Everybody says so!" This was her eternal retort, and he could not bear it.

"Everybody says so many things."

"Well, I know you never believe what I say, but there's our own children to think of."

"I think of all children," he said patiently. "Long ago I fought against Median being a cattle town because of children. I don't want the saloons here now." But he had felt goaded by her stiff figure, all its angles sharpened as she sat under the lamplight, one of his socks spread over her left hand, her right weaving the long needle in and out. "I don't want saloons, and yet I don't think it's right either that the state should tell a man he can't drink in a free country. It's a thing that has to be thought out, and I'm only doing this as a step toward that final thinking. Saloons have got to get out of Median, and I can't think of any other way to get that done for the time being except by prohibition. But maybe the next thing I'll work on is how a full-grown man can get a drink if he wants it."

She looked at him, her eyes round with indignation. "Shame on you, then!"

"All right, if you say so," he retorted and grinned at himself. It was his eternal retort, and he wondered if she knew it was. But such things they could not talk about, for she was humorless.

Then his irrepressible pity made him remorseful. She was so good a keeper of his home, scrupulously just to his sisters and carefully as kind to them as to her own children. And never had she let him know she felt a lack in him. His faults she might flare against, but then she made amends which he could scarcely endure because that way remorse compelled something beyond the power of his affection, and beyond he could not go.

But it was a marriage. It had become a marriage. Love was a single bond, but marriage could be a web woven of a thousand threads, none strong enough alone, but together as strong in time as love could be. He had come to believe that.

His eyes fell on Evan's name again. Evan's marriage had held by that single golden bond. At any rate, held—he had never heard a whisper of it, good or bad, and here in Median people had forgotten how Evan had found his wife. In his letters Evan always said, "Judy joins me in good wishes to you and yours." But that was all. "Judy joins me—" Evan saw Judy every day. As often as he saw Katie, Evan saw Judy.

"Pshaw!" he said aloud and folded the bill abruptly and thrust it into a drawer.

31

"WHAT shall you do next, Father?" Jonathan put this question openly one day in early spring. Clyde had spent the winter with them, penniless and making no move to earn anything. He slept at night on a pallet in the sitting room and lounged in the kitchen all day if it stormed. Through it all Katie had not once been impatient with him. Clyde liked her tolerantly, never forgetting for a moment that she was plain. Privately he wondered how Jonathan slept with her. 'Tis no wonder I have such a few grandchildren, he thought wickedly. Damn it, I admire Jonathan's stren'th of mind. He longed for someone he could say this to and laugh, but there was nobody in Median who would laugh at Jonathan. He felt a little ironical about his son. Now Jonathan was fixing to build a church.

"I never knew you was religious," he said.

"I'm not much," Jonathan said honestly. "But a church is a good thing in a town."

"Eh, I reckon," Clyde said. "I haven't been in a church since I heard old Clemony in Dentwater. Last preacher I see was a humped little chap out our way as called himself a rainmaker. Give him a try, I did, but there wasn't no rain. Guess he hadn't the trick. Folks say some do make rain, though, with sulphur or somethin', but he only had his prayers."

"A humped little fellow married Katie and me," Jonathan said. "After he was gone I took texts off the trees like apples."

"Same chap, likely," Clyde said. "He was always nailin' up somewheres as how you had to be born again."

He went on talking and talking. He sat in a warm room and talked all winter long.

"I'm waitin' for somethin' to open up," he said.

He waited through the summer, through winter again, until the verge of another spring. Then rains fell and all that had been waiting in the soil sprang early into life, and suddenly one day he was ready to be gone.

"Guess I'll be goin'," he said, "if you can spare me fifty dollars, Jonathan."

"I suppose I can," Jonathan said, not looking at Katie. He drew it out of his small savings and gave it to his father, and with this in the suit of clothes Jonathan had given him, he took the train westward. "It'll be kind of good to see my own land again," he told them. "Well, good-by all."

Clyde had trimmed his beard and parted it in the middle and pulled his hat over his dark eyes and let a red scarf Ruth had given him for Christmas fly at his throat. He waved to them gaily from the platform. He looked ten years younger than when he came—a young man still, Jonathan thought with disgust.

That night the house seemed full of room without his father's restless presence.

"A miracle you've been to that man, Katie," Jonathan said that night. "Don't think I haven't seen it all these months or that I haven't wondered at your goodness." He was somewhat dashed by her reply.

"Oh, I don't know, there's something about him I kind of like!"

But a strange good thing came out of Clyde's stay. Some terror went out of Ruth forever. She had been afraid of her father in memory for years because of the quarrels he had made in those nights upon the prairie, when she lay listening, because she could not help it, on the pallet beyond the blanket that curtained her parents' bed.

"Give over, do!" she could hear her mother's sharp whisper.

"Eh, what's the matter now? It's a headick or bellyache or somethin' every night—a sore toe, maybe, or a finger boil now."

"Be quiet, Clyde! You'll wake the children."

"Let 'em wake!"

"Clyde, for shame, what'll Ruth think?"

"She'll know, soon enough!"

But Clyde alone she grew used to through these months and no longer feared. He teased her and grumbled at her, and she came to mind neither.

"Eh, your hair's pretty, too, like hers was!"

"But Mother's hair was fair, Father, and mine's dark."

"Don't tell me what her hair was, for I know. I've wrapped them yellow braids of hers around my neck on a cold night like a muffler. When we was married she could sit in her hair like a cloak, and if I'd knew she was goin' to die with a child of mine I'd ha' let myself burn up before one of you was born, but a man don't think of it at the time."

She did not insist on what she knew, that her mother's hair had been as fair as Jonathan's, and soft and straight like his. Instead she laughed at him, and he made constant fun of her shyness with Matthew. When on Sunday afternoon Matthew came to see her, Clyde would open the door himself.

"Come in, lad! She's been waitin' for you all day. Couldn't eat no dinner, our Ruthie couldn't, and she's got on her best dress."

By now Ruth could not be found. Then he would shout at Matthew, "Sit down and wait, I'll find her!" He stormed through the tiny house, searching under beds and through closets, and from somewhere pulled Ruth out, half-crying and half-laughing, and pushed her by the shoulders and then shot her into the sitting room.

"There she is, lad!" he roared and banged the door upon them.

"You're terrible," Katie had said. But she had laughed, too.

And Jonathan, who could never have done the thing himself, knew nevertheless that it was what these two shy creatures needed. Behind that closed door Ruth would be blushing and wiping away tears and trying to laugh, and Matthew would have his chance.

He was not surprised when, the Sunday night after Clyde's going, Matthew came out of the sitting room to where he and Katie sat in the kitchen, his shoulders very straight.

"Mr. Goodliffe, sir, if you are willing, Ruth says she will have me."

Jonathan looked up from his paper and let his eyes twinkle. "I've been willing all along, Matthew," he said. And then he rose and went into the sitting room to find Ruth alone, twisting a curl of her hair around her finger.

"Well, Ruth!" He kissed her crimson cheek. It was hot under his cool lips. "I'm glad you've come to this. It's the right thing."

"Do you really think so, Jonathan?" she whispered.

"Sure of it," he said. "Matt's a fine gentle chap, and he'll be good to you, and you to him."

To Katie that night he said, "If my old Dad did this, I'll forgive him part of the nuisance he's been to you in the house—and to me always. A queer thing it took him to do it, though."

He put out his hand for hers in a gesture he did not often make. She quivered a little whenever he did it.

"There's something in him that makes folks easy-like," she said, and longed to tell Jonathan that she loved him. But between them those words had never passed.

Clyde trudged over the land, newly green, his big bundle on his back. The Santa Fe railroad came within twenty miles of his claim, and he got off at Garden City, a string of one-story houses along a wide unpaved street. He left it behind in a few minutes and tramped to the southwest. He was full of sleep and good food and restlessness and impatience. All of the old strength was in his blood again.

Everywhere over the land the firm, strong spears of buffalo grass were pushing up through last year's sod. The long drought was over. The earth was damp beneath his feet. It would have been mud had not the sod held it firm under its ancient roots. The sky was blue, but there were great white clouds rolling away to the Rocky Mountains. He had never seen the mountains, but they were there all the same. Some day he'd go to them, maybe. If farmers came cutting up the sod and planting their diddling crops, he'd go on West.

He yawned at the midday sun after he had eaten the bread and salt meat he had bought in Garden City, and then he lay down and slept for an hour. The warmth, the smell of the young grass, and the wet earth stirred him awake. He did not open his eyes at once. His blood rose uncomfortably.

Oh, I s'all have to get married again, maybe, he thought. When Mary died he swore marriage was a curse to man. But later it had come to him that not all women were like Mary. There were women who cared for men and not for whether they had babies or not. If a man had one of them in his bed every night, things would be different. He climbed slowly to his feet, unable to bear the physical weight of his desire.

"There's no good teasing myself with thinkin'," he muttered. He shouldered his bundle again and went the eight miles left. But the sun beat upon him warmly, and the stillness could not take his mind off his need. He grew peevish with himself.

Dang me if I couldn't have stayed in the town and come home tomorrow if I'd thought of this, he thought angrily. He had gone months in Jonathan's home with no violent need. Everything there had made him think of Mary, and since she had died he had thought of her as an angel and desire for her was gone. Or maybe, he thought, it was the books in Jonathan's home. He never liked books about. They cooled him down and made him feel ignorant. But here there was nothing, only him between earth and sky.

He plodded along angrily, aware of his body's need, and so came to his own sod house. It looked like a lump of earth in the midst of the green prairie, but it was still standing in spite of two winters and rain. He hastened to it, and to his indignation he saw the door was open.

"What son of a bitch has settled hisself here while I've been gone?" he yelled. He threw down his bundle and tore off his coat and made for the door.

Someone was standing at the stove where Mary used to stand. It was a woman with a crop of red hair down her back. She turned as he charged in.

"Hello, Clyde," she said.

He dropped his flailing arms, and his breath caught in his lungs.

"Jennet! It's never you!"

"Why not?" she said. A spoon was in her hand, and she licked it with the end of her red tongue. There was a great bruise over her left eye. "I've been here off and on all winter. Hope you don't mind."

She was not nearly as beautiful as once she had been. Her face was pallid and her hair burned dry and carroty. Her green eyes were still jewel-like, but the lids were tired. She put the spoon back into the stew she was cooking and began to braid her hair. She laughed a single hoarse note. "If I'd of known you was comin' I'd of cleaned myself up—maybe."

He was so dazed with the opportuneness of her presence that his head whirled. "I don't know anything as I'd rather have come home to than you, Jennet."

"You can make it permanent, if you want." She turned her back on him while he took this in.

"The Englishman'd split my head," he said.

"Reckon not." Her back was to him still. "I've left him."

"For good?"

She gave her short laugh. "For marriage," she said. "Is it the same?"

His throat was thick. " 'Twould be with me, Jennet."

"All right," she said indifferently. "But nothing don't begin before."

But in the night she yielded to him suddenly, and he cried out with happiness.

" 'Twill be fun to marry one like you," he panted.

Before the young minister Jonathan stood with Ruth clinging to his arm as she made her marriage promises. The wedding had waited through the spring until June before a minister stopped in Median. He was a young missionary on his way westward to the Indians.

But the long wait had determined Jonathan that the church must be next in Median. Upon the map he and Evan had once made together he had drawn a firm pencil line through schoolhouse and post office. These were done. He had the choice now between courthouse and church next. If the big county were to be divided, as there was clamor for, Median might be the new county seat. Courthouse, maybe, then should come first. Meanwhile they could go on having church in these two schoolrooms where he and Katie had been married, too.

But he liked this Paul Graham. There was none of Joel's fanaticism in his quiet gray eyes. He looked rugged and good. And since Jonathan never thought of anything near Judy without thinking of her, he wondered, as he often had before, in some sad secret abstraction, whether Joel had put into Judy some of the shifting sand of his being.

Katie was gray rock, and Judy silver sand. He still saw Judy more clearly bright than he saw anyone. Katie's face, which he saw every day, was a blur when he thought of Judy's face, which he never saw and doubtless would never see again. He dragged himself out of the slough of memory back to this moment of another marriage.

Just now the young minister's face was flushed. This was his first wedding, he had told Jonathan, and he stammered over the words until Ruth was suddenly set at ease. He minds as much as Matthew and me do, she thought.

Matthew, she now knew, was even more shy than she. The discovery had given her a sedate pleasure, and she blamed herself at heart for what she called to herself her dilly-dally. Now, as Paul Graham pronounced the final words, she slipped her left hand from Jonathan's arm and her right into Matthew's and squeezed it gently. He had bought his farm, though it was heavy with mortgage, and had built a two-room house upon it, and they would go there tonight. Sue had put white organdie curtains in the windows for a wedding present.

The Parry family kept almost out of sight until something needed to be done, and then they were there. That was because Jonathan kept sending their letters for them to Beaumont in France. Jonathan did things for everybody. People came to him about their children from all over the county, and in Median nothing was done without him. He had been better to Ruth than anybody and had made his home hers. She thought she ought to take Mary with her anyway, but he was not willing.

"You'll have your own children," he said in his dry quiet voice.

Martha Cobb played the wedding march on the school organ, and she stepped down the aisle. She felt the beat of her old shyness creep up out of her bosom as she faced the people. There were so many people in Median when they all came together.

"I shall miss you, Ruth, my dear," Jonathan had said, but he did not. Whatever Ruth had been, she had by her very presence kept Maggie a child. Now, without presage, or so it seemed to Jonathan, Maggie from being a fat little girl rose up from her bed one morning a plump young woman whose solid flesh had properly distributed itself into rounded hips and breasts and full white arms. By night, or so it seemed to him, as he looked back, every male under twenty-five in the county had known it.

For the first time there was quarreling between the women in his home, Katie scolding Maggie as she scolded all of them, but Maggie would have no more of it. Jonathan was distracted with the discord because he believed it of no importance when women quarreled, and more because he had made up his mind that Median must be the new county seat. This decision he had come to because he wanted order in the new county, and because Median shopkeepers, headed by Lew and Henry, the old-timers, wanted business.

"And don't you look to gettin' the county by any of your peaceable means, Jonathan," Henry Drear said sternly. "Women ain't gonna be no use here. I'm sendin' East for two dozen rifles on my own hook. We'll need 'em sure. I know that there town of Ashbee."

"I'll get the money for the courthouse if you'll get the election for Median," Jonathan said.

To Paul Graham he put the matter plainly. "Here's Median wanting a church and a courthouse. Our souls need the church and our pockets the courthouse. Give us time and we'll have both, but sermons'll go down better if our pockets are fuller, especially after the drought. But I want you to stay here and hold down our souls till we're the county seat."

"But I volunteered for the Indians," Paul said. He saw in Jonathan a slender, shabby man who was neither young nor old, because he had never been young and would never be old. Jonathan was energy made human, a dogged power of a man who had Median by the nose.

"I never took much stock in Indians," he now said. "It was a good sensible thing to get them herded together so they can be taken care of. Every human deserves to live once he's born. But so long as there's the souls of folk like we've got in Median, it's folly to bother about Indians. Why, these people here are what the country's made of!"

"God sent me to the heathen," Paul said.

"Indians aren't solid heathen," Jonathan retorted. "They're what's left of something that's gone. Save 'em, of course, if there's enough salvation to go around, but why shouldn't salvation come first to us? You can preach in the schoolhouse, and when we get the courthouse, I'll put my mind next to the church."

"Median's a city whose maker and builder is you, not God," Paul said, his smile faint.

"When I ask you, I'm asking God to help," Jonathan retorted.

In the midst of all this to go home and find Katie and Maggie in quarrel was sore on his patience. He lay at Katie's side at night listening to her story of the day.

"I want we should get Maggie married as soon as we can. She's not like Ruth. She's like your old goat of a father, and her mind's full of nothing but men, though she ain't seventeen yet. And the way she answers me back—I slapped her face today, Jonathan, she'll tell you I did, and I want you should know how it was. Let her say what she wants, it was like this. I told her to clean up her bedroom. She don't do a thing she don't have to. Well, she didn't, and I did it myself, and there was a letter laying on the bureau, open. I didn't read it, but I saw the first page. She's going out at night from her window down to the drugstore, after she says she's in bed."

"She can't come to much danger in the drugstore," Jonathan said mildly. The new drugstore was kept by a Methodist from Iowa.

"But it's night!" Katie cried.

"Oh, all right, my dear," Jonathan said, sighing. There was magic in the night for some, maybe. "I'll speak to Maggie."

He spoke to her the next day, calling her into his schoolroom office, as he would any pupil who needed it.

"Sit down, Maggie," he said. He looked at her as he would at another girl and saw her young body bursting out of its faded gingham dress. "Seems to me you need a new dress, child," he said.

Her impetuous face brightened at every point, the blue eyes bluer, the full lips parting, her red hair seeming to crinkle. She had hair strangely alive to the rest of her being.

"Can I, Jonathan? I need 'em something terrible. I haven't gained weight, but I've just—*grown!*" She gestured toward her breast, and he saw a bright scarlet flying up her neck.

"You mustn't wear that one any more, anyway," he said.

"You've come to a place, Maggie, my dear, when you must be careful how you show yourself—that is, if you want to catch the right sort of man. And it's no good pretending you don't, for what every woman is set upon in her heart is how to find the man she'll marry, and every man is thinking about her whom he will—love. Don't behave so he can't see you when he looks at you because you've made yourself like somebody else."

Maggie's full young breasts began to heave, and her bright blue eyes were full of warm quick tears. She had not prepared herself for gentleness after what she well knew had been her impudence to Katie. But how could she explain the brimming of her being these days? Her veins were too full; she could not keep her voice low or her laughter soft. And she was alternately excited and frightened by the changes in her body which she wanted to hide and yet at other times to flaunt without knowing why.

"Katie'll think it a lot of trouble to fix me new dresses, though," she said.

"Katie has a lot to do," Jonathan said sternly. "She cleaned your room for you yesterday when you should have done it. There's no reason why she should make your dresses any more. Go to the store and pick out your cloth for two dresses and tell Lew I'll pay for it. Then after school take the stuff over to Parry's and tell Sue I sent you to be taught how to make them. Now go along and don't let Katie clean your room again."

"All right, Jonathan." She hesitated a moment as to whether she would not go over to him and kiss him. She longed to pour out her strong affections whenever she could. But she had never kissed her brother or seen him kiss anyone. He was familiar to her as no one in the world was so that she gave him not a thought, taking his presence and his absence equally for granted. Now, with the intensity with which she saw everything these days, she saw him, a quiet reserved man, whose hair and skin were sunburned and wind-bitten to the color of sand. Only his eyes were vivid. She longed to speak to him, to say something to show him how different she was now from the fat troublesome child she had always been. But she did not know how to begin, and then he glanced up at her from under his sandy brows and said in his decisive schoolmaster's voice, "That'll do now, Maggie."

"Everybody obeys my brother Jonathan," Maggie said proudly. She was having a chattering good time with Sue, who said little and listened well. The excitement of the green-and-red checked gingham skirt pinned to her knee flew to her tongue. But there was more than the new dresses. Yesterday when she went into the store a strange thing happened. She had a letter. Never in her life had she received a letter, and now she could not believe it.

"Come yesterday," Lew had said. He was well. "I thought I'd give it to Katie or somethin', but they don't keer a crumb about me onless I'm about to die. Got to have my ol' bellyache to get my family together these days."

"I'll take my letter," Maggie said and put it in her pocket. She could scarcely choose her goods for thinking of it, and when she had the stuff measured and folded under her arm, she walked away from the town toward the prairie, her hand in her pocket on the letter. When she was well away she sat down beside the dusty road and took out the letter. A big loose handwriting sprawled her name across it. She tore it open and read it slowly. It was from someone she had never heard of, a George Tenney.

> DEAR MAGGIE:
>
> You will be surprised to get a word from me as you will hardly rember me but ask your brother Jonathan does he rember George Tenney used to giv you brekfeast on the ship. Well Maggie now you are grown up nearly. I had it hard at first but struck good luck a year gone and am in clover. So thought of little Maggie I used to know. Is your hair still red I will come to see for myself one of these days soon.
>
> Yours resp'f'lly,
> GEORGE TENNEY

But she had had no chance to be alone with Jonathan. He was in one of his "jobs," as he called it. This one was to make Median a county seat. When he came home at night he told Katie what was happening, and they talked long after she had gone to bed. She lay with her letter under her pillow. She had once got up in the night, sleepless with moonlight and, putting on her clothes, crawled out of the window and gone to Hale's drugstore. It had seemed exciting, though no one was there except Mr. Hale himself, surprised to see her. While he mixed her a strawberry soda he said, "Does your brother know you're out, Maggie?"

She had lied and said something about studying late. When three men came in and banged their fists down for root beer, he had kept his eyes on her and at last he said, "You git along, now, Maggie. It's late."

But she did not need to crawl out of the window any more now. The letter under her pillow was enough.

Sue was ironing the sleeves of the dress with a potlike iron full of hot coals.

"I don't know about eve'body," Sue said. "I know I obey him on account of I can't pay back what he did for Beaumont."

"Who's Beaumont?"

"Beaumont's my son."

Sue set the iron on the stove and went to a bureau and opened the top drawer and brought out a package wrapped in white paper. She took from it a photograph of a young and foreign-looking man in a frock coat, with a narrow moustache curled upward. His hands, even in the picture strong and supple, clasped hat, white gloves, and a thin walking stick. In the buttonhole of the coat was a white flower.

"This is Beaumont," she said. "He's in Paris, France."

"What's he doing there?" Maggie took the photograph into her thimbled hand and stared at it. The young man scarcely looked black at all.

"He's goin' to be a brain surgeon. Not goin' to do anything else but just brains."

"He don't look like any of you," Maggie said, still staring.

"He ain't," Sue said. She put the photograph back into its papers, into the drawer, and went back to her iron. She wet her fingers and touched it and when it hissed she began ironing.

"Is he coming back here?" Maggie asked.

"I don't want he should ever come back," Sue said quietly.

"Then will you go over there?"

"I reckon I cain't."

"But you'll never see him again!" Maggie's blunt voice put boldly into being what Sue knew but had never spoken.

"I reckon not," she said.

Maggie sat silent for a few minutes. How would anybody behave to a man who looked like that when you knew he was only one of the Parrys? The Parry children had finished the grades in school, but then they had gone to work. Melissa hired out, and Pete helped his father, and next year Gem would stop school.

"I guess I better go home," Maggie said. Her letter crackled in her bosom as she stooped to pick up threads from Sue's rag rug. She knew every word of it, but she longed to read it again. "I'll be back tomorrow right after school," she said joyously. If he was coming any day, she must have a dress made and ready.

32

JONATHAN, the school closed for summer, turned heartily to the next work for Median. An idle day was beyond his endurance. His life was good enough when he came home at night after a day's work. But the small house was a cage when he did not get away from it. Katie's voice, not unpleasant in itself, carried a peculiar vibrating penetration that pierced wall and door so that every room was full of her presence. Without knowing, he was compelled to escape it.

From the empty schoolhouse he drew together the web of affairs in Median. Young Graham had gone to his Indians for a year of trial. That had been his compromise with Jonathan.

"Suits me just as well," Jonathan had said. "It gives me a year to get this county-seat business out of the way."

Actually he was resolved to do it in this summer. He set tasks for himself of heroic size and lashed himself to finish them.

Today, the third of July, the men he knew best were coming in to plan the campaign—Lew and Henry and the three Hasty men, Samuel and his two sons, Bill White and his eldest son Frank, and he had asked Matthew to come in if he could leave. They came one by one, these men whose faces were better known to him than his own—the old-timers, he thought, pushing chairs forward for them. They were solemnly silent before the idea of a meeting, talking with quieted voices of crops.

"Folks say there's grasshoppers to the west—"

"I 'member the hoppers in seventy-four, et up the fence posts even, and out in the cornfields the noise was like cattle chewin'. And I picked up a fork, I 'member, out in the barn, and they'd chawed the handle too rough to hold. But still the next year Kansas apples got a gold medal in Philadelphy."

"I was back near Salina then. Poor man's diggin's, it was."

They were waiting for Jonathan. He sat at his desk before his papers. He shot up his sandy brows at them.

"Well, folks, we better begin. First question maybe is where's the county line to be drawn. Shall it go thirty miles west of Median and take in Hyman, or do we let Ashbee have that?"

Matthew came in, but nobody spoke while they considered the map Jonathan held up.

"If we let Hyman go, Median'll be plumb in the center of the new county," Jonathan said.

Matthew coughed, but nobody paid him any heed. "I don't know as it means anything," he said mildly, "but my farm's just the other side of Hyman. Yestiddy I was ridin' after a colt that broke loose, and about five miles off I found him in a sinkhole—leg broke. But there was water in the hole, and the water was slimed with oil. Leastways it looked like oil." His voice sank into silence. The room was full of silence. A cicada outside the window sawed its two notes suddenly and ended in a long wheeze before anyone spoke.

"Anyone else know?" Jonathan asked.

"Not a soul," Matthew said.

Oil! The men looked at each other, their faces carefully skeptical.

"Couldn't have been planted, could it?" Henry Drear's voice was husky.

"I don't see how," Matthew said. "Besides, nobody's ever said a word.

The man that owns the land himself don't know what's in that sinkhole."

"Wasn't he there to help you get the colt out?" Samuel Hasty asked. His meager little mouth worked.

"No, he wasn't at home yestiddy, his wife said. I borried some rope from her and got down in and roped the critter and crawled out again and hauled him out. 'Tain't but a young colt."

"Reckon we better draw the line west of Hyman," Lew said.

"The question is how far west?" Jonathan said. "Does the oil run east or west? We might cut the best part off, whatever we do."

"Put it ten miles west," Henry said.

"Put it twenty-five," Lew rejoined.

Jonathan was studying the map. "The river runs thirty miles west and south. Likely it's the boundary. Let's say thirty miles."

He glanced about a circle of nodding heads, and slowly he drew a firm pencil line. Then he put down the pencil and lifted his head.

"The next subject for discussion is the manner in which votes shall be collected as between Ashbee and Median."

Henry Drear grunted. "Jonathan, you let me tend to the vote-gettin'. Folks take their votes serious. It's a life-and-death business. You set the day, and I'll git me a gang and round 'em up."

Jonathan frowned impatiently. "I don't want Median votes got like that. Nobody'll be satisfied, and there's no luck to a thing when nothing but anger comes of it. Median's a decent place, and it's more important to have it so than to get the county seat."

Henry's chair came down on the floor. "If the world was half saints and half sinners, I would agree to that, Jonathan. But it ain't. It's full of sin, and I ain't pertendin' I'm not one of the sinners. I ain't converted. I never was baptized. I go to gospel meetin's, but I don't convert. I come out like I went in. You let me handle this-hyere votin'."

"What's the vote here?" Jonathan's quiet voice was steely with stubbornness.

Men looked at each other.

"I'm all for peace if you can git away with it," Lew said. "But I'd say keep the guns handy."

"My idea, too," Samuel agreed.

Jonathan waited. No one else spoke. After a moment he went on, "The next question is the date of the election. Ashbee wants it a month from today."

He waited again. The men were full of their own thoughts.

"Let 'em have what they want there, since they ain't gonna git nothin' more," Henry said. He rose as he spoke and pushed back his chair and spat into the spittoon near by. "I guess I gotta be goin'," he said.

"No, you don't," Lew said, his voice firm and his words slow. "We'll start fair."

Every man in the room, except Jonathan and Matthew, rose and moved toward the door. But Lew's great body filled it first.

"We'll all line up outside the schoolhouse," he said. He drew a pistol from his pocket. "When I fire we'll start. It won't pay anybody to start first."

He heaved himself down the steps, the pistol hanging from his hands, and waited until the half-dozen men were in a line. He fired it, running as he did so, and down the main street of Median they ran, every man for his horse.

Jonathan and Matthew sat in their chairs. They had not moved. Jonathan arranged the papers upon his desk into their usual straight piles.

"Any reason to think there is oil on your land?" he asked.

"I don't know yet," Matthew replied. "There's no reason against it. The sinkhole ain't but about half a mile from my line post."

"Oil's a tricky thing," Jonathan said musingly.

He tried to imagine Matthew and Ruth rich with the sudden fabulous wealth of those who found the treasure of oil in their earth. What would these two simple people do with money? If he had money he would build Median a church and a hospital and himself a roomful of books and add a study to his house where he could be alone sometimes in the evening.

"Shan't you buy a piece of land around there, Jonathan?" Matthew asked.

"I haven't time to bother about getting rich," Jonathan said. He smiled faintly. "Reckon it'll be easier for me to get the money I want from other folks when they get rich."

But he couldn't ask anyone else for a roomful of books for himself. "Haven't even much time to read," he thought.

He stirred in his swivel chair. "Well, reckon we better get back to work, Matt."

"Ruth and me haven't had much luck yet," Matthew said. He stood up, a tall stooped young man with an Adam's apple so large that he looked like a crane. "One of the cows tried to jump the fence last week and tore her belly open. We killed her quick and made beef, but she was a good cow and just come fresh. It's too hot to keep meat now, and I couldn't get rid of much of it. Ruth's tried to salt it down, and I brung some to Katie today."

"That's bad about the cow, though thanks for the meat," Jonathan said.

"I've done some carpenterin' for Stephen Parry on a house, though," Matthew went on. His toneless voice was part of him.

"Well, it takes energy," Jonathan said briskly. "I don't believe much in luck."

"I don't know about that," Matthew replied with doubt. " 'Twasn't any energy put that oil in the sinkhole. 'Twon't be energy that'll put oil in my land."

Jonathan laughed. "You've got me there. Well, then, good luck, Matt!"

"Thanks, Jonathan," Matthew drawled and, gathering up his long legs, he went away.

Six men crawled down the slimy black sides of the sinkhole. Lew's face was purple veined with black. He had not ridden horseback in a year, and his heart was beating as though it would burst out of his breast. But he lowered himself down into the hole.

"Ain't no doubt about the way it looks," Henry said. He dipped his hand into the iridescent black water and smelled it. The water was foul and stagnant, but stronger than the foulness was the penetrating reek of oil.

They smelled it, one after the other, and then they examined the sides of the hole. The earth was damp but not with water.

"It's like putty, it's so full of oil," Samuel Hasty said.

Two men clambered out quickly and mounted their horses.

"Hey, there!" Henry yelled.

They clawed the slimy banks and pulled themselves up by the strongly rooted grass, each man thinking only of himself. Not one saw that Lew was left behind.

"Hi, Henry!" he shouted. There was no answer. He heard the clatter of horses over the hard sod. "Sam'l!" he shrieked. He scrabbled at the slippery earth, but his vast body it was impossible to lift. He made one last great straining effort and felt a strong hot fiery flash inside his skull. Thought and knowledge were wiped away in an instant, and he fell backward into the oily, rainbow-surfaced water.

"You'd ought to tell Hans you found that oil in his sinkhole," Ruth said when they were eating their dinner of beef stew and cabbage.

Matthew's mouth was full of dry salt-rising bread, and he took a gulp of milk to down it before he could speak. "Never thought of it," he exclaimed.

"We'd surely appreciate it if somebody'd tell us if 'twas ours," Ruth said with wistfulness. Dreams unfinished and suppressed were in her dark eyes and in the faint color on her brown cheeks.

If they found oil she would add a parlor to the house, and they would buy a buggy and a team of horses instead of the mules, and she would buy an organ and a big doll for little Mary and for Maggie new clothes and Katie a fur muff and for Jonathan a gold watch. She loved to give presents, but never in her life had she walked into the store and bought anything. By some overlooking, no one had ever given her money and let her buy with it. Her mother and then Jonathan and Katie had bought and given to her, and now Matthew went to the store on Saturdays. Even if she went with him, he did the buying. She never had money in her hand to exchange for what she wanted. I could have it if I'd only say so, she thought in her defending heart. But she could never say so, dreading to explain, to be thought silly.

"I'll go right away before I start the afternoon's work," Matthew said.

An hour later he and Hans found Lew's great bulk head and shoulders under the rich water.

Hans, a kind and melancholy German, groaned, "I'd do midoudt oil forever before it happens on my place."

The two men could only heave the head out of the water.

"I'll have to get Jonathan," Matthew gasped. "Can you stay here, Hans?"

"Sure," Hans said. He took the end of Lew's shirt and wiped the oil from his face.

Matthew climbed out and upon his mule galloped to Median and went to the empty schoolhouse. Jonathan was back at his desk.

"Lew's drowned," Matthew shouted. "He's in the sinkhole. It'll take a lot of us to get him out."

Jonathan leaped out of his chair. "They didn't go and leave him!"

"Must of."

"I wish you'd never found the danged stuff, Matthew. It makes men act like beasts."

"What'll I do, Jonathan?"

"Round 'em up. Get the hotel surrey and take the back seats out and lay a quilt down to put Lew on. I'll have to tell Katie. Then I'll join you. But don't wait for me. Get the others. My mare's fast. I may catch you anyway."

He strode out of the schoolhouse into the clear July afternoon. How would he tell Katie, and how comfort her? He longed to have love to aid him so that he could open his arms and make amends. But to begin a course so strange to them would only make misery for them both. He sighed and, entering the door, smelled cinnamon and the fragrance of baking cookies. He went toward the kitchen. She was there at the table, cutting the dough quickly into stars and hearts. Through the open window he could see the children playing together in the back yard under a tree. She looked up, astonished to see him, and he began to speak quickly before she could ask the reason.

"Katie, there's bad news, my dear."

Her mouth opened, and her round eyes grew rounder.

"Wait," he said. "Do you want to take the cookies out of the oven first?"

"I better," she said. "They're done, anyway."

He stood while she emptied the pan of brown hot cookies upon a clean towel. The watchful children ran to the window.

"Mom! You said we could have some!" This was Mary, who called her Mom as her own children did.

She picked up six and gave them two apiece. "Don't ast me for any more," she said. Then she turned back to Jonathan.

"Your father's—passed away, Katie."

She sank upon a chair. "Oh, Jonathan!"

"In a queer terrible way, Katie—"

He had not told her that Matthew had found oil. The fewer people who knew it the better, he had thought. But the real reason was that he did not want her to urge him to buy land. He was a schoolteacher, he had been thinking wryly when Matthew came in, a speculator in human beings, not in human wealth.

"Shame on those men," Katie cried. "That Henry Drear, too, that Pop always stood by!" She choked and lifted her gray calico apron to her mouth and held it there. Over it her eyes filled with tears.

He made a step toward her, feeling he must make some response to her sorrow for Lew's sake, too.

"I was fond of him," he said in a low voice. He patted her shoulder gently once or twice. "I'm going to miss him myself, Katie, a great deal. I've got to hurry, Katie."

She fumbled for the slit pocket in her skirt and found her handkerchief and blew her nose loudly.

"I'll have to tell Maw," she said heavily.

He tiptoed away, his heart thick with sorrow and pity which he could not express, because between them there was no path of communication. He could only use the common ways in which he would have helped her had she never been his wife. And yet he longed to come nearer to her in her need. He knew her, if not with the illumination of love, nevertheless with the sober knowledge of the days and nights they had lived together under the same roof. But that life had been bounded by what could be said and heard and done. All that lay beyond these boundaries they had not shared. He thought sometimes that only in himself was there the beyond, and that her complete life was in what she did and said as she kept the house and in the afternoons went around two sides of the square to the store. But there was no time now to think. He hastened away.

Two hours later he helped to lift the lifeless mass of Lew's dead body off the surrey and carry it through the store into the back room and lay it upon the couch. Sue was waiting, for it had become her service in Median to prepare the dead for burial. Mrs. Merridy was there, and with her the twins.

"Get Joe and Jack out of here," Jonathan said to Katie sternly over his shoulder.

But she had shaken her head. "Maw wants 'em to be here," she whispered back. She held her handkerchief to her mouth as they laid Lew down. Mrs. Merridy sobbed loudly, but the twins did not move.

But Sue had heard this command. "Go out from here, all of you," she ordered them, but her full soft voice made the words gentle. "I must do what I can before he gets his mortal rigors too set."

They tiptoed out as though Lew's deaf ears could hear. Katie held her mother's arm, but Jonathan put a hand on each boy's thin shoulders, as tall now as his own. They were pupils in his school and Katie's brothers, but he had never given them much heed. They were, he had always thought, commonplace boys, exactly alike, from dusty brown hair to bare feet. But now he saw them acutely as Lew's sons, robbed forever of Lew's hearty, happy presence.

"Come along over to our house," he said. "Jonnie and Lula and Mary'll be glad to have you." He turned to their mother. "Will you come, too, Mrs. Merridy?" He had never been able to call her mother.

"No, I want to stay here with Lew," she moaned. "Sue'll be here—I don't want nobody else."

So they had left her, and after supper the children played out under the trees in the square. Katie went out to speak to them sharply two or three times because they grew too noisy.

"Why not let them be happy?" Jonathan said.

" 'Tain't decent, with a death in the family," she said indignantly. She was so exactly as she always was that he wondered how much she felt, or could feel.

In the night he thought he heard her crying. Something waked him, and it was Katie, sobbing. He moved from his side of the big double bed where he lay by long habit in a narrow stillness as he slept, and put out his hand. It touched her hair.

"Are you awake, my dear?" he asked.

"I been thinkin'," she replied. Her voice was firm. Perhaps she had not been crying, after all. He waited for her to go on.

"Jonathan, there's something I want you should do."

"I will if I can, Katie," he said gently.

In her fierce independence she had asked of him very little. He thought sometimes that it would have been easier for him if she had seemed to need him more than she did. A clinging, gentle woman might have wakened in him a deeper tenderness. But he was not a whit prepared for the stupendous act she now asked of him. Her voice came out of the darkness at his side.

"I want you should take the store."

His ears heard, but his mind refused belief. "I couldn't manage school and store both, Katie."

"You could give up the school."

"No, I couldn't!" His cry was sharp in the night.

"Why not?" she asked. "I wish you would, Jonathan. I've often wished you would. Even if Pa hadn't died, I've wished you would. It makes me mad the way you have to listen to the trustees and the way you're at everybody's beck and call, and you got to take what they feel to pay you. Last year they cut you a third, and you couldn't say anything. You haven't any independence—you belong to the town. But in the store you'd have nobody to be your boss."

"I couldn't," he gasped. He forgot that it had ever been his thought to comfort her. She needed no comfort. It was he who would need strength to withstand her. He could hear in her voice the strong stubbornness that meant one of her ideas had taken her narrow mind in its hold.

"I do hope you won't push me, Katie," he said, trying to be stern. "For I won't be pushed in this. A man must do what he likes best to do, and schoolteaching is what I've always wanted. Why, even in Dentwater I used to plan a school. I never thought I'd have it here in Median, but now that I have, my life is here."

"Then you don't care if a bunch of men says they can't pay you what you earn," she cried angrily.

"No, I don't," he said, "not when I know it's a bad year and nobody's gotten what he earned."

"Well, it's me has to feed you all just the same," she retorted. "If you was in the store you'd get easy twice as much. Pa said last year was his best year. He laid by more'n he spent."

"I don't want more money, Katie," he said gently. "I can pay my bills. If I can't, Median folk'll trust me. Why, I don't even want to buy up land for oil. I just want to live the way we are. I'd rather put in my extra time the way I did to get the post office. If we win the election for county seat, I'm going to get us a courthouse this summer. I made it a promise to Drear that he could say Median would put up its own courthouse if it was chosen."

"You're ready enough to work without pay, but somebody pays!" Her voice was bitter. "I pay and the children pay!"

"But you have what you need, Katie!" he cried. "What would you do with more money?"

He asked it honestly. She did not read, she played no instrument of music, clothes could not change her or give her vanity.

"I'd like money in the bank," she said. "If anything happened to you—"

He interrupted her. "Nothing's going to happen to me. I shall live a very long time."

In the darkness of midnight he felt infinitely weary. In the darkness he and Katie must lie, side by side. It was a very long time until the day could break. They did not speak again.

33

AND YET each time when the day came it was good. Jonathan was a man born to enjoy small cheerful things. Good food, sunshine, the slant of the plains toward the sky that his eyes never failed to see, the welcoming solitude of his office chair, the papers on his desk, a book he bought secretly to add to his shelves, a schoolbook sent him sometimes, and this always flattered him though he knew it was sent to hundreds like him, the sight of his son Jon running out of the house to meet him at night—the days were lively with such cheer.

Lew's funeral was hardly over before Katie went at him again.

"What's to be done about the store, Jonathan?"

"It can be sold," he said firmly.

"Well, it won't be," she said. Katie's chin, of no particular shape, could look like a cliff under her plain mouth.

He did not answer. In his own quiet way, without being aware of it, he could be as high-handed as Clyde.

When after weeks he saw Katie would never sell the store and was trying with her mother to manage it herself, he said mildly, "I'll keep the books for you, Katie, and make the inventory and orders."

"That'll be a help," she said.

But she did not give up, and he knew she had not. Between her and her mother he felt a snare set for him, and he walked warily; and yet, though he did not know it, he had Mrs. Merridy to thank for what peace he had.

"Don't you nag Jonathan," Mrs. Merridy told Katie. "He's the kind that comes quicker without. Now Lew you could nag, for he'd do anything to git rid of you. But Jonathan goes his own way."

"It'll come around my way one of these days just the same," Katie said. "I shan't rest until he's in the store."

Outside of his house Jonathan gave no thought to the submerged strife between him and Katie.

The dark rainbow promise of oil was being fulfilled. Fourteen great derricks had sprung up around the sinkhole in which Lew had drowned. American House was jammed with beds for men who had come out of every place in the country where rumor had chanced to be blown. Even in the days when wagons were going West there had not been so many travelers. These were all men. If a woman came, she was an oddity and she knew it. But the bulk of the oil land was not for sale. The Sunflower Oil Company had bought it. No one knew who were the men who made it. Hans Rourse said, "Somebody comes to me after Lew is *todt* in my sinkhole—a nize man knows Lew good, he sayed. 'Ain'dt it awful how Lew dies,' he sayed, and he was Lew's friend. So I sayed, 'Yes, is awful, for sure.' An' he sayed, do I want to sell the sinkhole and maybe ten-twenty acres around. He sayed maybe is there oil there and if iss, I will get twenty-five per cent. So I sayed, 'Ya, I don't vant a sinkhole nohow a man drowns in and maybe next my good cows.' And so I put my name on his paper."

The same man came one day to Matthew's door at noon. Matthew and Ruth were at dinner. They were eating their first green corn, and Matthew had a great ear of it in his hand when he opened the kitchen door.

"Good day," the man said. His dark eyes were soft with a smile. "May I have a word with you?"

"Come in," Matthew said. "We're eatin', and you're welcome to jine in. That's my wife. Cobb is the name."

"How do you do, Mrs. Cobb," the man said. "I'm glad I can speak with both of you. A man's wife is a useful partner. I'd like to have an option on your land for oil, Mr. Cobb. I'll pay higher than the usual terms—say, fifteen dollars a year, and if we strike oil, a fourth of the proceeds are yours. Does that seem fair?"

Ruth looked at Matthew. Others had offered them five dollars a year, and eight and ten.

"I—it is more than we've been offered," Matthew said, hesitating. "Won't you sit down, stranger?"

"Thanks, no," the man said. "I must be on my way. Then you will take it?"

Matthew looked at Ruth. "Can't do no harm to take the highest bid, can it?"

"I guess not," she said faintly.

"All right," Matthew said.

"Then will you sign this paper?" The man held a folded paper toward him. "Read it first, please. I wouldn't want you to sign what you hadn't read."

Long legal words heaped themselves before Matthew's eyes. "I guess it's all right," he said. "I don't make much sense out of 'em, but I ain't puttin' out any money, am I?"

"Of course not," the stranger said quickly. "It's the other way. As soon as you sign that, I put out the money."

He took his purse from his pocket and counted fifteen dollars.

"And here's a pen," he said, "one of those newfangled ones that holds its own ink."

Matthew shifted his corn to his left hand and wiped his fingers on the seat of his jeans.

"Works, does it?"

"It's inclined to be balky." The man laughed a rolling gust of laughter.

Matthew signed his name and took the money and the man folded the paper quickly and put it in his pocket. Then he tipped his hat to Ruth and smiled his pleasant smile.

"Good day," he said and was gone. They saw him leap on a chestnut horse and gallop away across the plains toward the east.

Matthew looked dazed. "Did somep'n happen to me or didn't it?"

Ruth laughed. "The money's in your hand, silly! What was the name on the paper?"

"Damned if I know," Matthew said ruefully. "I ought to of looked, oughtn't I?"

"Oh, well," Ruth said easily, "it doesn't matter. We have the money. Oh, Matthew, suppose they should find oil on our land!"

"What'll we do with the money?"

"Matthew, could I have a piano?" she whispered.

"Shore you can!" He stooped to kiss her and then sat down.

"It's silly when I can't play," she said.

"You can learn, can't you?" he retorted. "We'll have to move if they find oil. Might buy us a house in Topeka. You could get a music teacher there."

"What'll you do in Topeka?" she asked anxiously.

"Might go into making furniture," he said slowly. "I always did hanker after woodwork. Something I could smooth to the grain."

They sat in silence a moment, the fifteen dollars he had in his shirt pocket the kernel of all their hope.

"Seems like we ought to share all this with somebody," Ruth murmured, looking out of the window.

"Jonathan ought to buy, but he won't," Matthew said. "He don't want to bother with gettin' rich."

"Then let's tell Jamie!" Ruth's brown eyes lifted.

"Good idea," Matthew said largely. "You know where he's at?"

"He's still at the Big Four Ranch, his last letter said."

"Then shore," Matthew said. "I guess we can afford a stamp now, cain't we, Ruthie?"

"I reckon!" she said and laughed. "Oh, Matt, ain't we lucky?"

"Wonderful," he said.

At the Big Four Ranch, lying on the grass at noon hour, Jamie folded Ruth's letter and put it into his shirt pocket and stretched himself. Who would have thought of oil in Median? He was taller than either of his brothers, taller now than Clyde, and blue-eyed and black-haired. Hard riding against sun and wind had made his skin coppery as an Indian's. His hairy young hands were as strong as steel traps.

"Quickest way in the world to get rich," he muttered.

He had a contract with Big Four to stay until winter, but he made up his mind now that he would break it. No contract had ever held him beyond his wish when all he had to do was to jump on a horse and lope across the prairies. He had the finest horse that he had ever had, chosen out of the wild horses that he had lassoed by his uncanny skill with the rope. The horse did not belong to him, but that did not trouble him. He took care to keep it in the height of condition. If I have me a good horse, he often thought, it's my freedom.

A man came to the door and yelled at him. "Hey there, you! It's a long way from quittin' time!"

Jamie grinned, rose, and, pulling his wide felt hat over one eye, sauntered toward the door.

"You round up them horses you finished off yestiddy," the foreman ordered him. He was swallowing the last gulps of a tin cup full of black coffee. "They're due to be shipped by the four o'clock. Got a rush order today from Indiana."

Jamie did not answer. He changed the direction of his saunter from east to southeast to stop at the bunkhouse. It was empty. All the men had gone back to work. He went to his bunk and opened the end of the straw tick under the blankets and drew out a small wad rolled in oilcloth. In it were his summer's wages and all he owned except for an extra shirt under his pillow. This he drew out and stuffed inside the one he wore. Then he went out again.

If I'm goin', I'll git started, he thought. He quickened his easy loping gait and came to a small fenced-in lot full of horses pushing and nudging each other.

"Come here, Lady!" he called. He had a fine voice, Clyde's voice, but rich and young.

A bay mare thrust her head against him, and he led her out by the long black hair of her mane.

"Stand there till I fetch the saddle," he ordered her. Scarcely a trace of England remained upon his tongue.

He came back almost instantly to the obedient mare and flung across her back a saddle so handsome that half a year's pay had gone for it. The mare quivered, but he buckled the girth without paying any heed and tested the stirrups. Then he leaped on her back. The instant she felt his weight she sprang forward and across the sod.

Within sight of the ranch house, he headed seemingly for the corral. But before he reached it he turned sharp east. Then, leaning low, he gave the horse her head. If he kept her to her speed, he could reach the homestead by sundown. His heart lifted as the wind sang in his ears. This was what he loved best in his life, a horse flying beneath him and he headed for a new life. . . .

He did not think of his mother from one day's end to another, but for one moment his heart jumped when he stooped to enter his father's door. There was a woman sitting by the stove, her chin on her hand as Mary used often to sit in the last days of her life. He saw a thick braid of red hair swing over her shoulder as she turned her head to him, and instantly he knew her.

"Hello, Jennet," he said.

"Hello, you," she said without moving. "Where'd you come from?"

"I better ask you that," he retorted. He came in. "I belong here in a manner of speaking, but what about you?"

She laughed suddenly and held out her left hand. A wide shining gold ring was on the third finger.

"Meet your step-maw," she said.

"You're lying!" he said slowly. Anger and admiration mingled in him for a moment, an anger vaguely for his mother's sake that Jennet, whom she always disliked, should be here, and rueful admiration of a man as old as his father who was able so to persuade a young woman. Then he laughed.

"Why, Dad's a reg'lar old geezer!" he cried. He sat down on the end of the table without taking off his hat. "How'd you come to leave His Highness?"

"I got tired of being chucked out when he thought he didn't want me," she said. Her mouth, which had been beautiful in sullenness when she was a girl, was now coarse. "I decided I'd show him. I'm a respectable married woman, now."

"Does he come around?" Jamie asked, staring at her.

"Your paw took his shotgun to him the only time he did," Jennet said. They looked at each other and broke into common laughter.

"Dad's an old goat," Jamie said and spat on the earthen floor. "Nothing downs him."

"He's talkin' about runnin' for land when they open up the new territory," Jennet said with a fresh burst. Her laughter was unchanged, the same hard, clear laughter that even in her childhood had carried no music in it.

"Why, he can't run with that game leg!" Jamie cried. "And he's never learned to sit his horse right."

"He's rigged himself up a seat on the back wheels of an old wagon," Jennet said. "And he's trainin' one of the colts into a race horse."

Across the grassy landscape they saw Clyde limping briskly toward them. Jamie leaped from the table and went to meet him.

"Hi!" he shouted.

Clyde squeezed his favorite son in his arms. "Where'd you blow from?" he inquired. Under his torn hat of Indian straw his hair flew in curly gray strands, but his eyes were as sharp and black as ever, and a red handkerchief was knotted about his throat. He looked younger than he had in years, and full of impudence.

"I'm goin' East," Jamie said. He pulled Ruth's letter from his pocket and held it out to Clyde.

Clyde spat in the grass. "You tell me what's in it. I don't read much any more. Haven't the time."

Jamie put the letter back in his pocket. "Oil's been struck."

"Never on their land!" Clyde cried.

"Next door," Jamie said. "And they're lettin' 'em try on their land."

"Dang me if I won't go that way instead of the Territory." Clyde limped faster to match his son's long even gait. "Beats all how opportunity fair crushes a man here. Oil spouts out on one side of him, and there's free land on the other. I'm all in a maze."

"How's things here?"

"Good so far as they go, but I haven't enough land. Three hundred and twenty acres don't go far. A man's got to think big here in this country."

"But how'll you manage land there and here?"

Clyde shot a look at his son. "Thought maybe you'd give your old dad a hand. You was always the one I count on, Jamie."

"But I'm goin' in for oil, Dad."

Clyde scratched his fingers into his beard. "Eh, well, I'll manage," he said stubbornly.

Without knowing it he had decided for land and against oil because Jamie would not help him. "I can do for myself," he said with such complacency that Jamie looked down at him and then followed the beam of his father's eyes. They fell on Jennet standing in the doorway, the sun shining on her red head as she shaded her eyes to look for them.

Jamie's white teeth shone. "I should say you can," he said. "A reg'lar billy goat, ain't you, Dad?"

"Well, I'm hearty," Clyde said, and his red lips were smug in his beard.

34

IN HIS office Jonathan sat with three other men counting ballots steadily, stacking them into packages and slipping rubber bands about them. The box on the floor to the left of him was Ashbee; on the right was Median. Outside the midsummer sun of an August afternoon beat upon a crowd of men and horses and wagons. The horses were stirring against the flies, and men fanned themselves with branches they had picked from the trees in the square.

Jonathan stopped counting and leaned out of the window. "Don't you chaps break those young hardwoods!" he shouted. "Cottonwoods don't matter, but I sent East for the others to plant around the courthouse." He pulled his head in as they guffawed and went on counting.

Henry Drear waited patiently, a rifle across his knees. "Ashbee's goin' to declare the election's illegal if we win," he said.

"They can't do that," Jonathan said, his lips still murmuring numbers.

"Ashbee can do anything," Henry retorted. "But I've got 'em fixed."

Jonathan paused. "Median isn't going to do anything illegal, now, Henry."

"You git along with the countin'," Henry said.

Jonathan went on counting.

"Say," Henry said, "some of the folks want to change the name of the town when we git to be the county seat. Median sounds kind of common."

Jonathan stopped again. "How can I count if you keep on with your dangety ideas? I won't have the town called out of its name. Median it was when I came, and Median it'll be when I go. It's a good sensible name that don't pretend to be big."

"They want to call it Mecca," Henry said doubtfully.

"Mecca!" Jonathan repeated. "Why, that's the name of a city in heathendom!"

"They say it's a place everybody wants to go like to heaven."

"Who wants everybody coming to our town?" Jonathan's voice was querulous. "I've a good notion to stop this whole business right here."

"Now, Jonathan, don't get cantankerous. I swear for a man your size—" He sighed and spat.

"Don't let me hear any more silly talk about Mecca, then."

Jonathan's look was so gloomy that Henry took alarm. "Don't it look good for Median?"

"Too many handwritings alike on some of the ballots."

"So long as they all say Median—"

Jonathan banged the table with his fist. "Danged if I'll be party to a fraud," Jonathan cried. "Looks to me like your handwriting, Henry. See here." His square dexterous hands sorted a dozen or more ballots of the same large irregular writing. All of them were for Median.

The men roared with laughter. Henry was not abashed. "Don't look alike to me," he said.

Jonathan swept them together and threw them into the wastebasket. Henry chewed the straggling brown ends of his long moustache.

"Look hyere, you can't—"

"Then we'll declare the whole election fraudulent."

"Oh, all right," Henry grumbled. He had risen, but now he sat down heavily and took off his felt hat and wiped his forehead. "But if Median don't git it, I'll turn the hotel into a whorehouse to spite your damn pigheadedness, Jonathan."

"Median's getting it," Jonathan retorted.

"Even without my votes?" Henry shouted.

"Even without your many votes," Jonathan said.

But Henry did not notice irony. He leaped to his feet and rushed to the window and fired into the sky.

"It's Median!" he yelled. "Median's got it. Median—Median—Median —hooray!" and throwing his gun on the floor he jumped out of the window and ran round the schoolhouse while the crowd yelled.

But at his desk Jonathan picked up a letter. It was very short:

> DEAR JONATHAN:
>   I shall be glad to see you for any cause. Shall we say on
> Saturday the eighteenth? Judy joins me in regards. I am yours
> as ever,
>
>   EVAN

At the end of the letter Evan had scribbled in his own handwriting, "Come to my house, Jonathan."

Upstairs in her big bedroom, Judy hid behind the rose satin curtain and looked out the window. The house was the same into which Evan had first brought her, but a new wing added to each side had made it into what the Topeka newspapers called "a mansion." Judy herself had taken on stateliness. Her hair was brushed high and lay in curls over the top of her head. But above the lace collar of her dress her creamy nape was still as soft as a child's. Her hands clasping the curtains were strangely childish, too, in their shape, and her lips had kept their purity, and her eyes were as dark as ever above the wine-red taffeta of her wide-sleeved dress.

"Do you mind if Jonathan comes here?" Evan had asked her last night.

"Why should I mind?" she had replied, lifting her lashes at him.

He was no longer disturbed by this sight of long lashes sweeping upward like the wings of dark butterflies. He knew the movement was meaningless because she used it to delay the necessity for thought before speech.

"No reason whatever, my dear," he retorted. "All the agony is over, and it seems a little ridiculous now."

Judy did not answer. But had someone been there who loved her, he might have seen timidity in the look she gave her husband. She was afraid of him because she loved him and because he did not love her. Where it was in their life together that Evan had ceased to love her she did not know. Much of the time when she sat alone in the strange stillness which was now her life, she pondered this matter, searching over the years to discover at what moment the thing had happened.

"I haven't changed," she murmured often to herself.

She was even as beautiful as ever she was. She examined her hands, her face, even shyly her body, alone before the mirror. No, she had not changed, and did not know that in this very fact lay the secret of Evan's change.

For it was Evan's curse that he had a gentleman's conscience, and that he had in his way loved Jonathan more than he had ever loved any human being. Never except with Jonathan had his mind met the mind of another human being. Even now, when he and Jonathan had been years separated, he found himself remembering the hours of talk with him, when as two young men they had told one another everything, had argued and quarreled, but always had trusted one another. With Jonathan he had been himself, his good self, large and honest and free. Jonathan had been his foil and his inspiration. He had whetted himself on Jonathan, handsome because Jonathan was plain, gay because Jonathan was sober, a tempest beside Jonathan's calm. He had continued to love Jonathan because Jonathan alone of all the people he had known made him his best. And he knew that he was at his happiest when he was also at his best. He laughed at his own tricks but despised them. He could not enjoy dishonesty.

As for Judy, he had ceased to love her when he understood that he could never hope for more from her than the beauty of her body. He enjoyed her beauty especially when they were in public places. Alone with her, its satisfaction was swiftly over. There were no depths to it. He found himself wishing often that under the lovely face he might also have found an exciting mind.

"Unreasonable," he thought now, looking down into the lovely face. For he had taken her in his arms suddenly at this moment in a quick shallow burst of passion, stimulated by the thought of Jonathan's coming.

"You're not sorry you ran away with me, Judy?" he whispered.

She closed her eyes and put her white hand against his lips. "Never, Evan—if only you love me!"

He kissed her swiftly. "Of course," he said, and let her go. What perversity not to love a woman more because she loved him so much! But Judy was in perpetual surrender, and he loved excitement.

He kissed her once again, lightly, his passion gone in a whirlwind as small and useless as a toss of leaves in the middle of the road on a summer's day. He smiled, pulled her little ear, glanced at himself in the mirror, and went away.

Her eyes followed him with their large dark gaze, and when he was gone she went to the window as she always did when he left her. If he left the house she watched him, and when he did not, she stared out into the street. But behind the curtain her childish hand held from her face she now saw a slender sand-colored man step from a hired hack and pause for a moment. He lifted his head and looked at the house, and the look seemed to fall upon her, direct as a beam from a lamp. She shrank behind the curtain and hid her face in her hands.

"Oh!" she murmured. "He's just the same!" She sat down on her rose-colored taffeta chair, and waited to see whether Evan would send for her.

Downstairs in the library, Evan and Jonathan looked at each other after many years. Evan saw Jonathan, but between him and Evan Jonathan saw Judy. Evan was Judy's husband. This was Judy's home. Through these rooms she moved every day. Her hands perhaps had arranged the bowl of roses on Evan's desk. A large silver photograph stood beside the roses, and he could not see the face it held, yet doubtless it was hers.

"Well, Jonathan!" Evan filled his voice with heartiness. He had risen to shake Jonathan's hand and then had sat down again behind his desk. He had planned to be formal and full of business, but the sight of Jonathan in his usual gray garb, sitting quietly before him, moved him to an impulsiveness he did not often feel in these days of his increasing success. He saw governorship clearly ahead of him.

"We'll take up where we left off, Jonnie." His fine smile made his face young enough for Jonathan to recognize him. His first thought had been how much Evan was changed. The even, early gray in his dark hair made him strange.

" 'Tisn't for anything past that I've come, Evan," he said calmly. "It's for a thing I want now."

Evan withdrew his smile. "What can I do for you now?"

"I want quite a lot of money, it happens," Jonathan said firmly. "It's for Median and not me. Looks as though we'll get the county seat unless Ashbee protests the election, and if they do, it'll help us to say we have funds for the courthouse."

Evan's smile glimmered. "You wouldn't let me have a cattle town. I might take my revenge now, Jonnie. I wouldn't put it above my doing."

"A county seat's a dignified, respectable thing," Jonathan said, "very different from a rumbling, tumbling cattle town. A county seat'll bring churches into Median and law and order of all kinds. The people that buy lots in the town'll be the better sort as have to do with such things." He looked steadily at Evan with his cool gray eyes.

He's forgotten Judy, Evan was thinking. He's an odd, cold chap, but I'm fond of him still, somehow, though he'll never be anything but the principal of a small-town school.

"Still building Median, Jonnie!" he said aloud. "How far have you got on that map we made together?"

"Schoolhouse is up, post office, and after the courthouse I aim to start the church. I've got a young chap in mind for the preacher, though just now he's out among the Indians. But I'll draw him back maybe with the church."

"Do you have children?" Evan's question was a thrust.

"A boy and a girl," Jonathan replied.

"Ah, you're luckier than I am," Evan said significantly. "Judy has never had a child."

The name fell between them like a stone, and Jonathan was struck to silence. For a moment he could not speak, try as he did. His heart, so carefully hidden even from himself, pounded under his gray coat; and Evan, watching him, saw a dull red creep into his colorless cheeks.

He still thinks about her, Evan thought with cool pity. He turned the big photograph frame on the table abruptly to face Jonathan. "She's changed very little," he said carelessly.

Jonathan did not move by a hair. His hands upon his knees he held there. But with all his heart he gazed upon Judy's face. She was very beautiful. In the richness of her evening dress and the jewels about her bare neck, he saw her as infinitely handsomer and more stately than he remembered her. How ill she would have fitted his small plain home, he thought suddenly. No, Katie was the sort of woman anyone would expect to see come out of his door, a busy housewife of a woman, her face clean and brown, but not one to look at twice.

"What's past is long gone," Evan said. He laughed a little. "I used to think Judy might be a bit skittish, Jon, as pretty girls often are. But she settled into marriage like a cat by a fire. Never has a thought outside the house, apparently."

He felt himself seized by an absurd desire to tell Jonathan that somehow his marriage had been a disappointment to him, as though disappointment were expiation of the betrayal of his friend.

"Judy's a strange woman, Jonathan," he said abruptly.

"Indeed," Jonathan said stiffly. He did not want to hear Evan talk about Judy. No, nor did he like to hear any man talk about his wife.

Evan saw the pale plain face grow stern. There was to be no expiation there! He laughed uneasily. "You're thinking that I made my own bed."

"I am thinking only about my business," Jonathan retorted. "Will you do what I ask?" But his heart was pounding all through his body. How dared this man be disappointed in his love? But had Judy indeed repented of what she had done? Did her coldness come from deep within her? "Does she still remember me?" his heart demanded. He gripped his heart with his will and choked it into silence.

"Well, Evan?" he asked and made his voice as dry as rustling winter cornstalks.

Evan put the picture back. "What's your proposition?"

"Ten thousand dollars, at six per cent, the new town lots to be security."

"Can you sell them?"

"In time we can."

"What time?"

"Ten years."

"What's the population now?"

"Three thousand two hundred and ten."

"That include niggras?"

"Why shouldn't it?" Jonathan's pale eyes flashed a cold spark, and Evan laughed.

"Still think a lot of niggras, eh, Jon?"

"No more than of anybody else, but as much."

Evan leaned forward. "Say, what's become of that boy you sent to France?"

"He graduated last year from the Academy of Surgery in Paris, France. He's married a young Frenchwoman."

"You don't say! But the French are *white!*"

"I believe so," Jonathan said very coldly.

Evan drew in his breath. "Well, it couldn't happen here."

"Beaumont himself rather proves it can."

"What do you mean?" Evan demanded.

"Beaumont's father was white."

"Come now, Jon—that's different, and you know it."

"I do not know it."

Jonathan's thin body was erect with embattlement, and suddenly Evan laughed. "You haven't changed a hair of your head, Jonnie!"

"I hope I have not on this subject at least," Jonathan said severely.

"Well, you haven't, and let's shut up. Now, about this money. You shall have it. I don't mind saying I wouldn't think of laying out that much for Median if it weren't for you, Jonathan. Median's not my kind of a town. Now, here in Topeka we've just issued bonds for the new trolley-car system, and that's a sound investment. Trolleys will be wanted as long as the city stands. But I doubt Median ever grows to the point of needing them. In fact, there's no real reason for Median to grow."

Jonathan broke in. "I have no desire to see Median grow only in size. What kind of people live in Median means more than how many there are. And we've a good kind of folk there now. They're honest—barring an old-timer or two like Henry Drear, who sees things always off the end of his gun the way it used to be when the country was wild. You needn't be afraid your money wouldn't come back out of taxes."

"As long as you're alive, I'll have my security," Evan said. His good smile made the words very warm.

"Thanks," Jonathan said. He rose. "I aim to live a long life."

"I hope so," Evan said. He pressed a bell and, when Marcus appeared, rose and followed Jonathan to the library door. "Good-by, Jonathan. I'm glad you came."

"Thanks, Evan."

The two men clasped hands for a swift instant and parted, each aware that they were not brothers as they had been, and so they were not sorry to part.

In the hall, Jonathan put on his coat quickly and took his hat from the Negro. He wanted to be away out of this house, and yet he could not keep from glancing about him and up the stair. It was so silent a house. Not a sound could be heard from the carpeted and curtained rooms. From all that ear told, it might have been empty. Marcus opened the door and bowed; and Jonathan, nodding his head, went out. Behind him the door closed softly.

But he stood before it with a strange hesitating clairvoyance, as though the closing had not been final. Was this all or not? He wanted to go, but he did not feel free to go yet. And even as he stood, the door opened again suddenly, and Judy stood there.

The moment he saw her he knew that this was why he had come, and that he could not have gone away without it. She was more beautiful than his deepest memory had remembered. She was a woman of cream and roses beneath her softly piled curls, her red dress a vase for her beauty. In her little ears were pearls, and on her white neck a fine gold chain, and he saw everything about her—every color and tint and shape, the deep sweet corners of her red mouth and her glorious eyes and her upflung lashes. He had never seen a pretty girl until he saw Judy, and he had never seen a beautiful woman until he saw her now.

She spoke at last. "Jonathan, I couldn't quite just—let you go."

He was speechless, gazing at her, and she put out her hand to him. "You aren't still angry with me, Jonathan?"

He shook his head and felt her hand in his hand that was trembling in a palsy at what it held. She looked this way and that and whispered, "I often think you loved me best, after all, Jonathan."

He could not speak. He put her little hand to his lips and then knew what he did and turned himself and ran down the steps and into the waiting hack. Then he took one backward look at the door. She was standing there, the hand he had kissed against her mouth.

"Get on," he groaned to the hack driver. As the vehicle clattered down the street, he bent his head and shielded his face with his hand, full of horror at himself. I'm not fit to be trusted near her, he thought. I love her still.

"Did you get the money?" Katie's voice, her face across the supper table, the children between them to be served and fed, were what he had every night. Nothing was better, nothing worse.

"Yes, I got it," he said.

Katie stared at him. "You ain't sick, are you, Jonathan?" she asked. He looked more than usually pale, and he had eaten almost nothing of the fried liver and potatoes.

"No, I'm—tired."

"I thought maybe a day in the city would liven you up," she said.

He smiled faintly at this. "Do you feel I should be more lively?" he inquired.

He had entered his home tonight under the fresh shadow of his strong debt to Katie. He owed very much to this hard-working good woman who belonged in his house and made of it a place suitable for a man like him. Judy would have been a bird of paradise, and what would a plain chap like him have done with her?

"I'm sorry I'm dull, Katie," he said gently. "I did hear some interesting things. There's to be trolleys in Topeka—"

"Just so's you ain't sick is all I care," Katie said.

But in the night, lying sleepless in the bed beside her, he suddenly longed to confess all his heart to Katie. It would ease him to share the weight of his love, to tell her that because he had loved another woman and today knew he still loved her and would now love her always, he would make eternal amends to her for having married her. He put out his hand, and then he drew it back and lay in long self-examination. Why should he want to tell Katie a thing too great for her to bear? She would never comprehend it. So long as she lived she would stagger under the knowledge.

Another man would leave Katie, he thought bitterly, but I can't—I wouldn't. I care too much for what I've built up here in Median.

Yes, he was the sort who could love a woman with all this power and agony, and yet he would not give up what he was to that love. He could not forsake himself even for love. He lay on, sleepless through the night.

But I'm never to be left alone in the room with Judy, he thought. If ever we meet again, it's never to be alone.

He rose early before Katie stirred and stole into the kitchen and lit the fire for her and put the kettle on and then made himself a cup of tea and set the table for breakfast. She came bustling in while he was busy and cried, "My goodness, you don't have to help *me*, Jonathan!"

But he knew it was her wry way of thanking him.

"Dad's married to Jennet," Jamie said in the manner of one who makes a joke.

Jonathan looked up from a pile of architects' plans he was spreading over the dining table. An hour ago Jamie had come riding up to the kitchen door.

"Jamie, what are you saying?" he cried.

"Sure, Dad's married Jennet Drear," Jamie repeated, grinning.

"He's never!" Jonathan said.

"That Jennet!" Katie shrilled.

"Seems she was there when he came in one night, and so it kind of —happened," Jamie said.

"How'd she come to be there at all?" Katie demanded. She remembered Jennet as one who was a plain little girl remembers an older and pretty one, with a prickling of old envy.

"Well, she came over from the next ranch where she lived for a while," Jamie said with the proper deceit before women and children. Later he might tell Jonathan the truth. His old childish admiration for his father made him laugh now at Clyde's marrying again.

Suddenly Jonathan gathered up his papers and stalked out. He wanted to be alone that he might comprehend why he was so angry with his father. He stepped through the shadows and moonlight upon the grass and went up the steps of the schoolhouse and into his office and lit the oil lamp on the desk. He threw the roll of plans upon the floor and sat down and, thrusting his hands deep into his pockets, stared across the room.

A map of Europe hung on the wall, and he saw off in one corner of it the small oblong that was England. His mother would have been alive now if they could have stayed there. She had died because his father was impatient of work and steadiness and all that which Englishmen knew was righteousness. And now even as an old man he had not the decency to stay a widower for her sake, who lay so small and forlorn in her little grave in these huge plains!

"Oh, my poor wee!" he cried silently. In the spot upon the map he saw the green isle where she belonged.

But, no, his father must marry a red-haired woman who had wandered in and out of western towns and mining camps and who knew what else?

And then in his fearful honesty he went deep into his hatred for his father and found its roots. It was that once again, as gaily as a boy, Clyde had taken the woman he wanted, a thing he himself could not do.

I'm a wicked and deceitful man, he thought, pretending I'm crying for my mother's sake! It's Judy I'm thinking of again—and always will, I reckon.

He sat a moment, his lips pursed together, and then he stooped and picked up his plans.

35

IT WAS nearly six o'clock of a summer's day of the next year when he heard footsteps upon the cinder path which led from his own house to the open door of the schoolhouse. He had been uneasily conscious that Katie would be sending for him at any moment to come to supper. She divided her day into the three crises of meals, and nothing disturbed her more fiercely than to be ready to "dish up" and he not there. He yielded to her in such small tyrannies, though now he delayed.

He thought for a second before he looked up that the step was Maggie's plump footfall. But this was not Maggie. He looked up, and a strange man stood in the door. The late afternoon sunshine of a summer day falling through a dusty western window showed him a tall man, broad-shouldered, strong-legged, his face shaven as though he were young and yet lined enough to show him not young. He was dressed in a new gray suit, which fitted him ill, and his step had been the heavier for his new yellow leather shoes.

"You Jonathan Goodliffe?"

The man leaned arm and hand against the door jamb.

"I am," Jonathan replied. He showed his cautious English origin. Anyone else in Median would have cried to the man to come in, but Jonathan waited.

"You don't know me?" the man said.

"I can't say I do," Jonathan answered.

"Ever see me before?"

Jonathan examined the sunburned face before him. "Can't say I have."

"Ever hear the name George Tenney?"

Jonathan stared again, and now the face seemed younger and familiar. "You were on the ship coming from England."

"I was, and I gave you my name and you never sent me a word about Maggie, though you said you would."

"I didn't take that serious," Jonathan said, smiling.

George Tenney stood, his arms still stretched across the door and gazed at Jonathan. "I'd ha' known you anywhere," he said at last.

"I daresay I don't change," Jonathan said calmly. "Come in," he added.

But now there were Maggie's footsteps, hearty and hurrying.

"Jonathan!" Her clear loud young voice shouted through the silence of the evening. "Supper!"

"That's Maggie," George Tenney said.

"How did you know?" Jonathan asked.

"I know Maggie," George replied. A shy peculiar look came over his face and he looked over his shoulder. Then Maggie came near and stood staring with young severity at the big man in the door.

"Well?" she inquired tartly.

George Tenney's blue eyes smiled down at her. "Walk under my arm and let me see if you're the right size," he said slowly.

Maggie took quick offense. Girls were valued and indulged in Median, being too few.

"I don't see as my size has anything to do with you!" she cried. The curly ends of her red hair sprang out about her face in the wind.

"It's got a lot to do with me—I'm George Tenney," he said.

He could not have asked for more than the vivid red that rushed into Maggie's face.

"Did you get my letter?"

She flung up her head. "What letter?"

"You didn't answer it, so I come to see for myself."

"I don't answer strangers," she cried.

"I'm no stranger," he said in his slow deep voice. "Walk under my arm, Maggie." She did not move, and he repeated the words, but now they were not a command. His eyes smiled at her.

She stood rebellious and unwilling and shy. But she was struggling to fit to this man the vague man behind the letter which she kept all these months. She kept the two for a moment, and then the real man grew strong beside the conjured shadow, and suddenly, without bending her head, she walked under his arm. He dropped his hand to her shoulder.

"You're just the size I wanted you should be," he said gently. With his hand still on her shoulder he turned to Jonathan. "I'll come and take supper with you, Jonathan, seeing as I'm to be one of the family."

"Maggie's too young for you, George," Jonathan said.

Throughout the meal he said almost nothing, while the children were there. He simply watched George Tenney as he ate and drank and made friends with one child after another, and deferred to Katie with "ma'ams" and "thank yous." He was pleased that to each child this man made a gentle new approach. To little Jon he spoke of work as gravely as he would to a man.

"Cattle's my business," he said. "I herd 'em up from Texas by the thousand. It's a mean job while it lasts, but the pay's good. But I don't aim to stay in it. I've got other irons in my fire—a ranch, for one thing, with hosses, and if your pa'll let you, I'd like you to come out and give me a hand some summer. You can take your pick of the colts."

"Can I, Father?" Jon asked, yearning. He was a stocky, strong boy, more like his grandfather Lew than he was his own father.

"Maybe," Jonathan replied.

George teased Lula about her blond curls.

"Store curls, I'll swear," he said. "They don't grow on your head. You've bought 'em and stuck 'em on with glue."

"I never!" Lula cried happily, pulling her curls to show.

"And them pink cheeks are painted on and real eyes ain't blue like yours. You're just a store doll-baby."

"No—no—no!" Lula screamed, laughing. "I'm real!"

"Come here and let me feel your sawdust," George said gravely. He pinched her little arm. "No, damn if she ain't real, Jonathan! I wouldn't ha' believed it. She looks like a store doll, but she ain't."

And while he was talking and teasing, his arm was about Mary, small and quiet and dark. He did not tease her or notice her overmuch, and she stood contentedly in that large shelter. Jonathan liked it that through the evening George was content to be with them all, and that he did not hasten to be with Maggie alone. There had to be talk between them before he would leave Maggie alone with this man almost old enough to be her father. Maggie was more quiet than she had ever been in her life, and no one could tell what she was thinking. When the younger children went to bed, she rose, saying to Katie, "I'll make the bread tonight, Katie," and went to the kitchen.

So the three of them were left alone; and Katie, her mouth set, took up her mending basket. Jonathan would speak, but she would listen and uphold him. She wanted Maggie married and out from her care, but only if this was the man Jonathan wanted in the family.

"I am old for Maggie," George Tenney admitted, "but still not old as men go. I'm forty to Maggie's eighteen. But I'm a young forty, and she's an old eighteen. Girls are women early out hyere. And I don't want some-buddy snappin' her up. I've thought about Maggie as mine a good many years now."

"It doesn't seem possible a man could remember a baby," Jonathan said.

"'Twasn't a baby but Maggie I remembered."

Jonathan pondered a moment on Maggie's life, a troublesome healthy child, a troublesome healthy girl, but to him no more. "You'd find her a handful," he said.

"I've broken hosses aplenty," George Tenney said. "Always by gentlin'. I never took a whip to one. And I'd rather do the breakin' than leave it to another—never liked a hoss in my life that another man broke."

"I don't like the cattle business."

"Nor I, and I'm gettin' out of it into hosses. I've got my ranch, and I own half a gold mine that's got pay dirt. I aim to give my wife a piano and her own carriage if she wants."

Katie looked up from the sock over her hand. "Maggie's that headstrong," she said.

"Yes, ma'am, I can see she is," George replied, with deference. Jonathan's wife was the respectable, managing, housekeeping woman common to the country, salt of the earth, he thought, liking her, and plain as all git out. He thought of Maggie's round pink cheeks and blue eyes and firm round body. He liked women to have body.

Katie, catching Jonathan's eyes, rose. They said as plainly as speech that he wanted her to go, and she went. When the two men were alone, Jonathan cleared his throat.

"George, in a manner of speaking, I stand in the place of father to Maggie."

"Your old man passed on?" George's hearty voice was full of respect for death.

"No, but he doesn't give heed," Jonathan said. "And for my dead mother's sake I must ask you if in your own opinion you're fit to marry a young pure girl. If you were her age I wouldn't ask it. But a cattleman's had—temptations. And you have had twenty years of it."

"Of temptation?" George bellowed out laughter. "Well, if I have, I've resisted most of the time. I won't say I'm a virgin, Jonathan, for I'm not. You couldn't hardly find a man that was—west of the Mississippi, that is. But I'm clean, if that's your trouble, and now that I've found my girl, anything else is over. There ain't but two kinds of women in the world, good and bad, and the bad uns are only temporary in a man's life."

He spoke with confidence in the simple God who had created woman and therefore knew his material, and Jonathan did not contradict him. Katie was the good. Jennet was the bad. And what was Judy except herself? But perhaps there was no other like Judy in the world.

"Well, I still say you're old or she's young, one or the other. But I reckon Maggie'll have to make up her own mind," he said unwillingly.

"I'm agreeable to leave it to Maggie," George said. He rose. "Will I go out to the kitchen?"

"I can send her in here," Jonathan said. He felt a faint repulsion toward the excitement he saw creeping into George's eyes.

"I'd rather go and find her in the kitchen," George said.

"Good night, then," Jonathan said abruptly.

Upstairs in the bedroom he shared with Katie he undressed himself and placed his garments in the careful order habitual to him.

Katie was already in bed. "You goin' to let him have her?" she asked.

"Maggie'll do what she likes," he said. He blew out the light and, wrapping his nightshirt about his knees, he climbed into bed and stretched his slender body and sighed. He was tired of love and all its ways. He had other things to do, and he would put this far from him. But he was glad to have Maggie gone early from his home. He could not cope with passion.

"You all right?" Katie inquired. She reached through the darkness and put her hand on his forehead. "You don't feel bilious, do you?"

"No, I don't think so," he said mildly. He felt suddenly grateful to her. "You're too good a cook to make a man bilious, Katie," he said.

"Oh, get out," Katie replied, but he could feel her happiness.

She fell asleep quickly after that, but he lay long awake, aware of what was in the kitchen beneath this room. He was not disturbed, but he fell into pondering on the distances that lay between man and woman. That abyss he would never cross. Never so long as he lived would he know what a woman really was. For into that heaven, too, the gate was narrow and the way strait. Not through many women did a man come into it, but only through one. And if that one were denied him, or if he denied her, then heaven was closed.

But perhaps other men were not like him? He considered this a moment and put it aside. I've no reason to think myself anything but an ordinary man, he thought.

He fell asleep at last, long before those two in the kitchen had parted.

George Tenney sat in the old kitchen armchair that was padded with plaited rags and held Maggie upon his knee. The range was hot with wood he had thrown in.

"We might as well be warm," he had said when he came in. Her bread was made, and she was waiting. Then he had drawn Maggie into his arms. "I'm glad you've growed into something hefty, my girl," he said. "I never did like little bits of kindlin' wood."

Maggie's cheeks were scarlet, and she laughed loudly. "I'm too big," she said.

"Not for me," George said.

"I've outgrown everything," she said proudly, "so my brother Jonathan told me to make myself two new dresses."

"Did you make this one?" he asked. He smoothed the bright green stuff over her round thighs. He was going to be very gentle with this young thing. She was hot as fire, he could see, and heady for any man, because she did not know herself what she was. Better for that kind to be married quick and young and to a man old enough to handle them! He was right to come before another man had begun the job. His smoothing hand crept up over her waist and her young breast. She caught it back.

"Don't!" she said sharply, and tried to rise from his knee.

But he held her firmly. "Wait," he commanded. "I'll never do that again if you don't want I should. I've talked with Jonathan, and he says you're to do as you like. So—will you have me, Maggie?"

She quieted. "I don't hardly know you."

"You know me, but you don't remember."

"But you only came back today!"

"Did you keep my letter I sent you as you didn't answer?"

She hung her head. "It's here," she said, and put her hand on her breast.

"Was that why you pushed my hand away?"

She did not answer, but her ready blood was beating. She was trembling into love with him. He was handsomer than any boy in Median, a handsome man, the sort of man she liked, with big shoulders and sturdy legs, and strong hands and a voice you could hear across a field. And she was only a girl, and sometimes she feared not such a very pretty girl. Her body began to ache, and she looked at him. And suddenly she hid her face on his shoulder.

He held her as though she had been three. "There," he murmured, "there—there—there! I ain't goin' to hurry, or force you in any way. You shall come along as you want to, my little Mags."

But she seized his hand and pressed it against her bosom where his letter lay.

"That's where it is," she whispered and held his hand hard upon her hot young flesh.

In a month there were left in Jonathan's home only the three children, his own son and daughter and his small sister Mary. George Tenney went away and came back twice, and the third time he and Maggie were married. The marriage was right. Jonathan liked the man better each time he came, though he had little learning and never in his life had read a book from beginning to end. But few men had in these parts, and Maggie herself was no great reader.

In that month she grew into a woman ready for marriage. Her nature was defined by love. She was prudent in spending the little money Jonathan could spare her, and she did not once quarrel with Katie. Instead, she busied herself with recipes and ways of cooking, learning willingly all that she had rebelled against before. Katie was generous and taught her and helped her with advice and bade her choose what she liked from the store. Maggie exclaimed warmly over this kindness to Jonathan one day as he weeded the vegetable garden.

"Though there isn't much there," she added practically. "The store's gone down something terrible, Jonathan."

He looked up from his beets. "Has it?" he said sharply. "How, Maggie?"

"Well, the stock's poor," Maggie said, "and Mrs. Merridy isn't there much, and the boys take what they want to eat, and old Mr. Cobb is real lazy. He only works when Katie comes in or Mrs. Merridy."

"I'll have to talk with Katie," Jonathan said. He deliberately did not talk about the store with her, feeling upon him the uneasy knowledge of her wish that he would return to it. But maybe he owed it to Lew. Besides, Median wanted a good general store. He put it off until after the wedding.

The wedding was in the new church. The small wooden building had been finished a few months ago under Stephen Parry. It now belonged to all the denominations alike, the Episcopalians who were few, the Baptists and Presbyterians who were more, and the Methodists who because they were most had two Sunday mornings out of the month. But Jonathan had seen to it also that a strange sect from Russia had the church to themselves once a month, too, though in the afternoon. They were Mennonites and farmers, and they had come to Kansas bearing in their hands little bundles tied in kerchiefs. These held their most precious possession, the seed of a hard red wheat.

Traveling preachers held the meetings of the denominations, but in his heart Jonathan dreamed of a church where one man would be the minister for all, and that man Paul Graham. But Median was not ready for it. He had sounded out the people and had been hotly accused of believing in state religion, in the English fashion.

" 'Tisn't that I believe state and church should be one," he denied, "it's that I don't see the good of waste. What's it mean but that our folk will build six churches and struggle to pay half a dozen preachers and all the time they're worshiping the one God?"

But he gave up for the time and satisfied himself by inviting Paul Graham to come and marry Maggie and George, and advise him about uniting Median's souls. He liked Paul more than ever, a pale, grave, slender young priest. Then he was startled because he saw Paul's eyes on his sister Mary, who was still only a child. He was so put out by this that he let the matter of church unity rest. Might it be better not to have Paul living in Median? He was perturbed on the day of the wedding because Mary looked so pretty and grown up in her long bridesmaid's dress, and he was so cool to Paul that the sensitive young man was alarmed.

"Have I offended you, sir?" he asked before the ceremony. He was gowned in his ministerial robes and waiting with George and Jonathan in the little vestry.

But Jonathan was unable to put his irritation into words. It was beyond him to say to Paul, "My sister is too young for a man to look at her as though she were an angel."

"Of course not," he said shortly, and decided that he would not press Paul to stay on after this wedding day. So the matter of Median's unity in religion was put off into the future by so human a thing.

Median was too big now to come entire to a wedding, and Maggie had invitations printed, the first that Median had ever seen. A new little paper was sweating its way into print once a week, and this was its first wedding. The editor was the boy whose mother had accused Jonathan of paying no heed to drunkenness in Median. Jonathan had discovered in him an aptitude for words, and out of it had grown the boy's wish to make a newspaper.

"Why not?" Jonathan had replied. "Median's big enough now for its own paper." He talked gravely about type and headlines and what news was, and now every day or two the freckled young editor came loping down the street.

"What'd you think of today's paper, Mr. Goodliffe? How'd you think I handled the new populist trouble?"

Yesterday he had said solemnly, "I'm going to cover your sister's wedding myself, sir," and all during the ceremony he wrote feverishly upon a pad on his knee. Jonathan, walking up the aisle with Maggie's hand on his arm, saw a bent brown head look up and stare and bend to scribble again upon the pad.

He went on to the slowly pacing wedding march Martha Cobb was playing on the little organ. Someday he must find time to think about a big organ for the church. It was a pretty church. What would his mother think if she could know that there was a church in Median? Or if she knew that the fat, naughty little girl whom she had so often scolded and sometimes slapped had grown into this young bride? But Maggie had changed very little. All she had been was simply increased in quantity. He felt the vague stirring of his dry humor and repressed it.

After the wedding was over and they were all in his house for cake and lemonade, he took George aside.

"My mother used to say Maggie needed smacking once in a while. Don't be too gentle with her."

"Don't you worry," George said, grinning. "I can keep the upper hand, at my age."

He saw them out of his door and on the puffing noisy little train that was to carry them westward. There were no more wagons these days. People went West from Median on trains, though Jonathan had never set foot in one of them. He put a ten-dollar bill into Maggie's hand as she kissed his cheek, and then she put her arms around him and kissed him again.

"You've done too much for me as it is," she whispered.

"Take it," he said. "What's it for but to use?"

"But you could use it!"

"I have what I need, I reckon." He pushed her away a little, not knowing he did so. The smell of her warm body, perspiring freshly, was sweet enough, but not for him. "Good-by, good-by," he said, and turned back to his own home.

Because he knew that he would never leave Katie he was glad when this earthy pair were gone from his house. He and Katie were a common-sensible pair, and both of them had been faintly ashamed before one another while George and Maggie had been in the house. The two could not hide their frank passion and their eagerness for marriage.

Yet when he opened the door of his house its stillness smote him.

One by one he was sending them away from him, the children his mother had left him, and soon it would be his own children, he thought. Then he and Katie would be left alone, with no one between them for a shield. When that day comes, I'll be old, he thought. Then he put old age far from him. I've a lot to do first, he thought firmly. He glanced at the courthouse in the middle of the square. They had had to take away some of his trees when the foundations were laid, but he had let only the cottonwoods be cut. The hardwoods he had transplanted.

They're permanent, he always thought when he passed them. Whenever he planted a tree now, and he had the school children plant them somewhere in Median every spring, he always planted hardwoods.

36

THE Sunflower Oil Company, Jamie discovered, was Evan Bayne, the new candidate for the governorship of the state. Jamie had been living these months in Ruth's house. He slept there at night and spent the days on his horse examining every acre of the surrounding country. He bought three hundred acres and options on three times as much before his savings ran out. Then he cast about for resources, and Matthew told him of the Sunflower.

Without capital to offer, he went to Topeka to find the manager and to proffer himself for a job in the company. None of his land had produced oil yet, but it might at any moment. For a young man his assets were good, even if he had no cash.

Evan, taking shrewd stock of him, thought so too. A handsome fellow, this brother of Jonathan's! There was no trace in him of Jonathan's mild English look and ways. He was tall and bold-looking, his closely cut black hair was rough with a curl that could not be shorn, and his mouth was firm. It suddenly occurred to Evan that his sister Laura was coming to visit him, and that the last time she had come she had declared that if he did not produce at least one eligible young man, she would come no more. She had no time to waste, she had said. . . . Was this young man eligible?

"I rather think I might be able to do something for you," Evan said. "I'm very fond of your brother." He shot his eyebrows up, watching to discover what Jamie knew about that.

Jamie's face did not show him. "Of course I wouldn't want you to do anything for me because of Jonathan. I'd expect to stand on my own feet."

"Of course—"

A young woman came into the room. She was dressed in the new mannish shirtwaist and skirt, and her intensely black hair was pompadoured about her pale face. She was not pretty, and when she was not introduced Jamie dismissed her. But as soon as she spoke he looked at her again.

She had a voice as deep and soft as the heavy string on a fiddle. It went to his spine.

"Did you ring, Mr. Bayne?"

"This is my secretary, Miss Power," Evan said. "Rachel, when's Laura coming?"

"Saturday, sir."

Evan frowned a little. Why not? If both birds were killed with one stone, or if neither, no damage was done.

"Come along to my house Saturday night," he said to Jamie. "We dine at seven. Afterwards we can talk. Rachel, be sure I have the last figures on Sunflower before then."

"Yes, sir." Again the deep, sweet voice.

"Suits me, sir." Jamie rose.

The dark girl held out a card upon which she had been writing quickly. "Your memorandum, sir."

His spine quivered again, and he looked down into a narrow, clever face, still not pretty, but wise enough to confound him.

"Th-thanks," he stammered. He went out, sweating a little. Gosh, I'd hate to have her around me all the time, he thought. He looked at the card. Upon it in the neatest clearest script he had ever seen was all the information he could imagine, name, address, and hour for Saturday's engagement. In small bracketed letters she had even written [Dress].

"Well, damn it, does she think I'll go naked?" he wondered. He thrust the card into his pocket and took it out again. There was something queer about that bracketed word. He sauntered along and went into a men's clothing shop and accosted a man who wore striped pants and a long coat and a high collar.

"What do you make of that?" he demanded, presenting the card.

The man took it and read it. "I should say it was a dinner appointment, sir, to be attended in evening dress."

Jamie grinned. "My evening dress is my nightshirt."

The man grinned. "This isn't that."

"Show me what dress you've got for a man," Jamie demanded.

In less than an hour he was fitted to garments he had not only never worn before, but had never seen or heard of.

"Nifty," the man murmured.

"I kind of agree with you," Jamie said, looking at the young man in the mirror.

Too handsome, Laura was thinking. Would I dare?

She was older than this man, perhaps by a year, perhaps by three. But she was small, and he so big. Besides, she did not want to marry anyone she knew.

"I hate oil," she said aloud. "It smells."

Over her white shoulder she smiled into Jamie's face. Not quite a gentleman, she was thinking, but then all the men she knew were gentlemen, and they tired her.

"It smells," Jamie agreed, "but how it pays!" His brown face broke into a shimmering smile, and she laughed.

"You don't mind money, do you!" she said.

"It's what I'm lookin' for most," he said.

"More than anything?"

"When I get it, I'll look for a wife," he said impudently.

This girl made him feel like his dad. She drew the billy goat out of him as no nice woman ever had done in his life. He must be nice because she was his boss's sister. But he felt bold. He had not been here ten minutes before Evan had told him there would be a place for him in the company if he could agree to certain financial details.

"You bet I'll agree, Mr. Bayne!" he had said. Then he saw that dark girl again at his boss's elbow, and he heard her deep voice.

"I have the memoranda ready, but you won't want to talk until after dinner, will you, Mr. Bayne?"

"No—in the library, Rachel."

She had slipped away, but at the dinner table she was at Evan's elbow again, her seat at his left. Jamie looked down the table at Judy.

Tonight when Evan introduced them she had bowed her head a very little in answer to his bow. He remembered when he had seen her last, but he did not tell her so. Now he wondered what she thought of this dark girl at her husband's elbow, whose violin voice, so seldom raised, was always heard when it spoke. Anyone could see that it was to her that Evan turned when he wanted anything. No use pretending that a man could have a girl at his elbow all day and not grow to depend on her in all sorts of ways—not that it was any of his business, now that Evan was his boss!

"Can anything good come out of Kansas?" Laura's pretty insistent voice was at his ear.

"Me," he said promptly.

"I thought you were English?"

"If I ever was, it's been forgotten."

"I met your brother once—he was very English."

"Yes, Jonathan's pretty much what he always was. He's stayed in Median. All the rest of us have scattered. Why, my old dad's just run for new land and almost got it, by Jiminy!"

"Not quite?"

"He has a game leg and his wagon broke down, or he'd have made it."

"And Jonathan's not going in for oil?"

"No, he's a schoolteacher. He doesn't want to be anything else. Median's grown all around him, but he goes on just the same."

"I'd like to see him."

"He looks the way he always has."

"Not like you?"

"You'd never know we were brothers."

"Maybe I'd like him better than you."

" 'Twould surprise me, but he'd be even more surprised."

She laughed her quick, falling laughter. "I like you rather well," she said. Her great coquetry was to seem guiltless of any coquetry.

Jamie leaned toward her. "Like me as well as you can, will you?"

"Why?"

"Because some day I might fall in love with you!"

"You are too quick," she murmured. "We haven't reached dessert, yet."

"Out where I come from we hurry," he said.

Katie at the sitting-room window looked at the clock. It was six o'clock of the November day, and the sky was already black. Across the dead lawn the light in the office of the schoolhouse burned. Jonathan was still working. It used to be that she could see him through the curtainless window. Then one day he said the light from the window was too strong, and he had moved his desk so that now she could no longer see it.

"Mary!" Her voice rose high to the last syllable. "Oh, Mary!"

"Yessum?" Mary's light and childlike voice floated through the floor from her room upstairs.

"Go and call your brother to supper!"

"Yessum!"

Katie sighed and put down her sewing and went into the kitchen. She wanted supper over because there was something she must tell Jonathan. She had to tell him because she was sick and tired of holding her tongue when people complained about the way he was running the school. Today in the store she had had her fill, with fat Mrs. Tenber wanting her to ask Jonathan why he didn't let her Theodore pass the sixth grade.

"Three times he's been through the same grade, Mis' Goodliffe, and still Mr. Goodliffe don't let him pass it!"

"I reckon he'd pass if he was fit to pass!" she had said.

She was not afraid of any Mrs. Tenber, but it made her sick to think of all that Jonathan did and yet anybody who felt like it could criticize him. Schoolteaching was a thankless public job. And at the last meeting of the trustees they had made it plain enough that Jonathan could never get a raise in salary, not if he lived to be a hundred. She had quarreled with Jonathan over that, not because she wanted more money, but because they had hurt him. He was so gentle, so careful to explain to her why they had felt as they did, that she knew he was deeply hurt.

"It's perfectly natural that now, with all these young chaps getting out of universities in the East, they wouldn't much want a chap like me, Katie. I can see it."

"With all you've done!" she cried. "Every child like your own, and you slaving away summer and winter, Saturdays and vacations and everything!"

"They don't ask me to do that, though, Katie. If I wish to do it, I can scarcely expect to be paid for it."

"Ain't experience anything?"

He knew she stormed at them through him, and so he could be patient with her. "While I've been getting experience I've been getting older, too, Katie."

"What I hate is folks thinkin' they have the say-so of you, bcause you're paid out of taxes. A miserable little pay, and it's not your own when you've got it! I wish you was in the store. Then you'd be beholden to nobody."

"I can't quit my rightful work, Katie."

Neither of them mentioned the money for its own sake, she because she did not want him to think she could not manage, and he because he felt uneasily that he was deepening that vague great debt to her of his marriage. Would it make it up to Katie, he often wondered, if he could provide her with more comforts? But how could he give up his school?

In his office now he was preparing again for the quarterly meeting of the school board. Times had changed very much from those days when as a young schoolmaster he had simply gathered together his pupils. Subscription school, it had been then, paid for by parents who wanted their children taught. Now the schools were public. People grumbled at taxes and then expected everything from the scanty dollars they paid. He loved teaching, but the sinew of his life now could not go into it. He had to spend himself upon this grinding down of every expense to meet an appropriation too small. In the sod house there had been so few books that each had been precious. He had scarcely thought of the possibility of new books. Now there were so many books required that they were no longer precious, either to study or to possess. There were too many new ones for every school term. Children came and went to school loaded with books and caring for none of them. But he was still angry when he found a child defacing a book with scrawls and drawings.

"A book is a treasury," he always said. "You must learn how to find the treasure. That is why you come to school." This was really the soul of his teaching. But it was getting out of date, his sort of teaching. People were wanting a lot of new things that should not be in a school. Girls could learn them at home in their mothers' kitchens, and boys could apprentice themselves to blacksmiths and carpenters. School was a place to acquire learning out of books which were the fruit of man's knowledge and thought. So he believed.

"Supper's ready, Jonathan."

He looked up and saw that Mary had run out of the kitchen in her cotton school dress. He spoke quietly.

"Mary, why do you disobey me again about not putting on your cloak in this weather?"

She looked astonished and then frightened. "Honest, I forgot!"

She was so stricken that he smiled at her. She looked so like his mother in these days of her new adolescence that he could never scold her. It always seemed when he did that he was scolding the dying creature who had found her way back to him. "I notice you never forget anything Katie tells you to do," he grumbled.

"She keeps after me," Mary murmured.

"And I don't, eh?"

"You're more peaceful-like."

He went on smiling without hearing her, his mind on his determination to refuse the demand of the trustees for a course in manual arts in the high school. It would come to a battle, but he would fight it and win it. He wanted the money for a new teacher of history. People here did not value history. The newspaper was all they wanted—yesterday was far enough away, and only today was important. But how could man measure himself if he did not know the history of his kind?

"I'll be along, Mary." Then he remembered her and tossed her his old mackinaw. "Here, put that around you."

"But you?" she asked.

"I haven't on a thin dress." He saw her face for the moment framed in the coat she put over her head like a hood. A prettyish girl, he thought, too fine-featured, perhaps. At least among the sturdier girls of Median she looked puny. He must think to notice how she ate. She was small, as their mother had been small, but she must not grow up delicate.

He waited for her to be gone, then he rose, turned out the gas lamps he had just had installed with all of Median beginning to use gas, and strolled into sharply cold darkness. There was a smell in the air of frost-bitten lawns and flowers, and it struck into his memory so sudden and sharp that he recognized it instantly. This was the smell of the night years ago when he had been dreaming of his marriage to Judy. But he had forgotten, surely he had forgotten by now.

Katie said, "Don't raise the window yet, Jonathan. There's somethin' I've got to talk about."

He hesitated, his hand on the window that had once been a quarrel between him and Katie until he had removed it by simply refusing to sleep in a room in which the window was not opened at night. Love of air he had learned in England, and he was stifled unless he felt it fresh and cold upon his face. "Jonathan ain't happy without he's sittin' in a draught," Katie said so often that he had ceased to hear it.

"I'm fair tired tonight," he remarked, but he sat down on the bed instead of getting into it. This room, meant for quiet and sleep, was in reality the storm center of his life. It was the only room where he and Katie were ever alone. Children, growing and gangling, noisy and clamorous, trailed and galloped and lounged in every other.

He knew before she began what it was she wanted to talk about. It was another battle in her long war against the school. Depending upon his mood and physical state, he was able to be quietly humorous in his defence, parrying and delaying, or else he was abrupt. He was not sure tonight which he would be. He watched her as she slipped her full cotton nightgown over her head. In all these years she had never undressed except under this great convolution of white stuff. She was writhing, screwing herself out of garments underneath it now, and there were small clicks and pulls of sound.

"Jonathan, Mrs. Tenber's awful mad again about that boy of hers not passin'."

"Is she?" He suddenly felt he would not be humorous.

"She's goin' to complain to the trustees."

"It'll do her no good. The boy's a fool. I told her she ought to put him to work in the machine shop or livery stable."

"Jonathan, you didn't!" There was a small crash of steel-stayed corset about Katie's feet.

"I did."

Katie stood an instant imagining Mrs. Tenber's state of mind. "I reckon she thinks if she pays taxes she has as good a right as anybody else to send her boy to school."

"Just because the country's a democracy is no guarantee that none of our citizens are ever born fools," Jonathan retorted. He felt he wanted to be angry and he became so. He pulled the sandy moustache he had decided to grow last year.

"The trustees can't realize it, either. Instead of facing the truth that men may be born free but they are never born equal, they propose to meet the problem of fools like this Tenber boy by putting a machine shop and a carpentry shop and what-not into my school. The town's full of such places, but, no, fools have to think they're getting an education while they are tinkering with their hands though they've got no brains."

He was so angry now that he was chewing the rough ends of his moustache. "This isn't just one boy, Katie, it's a situation—a battle—and I'm going to win or get out."

"Then I'll be glad if you don't win," she retorted. "Schoolteachin' is a poor thankless business."

"Teaching is the highest job a man can do," Jonathan said firmly. "But they don't let me teach any more in these newfangled days. When I began in the sod house I was able to teach. I could put my whole mind to it, and I turned out sensible people from the raw ignorant boys and girls I got. Now I'm supposed to supply mechanics and carpenters and blacksmiths instead of scholars and civilized people."

He rose and flung open the window, and the cold air hit him like a wave of sea water. Upon such a night his mother had come home, and all his life was changed. The wind had been cold that night. He turned to Katie. "Here's a promise, Katie. If I can't have the kind of school I want, I'll give it up."

"And take the store?" She was braiding her tight brown pigtail of hair.

"And take the store," he said.

But he had no intention of letting it come to that. He was full of stubborn zest for his own way. He got into bed and lay very stiff and straight as he summoned before the tribunal of his mind one after the other of his school trustees.

Abram Hasty owned the mill now that old Samuel had died of apoplexy—a curious way for that wire of a man to die, but his veins were petrified with the whisky he had drunk for years instead of water. Abram had grown into a stolid pigheaded man who made a good thing out of the mill by putting in machinery. But Abram still remained nevertheless one of the stupidest of his pupils.

I can down him, Jonathan thought.

He ran his mind hastily over the others. Faience, the president of the new little Median Farmers' Bank; Riggs, the postmaster; Baker, the head of the livery stable. Not an educated man among them, Jonathan thought triumphantly. Not one who knows a Latin verb!

By his side Katie sniffed as she breathed. She suffered with hay fever and, though the hard frost had cured its cause, she kept for months the habit of sniffing.

"I hate your being at the beck and call of every taxpayer," she said.

"I'm not," Jonathan said flatly. He hated Katie's sniffing, but not for anything would he have mentioned it. Instead he said suddenly and inexplicably, "Put up or shut up!"

"Why, Jonathan Goodliffe!" Katie cried.

"I say that no more for you than for me," he retorted. And without further explanation to her or to himself he turned his back on her and went to sleep.

37

WHEN Jonathan saw the hack stop in front of his house, he recognized it as one of those that stood usually behind the railroad depot. Then he saw his brother Jamie leap out of the hack and turn and put out his hand to help a slender woman step down. They went into the house, and after a moment Katie came out of the door, her apron over her head, and he hurried from his office and met her halfway.

"Jamie's brought his girl," she cried. The wind twisted her skirts about her thin legs and big feet.

"I didn't know he had a girl," he shouted against the wind.

"I reckon it's only just happened!" she shrieked. "It's a Miss Bayne—Laura!"

He caught the name like a blow and set his teeth. Evan's sister, that fierce child of a girl he had seen years ago! Yes, she would be grown and not too young—older than Jamie. Buy why did she want Jamie? He stepped into the little hall.

"Smooth down your hair," Katie said. "You look wild."

He smoothed it down hastily. . . . But would this marriage bring him nearer to Evan? He did not want that.

"Howdy, Jonathan!"

Jamie was at the door of the sitting room. He was dressed in new city clothes from head to foot. Jonathan surveyed him, delaying. "You're looking very fine, aren't you?"

"I've struck oil," Jamie said, grinning. "A good deep well of it. Queer thing is, it ain't a hundred feet from Ruth and Matthew's cow pasture. I bought next to them."

"They never struck any."

"Not a drop. I've been all over their land myself. It's the dangdest thing I ever see."

"Hmph." Jonathan pulled his moustache. "Maybe the rest of you are draining it off of them."

"Maybe, but if we are, it's all legal." Jamie's bold blue eyes were calm. "Sure is bad luck for Ruth. I wisht it wasn't my own sister."

"Bad luck for anybody," Jonathan said dryly. Then he heard the rustle of a taffeta skirt and braced himself. Laura came to the door.

She put out her hand to him. "You don't remember me."

"Yes, I do." He took a long slender hand into his for a second.

Jamie grinned. "'Tisn't only oil I struck." He pulled her other long slender hand into his arm and patted it. "Laura and me are going to be married, Jonathan. That's what we came to tell you."

"I came to see Jonathan," Laura protested, with her pout that was still girlish enough to be pretty. "You made an impression once on a certain young thing, Jonathan. She was smitten for a while with a grave young Englishman—long enough to look twice at his brother."

"Hey! Which one of us is the lucky man?" Jamie inquired loudly. He was proud of her being a lady.

But he was proud of himself, too, these days. Luck was roaring around him. Money was pouring into his bank account, and Evan was talking of making him a vice-president of Sunflower, so that if he himself should be elected governor, Jamie could take over the company.

"Come in and sit down," Jonathan said. He was master of himself now, and he led the way into the sitting room and nodded when Katie went out to fetch coffee and cookies. "Well!" He looked from one face to the other. "When's it to be?"

For in this moment his mind had leaped ahead to their marriage day, where he and Judy must meet. Not once had he yielded to any imagination which would have made possible his seeing her again. But that his brother should marry Evan's sister was beyond imagination.

"After Lent," Laura said. "I have to go home and tell Mamma and get my trousseau."

"Your mother still living?" After Lent was a long time away, but the longer the better.

Laura gave a little scream of laughter. "Mamma would be furious if anybody thought she was dead!"

Jamie shouted, and Jonathan smiled dryly. "Give her my respects," he said.

He had a strange wry tingling of the blood at the relationship between these two because somehow it brought closer the separate orbits of his life and Judy's. Then he recognized this as the cause of his secret excitement and put it sternly away. Even if he met Judy face to face, what could it mean to him? He turned abruptly to Jamie. "Tell me about Ruth. Is she taking it hard that they don't find oil?"

"Ruth feels it right smart," Jamie said.

Laura was thinking, He's so handsome, and when we're married, I shall teach him manners and I will throw away that suit he's wearing. It was patterned like a checkerboard. But he was growing handsomer every day. The city was grooming him. She had taken him home and paraded him before her friends, complacent when they chorused their admiration. "I declah, honey, he's just beautiful!" "Laura, *how* did you—" "Laura, he just makes my haid *swirl!*"

Her mother, ninety-one years old, had stared at Jamie for a long time. "A very pretty man!" she declared at last. Her voice was silvery with age and self-will.

Laura took out her fencing weapons. "A man's a man for a' that," she said lightly.

"I suppose so," old Mrs. Bayne said. She had blinked her old eyes once or twice. "But what are you going to *do* with him when you've married him, Laura?" She behaved as if Jamie sitting not ten feet from her were cardboard.

"Keep him," Laura said sharply.

"My child, you always were ambitious," her mother had said. . . .

"I got the better of Mother," Laura thought and gazing at Jamie, her eyes grew liquid with love.

Jonathan caught that look and was as uneasy as though he were eavesdropping. "Excuse me," he said. "I'll step out and help Katie."

Neither of them noticed his going.

"Come over here by me, Jamie," Laura commanded. She still had to tell him when she wanted him to kiss her. He rose, shyly, very tall and full of beauty, and came over to her and took her in his arms. She gave herself up to the breathless luxury of giving herself up. "Love me?"

"Sure do."

"Are you a one-woman man, Jamie?"

He grinned down into her face on his breast. "How do I know?"

"Your dad sounds an old rake."

He laughed, and she dug her nails softly into his neck. "Feel my claws?"

"Like a tiger cat's!"

"I'll dig them into you if you ever stop loving me!"

"I'll remember that."

"Even when I'm an old woman and you're still a handsome young man, you'll have to love only me—oh, Jamie, you'll always be a handsome young man as long as you live, and that's what I've got to face."

He laughed again, not knowing quite what else to do, and she wrenched herself out of his arms.

"I wonder if Jonathan still loves Judy? I wonder if that's what is wrong with Judy? Even if she doesn't love anybody, if he loves her, and she knows it? Love is such a *poisonous* thing when it goes on and on after you want it to stop! It poisons lover and beloved."

He had not the slightest idea what she was talking about, and she knew it.

"Oh, well!" she said and threw herself into his arms again and closed her eyes. He was male, bread to her heart and wine to her body. What a curse to a woman was intelligence! How unnecessary and useless and unwanted in the life of man and woman! At this moment of her passing youth, it was the only life she wanted.

The door opened. Katie was back with the cookies and coffee. Behind her came Jonathan, his eyes cold, his lips set. With him were his children. He had brought them here to keep beside him, and when he sat down, he held them in the circle of his arms.

. . . Weeks later Laura ordered Jonathan to come to her wedding.

He smiled faintly. "Well, Laura, I'm a very plain chap, and Evan's a great man now."

"Nonsense! Evan doesn't forget his old friends. There's such a snobbishness about men like you! You're always thinking you're too good for people who are what you call 'great'!"

Jonathan knew she was baiting him, but still there was truth in what she said, and he was always confounded by any atom of truth.

"Maybe you're right at that," he agreed. He examined himself. "Reckon maybe I do like plain people because I feel good enough myself when I'm amongst 'em."

"Ah-ha!" she cried, shaking her pointed forefinger at him.

"Leave it to you to drag out my innards into the open air," he said good-naturedly. He liked Laura now and marveled at her folly in marrying Jamie. She read Dante in Italian, and he had never been able to persuade Jamie to read anything.

"I haven't finished," she said impudently. And then she leaned forward and dragged out his heart and stared at it thumping and leaping in her hand.

"You do love Judy still," she said.

"Reckon I'll always love Judy in a curious sort of way," he answered in a low voice. Not to another soul than to this impetuous, clever woman could he have said it. But once the thing was in words, he felt relief. There it was, out. His heart suddenly lay still in her hand. She took pity on him and put it neatly into his breast again.

"Dear Jonathan," she murmured. "You needn't come to my wedding, if it hurts you."

" 'Tisn't the hurt," he said. "It's just—the uselessness of hurt. But I'll come."

. . . That was it—the uselessness of even looking at Judy. And yet he looked at her quietly and freely all the time Jamie and Laura were being married, and in all the city church full of people he saw only that beautiful woman standing by Laura's side. She was dressed in some sort of soft stuff the color of cream, and she wore a big black hat against which her pallor was pure beauty. He knew that all she wore cost a great deal of money, more than he earned in a year; but for that he cared nothing. He wanted simply to look at her, without memory of the past, without thought of the future, without passion or possession. And as he gazed it came over him that she was as much his life as she had ever been. Whatever she was and was not, the mysterious form that the elements had taken to shape her being was the one form that he loved or could ever love.

He became aware of the small snifflings and twitches at his side that were Katie's sign of being, and he returned to his daily life.

"There's a terrible draught!" she whispered.

He glanced about the church. "I can't see where from. Everything's shut tight."

"I feel cold."

He lifted her coat from the back of the pew and held it for her to put on. At the same instant the wedding march burst into pealing music, and the bridal party turned and paced down the aisle. The instant was near when Judy must pass within very reach of his hand if he should put it out. Surely she would see him. He felt sick and giddy. If she should look at him? . . .

He kept his eyes on her approaching face. Her head was bent, but just before she reached his pew she lifted her head suddenly and gazed straight ahead, seeing no one. He saw her face foreshortened and still so innocent.

So the moment passed. She did not see him. Light went with her, the music faded, and people began to stir.

"Well, it's over," Katie said half-aloud. She wiggled her foot into the new shoe she had slipped off.

"Yes, I reckon it is," he agreed. "Let's go home."

He was very gentle with Katie that night. She complained of headache and cold, and he made some ginger tea and heated a brick. It occurred to him as he put the brick to her feet that she was very thin. It was so seldom that he noticed such things that he was ashamed now.

"Aren't you all right, Katie?" he asked.

" 'Course I'm all right," she replied.

She looked away from him, and he said no more. Between them the primary silence had never yet been broken. But that night he lay, long awake, astonished at the passing of life. Katie, whose small adolescent breasts had seemed shocking to him so short a time ago, this Katie had been his wife for all these years, and now she had reached the end of youth. He thought of Judy, changed only to greater beauty. He put out his hand and felt Katie's shoulder blade through the yoke of her nightgown. At his touch she woke.

"Did you lock the kitchen door?" she asked.

They had never locked doors in Median until recently. But since the panic in the East, panhandlers had come westward on freight trains and on foot, and there had been robberies everywhere. Even in Median people were beginning to lock their doors.

"I think I did, but I'd better make sure."

He climbed out of bed, fumbled for his carpet slippers, and lit the candle. Upon the stairs a cold small wind folded his nightshirt about his bare legs. The door must have blown open. He went on, shielding the candle with his hand. A good thing he got up, he thought, for the door stood wide. He peered out for a moment into the darkness. But there was nothing to be seen except the trees in the square, ghostly in the corner street lamp. When he had planted them they had been saplings. He shut the door and locked it fast and went back to his bed.

38

"You can't go against the times," Abram Hasty said. Then he added, "sir." Jonathan had all but beaten the word into him years ago.

It was the last meeting of the school year, and the question of manual arts, long argued, always delayed, had come to crisis.

"You're such a practical man, Goodliffe," Faience said courteously. Faience had come from Virginia. "I don't know anybody the town owes more to than you. Why, folks tell me you have started pretty nearly everything we have that's any good. But your attitude on the new education astonishes me."

"I've been a schoolteacher long enough to know what you can educate and what you can't," Jonathan said. "A schoolteacher's job is to sort, and sort more clearly as the grades go higher. Everybody ought to read and write, we'll say—though I don't know even that does everybody good. But not everybody ought to go on to higher mathematics and Latin."

"Exactly," Faience said, "so the manual arts allow education to those who shouldn't. It gives the right emphasis to education in a great democratic country. It says to the common man, 'The work you do with your hands is as worthy of a graduating degree as is the learning of books.'"

Jonathan put doggedly aside this river of words. Faience was the new mayor of Median, and everything was practice for speeches the mayor must make. "But manual arts are better taught where they're really practiced. Makin' little useless things that don't sell, that aren't wanted, that's not education for anyone. It's unreal."

"Still, seems as if fellows ought to have a chance at a diploma even if they can't memorize things outa books," Abram Hasty said.

Jonathan turned a pale sand color. His eyes glittered, and his blood was icy around his heart. Pure anger always made him cold. There was no rise in the level of his voice.

"Very well, I'll tell you what, gentlemen. I offer my resignation if there's to be carpentry and blacksmithing and basketry in the school. It'd be dishonest of me to stay."

"Now, Mr. Goodliffe," Abram protested. He was a big, hairy, coarse-fleshed man, but he had always been afraid of this slender, firm figure. He had secrets in books that Abram could never learn. Even money had not been enough to free Abram from distrust of the learning he had not been able to acquire or use. School for him and for Sam had only taught them enough to make them afraid of an educated man.

Jonathan rose and pushed his chair under the desk. He held his head high, and from under the sandy shelf of his eyebrows his eyes were agate-colored and full of cold light.

"I'll withdraw, if you please, while you talk it over. I'll hand in my resignation if it's decided against my opinion as a schoolmaster. Good day!"

He stalked out, his shoulders stiff, and so went across the lawn and into his own house. In the quiet of midafternoon in May it was empty. The children were at school, and Katie was at the store. He stood a moment not knowing what to do. Then he turned and went out again, down the street and toward the store.

Upon the single main street of Median which ran into the square and around it, a colored boy was selling newspapers. Jonathan stopped. It was Parry's youngest boy.

"Link, why aren't you in school?"

The boy's face was framed for impudence, but now he looked alarmed. He shifted the papers under his arm and wet his full lips. "I just got to earn me some money, Mr. Goodliffe."

"What for?"

"Circus comin'."

Jonathan gazed at him sternly. "When?"

"Sat'dy, suh."

"You know I ought to punish you for truancy?"

"Yessuh!"

Jonathan kept the moment long and miserable. "Give me a paper," he said at last, "and keep the change."

He gave the boy a dime and hastened on, shutting his ears to thanks. Circuses! So Median was big enough for circuses to find it worth while to stop. The town was getting too big—nearly six thousand people by the last count. He unfolded the paper as he went and came face to face with Evan upon the front page. The smiling dark eyes looked at him from under the handsome silver-gray hair. "Evan Bayne for Governor," the headlines shouted. He stared at them. He was neither sorry nor glad. All that the words meant was that Judy was going farther away.

No, I'm danged glad, he thought.

It separated him, sent him deeper into Median. Here in Median was his life. If the school were taken from him, he had the store. He'd make it a good store. He folded the paper and marched to the door of the store and went in, seeing it for the first time as something possibly his own. It was empty. He called, "Katie!"

She came out of the back room, two pencils stuck in the knots of hair on top of her head. "Jonathan! Why, what're you here for this time of day? We're taking inventory—"

She looked tired, and his heart, quivering in his bosom, leaped to her. This faithful woman was his home, his dwelling place in Median. Her good and honest face, her plain figure and working hands—these were his possession. His, too, her being, framed for loyalty and devotion and forgetfulness of self. How could he ever repay her all he owed to her? He knew. He held her reward in his hand.

"Katie, I've as good as resigned from the school."

"Jonathan Goodliffe!" She clasped her hands together with one loud clap. "Oh, I hope you didn't do it for anything I said!"

"No. They're going to put carpentry and blacksmithing and stuff like that into my curriculum. That's not school."

"Oh!" She sighed. Her hazel eyes were suffused. "If you knew how I've prayed!"

He had seen her by their bed every night, praying, her nightgowned figure kneeling, her head bowed on the counterpane. The soles of her large bare feet were repulsive and pathetic to him, but he always stopped any noise he was making until she rose.

"Well, here's your prayer answered," he said. A faint smile was upon his lips for a flickering second. "Though I've never thought of myself as able to give the answer to any woman's prayer!"

She laughed because she knew he meant to joke.

"I might as well begin," he said, and went behind a counter. He might just as well, for he had nothing else to do. To Katie now he paid his debt in full.

For the first time in his life he put much thought upon the matter of his marriage. It could have nothing to do with love, for what people thought of as love was certainly not between him and Katie. But other things were.

There were the children. He had made up his mind that they were ordinary children without a glimmer of the flame that was in Beaumont. But he did not blame them for that. He had not found it in any other child of the hundreds he had taught. And why should he think there was any source of it in himself or in Katie? Judy might have transmitted it from something Joel had. But others had not given it to Katie or to him.

I'm a common chap, he thought, and it would take something very uncommon to make my children anything else.

They were all the same, good and common. In church every Sunday he saw Ruth and Matthew, faithfully worshiping God in spite of disappointed hope. He had ceased to ask them whether they still had hope of oil. Matthew went on farming, and Ruth kept her house.

Once a year Maggie came home with George. In two years she had had two children, but they had not changed her. She was still impatient and high-tempered, but George kept her in bounds. They were well off, although they took care not to talk about it before people. Maggie was shrewd and a manager. She liked good clothes and good food, and she had both. George had put off leaving the cattle business until Maggie nagged him to it by complaining of the way he smelled. The crisis came one night when she climbed out of their bed and flounced herself into the spare room.

"And here I stay until you quit smelling like a farm hand," she said.

George had got himself a job in insurance the next day, for he was perpetually infatuated with the vigorous, plump-bodied, red-cheeked girl he had made his wife. Now she wanted him to move East, and sooner or later he knew he would do it, though he loved the West.

Yes, they were all good plain people.

Jonathan found that he even enjoyed the store once he knew it was his fate. I've shopkeeping blood, he thought, remembering his mother's small and fragmentary shops. Not that I wouldn't have enjoyed something else more if I could have had it the way I wanted.

Denied that, he was cheerful, and he arranged everything the way he liked, and this was pleasant. He asked no one anything, and that was good. If he had none of the high moments of the spirit that once had been his when he looked down into scores of young faces waiting for him to speak, he had solid moments of content. He liked to search out the thing he had to fill a need. When someone came in to ask for anything he liked to say,

"I have it." He liked to think he had everything in the store. To a woman coming for a dress, a child for candy, a man for a scythe, boys wanting rubber to make slings or string for kites, he wanted to be able to say, "I have it here." It was his ambition to have in the store what anybody in Median could want and to have it before it was asked for. He had wire screening before people thought of flies as anything but inevitable, or of any preventions for them except a branch broken from a tree and waved over the dinner table. He had rubber hot-water bottles, and hot bricks and warming pans slowly disappeared from homes in Median.

At American House, Henry Drear was growing too fat to walk and Mrs. Drear had colored men in the kitchen which she had made into a new dining room. Rows of rocking chairs stood on the porch now, and Henry Drear was always in one of them asleep. People passing took for granted his great body, hands folded across his belly, and head lolling on his shoulder.

At night Jonathan locked the store and went home and talked over the day with Katie. When he had been in the school there had been little to talk about with her. But now there were the things she had known all her life—the price of cloth and ribbon, the quality of carpets and the brands of groceries, the colors of hats and curtains and the styles of dresses, the quantities of furniture and underwear and overalls and shirts and haberdashery and hardware and the vegetables and baked goods that women brought in to sell. These home products were his bane, but Jonathan wanted to sell food, and he could not refuse to take eggs when a woman had no money to pay for a dress she needed.

In all this Katie's instinct was needle-fine and sure as money in his pocket after a sale. She was so average that she always knew what the average wanted, and he trusted to her completely when he ordered his stocks. They disagreed on two things only—wallpaper and books. He disliked wallpaper, but Katie said they must have it because it was coming into style. People were building little bare frame houses that wanted paper on the thin walls. So against his will he did his share to put upon Median walls the large flowery patterns that offended his sense of decent quiet.

"Stands to reason it's silly to paste up sprawling ribbons and flowers and scenes to stare at all day," he told Ruth sternly when he found her lingering over the table of wallpapers. He put it in the back of the shop, and time and again he told people, "You don't want that stuff." But they did and so did Ruth, and at last he said, "Well, have your way in your own home." But in his own he had plain limed walls and was firm with Katie except for the new parlor he put on the house that year.

There was no doubt that storekeeping paid him more money than teaching. The only thing in the store that never paid at all was books. He kept a small stock of them, old writers and new, on the chance that they might be wanted. But they seldom were. Even Charles Dickens, whose stories his mother had loved so well, was dead upon his shelf in Median. Jonathan read a volume sometimes, snatching a few pages when on a rainy afternoon the store was empty for an hour or so, but not in months did any other hand than his touch those books. He kept them, wondering why he had spent so much of his life in teaching people to read, and where they were whom he had taught.

And so in this life he and Katie grew together. It was her life, and he went into it. And the long unspoken friction between them was gone at last. She was jealous of no one and nothing now, for she and he were together in the store. She approved of him fundamentally at last, and he found peace in this approval. It made him free. He had done something he ought to do for her. He had done what she wanted him to do more than anything else. And so, his love expiated, he found his marriage better than it had ever been, a solid, everyday comradeship in which he and Katie took common share of the sources of their money and food and goods.

The store was a success and, because it was, it made all his life seem successful. He put a bathroom into his house, though it did not occur to him yet to take away the outdoor privy. But the women no longer used it. It became private to him and to Jon. This was a relief, for it had always been horrible to him to meet, coming to or from that small apartment, Katie or Lula or Mary. He ignored them as though he had not seen them. Now he merely ignored Jon, and he did not need to pretend to be examining the blight on the old lilac that screened the privy.

Median made a Chamber of Commerce the fourth year he had the store, and he was its first president.

39

ON AN August day in a hot summer Jonathan sat in the office. It was early afternoon, people were still loitering over noonday dinner, and the store was empty for the moment of customers. The mixed odors were strong, of pickles and cheese and dry goods, for he had ordered doors and windows shut against the heat. Behind the counter old Cobb was checking stacks of calico.

In the silence he heard the street door open and shut, and then Jon's voice.

"Where's Pop?" Jon demanded.

"Here!" Jonathan called. "And don't you call me Pop. It's no way for a boy to call his father."

"Want me to sweep the store, Dad?"

Jonathan looked up from his ledger. He wore small steel-rimmed spectacles to which he had fitted himself from the gross or two he kept in stock.

"If you get clean behind the counters better than you did last time."

"Didn't I?"

"No, you didn't." Jonathan's voice was kind but dry.

"Well, I will." Young Jonathan took the broom from the corner of the office and lingered. "Dad!"

"What, Jon?"

"Would you mind if I joined the Navy?"

Jonathan snatched off his spectacles. "What're you talking of, boy?"

"I'm sick of this little town."

Jonathan's eyes were upon his son's eyes, exactly like his own. "Why?"

"Everything's always the same here."

"No, it isn't. Every day is different. I've been here over thirty years, and no day has been like another. When I think of Median as I first saw it when I was your age and now, it's like a different world. Even the prairie is different."

"Everything's the same to me." Young Jon's eyes were hostile, but they did not drop before his father's and Jonathan liked that.

"Where do you want to go?"

"Manila."

"Manila!" Jonathan cried.

Upon Jonathan's earth Manila had of late been a place well defined because it stood for the chief cause of an inner discontent. He seldom discussed politics. He had early discovered that men were as irrational about politics as they were about religion, and he hated irrationality. But of all that he had disapproved in his time he most disapproved the push west across the Pacific. "West, west," he would mutter to himself, "as though heaven were there!"

The Sandwich Isles he had considered the ultimate folly of a people with already more land than they could conquer. Now these other islands were being talked about.

"Whatever has Manila got to do with you?" he asked, his voice so chill that young Jon longed to answer nothing. But he had the stubborn English blood in him, too.

"I'd like to travel a bit," he said quickly. "You came across the sea when you was my age, Dad. But I've only been to Topeka a couple of times."

Jonathan considered his son. He loved him, but the boy was not altogether his own. Half of him was Katie's, and he never forgot that. It was a strange piteous thing for which he could not blame his children that he knew still that he would have loved them better had Judy been their mother. He was the more carefully just to them.

"Do you want the Navy or only to travel?" he inquired.

"I don't feel any real call to the Navy," young Jon answered, considering. He suddenly noticed his bare feet and maneuvered the broom in front of them. "I'm just tired of Median."

"Tell you what I'll do," Jonathan said. "I'll give you a trip to Washington. I'll go with you. I've always wanted to see the capital of this country. That's what you want to see—not some place on the other side of the world that's none of our business as Americans."

"I'd like Washington all right," young Jon said cannily. "But what if I still want to join the Navy when we get back?"

"You shall go," Jonathan said. "It'll be against my judgment, but if you're going anyway I'd rather you went with my yes than with my no."

He was aware for the first time that this son of his had grown too big for him to command. How strange it was that merely by passing of days a small creature too helpless to feed itself should grow into a man! In his mind's eye he saw Jon always that little creature. But he was mistaken. Jon was a man in size and will. His eye moved over the broad-shouldered, brown-faced, sandy-haired boy. Then he saw his feet, and Jon trembled. But instead of being angry Jonathan smiled.

"Here I was thinking how quick you'd grown into a man. But those bare feet comfort me. You're still a little boy, and in a way I'm glad."

A scolding Jon would have taken and rebelled against it silently, but this kindness undermined rebellion and made him furious. He began to sweep the floor, his young mouth set. He was no child, and he would go barefoot no more.

And Jonathan, not knowing that he had ended his son's childhood, went back to his neat rows of figures that by care and calculation showed always a profit, a reasonable, righteous, earned profit.

He grew quietly excited throughout the next month about going to Washington. He bade young Jon come to the store, and he fitted him to a new blue suit and brown shoes, and himself to a new gray one. Out of his stock he took two new suitcases, some socks and shirts, and two ties. Secretly he was troubled by young Jon's choice of the gayest design. Left to himself, he would have stocked only ties of small and sober patterns, but this Katie would not allow.

"Men have to have fancy ties," she always said. "Don't know why, but Pa used to say a man always feels he can let himself go on his tie. So we got to have all kinds on hand."

Jonathan chose the quietest for himself. Without knowing he did, he estimated the men of Median by their choice in ties. Faience he distrusted because he liked flamboyance in ties. It was not suitable for the president of a bank. He had often considered putting his account into the state bank in Topeka.

That night before he and Jon went to Washington he inquired of Katie as they lay side by side in bed, "Has Jon a kink in him somewhere, would you say?"

"What kind of kink?" Katie asked.

"Wildness or something."

"Not as much as most boys, and you ought to know it," she retorted. "When I see the way women worry over their sons going to poolrooms and saloons, I'm thankful for our Jon."

"Ah, well," Jonathan said mildly.

They started to Washington on a September morning the day before the opening of school. He had planned the time to be away because he could never see the children crowd into the school without a quiver of his heart. He had planted a quickly growing hedge between the house and the school, and every day he walked around the square rather than pass the school-house. But nothing could shut out the rising of their voices when in the custom which he himself had set they sang, "My country, 'tis of thee . . ." After they had sung, he used to stand looking over the great roomful of children, healthy and eager and restless. It had been the most exciting sight his eyes could fall upon. And he had always said the same thing. "We begin by singing our national anthem. That is the way we should begin, for America gives you this school. Boys and girls, America treats you the same. America built this house and gives you books and hires teachers to teach you how to learn and how to grow into good men and women. That's all your country asks in return for all you are given—"

On the day school opened this year, he and Jon were on the train, rushing eastward. He sat by one window and young Jon by another, and across the space he talked to Jon of this country and for the first time of what he could remember of England.

"A different feel to it there, and when first I came here, Jon, I felt let loose and lost, and I didn't like it. In England everything was close around you, and you knew where every path went. But when we first came to Kansas there wasn't so much as a path. Sky and earth, and wherever you were it went on the same forever. Now I'm used to the size, and I doubt I could go back to closeness. I'd feel it too tight, maybe."

Young Jon listened politely. England was a name and no more.

When they reached Washington, Jonathan bought a guidebook at the hotel desk and marked what must be seen, and at the end of each day checked what they had seen. What effect the city had on his son he was not able to tell. Young Jon's sunburned face, always darker than his hair, showed no change. But neither did Jonathan's. Seen together, anyone could have told that they were father and son, and could have told, too, that they came from the West. Their voices had contended against wind and dust, and when they spoke their consonants were hard, as they must be when human voices contend against the wind and call across distances. Jonathan still carried the echoes of England in his speech, but Jon had the plain Kansas burr. They talked of what they saw, without communicating what they felt. They walked miles over hard pavements and up and down stone and cement stairs and floors and grew footsore as they had never been in their lives. They stared until they saw so much that nothing had any meaning, and still they kept on going, buying their food hastily wherever they happened to be and dropping into their cheap hotel beds at night too tired to speak. Jonathan had had ideas of teaching young Jon something of history and government, but he was too busy to teach or Jon to learn. They crammed their minds through their eyes.

They left Washington on a rainy night at midnight. Young Jon curled himself upon a seat, but Jonathan could not sleep. He sat upright and thinking.

He knew now that his was a great country. But he had known it in Median. There was never a day when he walked down a Median street and looked beyond it into the endless prairie that he did not know his country great. Washington had showed him a great nation as well, a vast civilized nation. Handsome buildings, great libraries and art galleries, magnificent streets, embassies and hotels and gardens and parks, and at the center of it, in a plain white house whose beauty was its plainness, there sat a plain American. They had seen the President by the merest chance on the day they went to visit the Senate. A heavy-set, square-faced man in a frock coat had passed through the hall, his silk hat in his hand. Whispering flew from mouth to mouth. "The President!" "Is that the President?" "That's the President."

He and Jon had stood gaping like everyone else. Afterward Jon had said, "He looks like anybody, don't he, Dad?"

And Jonathan had answered, "That's the glory of him."

He went back to Median proud of all that he had seen. Yes, it was a great country, and he was part of it. Men like him chose a common man and bade him go to Washington and run the nation for them, and so long as they willed, he obeyed them. When they willed, they sent him home again, and he went back to some little place like Median and was no more than anybody else. It was a glorious idealism, its only weakness the weakness of the individual.

He talked about this to Katie the night he came home, without expecting her to know what he was talking about, but having to talk.

"It was a beautiful sight, that city, but terrible, too. It made you take thought who you sent there. Only the best is good enough. And how'll we find the best in a country as big as this and people living so far apart? What is the test of a man when there's no guidepost to where he is, no class to define him, no standard of birth or race or religion to measure him by? Is democracy too big?"

Katie waited for him respectfully. This was men's talk and beyond women. She wished young Jon could hear his father. It was so educational when Jonathan talked like this. When she was sure he was through and not going to say anything more, she remembered something she had had on her mind.

"The long underwear stock is kind of low, Jonathan. I was pickin' out two new suits for you today, and I noticed we don't have enough."

"I'll order some tomorrow," Jonathan said. He was back in Median.

But he kept his word to Jon. A year later Jon went to his father on a Sunday after church, in that empty pleasant hour after worship and before food. He had grown much in this year. There was no possibility of bare feet now. He would have been more shocked than his father.

On this Sunday, at this hour, Jonathan was walking among the trees in the square. He made it his business to examine them and keep them sound. He was searching down a borer in an elm when he saw his son coming through the shadows. Jon had on his Sunday suit of dark blue, and he was a sturdy fellow. Jonathan was proud of him and pretended not to see him.

"Hello, Dad."

"Hello, son. That you?"

"Yep. What you doin'?"

"Chasing a borer. Got him, too."

Jonathan took out his pocket knife and opened a small winding tunnel. Young Jon watched him find its end and dig out a fat white worm and crush it carefully.

"That's the end of a nasty thing," Jonathan said.

"Dad!"

The sound of Jon's voice made his father wary. Something was about to be asked.

"Yes, son?"

"I'd like to remind you of something you promised me."

"If I promised, I'll keep to my word."

"Remember you said I could join the Navy?"

Median rocked a little about Jonathan. The boy hadn't forgotten!

"Yes, I remember."

"I don't want to join the Navy now, but I want to go away."

Jonathan kept on walking and looking at the trees, sharply aware of his son at his side.

"I want you to be anything you want to be, Jon. It's the beauty of America that a man can say that to his son. You don't have to be a store-keeper because I am one. It doesn't matter what you're born. It doesn't even matter how much money I've got. You can work up to anything. Have you thought of that?"

"I'd like to get away from Median, Dad."

"You can go anywhere you like to college." There was a blight on a chestnut, and he took a leaf apart to examine its disease.

"I don't want to go to school any more, Dad."

Jonathan dropped the leaf. "You don't want to go to *school!*" he repeated. "Why, I never heard that before!"

"I didn't want to tell you, because you set such store by school," Jon confessed. He was very red and afraid.

"I can't imagine it," Jonathan said slowly. "When I think how in Dentwater I longed and ached and suffered for school—and here it's free!"

Jon did not answer because he did not know how. Why was it that the old, in their youth, were so different from the young? He waited.

"If you don't want any more schooling," his father said, so coldly that he knew he was angry, "I reckon it doesn't matter what you do. A farmer, a sailor, a blacksmith—"

Jonathan pulled his moustache. Common folk were common folk. It was the one weakness in the democratic idea which no one heeded.

"I want to go to Nevada," Jon said. "Reckon I'll go to the gold mines."

"Go where you like," he told his son shortly, and knew that it would do him no good, whatever Katie had for Sunday dinner. He would not be able to eat it.

The desolation he felt when he saw the train carrying his son to a new West was broken before it was two days old. Clyde came back to Median. Jonathan in the hurly-burly of a Saturday morning heard the news from Mrs. Drear, running into the store with her apron about her head.

"Jonathan, you come over to the hotel quick. Jennet's come back and your old man!"

Everybody knew long ago the story of Jennet and Clyde, but no questions had been asked after Mrs. Drear had said flatly, "I'm thankful to any man that's put a wedding ring on Jennet's finger."

That it happened to be Clyde Goodliffe was strange, but she was still grateful. Besides, Clyde was now respectable in Median because he was Jonathan's father.

"Whatever!" Jonathan leaned across the counter to whisper, in his hand a slab of cheese. "I'll be over. Is he all right?"

"Looks the picture of a hearty, wicked old man," Mrs. Drear said and laughed.

But Jonathan did not even smile. "I'll be over." He filled a basket hastily with packages and called to one of the twins who were now clerks in the store.

"Joe! Carry this out to Mrs. Johnson's buggy!"

Then he hurried across to the hotel. His father had not written to him in years. Twice a year he wrote out of duty, but he had long ceased to expect answer. What news he had of his father was from Jamie, to whom Jennet sometimes wrote. He went into the hall of American House, now called a lobby, and to the bar made over into a desk space. A young, smooth-faced man stood there. Jonathan knew him as a boy he had taught in fifth grade.

"What room has my father, Hal?"

"The room over the kitchen—twenty-eight, it is."

The rooms in American House had in recent years been numbered, but more often than not they were still called by old location.

Jonathan mounted the stairs and went down a narrow carpeted aisle and knocked at twenty-eight.

"Come in!" Clyde roared.

He opened the door upon his father and Jennet. They were sitting in rocking chairs, each of them, and a basket full of yellow oranges was upon the floor between them. Oranges were beginning to come in from California, but they were still luxury. Try as he would to accept it, he was shocked by Jennet in his father's room. And yet he saw at once that every trace of girlishness had left her. She was a woman of middle age. What had been willful on her face was changed into firmness; what had been wistful was gone; and what had been gay was now only humor.

"Well, Jonathan!" Clyde leaped to his feet and seized his son's hand and shook it. And in that moment Jonathan saw that his father had dyed his hair and his moustache. They were blacker than they had ever been, and he had cut off his beard, and under his chin his neck was corded. For the first time in his life Jonathan saw his father's chin. It was not at all the chin he expected. Instead of being bold and jutting beneath the bushy beard, it was narrow and receded a little; and in this instant, beholding it, Jonathan lost all fear of his father forever.

"Hello, Dad," he said coolly, and to Jennet, not shaking her hand, "How are you?"

But Jennet laughed, and her laughter was not changed. "You don't hold it against me that I'm your stepmother?"

"Certainly not," Jonathan said with all his dignity. But he knew he would never forgive his father. Mary's little ghost came creeping to his side and stood looking with disdain at this red-haired woman in a golden-brown taffeta suit, cut too tightly across her bosom and her thighs.

"You're looking well," Jonathan said to his father.

"Never was better," Clyde said. He sat down and nodded at the oranges. "Help yourself."

"No, thanks," Jonathan said. Then he asked, "Are you staying long?"

Clyde peeled the skin in strips from the ripe yellow flesh of an orange. "The rest of time," he said. "Jennet and me've sold out and put the money in the bank. We made out well. And we've come home to help out the old folks."

"You mean—"

"Pa and Ma need help," Jennet said, "and Clyde and I are going to take over American House."

"Ah?" Jonathan said. He was suddenly glad that young Jon was gone. It would have been too hard on a decent boy to have this rakish old man for his grandfather. I needn't stay long, he thought, there'll be plenty of time.

But there was very little time, after all. For Clyde in his restless old age after two weeks of Median decided suddenly to go back and see what England was like now.

"There's all that money in the bank, and it's now or never," he said.

Jennet was willing because she was tired of him. But she was always good-humored with this man who had made her a wife.

"Good idea," she said, and saw to it that he set off with what he needed in two new carpetbags.

He reached England. This they knew because Jennet had a letter which Clyde told her to show to Jonathan to save him the trouble of writing another. And Jonathan, reading it, saw for the first time how little educated his father was. A child might have written these large, uneven penciled words. There was neither spelling nor punctuation. But still Clyde made himself plain. He was full of disgust because nothing was changed in England. The only news was that Edward and Millie had six fine children, to whom, it seemed, he preached the greatness of America until he had them all discontented. He ended the letter with a smack on Jennet's lips. "A fond kis as you no wat I like my girl."

Jonathan folded the letter abruptly on the words and handed it back to Jennet across the same counter over which he had once sold her a red dress, and she laughed.

"He's having a wonderful time, but he always does, don't he?"

"So it seems," Jonathan said dryly.

And then they heard no more and months passed and Jennet had time to turn American House over and over with paint and wallpaper and a new quick lunch counter, and still there was nothing from Clyde. She began coming over to the store every few days to ask Jonathan if she ought to do something about Clyde, and then suddenly one day in January Katie brought a letter to the store because it had an English stamp upon it and an unknown handwriting. It was Edward's handwriting. Jonathan read it behind the meat counter. It was high enough to hide him, for he had just this year put in ice refrigeration beneath the meat.

DEAR BRO. JONATHAN:

I take my pen in hand to tell you the Sad news. Our father passed away the sixth of December. Walking on the railroad track. Though we had warned him it is not safe as trains are frequent here, but he was used to America and an unmanageable old man. Said English trains was so slow he could run faster than them. He met his Sad end by a train and was mangled very bad. We buried the remains in Dentwater churchyard. Old vicar is gone, but the new vicar did the burial nicely and Millie says tell you everything was done.

We are all well. Business fair to good. We have four sons and
two girls the eldest married and two boys in business. Millie sends
her best and so does

Your aff. brother
EDWARD

He handed the letter to Katie, and she read it. He met her eyes.

"Dad would be the one to go back to England and get himself buried
safe in Dentwater churchyard," he said bitterly. And he thought of his
mother and of her little grave here in Median that he kept tended carefully. Now all he had done was not enough.

"I'm going to put up a new tombstone for my mother," he told Katie,
"one with an angel on it."

He stood before the angel on his mother's grave a few months later.
The angel was very nice, a pretty thing of Vermont marble. But he was
not excited by it. Indeed, he did not know what was the matter with him
this April. He had been ill in March with a heavy bronchitis that left him
tired and thin, and had gone this morning to see the doctor. He had been
proud that he could go to a doctor in Median and had entirely pooh-
poohed Katie's anxious suggestion at breakfast that he go to a doctor in
Topeka.

"It's a pretty pass if a man doesn't trust the doctor in his own town," he
had exclaimed.

His temper was distinctly not as good as it used to be, and he knew it.
But there was no one in the house any more except women, Katie and
Mary and Lula, and being the only man gave him some privilege.

So he had listened to young Dr. Peter Hall, and he took pride in the
shining new offices. Very gravely he had breathed in and out under the
stethoscope and had allowed the young man to thump him soundly.

"You need a rest," Peter Hall said affectionately. When he had first
come to Median he had been told to go and see Jonathan Goodliffe.

"No use your figurin' to settle down here in Median withouten he likes
you," the postmaster had chuckled.

"That's so," men had agreed. They were hanging about waiting for the
mail to come in.

"Rest!" Jonathan now exclaimed. "What from?"

"Well, sir, you're not as young as you were," Peter hinted.

Jonathan did not answer this. Secretly he had been dismayed for some
time at the new feeling he had nowadays that life was passing and he had
nothing more ahead except one day after another. This feeling had returned
upon him heavily as he buttoned his clothes and waited for the prescription.

"A month off is what you need," Peter Hall said.

"A month!" he had exclaimed. "Doin' what?"

"Play," Peter had said smiling. "Indulge yourself, Mr. Goodliffe."

Play! He had come out of the office feeling that he was sentenced.

"Danged if I want to go home and look at Katie, though," he muttered into the warm spring sunshine and was aghast at his wickedness. Remorse had led him here to the cemetery and the comfort of looking at the new angel on his mother's grave.

"I would like to indulge myself," he thought solemnly.

But what would such indulgence be? Was there really anything more that he wanted? Median had grown into a handsome town. It would be easy enough now for the citizens to go on and put in what they wanted. There was talk of a park and a swimming pool. Some of the young fellows had wanted a race track but he had put his foot down on that in town meeting.

"Racing brings in a lot of trash," he had declared. "I fought once against Median's being a cattle town for the same reason." When he had finished what he had to say, the council had voted against a race track.

"Don't know why I shouldn't indulge myself a little," he thought. "I'm not needed any more like I was, I reckon."

And then into his heart crept the old small serpent of desire. The angel on his mother's tombstone began it and the fragrance of the violets in the grass at his feet went on with it.

"It's Judy I'm still thinkin' of," he murmured. "Judy, my dear!"

Yes, this could be the only indulgence he craved, the delight of seeing her again, of talking with her and perhaps holding her hand.

" 'Tisn't as if I'd want anything of her," he thought. "Except to hear from her own lips—"

Except to hear from her own lips why she had run away from him that dreadful day, except to know if Evan treated her well, except to find out, once and for all, how she was!

He lifted his face in the sunshine and closed his eyes and standing so, with his hands clenched behind his back, he felt tears burn under his eyelids.

"I've lived mortally alone, Judy!" he murmured.

Then struck with fear lest someone had heard, or seen, he opened his eyes and looked around. Nobody was near. The little cemetery lay, a place of peace, beside the church and shielded from the street by trees. The quiet graves were all his company. He wiped his eyes and felt better. His heart loosened, as though something tight had slipped away from it.

"And I don't see why I shouldn't go to see my love just once," he thought. "It wouldn't hurt Katie if she didn't know."

But it was impossible to break in a day the habit of years. He would have to get himself ready for it, think about it for a few weeks perhaps, dream of it, plan it.

"I shall just put Evan aside, too," he thought. He was walking slowly homeward through the streets. It was noon and Katie would fret if he were late to dinner. "And if Evan comes in, why, I'll just tell him the truth, that it's due me after all these years, to hear her voice." He lifted his head as he thus made up his mind, and hastened his step.

It was at this moment he heard Lula's piercing voice shriek at him down the street.

"Dad—Dad—where've you been? We couldn't find you nowhere!"

"Why, Lula girl—" he broke into a little trot to meet her.

"Dad—Dad!" Lula sobbed. "Mother's fallen on the kitchen floor!"

He hastened down the street, Lula's hand clinging to his, and pressed her with questions. But she knew nothing of how it had happened. She had been upstairs in her room, "reading with my ears stopped with my fingers so I wouldn't hear nobody call," she sobbed remorsefully, and Mary had come and pulled her shoulder.

"I heard somebody crash down, like, in the kitchen," Mary had cried.

"We ran downstairs together and there Mother was lyin'," Lula sobbed, "and she don't know anything."

He dropped her hand, hurried to the back door and into the kitchen. Katie lay on the floor, and Mary was kneeling beside her. She had put a cushion under Katie's head and an old afghan over her, but Katie knew nothing of it. The dishes she had been carrying clean and ready to put away lay smashed on the floor around her. Lula began picking them up, still weeping.

But Jonathan stared in horror at Katie's closed eyes, and at her thin face, dark with blood.

"What in God's name—" he gasped.

He stooped and lifted her inert body, and her heavy hands fell like weights to her side. He carried her into the sitting room and laid her on the couch.

"Mary, telephone the doctor!" he flung over his shoulder.

Now he lifted Katie's hand that had slipped from the couch and put it on her breast. And then, because he could not bear the torture of her gasping breath, he went into the kitchen and pumped a basin full of cool water and found a clean towel and came back and bathed her hot, dark face. It was the most intimate service he had ever given her. The peculiar independence which was her being had taken its pride in doing everything for herself as well as all she could for her family. Now, as he sponged her forehead and her cheeks and wiped her twisted mouth, he felt awkward and shy and touched to tears. Poor Katie, who never in her life before had been helpless!

"Dear wife," he whispered. But she could not hear him now.

"My God," Peter Hall exclaimed, "her blood pressure—"

His mouth clamped shut, and he began his examination. He knew the signs so well. These swift, hard-bitten, thin-bodied women, driving themselves under the whip of their own restless energy, intoxicating themselves with their own ferment! He was fond of Katie, and he liked the kindly lash of her tongue. His own mother had been just such a woman, a prairie woman, lean and hard and direct as the prairie wind.

"Stroke," he muttered.

"You mean, she'll be helpless?" Jonathan whispered.

"If she lives," the doctor said.

He rose, and they stood looking at Katie. Mary, standing behind them, put her apron to her face and began to sob, and the doctor turned.

"You'll have to take her place, my girl. This woman'll never work again."

"Then I know she'd rather die," Jonathan said.

"Yes, but maybe she can't, after all," the doctor replied, "and I doubt she'll ever so much as lift her own hand again."

Jonathan's mouth was dry. "What'll I do?" he asked.

"Put her to bed and feed her, care for her, like she was a baby," the doctor said sadly. "It's all a man can do except to wait and see what nerves and muscles may come back. I'll help you lift her to her bed."

He put his hand beneath Katie's arms, and Jonathan took her stiff inert feet. One of her slippers fell off. Only this morning he had seen her thrust her feet into the carpet slippers she wore around the house in the morning and had thought to himself that she needed a new pair, and he would give them to her for Christmas. It was always hard to find things to give her. She needed so little, and now she would not need even slippers. They laid her on the bed.

"Mary can put on her nightgown, can't you, Mary?" Peter Hall said.

Mary nodded, and they left her. Out in the sitting room they sat down.

"Did she never tell you she felt badly?" he asked.

"She never talked about herself to anybody," Jonathan said faintly. He felt himself trembling, and his throat was dry. He kept asking himself, now what was he going to do? If Katie was going to be like this, what would he do? What would any of them do without Katie?

The doctor coughed. "I ought to tell you, Mr. Goodliffe, as your family physician, that I'm afraid your married life is over."

Jonathan stared at him, not comprehending. Then he understood and blushed as he had not for years. "Th—that's all right," he muttered. "Th— that's the least of it."

"Well, I'm glad you take it that way," the doctor said solemnly. "It's not that way with most men. You're a decent man, Mr. Goodliffe."

He wanted to tell the doctor that it wasn't that he was decent—though I hope I am a decent man, he thought to himself in the silence. But how could he say that what he had spoken was the truth and yet make the doctor realize how good his marriage was and how fond he was of his wife? Marriage was a manifold thing, he thought gravely, and in the variety possible between man and woman he had been happy with Katie in his way. By her conquering goodness Katie had made him content.

"It's just that we had much more," he said firmly.

The doctor bowed his head.

"You've had a real marriage, Mr. Goodliffe," he said.

"Maybe I have," Jonathan replied.

Night and day, thinking of a thousand small and sorrowful things, Jonathan watched beside this silent and inert woman. He moved the couch in from the sitting room, and on it he lay through the long hours of the night, listening for the slightest movement from the bed. But there was no movement, only Katie's breath, coming and going, catching, unsteady, and going on again. Sometimes he rose, conscious of a change in the direction of the endlessly blowing winds of spring outside the house, or in the warmth and cold of the April air, and he changed and adjusted the covering over her according to the need of his own body. In the morning he rose and while he was alone with her he washed her face and hands and brushed her dry mouse-brown hair that had as yet no gray in it.

But the bathing of her body and the changing of her garments he left to Mary and to Lula. He could not bear in her unconsciousness to see the nakedness her painful burning modesty had always hidden from him. If she had known, she would have suffered because anyone must see her, but even so he felt that she would choose the girls rather than him. So he went into the sitting room and waited and came back again and sat beside her and waited.

She might be conscious again at any moment, the doctor had said. When that moment came he must be there. He did not leave the house for an instant. Unwillingly even did he leave the room where she lay to answer a knock on the door and the many inquiries of neighbors. Hour after hour through the days and the nights he waited.

On the fifth day, at three o'clock in the morning, the moment came. He leaped from his couch at the sound of her louder breathing. He turned the wick high on the oil lamp on the table by the bed, and he saw her eyelids lift, and then in her eyes he saw the rising terror of her awakening mind. For the first time in all their life together he bent and gathered her in his arms and held her.

"You're going to be all right, Katie," he said in a loud clear voice, so that she might hear. "I'm going to see that you're all right, my—my dear. You needn't be afraid of—of anything. I'm here. I'll take care of you, night and day."

This he kept saying with the tears streaming down his face and into her hair that was against his lips, when suddenly she died.

He laid her down and looked involuntarily at the clock on the mantel. A lifetime was finished, and he felt it was his own.

40

THE BRIEF hour beside the angel on his mother's tombstone was now nothing but a dream. He thought of it sometimes and felt it as heavy upon his conscience as an actual sin.

"If I hadn't been dreaming in my own wind that morning I'd have been at home, maybe," he mused over and over again, driving remorse into himself until he felt himself bleed within. At least, he would have been at the store where he could have been found. For an hour the girls had let Katie lie, searching for him before they went for the doctor.

He had made sure Katie's death was not caused by the delay. "Still, that doesn't excuse me," he thought with gloom.

He knew what the sin was. He had been dreaming of Judy. Nothing else would have delayed him. To have pursued the dream now was no longer possible. It was over again, he told himself.

He went grimly back to his life in the store, and Mary and Lula kept the house for him. He sat down at table with two women instead of three, that was all. And he slept alone in his bed.

The summer dragged by, full of heat and drought. It was a year of grasshoppers. Business was bad and he had much idle time. Without missing Katie he was lonely. Then in August he had a letter from Jon.

"I'm here, Dad, and I plan to settle in San Francisco. Got myself engaged to a very fine girl, Isabel Dent, and we hope to marry next month. Her father will give me a job in the railroad business."

Jonathan wrote back with some bitterness. "Why shouldn't you come and help me in the store? You can have it, if you wish. I'm thinking of a holiday."

He had not thought of a holiday, but as soon as he said it, he knew he still wanted one. Jon wrote back promptly. "Why didn't you say so before, Dad? Sure we will come, if you'll come to the wedding."

But he did not want to go to the wedding. He was done with marriages and lovemaking. He wanted to go away alone.

"Where'll you go, Dad?" Lula asked fearfully when he spoke of it. She could not imagine this house without him, nor the town. It was impending catastrophe.

He felt his imagination grow reckless. He'd go as far as he could, away from everything.

"Where do you want to go, Dad?" Lula pressed.

"Go?" he repeated, searching his heart for its longings. "I'm goin' away off—I'm going to England. And maybe I'll never come back."

"Oh, Dad!" Lula wailed. And across the table, Mary, his mother's child, looked at him with sad dark eyes.

But he shut his lips and gave them no promises. If he did not do what he liked now, when would he? The image of Judy framed itself before his eyes and he stared at it.

"Not you," he thought, "not you!"

For he had begun thinking of her, to his shame, even at Katie's funeral. He had stood aloof in the midst of his family, solitary in his being. He was free, and he was afraid of freedom.

I'll have to get out of this, he had thought, looking down into Katie's grave. "I'm acting out of something that's not the man I am. I'll go away for a bit and get my own nature in hand again."

It was then that he had thought suddenly of England. But there had been delays, one after the other. Paul Graham came to Median as the rector of the new Episcopalian church. The churches in Median had been built as Jonathan had foreseen. There were now four of them. But Jonathan had grown more tolerant of men's souls. "There is only one God," he had said to Paul one day, "but men do not know it yet. You'll have to tell 'em, Paul."

He liked the older Paul better even than he had liked the young missionary, and he made no objection when early in the autumn Paul told him frankly he had come back to Median because he wanted to marry Mary, and Mary wanted to stay here. Mary was long ready for marriage, a fragile fair girl with his mother's tenacity under her fragility. But this wedding had been a cause for Jonathan's delay. It was not decent to have a marriage so soon after Katie's death, and yet he was not willing, out of his sense of duty to Mary's mother, to go away without seeing with his own eyes how happy she was with Paul. He had given Mary to Paul on a February day at a quiet wedding in the small new rectory and had felt the last duty to his mother finished.

It had been difficult to arrange his own affairs. Martha Cobb and the twins could manage in the store, and after some thought Jonathan had invited Matthew and Ruth to live in his house with Lula. It would do Ruth good to come to Median away from that lonely, heartbreaking farm, set like a dry island in the midst of a sea of rich oil.

But the real reason for his delay, month after month, after Mary's marriage had been none of these things. Judy, only Judy had held him. And yet he could not blame her, dear soul, since she knew nothing about it.

In May, only a month after Katie's death, Laura had come to him. She and Jamie had been in New York at the time of the funeral. Evan had sent Jamie there to put some new stocks on the market. But as soon as they came back to Topeka, Laura had come flying out to Median in a new bright yellow automobile, with Jamie driving. They had been kind, too kind about Katie, and Jonathan had soon wished them gone. And then Laura, in one of her commanding moods, had sent the others away, declaring that she must and would speak to Jonathan alone.

He had dreaded what she might say about Katie. Instead, she had leaned forward in her low chair in which she sat and clasping her ringed hands about her knee, she had said abruptly, "Jonathan, Judy is most unhappy."

He had given a startled cry. "Eh—is she?" He was ashamed of the cry the moment it came hurtling out of his mouth.

"You still love her, God bless you," Laura had exclaimed. "Now, Jonathan, you must tell me what to do for her."

He had sat motionless in his old Windsor chair, his eyes upon Laura's pretty, painted face. She talked with impetuous shrugs and rustlings of her taffeta ruffles and little frowns and grimaces, her hands clasping and unclasping.

"I'm furious with Evan, Jonathan—but it's really that Rachel Power's fault. She's inveigled Evan into making her his mistress. It's been going on for years, so long that he doesn't even deny it. They're together all the time in his office. Oh, dear—Mamma used to say when he first took that woman into his office that it would end this way. Mamma said Nature always took advantage of such a situation—"

"Wait!" Jonathan had commanded her. "You're saying a serious thing."

"Do you think I don't know it?" she cried.

"Is there proof?" he had asked.

"Everybody knows—"

"Everybody doesn't always really know," he had insisted.

"You wait," she had commanded him in return. "Don't forget, Evan is my brother. I'm not afraid of him. I asked him, and he wouldn't deny it. Do you know what he said? He shouted that he'd dare anyone to let it make a difference in the way they treated Rachel. He's simply going to carry it off with his usual high hand, forcing her down all our throats as his secretary."

"What does that mean?" Jonathan asked, and his hands gripped the sides of the Windsor chair.

"It means that Rachel will stay in his office all day and go with him on all his trips as his secretary and sit at his table in his house. And no one can say a word, least of all Judy."

"Why is she helpless?" he asked sternly.

"She seems to have no close friends, except me," Laura replied.

"Has he been cruel to her?" he asked. He thought of Judy as he had first known her, young, gay, at ease in the world, pouring her music into the old accordion.

"If you mean beating—no," Laura said. "But Evan is cruel. He thinks only of himself."

"Many men do that," Jonathan said. His lips were tight, and his eyes were pale and bright.

Laura leaned forward again. Her small, intense face was burning. "Jona-

than, of course men think only of themselves. Jamie's a selfish man—don't
I know it? But there's a place where even Jamie has the sense to know he
has to think of me, for his own sake. Well, Evan hasn't that sense. And
Judy can't talk with him. Judy never talks with anybody. She's like anything lovely—she simply *is*."

He quelled the rush in his heart. "This—this other woman—"

"Rachel Power—"

"She's different from Judy?"

"Different as night from day. She's as selfish as Evan, smart enough to
use her love. And he heeds everything she says because she's so smart."

"I'll have to go and see Evan," Jonathan said.

Laura laid her narrow hand on his. "He'll listen to nobody else, Jonathan. I know my own brother. He'll listen to you maybe because he's never
confessed even to himself that once he injured you."

He had not answered this, and he had drawn his hand gently away.

But Evan had not listened to him, either. When that brief, hard interview
was over, Jonathan knew that he and Evan would never meet again. The
words they had spoken to one another were an end.

"I come to say something direct, Evan, for the sake of what's past."

"Say what you like, Jonathan."

They were in Evan's office. Rachel Power had been there, a tall, dark
handsome woman in severe clothes, and Evan had sent her away. She
had returned Jonathan's look with quiet arrogance and then had closed the
door softly behind.

"Evan, I am told that Judy is unhappy."

He had thrown this at Evan, and Evan had hid his surprise behind a
quick smile. He tilted back in his chair. "Now where did you hear that?"

Evan was successfully rich, but the signs of disappointment were upon
him. His handsome eyes had hardened and his lips sneered through the
smiles. He had run twice for governor and had been defeated, the first
time by the Populists, and the second time no one quite knew why. He
had flung away politics then and had devoted himself to making money.
Now he held the reins of half a dozen utilities and industries in his hands.

He's like a man with a lot of horses tearing away and nowhere to go,
Jonathan had thought shrewdly, looking at him.

"Don't matter how I heard," he had said aloud. "It's this I want to
say: What's gone is over. I've had my life and I'm content. I'm goin' to
England now."

"To stay?" Evan broke in.

"Maybe," Jonathan said. "So, Evan, I want you to remember you owe
it to me—to—to keep Judy happy. That's all."

Evan sat still. "Why, damn you, Jonathan," he said slowly. "I don't owe
you anything." He rose and leaned over the desk on his hands. "I owe no
man anything—nor any woman!"

Jonathan rose, too, a slight medium figure in his new pepper-and-salt suit. "When you marry a woman you take on a debt, Evan—if you're a man."

"Judy has had everything she wanted," Evan said.

"You can't be sure of that until death do you part," Jonathan said gravely and took up his black felt hat and went away.

He came down early one morning a year later to make his own breakfast. Since Katie's death he found himself in the habit of waking just before dawn. He lay usually until daylight, listening to the twitter of birds in the ivy that climbed about his window. When the day silenced them, he rose, washed, and dressed and went down. It was six o'clock and he heard Bill Hasty, Abram's boy, throw the morning newspaper on the porch and go whistling on his way. He opened the door and reached for the paper. The wind had unfolded it and great black letters leaped at him. EVAN BAYNE KILLED BY WIFE'S INSANE FATHER. He gripped the paper in two hands and stood staring at the news, and the cool autumn wind blew his thinning hair.

In an instant he had it all as clearly in his mind as though he had been there. Old Joel had been sent home from Honolulu to his daughter. He had been found wandering on the streets, a beggar. Joel had been in Judy's house less than a week and yesterday he had walked into Evan's office, had shot him and killed him instantly.

Jonathan took the paper into the house and burned it in the kitchen stove. Then forgetting he had not eaten he went upstairs and put on his best suit and told Lula to get up.

"I'm going in to Topeka," he said. "I don't know when I'll be back. Evan Bayne is dead."

. . . The black butler opened the door but Laura was there instantly, rustling out of the drawing room in her black taffeta.

"Oh, Jonathan, how I prayed you would come!"

"Where's Jamie?" he asked stolidly.

"At the office, looking after things. Jonathan, it's so terrible." She seized his hand and pulled him in to the drawing room. "Sit down—let me tell you. It all happened in a minute. I can't get Judy to move. She just sits there in her music room staring at her hands." She glanced at a closed door. "And her poor old father—crazy as a loon. They have him in a padded cell in the hospital, waiting trial."

"They'll never prosecute," Jonathan said.

"How can they?" she cried back. "He's just an old ghost. And he keeps telling everybody God made him do it. Nobody even knew he was in the building. He just walked into Evan's office."

"Nobody with Evan?"

"That Rachel Power, of course. She says he tried to shoot her, too. But she grabbed him—he's so weak and old."

He did not speak. He was listening beyond Laura's voice. She saw it and said, "Dear Jonathan, you want to see Judy."

"No, better not," he said indistinctly.

"I will send her to you," she said and went away.

And in the next moment the door opened. He saw Judy standing there in her soft full black skirt. "I knew you would come, Jonathan," she said.

"Of course," he said and took her hands. They were as soft as ever and crushed so easily—how he remembered!

"I didn't want to go away, Jonathan, because I knew you would come as soon as you could."

They sat down on a satin couch, and he went on holding her hands.

"Poor Papa," she said gently. "He thought he was doing right. You know how he is, Jonathan. He told me over and over, 'I did God's will, Judy, and God helped me.' He was so pleased with himself, poor Papa. They won't kill him, will they, Jonathan?"

"No, Judy." She was so beautiful in his eyes, so frighteningly beautiful! Her lovely bright hair, shining about the black frock, her creamy skin and the dark sweetly lashed eyes!

"And you, my darling dear," he said with unutterable tenderness, "how are you bearing it?" He had her hands at his breast, fondling them, kissing them. He could not help it, after all these years. And she did not pull her hands away nor turn her eyes from his face. But large clear tears came rolling down her pale cheeks. "I loved Evan so," she said. "It never mattered what he did—I loved him."

She spoke with such innocent honesty that he felt his blood stop. He put her hands down gently on her knees.

"Did you, Judy?" His voice sounded small and weak in his ears. "Then, how can I help you, my dear?"

She gave a sob and leaned her head against his shoulder. "Oh, be my friend—please, Jonathan!" He longed to put his arm about her, but he sat rigid.

"That I will, Judy, always. Count me for that, my dear," he said and forced false cheerfulness into his voice.

And she lifted her head and wiped her eyes, and he sat rigid while she talked softly, sobbing now and then. "They sent poor Papa back from Honolulu, Jonathan. They sent him back because he was destitute. He was begging in the streets, they said—begging and preaching. Jonathan, I want him to come here and live with me, and I'll look after him. I haven't anything else to do, now."

"We'll have to see, my dear," he said. His voice was trembling again, but he mastered it. "It'll depend on others, I fancy—not on you and me."

Distress flushed her sweet pale cheeks. "But, Jonathan, you tell them."

"I will, my dear," he promised and suddenly could bear no more. "I'll go now, Judy, and see your father and find out how things are."

"Oh, thank you, Jonathan. I feel safe again, now you're here." She dried her tears with a wisp of lace and muslin she took from her belt.

He went away without touching her hand but she did not notice this, and seeing her absent eyes when he said good-by he felt a shock that chilled his heart. The brief flame kindling out of the old smouldering fire of his love died suddenly to its final ashes. He knew, in the instant he closed the door, that she had never loved him. If she had loved him even when he was young, she would have come into the sod house with him in the days of his grief, and she would have stayed with him.

"As Katie did," he muttered bleakly.

Instead she had run away with Evan and all these years she had been Evan's wife. Today when Evan was dead, even when it was plain that Evan had ceased to love her, she still had no thought for him whom she had left so lonely long ago.

"Though I've loved her faithfully," he thought with stark bitterness.

No, Judy had come to him even today counting with simple unthinking selfishness upon the faithfulness of his love. But he understood now that she had thought only of herself. Well, he would help her and go away.

"I'm cured, I hope," he thought.

But he felt a wound within him, a bottomless loss, a grief for something that never was except inside his dreams.

"Best to know," he told himself.

He buttoned his coat and plodded down the street to fulfill his last promise to her.

At the city hospital he asked to see Joel. "I'm a friend of Evan Bayne's, and Mrs. Bayne asked me to come," he said simply.

A male nurse led him into a barred room, and there old Joel sat bolt upright in a wooden chair in the middle of it. He lifted his head at the sound of the door and rose when Jonathan came in and stood tall and spare in his rusty black suit, taller than Jonathan remembered him, his white hair hanging to his shoulders.

"You don't remember me?" Jonathan asked.

"I do not, I am sorry to say," Joel replied in a resonant strong voice. The bright mad eyes did not look at him. "Are you sent to me from the Lord?"

Jonathan smiled. "Perhaps I am," he said. "I'm Jonathan Goodliffe. I was a lad in Median when you came there to preach, years ago."

"The Lord sent me there," Joel declared with energy. "The Lord has sent me to many places." He stood towering over Jonathan, his eyes fixed on space above his head.

"And the Lord told you to kill Evan Bayne?" Jonathan asked quietly.

The vague blue eyes glittered, wavered, and fell to Jonathan's face. Joel put up one hand and clutched his hair. His hand, thin and fine as a shell, was crusted with dirt. "The man wouldn't let me see Judy—he wouldn't even tell me where Judy was." Joel's voice was suddenly weak and childish and all the resonance was gone. "I was coming home to be with Judy, and the man behind the desk said, 'Put the old fool in the asylum.' "

"And what did you do, Mr. Spender?" Jonathan asked. His voice was quiet and kind, and Joel answered at once.

"I hastened out of that room, and the woman outside the door put a pistol into my hand, and I listened to the voice of the Lord."

"What did the Lord say?" Jonathan asked.

"She said, 'Go and kill that man!' "

Joel drew himself up to his full height and thrust out his hands as though in invocation. "Blessed be the name of the Lord!" he shouted.

"Mr. Spender, sit down and rest, sir," Jonathan said. "I will try to take you to Judy."

Obediently as a child the old man sat down. Jonathan took this strange conversation to the nearest police station, and in less than half an hour he stood listening, with a police officer, to the dark handsome woman locked behind the mahogany doors of Evan's office.

"He wouldn't marry me," she said sullenly, in her deep and strange voice. "He loved me, but he wouldn't marry me. He said it would ruin him if he divorced his wife and married me. People wouldn't trust a divorced man with their money. He said I had to go on as we were. He made me sit at his table, obey him, work for him. He used me like a servant. I'd bought that pistol weeks before. When that crazy old man came out talking about God—I took the chance."

"Take her to headquarters," the officer commanded his men.

So Evan's life had ended, a bitter frustrated history, Jonathan told himself sadly. But he thought most of Judy.

I can understand my poor dear, he told himself. In some queer way, I still love him, too.

But he made up his mind to go to England at once.

The ship ground against the wharf, and the gangplank was flung down, and people pushed ahead of him. It was the habit of his whole life to let them pass him and go on. Then, as he was about to move forward, he felt his shoulders strongly grasped and held.

He looked up astonished and saw looming above him a tall, dark-faced man and knew him instantly.

"Beaumont!" he gasped. "However?"

"Mother told me to meet you, sir, and here I am. This is my wife, Michelle."

He felt his hand taken between two soft ones, he smelled a delicate perfume, and a woman's pretty face under a little lace hat leaned forward impetuously and kissed his cheek.

"Ah, Mr. Goodliffe, you who are so good—now I can see you!" Her warm woman's voice spoke with an enchanting accent. He was too be-wildered with surprise and pleasure to speak.

The more he looked at them, the more shy he was. They were so beauti-ful, their garments rich, their faces happy with the careless happiness of those who have no secret cares of their own. They took his arms and bore him away between them; and a porter, unseen until now, seized his bags. Protesting and pleased, together, he was carried off to a hotel which he saw from the very flunkeys at the door was an expensive one.

"I say," he remonstrated, "I can't stay here, Beaumont. It's not my kind of a place."

"You're our guest," Beaumont cried with joy. "To think I have the chance!"

They swept him along with them into an enormous mahogany-lined lift and then along wide halls into a suite of rooms facing the sea. Beau-mont threw open the door of a huge bedroom, and the bellboy put his bags down, and Beaumont gave him a tip from which Jonathan averted his eyes.

"We'll have lunch in twenty minutes," Beaumont announced, "and we'll wait for you in the parlor. We have everything to talk about—not a moment must be wasted, *mon cher!*"

Jonathan understood not one word of the French into which these two fell as naturally as they breathed, but he understood them. He had never seen two such glorious creatures. In the cab he had sat between them, looking from one face to the other, silent while they poured out talk, and thinking that Beaumont had fulfilled his whole promise as he could have done only in the air of a country where he was free as France could make him free. Jonathan thought with sorrowful contrast of Stephen and Sue in Median, living out their lives humbly under the shadow. But upon Beau-mont no shadow had fallen.

I got him out in time, Jonathan thought with thankfulness.

And Michelle had dispelled even the chances of memory. She was a lovely creature, her auburn hair curled about her pretty vivid face and her violet eyes dancing and gleaming with light. The love between her and Beaumont was open, and neither thought of hiding it.

He stood alone in the huge bedroom and caught a sudden sight of him-self in a great panel mirror behind the door. He had never seen himself from head to foot all at once, and he was startled and abashed. What did that brilliant pair see in this middle-sized, common-looking chap that was he? He turned away from himself and tiptoed about the room. Everything in it was big and solid, nothing was makeshift. On this little isle people built to last for eternity. Centuries could not destroy such stuff. He thought of the makeshifts of Kansas, the quick wooden buildings thrown up in a few days, the shoddy furniture of mail-order catalogues.

It's because America is so big that folk can always move somewhere else, he thought. Here they know they've got to stay.

Beyond the bedroom was a bathroom so immense that he was struck with admiration. Even America had no such bathroom. The tub was enormous, built upon the floor like a monument, the plumbing massive and too firm to admit of improvement. This bathroom would endure as it had been installed, let invention be what it might.

He inspected everything, gazed out of the window, and then inexplicably changed his tie. He had put on a plain gray silk tie in the ship's cabin this morning. Now he took it off and put on the gayest one he had, a narrow maroon satin stripe. Then he opened the door into the other room and stood there smiling at them with love in his heart.

An hour later, in the great orderly hotel dining room, he told himself that this could never have happened in America. He had hesitated half-fearfully at the dining-room door, between Beaumont and Michelle. Beaumont looked prosperous and proud, a man obviously of the upper classes. But there was no need for hesitation. The steward had hastened forward.

"Yes, sir—Dr. Parry, please, your table is reserved."

They had followed him and seated themselves at a table where a high window gave toward the sea, and he had eaten the best meal of his life, English food, roast beef from a hot service wheeled to the table and carved by a white-capped, white-aproned cook—Yorkshire pudding and gravy, mashed potatoes and boiled cabbage, a green salad and plum tart. His heart was warm toward this country of his ancestors. He felt foundations firm under him. People knew where they were. Every man had his place.

And all the time he listened to this pair. They made a duet, wanting to tell him everything at once. Yet he could scarcely listen for looking at them.

"I wish your mother could see you, Beaumont," he interposed.

"I wish we could see her," Beaumont said eagerly. "We've thought often of going back to America, just for a visit. I'm still an American. We think of that often, eh, Michelle?"

"How often!" Michelle echoed. "I long to see my dear good *belle mère* and my good *beau père* and the brothers and sisters. Gem—it is such a sweet name!"

"We will talk of it later," Jonathan said quietly.

They did talk of it later, but he had first to hear of Beaumont's great achievements as a surgeon of the hospital where "he reigns supreme," Michelle said proudly. She put her white hand on Jonathan's arm. "I must tell you what he will not—that he is a *vairy* great surgeon. Oh, people come from everyw'ere—only for the brain, you know. Last mont' a prince from India, dying of the tumore, and my Beau cut it away and mended the brain again, and the prince grows well. If he liked, my Beau could be a great musician, but he chooses to do what helps so many people!"

Beaumont laughed, his white teeth shining in his dark face, and his dark eyes tender upon his wife.

"It is my turn, Michelle," he said, and then he told Jonathan in a few deep words what Michelle had meant to him.

"We loved each other so soon after I came," he said. "How it would have been for me without her I cannot imagine. She was my home, my love, my security, my refuge. She comforted me when I was discouraged, praised me, scolded me. I was not lowly or alone because of her."

Michelle's eyes were wet. "And was it nothing for me to have you, too, all those years?" she said.

In the presence of this love Jonathan's heart began to bleed from the old heart wound. Ah, he had always known that love was like this, even if it could not be for him. "I thank you, my dear," he said gently to Michelle. "And you, Beaumont—you've grown to your height, my son."

Yes, this great brown fellow was his son, the son of his spirit. He looked at the big, dexterous, life-saving hands. "You must never come back to America, Beaumont," he said slowly. "Never—never."

Beaumont's face quivered. "Is America the same?"

Michelle was suddenly quiet. Her luminous eyes moved from one face to the other. Ah, these two, Jonathan thought, so happy, so rich in one another, they knew the shadow over there across the sea! They did not live in it, they were free; but they knew it was in the world with them.

"America has not changed in her heart," Jonathan said in his quiet sad fashion. "The body has grown. How the body grows! You would never know Median, Beaumont. The courthouse, the churches, the post office, the fine school—I'm not the schoolmaster now, you know—"

"I can't imagine you not a schoolmaster," Beaumont said. The tenderness in his deep, gentle voice broke over Jonathan's heart.

"I tend the store now," he said. "But I daresay your mother's kept you up in Median news."

"Yes," Beaumont said simply.

They were still thinking of the shadow over there. In silence Beaumont leaned forward, his hands hung between his knees, his head drooped. It was an attitude of unconscious memory, the memory of Stephen, his stepfather, and of Sue his mother.

"If America doesn't change," he said—with somberness—"if her heart doesn't grow to comprehend the brotherhood of man, she'll be torn in two when the big war comes."

"The big war?" Jonathan repeated blankly. He had not thought of war for years. That minor splash in the Pacific had been soon over, and Admiral Dewey had come home to be made into a hero of clay and then broken into dust again by a childish people.

"There'll be lesser wars first," Beaumont said. His voice was the prophetic tolling of a bell. "There'll be a war in Europe in the next five years, but it'll be a lesser war. Maybe there'll be a couple of wars like that. But the big war is coming, the war for the brotherhood of man."

He had dropped back into the speech of his childhood. Michelle looked frightened. "Beau, what are you saying!" she cried.

Beaumont shook his great head. "No, we won't go to America, you and I, Michelle. We'll live in the sunshine of France. But I'll never see my mother again."

They stayed together four days, talking a little less each day but feeling closer together. In the evenings Beaumont went to the piano and played, and sometimes while he played he threw back his head and sang. When the great rolling voice poured into the room, Michelle slipped her hand into Jonathan's and squeezed it. "You see why I adore him," she whispered, and Jonathan nodded. Most of these songs he had never heard, but sometimes, a few times, Beaumont sang the slave songs of his childhood, and tears came into Jonathan's eyes. Ah, Beaumont must never come back!

On the morning of the fifth day Beaumont was summoned to Paris by cable. The only son of a cabinet minister had been caught in a motor accident, and his skull was crushed. There could be no delay.

"Come home with us, sir," he begged Jonathan, and Michelle's soft hands clasping Jonathan's pulled him toward France.

But Jonathan refused. "No, I came back to see England, and it was rare luck to be met by you and Michelle. I'll never forget these days. In a way, they're better than any of my life."

"We'll meet again," Beaumont said.

Jonathan smiled and did not say what he knew, that such meeting could not be sure. Once in a lifetime it was lucky enough.

41

IT WAS not many days before he knew he did not want to stay in England. He found no such companionship again as Beaumont and Michelle had given him. The great hotel was too fine for him left alone. He took the train to Blackpool and was met at the station by Edward and his two eldest sons. He saw the three medium-sized, soberly clad figures and knew them at once. Edward had settled into thickishness at the waist, and his long gray moustache was yellow at the fringes.

"Well, Jonathan," Edward said, and they clasped hands.

"Well, Edward," Jonathan replied.

"This is Tom, my eldest, and this is Ed." Edward pointed his stick at his two sons.

"Fine lads," Jonathan said heartily.

The men took his bags, and the brothers walked ahead. "We'll take a cab for once," Edward said.

"Don't for me," Jonathan replied.

But they crowded into a cab and rattled off and stopped in front of the store. Nothing was changed. Jonathan knew the rooms as soon as he stepped into them, and knew Millie, too, stout and middle-aged as she was. The younger boys were apprenticed at shops, but the house still seemed full of Edward's children.

But after the first day it was hard to talk. Edward and Millie talked while he listened, and he saw the picture of their lives—the petty troubles with rival shops, the competition of too many people trying to earn their bread in the same spot, the careful watching of tiny profits. It was a decent life, but how small! His own life in Median, he now saw, had been filled with immensities.

Of that life, to his amazement, they asked no questions. When he spoke of it, Edward lit his pipe and let his mind wander and Millie said, "Well, I never," her eye on her knitting.

Once she stared at him and when he paused she broke in, "Jonathan, remember Connie Favor?"

Jonathan blushed against his will. "Yes, I do—just."

Millie smiled. "She was sweet on you—she'd have gone to America for the asking."

"I was only a lad," Jonathan said stiffly.

Millie laughed. "Ah, well, she married a chap as went to Australia—lives on a sheep farm now."

He gave up talking of Median after that, and in a few days he had had enough.

England was small, too small for him, and he knew he did not want to stay in it. All against his will America had stretched his soul. He thought much of Median, in the narrow streets of Blackpool, and he longed for the wide plains and wider skies of Kansas. There's room to grow there, he thought.

On his second Sunday he tramped off to Dentwater. "Don't expect me until you see me," he told them.

He took the familiar road along which he and Edward had climbed into the coal cart when they went to see Clyde off to America. Nothing along the road had changed. He came to Dentwater, and saw it had not added a house or changed a chimney. England's a damned finished kind of place, he thought, looking over the village. He tramped to the cottage that had been his home and stared at it and did not ask to enter. A surly old chap tilled the garden plot and looked at him suspiciously.

"I lived here once as a lad," Jonathan said to excuse his presence.

"Eh, you're not the only one," the man retorted. "It's changed hands often, this place has. Chimney smokes."

"I don't remember that," Jonathan said. "But I do remember that from that window up yonder, if the day was fair, I could see the sails of ships upon the Irish Sea."

"Attic's full of stuff now," the surly man said.

He left the cottage then and walked down the street to the school. It was no longer a school. Two ancient and withered old men sat on a bench outside the door into which he had gone so eagerly every school day.

"What's this place?" he asked them. One of them was deaf, but the other took his pipe out of his mouth and said, "Dentwater Almshouse," and put the pipe in again.

"It was a school in my time," Jonathan said and had there been answer he would have asked next of his old schoolteacher. But there was no answer, and he went on and took his lunch at the small public house which had been such a cause of quarrel between his mother and father. The faces were strange, and he did not remind them of Clyde Goodliffe. He drank his glass of ale and ate his cheese sandwich, and when this was done he went down the street and into the empty church and sat a while. A young curate came in, not yet out of pimples. "Anything I can do for you, sir?" he asked.

"I came to this church as a lad with my mother," Jonathan said. "The rector was old then, and his name was Clemony."

"He's in the churchyard," the young priest said. "Maybe you'd like to see his grave?"

"If you please," Jonathan replied.

He followed the fluttering robes along the mossy churchyard path and stood at the foot of two narrow graves. He remembered as clearly as though he had been in church this morning the old vicar and his flying white hair, preaching the brotherhood of man. What was that old Clemony had said about the blacks in India? Jonathan could only remember that tears had streamed down the prophet's cheeks as he cried out to the staid and wondering people in the little village of Dentwater. . . . Beaumont and the big war! Against the vague trouble of his own mind Jonathan saw the faces of Stephen and Sue Parry, dark with sorrow.

"Where's Clyde Goodliffe's grave?" he asked abruptly.

"Here, sir," the curate said.

And in a moment he stood beside his father's grave. It was hard to believe that under this still green sod lay the restless bones of that wild-hearted man.

"You knew him?" the curate asked.

"Yes," Jonathan said and shut his lips.

"He'd come all the way from America, and his family is mostly on the other side—one son in Blackpool, I believe," the curate said.

"Aye," Jonathan said and turned away. He was glad that he had not brought his mother's dust here into this shadowy old churchyard. Let her lie where she was in the bright western sunshine.

He put some money into the church box, thanked the curate, and went away. He knew now he could not live in Dentwater, and if not in Dentwater then not in England. Yes, England's made and finished, he thought, and hurried his steps along the road he had come. A man can't do anything here but live out his time and die.

He took passage within the week for America.

. . . On the ship crossing the ocean he found he could not sleep for eagerness. He rose at dawn and went on deck where he could feel the ship's speed and see the parted waves flow from its sides. And while his body was carried forward to its home his mind roamed backward over the years and to his first voyage over these same waters.

"I ought to thank my dad, I reckon," he told himself, thinking of the unwilling lad he had been. "I'm glad now he pulled me up out of Dentwater. I wish I could tell him so."

He had been pulled up out of a small place and set in a large one. He thought with joy of Median. It was the core of all his being.

"It's the kind of a town I like," he thought fondly.

In a queer way his father had been right about life and his mother wrong. No, they had both been right in their own ways. But they had never been fused. Not all their passion toward one another had fused their eternal difference, he the wanderer and she the homekeeper.

"Reckon I'm the mixture," he thought with some astonishment. For was he not the fusion? He stared down into the clear green waves and pondered himself. Homekeeping he was and he had made a town his eternal home. But the town he had set in the midst of land as wide as any sea.

"A love of a town," he thought fondly, and knew when he said the words that Judy had lost her power over him at last. It was not Judy now who drew him, but Median, the creation of his being.

He found himself hungering for the first sight of it. He could not bear a moment's delay between ship and train, and seated by the window in a day coach of the first train westward out of New York he watched the rugged hills of the East shorten and smooth into the plains and his heart began to beat fast. He knew better than he knew any human face the outlines of his town, the comfortable solid shape, rooted in the prairie and open to the sky. He was glad that Median would never grow into a city. He had protected her from the ravages of cattlemen and had forbidden her to the coarse men who might have spoiled her with gambling dens and racecourses. Median was now what he had planned she should be, the seat of a prosperous farming county, a town where laws were made and enforced without cruelty, a center for homes and a place of rest for the old. All around her, except to the south where the oil wells stood, the wheat grew unbroken, green in spring and yellow at harvest, the fine hard red wheat brought from Russia by peasants. It made the country's finest flour.

His mind dwelled with rising love upon every aspect of his town. He was proud of his own neat white house with its green shutters and of his good store. Jon was there now looking after things. His son's children would be born there in the town, too. Median was a good town for children, just as he had always planned.

He was to reach there in the midafternoon of a Saturday and he had told nobody of his coming. Again and again he had imagined his homecoming. He would get off the train casually, and say hello to old Jackson, the ticket agent, and then walk down the street to his house and go in. Maybe the children would all be out somewhere. They'd come home and find him. "Hello," he'd say. "Well, I'm back."

When the train passed the last station, he reviewed all this in his mind and found his heart beating so hard that he was alarmed. He walked down the aisle and poured himself a drink of water. It was stale and lukewarm.

"Next time I drink it'll be from my own well," he thought. That water was the best in the world, clear and cold and pure.

But his heart kept on beating hard and he had to bear it while the train pulled in at the station. He fumbled over his bag and forgot his hat and hurried back to his seat for it. He got off finally and for a moment stood bewildered. He was the only passenger for Median, and almost immediately the train shrieked and went on again. The sun was so bright he was blinded. He had forgotten how bright the sun could be in Median. He stood uncertainly, looking about him. Then suddenly he heard voices cry out.

"There he is!"

And down the platform a host approached him. He stood smiling sheepishly, recognizing them all. Why it looked as if the whole town had turned out to meet him!

"How'd you know I was coming?" he demanded as they drew near.

"We cabled Uncle Edward," Jon said proudly. "He told us the ship and of course we knew you wouldn't waste time in New York. We have met every train anyway."

He was in a mist of happiness. The whole town wanted him back!

"I was going to slip in and surprise you all," he said.

"You're the one that's going to get the surprise, Dad," Jon said.

"Where's Isabel?" Jonathan asked. He began to suspect some extravagance of welcome and to guard against his heart melting under it, he looked severe.

"At home, getting ready enough cake and ice cream to feed the town," Jon said joyously.

But there was no more time for such talk. They were pressing around him, all wanting to shake his hands. Faience, who was still the mayor, took his bag.

"I can carry it," Jonathan said. "I've carried it a couple of thousand miles."

But no one answered anything he said. They were full of a superb secret.

Jackson locked the railroad station and came with them and they swept up the main street, the young people singing and yelling and the children blowing whistles.

"I never knew there was so much noise in Median," Jonathan cried.

"Never was before!" a voice shouted back at him.

Up Main Street they went, beyond the courthouse, beyond the church.

"Where are we going?" Jonathan asked.

"Never mind," Faience said, laughing. "We're just going!"

They crossed the street, swarming around Jonathan, treading on his heels. Then they paused and he stood still. There in a big empty space where years ago he had planted hardwoods on the edge of the town he saw the foundations for a big building. Walls had been laid to the level of the ground, but only in one corner had they reached above the level.

"What in time—" he began.

"Hush!" said Jon.

He stood silent and the crowd drew back from him. He looked down and saw at his feet a great white marble stone, cut square and polished smooth. There were letters on it—he read his name.

"The Jonathan Goodliffe High School."

He began to tremble and he felt his son's steadying hand on his arm. The mayor stepped forward and drew a paper from his pocket and began to read and the people listened.

"Friends and fellow citizens of Median," the mayor said in a loud voice. "We are gathered today to perform a most significant act—"

Jonathan stood rigid, his eyes on the stone. There upon the eternal marble, he went on reading—*"named in honor of Jonathan Goodliffe, the man who more than any other made and shaped the town of Median into a goodly home for us and for our children."*

The mayor's voice rang out through the trees. "We have laid these foundations for our new high school, the school which we dedicate today to Jonathan Goodliffe, the man whom we all delight to honor. We deliberately choose to express our love and gratitude now, while he is alive and active among us. We want him to know today how Median feels."

Median had made a monument for him! His heart dissolved and he would have wept had he not fixed his eyes sternly upon the shadows dancing over the mayor's bald head and shaven cheeks. A bird sang shrilly in the hardwood under which they stood and a boy threw a stone into the leaves and it flew away. Of course he did not deserve all these things Faience was saying. He had simply lived in Median and done his duty.

The mayor was finished. He stooped and picked up something and put it into Jonathan's hand. It was a shining silver trowel.

"Will you lay the cornerstone of our new school, Jonathan?" he asked, his voice natural again.

"Yes," Jonathan said. "Of course—yes—"

But the big white stone blurred through his tears. Two men stepped forward—his son and Steve Parry.

"I saw Beaumont," he muttered to Steve. "I want to tell you—"

"Later, Mr. Goodliffe, sir," Steve whispered.

They heaved the stone up before him, and Steve took the trowel and filled it with mortar, and put it back into his hands again, and somehow he smeared the stuff on the wall and together Jon and Steve placed the stone.

"The cornerstone is laid," the mayor announced.

It was over. They were all gazing at Jonathan. He looked away, but wherever he looked, he met the eyes of Median warm upon him. Unutterable shyness rushed over him. He tried to smile and felt his face stiffen.

"We talked over a dozen things we wanted to do for you," Faience said tenderly. "Some of the people wanted a bronze statue."

Jonathan felt his tongue unloosen. "Nonsense, that," he said sharply. "Waste of money and for what?"

They roared with laughter and he smiled and felt his blood begin to flow again. He flung his hand toward the foundations and tried to make the gesture careless. "The school's the thing," he declared. His eyes twinkled. "I shall plant some ivy at this corner and let it grow. I'm a common chap—no reason why my name should be on the school more than anybody's."

They shouted laughter again, they hugged him and all but smothered him with their joy in him.

"He's just the same!" they cried to one another. "Jonathan Goodliffe, you haven't changed a bit!"

"The same old screw," he agreed. "Why not?"

They carried him down the street in the heart of the crowd and Jon went ahead to tell Isabel he was coming. But Jonathan turned his head and looked back. It was odd to think that his name would be there upon the cornerstone, forever! Long after he was dead and buried, his body dust, his name would be carved solidly in the midst of Median. Generations of children, coming and going, would read—*Jonathan Goodliffe*.

"It's queer how I like it," he thought. "I like it wonderfully well."

Voices In The House

THE big house stood on the top of a flattened hill outside the town of Manchester, Vermont. It was an ancient house, built nearly one hundred years before the last Mrs. Winsten died and before William Asher married her daughter Elinor and changed it to the Asher house. It was not entirely changed at that, old Vermonters still called it the Winsten House and always would. William did not resent this for he liked the house as it always had been. He was not afraid of losing his identity, it did not occur to him that such a thing could happen. He was large enough in mind to be himself under all circumstances, and so to enjoy Elinor's heritage and make it his own. There was an Asher house on Long Island which he could have had, as an only child, had he wanted it. But he had learned in his childhood, in the soft green summers in Vermont, to love the town of Manchester and the graceful mountains about it, and he sold the Long Island house without compunction when his parents died.

The Winsten house itself had been built so large and solid that the following generations of the family had not added so much as a wing to it. Before its founder, Adam Winsten, had died, in the early years of the nineteenth century, he had needed a big house, for he begat a family of twelve children, nine of whom lived to grow up. Most of the grandchildren, however, had gone West. The house, huge as it was, could not contain them, and in the west, grown rich on gold and railroads, they had all but forgotten that they had come from Vermont. Yet in the earlier century there was always one Winsten to live on in the house, and old Mr. Winsten, the last of them and Elinor's father, as lean and wintry before he died as an aging elm tree, had been an Adam, too. But none of his sons wanted a house so big that new servants would not stay after one look at the stretching roofs, and none, neither son nor wife, wanted old Bertha, the cook who had lived in the house for as long as any of them could remember.

In the end the children all went away except Elinor, the youngest, and she stayed on with her mother and old Cousin Emma, who had always lived in the big house. It was during these years in the summers that William fell in love. He and Elinor were married soon and very quietly after Mrs. Asher died of a stroke one spring day, when she had worked too long over her rose beds. Cousin Emma announced after the wedding that she had always wanted to live in New York, and now she would do so, since Jessica, who was the dead Mrs. Winsten, had willed her enough money.

This left the house to Elinor and therefore to William who liked the idea of living in it. The Ashers had always been merely a summer family, so far as Vermont was concerned, and William loved Vermont and hated being a transient. New-fledged from Harvard Law School, he had opened his first small office in Manchester and there it still was, for sentiment's sake, for now, years later, as a successful lawyer, he was compelled to have his main office in New York. Between New York and Boston it had been difficult to choose, but the Ashers were a New York family and to continue his business life there made a nice balance between the past and the present.

The big house remained exactly as it had always been. On the outside it was white clapboard and green shutters, but underneath the wood the walls were of brick, and so the windows had deep sills. The house stretched long and not quite symmetrical, two wings on one side and three on the other, all set back some feet from the central part, which was three stories high and severely plain except for the carved front door. A long driveway of elm trees, now so old that William had them regularly inspected and reinforced every autumn before the winter winds came down from the mountains, led to the lawn before the house. The first Adam had planted the elms widely apart so that the driveway was spacious and lent its space to the house. When the front door opened it revealed the same instinct for space within. A wide hall ran straight through the house to a glass door at the back, which opened upon an enclosed garden. Double stairways joined above the door, and to the right and left were what had always been called, since the first Adam's day, the east and west parlors.

The furnishings were still fine, the pleasant mixture of an old family who bought the things they liked in each generation and put them together without thought of periods. Elinor had considered the rooms overfurnished when she became the mistress, and she had invited her brothers and sisters, scattered over distant states, to take certain pieces for their own homes as mementos of their common childhood. The mahogany velvet-covered chairs and sofas and the special pieces which had always been in the house, such as the long French mirrors between the front windows in the parlors, of course no one thought of taking away, any more than they would have thought of digging up by the roots the old syringas and lilacs, or the vast elms themselves. Certain things belonged in the big house and the Winstens had proper respect for them.

The house had not seemed strange to William Asher when he moved into it as a bridegroom, that late spring day, now twenty-five years ago. He had been in and out of the house every summer of his youth. Elinor's brothers had been his friends and in that sense he had grown up with her, only gradually aware, as summers passed, that he was falling in love with her. Thus, too, he had grown used to Bertha, and her husband, Heinrich, who was the butler, and it was not strange to have them as his servants after his marriage. It had not been so easy to get used to their daughter

Jessica, however, born to Bertha and Heinrich the year after he and Elinor were married. For the two stout elderly servants to have an unexpected child was preposterous, they felt it so and were embarrassed and confounded. Elinor had laughed a great deal, but she gave them permission when they asked to name the child Jessica, after the dead Mrs. Winsten, her mother. And so the strange little Jessica had grown up in the kitchen, on the fringe of the big house, although William was scarcely aware of her existence, except to wonder sometimes, when he caught a glimpse of her, what would become of her. She was a servant's child and yet it was difficult to think of her as such. She was quite exquisite as she grew out of babyhood, very slender, her eyes electric blue, her fine spun hair as yellow as the traditional gold.

Once years ago, when he came home, William had walked through the unlocked door to find Jessica in the east parlor, a child then of seven, but with a duster in her hand, for Bertha was already teaching her to help. She was not using the duster, however. She was sitting on one of the rose velvet chairs, her eyes unseeing and bright, her lips upcurved in a vague sweet smile, as she gesticulated with the hand that held no duster, a delicate child's hand, white and soft and not at all a housemaid's hand.

When William stared she recovered herself with a gasp.

"Oh, Mr. Asher, I never heard you," she whispered. She jumped from the chair and ran to the kitchen, while he called to her not to mind. She was only a child, and although he had been afraid of children until his own were born, he did not like to frighten so tender and pretty a little creature. But she did not return. The next week Bertha sent her away to a convent in Canada, an English convent, where the nuns, she told Elinor, would be more strict than French nuns.

"Jessica is so little to be sent away," Elinor had said half remorsefully when she told William.

"Too young," he agreed.

Nothing could change Bertha's mind, however, and they let Jessica go. They were young themselves in those days, they were deeply engrossed in their own life and love. Jessica came home sometimes in the summers, yet never to stay long. Bertha found her troublesome and when Heinrich died in the year that Jessica was ten, Bertha let her spend even the vacations in the convent, until she was old enough to leave for good and work as a maid in the big house. As a maid, they were all used to her now, although, as Elinor said, Jessica would never be as steady as Bertha and probably she needed to get married. Still, as Elinor had said again only this morning, who was there to marry Jessica except Herbert, the chauffeur and houseman, who had come seven years or so ago, after a succession of unsatisfactory substitutes for Heinrich? He had fallen in love with Jessica at once in his slow stubborn way, and for love he had stayed on in the big house, in spite of her persistent, half-laughing, half-angry refusals.

This servant gossip, as William called it, was merely mild diversion and subject for Elinor's sprightly and humorous description when he came home tired from the office. He listened, only partly heeding, as a form of relaxation, while she put the children to bed. Now of course the children were grown up, Winsten married and Edwin and Susan away at college. He and Elinor were alone again in the big house.

The train, swinging between the Vermont hills, stopped with a jerk at the station, and William gathered his papers together, slipped them into his black leather briefcase, and prepared to get out at once. Elinor had given him the briefcase last Christmas, and it had then been brown. The difference between brown and black, in a lawyer's briefcase, is delicate but profound, and William, gazing at the new briefcase, had betrayed his own doubt.

Elinor had laughed. "Give it back to me," she cried, her blue eyes sparkling in frosty mirth. "Give it back to me, William, and I'll exchange it for a black one. You've had black ever since I knew you and I wondered what effect change would have upon you."

"It is not a question of the effect on me," he had replied. "I am concerned with the effect on others. Clients expect a certain sobriety."

To this Elinor had returned nothing but her smile, sweet beneath the sparkling eyes. He was relieved, however, when a few days later he had found the handsome black briefcase, his initials impressed upon it in pale gold.

Herbert had asked for the day off, which explained the coming home by train. It was pleasant to look out of the car window, however, and see Elinor, waiting for him on the platform. She was here to meet him, driving the car herself and she was still, after twenty-five years of marriage, a pleasant sight to him. She had come in her own car, a small dark green convertible, which however she never converted. Today at the end of summer the windows were rolled down, but the top remained fixed. She sat in the front seat, smoking a cigarette in the offhand dainty sort of way which was natural to her, a slender, rather tall woman, who had never cut her blonde hair. It was soft, almost straight, and now, although she was only forty-five, it was growing white, and because it had been so blonde, he scarcely noticed it, knotted heavily at her neck as she had always worn it. Had she not been so dainty, so thin, so fine-boned, she might, he sometimes felt, have looked a slattern. As it was, the slight disorder always apparent about her person seemed accidental. He had learned not to point out that the top button of her white silk blouse was open, revealing the glimpse of a bosom surprisingly young. He knew that to remind her was to risk a smile, a shrug, certainly not the button buttoned. A pin, one of the many brooches he had given to her, would have taken the place of the stitch or two needed to tighten the buttonhole. She would probably never take the stitch, he now knew.

"Herbert not back yet?" he inquired as he got into the car, his eyes averted. She slid over, yielding the wheel to him. It was accepted between them that he was the better driver because he was more steady and because the late afternoon traffic did not annoy him. Manchester in summer was a tourists' town, highly refined, of course, but tourist in spite of that. The Equinox Hotel was filled with the best people, but Cook's tours in buses screeched in the streets while others found less expensive hostels.

"I came alone because I wanted to tell you—Jessica has decided to marry Herbert," Elinor said.

"No!"

"Yes, she has at last. They were away all day together."

He swung down the street to the right, and after some blocks turned into a road which after two miles of silence and green, gave into their own lane.

"After seven years," he murmured, amazed.

"I always knew that Herbert would get her in the end," Elinor said.

"I wonder if she really wants to marry Herbert," William mused, not caring. It was a delight always renewed to drive toward the massive house on the hill ahead, and he slowed the car.

"Don't talk about Herbert as a husband," Elinor said, rather sharply.

William smiled. Elinor was too fastidious, she did not like Herbert, and the less because she could really find no fault with him. He was an exemplary character, faithful, honest, silent, hardworking, and burning with secret energy. It had not taken her long to discover that this energy was directed to a relentless pursuit of Jessica.

William remembered. "Six years ago this summer, I believe it was, you told me that Herbert was in love with Jessica and that she hated him."

Elinor reminded him. "You said that it was a pity he wasted his efforts, and I told you that if he kept on he would win."

He turned his head to glance at her profile and saw it enigmatic, her delicate lips severe, her eyes doubtful, her eyebrows lifted. The wind was blowing back soft strands of her hair leaving her forehead bare. She had a high forehead, not knobby, but intelligent and beautiful. The look meant that she preferred not to talk about the matter any more. He fell silent, knowing that when she was inclined she would talk, explaining herself fully without being urged.

He swept the car gently into the driveway, stopped it at precisely the proper spot, opened the door for Elinor, and got out on the other side. At this moment Herbert came from the house by the pantry entrance and took over the car. He was still in his best double-breasted blue suit.

"Good evening, Mr. Asher," he said.

"Good evening, Herbert," William replied. He paused, his foot on the lowest step to the columned porch. The columns had been added to the house only fifty years ago by Elinor's grandfather. "I hear you're to be congratulated," he went on.

Herbert's face did not deepen its usual brickish red. "Jessica gave me her word today," he said. He had a lipless mouth but his small greyish eyes were not unkind.

"Well, well," William said. "You've been very faithful."

"I never looked at another woman," Herbert said. His voice, flat and firm, suited his square-set body. Dutch ancestors somewhere, William thought, had given him the blockhouse build, the thick hands.

William smiled and mounted the steps and Herbert drove the car away to the garage. Elinor was already in the house, she had run up the marble steps while they talked, as light and fleet as ever she had been. He saw no glimpse of her, however. She was already in the kitchen or upstairs or in the garden and he entered his silent house. He did not mind the absence of his children, knowing that they were at the unreachable age, lost in a time tunnel out of which they would emerge when they were fully adult, as Winsten was beginning to do. He could talk to his elder son as to a man, but Edwin was still impossibly young and opinionated. Susan as a woman he felt he did not know and the child she had been was gone altogether. He took Elinor's word for it that she was all that he hoped she was and meanwhile he enjoyed the fact that she was certainly very pretty, although he regretted that she had not inherited her mother's permanently slender figure. Susan looked like his side of the family. She was dark and inclined to be plump, and she would have to look after her diet, as he had learned to do. He had once let himself get fat in his thirties and it had taken Elinor's repulsion to alarm him enough to bring himself down. Not so long as he lived would he forget that midnight scene.

"You don't love me as you used to, Elinor." He had said that because she turned her head away.

"Oh well—" she had murmured.

Desire, rising toward high tide, had suddenly ebbed. He seized her chin. "Look here, tell me the truth!"

She had been ashamed to tell him but she did it somehow, because he forced her, and that night for the first time he began to understand the difference between himself and Elinor, the dividing difference, indeed, between man and woman. Her passion was a secret silver spring permeating all her being, connecting nerves and feelings, while his was a river, separate and strong. The river flowed in him independent of all else, determined upon its own course, but anywhere the spring in her could be stopped by distaste, by moods, by thoughts she concealed.

The boys took after the Winstens, through some perversity of inheritance they were tall, fair and extremely handsome, unnecessarily so, especially Edwin. But Susan had dark curly hair. He was very fond of Susan, with a peculiar secret fondness which he excused on the grounds that she was his only daughter.

At the top landing he met Jessica. She appeared at her usual speed, a slight creature, flying down the long wide hall, her pale green uniform fluttering, her white apron ruffling and the bows at her back all ends and ribbons. She was only twenty-four and looked much younger.

"Don't hurry, Jessica," he warned her. "You'll fall down the stairs one of these days."

"Oh, I don't mind what happens to me, Mr. Asher," she replied. Her hands were full of fresh towels, she was putting away the laundry, and the smell of clean ironed linen was about her like a fragrance. She was shining clean, her blonde braids wrapped tight about her head and little damp sweat curls encircled her face.

"Always in a hurry," he grumbled. "You make me tired just to look at you. So you are to marry Herbert, after all these years!"

She laughed suddenly. "Oh, that man! I have to get rid of him somehow. It's Mother's doing, really. She says it's time. I might as well marry him as anybody."

She was a creature so childlike, though woman grown, that instinctively one felt playful merely at the sight of her. Her uniforms, pale blue or pink or green, her little ruffled white aprons and caps, made her as unreal as a servant on a stage.

"I don't know that you can get rid of a man by marrying him," he said rather more seriously than he felt.

"Oh, at least he won't keep asking me," she retorted. She spoke English with a clear pure accent, the result of her years in the convent. Bertha still had a guttural German edge to her tongue and Heinrich had never mastered the English language at all. But this child of theirs spoke with a silvery sweet voice and a carved beauty of words. He had once said to Elinor that Jessica had come from the convent speaking English like an angel and she had said, "Do angels speak English?"

"Tongues," he had replied, "of which English is doubtless the most beautiful." He liked good English, he was somewhat precious about literature, and often felt that had he taken the time he might have been a writer.

"Well, I suppose you know what you are doing," he now grumbled to Jessica who stood with her arms full of the fragrant linen. "All young people seem to think they do, anyhow."

He went on to his room where everything was laid out as usual for his bath and change. Jessica did that for him and for Elinor and they would miss her, unless, of course, she kept on working, which he supposed she would not. Herbert Morris would not want his wife working even though he would probably ask for a raise on the strength of getting married.

He averted his mind from the thought of Herbert Morris married to Jessica. There was something distasteful about the involuntary picture which crept into his mind like the unrolling of a secret film, that solid brutish body fastened upon the pale delicacy of Jessica. He was shocked at his own imagination. Civilized as he believed himself to be, the antics of the human brain were distressing. He had no wish, indeed, to imagine Herbert Morris in any way whatever, and he felt only the utmost repulsion toward the fellow except as he daily appeared, respectable and decent in his chauffeur's uniform, or houseman's coat. So far as he was concerned, this was the only Herbert Morris there was. Nor, for that matter, did he have the slightest interest in the pale delicacies of the maid Jessica. He was, he believed, a man of clean heart and this by choice and taste, yet here was his antic mind, and if his mind could so exhibit its inner lawlessness, the inward brute, he supposed and most unwillingly acknowledged, what must other minds be, less controlled than his?

It did not bear consideration. He dismissed the matter by turning his thoughts firmly to the clear and bodiless aspects of the law. He was at this time involved in an interesting case which concerned the claims of two inventors, who unfortunately had produced almost identical improvements in machinery for the treatment of drying woolens. Independent of each other and unknown, the two minds had followed strangely similar paths. Which had begun first the thought process and how inexorable was it that one had been shrewd enough to reach the goal of the patent office first? In such cool rumination, he finished the changing of his garments and went down to dinner with a mood both pleasant and calm. Jessica and Herbert were only servants again.

Immediately he received a shock. As he came downstairs, his step noiseless upon the carpet, he saw Jessica. Taking advantage, he supposed, of the space of time before dinner while she waited for them to appear, she was in the east parlor, sitting in the rose velvet chair. It was not only this. She had taken off her apron and her cap and she had moved the chair so that she could see herself in the long French mirror between the windows. She had even changed her hair somehow, it stood about her face in a fluffy yellow cloud, and she was talking in a low musical conversational voice almost distinctly. He paused on the stair, remembering with some indignation, the same scene years ago, which, he supposed, had made Bertha decide on the convent. But this was worse. Jessica was actually speaking words of love to some unseen person.

"But, my darling," she was saying, "don't you see that I love you? Everything I do is for you. This house, the gardens, myself, would I care for it all as I do if it were not for you? Would I stay here when I could be in England or France or Italy, if it were not for you?"

She laughed softly for someone, shook back her hair and reached out her arms.

This was monstrous, he thought in consternation. He was very glad that Elinor had not seen it. He came forward firmly, and Jessica hearing his step turned with a flying movement of terror.

"Oh, it's you—" she breathed.

Her face went absolutely white, a bluish white, she snatched at her cap and apron and put them on with swift and trembling hands.

"Were you imagining yourself in a play?" he inquired not unkindly.

She looked at him as though she did not comprehend. "Please, please don't tell anybody!" she whispered.

"Then you think you were doing wrong?" he asked.

"Please!" she begged.

"You are very foolish," William said severely.

Again she threw him that fearful uncomprehending look and fled away, kitchenward. He stood frowning for a moment, pursing his firm mouth, then he decided to let the moment pass. What Jessica was saying before the mirror was too silly to repeat even to Elinor.

In the kitchen Herbert and Bertha looked at Jessica as she dashed in, her cap awry, her apron crooked.

"You look like somebody was chasin' you," Herbert said in a fond effort to amuse her.

"I ran downstairs too fast," she said, trying to control her quick breathing.

"Always she runs," Bertha complained. "What for? It don't make some sense."

But the atmosphere was benign. They were not going to scold, Jessica could see, not today, and turning her back on them she began to place the bouillon cups on the silver tray.

Her life was distinct and separate from the rest of the house, a life within a life, and the two worlds meeting only at the points of service had nothing to do with each other spiritually. Bertha, large, sensible, firm-faced in her grey cotton uniform, sat at the kitchen table, slicing roast beef for Herbert. Jessica still did not sit down. On every table in the kitchen the dishes were in disorder, but the oblong center table was set with straw mats and the red handled kitchen knives and forks. Herbert sat at the end which had been Heinrich's place when he was alive. Upon the day, now six years ago when Bertha told Herbert to sit there, he knew that she was on his side. Six long years it had taken to persuade Jessica that he was going to marry her, seven years he had been after her, but now that he looked back, he felt that if Heinrich had not died, he would still have been in pursuit and she would still not have given in. Her father was always on Jessica's side, no matter what she wanted.

"Sit down, girl," he ordered her.

Jessica sat down and began to eat daintily from the plate her mother had piled too high. Never could her mother learn that the sight of too much food sickened her and long ago she had ceased complaining.

"Miss Elinor told me I should fetch up a bottle of champagne to wish luck," Bertha said now.

She got up, heavy on her feet, and waddled to the refrigerator where the bottle was cooling.

"Ah," Herbert said wiping his mouth with the back of his hand. "That was nice of her. Next to beer, I don't know but what champagne is as good as you can get. A cold glass of beer is always my favrit, but that's not saying I'm against the champagne for once."

"Jessica, liebchen, eat," Bertha commanded. "It iss a big day for die alte mutter."

Jessica looked up, uncertain, quivering, slight, conscious of the two faces turned toward her, each with its peculiar and terrifying yearning, as though, she thought, she were a mouse and they were large affectionate cats. She smiled a quick and brilliant smile, her armor of defense.

"Oh, I'm eating, Mother," she cried in her high sweet voice, and she continued to smile while her mother poured the sparkling wine into the second best goblets.

They held their glasses high in the German fashion, Herbert self-conscious, embarrassed, unable to share in Bertha's open sentimental mood.

"Here's to you, my children," Bertha said. "Be happy, dear ones, and give me grandchildren. Herbert, be good to my liebchen, and Jessica, you be a good wife like I teached you."

They drank, Bertha solemnly and slowly, Herbert in gulps, and Jessica in quick sips.

"Ah," Bertha said, setting down her empty glass. "I think of der lieber fater. How happy today would he be, Jessica!"

"Don't talk about him," Jessica said sharply.

"No, no," Bertha agreed. "Nothing sad today. It is right. Eat now, liebchen."

She took her own knife and fork again and cut the roast beef upon her plate into large square bits and began solidly to eat her dinner.

Herbert did not talk while he ate. He had grown up on a farm where conversation was not to be thought of with food. He clutched his fork upright in his left hand while he sawed the beef with his knife, held in his right. Jessica looked away. When they were married she would tell him that the fork was not held so. But then he had not had the opportunity to learn such things that she had. She waited at the table and saw how people held their forks, people who knew.

Mr. Asher used his fork and knife so nicely, eating in a way that was never repulsive. She had always liked Mr. Asher, even when she was only a child. His marriage to Miss Elinor was a real romance, like in fairy books, the handsome dark young man, well mannered, his voice pleasant, and nothing repulsive about him. She looked at her plate steadily now while she ate, taking the smallest bites, careful not to look at Herbert or her mother, who were repulsive when they ate. But she was twenty-four already, and no one else had asked her to marry him, because she had never let anyone ask, for who had there been except butcher boys and grocery clerks and shopkeepers? Herbert, too, she had tried to prevent from the very first, six years ago, but he was not to be prevented. He was always about and he simply kept saying the same thing over and over again, and her mother telling her that she must marry somebody and so why not Herbert because he was solid and good. They could live on the chicken farm and Herbert would look after things in the evenings. It would make a home for all of them, even for her mother when she got too old to work any more.

"Dondt pick, Jessie," her mother said sharply at this moment. "You eat good now, like I tell you."

Immediately all appetite left her. When she was small, a pale little girl, always too thin, her mother had pushed food into her mouth and held it there, her big flat palm tight over her mouth to keep her from spitting it out. Once she had bitten her mother's palm and her mother had slapped her mouth until it bled, and then her front teeth were loose for a while. Yet she knew her mother loved her. Her mother loved her terribly, terribly, and that was why it was so wicked not to love her back.

Herbert held a fork full of food, poised, "You want to put some meat on your bones. You'd feel a lot better."

"Oh, I feel well enough," she said, laughing.

The bell rang from the dining room and she darted up and flew to the door. "Ah, they're ready," she cried.

"She'll settle down once she's married," Bertha said.

"She'll have to," Herbert said.

"Her father was flightylike," Bertha went on, "he was immer so qvick changing, and fussy, too. I settled him, when we was married, ya, yust like I settle Jessie too, when she comes here. She lissens to me, and she lissens to you, you vill see."

"All the same," Herbert said, "I'll be good to her."

"Sure," Bertha said, "I am good also. Vy not? She iss all I have."

Autumn was the season that William liked best of all the year. He had never been an enthusiast for spring, although it had been spring when he fell in love with Elinor. Because it was spring he had distrusted the violent attraction he felt the moment he saw her that summer when he was twenty-two, especially as he had seen her every summer for years before without thinking of love. He had even been mildly in love with someone quite different the summer before. Marian Heyworth was a neighbor, a nice girl, he still thought, when occasionally he remembered her, not with any interest but with placid wonder at the turn his life had taken. The Heyworths had owned a summer place next to theirs in Manchester and Marian was decent about Elinor after the first shock. Indeed, it had been her accusation that had revealed to William the full enormity of his new passion. He was of a dogged nature, however, and when she faced him with the truth he acknowledged it.

"I think you're right, Marian," he had said. "I regret it very much but it has happened."

He had never regretted it, of course. Elinor was not only his wife, she was still his beloved, a very rare combination, he believed, after so many years. But he had not allowed himself to speak his love until after the summer was well begun. In the dogdays, hot and humid, on a particularly uncomfortable day when they had paddled down the upper reaches of the brook near the house, he had proposed and been accepted promptly. Elinor had not seemed surprised. When he inquired why not, she had said in a matter-of-fact voice, "I've been expecting it, William. Marian told me that you had told her."

He had been shocked at this frankness between the two girls he knew best but he said nothing. Men would never have spoken of such sacred matters but he knew now that to women nothing was sacred. He winced when he thought of it, but he knew it was true. Elinor's bridge parties confirmed his conviction. Quite against his will he had sometimes overheard the remarks of the seven women in and about Manchester who were her best friends, whose seven husbands were also his best friends in the country club, and he was always shocked. He did not believe that Elinor was so wickedly frank as the seven unwise wives, but he did not dare to ask. He simply went on believing that she was not, because he considered her unique among women and very near perfection. Her graceful head, poised upon a rather long slender neck, the soft silver-gold knot of hair at the nape, to this day sent a ripple of delight through his blood. He could not keep from touching her when he passed her, his hand smoothing the hair to the contour of her head, or pressing the firmness of her small breasts.

Autumn, then, was his favorite season, the early autumn, beginning, here in Vermont, somewhere in late August and ending with the first snowfall. In his way he was an outdoor man, not hunting or shooting, but enjoying the shallow curves of the pleasant mountains, the change of color upon the trees. This morning when he came downstairs he saw a tiny grey feather lying on the rust brown carpet of the living room and he stooped and picked it up. It was the feather of some small wild bird, the wind had blown it in when the door was opened, perhaps by Jessica when she was sweeping. But how delightful to live in a big house where yet one could find upon the carpet the feather of a bird! He put the feather between the leaves of the book lying on his special reading table, the current book which he now read as he waited for Elinor to come down to breakfast. It happened to be Proust, and it pained him to realize how remote the story was, how far from France today, or from life in any part of the world, indeed. He felt the permanent hidden nostalgia that all men of his age feel, he supposed, for the era they knew as young men, the safe, assured, happy years which unaccountably had simply ceased to be. In his way he had been a young radical, alarming his parents as today he was alarmed by Winsten and Edwin, not because they were radical, far from it, but because they were so conservative, so prudent, so dangerously careful not to ally themselves with the slightest possibility of revolt. Two safer young men than his sons never lived, and he hid from them his own doubts and queries, as a liberal. He still classified himself as a liberal, a conservative liberal, of course, but certainly a liberal, a point of view which disgusted his sons. Susan so far had shown no interest in politics or the world, or in anything except herself and her chances of marriage. It mortified him sometimes to see how single-mindedly she pursued her quest of a mate. Surely Elinor had not been so obvious or so determined. Above all, Susan detested, despised was her word, the women who in the past had devoted their lives to feminism, or as he preferred to put it, to the equality of the sexes. His own grandmother had been a friend and helper of Elizabeth Cady Stanton but Susan begged him not to remind her of it. Among the family photographs was a picture of the two ladies taken together, in hooped skirts and side curls, and Susan, coming once upon the likeness of her ancestress had expressed fierce scorn.

"Women like that have set us back so far with men that we can't mend the damage!"

"Explain yourself," he had demanded.

"Don't you see, Dad?" Susan had cried. "They made men hate us!"

"Rubbish," he had retorted. "I don't hate any woman."

"You wouldn't like me to be a lawyer, would you?" she asked too shrewdly.

"I don't think you'd make a good one," he countered. "You haven't a logical mind."

"There," she said in triumph, "I told you! If it hadn't been for the Stanton woman and her kind you wouldn't have thought about my mind and I'd have been what I liked."

"Do you wish to be a lawyer?" he had asked after a digesting pause.

"No, of course not," she had said with outrageous calm. "That was just a catch."

He gave up. He could make nothing of this generation. Serious conversation was impossible with them. They sacrificed their very souls for a wisecrack, a form of speech which he loathed as destructive not only of sensible communication but of civilization itself.

Elinor came down at this moment and he put down the book and showed her the minute grey feather.

"See what I found upon the floor, blown hither by the autumn wind."

She looked at it and smiled absently. "It's only a sparrow feather, I'm afraid. Probably two sparrows had a fight—they're always quarreling in the gutters under the roof."

He put it back between the leaves without reply. There were times when she caught his moods perfectly, replying so delicately true that he could not refrain from taking her in his arms. At other times, as now, she refused compliance. He understood exactly what she meant. Her mood this morning was remote, she was to be let alone, he must not kiss her close, she was off somewhere in the day to come, living ahead without him, and he might or might not know about it. It had taken him a long time, at least ten years, to comprehend that marriage consisted largely of mutual consideration of the other's mood, selfishly perhaps, in order to keep within the circle together. They had clashed a good deal in the early years, because he had taken it for granted that a wife was supposed—not, of course, to obey her husband, but at least to consider him before she considered herself. He knew now that Elinor with all her delicacy was of tougher fiber than he, that she could do without him better than he without her, and that she could be most cruelly stubborn about letting him suffer it out.

He suspected that what was true of Elinor was true of all women. They could and did manage their own lives, either openly and above board as Elinor did or else secretly. Yet he was completely happy with her, sometimes to his own surprise, and he was still infatuated with her, although there were times when she made him thoroughly angry.

They sat down at the breakfast table, a rite which he always enjoyed so much that he felt sorry for his friends whose wives did not rise from bed in time to share this hour. Elinor enjoyed it, too, and did this morning, for in spite of the remoteness of her mood she got up to kiss the top of his head when it became apparent that he was not going to kiss her. He had learned to leave her alone when she was remote, and here was his reward, that she would, as now, come fluttering back, even if only for something so light, so scarcely felt, so almost worthless, and yet so valued, as a kiss on top of his hair. He restrained himself from seizing her while she was near, and was again rewarded by her kindling gaze when she sat down.

"I do like that grey suit with that maroon tie," she exclaimed.

"Thank you," he said calmly. "I rather like it myself."

Breakfast then went its usual way. They had faced each other, had taken temperatures, had renewed their mutual approval and understanding. He left the house for his Manchester office a few minutes later, and in spite of her somewhat warming good-by kiss, he was able to put his entire mind on his work. His marriage was entirely successful and therefore safe.

The house which he had left in such peace in the morning was in a roil when he returned to it in the evening. Elinor met him at the door with her finger on her lip and a warning glance toward the kitchen.

"What is the matter now?" he inquired in something less than his ordinary voice.

"Bertha is angry at Jessica again," Elinor sighed. "Neither of them will talk about it. Jessica is upstairs with her door locked, and Bertha is glowering over the stove."

He was not as patient with servants as Elinor was, although he recognized that this patience, inherited from the Winstens, was rewarded by the clinging loyalty of Bertha. Forty years had imbedded Bertha deeply into the family, like a pearl in an oyster, as valuable generally and yet as irritating, he sometimes felt, as the pearl must undoubtedly be.

"Herbert didn't say anything," he said, considering. Herbert all the way home had been simply the block-backed figure in the chauffeur's seat.

"Perhaps he doesn't know," Elinor said.

"Come, come," he said, putting his arm about her. "You must not let servants upset you." He was glad he had not told her of the scene of Jessica before the mirror.

"I don't think so of Bertha and Jessica," she replied.

"Once you let servants become human beings," he retorted, "you are in for trouble. There are other cooks as good as Bertha."

"Poor Bertha," Elinor said, but she relaxed pleasantly in his arm as they walked toward the living room. There she had set out the tray for cocktails, a task which was Jessica's but which she had performed as a matter of course when Jessica locked herself up.

"Shake it well, my love," he said. She had taken the frosted cocktail shaker. "Meanwhile I shall tidy myself a bit. I am sorry I am late."

When he came down again, tidied, Herbert was waiting in his white coat, and the house to all outward appearance was as usual upon a fine autumn evening. The doors were open to the dining room, two places were set at the table. He had thought, when the children went away to school, that he and Elinor would be lonely, the house so large and, always before filled with children, now so silent, so seemingly empty. He had discovered after a very few days that his apprehensions were unnecessary. The house was delightfully quiet, he did not miss the loud young voices, the poundings of footsteps upon the stairs, the shouts from the upper windows. It was pleasurable to wander through the rooms, orderly at last, to find a book where he had put it down, and no litter of comic magazines. Only at night sometimes, when sleepless he prowled about the house, did he see the small ghosts of the living children, Winsten at ten, a blond slip of a boy, always leaping, running, darting through the halls; Edwin, the brown boy, deep in a chair in the library, a particular chair, his head bent over a book, his features foreshortened. Many a time when he himself had sat in the chair it was still warm from the body of his son. And the ghost of Susan, flesh of his flesh, yet female and alien to him eternally, they all came back in the night, the children they once had been, and he yearned over them and then he felt old age loom near because they were gone. For though they came home at Christmas and in the summer, it was no real homecoming. The house for them was now only a brief stopping place on the way to the final destination. They were not lost to him, for he had had them, newborn and helpless, the little children learning to walk and talk, and then impetuous school children, and turbulent in adolescence. Those were the children he kept and he did not miss the tall and gawky young adults who came back so briefly to use his house as a place to bathe and change before dances and dinners, a place where they slept and ate without paying for it. He had wondered sometimes as they grew what they thought of him and their mother, and whether they missed at all the early closeness. Watching them, he had decided that they missed nothing, and that they did not think. They were on their way to unknown places, blown by the winds of their own desires.

Still, this was only his night mood. In the morning he woke up, rested by silence, and when he was bathed and dressed his reflection in the mirror was not at all that of an aging man. Quite otherwise, he looked what he was, a man in the prime of his life, his hair scarcely grey except at the temples, and without a hint of baldness. But he inherited his thatchy hair, a brush until he had found a barber in the city who knew how to subdue it by skilful cutting. . . . No, he did not miss the children. Being alone with Elinor renewed his ardor.

"Are you thinking of the children?" Elinor inquired too shrewdly.

"How did you know?" he asked. He was accustomed to this second sight, this intuition, telepathy, whatever it was that she possessed, but he no longer feared it or resented it, as he had once done when they were young. He had yielded himself to his marriage years ago, and now there was nothing in him to hide, not even the will, once so stubborn, to maintain at least his own individuality.

"I know your father look." Her voice was tender with that special tenderness of which he had once been so jealous, because, it had seemed to him in the years of his youth when he could never possess enough of her, that she loved the children more than she did him.

"I was wondering if they miss us at all," he said.

"Of course not," she replied. "If they missed us it would simply mean that they were in retreat."

He went on to confess his guilt. "Then I suppose it is not wrong that I do not miss them. It seems pleasant to be alone with you in the house, as we were before they were born."

The house then had seemed to him far too large, and he had been eager to see it filled with children. Now it did not seem too large, perhaps because of the small and lively ghosts whom he could summon by a moment's memory. Life had been lived here and was therefore still alive. Yet he and Elinor were very different from the two young creatures who had come here newly married. They were facing life again, but what life? He had not been quite sure, when the children left, what adjustments aging lovers must make, and whether his reviving ardor would be acceptable to her. But he had faith in her. That was his comfort. He knew men who dreaded getting old with their wives. How fortunate was he that still above all other companions he found Elinor the best, not merely because he loved her but because her mind met his own. She was not a learned woman and she pretended no interest in the law, for which he was grateful, but her judgments were fresh, her approach to human beings was original and direct, and she never lied to him.

"Do you not miss the children?" he asked somewhat tentatively. He had avoided the question until now.

She gazed for a few seconds into the clear amber drink she held aloft, examining its color with pleasure. A sensuous creature, he thought, finding an absorbing delight in shape and color, and never ashamed of physical enjoyment, even of food. Her literalness, her natural lack of shame, perhaps, were what kept her younger than her years. Nothing dried the blood like false respectability, a tendency toward prudery against which he himself struggled because he dreaded the possibility of seeming ridiculous. He could never, for example, have belonged to one of those organizations which compelled its members to garb themselves in pseudo-Oriental robes and when, as had happened last week in New York, such an organization held its annual meeting in the city, so that he was compelled to see the antics of bedizened elderly men, potbellied or lean-shanked, one or the other always equally silly, he went far out of his way to avoid them.

"I do miss the children," Elinor said, "but not as much as I should. I wonder why?"

"We have not seen a great deal of them in late years," he said. "They lead their own lives early nowadays."

She said reflectively. "I think the real break began when we got the television and they took to spending their evenings in the television room without us."

"The other day," he said irrelevantly, only it was not irrelevant, because television men had been photographing the neo-Oriental crowds on the streets, "there was some sort of jamboree in New York, and I was ashamed to take Michael Cotman up the Avenue. I felt I couldn't explain."

"One of the animal orders?" she inquired, lifting an eyebrow.

"Something of the sort," he replied. Cotman was an English lawyer, representing his own firm in London, a middle-aged, good-natured man who asked no questions of anything he saw in the United States and expressed no opinions. His assumed acceptance of all he saw was alarming to any conservative American, such as William Asher considered himself to be. It could mean anything.

Herbert came to the door, immense in his white duck coat.

"Dinner is ready," he announced.

Elinor rose, putting out her hand for William's arm.

"Come, my love," she said. They marched into the dining room with playful formality behind Herbert's shielding back.

"I have always been so grateful," Elinor said, while William pushed her chair gently under her, "that you are exactly what you are."

He sat down, smiled at her above the bouillon which Herbert set before him, and meeting her eyes he saw there her love for him, shining like a mild and steady flame. A very lucky man, he thought, to live so well into middle age as he now was, and still see that light, which would last, he trusted, until the end. He bent his head and then in the continuing silence he heard quite clearly the sound of distant sobbing.

William put down his spoon.

"Can that be Jessica?" he inquired. Herbert had left the room.

"It is," Elinor said, and then she added with unusual sternness, "She should be ashamed to cry so loudly."

"But, my dear," he remonstrated.

"No, really, William," she broke in. "When a woman cries out loud I can't feel sorry for her. It's indecent. What if we all did that? The world would be bedlam."

She rose and closing the window she cut off the sound. He did not answer. What did she mean by all women crying? He had never seen her shed a tear. He supposed that she had been too happy. He still could not fathom her entirely, even after twenty-five years of close living. It was simply one of those things she said, tossed off, meaningless except that when he pondered them, he felt them edged. He finished his soup in the artificial silence and Herbert came in and took the bowls away.

The bright autumn weather held. It was far too dry and the hardy chrysanthemums which he always enjoyed were small and dull, a disappointment, but not to be helped. He was very busy, for scandals had broken out in the city administration and he had the task of trying to decide whether he would defend the accused, and yet it was always difficult to decide whether he should, when it was obvious, as he thought it was, that the accused were guilty. The guilty had their rights, nevertheless, and it was a point nice to define, where their rights were fulfilled and where their guilt must stand.

He was face to face with the men, whom he was careful not to call the guilty, for that had not yet been proved, one morning in New York in late September. It was necessary for him to see them, in order, as they said, to get their side of the story which was, simply enough, that plenty of men had done what they had done and had not got into trouble and so in fairness, why should they?

He gazed into three fat smooth faces, glazed with years of good living and liquor, and tried not to recognize their racial origins, all different and yet all symbolic of the roots of evil in the political system of the greatest city in the world. Not that race or national origin had anything to do with it, he well knew, but the environment which society had forced upon the origins had a great deal to do with it. City slums, gang fights, prejudices and blows and finally crime had created the three he saw before him, whatever their racial origins. He felt remote and clean, a grey Vermont figure as he sat behind his desk and looked at them steadfastly.

"It all depends," he said, "upon what you want of me. If you will be content to have me fight for your right to plead your case, to be heard, to present every extenuating circumstance, that I can and will do. But if you expect me to prove you innocent, you will have to convince me first of your innocence."

The three fat faces looked blank. The big one coughed and spoke. "We know lawyers like you cost money and we'll pay." He had a strangely good accent, not an ignorant man, William decided, contemplating him with his usual high cool gaze.

"Certainly I expect to be paid for what I do," William agreed, "but I repeat my question—what do you want of me?"

The small fat one, the one in the middle, leaned forward coaxing. "Have a heart," he said in a husky pleading voice, a spoiled child voice, a babyish mouth, pouting and pretty. Somewhere along the way from the cradle his mother had yielded everything to the baby face, the pretty mouth. He was glad again that Elinor had been too intelligent to be a yielding mother. He had thought her sometimes harsh, but she had loved the children cleanly and without self-indulgence. Her honesty had remained inexorable.

"You do not convince me," William said coldly at last.

They had settled upon the defense, after he had spent the morning explaining to these three, who had never understood before, that innocence was a quality entirely apart from their rights as citizens. Guilty they might be, and he did not wish to know whether they were or not, for that was for the judge and the jury to decide, but they had their rights.

The fattest one, the swarthy, greasy, silent one, had given a retching sigh. "I guess it's the best we can do."

It was hard for them to believe that he could not be bought, coaxed, persuaded or in any way moved from his impregnable position. They accepted what he said because they trusted him and knew he was able but they could not understand him. That he did not refuse to defend their rights, that he did refuse to defend their actions, here was confusion. He saw it in their jowlish faces. They rose together, bewildered between humility and braggadocio, and left him cursing himself for a fool. Months of sifting evidence lay ahead of him, dividing strand from strand, protecting, in a sense, men whom he despised, and yet this was the honor of the law, before whom none was guilty until guilt had been proved. He had defended murderers up to the electric chair itself, and there he had left them, knowing his duty done.

He went home at the end of the week, feeling that he would have been exhausted except for the grimness of the task ahead of him. He could not afford weariness now for months to come, in the dissection of the underworld of this vast city which was to be his task. Thank God, he thought, for his peaceful distant home, for his quiet wife, for security of the heart.

Jessica opened the door when he came home, dimpling at the sight of him, pretty in a fresh blue uniform and white ruffled apron. There had been no more sobbing from upstairs and the wedding, he understood, was to be soon. She took his hat and coat, and tempted as by a child to a pleasant remark, he asked,

"When is the great day, Jessica?"

Her brightness did not falter. "Next Saturday week, sir. It's Herbert's birthday."

"A very special celebration, eh?" His foot was on the bottom stair. Upstairs he heard Elinor singing as she busied herself somewhere.

"He says," Jessica agreed from the coat closet.

He went on up the stairs and at the landing, which turned sharply less than half way, he chanced to look down over the bannisters. There to his astonishment he saw Jessica again pausing in the east parlor on the way back to the kitchen. It was the third time, once when she was a child, once as a girl. Now she was a woman and again she seated herself in the rose velvet chair in front of the long oval mirror, and in the mirror he saw her reflected face, smiling, not indeed the bright childish smile he knew so well, but an affected grimace, as though she beheld in the glass a stranger. Her right hand caught up her short fair hair and held it on top of her head in a new coiffeur and her left hand waved as though she held a fan. She spoke silent words, twisting her pretty mouth, and her large blue eyes were fixed in strange enchantment upon herself. What habit was this?

He was really startled now, and for a moment stood staring at her. Then deciding not to betray his observation, this time even to her, he tiptoed to his room, leaving her there with herself, a fancied self, a stranger certainly to him. Was this the way she always behaved when she thought no one was looking? When he and Elinor were away, when the house was empty, did she make free with any room she chose, imagining what she chose, forgetting her proper place as a servant? He was outraged at the possibility and closing the door of his room, he paused to consider whether it was his duty to tell Elinor at once. The distant sound of her voice was still to be heard, her good contralto, a voice he had often thought might have been trained to rich quality. Again he decided against mentioning the matter. Elinor might take it far too seriously, and Jessica was so soon to leave the house forever. Bertha had decided that. Jessica was to go to the farmhouse and be a proper wife, and Bertha would have a place to spend her vacations, a place to live when she was too old to work. There was no use in making an upset these last few days.

He changed into his usual dark trousers and wine velvet jacket and then went to find Elinor, trying not to feel troubled. The singing had ceased, but he found her in the small linen room looking, so she explained, for a certain lace scarf which she wanted for the small mahogany chest in her bedroom. He stood waiting, enjoying her looks, and now glad he had not disturbed her calm. Whatever she had been doing in the day it must have been pleasant, for her face, expressive, mobile, was fresh and handsome. She had put on a silver grey teagown which he liked, and she wore at her bosom a pearl pink velvet rose. They embraced, and for once he wished that his home was not so far from New York. The hope that Elinor might be willing to come with him when he had to be in his city office, now that the children were grown, was not fulfilled. She disliked the city, and he continued his contriving of time, his arranged life, wherein the study he needed to make for his cases could be done in the Manchester office, or here at home, quiet days whose fruit, he hoped, was the soundness with which later he argued for his clients.

"It was cheerful to hear you singing when I came into the house," he said.

"That tune has caught itself in my mind all day," she replied. "A tag end of that song we heard at the theater a month ago. But why was it in my mind?"

She did not expect an answer and he did not give one. She found the scarf and placed it and they went downstairs together. The living room was empty, the rose velvet chair was in its place, and the mirror reflected merely themselves, arm in arm.

The next morning Jessica waylaid him at the door to the library. He had brought home with him in the black leather briefcase a mass of documents, letters, newspaper clippings, material his junior partners had been collecting for him during the last week, and now it remained for him to digest this until it was as familiar to him as the history of his own life. He had risen early, oppressed during his sleep by the faces of the three men whose rights he had chosen to defend.

"Please, sir," Jessica said.

William stopped to look at her sternly, mindful of yesterday. "Yes?"

Jessica twisted her apron with one hand and the other flew to her pink cheek. "Please, Mr. Asher, sir, don't think you must come to my wedding. I know Mrs. Asher will think so, because of my mother, but I don't mind a bit—indeed, sir, I'd rather you didn't."

He was impatient with her. "Yes? Oh well, I'll speak to Mrs. Asher about it. As a matter of fact, I shall be very busy about that time."

"And sir," she pleaded, for this was not at all, as he could see, though puzzling enough, "could you not do one more thing? You are the kindest one in the house—yes, sir, I don't mean that the mistress isn't kind, but she's for my mother, if you know what I mean and I can't blame her for that, for Mother has been here so long and all, long before I was born, of course, but might I come back afterwards, sir, and do my work here just as if I wasn't married?"

This was quite outside his province. He never meddled in the house, especially when the servants were really Winsten property, Herbert having come through Bertha, and Jessica belonging to Bertha. Besides, what about yesterday? That sort of thing could not go on unchecked.

Jessica saw his surprise, his doubt. Her violet eyes implored, lovely, yes, he saw unwillingly, with long amber lashes shades darker than her hair. Poor child—such beauty meaningless, he supposed.

Jessica hurried on. "If it isn't presuming, sir, this house is really my home." The violet eyes swept the handsome old rooms. "I can remember when I was such a small thing, really not more than three or four years old, I used to push open that door, sir," she pointed toward the pantry entrance into the hall, "and I'd stand there, pretending it was all mine. It was naughty but that's what I did. And when I was a bit bigger, more bold, I daresay, I used to come in when the family was away and my father out in the garden and Mother in the kitchen, and I'd sit down in that chair there"—it was the rose velvet chair—"and pull it up to the mirror and see myself here in the midst of the beautiful rooms, and I'd pretend again. Oh, I was naughty all right and that's why Mother sent me to the convent when I was only seven because she found me doing that and she said I was getting above myself. But it was only that I loved the house so much, and the family, and I still do and must always, because it's been my home, like."

He was astounded at all this and very uncomfortable indeed. Pretending it was all hers! Did she forget he had seen her at it himself? "Well, Jessica, I can speak to Mrs. Asher——"

"Oh, please, but not to tell her what I've said! For it is presumptuous, I know that, and she might not understand, being one of the family, but you, sir—"

He was very unwilling to admit an understanding that Elinor did not share, especially to this girl who was so unsuitably a servant, for he guessed there were all sorts of delicacies and moods here which could not possibly do her any good, her station being what it was, not that he believed in station as any sort of permanence, but it took an energy he doubted she possessed to get out of the estate to which she was born.

"Well, Jessica," he said with determined coldness, "I will do the best I can, but if Mrs. Asher decides your mother would be too much hurt by our not coming to the wedding, you must forgive us if we are there. As to the rest of it, you'd better wait a bit after the wedding. It might come about quite naturally during the holidays, say, when the children are all home, that we'd need extra help, and we'd call on you."

She glowed far beyond the faint hope. "Oh, thank you, Mr. Asher." Her thin hands flew together.

"It's no promise, mind you," he told her.

"Oh, I'll understand," she breathed.

He went on toward the library and forgot her in the immensities of the city corruption. By the end of the day, when he remembered again, the incident seemed slight, not worth repeating to Elinor. He had learned long ago that the peace in a home is kept as much by forgetting as by remembering, and Elinor might be annoyed that Jessica had made so strange a request as to come back to work instead of staying at home, a request so calculated to annoy the far more important Bertha. Nevertheless, the forgetfulness was not so complete that, days later, when Elinor reminded him of the wedding he told her that he would not be able to go. This was true. Even had Jessica not spoken, he would have been hard put to it to be at home, certainly not at two o'clock.

"My dear," he said, "I cannot leave the city at all next week. I shall have to go in early Monday morning and you won't see me again until Friday or even Saturday. We shall be preparing our briefs, the other men cannot possibly do this without me, and I could scarcely attend the wedding even if it were Susan's."

"Bertha will be hurt," Elinor observed, "especially as the children aren't here, and the rest of my family is so scattered. My brothers and sisters are nomads—I don't know why. I hope the children won't be so. I suppose Cousin Emma will come."

"I am sorry you have a nomadic husband, too," he said lightly. It would have been easy to tell her now what Jessica had said, but it seemed not worth while, the mood of a servant girl, which it had only made him uncomfortable to share for a moment. He was glad that Jessica was going and he would not help her to return. He was not pleased to think that she considered this house, now his, as her home, even her spiritual home, so to speak.

Thus the wedding took place without him and when he came home late the Saturday after, tired and tense with the rising energy that he always felt when a major case proceeded towards its climax, he forgot that Jessica was gone. It was only when Bertha served the dinner alone that he remembered. He felt compelled to be kind.

"Well, Bertha, not a daughter lost—a son gained, eh? I am sorry I couldn't be at the wedding."

"Herbert will be back next week, sir," she replied. "I toldt him a week is plendy. Heinrich and me, we tookt only two dayss. But Herbert sayss the chicken haus shall get a new roof and he makes it in the honeymoon."

"Good," he said heartily, but somehow feeling it not good at all.

"The wedding," Elinor said when Bertha had left the room, "was really pitiful. There was nobody there except Herbert's brothers and sisters and Cousin Emma. Her chauffeur drove her from New York. It was sweet of her to come, but she kept saying afterwards in such a loud voice that she didn't like Herbert's looks."

"Did Cousin Emma go straight back?" he inquired, for conversation.

"No, she spent the night here, and I had to assure her that Herbert was really just the sort of person that Jessica needs. Jessica is rather flighty, William. You don't notice it, being away so much, but sometimes she is quite wearing. Well-trained servants should never impose their moods, my mother used always to say. Heinrich and Bertha never did. Heinrich might have, he was inclined to be the soft sentimental German type, but Bertha kept a firm hand. I know my father had only to look hard at Heinrich when he fumbled something and Bertha took over."

"How is Cousin Emma?" he asked, still in abstraction. He should really have spent Sunday in the city. The single witness upon whom much depended was under guard, but could the city be trusted?

"Fading," Elinor said gently and then she went on, "I often wonder what Cousin Emma has had out of life. She kept talking about Jessica as a little girl. It seems she took notice of her when she visited us. Still she likes to live in New York, 'the city of lonely women,' she calls it, where she can enjoy music and lectures and art. She is getting queer, I suppose, though so sweet."

"Queer?" he echoed.

Bertha was serving a delightful baked scrod.

"She leaned towards me the way she does," Elinor went on. "She tapped my wrist. 'I have a beautiful Turner painting,' she whispered. Now where could she get a Turner, William? They cost thousands. So I said, 'Have you, Cousin Emma?' And she laughed without making the slightest sound and went on. 'Yes, in the Frick gallery. I sit there every day for hours and enjoy it. Nobody knows it's mine, but it is. I own it—in here,'—and she tapped her old caved-in bosom."

Elinor's father had made William one of the trustees of Cousin Emma's small inheritance. "I must look into that," he said, troubled. "It may be she is getting incompetent. She lives alone, doesn't she?"

"In that old hotel," Elinor said. "I'd go to see her oftener but it's such a distance."

He looked at her half humorously, "A distance I travel weekly in order to live with you."

She acknowledged this fondly. "Ah, I know! I ought to take the house in town that you wanted now that I don't have the children as an excuse. But I still hate the city!"

He had accepted this years ago, when she declared that she could live nowhere but in Vermont. "Never mind, my dear," he said. "The roads are wonderful, the highways come almost to our door, and it is much easier than it used to be for me when the children were small. Then, too, I acknowledge that in this native air of ours my brain cells function well."

Nevertheless a few days later in a lull for new evidence he took an hour away from his city office and went to call upon Cousin Emma, his secretary having made the appointment.

He found her in a small overstuffed apartment, a lank agitated old lady, a tall figure draped in chiffon of a faded blue, the color of her eyes, and she was guarded by an elderly hotel maid, who opened the door and later brought in the heavy silver tea tray.

"It is very nice of you to come and see me, William," Cousin Emma said. "I hope there is nothing wrong with my affairs."

"Not at all," William replied, taking his seat opposite the yellow bro-caded satin chair. Gas logs burned between, and there was a reek of gas in the air. He must speak to the superintendent. The kind old lady might be suffocated some night, accustomed to the atmosphere, as he could see, and every window shut. The gas logs looked old enough to fall apart. He went on.

"Elinor told me you had gone up for Jessica's wedding and I told myself it had been a long time since I came to see you—too long. After all, you are, in a manner of speaking, my ward, you know."

She gave him a sweet withered smile. "I am quite well, William. It was a jaunt for me to get up to Manchester for the wedding, but Bertha had written me about it and I felt some of the family should go. As it turned out, only Elinor and I were there. I remember Jessica so well before she went to the convent—such a beautiful little thing and so gifted. Really, William, it is a pity. I came upon her one day years ago, in the long east parlor. She was at the piano, singing very softly, touching the keys quite in harmony, and the most heavenly clear little voice. I ought to have taken her straight out of that house and educated her in music. But—" Cousin Emma leaned forward in her enthusiasm, "she paints equally well, or could have, if she had been taught. I remember once when she was home at Christmas she gave me a water color she had done for a present. She used to make little gifts for me because she knew I was fond of her and she gave them to me secretly. I found the water color rolled up and tied with a holly ribbon and hidden in my bureau drawer. I still have it somewhere—"

Her eyes grew vague, thinking where it could be.

"And that man," she said suddenly. "He is so very thick."

He knew she meant Herbert. "Nevertheless very stable, if solid," he suggested.

"Oh, I don't know," Cousin Emma said, suddenly distracted. She wrung her long thin hands. "Do you want some more tea, William?"

"One more cup," he said to please her. "It is delicious tea."

She was very pleased. "Oh, do you like it? It is special but so few people would know. I get it from a Chinese shop, such a delightful place. I imagine, you know, William, that I am travelling quite around the world, all the while I am living here in New York. The other day I found a real Italian fiesta, two streets downtown shut off from traffic, and there were hundreds of lights festooned across them and the quaintest bazaar going on. I had gone to buy this very tea when your secretary telephoned you were coming. I often wish I had brought Jessica here with me, William. I believe she would have been glad to come. You know, Bertha was too strict with that little child. I used to see her snatching her by the arm. It wasn't wrong for the little thing to steal about those big empty rooms. Nobody knew except me, really. Everybody else was so busy."

"Yet Bertha loves Jessica very much," he suggested, without telling her what he thought of Jessica's behavior.

Cousin Emma made a grimace of distaste. "Oh, don't talk to me about love, please, William. It's made such an excuse. That is the way my own sister Jessica used to begin—'You know I love you, Emma, but—'"

She laughed shrilly. Elinor's mother was a woman gentle and beloved, William believed, except by Cousin Emma.

Yet he could detect no signs of madness in the old lady. She had always been wilful, difficult, frustrated he supposed because she had never married, although she had had chances enough, he had been told, and he did not know why she had not accepted any of them. So far as he knew, there had never been a tragedy. He rose after a third cup of tea, relieved that no new problem must confront him just now.

"You are going to be quite rich this year, Cousin Emma," he said by way of parting cheer. "Your stocks are rising. Dividends are inevitable."

But she was not cheered. "Oh, don't speak of that," she cried. "It's only this horrible talk of another war. I'd rather go to the poorhouse than get rich from it." She fumbled for a bit of ragged newspaper in her black velvet handbag hanging from her wrist and put up her pince-nez to her eyes. "Making atomic bombs!" She put down the glass and gazed at him with reproach. "And you talk to me about dividends!"

"Forgive me," he said contritely. "I'd forgotten how you follow the news."

"If I weren't so old," she said dramatically, "I'd pour out my blood. But they don't want it. It's too old. Why not? Does blood change?" She held out her withered right arm, the lace sleeve falling back.

"I suppose it does," he said. "I suppose the doctors know."

She let the arm drop upon her knee. "I am very glad I never married. I thank God I never had a son. I couldn't have taken the suffering now." She leaned forward. "What are you doing about your sons?"

"They will have to do what other young men do," William replied.

"There, you see," she exclaimed. "They are in for a lot of suffering, and you, too. That is what marriage brings. I do wish I had told Jessica to come here. I didn't think of it, not until I saw her standing up by that thick fellow. Bertha is thick, too. I don't know why I didn't command Jessica to come and live with me. She could have gone to the galleries with me. I have a wonderful Turner there—quite my own, although nobody knows."

Was this the tinge of madness? No, he saw nothing but the old wilfulness. Cousin Emma was entirely sane, merely wilful in her fancy, as she had always been, delighting to bewilder.

"That is pleasant," he said. "Now I must be going, Cousin Emma. A most delicious tea—I shall have to tell Elinor."

He pressed her long bony old hand, and went away. Nothing here but the irresponsibility of age, he thought, the determination not to be what people, he or anyone else, expected. It would have been very bad for Jessica to live alone with this, much better, indeed, for her to tread the ordinary path of woman, to marry, to have a home of her own and children in due time. That way lay health and sanity and companionship. For there was a companionship, he felt sure, in the mere sharing of a common life beneath one roof. Love was the glory of a marriage, the cup running over, but marriage itself was the necessity. He doubted the enthusiasm of Cousin Emma, he doubted the talents that she saw in Jessica, there was nothing to warrant such gifts in the stodgy heritage of Bertha and Heinrich. The nuns perhaps had given her taste, but it might be forgotten, if it still existed, in the growing of her normal life. He dismissed Jessica, somewhat impatient that quite without his will or interest, she appeared so often and so irrelevantly in his life.

AT CHRISTMAS time Susan brought home a dog. William, riding in the car half asleep with fatigue, his eyes closed behind Herbert's stolid back, opened them to see his daughter in the frosty dusk. She was waiting for him at the gate, between the elm trees. He saw her short strong figure, swathed in a white fur jacket, and then he saw a huge black dog of an unknown breed, pulling savagely at a leather lead she had wrapped about her right hand. He stopped the car and opened the window.

"What's that animal?" he shouted.

"It's not an animal, it's a dog," she cried back at him. "His name is Pirate!"

"I can't get out," he grumbled. "I can't ask you in. He looks as though he'd chew one up."

"He's only young," she retorted, struggling against the plunging beast, now furiously barking at the car, at the night, at everything, William thought, most of all at him.

"Whatever possessed you to bring him home?" He was compelled to shout because the dog had a deep bass roar that echoed through the woods.

"He's immense," she cried. "He eats two pounds of meat at a meal!"

"Two pounds! He looks as though he'd think nothing of fifty!" William retorted.

He could not get near her and he called gloomily through the half darkness. "I'll see you later when I'm safe in the house. You don't bring him in, I hope."

"He insists on it," Susan screamed and braced herself against a tree.

"Horrible," William muttered and closed the window. "Go on, Herbert. The night air is cold."

To all this Herbert had made no remark. He seldom spoke unless spoken to and this, William thought, was his greatest virtue. Secretly he was astonished at other changes in Herbert during the last weeks since the wedding. Always a cautious and even slow driver, Herbert had begun in a stealthy fashion to speed. Tonight he had crept out of the city at a sober rate, and as he approached the parkways he had properly increased his speed. Nevertheless after a while William had stirred from a half doze, aware of a faint giddiness, and peering into the front seat he saw the speedometer edging eighty.

"Good God, Herbert!" he cried sharply.

Herbert gave a violent start and the car swerved dangerously close to the other lane.

"Keep your eyes on the road," William had shouted. That was another folly the man had. When addressed he would turn his head, leaving the car to manage for itself. "You'll get arrested!"

Herbert dropped so suddenly to fifty that the car seemed to stop with a jerk. "Sorry, sir. My mind was wanderin'."

"Never let your mind wander on the road," William said sternly, and he did not doze again for an hour.

Now entering the house he kissed Elinor at the door and began to complain. "Herbert very nearly had an accident this afternoon. He was driving at eighty miles an hour."

Elinor replied with proper concern. "I can't imagine it."

"He was," William insisted. "I spoke to him and he said his mind was wandering."

The door to the pantry opened and to his astonishment he saw Jessica come in, dressed in a blue cotton uniform and ruffled white apron. She dimpled at his surprise as she took his coat and hat. "It's only for the holidays, sir, but it will give me a bit of change."

He remembered now that he had said something about this, and his exacting conscience was roused. "Look here, I had nothing to do with it. In fact, I forgot all about it. You'll have to thank Mrs. Asher."

Elinor stood waiting, looking, he thought, somewhat aloof.

"It's lovely being back, Madame," Jessica said with a strange pleading urgency. "Indeed I do thank you."

"It will be a help to have you here while the children are at home," Elinor said. Her voice was cool and kind.

William turned to the stairs and felt her hand tucked in his elbow. They mounted the steps together and in silence. When they reached the upstairs sitting room they shared, the two bedrooms opening from it, she sat down. This was a pleasant room furnished in the opulent but unadorned style which he liked and which seemed native to the Winstens. There was no bric-a-brac. There were no ruffles or dust catchers of any sort. The curtains were a plain clear blue satin, very heavy, and the old Persian carpet caught the same blue in its multifold regular pattern. Blue became his wife, her eyes very blue under her silver blonde hair. He sat down to fill his pipe before undertaking the task of washing and changing. The house was still, but from outdoors he could hear the harsh bass roar of the dog's barking.

"Is Winsten's family here yet?" he asked.

"Madge telephoned that they couldn't make it until tomorrow," Elinor replied. "Edwin came, but he went out at once to see Vera. Susan arrived on schedule, with a young man and a dog."

"I saw the dog," he replied. "A vile beast."

"You can't say that publicly," she retorted. "The young man gave it to her."

"Where is he?"

"Asleep, I believe. He ate a great deal of cake and a plate full of sandwiches, declined tea and drank two highballs and then said he was sleepy."

"Have we seen him before?" William inquired.

"No, dear," Elinor replied. "He's quite new."

"What's he like?"

Elinor considered. "A good deal like the dog—large, rough, a plain family, I judge—oh, very plain—but Susan tells me the girls think he's wonderful."

This made him think of something. "Why is it this generation of young females likes them in the rough? If I remember, you used to keep me right up to the mark. Now the more the young men talk out of the corner of their mouths, swear, sprawl, generally act like gangsters, the more girls like them."

Elinor considered this. She sat gracefully composed, a figure as aristocratic as could be designed, perhaps, in a democracy as new as America, her narrow feet, encased in silver slippers, crossed beneath her long skirt of fine black lace over some sort of a cherry-colored stuff, satin, he supposed, since it did not rustle. She disliked rustling garments.

"I don't know," she said thoughtfully. "I do know that I detest Susan's young men. I only pray that she does not marry any of the ones we have seen."

"Vera, on the other hand—" he said, thinking of Edwin.

"Oh, Vera, of course, would be wonderful," Elinor said at once. Then hesitating, reluctant, she went on, "I have a mad sort of notion that I ought not to put into words."

"Do," he urged. "Between us, we have said a number of mad things."

"I wonder if Jessica has some ridiculous notion about Edwin?"

He was startled indeed. "Now that really is mad," he said. "Jessica, trained by Bertha, could scarcely so forget herself! Besides, Edwin is only a kid—what's Jessica?"

"Twenty-four—"

"Well, then twenty-one to twenty-four."

"Edwin is very handsome, and I would feel happier," she went on, "if Jessica were not so pretty—oh, so what people used to call refined, you know—delicate, perhaps, and certainly far too sensitive for a servant."

"What did you see?" he asked, unwillingly troubled.

"Jessica laughing, her hands on Edwin's shoulders, and he looking down, blushing—"

He was so much upset by this that he felt he ought to tell her something which until now had not had a shape definite enough for words, not the posturing before the mirror, but something he had not expressed even to himself.

"You know," he said with uneasy reluctance, "Jessica has a very odd way with any man."

She looked at him with eyes suddenly direct. "What do you mean, William?"

He did not know how to answer. Put into words, it seemed too much beyond the truth. He laughed but with constraint. "There, I don't know what I mean. When I try to explain, the thing escapes me. Perhaps it's a way she has of looking coaxing or wistful. It has always made me uncomfortable and I escape immediately. I'm sure she's too innocent to know how she looks."

"No woman is so innocent," Elinor said, quite without rancor, he decided, after he had stared at her.

"We are born wise," she said, now, he believed, half teasing him. "It's our only escape to freedom. The more enslaved women are, the more wise we become."

"You aren't enslaved," he declared.

"Then I am not wise?" she demanded.

She had slipped into the remoteness where sometimes she lived for days at a time. He knew the mood so well, and long ago he had learned merely to smile, to accept, and if possible to love her more while he waited. He replied, "Though I am a lawyer considered famous in a mild way I know better than to let you engage me and I shall go and wash the city from me and change into something comfortable. As for Jessica and Edwin, no, I will not believe it, but I shall keep my eyes open."

"It reassures me," Elinor said, "to have you say that even you feel Jessica makes a special approach. So long as it is to all men, my dear—"

"Make the best of it," he replied tranquilly. He felt too tired to be serious.

The trial in the city was not going well. That star witness, that treasure store of evil knowledge, had been allowed to escape long enough to be bribed by the devil only knew what, so that he had refused to divulge what he had promised to tell and he was now behind prison bars where he was entirely safe, but entirely useless. The city would have to pay for a long renewed examination of facts hidden inside that solid skull to which there was no combination known that might force the lock and lift the lid.

He forgot his family while he bathed and shaved again, for his beard grew apparently upon city soot and dust so that he must needs shave at night as well as morning if he was to present a cheek smooth enough at bedtime to tempt Elinor's lips. Then he heard a door open and slam shut again and a clatter upon the stairs such as neither of his two sons had made even in their liveliest childhood. It was, he knew at once, Susan's young man, the Pirate, he thought, the giver of the dog so like him that even Elinor the merciful, the tolerant, the more than kind, saw the resemblance.

The resemblance was plain enough to him, too, when later he entered the east parlor. The dog was lying on the rug before the fire, where no dog had ever lain, for William was not a lover of dogs and when the children had clamored for those animals in their childhood he had permitted cocker spaniels but only outdoors. He was sensitive to the smell of dog and the room was full of it.

"Susan," he began, impetuous with horror, seeing his daughter vaguely in a yellow frock billowing about her slender waist and brown shoulders.

"I know, Dad," she said, "but Pete says that Pirate simply has to be indoors or he'll howl all night."

An immense young man rose out of his own leather chair, a length of male flesh and bone, hollow eyes pitch black under heavy black brows and stiff black hair surely never brushed nor combed and needing to be cut. The fellow wore a dark suit of some sort, but the coat was carelessly unbuttoned over a rumpled blue shirt in which he had undoubtedly slept. His high cheek bones were red, his red ears were too big and the hand which he now thrust out briskly was enormous and hairy.

"Mr. Asher?" he bellowed.

"I presume," Susan said pertly. "Don't you know the proper address, Pete? Dad, he's Peter Dobbs."

But Pete had never heard of Livingstone in Africa, and the mild joke escaped him.

"I'm pleased to meet you," he said with a loose southern accent. "I've heard a lot about you. I been readin' the papers since I got to know Susan. I really admire the way you been cuttin' circles round the gangsters. Too bad they let Bergman escape, if you call it that now he's in jail."

The dog leaped up and braced his forefeet. The thick black hair on its back rose at the sight of William. He growled like a bass drum.

"Shut up, Pirate," Pete said carelessly. "Lie down, dawg! He's just not used to you all yet."

"I doubt that I shall ever be used to him," William said with tartness.

"I reckon you will," Pete said comfortably. He folded himself in the leather chair again.

"Pete, get up," Susan said imperiously. "That's my father's chair."

"Don't disturb yourself," William said with bitter courtesy.

"Get up, I tell you," Susan repeated.

Pete got up, amiable, to take another chair. "I don't care wheah I sit, just so the chair's big enough. I don't like anything tight."

"Sit down, Dad," Susan commanded. "He really doesn't care. He's good-natured but you have to speak plainly to him. He doesn't understand anything else. It makes him awfully easy to get on with."

She spoke these outrageous words in her calm contralto, a pretty voice, a soft resonant sweetness under its attempted curtness. William sat down, feeling helpless. The huge dog collapsed on the rug again and he found himself staring into its furious eyes. They were fixed upon him under lowering brows, red in the reflected light of the fire.

"That dog looks bad tempered," he said, somewhat sourly. Privately he made up his mind that he would speak to Susan alone at the first moment and command her to remove this wild animal from his hearth.

"He ain't bad tempered," Pete said. "He just looks thataway—cain't help it."

"Like you," Susan said without a smile.

Pete guffawed in admiration. "You sure have a mean little tongue! Some day when you stick it out at me I'm goin' to take out mah knife like this—" he took a large clasp knife from his pocket, and flipped open the blade, "—and I'm goin' to cut that little tongue right off and give it to Pirate to eat up."

William listened to this in horror. He felt unable to cope with it. Gangsters in a courtroom in a vast wicked city were all very well, but he did not expect to find a monster in his own house.

"Where is your mother?" he asked Susan. "Tell her I'd like my dinner."

"We are waiting for Edwin," Susan replied without stirring. "Mother said he telephoned at the last minute that he was bringing Vera to dinner."

Commotion in the hall signified Edwin's arrival and a moment later they came in, his tall younger son, blond as all the Winstens were, and with him the equally tall Vermont girl, the daughter of the local banker, Vera Bates, a silver birch of a girl, severely beautiful, whose lips, though thin and straightly cut, were tender.

He rose gallantly, this was his kind of a girl, a reassuring youthful creature whom he would delight to welcome into his house and family. The dog rose again to growl, but Vera stooped and smoothed down its rising scruff and the belly growl subsided. The beast snorted and sank down again.

"Your inestimable charm," William said, and putting out his hand, he felt her cool palm against his.

"Good evening, Mr. Asher," she said very correctly.

"Good evening, my dear," he replied, "and you, Edwin, are looking very well, my son."

He felt happy again. There were also these young people, and the soundness of a great country was that, however unpleasant parts of it were, and however uncouth certain sections undoubtedly were, there were to be found elsewhere one's own kind, those of whom he could be proud.

He felt mildly sorry for Pete, the uncouth and unpleasant, and when they were all seated he leaned toward him.

"What sort of dog——"

At this moment Elinor came in from somewhere, the pantry perhaps, for she was concerned about her table, fastidious over the serving of food. She pressed Vera's hand gently and sat down in the chair left empty for her, the rose velvet. William rose and pushed the small needlepoint footstool toward it.

"Thank you, dear," she said.

He sat down then and surveyed his family with a loving care and found them good, and feeling sorry again for Pete, whom he could never count among them, he leaned once more toward that uncouth young man who had remained sprawled in amiable silence.

"What sort of dog is Pirate?" he inquired, not knowing what conversation could be made that would include this incongruous pair.

"He ain't any sort of dawg," Pete replied without embarrassment. "He's just a mungrel. We got plenty of dawgs like that in my dad's place. I took to Pirate because he's big. He's smart, too. He kin learn. He'll do anything I say. Hyeah, Pirate—"

Pete snapped his fingers and the dog sprang up bristling, its glittering eyes alert, its sharp ears cocked.

"If I told him, he'd spring at anybody in this room," Pete said proudly.

"Oh—"

The half strangled cry came from the doorway and they turned their heads simultaneously to see who had made that cry, so strange, so stifled. It was Jessica. She had come to announce dinner, and now, facing the dog, she stared at it in terror, her hands knotted at her throat. The dog rose stealthily to its feet, its eyes fixed upon her.

"Lie down, dawg," Pete commanded.

"Jessica," Elinor said, warning.

"Yes, Madame." The hands dropped. "I—dinner is served, please."

Jessica disappeared. They rose and the dog did not move.

"Come here, Pirate," Pete commanded.

The dog followed him into the dining room.

"Lie down there," Pete commanded, pointing to the spot beside the closed French doors.

The dog hesitated.

"Lie down, I say!" Pete bawled.

The dog collapsed heavily and Pete sat down and grinned at them all. "Like I said, he'll do anything I tell him."

Jessica did not come in again. Herbert served the dinner, rather better, William noticed, than usual, and paying no attention to the dog, who growled every time he came in until Pete yelled at it. It was true. The dog obeyed.

"You'll have to teach me your magic," Susan said to Pete. They sat side by side and the dog lay on the carpet behind them.

"No magic," the young man replied. He was comfortably ladling food into his mouth with a strange combination of knife and fork working together as a conveyor. "He listens to one person at a time, 'at's all. Whichever person he belongs to, 'at's the one he listens to."

"How will he know he belongs to me?" Susan asked. "When I'm gone, he'll turn to you."

William heard this with alarm. "You aren't leaving the dog here!"

Pete lifted his huge head from his plate. "Susan's Christmas present," he explained.

"Oh, no!" Elinor cried.

Edwin lifted his handsome eyebrows at Vera, who answered by the slightest drop of her eyelids. Neither spoke.

Susan turned impetuously upon her mother. "He won't bother you, I shall take him back to college. The charwoman says he may stay with her if they won't let me keep him at the dormitory."

Elinor did not reply. Long ago she and William had agreed that not at the family table would they contend with their young, and certainly not, her firm face declared, before this stranger named Pete.

Her eyes met William's down the length of the table and he responded at once. "The weatherman predicts a white Christmas," he said with proper pleasantness. "I hope so, for Winsten's children will enjoy the snow so much."

"I'll have to get out the old sleds," Edwin suggested. Edwin always joined loyally in any necessary turn in the conversation.

"Do," Elinor said heroically. "We haven't used them for so long. It will be something new for the children to have a white Christmas. They were too small two years ago to remember. I don't believe that even little Billy can remember that far back, do you, William?"

"Certainly not," he replied. And behind the loyal conversation he was thinking that tomorrow the unspeakable Pete would be gone. What was the fellow's last name? He had forgotten—not that it mattered! And as soon as he was gone he would command Susan to put the dog outdoors where it belonged.

Pete went in the early morning, flinging himself tousled into a car so old that nothing like it could be seen, William felt sure, outside the circle of the Ozarks. He surmised that under the wrinkled top coat and the same suit of yesterday Pete might still be wearing his pajamas. He watched all this from his bedroom window, wakened by the noise, but prudently not appearing until this voice in his house was gone. Susan he now saw come flying out of the door when Pete started the engine into a gasping roar of noise and smoke. She was frankly in her red wool dressing gown, a scarlet figure, her dark hair down her back, surprisingly long since last spring when she had decided to let it grow. William closed his eyes lest he see his beloved daughter kiss the unshaved and altogether repellent young male in the driver's seat, and then he opened them quickly in the hope that he could see for himself this was not to happen. It did not. Pete reached out a long arm from which a pajama sleeve could be seen distinctly from underneath the top coat, he squeezed Susan hard enough to make her shoulders disappear, but there was no kiss.

"Thank heaven," William breathed, and climbed back into bed to sleep for another hour.

Sleep was impossible, he quickly discovered. He had ordered Herbert last night when he went to bed that as soon as Pete left the dog was to be put outside, and Herbert now obeyed. The creature was asleep on the hearth rug again and Herbert went in masterfully and seized its collar. He was a man brutishly strong and the dog felt himself lifted up and half choked. He growled and could make no sound. The man was astride his back dragging him as he walked. A moment later the dog felt itself pushed through the door into the cold and the door was locked upon him. It flung its body against the door, bellowing, and this was the noise that William now heard, the uproar, the howls of a wild animal, and then he heard the dreadful sound of clawing upon the oaken front door, the pride of the house, the door so old that tradition said it had come from a massive oak upon the mountain side, already hundreds of years old when the Winsten family settled here in Vermont. He leaped out of bed, hastened into his wool dressing gown and met Elinor and Susan upon the stair, Herbert and Jessica converging upon them from the pantry and Bertha panting behind from the kitchen. William threw the door open and the dog hurled itself into the house.

"Absolutely this will not do!" William shouted. He turned on Susan, his pale eyes so furious that for the first time in her life he saw she was afraid of him. He took advantage of her astonished terror. "I will not have that dog in the house." He shouted in a way that surprised himself. "Get the beast out and keep it out."

Susan ran into the east parlor. The dog was on the hearth rug again, its enormous body pressed down, immobile with determination, its head on its great paws, seemingly docile, but its eyes were baleful as he glared at them all.

"Pirate." Susan fell on her knees beside him. "Good dog, Pirate."

The dog lifted its head at her and bared its teeth.

"Susan, come away," Elinor cried. "It's dangerous. Oh, what shall we do, and the children due in less than an hour?"

It was true. Winsten's train would arrive before nine o'clock and it was nearly half past eight.

"I shall send it away," William said firmly.

Susan screamed at him. "I won't have him killed! He's only strange. He knows Pete has left him. He's frightened of me because I'm strange to him, too, now that Pete isn't here. He's always seen us together."

"The dog can't stay here," William said, inflexible, but his heart, to his own disgust, began to melt in him. There were actually tears in his child's brown eyes.

"Oh dear, oh dear," Elinor murmured.

It was Jessica who now surprised them all, Jessica who was always so timid. She stepped forward from the rank of servants where she stood between Herbert and Bertha and she said quite clearly, "I'll take the dog, Miss Susan. I'll take it home. I've changed my mind, please, about staying. Mother can manage." She looked from one surprised face to the other, and fastened on William. "Please, sir, it's that I don't feel quite well, all of a sudden. Herbert didn't want me to come in the first place—he said it would upset me and it has somehow. But we could do with a watch dog. The house is so lonely. I'm often quite frightened. I daresay it will get used to me when it's alone with me there."

Was this not solution, with the train time so near? They looked at each other uncertainly. Herbert did not speak.

Elinor turned to Bertha. "Can you really manage?" She saw that Jessica meant to leave at once, only why, when she had begged so earnestly . . . ?

"Herbert helps me," Bertha said.

"Of course you may all go home after the dinner is served tomorrow," Elinor said.

"*Ya, gewiss,*" Bertha agreed.

So it was done. Once more Herbert attacked the dog. He flung one leg over the dog's back and seized the neck with such strangling force that the creature could not turn its head, could scarcely breathe, its choking a mere guttural mutter in the throat. Herbert dragged the dog out between his clenched knees.

William opened the front door and they all stood watching the man clutching the dog, mastering it by a force as brutal as its own, until they reached the old Packard taxicab which was Herbert's private conveyance. He lifted one hand to open the door, and the dog, loosened, snarled and turned his head enough to snatch the man's arm. Herbert kicked the dog's belly and in a rage he lifted the animal with his hands and one knee, flung it into the vehicle and shut the door.

"I won't come in the house," he called. "My arm is drippin' blood."

"You must go to the doctor," Elinor called back.

"How can Jessica drive with that beast?" William shouted.

"She's safe enough in the front—there's a thick glass between. And I don't need no doctor. The dog's not mad—only mean."

They stepped back into the house and through the window William watched the dog flinging itself against the doors and the glass, barking in a frenzy and then howling long screams of fury. In a few minutes Jessica came from the back door, neat in her long blue cloth coat fitting her slender figure, a little blue hat close to her head, looking as usual so unlike what she was, a servant. Without a glance at the dog she climbed into the closed off front seat and drove away.

It was over, the house was restored to decency and Christmas peace. William went upstairs and bathed and dressed and came down again shaved, composed enough for the day. Elinor and Susan were already in the dining room, waiting for him.

"Where is Edwin?" he asked. He pushed Elinor's chair in behind her, a habit so ingrained that he no longer noticed what he did.

"Would you believe that he is still asleep?" Elinor replied.

"I'm glad he is. I wish I were," William grumbled. "What a way to begin Christmas Eve!"

Susan, he was glad to notice, was entirely subdued. She had on some sort of negligee, a rose-colored wool. He disliked negligees at breakfast, but he did not mention it, since of course she knew it. She was drinking her orange juice slowly, as though it were hard to swallow, and she looked pale.

Herbert came in with the coffee. Bertha had bandaged his wrist neatly.

"I don't see how Jessica can possibly manage that dog when she gets home alone," William said.

"I told her to leave him be, Mr. Asher, sir," Herbert said. "I told her to leave him stay in the back of the car until he was starved quiet. When he's weakened enough, I'll handle him. I'll teach him who's master."

Susan lifted her head for protest but William met her eyes sharply and at once. Their gaze was a clash, he did not yield, and her eyelids drooped.

"A very good idea, Herbert," William said.

"Thank you, sir," Herbert replied and poured a cup full of coffee.

THERE was enough going on in the world outside his family, William Asher told himself somewhat sourly one April evening, while he knotted his tie in front of the mirror in his dressing room, without having something going on again in his own family. He had the same feelings of resentment that he remembered having when he was a boy, more than a boy really, quarreling with his own father in a subterranean fashion, because he wanted to stop being merely summer people, and become bonafide citizens of Manchester, in order that he might see Elinor every day. He was then learning to play the piano, had been learning for some years, and he played well enough to accompany Elinor while she sang, unless she chose something difficult out of German opera, which he did not feel suited her voice, even then. She had learned better as time went on, and he still enjoyed playing her accompaniments, though of course when they married and had the children that sort of thing had to wait. One of the pleasures of having the children out of the house at last was that Elinor and he had begun music again and he was delighted to find that his fingers were still nimble and her voice still lovely, though much lower in register than it had been when she was young. And again he remembered, that the summer before they were married, he had a strange infection in the palm of his hand, a swelling from within, there being no sign whatever on the surface skin, but simply first a soreness that mounted in a few days to a deep-seated agony centered in his hand but pervading his whole being. The fury of it was that he and Elinor were to perform at the summer concert, the big affair of the season, and he could not do his part, and in addition to his aching, throbbing palm, he had to see her on the platform at the town hall with another accompanist, a man older than he by four or five years and the personification of his intense jealousy for years thereafter, even when he and Elinor were married. Why not say what was true, staring at his own face here in the mirror, that he was still jealous in a strange silly way of Lorenzo Marquis? Marquis had continued as one of the summer people, and every year William had to endure the man's complacency about his own success. Marquis was by now several times a millionaire and had been deeply insulting the last time he came to dinner, he and his fancy third wife.

"Well, the house looks exactly as it used to," he said, and Elinor had replied somewhat tartly. "That is why we like it," which would have been well enough except that then Marquis said, "I like you—you haven't changed, either. William must be easy to live with," and then with a coarse look of admiration at the blonde young girl he had recently married he had said, "I seem to go through 'em fast, don't I, Tootles?" Tootles had merely smiled. She was a sleepy beauty, not needing to speak.

That early summer William had been the more angry because the swelling in his hand had come from within. It was not a wound, he had not fallen and cut his hand, he had not misused a tool, no knife had slipped. Simply from within himself somewhere had come this senseless painful infection which had robbed him of joy with Elinor.

Now in April, years later, he remembered his hand because he and Elinor were planning an Easter vacation to Atlantic City, where the sun was said to shine at this season, and he felt, as he had felt long ago, that something was wrong within him. Certainly the sun did not shine in Vermont. The persistent grey of the sky above his house had got him on edge. He longed to see the hard clear blue of a sea still cold, a clear blue sky and clouds, a clean chill wind, people in bright garments of spring, pacing the boardwalks, an Easter crowd.

He needed the change after a hard winter in which there had been weeks when he could not come home at all. And while this was going on, the scandal in the city now growing deeper until he was compelled to probe into the very sewers of humanity where life was horrible in its fertility, its growth, its vitality consuming the healthy life of the innocent, a cancer fastened upon the corporate frame, while all this was going on until he was sick to the core, something of the same sort was taking place far away in what he had always liked to think was the singularly pure and innocent state of Vermont, in the sacred spot which belonged to him and to Elinor, in his own home.

The disturbance centered ridiculously about the black dog, the enormous animal which Jessica had taken home with her on Christmas Eve. He had not thought of the beast again, and the holidays had been delightful, the snow had come, and for the first time, he recalled, he had enjoyed the pleasures of being a grandfather. Until now he had been ashamed that he somewhat resented at his youthful age the fact of a third generation already springing up around him. He had married early and so had Winsten, and Madge had been quite willing to have children at once, in the shameless fashion young women did these days. When he and Elinor were married the prompt arrival of Winsten a bare twelve months after the ceremony had been a source of embarrassment to the whole family, implying, quite unjustly, that he, William Asher, as correct a young man then as ever lived, was a brute of unleashed passions. Winsten and Madge, on the contrary, had been proud of their early marriage and had been only the more so when less than a year later a boy was born. At Christmas Madge announced herself again pregnant, and quite unnecessarily, to every one who came into the house.

"Yes, yes," she had cried, her round face, pink and white, all laughter. "Isn't it wonderful? In July, the twelfth—" There it was again, she named the very day, implying a dreadful planning, inviting the prurient to imagine the very night—or day for that matter, for he had once seen something here in this house which revealed to him that Winsten did not wait decently until night, but if he felt impelled, simply——

He turned away from the mirror where he had been standing. At any rate, the children had been beautiful in the Christmas snow, the boy in his scarlet coat and leggings, and the little girl, still a baby and scarcely able to stagger, in her bright blue costume and the little white fur tippet she was so proud of, her eyes blue as bits of sky when she stood up on a snow bank, outlined against the sky itself. He had understood then something of the wonder of continuing human life, the beauty of it in health and goodness here in his home, in blessed contrast to the spawn of city filth. He would at least keep his own in health and goodness, and if every man did as well, corruption would die.

Yet a corruption had appeared here in his own house, an infection from within, with which it seemed he had nothing to do, and yet which could and did bring unease to the whole.

He frowned, put on his coat, and went downstairs to dinner. A pleasant air of spring pervaded the rooms, although it was far to cold to open the windows, and there was as usual a fire burning upon the hearth. But Elinor had put early daffodils in bowls upon the table, and she wore a taffeta dress of April green, not new, he recognized, but still too cool for winter and therefore it was spring. She sat down, he pushed her chair under her, and took his own place. There were daffodils between them, very low in a silver dish, so that he could see her face. There it was, the remote look, the wistful distance, her cheeks a trifle pale, and her mouth red only because she had made it so. Something was wrong, but he delayed facing it. He would have his dinner first. He had planned to tell her the exasperations of his own week, for he could not come home except on Friday nights, as this was, and he must be back in the city by Tuesday morning.

"When this dirty business is over," he said somewhat harshly while Herbert served the soup in small broth bowls, "I shall take a month off and not go near the city. I am glad we have the few days next week at the sea."

The plan was that Elinor should meet him and they would leave the city together, so that actually it would be two weeks and perhaps more before they were home together again. He would miss her until then, but these were the last crowded years before his retirement. He had set that year for himself. After it he would be on call as a consultant for difficult cases, but he would do no more of the frontal attack that he was doing now. Younger men, perhaps Edwin, who had decided suddenly to be a lawyer, would take his place. But he would not take Edwin into the firm until he had proved himself in another. No nepotism—he loved his family too well, he was jealous for them, nothing must assail his children before each attained the top, alone. Marquis had ruined his only son, the boy was a man of twenty-five, still living on his father's absurd allowance, five thousand a month, pretending to write a play, a book, something. Marquis had provided a salary for him for years on his own radio station, but the boy did not know it. That had to stop when the employees had revolted.

"I don't know whether I ought to leave home just now," Elinor said.

"Why?" he demanded.

"I don't like the way Susan is behaving," Elinor said.

Her eyebrows lifted. Herbert was in the room. He had gained weight absurdly during the last few months, and his house coat was so tight that he was breathing in short gasps loud enough to be heard.

William noticed it and smiled slightly. "Looks like marriage agrees with you, Herbert," he said, helping himself to lamb roast.

Herbert, were he not addressed, could maintain silence for days on end, but a friendly comment could unlock the sealed gates within him. He stepped back, set the meat platter upon the silver trivet on the buffet and spoke, first coughing behind his thick right hand.

"Jessica ain't going so good," he said in his rather thin voice.

"No?" William said. It had been a mistake to notice Herbert.

"I was thinkin'," Herbert said, lowering his voice, "that I would like to have a talk with you and Mrs. Asher tonight, if you have the time."

William inquired of Elinor silently by a look of secret exasperation, conveyed by his uplifted eyebrows.

"Oh, certainly," she said, "as soon as dinner is over, Herbert, while we are having our coffee. Then you won't be so late getting home. Jessica must feel nervous there alone at night until you come."

"She has the dog," Herbert said.

No more was said, they finished their dinner and withdrew to the living room. There comfortably seated William sighed. "I wish we needn't go through with this. Have you any idea—"

Elinor interrupted. "I know that things haven't been right since Christmas. Bertha has cried a good deal in the kitchen, but I have been too much of a coward to ask why. I've even pretended not to notice. But of course I've known all along that it had to come out."

William grunted as he lit his pipe. Talk about servants was always distasteful. One paid for peace in the home.

"What's wrong with Susan?" he demanded. He had put this off, too, until the meal was over, but now they might as well face everything at once.

"It's Pete," Elinor said. "He has never forgiven her for letting Jessica have the dog. They are quarreling all the time, and it takes her mind from her work. I don't like the way she looks. She is actually getting thin."

"I wish she'd forget the fellow."

"I think she does, too, but she can't. There's something—"

Herbert came in with the coffee and she broke off. He set the cups carefully before her on a small table, his big hands trembling slightly, as even William could see.

"Very well, Herbert," Elinor said.

The man stood then between them and stepped back somewhat so that they saw his face, that fat flabby absurd face, the pinched nose, the small lipless mouth, the lashless little grey eyes, the stiff black hair which no brush or lotion would smooth down. A common fellow, William thought, a shape of ordinary clay, hiding what low passions—

Then came the horror. Herbert did not speak. Instead he began silently to cry and this with only the slightest disarrangement of his pudgy features. The tight mouth twitched, out of the little eyes tears rolled down the pasty cheeks and fell upon the white starched house coat in grey and viscid spots.

"Oh, Herbert, please don't," Elinor murmured.

Herbert sniffed and felt for his handkerchief and not finding it, he wiped his nose with the back of his hand. William looked away, resisting the thought that he ought to offer Herbert his own clean handkerchief. He could not do it. Instead he gazed into the fire while Herbert went on sniffing until he was able to speak, sobbing short gasps.

"I give her—everything, Mrs. Asher!"

"I'm sure you do," Elinor said, comforting while William sat motionless gazing into the fire.

"Two vacuum cleaners, one upstairs, Mrs. Asher, on account of she ain't strong and it was heavy liftin' the machine here up and down—"

"Very kind of you," Elinor said crisply.

"She don't like the livin' room rug, she wants an all over like this one here—two hundred dollars, Mrs. Asher, ma'am."

"I hope she will appreciate it," Elinor said.

The sniffling began again. William glanced swiftly and saw the massive face trembling in a jelly of pain.

"She won't let me come near her—"

Ah, here it was—the eternal accusation between man and wife!

"Night after night—my health's gettin' ruined—"

Elinor took hold resolutely. "It's very strange. Does she give a reason?"

"No reason, Mrs. Asher. Just says she—can't."

"I simply don't know how to advise you, Herbert," Elinor said.

"No, ma'am, nor you, sir, I don't expect it. I used to handle it myself before. She hasn't no real stren'th."

"Before what?" William asked, suddenly turning his head.

"Before she got the dog," Herbert sobbed. "It's that beast, sir, it lays between us on the floor—she would have them twin beds before she'd marry me. He lays there, ready to jump at me—she just calls him—"

"What a dreadful thing!" Elinor whispered.

Herbert stood, his heavy head drooping, sniffling unevenly, trembling from head to foot.

"Why don't you get rid of the dog?" William demanded. Here was a hideous thing to go through with after dinner in his own house! His quick imagination, the bane of his soul, uncontrollable, created the bedroom scene, the lustful man, the terrified woman, that red-eyed beast between, its scruff standing.

"She says if I do, she'll—leave me." Herbert's voice rose into a squeak of final agony.

"That's ridiculous," Elinor said in a voice of hearty common sense. "She'll probably respect you for it."

"I daren't—take the chance. She's queer in some ways you wouldn't expect."

Elinor sat up in her chair. "Herbert, stop crying, please. We can't discuss this sensibly while you stand there looking like that. If you cry before Jessica, it will really make her despise you. No woman could bear it."

She spoke cruelly, her voice hard and clear, but it was relief to hear it like a knife of steel, cutting through the mush of the clogged atmosphere of Herbert.

It did no good to Herbert, however. "Hankishiff," he muttered in a strangled voice and rushed from the room.

Neither of them spoke for minutes. Then Elinor poured the coffee. "Sugar?" she asked.

Sometimes William wanted sugar, sometimes he did not.

"Clear and black," he said and took the cup.

She had broken the brunt of it and he should say something.

"A horrible revelation," he said drily. "Revolting, repulsive, it should never have been made. We can do nothing about it."

Elinor did not answer at once. Then she said, "I do feel sorry for Jessica."

He was surprised, for he had thought until now that she had some impatience with Jessica, an unrecognized jealousy he might have said, strictly to himself, because Jessica was pretty and because she had seen this young and pretty woman put her hands on Edwin's shoulders, appealing, in Jessica's own way, to every man, something which Elinor herself had never done and could never have done simply because of her own straightforward soul, and not because she did not know, as of course she did, that her own high beauty was far beyond anything, even now, that Jessica possessed.

"Still, you know," he remonstrated.

"There's no 'still' about it," Elinor broke in sharply. "I know exactly what you are going to say and I am surprised at you, William, for you so seldom say what any man would say."

"What was I about to say?" he inquired with purposeful mildness.

"You were going to say that after all Herbert is her husband, that it is right and natural that he should expect to have sexual intercourse, and what does a man marry for?"

He was too honest to manufacture anything else. It was true that he had been about to say this, although certainly not in such bold words.

"You put it very crudely," he said with dignity.

"I put it as it is," Elinor said. "It is a crude business."

"But the dog—" he protested.

"I'm glad Jessica has the dog," Elinor said almost rudely.

He was amazed at her. He put down his coffee cup and gazed at her. This aspect he had never seen and he did not like it. Where might a man find security if not with his wife after twenty-five years of marriage? A woman ought not to reveal new aspects after that. It was unfair, disturbing, upsetting the very citadel of the home.

"My dear," he said, "you sound bitter."

"I feel bitter," Elinor said vigorously. She poured herself a cup of coffee, and it occurred to him that all this time she had not lifted her head to look at him.

"Why?" he demanded looking at her bent head.

"That Herbert," she exclaimed, "so soft, so fat, so demanding! I know exactly how Jessica feels. Every woman does."

This was frightening. She made it personal, she dragged it here between them, something obscene, the sort of thing a decent man never faces, certainly not in himself.

"Let's not discuss it," he said.

They sat in silence then, drinking their coffee.

All this distracted William's mind from Susan, and it was only when Elinor spoke of their child again a week later at Atlantic City that he remembered there was also Peter Dobbs. They were sitting in a warm corner of the sandy beach, sheltered from an inconsiderate west wind by the boardwalk. It was too cold to think of going into the water, which nevertheless looked temptingly clear and mild, the surf small and guileless. He was not a strong swimmer and he did not like the crushing surf of summertime; it was one of the lesser cruelties of nature, he thought, that in the winter when the water was too cold for the human frame the sea was often smooth, the waves subdued at least when the sky was cloudless as today it was, whereas in summer some tempestuous aspect of the moon compelled the tides to restlessness. Eve, made from the rib of Adam, was only the legend of the perverse and female moon torn from the side of the newly created globe of billions of years ago, and the gaping wound of the

Pacific basin, raw basalt at the bottom, was still as unhealed as man himself. And here was the moon as he had seen it last night, whirling above the yearning earth, remote and unreachable, never again to be joined, and yet pulling the earth's tides toward herself, only to reject them again and again in the ceaseless rise and fall of the rhythms of untiring creation.

Lying on his back, his eyes closed to the sun, he felt those rhythms in his own being and he reached for Elinor's hand. She gave it willingly and he pressed it against his cheek, a miracle today as it had been years ago; not the same, for the hand had changed, grown harder, perhaps, certainly more firm, but still his Elinor's hand.

"Susan wants to come down," Elinor said.

"Did she telephone?" he asked.

"Yes, this morning while you were still asleep. She wants to come down tomorrow. She says she has to talk to us."

He sighed and pressing her hand he let it fall to the sand. "Then I suppose she must."

"I think so."

It was extraordinary how children could continue to intrude. One expected it when they were babies, and Susan would have been the first to insist upon her womanhood, did he call her still his child. Nevertheless for him the carefree morning was over, though it was two hours until they could go into the hotel for lunch. He could not feel alone with Elinor any more until Susan had come and gone, had made known her new problem, whatever it was, for the lives of the young were, it seemed, thorny with inexplicable and insoluble problems. The entire web of his law practice, fraught with the crimes underlying the life of the greatest city in the world, was not as agitating as the militant demand of the problems of his three grown children, Winsten, the young father, Edwin, the lover, and Susan, the eternal female. Or perhaps it was only that he could get up from his desk, close the door of his city office and walk away, whereas these three who were his children, inescapably his own being, continued in him and were forever in his home, their childish ghosts persistent in his very blood. He could no more escape them than he could escape himself.

Nevertheless, he was not prepared even by a day and a night of wondering what was the matter now with Susan. She appeared the next morning, nearer noon than dawn, whirling up to the hotel entrance as he could see from the window where he had gone to examine his second best tie, a dark blue and gray stripe of which he was fond but which he suspected of becoming threadbare. He was not a vain man but Susan was critical of him as a possession. There in the hotel driveway he saw her small dark red convertible, which she had teased out of him as an early graduation present, and to his unutterable horror he saw Peter Dobbs leaping over the door, one long leg after the other, then opening the door for Susan.

"Elinor!" So he shouted through the connecting bathroom. "She's brought that fellow from the Ozarks with her!"

"Oh no!" Elinor cried back, but she came, looking quite pretty in her pink silk slip, and he wondered why it was that the face of a slender woman must fade first. Elinor in her pink slip was otherwise still a young girl.

She stood behind the curtain, drawing it across her as a screen, and he saw the nape of her neck, the little silvery curls there, threaded with blonde hairs. He remembered that when they were first married the little pale gold curls on the nape of her neck were irresistible, and he bent forward suddenly and kissed them again now.

She turned to smile at him brightly. "Now, William, we must get dressed quickly. She'll be running up here—"

"Of course!" he grumbled. He considered explaining to her that the kiss he had given her was not the beginning of something at this moment, but a souvenir from their bridal morning. Another time he might have explained, but the fear of Susan bringing that great black-haired fellow upstairs made explanation impossible. Besides, Elinor should have known. But she still suspected him, as he supposed all women suspected all men, of the potential and instantaneous passion which he had not known how to manage in the early days, but which now, alas, or perhaps luckily, he was quite used to curbing, subduing or allowing, according to the faint hints she permitted to escape her. There was nothing actually stereotyped about their love. She could and did often surprise him. But it was a cat and mouse business, and sometimes he felt that more often than he knew he was the mouse.

Susan was by now actually at the door, but Elinor was dressed and looking composed, although the top button of her blouse was unbuttoned as usual, and he felt sensitive about that black beast of the mountains observing such a detail. To Susan it would not have mattered, but he preserved the jealousy of his generation and yet still he could not mention it to Elinor, although she was so calm he guessed that she knew what he was feeling and would have none of it.

There was no time, however. The door burst open and they stood there, the young and healthy creatures, gay with their news which was obvious to anyone looking at them. They were in love, some sort of love at least, and William felt his scalp prickle. Elinor was looking at them strangely, her blue eyes intense.

"Mother and Dad!" Susan cried dramatically, "Pete and I are engaged. We thought we'd better tell you."

"Come in," William said. "I should think you had. When did it happen?"

Susan shrieked laughter. "Oh, Dad, as though it just happened!"

They came in, and he noticed that Elinor said nothing. She sat down on one of the two stuffed chairs, and the two young creatures sat on the narrow sofa. Entirely shameless, Pete wrapped his long right arm about Susan, and she caught his right hand under her left arm and held it pressed to her waist.

"It's such a relief to have it over," she cried in the same excited voice. "I didn't really know my own mind until he asked me, at last, day before yesterday. I did and I didn't. When I thought he never was going to ask me, I thought I didn't. The rest of the time I did."

William listened to this and for the first time since he saw his daughter born, red with her recent efforts and rebellious apparently even against birth, he found her repulsive. The nakedness of the triumphant female nowadays was nothing less than repulsive. What hidden aspect of Elinor had taken this modern shape in their daughter? Elinor at least was modest.

"Why don't one of you say something?" Susan demanded.

William refused to answer this but Elinor was heroic.

"How nice," she murmured through pallid lips.

Susan and Pete burst into a duet of loud laughter. "Oh Mother," Susan sighed, drunk with laughter. "Isn't she priceless, Pete? Isn't she wonderful? Nice! Didn't I tell you?"

"Yeah," Pete grunted. His black eyes were glittering bright; for the first time William saw him awake.

He felt an immense anger. "I wonder if you two have any imagination," he said sharply. "I wonder if, short of waiting a quarter of a century, you can imagine how it feels when a child who has absorbed time and funds—not to mention love—suddenly turns up with a perfect stranger to whom she announces herself engaged. Does it occur to you," he went on magisterially, gazing at his daughter, "whether we might perhaps ask, as a return for benefits received, that we be given some opportunity of acquaintance with the stranger before we are compelled to accept him as our son-in-law?"

The sound of his voice was impressive, even in his own ears. He had never heard it more so when he pleaded his cases before obdurate judges.

Susan looked puzzled. She opened her dark eyes wide, a trick he remembered from her childhood, when, compelled in due course to reprove her, she had looked up at him with these same large eyes. She leaned forward in the circle of Pete's arm.

"Are you serious, Dad?" So she inquired, wondering, as he could see, quite genuinely.

He was about to protest his seriousness when Elinor broke in.

"Of course he's not serious. It's a shock and he doesn't know what to say. It's none of our business. If you choose Pete, it's welcome to you, Pete."

She smiled her warmest and most charming smile and William stared at her, stirred by her reasonless desertion. Had he not been protecting her? What did it matter to him whom the children chose? He was used now to doing without them. This Susan was not the small dark exquisite child, so plump and fragrant, who used to curl into his arms before she went to bed. She had left his house, in spirit, long ago. Her heart was not there. He had read of countries where the daughter was never considered a permanent member of the family because when she married she belonged by the heart to a strange man's family. Therefore why educate her and why spend upon her the treasures of parental love? He recognized this sympathy with dim guilt as a subterranean jealousy which disgusted him. At what age, he inquired of himself, did the beast in a man finally surrender unconditionally?

"What are you thinking about, Dad?" Susan asked curiously.

"Nothing that you would understand," he retorted. He gathered himself together with effort.

"Has he an income?" he inquired, not looking at Pete.

"Gas station," Pete said amiably.

"He owns it," Susan said proudly.

It was the second blow. A gas station? For this he had tenderly nurtured his daughter, had even paid for lessons on the violin, enduring without articulate complaint the primary years of wailing discord, until she was at last very good indeed. "I suppose you know," her music master had said to him only a few months ago, "your daughter can do about as she likes with music. She is very near the professional level."

With frightful control he put the next question gently. "Where is this gas station?"

"Highway near my home," Pete said. "Lots of tourists to the Ozarks nowadays."

Elinor spoke with pale lips. "Shall you like to go so far away, Susan?"

"Yes," Susan said robustly. "I shall love it."

There was nothing much to be said after that. Elinor, who had envied the parents of Winsten's wife the long pleasure of a carefully arranged wedding for a bride, was silenced. She was probably thinking, as he was, William imagined. What was the use of a beautiful and expensive wedding, when the next step was to a gas station?

"Oughtn't we to have lunch?" Elinor asked. She glanced at the small circle of diamonds on her wrist that held the watch he had given her upon their twenty-fifth wedding anniversary. "The dining room will be crowded if we wait."

"We're starved," Susan agreed. "At least I am, and Pete is always hungry."

"Always kin eat," Pete agreed, unfolding himself from the sofa.

So they went downstairs, and William was glad not to be alone with the strangers. Susan was a stranger, too, he had lost her finally this morning, and all that he had left was the ghost of the child she had been, that and nothing more. He sat down at a small round table at which they were all crowded, and examined the menu carefully. Rejecting the array of seafood and steaks he chose baked beans and brown bread and ate them, after a long wait, in complete silence, listening not to the chattering rise and fall of the voices around him but to the rising thunder of the surf outside. The tide was coming in.

The moment William reached home on Friday, as though he had not been disturbed enough by Susan, Herbert waylaid him in the hall.

"I'd like a word or two with you, sir, if it's convenient."

It was not convenient. William was tired, the week in his office had been peculiarly exhausting after his absence, and he had wondered on the way home whether he were getting too old for the grind. All those hours Herbert had sat in the chauffeur's seat, speechless. Now liberated by his white house coat he wanted time from his employer. Time, William felt rebelliously, was the one treasure he had left. Money was of little worth, half of his wage went to supporting a government he could not approve, and his children had left him. Time, and especially time with Elinor, was what he could not spare. But the demand of one's inferiors could not be refused, as he would have refused curtly enough any man who was his equal. He hired secretaries for nothing else than to protect him from requests for his time, but at home he was defenseless.

"Very well, Herbert," he said with grim patience. "We had better go into the library at once. We have fifteen or twenty minutes before dinner."

Herbert followed with noiseless and solemn tread and when William had sat down he closed the door and stood against it. There he began soundlessly to weep as he had before, his big flat face quivering and trembling and his tight lips twitching. This could only mean Jessica again!

"Come—come," William said, repelled anew and trying not to be impatient.

Herbert sniffed stealthily, searched for his handkerchief with the same stealthy air, found it and wiped his face.

"You know the black dog, sir?"

"Yes, I remember the beast," William replied.

"Well, that dog, sir, it seems she's got to care for it more than any earthly creetur, more than her mother or even me, her lawful husband."

"Sit down," William said.

Herbert turned and locked the door. Then he tiptoed three steps forward and sat down on the edge of one of the straight oaken chairs. His flabby jowls trembled again and William looked away.

"That black dog," Herbert said, clearing his throat, "bit a little kid last week. It was a farmer's kid next to our farm. She come over to git some eggs. They take eggs off us onct a week. She's about seven or eight years old. The dog bit her in the thigh. It wasn't the first time, either. He bit her onct before on the hand."

"I trust the dog isn't mad," William said gravely.

Herbert did not heed the interruption. He went on, his voice dreadful and whispering. "I told her—Jessica, that is—that we ought not to keep a dog that bites kids. When we have a kid of our own—did I tell you she was expecting?"

"No," William said.

"Yes," Herbert said, "she's due in June. I told her we ought to get rid of that dog when it bit the kid the first time. She wouldn't hear to it and I let it go. She was pregnant and I thought it was a notion. Now the dog has bit the kid again, and the kid's father says he'll sue me. It's a real deep bite. The kid is in the hospital to get it cauterized. Can I be sued?"

"It depends," William said cautiously.

"On what?"

"Let me consider it for a few days," William said.

"The kid's father is liable to sue me for a thousand dollars maybe," Herbert said.

"I'll let you know," William said. It was absurd that he should take his priceless time for a dog bite. He felt his anger rise against Pete, who had brought the savage beast to his house and now he could not be rid of it.

Herbert wadded the handkerchief into a ball and dabbed at one eye and the other. "You probably think it's queer I cry, sir." His voice slid into a hysterical squeak. "It's not just the dog now. It's her. I don't know what to make of Jessica, sir."

"What's the matter now with Jessica?" William asked, not wanting to know. He glanced at the locked door. A moment more and he would get up and unlock it.

"She's turning on her mother to hate her, like," Herbert said, his voice falling to a whisper. "We can't make it out. Her mother considers her like the apple of her eye, you might say, if you understand that saying, sir. The old lady spends her spare time with us, naturally, and we have fixed up a room for her upstairs, a nice corner room, which is only right, since the house is hers until after she dies, it's in her will to come to Jessica and me, of course, after that, but I had expected to have the old lady with us when she gets too old for the job here which I figure might be any time, and then I figured maybe Jessica and I could work here and the old lady could take care of the kids we might have by then. I don't want a lot of kids, two is plenty, and then I thought I'd let Jessica get herself tied, which she wanted to do in the very beginning."

"Tied?" William inquired.

"Her toobes," Herbert explained, "so she won't get pregnant. You can get a doctor to do it, if she's nervous. She is nervous and that's the truth. The doctor says so himself."

"Indeed," William said, once more deeply revolted.

"I wouldn't hear to its being done right away," Herbert went on. Voice and face were solemn and the tears drying on his cheeks had left the glistening wake of snails.

"No—no," William said unhappily. "I feel sorry for Bertha," he added. "Someone should talk with Jessica. Perhaps Mrs. Asher will do so."

"Would she?" Herbert asked eagerly. "That's what I wanted to know could I ask. It would bring Jessica to her senses, like. She's that fond of Mrs. Asher's family."

"Very well," William said. He got up determined to unlock the door, but Herbert hastened toward it first. He turned the key and stood impressively holding the door wide, while William passed through, bestowing a slight nod of acknowledgment.

Upstairs he found Elinor putting dried lavender from last year's garden between the garments in her bureau drawers.

They kissed, and he sniffed the clean fragrance. How many women, he wondered, put lavender between their garments nowadays instead of some French sachet? He disliked all French perfumes, though once he had thought them enchanting. Vermont had made the change. French perfumes were foreign here.

"Has Bertha complained to you of Jessica's behavior?" he asked.

"She has been grumpy," Elinor said, "but she has not mentioned Jessica."

"Herbert tells me Jessica has turned completely against Bertha. He took me into the library and locked the door and confided to me a mixture of complaints. I won't go into them all, but somehow I promised that you would speak to Jessica."

"Oh dear," Elinor said.

"I'm very sorry," William said. "I don't know how it happened. I wanted to get rid of him, I suppose."

"Well, I'd better hear Jessica's side of it first," Elinor said sighing. "Bertha gets so upset and then she goes to bed. I can't have her going to bed this weekend. Edwin is coming home tomorrow."

"What for?" Were they never to be alone?

"Have you forgotten it is his spring vacation?"

He had forgotten. Now that Winsten was fairly stabilized in Boston in his own small house with wife and children, now that Susan had gone blithely to the Ozarks to visit Pete's family, for that was where she was, an unthinkable liberty, but she had laughed when he suggested some sort of a chaperone, he had supposed that he and Elinor could live in some peace for the next few weeks. He had even thought of persuading her to go to New York with him for some of the last theater of the season.

"I think Vera will decide this week whether she'll marry Edwin," Elinor was saying.

"It is high time," William said. He wanted to get them all settled, all his children.

"Wouldn't it be nice," Elinor now said, "if we had robots in the house instead of servants?"

He sank down upon a chair. "Robots? They'd develop some devilish temperament of their own. What is Herbert or Jessica but a handful of chemicals mixed with a lot of water? It's the proportion. When everything is all in some damned relationship to everything else, something new emerges, a creature, a personality. It's fission. Even the atom won't explode until the combination is just right—"

Elinor stood listening, her arms hanging at her sides. "You're low, aren't you?"

"Peace," William said. "It's all I want."

A fine strange thing, he thought, the way human beings destroyed their own peace while most earnestly desiring peace above all else, and destroyed it in secret subterranean ways, obstinately maintaining their own wilfulness, as Jessica was doing, the upheaval in that small farm dwelling he had never seen reaching even into his own stately house. And why had he and Elinor not the courage to repudiate these creatures who disturbed them so causelessly? He watched Elinor as she moved about the room and understood her as he understood himself, that neither of them had the courage to be ruthless. They could not, out of something that was not weakness, he believed, cut off a human being who was helpless within their periphery, as surely Jessica was. Jessica was a child, innocent and gentle, between the two monoliths of Bertha and Herbert. She must be rescued, she could be rescued.

"Cousin Emma said that she wished she had taken Jessica to New York with her, before that marriage," he said suddenly.

Elinor sat down to ponder. "It might have been a good thing, but it is too late. Jessica is married."

"I have a feeling that we ought to get together today and see exactly what her circumstances are," he said. "I'd like to have the matter settled in my mind. It is very difficult to deal with Herbert when he stands and blubbers."

"He's disgusting," Elinor said vehemently. "A man in tears turns my stomach."

William found himself moved to defense. "I suppose there are times when a man must weep also."

"Weeping should be done in secret," Elinor said.

It occurred to him again that indeed he had rarely seen her weep and not for years. He asked with intense diffidence and after a long moment, "Do you weep in secret, my dearest?"

She was evasive as always when he approached the depths between them, which was the Vermont in her, he supposed, or perhaps only the Winsten, so long in Vermont. "I learned long ago not to weep about anything," she said.

"Did you once?" he pressed.

"Perhaps," she said almost with indifference, "when I was younger, before I understood life."

He went no further, a natural fear or shyness preventing him, or perhaps only the reluctance of the aging to turn up one's own past, as buried, as irretrievable, as the centuries before one's birth.

He got up with energy enough to dismiss it all, saying, "At any rate, let us go and see Jessica."

"Shall I tell Bertha?" Elinor asked.

They looked at each other uncertainly and he laughed. "We are absurd, the matter is of no importance, the quarrels of servants, and we feel as though we were discussing the affairs of nations. Tell her by all means and what if she does go to bed? We'll do for ourselves."

His hardihood decided her. "You must come with me, for she is afraid of you at least and she thinks nothing of me, because she saw me the day I was born."

They went together down the stairs and into Bertha's kitchen where she stood before the stove, her thick legs planted wide, upholding the mountain of her body. She did not turn her head when they came in, and their courage dwindled. But William felt Elinor quail first, and he summoned his remote sense of humor. What, must two educated resourceful cultivated persons be cowed by the mass simplicity of a Bertha?

"Bertha," he said decisively, "Mrs. Asher and I have been talking about Jessica. We would like to go and visit her today and see why she seems so unhappy with Herbert."

Bertha began to weep, not turning her head and continuing to stir gravy in a skillet. Her huge frame quivered, haunches, shoulders, the massive neck. "I losted my home," she moaned. She dabbed her eyes with her huge red hand. "She's turned against me, mine own childt! She don't vant I shouldt come home even for Sunday, no, and she says she don't vant I shouldt come home on birt'dayss, and not on Christmas yet. She tellt Herbert I beated her hard venn she vass liddle."

She turned slowly, her big face a wreckage of sorrow, she demanded of Elinor, "Didt I effer beat her, Miss Elinor, you tell me, only venn she vendt into your haus, the parlors, and like she vass one of you? Ya, I see her, and so I muss beat her. It iss not her haus, I tellt her, you shtay in kitchen vere ve belongs, not im haus. Only so I beat her, because she dondt lissen. She goes und she goes, sitting on welwet chairs, playing pianos, looking in mirrows, so I beat her."

William listening, caught the gleam of a thread of reason, a quick illumination. This then was the explanation of Jessica posing before the mirrors. Even as a child she had begun to live the dream of herself in the big house, not belonging to the kitchen and therefore not, oh never, to Bertha, the cook, and scarcely to Heinrich the butler. She was somebody else, a lovely girl, somebody perhaps even belonging to the family who really lived in the big house, who owned it, certainly as she could not except through dreams. His sensitive mind, his swift imagination, the qualities which underlay his work as a lawyer and made him understand why crimes were commited enlightened him now, and he was warm with pity for the little child beaten for her dreams, incurable dreams which she still wove. He was glad that he had not told Elinor about the scenes before the mirror.

Bertha was talking through thick sobs. "Can I let her get out of kitchens and maybe Misses Winsten fire me and Heinrich? Only so I beat her, maybe *ein, drei, vier* times, not effery day like she tells it now. She tells it to Herbert and he lofs her so silly he beliefs it. He don't want me in mine own *haus,* nieder."

"Herbert?" Elinor repeated, mystified.

"Ya, him," Bertha said, and seizing her large apron she wept into it, the gravy spoon uplifted like a signal above her bent head.

"We will go and see for ourselves," William said sternly.

"Don't cry, Bertha," Elinor said. She patted the heavy shoulder. "Oh, please don't cry! You'll always have a home here, Bertha."

William looked at Elinor, aghast. She had committed them! She had promised an eternal home to Bertha, the aging, pig-headed, tenderhearted, bad-tempered old woman who was slave and tyrant together. Aghast they stole from the kitchen, and faced each other in the living room.

"Still, we can't turn Bertha out in the streets, William," Elinor said.

"No," he agreed. That was the trouble with life. The old and the poor, the ignorant, the helpless, the young, even a beast, could not just be turned out into the streets when they became nuisances. They had to be sheltered, though under one's own roof.

They were diverted at this moment, if not cheered, by the early arrival of Edwin, neat and debonair in his usual fashion. It occurred to William to recognize now the value in this second son, the calmness of his young face, the competence of his manner, the composure unusual for one so young.

"Let us take Edwin and Vera with us when we go to see Jessica," he suggested, turning to Elinor.

He explained briefly, and Edwin nodded. "It sounds queer, I'd like to go. I've always been fond of Jessica, in a way. She's never seemed quite like a servant. If she wants to leave Herbert, she might come to Vera and me when we're married."

Elinor clasped her hands in joy. "Has Vera really decided? Oh, Edwin!"

He nodded. "She really has. She decided last night. She said she wanted it settled before she came today."

"Oh, darling," Elinor said fondly. She seldom kissed her grown children but now she went to this reliable son and kissed his cheek. "I am so happy. I dearly love Vera."

He blushed, his blue eyes shone, he embraced her warmly. "She adores you both," he said, his calm young voice cracking a little. "I am really bringing you another daughter."

The affair of Jessica disappeared in the mists of their immediate content and they allowed him to leave them again almost immediately that he might fetch Vera.

"Now we must wait until tomorrow to see Jessica," Elinor said happily. "I wonder where Edwin's wedding will be? I suppose they'll want it in Manchester, in the Episcopal church."

"Just so Vera's father doesn't want it in his bank," William said with returning humor. A happy marriage was a good omen for the whole family, a young and happy marriage, as his and Elinor's had been and had continued to be, even when youth was gone. Unusual sentiment warmed his heart and he felt moved to turn and take his wife in his arms and kiss her full on the mouth.

"Why, William," she cried.

"I suddenly remember myself when young," he explained.

She wavered for only a moment and then she yielded gracefully to his arms and returned his kiss, without ardor but with full consent.

Thus the next morning after an evening made delightful by the tactful tenderness of Edwin, who somehow made his parents believe that he was in no haste for them to retire early, they rose from the breakfast table and prepared to visit Jessica. Vera liked the early morning, she never lay abed after the fashion of Susan, and she had already taken an early walk with Edwin before breakfast. Fresh as a single-petaled rose, her straight blonde hair bright and smooth, her fair skin delicately pink upon her cheeks, she presented as nearly a perfect picture of the desirable daughter-in-law as William could imagine. He could imagine, too, exactly the sort of wife she would make for Edwin, a loyal, faithful, steadfast woman, pretty enough to be pleasant and not so pretty as to be dangerous under any circumstances.

Her well-cut blue suit was smart enough, expensive of course, but worth the money and it would wear well. Everything about Vera would wear well. There was nothing sportive in her. Though she had given her promise to Edwin only day before yesterday, a scant thirty-six hours ago, yet already there was about her the air of the faithful wife. He was glad that Edwin deserved her. Vera was too pure a gold to be given into hands less honorable than Edwin's. It was all very suitable, and this was perhaps praise enough.

They set forth in the old grey car, the country car they called it, Edwin driving, and after half an hour or so, they left the macadam and turned down a rutted dirt road, which led them some miles across a low mountain into a spreading valley. Herbert and Bertha had seen them off, Bertha on the verge of recurring tears, and Herbert giving solemn directions regarding Clayton Corners where anybody except himself would take the wrong turn, five roads meeting together as they did, the center of a star.

"You take the worst road, sir. I been aimin' to get that road fixed but the township is short of funds—always is."

The worst road was entirely obvious and they chose it unerringly for another five miles to draw up before the house which they recognized from Herbert's description.

"We must be careful of that miserable cur," William exclaimed, peering from the window.

The dog, however, was chained. They saw it at once. The immense black frame crawled out of the large kennel, it rushed the length of the thick iron chain, roaring at them, bellowing until the hills echoed.

Almost immediately Jessica opened the front door and came out to meet them. She was beautifully dressed, pregnant as they could see, but the soft wool stuff of her suit, a full skirt, a smart little jacket falling over her waist, concealed the harshness of her shape. Her face was thin, her blue eyes were ethereal and ethereal was her smile as she held out her hands to them.

"Oh, how welcome you are," she cried in her pretty voice. "I feel as though you were my own family, coming to see me at last!"

She came forward. Elinor kissed her upon a sudden impulse and William found himself holding both her hands. Vera and Edwin stood to one side, waiting, and Jessica turned to them.

"Mr. Edwin," she said uncertainly.

"You remember Vera," Edwin began.

"Oh, I do," Jessica interrupted him. "I do indeed remember! It is good of you to come."

"We are to be married," Edwin said somewhat abruptly.

Jessica looked bewildered for a moment, almost hurt.

"Married? Are you—" she hesitated and laughed softly. "Of course you are, I forget you are a man. I always think of you as a boy."

Jessica's sweet blue eyes lingered wistfully upon Vera's quiet face. "And how old are you?"

"I am a year younger than Edwin," Vera said quietly.

"Oh, that is so wise," Jessica cried softly. "It is always wise to be younger —not too much, but just a year or so. Come in, come in—"

They did not know what to make of her manner, she threw a light contrived fascination over all she said and did, her narrow hands moved here and there, now at her throat, now at her hair, and she smiled incessantly, a bright and brittle glitter about her face, her great blue eyes shining. She was like a foreigner, come from a country they did not know, whose customs were not theirs, whose thoughts they could not fathom even through the common language.

"Come in—come in," she repeated in a sort of floating ecstasy, and she led the way into the house, a farmhouse, but strangely unlike what William had imagined. The front door gave into a narrow hall from which a straight flight of steps led up to the second floor. The conventional rooms, parlor to the left, dining room to the right, opened from the hall. They entered the parlor, and William looked about him, seeing vaguely familiar settings. Suddenly he understood the strangeness of the room. In her way this astounding creature Jessica had tried to imitate his own home! Between the windows opposite the door hung the mirror, the two wall candlesticks, underneath which was a really good imitation of his walnut escritoire, at either end of the room were the tall book cabinets, not so

large, of course, as his and certainly not antiques. Upon the mantelpiece
were china figures, though not Dresden. His eyes met Elinor's and they
exchanged amazement and pity.

"What a pretty room," Vera said.

"I don't like the carpet," Jessica said eagerly. "It's a cheap thing. The
one I want costs two hundred dollars. Herbert says we can't afford it."
She laughed, her eyes suddenly diamond-hard. "But I'll get it! I don't
worry any more about such things. Would you like to go upstairs and see
all the rooms? The house is much too small, of course, but we are planning
to build, and then this house will just be used for the servants. I have the
place chosen, up on the hill."

She parted the net curtains hanging between the blue velveteen draperies.

"I want to see you, not the house," Elinor said with sudden firmness.
"Sit down, Jessica."

"Vera and I will walk about outside," Edwin said. They had not sat
down.

"Oh no, indeed," Jessica cried in her highest most silvery tones. "You
must sit down, Edwin. There is nothing hidden from you. I have never
had secrets from you, have I? Never!"

Edwin, astonished, sat down. They all sat down, bemused by unreality.

"When do you expect the baby?" Elinor asked quietly.

"Oh, I don't know," Jessica said. Her strangely innocent face turned
upon them radiantly. "I don't think about it, Mrs. Asher. It seems so useless,
just having children. Children have children have children have children
—isn't it all just useless? Over and over and over and over! And what is
there here for children? No streets to walk upon, no shop windows, no
movies, no drugstores, nothing to amuse them. So I just don't think about
it."

Elinor interrupted this. "Your mother tells me you have quarrels with
her."

Jessica flung up her hands. They were very white and thin, the nails
painted a shell pink. Who, William wondered, washed the dishes and
scrubbed the floors? Herbert perhaps, fatuous as he was, or Bertha, on
the rare days when she came home. Only now she was not to be allowed
to come.

"Indeed I don't quarrel with Mamma," Jessica declared. "I have simply
said I will never see her any more, as long as I live, that's all."

"You are living in her house," William said abruptly.

"Only until we build upon the hill," she said brightly. "Then this house
will just be used for the servants."

"Your mother?" he asked grimly.

"Oh no," Jessica said. "I will never see her again." She leaned forward,
her cheeks suddenly scarlet. "I don't suppose you ever knew, Mr. Asher,
but my mother used to beat me terribly. She is a very cruel woman."

"Jessica, I don't believe you," Elinor said. "In all the years that Bertha has been in our house I have never heard anybody else say that."

"That's because you are the family," Jessica said and then words burst from the pent spring within her, her eyes widened, the lids snapping, as she looked from one face to the other. She rushed on, the clearly articulated words like a ripple of falling crystals. "She used to beat me and hold her great fist over my mouth so I couldn't cry! She beat me until I felt as though my very bones were split and my poor father was helpless. He would stand there wringing his hands, he would get down on his knees, speechless, because he didn't want the family to hear, and just on the other side of the pantry door, you were all sitting in riches and safety, while I was being beaten, and all in such quiet—"

The terrible drama was displayed before them in the frightful intensity of Jessica's being. She flamed, she quivered, her eyes were wild and immense, her voice as edged as the high string of a violin.

"I cannot believe it," Elinor insisted.

"Oh, you never could believe," Jessica cried. "None of you have ever believed me, only Edwin—Edwin, my darling!"

She turned and gazed at Edwin, melting, her whole frame relaxing, softening, yearning. "You knew, didn't you, Edwin? I told you everything."

Edwin stared. "I don't know what you are talking about," he said in a clear voice.

"Oh yes, you do, my darling," Jessica said, coaxing him. The white hands fluttered toward him, they clasped each other. "Don't be afraid, you will have to tell your bride, and now I can tell Herbert. I have kept it all a beautiful secret until now. But Herbert will have to know at last."

"Jessica!" William said sternly, seeing his son's face.

She paid no heed to him, the words flowed on, softly, freely, swept upon her apparent love. "Don't you remember, Edwin? Can you forget? Don't you remember the long lovely day we spent together in the hotel in New York? I met you there, do you remember? The one day, my one perfect day in all my life! Ah, don't be afraid to remember!"

Edwin leaped to his feet. He turned to Vera, his face white, even his lips dry and white. "Vera, I assure you, I don't know what she is talking about."

Vera rose, too. "I know you do not." She put her hand in his arm. "Let's go outside and wait." But she was suddenly very pale.

They went out and Elinor watched them, and Wiliam appalled and dazed, glanced at her, and then stared at Jessica. Jessica was smiling gently, her eyes upon the floor, seeing nothing.

"Poor Edwin," she said softly, "he has not the courage to say he remembers. But I shall never forget—never! It was I who refused him at last, Mrs. Asher. I knew that the family would never accept me. And how could I live in the house, with my mother in the kitchen? Of course I could have dismissed her. That could have been done. But I refused my love. Now I know how wrong that was. Love must never be refused, lead where it may. I have lost everything, except that one lovely day—with him. And I shall never see my mother again."

"Jessica, you are lying," William said. "You know that there never was such a day." He made his voice loud, to penetrate the charm.

"Oh yes, indeed there was, and indeed and indeed," Jessica said softly, positively. She laid her clasped hands upon her bosom. "It is here forever."

"William, let's go home," Elinor said. She rose and did not put out her hand. "Jessica, I, too, do not believe one word of what you say. But you must never again tell such lies. I shall tell Herbert myself that I think you are either very ill or very wicked. I feel sorry for both Herbert and your mother."

She walked from the room and William followed. He turned his head once to look back. Jessica sat with her hands clasped on her bosom, smiling, as though she did not see them go. There was something very wrong.

Outside, the four of them climbed into the car and drove away in silence. For what was there to say? What was Vera thinking and what lay in the mind of Edwin, his son, and did Elinor doubt her son, in spite of denial, as women always doubted men? Ah, what a maze of trouble, William thought, and there could never be peace in a world where there were such troublemakers as Jessica, a woman of no worth whatever, one could say, and yet a source of confusion and misery to them all.

A mile beyond the house Edwin stopped the car and jerked at the brake. He turned half around in his seat and faced them. "I am so stunned I don't know what to say. It's all utter fantasy. I don't know what she's talking about."

Elinor interrupted. "When she stood with her hands on your shoulders that day in the hall, what was she saying?"

"What day?" Edwin asked, bewildered. "She's had a way of putting her hands on my shoulders ever since we were kids. I always tried to stand out of reach."

"Why didn't you tell her to stop it?" Elinor asked in a hard voice.

"I didn't want to hurt her feelings—you always told us not to—" Edwin retorted.

Vera sat, silent, her head drooping.

"Had you any intimation," William asked slowly, "that she was in love with you?"

"I never thought of such a thing," Edwin said bluntly. "It's revolting," he added passionately.

He gazed at them, suddenly haggard. "How in hell am I going to prove she was lying? If you don't believe in me, who will?"

Vera turned her graceful head. "I believe in you," she said distinctly.

"Oh Vera—" his voice broke.

"We all believe in you," William said in a practical voice. "I think

Jessica has gone out of her mind. She's making things up. Maybe she thinks what she dreamed about is real. We had better just ignore the whole thing."

"Certainly," Elinor said. She recovered herself as he spoke and leaned to touch her son's shoulder. "It has nothing to do with you, Edwin. I do think simply that poor Jessica must have medical attention. I shall speak to Herbert and Bertha. Now drive on home."

They drove in silence, but who knew what was going on in the minds of those two, sitting in the seat in front of him? Yet long ago William had learned that the safest way to deal with the inexplicable was to ignore it until it became explicable. The subconscious mind worked beneath the routine of daily life, the blessed necessities of food and drink, fresh air and sleep and above all of work. What madness indeed might take place between human beings were there not the command of work to be done, the body to be fed and clothed! It occurred to him when they reached home to explain Jessica in this fashion to Elinor.

"Do you think it is mere idleness that afflicts Jessica? She has too much time on her hands—maybe she always did have."

"She wouldn't have so much time if she took care of the house properly," Elinor said tartly. "Herbert tells me she will not wash his clothes any more. He has to hire a neighbor woman to do them. And you remember he has bought two vacuum cleaners—that's more than you have done for me, William."

She looked at him with suddenly twinkling eyes.

"Herbert is a fool," William said.

Nevertheless this folly could assume vast proportions. Herbert, Elinor said, believed everything Jessica told him. He listened at night to her pretty voice making hideous disclosures and in the morning he stared at Bertha in a way that made her afraid of him.

"Herbert looks at me so, too," Bertha had told Elinor only last night. "I dondt like how he looks."

"Jessica is too clever for Herbert," Elinor now said. "He believes everything she says because she speaks good English and he never got beyond the fourth grade. Sometimes I think we had better send the whole lot of them packing, I don't care how long they've been with us."

"We must wait until after Jessica has had the baby," William replied.

"And," he added after a moment's further thought, "they work as well as ever. In fact, I don't know that Bertha has ever cooked better than she is doing and Herbert is certainly trying. He actually asked if I would like him to brush my shoes the other day."

So they would wait for the birth of Jessica's child.

Vera's visit lasted a week, and nothing more was said about Jessica. In her calm way Vera planned her wedding, setting the date forward to early July instead of, as she had planned before, making it in September.

"Edwin needs me," she said simply, her eyes blue and calm.

And William, divining some lingering uncertainty in Edwin, suggested what he had only been thinking of, that Edwin should come into his law office after the honeymoon and get his apprenticeship through practice, taking his work at law school after a year, or possibly two.

"It won't hurt you to know something before you go to school again," he said to his son. Inwardly he felt it would do Edwin good to be self-supporting for a year or so after his marriage. Thus they united as a family to mend the breach that Jessica had made.

"WHEN is Jessica to have her baby?" Elinor inquired of Bertha.

Bertha shook her massive head. "I don't know nottings—" she said stubbornly. "They tellt me nottings—*nichts, nichts!*" She and Herbert seldom spoke. The kitchen, which had been a companionable place, became a room of solitude and hostility. Herbert ate his food in the pantry, serving himself.

When Elinor asked Herbert he, too, shook his head. "Doctor can't seem to tell," he replied evasively. "Any time in the month, I guess."

The weeks went by and the child was not born. One morning, however, Herbert did not appear for breakfast. A telephone call later in the day explained the reason.

"Jessica has been took," Herbert bawled into the mouthpiece. "I'm at the hospital. She had a hard time and I thought I lost her. It's a girl. Doctor says there can't be no more. He's tying her toobes right away."

"Oh, Herbert, that's too bad," Elinor exclaimed.

"It don't matter," Herbert said. She could almost hear him wiping the too ready damp from his face and neck. Herbert sweated easily, summer or winter, an emotional effluvia that had nothing to do with heat or cold. "I guess I won't be at work for a couple days," he added.

"Never mind," she said. Really it would be a relief. She put up the telephone and went out into the kitchen. Bertha down on her hands and knees was scrubbing out the oven.

"Bertha," Elinor said gently. "Herbert just telephoned. You have a little granddaughter. I'm so glad."

Bertha sobbed suddenly. "It dondt do me no good."

"Yes, it will," Elinor said, filled with pity. "As soon as she is big enough Herbert can bring her here to see me, and then you will see her, too."

"Herbert dondt let me," Bertha muttered, thick with tears. She inserted her head into the oven and reached for the far corners and her voice came out hollow. "Herbert, he hates me, now, too."

"Oh, Bertha," Elinor said impatiently. She left the room, and did not speak to Bertha again all day, waiting until William came home.

"They seem determined to hate each other, the whole lot of them," she declared. "I feel sorry for that poor little baby."

"A girl again," William said thoughtfully.

He was reassured, however, by Edwin's wedding. Bertha and Herbert responded to the family's crisis, a wedding demanded co-operation. Winsten and Madge came with the children, Susan had come from college, and Ozark Pete, as William was beginning to call him privately, arrived the day before, at Susan's command.

The big house was full, there was no time for any but their own concerns, and William relaxed, a boon he deserved, for he had brought to triumphant conclusion his engagement with the city criminals. The three rascals whom he defended, not for their worth but for their rights as citizens, however mean, were discovered to be only minor in comparison to the real murderer, who was apprehended, through the confessions of the fat-faced man among the three. The prime criminal being safely in jail and destined for the electric chair, the three minors were out on bail, severely warned by William who promised them no further defense except upon good behavior. Now he was ready to forget evildoers and bask in the pleasant goodness of his family. It was June, the house was open at door and window, and his small grandchildren played outside happily. He was pleased by the deep devotion between Winsten and Madge, and not too much annoyed by Madge's air of triumph at having come to the wedding upon the eve of the birth of her third child.

"He can be born anywhere," she said recklessly, bursting into laughter. "It might be fun to have him born right here in his grandfather's house."

William merely smiled, praying inwardly that it might not be so. Meanwhile the weather reached perfection. Edwin had come home from college with honors enough to please his parents. So far as William could see, there was no cloud between the young man and Vera, and at the proper time the family set out for Manchester, where the wedding was to take place at two o'clock in the afternoon.

No, there was not a cloud between the two. Edwin came quietly into the nave of the church with Winsten, his best man, as handsome young men as one saw nowadays, William thought, the minister approached from the opposite door in full regalia, and the organ, changing from its wistful strains of "Oh Promise Me," until the solemn joyful wedding march, gave warning that he must with all others rise to his feet. Only Cousin Emma, because of arthritis remained seated on the front pew with Vera's mother.

So William watched again the unfailing pageant of life, the touching powerful procession, his two small grandchildren, scattering rose petals before Susan in gold gauze as the maid of honor, the following brides-maids in pink and ivory, and at last the tall white bride, so young, her hand upon her father's arm. William had been through it with Winsten and yet somehow this time he was moved more deeply. Vera had refused to believe evil of his son, she had stood by him steadfastly upon his word, a noble young girl, ready to become a noble wife.

He was somewhat disturbed in spite of himself, however, by the statuesque coldness of Vera's face. White as marble, she moved slowly forward, and she did not look up to meet Edwin's ardent eyes. Gazing now at his son's face, he wondered if in the strongly focussed, expectant eyes he did discern something like anxiety. Could it be that Jessica had indeed destroyed something between these two, even though there was not an iota of truth in what she had said? Were there even a trace of truth he could not have blamed his son. A boy growing always too quickly for himself is not to be blamed.

He remembered at this moment, most unwillingly, an incident in his own youth. He, William Asher, in love with the girl Elinor, had nevertheless been compelled to confess to her in the lovely and dreadful week before his marriage, that he had once been such a fool in his Senior year at Harvard as to let himself be taken by a gang of college mates to a hideous house on the edge of Cambridge, far from the Yard. What he could not confess was that she herself was partly to blame, the long engagement she had demanded, her gradually increasing yet always delicate warmth, the weariness of their slowly approaching wedding day, his fear of himself, lest the controls break and he offend her at the very outset of married love, how could he explain to the virgin Elinor these darknesses? His experience had been ugly enough so that he fled the place early and alone, but nevertheless there remained something to be told, and Elinor had listened, as white as Vera now was, and as hopelessly pure. He still remembered her forgiveness, the moment of his deepest self-abasement, for years not allowed in his memory until now suddenly it came back whole, his resentment increased because in spite of the years he had never let her know she ought to share the blame with him.

He felt profound pain now for his son, and wondered if at any time it would be possible to hint that Edwin must never ask Vera to forgive him, even if what Jessica had said had been wholly true, lest by asking forgiveness he confirm her doubt of him.

Upon this he brought himself up with a start. The two were making their promises while he was so unfaithful to Edwin as to act in his thoughts as if Jessica had been telling the truth instead of, as he truly believed, merely the worst of falsehoods, to be explained only by the sort of inexplicable madness that sometimes besets a woman.

Winsten put the ring from his vest pocket into his brother's waiting hand and Edwin placed it upon Vera's finger, speaking the ancient and beautiful words, and now they were spoken, the two knelt to receive the benediction, the prayer for their lifelong faithfulness. William had perfect confidence in the quality of his son, born to be faithful to duty as well as to love. But would Vera make demands upon him beyond that which a man could bear? Jessica had cast a cloud upon them, nevertheless, he thought gloomily, a cloud even upon him because he would never know what Vera might do to his fine son, and he might have to wait for years to pass before he knew, and then only by watching Edwin, whether he held up his head in self-confidence as a man could do only when he was sure of his wife's approval as well as of her love. But if he saw Edwin's proud head begin to stoop, if he saw that dreadful downward look of the man betrayed by his marriage and wounded by his wife's superior purity, then he would know.

The wedding march burst forth with the peal of bells, and the two marched toward the open door, and Edwin held his head high enough. But Vera's face was still white and cold.

Elinor was sleepless. William, waking from what he realized was only light slumber, saw that although she had shut the door between their rooms, the door, shrunken with age, left a good half inch beneath it open and in this generous crack he saw light cast by the yellow lamp shade of Elinor's bedside lamp. Lying exactly as he had waked, flat upon his back, head thrust back, he listened and heard her footsteps prowling about in velvet slippers. He turned enough to see the illumined face of the clock upon the small table beside his bed. It was three o'clock, that dreadful hour at which the hidden worries of the day creep out like beasts of the night, to snarl and spread their poisonous forebodings. He sighed and got up, thrust his feet into his slippers and put on his bathrobe. He had left the cord of the belt in a knot and he fumbled at it, impatient, and then let it go as it was. He knocked at Elinor's door. There were times when she did not wish to have the door opened, and he had learned this early.

She did not now reply to come in. Instead he heard her inquiring voice, rather high, "Yes?"

"Are you sleepless?" he called back.

"Come in," she said after the briefest pause.

So he went in. She was lying now on her chaise longue holding about her a soft silk quilt.

"Can't you sleep?" he repeated, staring at her. Her long hair, looking silvery blonde as it had in her youth, was braided in two braids and these hung over her shoulders. Her face without makeup was white between them and he thought she looked exhausted.

"I keep thinking about Vera," she said abruptly.

"Why Vera?" he asked stupidly.

"Does she believe what Jessica said or not?" Elinor asked, not of him, but anyhow.

He sat down on the end of the chaise longue. "Can we do anything about that, my dear?"

"I keep wondering."

He would have liked to go to bed, remembering the work piled upon his desk for the morrow, but he knew her tenacious mind. He had taught himself to turn off his own mind, he could delay further thought until he felt ready to begin it again, but she pursued conclusion without stop, although when she reached it, he reflected, she never thought again of that single pursuit. The answer, when she found it, was final.

"I am afraid of what Vera is thinking," she said gently.

The words, so cool, so absolute in their gentleness, brought him a violent shock.

"Will you never forget?" he demanded. "Haven't all these years meant anything to you? Haven't I proved my faithfulness?"

"Of course they do—of course you have," she replied, her voice, her eyes caressing, "but will Vera know?"

He saw what she meant, he thought gloomily. Vera was at the point where he and Elinor had been twenty-five and more years ago. It was Edwin's wedding night, alas!

"I thought it was all dead and buried decades ago," he groaned.

"It is," she insisted, "but don't you see that it has only begun for Edwin and Vera tonight?"

"Has that anything to do with us?" he demanded.

"They are our children and we want them to be happy."

"We've been happy—can't we trust them to find their own happiness as we have?" he urged.

She did not reply, she thought this over, there was reservation, he felt it, he saw it in the silence in the closing look of her face.

"I suppose only I understand how Vera might feel," she said at last.

"Come," he said with impatience, "after all these years, is there still something you have not told me?"

They looked at each other and the years faded into unreality. What was real was their wedding night when even in the midst of his hunger and ardor, he had seen tears in her eyes. She was so beautiful, the delicately strong, the exquisitely slender girl who was at last his own. Her pale gold hair that night was spread on the pillow like a wide halo, he had spread it so, marvelling at the length, the fineness, the living touch of it in his hands. In those days there was everything to know upon his wedding night. He had never seen her hair down, he had never seen the contour of her breasts, the shape of her waist, the roundness of her hips, the long grace of her legs, her narrow feet. He had never even seen her ankles bare. Absorbed and trembling, rapt in passion and wonder, incredible that all was now his, he had not seen her tears until the light from the lamp fell upon her face and he saw them shining in the blueness of her eyes.

He had fallen back. "What is wrong?" he demanded.

"Nothing," she had faltered.

"But something," he had insisted, and pausing, harnessing and holding back all his onrushing love, he had probed and questioned, had wrenched from her the truth that she could not forget this was not the first time for him, for there had been that other woman.

Why had he told her? If he had not been so utterly truthful he would have concealed the whole wretched meaningless episode, the college prank, to which he had yielded because of her intolerable delay, the act so suddenly repulsive to him even in the doing, so miserable to remember, which indeed he was determined to forget. He had explained all this again to her on his wedding night. She had seemed to understand. But now so many more years later he saw that she had not understood! And would not perhaps ever understand. It was a sacrilege to have brought into that magic hour of first love, yes, that holy hour, the folly which he had felt himself childishly compelled to confess to her.

"My God," he cried out now, "how I wish I had never told you!"

"Do you?" she asked. "Do you really wish you had not told me?"

"You have never forgotten," he accused her.

"I forget nothing that has happened between you and me," she replied.

"And not satisfied with never forgetting," he cried out against her, "you transplant your memory to your own son and his young wife!" He got up and walked about the floor. The cord he had not been able to tie was a nuisance again, his bathrobe did not stay together, he had to stop under the light to discover the mischief.

She got up automatically, then, and untied the cord for him, her thin fingers nimble and dexterous where his fumbled. She tied the belt securely about him and lay down again and drew the quilt to her neck. He accepted the service without thinking.

"Vera has grown up in a more sensible age than we did," he went on. "The war made women more sensible, at least."

"By sensible just what do you mean?" she inquired.

He was unwilling to analyze and then he did so, against his will. "I mean simply that man and woman cannot be judged by the same standards. That is as old-fashioned as Adam, but the truth remains ever new."

"Then you think Edwin is guilty?" she said too quietly.

"Guilty?" he repeated. "I don't know what you mean. If you mean is Jessica lying—yes, I do—that is, I think she is."

"You think she is," Elinor repeated.

"How does anyone know anything?" he replied, irritated. In some absurd far-reaching illogical fashion Jessica had woven even his abortive folly into the web which now caught even his son into its meshes. Had he not gone to Rose Schwenk's place, Elinor would not have believed Jessica, it would have been incredible that her son and his could have stooped to a servant girl, even though the girl was Jessica. But now!

And all this was taking place in this present year, this most modern year, the papers full of divorce and scandals, where sex was reckoned as only an appetite, scarcely to be confused with love. Here in his home, in Vermont, in a valley encircled by green mountains, he and Elinor were living in an age the world had forgot. Such was the power of love.

He turned to his wife, his face set, his jaws white, his teeth clenched, and he held out his arms.

"I will slay myself for you," he muttered. "I must have your faith as well as your love. I will not be betrayed by your distrust in me. For if you do not trust me, then all else is dust upon my head, ashes in my mouth."

His black and bitter eyes compelled her, she was overcome by his despair, and she rose instantly from the couch and went into his arms and he held her, his cheek upon the top of her head, upon the soft crown of her hair. No words—no words—only this, and let it be enough, at least for tonight, and at least for themselves in their generation. The young must learn in their own fashion, for no one could teach them. Love must be learned afresh by every human heart, newborn and alone.

"I want to go and see Jessica and her baby."

This was Madge at breakfast, surrounded by her young, a proud madonna, her husband on her right hand. Elinor was late, a most unusual accident for which William was grateful when he entered the dining room promptly at half past eight. He had not dared to open her door, but listening outside he had heard no sound.

The sun was bright after a light rain just before dawn, a gentle roll of thunder introducing the sudden cloud. Herbert was zealous with buttered toast for the children, and Madge was announcing her intention to him as William entered the room.

"Good morning," William said. He sat down and received the sticky kisses of his grandchildren, who had been instructed, he felt sure, by their mother, to kiss their grandparents morning and night without fail, and at any time between. Madge was a demonstrative wife and mother, believing that kisses and endearments were the cement of family life.

It was impossible not to appreciate the picture she made as a young and blooming mother, his daughter-in-law, although he averted his eyes when Winsten picked up Madge's plump little hand and held it to his cheek. Winsten was uxorious, and this was repellent, but he was glad his son was happy. Both parents adored the sight of their children kissing their grandfather.

"That's right, darlings," Madge cooed. "You must always love Grandfather."

"Yes, indeed," William echoed sincerely enough but conscious of the coolness of his words and tone in contrast to Madge's rich enthusiasm.

Herbert did not answer Madge's announcement. He left the room murmuring about more hot toast, and Madge went on comfortably now to William. "I do feel I should show some interest. After all, Jessica grew up in this house, and this is her first child. Then, too, I might be of help. It is very sad that she will not let Bertha even see the baby. I might be able to say something."

"I shall be glad if you can raise Bertha's spirits," William said. "It may do Jessica good to see someone so entirely normal as you are, Madge. I confess I cannot understand Jessica."

He pondered whether he should tell them of Jessica's extraordinary outburst about Edwin and then decided that he would not. Even though it was all in the family, one never knew how Madge might take it. There was no jealousy between the two brothers, he believed, but Edwin now had a wife, and granting that Vera was altogether different from Madge, William was not sure that this removed her from the possibility of jealousy, her own or Madge's. He was not used to having two daughters-in-law, nor was Madge used to having a sister-in-law—beautiful and young, whose figure as yet was unspoiled. He imagined that Vera would never allow her figure to be spoiled, whatever the number of her children, and this in itself might be a source of jealousy one day, for Madge was the mother type who believed that babies should be breast-fed, and she would think it indecent to consider the contour of a woman's breasts more important than their use for motherhood, or indeed for any other use at all. Winsten, William thought, glancing sharply at his son, looked completely fatuous, a thin intense young man, devoted in fatherhood. What sort of husband was he? Well, Madge had made him whatever he was. Madge was inexorably maternal, her soft massive love absorbed all about her. It was only with the greatest firmness that William himself refused to be absorbed. He loved his grandchildren, sticky though they were with morning marmalade, but he refused to consider them more than a sideline in his life. He was determined to be something more than a mere grandfather, however Madge might view him. It occurred to him that perhaps the only way Winsten could be his young wife's lover was to embrace her first as the mother of his children. A revolting possibility, William thought, averting his mind from the scene. He finished his breakfast hastily, making only a few ordinary remarks and grunting occasionally when the children put a question to him. Then he got up.

"I shan't wake your mother," he said to Winsten at the door. "Ask her to telephone me when she gets up."

He left them with a propitiatory smile, a kiss tossed off his moustache to the children, and was glad to get away. Herbert had made a quick change and was the chauffeur again, immobile and silent at the wheel. William was going this morning only to Manchester, the city office being in the usual summer slackness. It was odd but true that city crime took a moderate vacation in the summer, too, growing brisk again in the sharpness of autumn air.

The green hills were pleasant, the sunshine spilled over into the valleys and he wondered if he should speak to Herbert merely in good humor and decided against it. There was something threatening about Herbert's tight small mouth this morning. So he sat silent and at peace, putting out of his mind the difficulties of human relationships, and meditating upon the gratifying aspects of the law, where all was according to pattern and precedent and one knew exactly what was right. A pity such patterns could not regulate the minds as well as the actions of men and women! He enjoyed the approach to the town, and noticed the attack of tourists, school teachers on a holiday by the busload. The car slowed and Herbert chose a side street and they drew up before the old red brick mansion which years ago William had made into his first law office, and from which he would not have departed now for any cause whatsoever, although he had almost no local practice any more. The older he grew the less change he wanted in his life. This alone made Jessica a menace. Remote as she was, a contemptible creature, yet the irrationality of her uneducated mind created a force which could destroy a rational and innocent universe however small, and that universe his own. He considered again the dismissal of Bertha and Herbert, a clean sweep, removing his household from the fatal orbit within which entirely by chance they were being drawn. For he did not believe for a moment that they had heard the last of Jessica. Yet constitutionally he distrusted clean sweeps.

The morning passed quietly at his desk and he was only uneasy at noon when he allowed himself to realize what he had been aware of all along, that Elinor had not telephoned. He ordered his lunch sent in from the nearby hotel and decided that he would not call her. That she had not called him meant either that she was still asleep, which he could not believe, or that she did not wish to call, in which case she had better be left alone. Long ago he had learned that it availed him nothing if his impatience compelled him to find out her reasons before she chose to reveal them.

He allowed the day to pass, granting himself only no delay after five o'clock. To his astonishment, when he went out to the car he found that the driver was not Herbert but Winsten.

"It's a surprise, I know," Winsten said, reaching to open the door. "Get in—it's been a queer day. Herbert had to go home. Madge thought he should."

William got in. "What's wrong now?"

"Madge wanted me to tell you alone on the way home," Winsten said. He steered his way carefully among clumps of tired tourists, waiting to get into returning buses. "Madge feels terribly sorry for Jessica. She thinks we ought to do something for her immediately."

"Well, well," William said, "let's get it over with."

The scene, reconstructed from Winsten's cautious narrative and propelled by his own dry occasional questions, was clear enough. He and Madge had taken the children with them this morning and had driven to the farmhouse. There they had found everything wrong. No one had answered their cries or knocks, and at last listening they heard the baby crying upstairs. Madge could bear it no longer. She tried the front door and found it unlocked.

"Winsten, you stay here with the children and I'll go up," she had commanded.

"What about the dog?" William interrupted.

"We didn't see the dog then," Winsten replied.

Madge had gone straight upstairs, although the steep stairs were difficult for her. She went to the door from which the baby's crying came, and then she heard Jessica weeping in low moaning wails.

She tried to open the door, but this door was locked. She shook the handle. "Jessica!" she cried, "let me in. It is Madge Asher. We've come to see you."

Then she heard the growl of the dog, the loud bass roar. "Jessica!" she cried again.

"I can't let you in," Jessica called back, her voice all broken with sobs. "I can't hold the dog."

The dog sounded vicious enough to make Madge pause indeed. She went down the evil stairs again and out into the yard, where Winsten was waiting with the children, and told him what Jessica had said.

"You get into the car and stay with the children. I'll go up," he said.

She obeyed him, for now she was honestly afraid. It was too strange. Why had Jessica locked herself in with the baby and the dog in that upstairs room? Or had she? Perhaps Herbert had locked them there. She got into the car with the children and Winsten searched the yard and found a heavy stick.

"Do be careful," she begged from the window of the car.

"I'm not afraid of a dog," he retorted.

He climbed the stairs and rattled the handle of the door. "Jessica!" he shouted. "It is I, Winsten Asher. What is the matter in there?"

She stopped her sobbing, and he supposed she must have taken the child in her arms, nursed it perhaps, for its crying stopped abruptly. Only the dog continued its horrible hoarse growling.

"Open the door," he commanded.

"In a minute, Mr. Winsten," she said in her usual sweet voice. "I just have to tie the dog."

What was this, Winsten asked himself. Could she not have tied the dog before? He heard her talking to the dog in her light coaxing way.

"Now stop, Pirate. It's a friend. You needn't be excited. It's Winsten. Don't you remember Winsten? He was always my friend."

A moment after that she opened the door and he saw an incredible sight. She stood there, quite composed, the child at her breast. Behind her was the dog tied into a huge kennel which stood between the twin beds.

"Come in, please, Mr. Winsten," she said gently. "I am not strong enough to go downstairs yet, and I keep Pirate up here with me while Herbert is away. There are so many tramps, especially in summer, and they all seem to know that I am here alone."

Her meek voice, her pure accents, calmed his astonishment, even his horror, for the dog was a dreadful sight, its meaty jaws slathered with foam, its red eyes rolling. Still, he could understand that she was afraid.

"Shall I call Mrs. Asher?" he suggested.

"Oh do, please," Jessica said almost gaily. "I am so glad she has come, it's very kind of the family."

So, much bewildered, he had gone downstairs again to fetch Madge, who was astonished, too, when he told her, and they left the children for a moment, locked in the car, and went upstairs together. Jessica had sat down in a rocking chair and the dog had ceased to strain against the leather thongs which tied it into the kennel, although its jaws still dripped and its baleful eyes still glowered.

"Do come in, Mrs. Winsten, dear," Jessica said warmly. "I was just sitting there crying all by myself I was so lonesome. I didn't recognize your voice. I couldn't hear you clearly else I would have let you in at once. I have always to tell strangers at the door that I daren't let the dog loose."

It was all reasonable enough, except that it seemed absurd and unreal.

"The front door was open," Winsten said.

Jessica looked vexed. "That's careless of Herbert! I beg him to lock the house when he leaves in the morning but he thinks I am just silly. He has no imagination. He cannot think how it is with me here alone all day, and now this child—"

She looked down at the child as it suckled, her eyes almost hostile, and Winsten had his first quick distrust of her. For gazing at that innocent face, the eyes closed now, the lips relaxing, Jessica asked in strange abstract wonder, "How could this child be born? I shall never understand."

Madge was touched. "Oh, my dear," she remonstrated. "You must not talk like that. When men and women love each other, babies always come."

Jessica looked up at Madge standing above her like a kindly goddess of fertility.

"Ah, but I don't love Herbert," she said clearly, coldly.

Madge turned to Winsten. "Go downstairs, dear, and see to the children. I shall be quite all right. I must have a talk with poor Jessica."

So unwillingly Winsten had gone downstairs and Madge stayed and she repeated their talk faithfully afterwards to Winsten when they were driving home.

"It is very wrong not to love your own husband, Jessica," she had said.

"Oh, I know it is," Jessica sighed. "I try and try."

"Did you never love Herbert?" Madge inquired. She pulled up a small chair and sat down and took the baby in her arms. Poor little creature, she thought, it looked like Herbert and was quite ugly.

Jessica drew her dress over her breast and leaned back and closed her eyes. "It's all so—disgusting!" she whispered.

"What?" Madge asked.

"To have to be alone with Herbert here in this room, night after night— when I don't love him."

Madge was shocked. "Why did you marry him?"

"Mr. William Asher said I must."

"My father-in-law?"

Jessica nodded, and large tears welled beneath her golden lashes and slipped down her pale cheeks.

"But why?" Madge demanded.

"I cannot tell you," Jessica cried. "Oh, I must never, never tell!"

She did not tell, she would not tell, she could only weep hysterically in a convulsion of sorrow. She clung to Madge with both hands. "Oh, you must never, never ask me, promise me," she cried. "You must never mention it even to Winsten. Only Edwin knows. Edwin knows everything. But Mr. Asher doesn't know that Edwin knows. Edwin was like my brother. Oh, he *is* my brother—we'll never change to each other."

Frightful vistas opened before Madge. Jessica was too pretty, she had always been too pretty, and older men could be very strange.

"But did he—" she began.

"Oh yes, yes, yes," Jessica cried in a rush.

"Tell me this," Madge said sternly, "how long did it go on?"

"Oh, years," Jessica said desperately. "When I came back from the convent I was only seventeen. I couldn't help giving in then, could I? It went on and on."

The dog began to growl suddenly and Madge gave a start.

"He won't hurt you," Jessica said. "It's only men he hates. I've taught him that."

The baby slept on peacefully in her arms and Madge could have cried. Poor little thing, what chance had it here in this house? What a tangle life could be!

"Please don't cry, Jessica," she said mildly. Her own life had been so happy that she had no notion of what to do now. She felt the firm universe, the little warm universe which was her own, begin to crumble about her. If Winsten's own father—

She got up and laid the baby on the bed and put a bit of the counterpane over it. "I shall have to think what to do, Jessica," she said. "I want to help you but now I don't know how. I have to think of the family first."

"Oh, yes," Jessica agreed humbly. "We must always think of the family first. I quite realize that."

She got up and stood waiting, looking so quiet, so sad, that Madge was overcome with pity in the midst of her daze. "Poor Jessica," she said simply. "It must have been awful for you, living there."

Jessica's eyes filled again. "I can't forget," she whispered.

Madge nodded and unable to speak she went downstairs and closed the front door and crept into the car. . . .

"I think it best to tell you exactly what happened, sir," Winsten said. He had taken the long road home, to give them both time. Now, his eyes upon the road, golden in the late sunshine, he did not turn his head even to glance at his father's profile.

William had pished and pshawed while the narrative went on. Now however he was in the stillness of profound wrath.

"This is just enough," he declared between set teeth. "Jessica is insane. There is no doubt of it. The idea, the very idea—"

He swallowed and coughed and choked. Winsten slowed the car and thumped him on the back. "Take it easy, sir."

"I know you wouldn't believe such a ridiculous hallucination," William said hoarsely, still stifled. "I'm not so sure about Madge. Women are infernally ready to believe the worst about men when it comes to sex. Even your mother—" His cough seized him again and threatened to strangle him.

"Here, here," Winsten said, pulling up to the side of the road.

"Choking—on my own spittle—" William gasped, purple in the face.

Winsten waited, thumping him gently and rhythmically on the back until he had control again of his wind.

"Well," William said, wiping his eyes, "that was a performance! I don't know that I ever had such a thing happen to me before. But I was never so angry before. Does Madge think—?"

"I don't know what Madge thinks in her heart of hearts," Winsten broke in wearily. "She's a creature of instinct, as all good mothers are. When she's pregnant everything is exaggerated."

"You don't mean she really believes I would demean myself with a servant girl!" William shouted violently.

"She doesn't believe anything exactly," Winsten said doggedly. "She just feels with Jessica somehow."

William shut his mouth firmly and folded his arms, and sat stiff and silent. "Let's get home," he muttered after a moment. "I'm going to talk to Herbert."

The contamination of Jessica in his household might be dreadful, indeed uncontrollable, if Madge were allowed to spread her feelings about. Something had to be done. He was not afraid of any woman, certainly not of his own daughter-in-law, and he would simply stop the whole trouble at its source, which was Jessica. Jessica could not be allowed to go on like this and he would tell Herbert so. Herbert was at least a man, and Jessica's husband.

He got out of the car at his own door and upon the terrace saw Susan and Pete; they were playing a childish game of some sort together, rubber balls attached to long strands of rubber and wooden bats. Each of them had such an instrument and they were laughing loudly. They did not see him and he passed them by. It was odd that Pete did not go back to his business, his garage in the Ozarks or whatever it was. He would be glad when Susan's wedding was over, too. Let them all get married and go away and leave him and Elinor in peace.

Herbert at the door took his hat and cane.

"Come into the library, Herbert," William said sternly.

"The dinner is just on the boil, sir," Herbert suggested.

"Never mind," William said in the same voice.

"I'd better warn Bertha," Herbert said.

William stalked ahead into the library and shut the door. He sat down in the highbacked oaken chair at the end of the long table of English oak and waited. In a moment Herbert came in soft-shod and closed the door and stood against it, his large face pale.

"Yes, sir?"

How could he begin, William asked himself, how could he repeat to Herbert the vile and foolish fantasy which Jessica had woven? Begin he must, and he did so firmly.

"Herbert, my elder son and his wife went to see Jessica today in the kindness of their hearts."

"Thank you, sir—" Herbert whimpered under his breath.

"While there," William continued sternly, "Jessica told a complete falsehood to my daughter-in-law concerning events she declared had taken place while she was in my house."

Herbert's head drooped, his fat face began to quiver.

"I could take legal steps for defamation of character," William continued, "and I would do so except that I believe Jessica to be mentally ill. I demand that you have a doctor examine her at once."

Herbert's face disintegrated, his eyes ran with tears, his tiny mouth trembled between his great cheeks, his chin shook like a dish of jelly.

"It's that black dog, sir," he sobbed.

"The dog?"

"Yes, sir. She don't let me come near her—weeks and months it's been. The dog stays between her and me day and night."

"Do you mean to say she keeps the dog there all night when you are at home?" William inquired, aghast.

"She keeps the dog because of me, sir," Herbert faltered. "She ain't afraid of no man—just me."

"What do you do to her?" William demanded.

Herbert pulled a large clean handkerchief from his pocket and wiped his face. "Nothing, sir, except I want my rights."

He folded the handkerchief neatly and put it into his pocket. Then he looked at William humbly, his face glistening with sudden sweat.

"Sit down," William ordered.

Herbert sat down on a corner of one of the heavy chairs and continued to look at his master with eyes piteous but dogged.

"Explain yourself," William commanded him.

Herbert cleared his throat and leaned forward slightly. "As man to man, sir," he began—

And upon this William, his eyes fixed upon Herbert's pallid and glistening face, saw unfolded before him a scene as old as man and woman.

The man, who only happened to be Herbert, advanced nightly upon the woman whom he had made his own with her consent, given for what reason could not be imagined, and nightly the drama repeated itself, Jessica's delicacy, her fantastic imagination, her thwarted longings, her melancholy inheritance shaped in remote ages in the Black Forest of Germany, concentrated now into a single blind determination. She would not yield to this man, she the woman. Oh, she had yielded at first, half laughing, flouncing at him, "Leave me alone, you dirty beast!"

He had left her alone then sometimes, cunningly trying to arouse desire in her by ways he knew, ways he had tried before on other women, ways he had heard men talk about—

"Don't touch me, *schweinhund!*" she had screamed. "I am not like that."

He had been cautiously patient, knowing that good women did not give in all at once. But what does a man do when a woman never gives in? What does a man do when a woman bites and scratches him so that he had to hold down her hands and thrust his arm against her throat so that she cannot raise her head and then must mount her hard so that her kicking legs and thrusting feet do not wound him in his tenderest parts?

"I ask you, sir," Herbert said, the tears starting down his cheeks again, "what do I do?"

"I cannot imagine your wanting to—to compel your wife against her will," William said, sickened to the soul.

"What for does a man marry?" Herbert asked, astonished. "A man pays, don't he? He gives her bed and board, so to speak, and everything else beside. I've give Jessica everything she ast for—"

He ticked off again on his stubby fingers what he had given her, the Beautyrest mattresses, the washing machine, the two vacuum cleaners, the almost antique furniture, the gold-edged mirror, the new blankets, the refrigerator, the electric stove, at last the carpet, yes and carpet even on the stairs.

"What do I ast back? Just my rights," Herbert said. His humility passed from him suddenly. William saw a man remembering his wife whom he was determined to possess.

"What's more, I'm goin' to have my rights," Herbert said, heavily.

"How do you propose to get them?" William inquired, his voice grim.

It was useless to explain to this male that there was no getting without giving. The subtleties of sex were beyond Herbert's comprehension. The delicate lessons which he himself had taken so long to learn Herbert could never grasp, nor even their necessity. Perhaps for Herbert they were not necessary. To take might be enough for this molecular soul surrounded so massively with body. But ah, Jessica was another material. William had mercy enough in his heart suddenly to be sorry for Jessica. He caught a dim glimpse of what it might mean to be a woman.

"I'll take my rights," Herbert said. His small mouth pursed into a tight knot. "First of all, I'll get rid of that dog."

William sighed. "Why don't you handle the matter a little gently, so that she won't suspect? Ask Pete to take the dog back. Say that it is getting too fierce to be with the child and you would be obliged if it could be taken away. Then Jessica will not blame you so much."

Herbert stared at him. "It's a good idea, sir. It takes a lawyer, I guess, to think of how to do things." He hesitated. "I wisht I could do it now, tonight."

"Why not?" William replied. "You might ask Pete at once. He will be leaving perhaps tomorrow."

Herbert got up. "Thank you, sir—Bertha will wash the dishes, I guess."

"Go now," William said. He did not want Herbert about the dinner table tonight. "Madge said your wife was in a bad way this morning. Get home to her. I'll speak to Susan. They can go with you, tie the dog in the car, and get their dinner somewhere on the way home."

"Thank you, sir."

He waited for Herbert to leave and then he went out to the terrace and there found Elinor with Susan and Pete. The game was over, Susan was shaking cocktails and Pete was lounging in the most comfortable chair.

"Get up, you big bum," Susan said cheerfully to her betrothed. "Don't you see my father?"

Pete got up, grinning. "Didn't know this was your chair—"

"It isn't, particularly," William said. He paused to kiss Elinor's cheek and took another chair.

She said, "I heard you and Herbert in the library, and I didn't come in."

"Jessica is in a bad way," William replied. "Herbert feels he must go home at once. Susan, he has a strange request to make but I concur in it for reasons I will explain later. He wishes that Pete would take away the black dog."

"Now?" Susan's dark eyes were large.

"At once," William said firmly.

He glanced at Elinor to see if her face betrayed the slightest change of knowledge. He saw nothing. The twilight fell upon her lovely hair and placid eyes. Madge might be honorable enough, after all, to say nothing except to Winsten, and his own son he could trust. As soon as possible he himself would tell Elinor the whole miserable fantasy, once the dog was gone, once Herbert had a chance to assert his will. He felt guilty in strangely hidden ways, that he was, so to speak, delivering Jessica over to the male, but perhaps that was what she needed. She had been spoiled all her life, catered to, indulged, nobody had ever made her do anything, beginning with gentle old Heinrich, and even Bertha with her sporadic slaps and tantrums, and certainly Cousin Emma. They had all made far too much of a child who though she happened to be pretty and vaguely talented was after all doomed, or destined, rather, to be nothing but a servant. Let Herbert beat her if need be, once and for all. He did not want to talk to Elinor until this was over. Elinor would somehow prevent it.

Herbert drew the grey car in front of the terrace a few minutes later and sat immobile.

"Well, Pete?" Susan inquired.

"I don't care," he said amiably, and so the two went off, and at the same moment Winsten came down, preventing William from being alone with Elinor.

"Where is Madge?" Elinor inquired. "I'm ashamed that I've slept all day. But I felt tired after the wedding."

"Madge isn't feeling quite herself," Winsten replied. "I have told her to go to bed."

"Oh dear," Elinor said, "is it, do you think—"

"I don't know," Winsten said, "it may be. We'll soon see."

His thin young face was worried, the perpetual father, William thought, not without relief that Madge could not appear.

"The trip this morning was too much for her," Elinor said.

"The children have been fretful this afternoon," Winsten replied. He poured himself a cocktail. "Where are Susan and Pete going?"

"Herbert wants the black dog taken away tonight." William said significantly. "I talked with him about Madge's impression of Jessica this morning. He thinks the dog has an unhealthy influence on Jessica—has thought so for a long time."

"How strange," Elinor said in surprise. "I wouldn't have suspected Herbert of so much subtlety."

"It may be only a notion," William said quietly.

Winsten said nothing. He stirred his drink slowly, his eyes downcast.

"Don't worry about Madge," his mother said. "It would be rather nice having a baby born here the way you all were."

"I'm only thinking about my job," Winsten said. "I ought to telephone the first thing in the morning."

"Well, not until morning," Elinor said comfortably. "Let's go in to dinner."

It was well toward midnight before William heard the car come up to the terrace. He had not gone to bed, pleading papers, and he had sat alone in the library working after Elinor left him.

"I shall sleep with one eye open," she had said. "I don't like Madge's looks. I think something is going to happen before dawn. Winsten has called the doctor. He's made a reservation in the hospital, at least." This was after she had been upstairs to see Madge.

"That's better," William said absently. "I hate nurses in the house—always did."

She laughed softly, and kissed him. "You dried up old lawyer," she said. "Babies mean nothing to you, I do believe."

"I like them when they're washed, properly dressed and looking like human beings."

"You always acted as though you had nothing to do with ours," she accused him.

"My part was somewhat vague," he admitted.

She shook him slightly. "Such talk," she scolded, but lovingly.

He smiled up at her and when she bent to kiss him again he held her down for a moment, his hand on the back of her neck.

"Have you been quite happy with me?"

"On the whole, yes," she said round and clear.

"I never forced you—against your will?"

He thought he caught the slightest flickering of her golden eyelashes. "Not really—"

"No, now, Elinor," he demanded.

"Oh, let's not talk about things at this late date—"

"Indeed we will," he said with sudden anger. "Come, sit down. Now when did I ever force you against your will?"

She sat down, opened her blue eyes very wide and began to take down her hair, pin by pin, and braid it before his eyes, growing younger by the minute as she did so.

"All right, stupid, if you don't know by now. Of course you forced me, not by raping me or anything so silly. Still, plenty of times a woman doesn't want to—but she does it anyway, because if she doesn't the man gets huffed, irritable, cross the next day with children, and it just isn't worth it—"

He stared at her and felt something collapse within him.

"Elinor," he stammered. "Elinor, you didn't—"

She gazed at him rebelliously. "Yes, I did, and you have made me tell something I didn't want to tell and don't want to tell, and now that I've told you, you are going to get angry with me. How unreasonable and illogical and emotional and ridiculous men are! You want romance, all the time, it's all to be love-making and sex, but it has to be to your tune and when you say so, and if the woman doesn't happen to be ready all the time, any time, and remember the bull and the cows, if you please, the bull always waiting and ready, damn him, but he has to wait on the mood of the cows as any farmer knows, and it's only the human female who has to deny her very nature and pretend and pretend, and then you can't believe the truth. Oh, you men, you must have nature itself the way you'd like to have it, you can't and won't face the truth—"

"Elinor!" he shouted, "have you lost your mind?"

She flung her braid over her shoulder and gave him a glorious and bewildered smile. "No," she said softly, "and I feel wonderful! I do believe I have wanted for years to say that. Now I've said it." She put her clasped hands on her breast. "Thank you, William, for giving me the chance."

She took a deep breath, not a sigh, but the breath of freedom, and he stared at her in stupefaction. "Why didn't you say it years ago if you wanted to?" he demanded.

"I didn't dare," she said strangely. "I used to be afraid of how you would feel."

"And you're not afraid of me now?" he said rather sadly.

She shook her head and the waves of her soft hair parted on either side and fell over her ears. "No, I suppose because the children have grown up. I can't think of any other reason."

"I don't understand you," he confessed. "In spite of loving you and you only all these years I don't understand you."

She rose and went over to him and putting her arms about him she pressed his head into her fragrant bosom.

"It was often completely right and wonderful," she whispered. "Most wonderful of all, it still is. Better really, because now it's just for you and me. It's so nice that God has arranged for younger women to take over the worry of having the babies."

He buried his face between her breasts. "Oh, Elinor," he muttered, forgiving her for everything. "I'll never have time enough with you."

"All the time there is," she said cheerfully. She bent to kiss him firmly but briefly upon the lips. "Good night, don't sit up all hours."

She pulled herself away and detected a speculative look that he permitted to creep into his eyes and she laughed. "No, no," she said airily, "not tonight, not with this house full of children, Madge likely to be taken to the hospital at any moment, and that dreadful dog coming back—"

She shuddered and went away quickly, pausing at the door to say one last word, "I do thank you, William—"

"Don't thank me," he muttered, going back to his papers, and forcing his mind away from her. All that stuff she had poured out, there was no telling how much of it was truth, and how much of it was thought up on the spur of the moment. There was something of Jessica in every woman.

Nevertheless he felt quite sleepless, and when he heard the car just before midnight, he tiptoed to the front door which was standing open, Madge had not gone to the hospital, and the upstairs was dark except for the night light in the hall.

"Be quiet, you two," he said in a low voice when the car stopped.

"What's wrong?" Susan asked with something just under her usual voice.

"Madge isn't feeling well," he replied. "What's that?"

For between the two of them they were dragging an immense dark body out of the rear of the car.

"It's the dog," Susan said, "Pete had to kill it."

"What an extraordinary day!" William muttered under his breath. "What are you going to do with it?"

"Put it here behind the lilacs until tomorrow, Pete," Susan said. "It will smell up the car."

Pete did not reply. He dragged the huge corpse along the ground by the forepaws, flung it behind the lilacs, and then came up the steps looking depressed. "I never thought I'd kill a dawg."

"Come into the library," William commanded softly. "What on earth happened?"

They tiptoed after him and he closed the door.

"I want a drink," Pete said. His dark face was somber and Susan looked at him with troubled eyes.

William went to a small cupboard in the panelled wall and took out a bottle of whiskey and three glasses. He poured a small amount of the liquor in each and they drank slowly.

"Well?" he inquired.

"You tell it, Susan," Peter said.

He sat with his knees apart, his head hanging while she talked, his full lower lip thrust out.

"Jessica was asleep when we got there," Susan said. "Herbert went up-stairs alone first, of course. He looked in and then he came down again. 'She's got the dog loose in there,' that was what he said: 'I don't dast to go in,' he said. So of course Pete said he would go up. We all went up, Herbert last."

She told it well, struggling as William could see with her own horror. They went up the stairs without making any noise, thinking, she said, that they would take the dog away without waking Jessica or the baby.

"Does she always let the dog loose when you're late?" she asked Herbert.

"She keeps him on a long rope, as a reg'lar thing," Herbert replied.

But Jessica had waked at once. "Is that you, Herbert?" she called.

"Answer," Susan commanded him.

"Yes, it's me," Herbert said in a placating mild voice. He held the door. "I tried to come in before, Jessica, but I heard the dog loose."

"You can't come in, Herbert," Jessica called back. "I have the dog loose on purpose."

Herbert turned his big pale face toward them. There was a naked electric light in the ceiling blazing down on them.

"Now what'll I do?" he begged.

"Tell her we're here to get the dog," Susan said.

The dog was growling horribly just inside the door. They could hear its rasping breath drawn in after each growl.

"Miss Susan is here with Mr. Peter," Herbert said placatingly. "They've come for the dog, Jessica. Mr. Peter wants it back again."

Jessica did not answer. They listened and heard nothing but the growling of the dog.

"Let me open the door," Peter said. "The dawg knows me." He flung the door open but the dog sprang at him. Standing on its hind feet it was as high as his shoulders and he grappled with it, holding its jaws shut with one hand.

Herbert closed his eyes and leaned against the wall, moaning, but Susan sprang forward and dragged the dog's hind legs so that it fell on the floor.

"Smart girl," Pete gasped. "Hold 'em down. I'll choke the life out of the damn beast."

"And that is what he did," Susan said in the library, facing her father steadfastly. "I held the dog's hind legs and Pete choked him dead. And then I heard Jessica. She was saying over and over, 'Kill them, Pirate—kill them all!' I was so angry when I heard it, and I yelled at her. 'You shut up, Jessica!' That's what I yelled. It was like a room full of crazy people, Herbert crying out loud and Jessica saying that over and over and me yelling at her. She was sitting up in bed all dressed up in a silk nightgown and a fancy bed jacket, pink sheets on her bed, if you please. Only the baby kept on sleeping."

"What did you do when the dog was dead?" William asked. His mouth felt dry as leather and he sipped the whiskey again.

"Pete dragged the body down the stairs and we stuffed it in the car and came home," Susan said.

"Yeah," Pete said in his heavy voice, "and I never thought I would kill a dawg. I always liked that dawg. I never should of brought it here. I should of left it at home where it belonged. She had that dawg all strung up tense like and ready to kill anybody. Why, the way that dawg was tonight it would have eaten Herbert alive. Lucky for him we went along."

"I suppose you saved his life," Susan said, "if it was worth saving. I doubt it. I despise men who cry. I never cry myself."

"Let's go to bed," William said. "I am exhausted."

He was waked the next morning late by Elinor's cool hand on his forehead.

"Wake up, Grandfather," she said gaily.

He dragged himself upward out of sleep. "Don't tell me Madge—"

"A little girl, named Elinor," she said too brightly.

"Another girl," he exclaimed, waking up.

"Too many?" she inquired.

"Depends," he said, yawning. He got up and shuffled into his slippers. She paused at the door and blew him a kiss. "You look tired. Would you like to stay in bed this morning? Herbert's not here."

"Oh no, I'll get up," he grumbled. "Herbert's not here, eh? Susan tell you about the dog?"

"She came in my room last night and waked me up to tell me," Elinor said. "Terrifying, wasn't it? I'm glad it's dead. Jessica will be better, I do believe."

"I don't know," he mumbled from the bathroom.

She did not hear him. She was already on her way downstairs, her spirits high because of the new baby. A girl was what she had wanted, he could see. His own spirits sank strangely. This was not going to be a good day. They had not seen the end of Jessica, not by a long shot.

It was the middle of the morning, however, before he knew the worst.

After breakfast, not having seen any of his children, he withdrew again into his library, taking care not to look out of the window to see whether the dog lay behind the lilacs. Susan was still asleep and Pete was probably the same. The young these days seemed able to sleep all day, a sort of escape, he felt, from the insoluble problems of the times. No one knew how to stop war, corruption in government was monstrous, women went crazy and dogs went mad, therefore the young slept.

At eleven o'clock when Elinor had just left for the hospital to see Madge and her baby, he himself declining to go before the baby was twenty-four hours old and the first rawness off, he heard a scream in the kitchen. The back window of the library opened upon the kitchen garden and the morning being warm he had opened it to make a current of air. He was therefore able to hear Bertha scream loudly again and then again. He flung down his pen, but before he could get up she came rushing into the room in her stocking feet as she always was in the kitchen, especially in summer when her feet swelled.

"Mr. Asher, sir, oh, Mr. Asher—"

She sobbed, her face was purple.

"Well?" he said sharply.

"Herbert, sir, he's on the phone, Jessica—she's gone someting awful—"

William picked up the receiver on his desk and heard a strange noise.

"Herbert!" he shouted.

"Oh, Mr. Asher," Herbert moaned, "please can you come quick?"

"I cannot," William said firmly. "I must first know what is wrong."

"It's Jessica, sir—can't you hear her?"

"I hear a dog barking," William said.

"That's her!" Herbert shouted. "She's down on her hands and knees going round and round the room. She's actin' like a dog, she's stark ravin' crazy. I don't know what to do. And the baby is hungry. I can't get her to feed the baby. She tries to bite it. I can't stop her goin' round and round barkin'—"

"Oh, my God," William cried. "I'll call an ambulance. Good gracious! Watch her, Herbert—"

But when he had called the doctor and told him and the ambulance arrived, it seemed there was nothing for it except to go with it himself, for the country roads were inexplicable and the quickest thing was simply to leap in beside the driver. A nurse and an interne with a straitjacket sat in the back by the stretcher.

He rode in silence while the lovely summer morning shone down peacefully from heaven upon the troubled earth.

"That was some dog lyin' there dead under them lilacs," the driver remarked.

"It is to be buried this morning," William said in a distant voice. It would be impossible to explain all that had happened, and he felt too exhausted inwardly to make an attempt. It was simply not to be understood.

"That's the trouble with living near a highway and keepin' a dog," the driver said amiably.

"Yes," William agreed, too exhausted to explain.

"It must have took a truck, though, to kill that dog," the driver suggested.

"I suppose so," William said vaguely and then uncomfortable.

The driver gave up and was silent until they drove up to the farmhouse. William got out, followed by the interne and the nurse and the door was opened by the driver. At the foot of the stair William paused. "Herbert?" he called. The bedroom door opened and they could hear a strange low growling from upstairs. Herbert came out with the baby in his arms.

"She's quieter," he whispered. "She's layin' under the bed."

William turned to the nurse. "You had better go up without me. She knows me and might get excited."

He was uncomfortable indeed. What if Jessica should recognize him and renew her charges? He sat down in the small parlor, now ill-kept and dusty. Herbert had made it a place to change his clothes, and his shoes and undergarments were scattered about, a piteous place, he thought, looking about at the touching effects that Jessica had tried to create, a little world for herself in which she had nevertheless gone mad.

They were bringing her downstairs now, in a white coat of some kind, the sleeves tied around her. He caught a dreadful glimpse of her as she passed the door, her head down slung, and her jaw slavering. She was muttering in her throat, a rasping guttural growl, and they passed the door without her lifting her head. He rose and stood by the open window and when they put her into the ambulance, she snapped at the interne's wrist suddenly, and he slapped her.

"You'd bite, would you?" he said not unkindly. He strapped her down upon the stationary cot within and the nurse took her place. The driver climbed into the seat and then shouted.

"Ain't you comin' back?"

William shook his head. "I will stay and see how things are here and the man can drive me back later."

The driver nodded and the ambulance rumbled away. The house was still. There was not even the sound of Herbert weeping. William went upstairs after a moment and found him sitting in the chair, rocking back and forth, the baby asleep in his arms. The room was frightful. Some sort of human battle had taken place. The bed clothes were tossed over the floor, the pictures had fallen from the walls, glass broken, and the curtains were torn from the windows. In the midst of this wreckage Herbert sat in the rocking chair, the baby in his arms, rocking back and forth and the child was placidly asleep.

"How did you feed it?" William asked stupidly.

"I mixed some milk and water and sugar and fed her with a spoon, sir," Herbert replied. He seemed calm but exhausted. "Do you want me to drive you home?" he asked.

"What about the baby?" William countered.

"Now that she's full she can just sleep in the back seat," Herbert said.

So with no more words they went downstairs, Herbert put the child in a rolled blanket in the back seat of his worn car and they went slowly away from the house.

"You'll understand I can't come back for a day or so, sir," Herbert said. "I'll have to get the baby into a home somewhere."

"Certainly," William said. "But wouldn't this be a good time to have Bertha retire and come here and take care of the child?"

Herbert's immense white face took on a look of rocklike stubborness. "I'll never have her in the house, sir, not while I live."

"But Bertha has done nothing," William protested.

"I don't know what she has done nor what she hasn't," Herbert said darkly, his little sad eyes on the rutted road. "All I know is that Jessica couldn't abide her and so I can't. Something she did to my girl, and I shan't lay eyes on her in my house."

"Does that mean you want to quit your job?" William asked.

"No, it just means I don't want her in my house," Herbert repeated.

"Is it not Bertha's house?" William suggested.

"It's to be Jessica's and mine as soon as the old woman dies," Herbert declared.

William was silent, there was no fathoming Herbert's mood. He would be glad to get home.

"Or again," Herbert said half a mile later, "it might be them nuns. Jessica was never willin' to give herself up to herself. There was somethin' about nature that she thought was dirty and that's the nuns. Still, it was Bertha sent her to the convent, where her father never wanted her to go. She liked her father, Jessica did. He was good to her."

William could remember Heinrich very well, a disorganized kindly man who without Bertha to direct him would certainly have ended as a drunkard or a beggar. But that was perhaps the tragedy of women like Bertha, the managers to whom the weak turn, upon whom they cling, and whom unfailingly they hate, and this, too, could not be explained to Herbert.

"Well," he said vaguely. "One never knows. I suppose the first thing is to get Jessica well again, if it's possible."

Then Herbert said the incomprehensible thing. "She ain't sick, sir, she's just tryin' to win."

"Win what?" William asked.

"What we went through last night."

He would like to have cried out not to be told what had gone on, but he saw it was necessary for Herbert to tell him. Sooner or later Herbert would insist upon telling what had taken place in that room after the guardian dog was dead, after Susan and Peter had gone away and there was no one left to stand between the man and the woman. It was plain enough as he told it. Even so soon after childbirth the endless war of the ages between male and female had burst into battle in that lonely room, far from any human habitation, so that Jessica screaming and crying could be heard by no one. No, and Herbert, too, was not heard, his slow temper rising at last to crisis when he knew that she was defenseless, and no one could hear the bellowing of the bull, alone at last with the weaker female. Jessica did not yield. She leaped from bed to floor, she clung to the curtains, struggling to throw herself from the windows, but he had nailed them shut. The curtains fell about her and she hid in them until he tore them from her. She clung to the table, to the beds, until he wrenched her hands away, pounding upon her knuckles with his clenched fists. He beat her with the rung of a broken chair at last until she fell writhing upon the floor, screaming with pain, and still as tireless, thin as she was, as though she were made of twisted wires. He imprisoned her beneath his vast body there upon the floor and held her down, his hands clutching her wrists, his tight mouth pressed upon her turned cheek, his loins fastened upon hers.

"And all the time," he said mournfully now in the morning light driving carefully along the road so that the sleeping baby would not be jarred from the seat, "All the time I was takin' only what was my rightful due."

William listened, fixed in solemn horror. There was simply no way to explain to Herbert that what he had done was worse than murder.

"When it was all over," Herbert was saying, "I lifted her up and laid her on the bed. I thought she had fainted and I was scared. I went in the bathroom to get her smellin' salts. She always had smellin' salts like Miss Emma. When I came back—" his chin began to quiver and he cleared his throat. "When I come back into the room she was on her hands and knees on the floor, swingin' her head low, and when I spoke to her, she—barked, like the dog."

William drew a deep sigh. Another five miles and they would be home.

"It is all incomprehensible," he said at last, "quite, quite incomprehensible."

But he had a dreadful fear that if he really tried, he could understand, and to understand was, for the moment, simply too much for him.

When he got home he looked involuntarily for the carcass of the dog. It was gone. Susan and Pete had buried it, then! Now perhaps there would be peace. He went upstairs to wash his hands and change his clothes for no particular reason except that he wanted to look as well as to feel differently, a change surely for the better. On the stairs he met Susan and noticed that her eyes were at once remote and luminous. He made no reference to the dog.

"Where is your mother?" he inquired mildly.

"She is in the herb garden," Susan replied and went on her way.

When he was properly changed into an old suit, newly cleaned and comfortable, he went in search of Elinor. She was as Susan had said in the herb garden, a square of greenery in the midst of the kitchen garden behind the house. She was on her knees, choosing slowly and with care a small bouquet of herbs, designed he supposed for the delectation of the meat she had planned for their dinner. He walked toward her, lighting a cigarette and pretending an amiable leisure.

She looked up. "Well?"

"Well, Jessica has been taken to the hospital—in a straitjacket." He said it gently, low enough so that Bertha could not hear. Elinor would have to tell her.

"A straitjacket!" Elinor cried in high concern.

He described the dreadful morning and she listened, frightened and yet unbelieving, as he could see. She knelt there on the ground, protesting in silence while he told her what he had done.

"Somebody had to do something," he said in final irritation. "Even Herbert agrees to that. The doctors will decide whether Jessica is or is not insane. I hope she is. Insanity is the only possible excuse for all that has happened. If she is not insane, she must be a devil of malevolence."

This made an impression, he was grateful to notice. The sparkling protest faded from Elinor's eyes.

"Oh dear," she sighed. She sniffed the herbs and rose to her feet. "I wish I knew whether it's the right thing."

"For the present it is," he said firmly. He himself felt a strange relief in the thought that Jessica was safely locked up.

"I suppose so," Elinor said. "Of course they have all sorts of ways of curing people now—even if she is insane."

"Yes," he agreed, and then very guardedly, he asked, "How's Madge?"

"Perfectly normal," Elinor replied. "That is, she is well enough physically. I thought she seemed a little queer with me. I suppose she is just tired."

He felt his cheeks grow hot. "I am tired myself. I have had just about enough of queer women," he said with unusual energy. "If Madge feels queer I had rather not hear about it. How is the baby?"

"I'm sorry you're tired," Elinor said. "As for the baby, she is simply adorable, the prettiest of all the babies."

"Then I am glad she is named after you," he said gallantly.

She flashed him one of her looks, fully appreciative, a little humorous, meaning isn't it rather late in the day for this sort of speech. He raised his eyebrows and noticed that her skin still stood the sunshine remarkably well. She had no wrinkles, not even a delicate tracery under the ivory surface. He felt gratified that he had been able at least until now to keep her life serene enough for beauty.

"I LOATHE men who weep," Susan said with unutterable loathing. "Thank God Pete is a real man. I would hate Herbert, myself, if I were Jessica, I swear."

It was evening, and William was waiting for dinner. Elinor was in the kitchen, Bertha had retired to her attic room upon hearing the news of Jessica, and Susan was setting the table.

"Ah," William said to encourage Susan and yet not to commit himself. It was all very well but there could be extremes either way. "Is Peter not coming for dinner?"

"No," Susan said. "He decided to go home this afternoon."

"Nothing wrong?"

"Not if you and Mother behave," Susan said firmly.

He avoided this portent. She wanted something and so it was she, he very well knew, who had sent Peter home. She wanted him out of the way while she took her parents in hand. How well he recognized the signs! He got up and sauntered toward the door.

"You'd better help your mother with the dishes after dinner, Bertha is prostrated."

"There it is again," Susan replied. "Getting prostrated! People are so soft."

And if anyone looked soft, William thought, gazing at her, it was this luscious creature who was his daughter, this girl with the tender air, her large brown eyes fringed with black lashes uselessly long and thick, her slender round figure, hinting plumpness that was like his own mother's, a voice as deep and soft as slumbrous music. But that was the fashion of girls these days and it all meant nothing. He had not the slightest idea of the real Susan since Pete had attached himself in his singularly lackadaisical and desultory manner to the family. Yet apparently it was to be permanent.

He seized upon an instant's daring, "Are you really going on with this preposterous marriage?"

Susan folded three stiff linen table napkins into fanciful shapes. "That is what I want to talk about tonight. I am glad that Bertha is prostrated. We'll have perfect privacy."

"Wait until after dinner," he begged, pausing at the door. "My digestion is not what it used to be. Peace, please, at our meal."

He left her, and somewhat heavily he went outdoors and walked back and forth upon the terrace, suspending thought. Long ago he had learned the trick of self-suspension, a defense against criminals pervading his inner life. He had been compelled to learn how to send them off into the outer air, their evil faces fading away like Cheshire cats, in order that he might return whole to his household to play with the children, to examine the defects of a reluctant furnace, to read a book he had laid aside the night before, or finally and most important of all, to make love to his Elinor. Now in the long summer twilight he exercised his habit and felt a refreshing inner quiet steal forth. The garden was lovely in the dusk, the early summer flowers bright against the stone wall. It was weather for roses, the only flowers whose name he infallibly remembered. Whatever happened within a man's house, the walls stood, the trees grew high and flowers bloomed.

But the foundations could be shaken nevertheless. The evening went on and Susan was merciless. The meal was pleasant, delightful so far as the food went, he made tentative veiled references to the exhaustion of his day, and yet he perceived that Susan had no intention of sparing him. The young were single-minded, they thought only of themselves. Glancing at his daughter occasionally between moments of enjoyment of a lamb curry that was really superb, he muttered within himself and strictly to himself that he might as well enjoy his dinner, for what was coming afterwards was inescapable. He knew the look of inexorable determination upon Susan's beautiful mouth, he had seen it first when she was less than a year old, in conflict then as now with him, beginning, he recalled, with the day upon which he had insisted that she eat her spinach. She had not eaten it. Instead she had brushed the dish to the floor with one swift movement of her then fat right hand. The hand now was very pretty, slender and well-kept, the nails coral red, and upon the third finger he saw for the first time a diamond ring, a solitaire of size. When she saw him looking at her hand she flashed the diamond in his eyes like a lantern.

"Like it?"

"I've seen others," he said drily.

"It's very nice," Elinor said, hastening to make amends for him by generosity.

"Where did Ozark Pete get the money for that?" he grumbled. There was no use being delicate with Susan. Girls nowadays did not know what delicacy was. Jessica had modeled herself on the young ladies of another day.

"You'd be surprised how much money you can make in a garage," Susan said complacently. "Besides, we bought it on time."

"Oh, Susan," her mother exclaimed.

"What?" Susan asked.

"But your engagement ring! On borrowed money!"

"I didn't want the small size," Susan said.

"Get what you want, get what you want," William said.

"Okay, Dad—"

"Even your English is corrupted," he grumbled. "A college education can't stand up against a garage, I suppose."

He saw he had gone far enough for the present. Her dark eyes burned with fury upon his face. He shrugged his shoulders slightly. "I won't quarrel at the table. There'll be no punches pulled later, though."

"None," Susan promised.

He rose from the meal and without conscience he left the table and dishes to the two women, and proceeded to smoke a quiet pipe in the east parlor. There in that peaceful place, all children and servants removed, he reflected upon the strange human phenomenon of modern times, the tough guy Peter, and millions more like him, uncivilized and ignorant, a magnificent body and no brain, or if a brain then so well concealed beneath mannerless behavior and uncouth speech that it might as well be non-existent. He felt sorry for his own sons, Winsten, the young father, molded in a pattern outworn, and Edwin, the intellectual, who could not survive, certainly, unless law prevailed. If ever law broke down beneath the assaults of revolution, inevitably it would be Peter who was the revolutionist and never Edwin, and certainly not Winsten, and Edwin would be liquidated. That was the modern word for murder. Winsten might be allowed to live if he conformed, and he would conform, fearful for his wife and his children. Edwin would never conform and so he would be killed. William savored the harsh old-fashioned word. Killed was the truth of it, and liquidated was the lie. Peter might hate to kill a dog, which was his slave, but he would not hate to kill a man more intelligent than he, more educated than he, who at some future and perfectly possible time might try to uphold the tables of the law when Ozark Pete wanted them broken. And could Susan not understand this possibility, and in the day to come would she stand beside the brute or would she choose the blood to which she was born? He did not know. A woman could not be counted upon when it came to love.

Somber thoughts upon a summer night!

"And why, pray, are you sitting in the dark?" Susan demanded in her velvet voice, so soft and deep and yet unrelenting.

"Thinking," he replied.

She did not ask what thoughts. Instead she went about turning on one light after another, until the large quiet room was blazing. Probably she did not care what he thought.

"I don't like to hurt you," Susan said sweetly in the midst of light. She sat down on the couch, leaned her elbow upon her hand and curled her feet under her. There in her apple green frock, short-sleeved and round at the neck, the full skirt billowing about her, she looked a child, a dreaded child, William thought, too well loved, too much indulged, too clever, too adorable.

Knowing through the experience of her years that she liked to arouse concern, he avoided this direct attack.

"By the way, I meant to ask, where did you bury the dog?" He acknowledged to himself the morbidity of the question, the desire to know once and for all that there was a definite end to the despicable creature.

"Pete took him out into the country," Susan said. "He threw him down the old marble quarry."

The old marble quarry was filled with water to an unknown depth. Long ago, in a generation past, it had been used as a swimming hole by the sons of farmers until a boy had drowned so deep that no dragging could bring his body to the surface. The quarry had then been forbidden.

"I am glad that the beast was not put into our ground somewhere," William said.

"That dog was too big to bury," Susan said indifferently. "Pete said it would have taken him half a day to dig the hole. Still, he was angry about it—a good dog spoiled."

"A savage beast," William said decisively.

Silence fell, light and tense, necessary to be broken quickly.

"What do you plan that will hurt us?" Elinor asked. She had come in while Susan was turning on the lights and had taken her usual chair. Now, contrary to habit, she was smoking a cigarette while she sipped her coffee.

"Perhaps we cannot be hurt," William said.

"Oh yes, you can," Susan declared, "but it can't be helped. I know you are disappointed in me, but I guess you understand that I am not going to finish college."

He had feared it. She had hinted as much at the seashore and when she came home he had noticed a finality in her behavior, a definite return, complete in intention. Neither he nor Elinor spoke. Susan tossed her short hair from her face and toyed with her ring.

"I shall marry Pete right away," she said.

"Oh, no," Elinor began, but Susan put up her hands.

"Mother, I don't want a wedding."

"Oh, Susan," Elinor cried.

"Pete would look silly—I know it. No, don't say a word, either of you. I know every word you would say. I know what you think of Pete. I can see him with your eyes every time you look at him. That's why I sent him away today. I want to wrestle with you alone. I know how you feel about him, I tell you."

The dark eyebrows leveled in a furious frown above her brown eyes.

"And you don't care?" Elinor asked.

"I do care," Susan said. "But I shan't let it change me toward Pete. I shall marry him."

"When?" William asked with dry lips.

"Any day, the first day we can," Susan said.

Silence fell again, and this, William thought, was the end of their children! For this, one built a house and made it home; for this, one worked and denied pleasure, waked in the night—he remembered how the child Susan grew thirsty always in the early hours after midnight, when he was in his first deep sleep. Night after night he had got up out of bed, groaning, to fetch the cupful of water, taking a small share of responsibility that Elinor might be spared, and yet it was not small for he was of the tense mind that once waked could not easily sleep again so that the brief service drained away from him an hour or more of rest. Year after year it went on, and a cup of water set at her bedside did not answer the purpose. She needed to make sure of his readiness and his presence. It was more than a cup of water.

"Tell me why you love Peter?" he asked in a coaxing voice. "If I could understand that, I might find it easier to have you leave us. For you are leaving us in a very total sense when you marry him."

He caught a hauntingly childish terror in Susan's eyes as he spoke these words.

"Oh, no," Elinor said quickly, "she can always come back. Marriage needn't be permanent nowadays. People get divorces."

He was amazed at this speech. Elinor had always been merciless toward divorce, always, she said, the woman's fault. She refused to believe that any man could not be held, as women put it, if the wife tried.

"I shall never divorce Pete," Susan said. "No matter what he does, it's permanent."

"Tell me why you love him," William repeated.

The question embarrassed Susan strangely and she did not reply. She bit her red lower lip, she examined her nails.

"He is not at all the sort of young man we had imagined you would choose," William went on. "I don't mind so much your leaving college unfinished. I realize that time is shortened these days for the young. With another war threatening it is quite natural, perhaps. But Peter is foreign to us, and so in a measure he must be to you, or so we imagine."

He kept his voice calm, his manner judicial and as far as possible unprejudiced.

"After all, we know you better than you think," he went on again, to give her plenty of time. "I don't believe in the Oriental fashion of choosing the persons whom one's children marry, and yet one does get to know one's child."

She said in a small choked voice, "You get to know me in a way—maybe you do. You know I don't like liver and onions, you know my favorite color is green, that I like to play tennis and don't like mathematics—that sort of thing. But you don't know what I am thinking—and feeling."

Her voice failed and she swallowed hard against tears.

"There are things we cannot know unless you tell us," he agreed gravely. He longed to reach out his hand to her, draw her to his knee as he used to do when she was a child, to stop her tears. But she was a woman now. Another man might do that but not he.

And Elinor sat silent, lighting one cigarette from another. Did she understand, ought not she to understand? He cast her a reproachful look which she caught and rejected. Manage this your own way, her eyes said. Well, he would. Susan could not be entirely remote from the child he had known and loved. She had not been too complex. She had been a direct child, ready of temper, quick with affection, not nearly so complex for that matter, as Edwin. She had never had his dark silences. It was only since Pete had come that she was changed.

"Where did you meet Peter?" he inquired and was shocked to realize that he had never asked the question before.

"At a dance, a blind date—"

It could happen, he reflected, as she went on with her story, in such times as these when all classes were churned together by war. Pete had come back from the Pacific, and before he went home he had stopped to see a friend, a buddy, in Poughkeepsie, a town boy whom Susan had met through her roommate, a nice boy who was going to Yale. Pete had fought beside him upon a distant island and he had once saved Pete's life.

Susan laughed now in the middle of the story. "It ought to have been the other way around. Pete is so huge, and Eliot is so small and—oh, exactly so! His father is the Episcopal minister but he's not the least like most minister's sons, although I guess he is going to be a preacher, at that. Anyway, Pete was barging up one of those hills on Okinawa, all ready to make a hero of himself when Eliot, who was scared to death—says so himself—was sneaking up behind, sheltering behind Pete, really, holding his rifle ready to shoot at anything he saw, and of course he saw the enemy first and potted him."

Her voice was suddenly normal and her eyes dried. "Pete will never forget that. Eliot comes half way to his shoulder and Pete can swing him off the ground with one arm."

She was amused.

"But you don't care for Eliot," Elinor said quietly.

Susan put back her hair with both hands, restlessly. "Oh, who could? He's such a shrimp. Pete's strong—if you could have seen the way he caught that dog! It was like fighting a bear. He clenched his fist around its jaws and bent its head back until I could hear the bones crack."

"Susan!" Elinor cried, shuddering.

Susan looked at her mother with strange eyes. "That makes you sick, doesn't it, Mother? It doesn't make me sick, though. That's the difference between your generation and mine. It's what makes me have to love someone like Pete. With him I let go, don't have to care how I talk or what I do. What you two can't seem to realize is that everything has changed. The world isn't what you thought it was—or what you told me it was. It's another world and nothing can stop that, and it's I who have to live in the world. Pete knows what I mean. He says it's only toughness that counts now and being able to fight for yourself. He's right. All the old soft stuff is gone."

"Yet Eliot—" William hinted.

"That was only an accident," Susan said quickly. "It doesn't change anything. Eliot says himself that he didn't plan it, he was scared to death. He says now he doesn't know how he did it, and he wasn't even thinking of Pete."

She leaped to her feet and walked about the room, swinging her wide green skirts. "It's such a rest to me to be with Pete. He doesn't care about anything—manners or small talk or any of the pretty-pretty stuff."

"He doesn't even care about being clean," Elinor remarked with caustic.

Susan turned on her. "No, he doesn't! It's not important to him. He likes dirt. I know what he means, too. When you've been bathed every day of your life and shampooed and scrubbed and made to wipe your feet when you come in and put on overshoes when you go out, dirt is wonderful! I tramped into his house with as much mud as I liked. If I wanted to bathe, I took a bath, if I didn't nobody cared. I could eat any way I liked, anywhere I liked, anything I liked, I could talk or not talk, swear if I wanted to—that's Pete's way and I like it."

"You have never really told us about Peter's home," Elinor said.

Susan looked at them, one and then the other, doubting, as William could see, whether she could trust them enough.

"Tell us," he urged, but gently.

She took the step against doubt and earnestly they tried to follow. "It's a shack of a house, you would say," she began, "but there are plenty of rooms, they kept building as the children came."

A wooden house lost in a forest of trees, two miles away from the highway and Pete's garage, a rough hillside farm, crops scraped from the earth by antiquated machinery, so that the children had little enough to eat and yet somehow on the energetic air and the pure water they grew tall and strong, though without a pound of flesh to spare, six boys and two girls. But Peter was the youngest of them all, so that the dilapidated house was empty when she went there, except for the father, the mother, and one of the sisters whose husband had been killed somewhere in Burma, which they thought was the name of a town, and the sister's children, three of them, all boys.

The house was one story, a string of rooms, the main one in the middle, the living room, dining room and kitchen all together, a long, ramshackle room full of broken down furniture that was worn to the shape of big lank bodies, the sinking chairs comfortable with quilts and milkweed cushions. There was no yard, a small vegetable garden came up by the house on one side and the fields on the other, and chickens and several grey geese ran over the warped wooden porch floor.

At first Susan had thought the house filthy, but as she stayed she discovered that it was clean in its fashion, without paint, the mattresses on the beds of fresh corn husks, or, since she had the spare room, of feathers. There were no books except the family Bible and a few comics, nobody thought of reading, there was no music except that which Pete made upon his guitar when he felt moved, and a bath was to be had in the brook a quarter of a mile away or in a wash tub in the woodshed. Old Mr. Dobbs talked of electricity but none of his family believed he meant it or cared whether he did. Mrs. Dobbs cooked on an old iron stove and washed the clothes outdoors with water heated in an iron pot over burning logs.

And yet, Susan said, she had liked it. It was peaceful there, the trees tall and silent, the mountain water clear, and no need to talk unless one felt like it. Pete's sister, Maryanne, was sad, but she went on living, dealing with her children swiftly and cleanly. She loved them heartily, and could be angry with them as heartily. There were no barriers between any of them. You always knew where you were with each one of them, and they were all strong and lean and healthy. Learning was not necessary, life was simple and easily lived. They admired her when she cut wild flowers and put them in a pitcher, even though none of them thought of doing it. In the evenings they sat together on the porch, not talking or else talking, if they wished. Nobody cared.

And what she could not tell her parents here in the east parlor was that in that mountain setting love itself grew deep because there was nothing else. To love or hate, to wake or sleep, to live or die, these were the simple alternatives and one made one's choice. The complications of civilization were as though they had never been.

"My generation is tired of civilization," Susan said at last in a voice strangely old. "We can't understand why we must do all the things we are told to do, even to die for something that is beyond our comprehension. We are tired of being pushed around. Well, up there in the mountains, I won't be pushed around. I'll just live, and with Pete."

They listened to her in utter stillness, amazed, wounded, confounded. Elinor put down her cigarette, her hand trembling.

"It isn't even back to the gutter," she said in a stifled voice, "it's choosing the gutter you've never known. It's rejecting a civilization. You aren't even modern enough to understand. But why, but why—"

She was not asking a question, she was crying out the mystery she could not comprehend.

William went to her side and took the trembling hand. "Don't grieve, my darling."

Susan whirled upon them, her eyes flaming. "Oh, you two, what do you know? Only something that is dead and gone. I'll be safe with Pete, do you understand? Whatever happens, he'll keep me safe. He's tough, he's strong, he isn't afraid of anybody. He's got fists and he's ready to fight."

"Oh, my God," William whispered. "Is life as simple as that?"

He turned away and unable to resist an escape he went on into his library and closed the door. There he sat down and put his head in his hands. His daughter's words had made the tomb of all in which he had believed. To have fists, to be ready to fight, to hurl one's self up a hill against an enemy, any enemy, the folly of such simplicity crushed his heart. And so where was intelligence fled, and who had killed in this generation the daring of the spirit, the courage of the mind? Would there ever again be the resurrection of human truth? Wherein had he failed as a man, and Elinor as a woman that their child, their treasure, could so choose to hide herself in animal retreat? Susan was as foolish as Jessica, her dreams as vain, her faith as surely to be lost.

He got up and began the long pacing across the floor which marked the thinking process in his most abstruse cases of the law. The child's reason was still there. Confused in her emotions, entangled by the subconscious fears of this generation at the endless prospect of wars ahead, a fear which now concerned women as much as men, women whose whole foundation must be in love and home, Susan still possessed her sane mind. If he could separate her for a time, even a brief time, from Pete, if they could all go away for a holiday somewhere, she and Elinor with him, go perhaps to England, where he had been told the young were steadier, older in the age of the nation than they were here, then she might yet be saved. She was too childish to choose now the course of her events. He made up his mind swiftly. He had business always waiting in England, he would make it imperative and insist that they leave at once, immediately, tomorrow if need be. And if she refused to go, he would compel her. His long dark face set itself in grim lines, the look that criminals had learned to dread, and he opened the door abruptly and faced his beloved foe.

"We are going to England," he announced. He stood there, dangling his pince-nez in his right hand. "I shall telephone for reservations on the *Queen Mary*. The sea voyage will clear our minds and give us time. We'll go to England and see whether the young men and women there are thinking in terms of fists and fights."

He looked from one surprised face to the other. "I don't ask for agreement. I shall demand obedience. We need perspective, all of us. I need perspective on you, Susan, for at present you appear a fool. The world is not so hopeless as you think. You have somehow happened upon a low level but there are others. Not all young men are Ozark Petes, thank God. Your brothers are proof."

Susan drew up the corner of her full mouth in a sneer. "Those two?" she muttered. "Do you call Winsten a man? He's a papa, just a papa—"

"Hush," Elinor said in a violent whisper. "Here he comes." It was indeed Winsten, returning from the hospital. He stood in the doorway, looking a little haggard, smiling at them with wan lips.

"The children have been good?" he inquired. He had put them to bed early, before he went.

"I haven't heard a word from them," Elinor replied. "Have you had dinner?"

"I dined in Manchester," Winsten said. He came in and sat down and lit a cigarette.

"How is Madge?" Elinor inquired. Someone had to ask the necessary questions. William stood where he had stopped, and Susan was pouting.

"She is in excellent shape. The doctor says we may go home at the end of the week." Winsten said gratefully. "They are getting her on her feet tomorrow. Seems strange, but everything is strange nowadays. We are all doing things we thought were wrong yesterday."

He smiled his wan smile again, caught a triumphant look upon Susan's face, turned to William.

"Have I interrupted something?"

Susan got up decidedly. "Nothing! I am going to bed. That's all. Just that and nothing more, my friends!"

She caught her circular skirt in her hands and danced out of the room on noiseless feet, and William watching her understood perfectly that she had no intention of obedience. He stiffened himself, his back straightened and he felt the angry blood rush dangerously through his veins. This was the sort of thing that brought blood pressure to the danger point, the technique of the young for hastening the death of the old. He forced himself to relax, breathing deeply, not heeding the hospital conversation going on between Winsten and his mother.

"Don't you feel well, William?" Elinor asked after a moment or two.

"Yes, yes," he answered impatiently. "Don't mind me. What were you saying, Winsten?"

"That it is fortunate I was born just when I was," Winsten said earnestly. "I escaped the last war and I'll be too old for the next one."

William got to his feet. "It's been an exhausting day, I think I do feel tired." He hesitated, remembering suddenly that now he would be leaving Winsten alone with Elinor, and Winsten with his usual sense of duty might feel it necessary, if his mother expressed anxiety, to repeat the absurd stuff that Jessica had said about him to Madge. Then he felt weariness creep over him like a pall.

"Good night," he said abruptly, and bending he kissed Elinor's cheek and felt her hand reach up to his face. Enough was enough, he thought, climbing the stairs, and today more than enough. It was a wonder he had strength to earn their bread.

Some time in the night, in the deep night when he was so sunk in sleep that Elinor's hand upon his face, smoothing his cheek, seemed only a dream left over from their earlier parting, he was impelled to waken. He heard her voice summoning him from afar.

"William, wake up, darling—William—William—"

"What—" he muttered, staggering upward out of the abyss.

She sat down on his bed, her silvery braids hanging over her bare shoulders. "William, are you awake?"

"Yes—yes—"

"No, you're not, poor thing. Oh, William, try!"

He hauled his consciousness out of the dark, hand over hand, opened his eyes wide by force and stared at her painfully.

"What's wrong?"

"I nearly didn't wake you," she whispered, "then I thought I must. I can't take the responsibility alone."

"Eh?" he demanded.

"Hush," she whispered. "Come to the window, William. Not a sound, mind you—"

He got out of bed and she seized his hand and they stole to the window and she parted the curtains.

"Look!" she whispered.

The light of the moon shone down upon the lawn in a pale mist. There in the driveway he saw a car, Pete's car. The young man was waiting motionless beside it.

"There is a light in Susan's room," Elinor said. "I have heard her moving about for the last half hour. I heard her go up and I knew exactly what was happening. I knew that Pete's car would pull into the driveway just like that. It is four o'clock."

He started impetuously for the door but she clung to him. "Wait—wait! It was such a beautiful idea that we go to England. But it is no use, don't you see? England can't do anything for her, William, nor for Pete. For us, maybe, yes indeed, but nobody can do anything for them, William, don't you see?"

"You aren't going to let her ruin her life!" he whispered hoarsely.

She put her arms about his neck. "We must let her go, William. We must just let her go and maybe then some day she will come back. If we try to stop her she will die before she'll come back."

He was too perplexed to refute what she was saying. What indeed if she were right?

She drew him gently back to the open window and they stood, waiting, and there hand in hand, their hearts beating with the sorrow that only the aging know, they watched the old, old play unfold itself, as it had for thousands of years. The front door opened softly and Susan came out, lugging two bags. Pete took them and put them in the back of the car, they moved noiselessly together, shadowy figures in the mist, they embraced and clung for one long instant, then they climbed into the car and slowly the car crept over the gravel of the drive and passing through the gate faded away into the night.

He became aware then of Elinor's trembling. She was weeping! He took her into his arms, pressing her close. When had she wept before? Not for years! He was frightened, and he hated Susan. Let her go—let them all go, so long as he held the beloved woman, who alone was his.

"I don't know why we ever had children," he muttered fiercely, his own throat constricted.

He felt her strangling her tears, choking back her sobs, struggling against breakdown. "Oh, cry," he begged. "What does it matter with me? Do cry, my darling!"

She shook her head and pulled away from him slightly. "I don't want—to—to cry. It's too devastating—now—at my age."

"Nonsense!"

"No, I know." She wiped her eye on her ruffled sleeve and swallowed once or twice. "I wonder—" she said after a moment.

"What do you wonder?" he asked, all tenderness.

She shook her head again and bit her lips and went on.

"I wonder if we'll ever be able to tell them that we watched them go—and let them!"

He smiled a bitter smile. "It would break their hearts. What, not oppose them? It would spoil all the heroics."

She laughed trembling heartbroken laughter. "I suppose you're right. We'll never tell them." And turning to him suddenly she threw herself into his arms and hid her face against his neck and cried desperately.

IT WAS becoming clear, William told himself, that Herbert was not what he had been. Usually he enjoyed the long ride to New York, especially in the spring when the dogwoods spread through the woods a foam of white. Now, however, the ride was more often than not an ordeal. Herbert, once so stolid and calm a driver, was becoming erratic and reckless. William, complaining yesterday to Elinor, had blamed the parkways.

"Once Herbert gets on the parkway," he grumbled, "he seems to think he can pass every car in sight. Fifty miles doesn't satisfy him. His rate is sixty, if he thinks I am asleep he gets as high as eighty. We've been stopped half a dozen times in the last year."

"It's not the parkways," Elinor said. "It is Jessica. He had me call the doctor at the asylum last week and ask if Jessica wasn't well enough to come home for good, so they can bring the baby home before she gets any older. She's almost three years old now, and she doesn't remember any home but the orphanage. It does seem a shame."

William was reluctant to talk about Jessica, although during the years that she had been put away, there had been talk, of course. He considered her dangerous, remembering what she had said to Madge, and though he had heard no more of it, Winsten and Madge seeming the same when they came home for brief visits, now no more at Christmas since the fourth child, a boy, had arrived. Still, they met once or twice a year, and he continued to feel an unconquerable reserve toward both Winsten and Madge, even when nothing was said about Jessica. If she were mentioned Madge showed only a mild interest, her children absorbing her entire attention and continuing as the sole theme of her conversation. He did notice, William told himself, that she was no longer so insistent upon the children bestowing upon him kisses of dutiful affection.

"What did the doctor say about Jessica?" William had inquired.

"He says that Jessica may try it for a while at home, if she wishes to do so."

"Does she wish it?" he asked.

"That is what we don't know," Elinor had replied . . .

The car swerved dangerously around a curve and he cried out, "Herbert, slow down!"

Herbert slowed down to an aggravating crawl but William did not speak again. The crawl would last only a few minutes. He allowed himself to be absorbed in his papers and the speed crept up. When a sharp siren blew, William rejoiced to see a state policeman. Let the fellow deal with Herbert as he would! He sat back, folded his arms and put on his legal look. Herbert maintained his speed stubbornly for a few seconds and then pulled to the side of the road. The motorcycle roared and stopped at the window.

"Who do you think you are?" the policeman bellowed at Herbert, who presented only his profile. "Can't you read? Don't you see what the signs say? Goin' seventy miles an hour!"

Herbert refused to reply. The policeman motioned to William to lower the window. "Hey, you, whyn't you tell him to hold down his speed?"

"I have repeatedly done so," William said in a quiet voice.

"Whyn't you fire him?" the policeman demanded.

"He has been with us a number of years," William said.

The policeman snorted. "He'll lose his license a number of years if this goes on!"

William smiled. "I am afraid he deserves to do so."

The policeman was only slightly mollified. "Where you goin'?"

"I am due at the city hall at three o'clock," William said. "I am legal counsel in the case of The City of New York versus Marty Malone."

The policeman hesitated. "I oughtn't to let you get by with this."

"Perhaps I can get a ride with somebody and leave the car and my chauffeur with you," William suggested.

The policeman continued to hesitate. "No," he said finally. "I'll let you go this time." He leaned on the front window to attack Herbert again. "But you, fatface, if I ever catch you speedin' here again, and I'll catch you if you do, you'll lose your job sure. You won't have no license again for a good long time. Haven't I spoke to you before?"

"Maybe," Herbert said tightly. His small mouth disappeared between his cheeks.

"Maybe," the policemen mocked, "maybe for sure, I guess! Well, it's the last time. Now take it easy."

He waved them on, and William said nothing. It was possible that Herbert could be frightened.

Late at his office, he hurried to his desk and found a telephone call from Cousin Emma waiting for him. He was about to put it impatiently aside when he remembered her extreme age and fragility and his responsibility and so he ordered it put through. Across the city wires the trembling old voice reached his ears shrilly.

"William, is that you?"

"Yes, Cousin Emma, what can I do for you?" He glanced at his watch. At least she would not be long-winded. She was able to keep only one thing on her mind these days.

"William, I have had a letter from Jessica."

"What does she want?" he asked impatiently. Jessica was less than important at the moment.

"She wants to go home, William. She says she can't stand the horrid place. She wants to see her little baby. She says the baby ought to come home. She doesn't think they are treating the baby right. The baby doesn't even know who she is."

"I should think not," William said drily. "She has never taken care of it."

"Well, she wants to now," Cousin Emma said shrilly. "I think you ought to get her out of that horrid place."

"I believe Elinor has called up the doctor," he replied.

"What did you say, William?"

"Have you got your good ear to the receiver?" he demanded.

"It's no better than the other one now," Cousin Emma said.

"I say," he repeated in a clear low voice, "Elinor has talked with the doctor."

"That's good, is she coming home?"

"If she wants to," William said.

"Well, she wants to," Cousin Emma said.

"Then I suppose she is coming home," William said.

"That's good, I'll write and tell her."

"Better wait," William commanded.

"Didn't you say she could come home if she wants to?" Cousin Emma demanded. "Well, if she wants to do so I suppose she can, can't she?"

"Yes," William said in desperation, "yes, yes, all right, Cousin Emma. You write to her."

He was irritated with the nonsense, and he hung up the receiver forcibly and plunged into the papers on his desk.

Nevertheless his irritation was touched with enough alarm so that he remembered the conversation when he reached home two days later and repeated it to Elinor.

"Jessica is coming home," Elinor said. "Didn't Herbert tell you?"

"Herbert isn't speaking to me, I think," William said. "He was stopped by a state policeman on the way down and I didn't exactly defend him."

"Oh, well," Elinor said comfortably. "I hope when Jessica gets home and the child is brought back that they can resume some sort of normal living."

They were not prepared, however, for the arrival of Jessica, Herbert and the child on the next Sunday morning while Bertha was at church. Bertha had become recently religious and was fetched every Sunday morning by a neighbor with whom she went to a church whose denomination she had never been able to remember, but where she found comfort enough to enable her to live through the week without having to recount with tears how wicked Jessica was to her old mother and how nobody at the orphanage really cared for the baby. She and Herbert did not speak, but otherwise their relations went on as usual. She made pitiful attempts to engage his sympathy, but his stubborn determination prevailed in his steadfastly ignoring her.

William, walking about the lawn with Elinor after breakfast, saw Herbert's new second hand yellow convertible car come dashing up the road, and swerve into the driveway. He turned his head away, expecting to hear it crash against the heavy stone pillars of the entrance. This it escaped, however, and Herbert brought it to an abrupt stop in a swirl of gravel. Jessica, it seemed, did not mind speed. She got out of the car holding by the hand a small exquisite child in a ruffled pink organdy dress and Herbert descended, smiling and proud. Jessica herself looked actually beautiful, William saw with profound reluctance. He had a horrible chill of fear. What if she should renew her false pretensions of a relationship here and now? She came forward gracefully with her usual modest air.

"Good morning, Mr. Asher, and Mrs. Asher, too. I am so happy to see you again. It's so lovely to be home at last. I told Herbert this morning that we must come over the very first thing and thank you for everything. I know they wouldn't have let me come home unless you had both insisted."

The pretty voice was sweeter than ever, deepened with an edge of sadness. Jessica's face, too, was more delicate, more thoughtful, and her large blue eyes were remote and gentle.

"Good morning," William said stiffly. But Elinor saw only the child.

"What a beautiful little girl!" she said, and kneeling down upon the grass, she took the child's small plump hand. "What is your name, dear?"

"Monica," the child replied.

"Monica?" Elinor repeated.

"I have always liked that name, Mrs. Asher," Jessica said, "though I never knew anybody called it. It came out of a book. It was an English story, I remember."

"Come and sit on the terrace," Elinor said kindly. "I shall find a cookie for Monica."

Thus in a moment they were sitting in the terrace chairs, Herbert smiling and yearning, the sunshine glistening on his fat white face. Elinor disappeared and came back with a plate of cookies.

"Take a cookie," Jessica said almost sternly to Monica.

The child put out her hand and took one carefully by the edge, and stood holding it between her thumb and forefinger.

William remained silent, wishing that he could escape. He had no small talk for such an occasion. It was impossible to forget the repulsive scenes of the past, and yet it was incredible that they had left no mark upon Jessica except the slight pensiveness which only increased her grace.

"I hope you are home to stay," Elinor said cordially.

"Oh, yes," Jessica said with eagerness. "The house seems so nice. Herbert has tried to keep it clean. I do want the downstairs papered, a satin stripe, I think, something like you have, Mrs. Asher, in the parlors. And I think I shall have the sofas covered in velvet, a pale green, perhaps—what do you think?"

"It sounds very nice," Elinor said with reserve.

"Of course, if I had not been ill, we would have had the new house built by now," Jessica went on, hurrying a trifle more than she had used to do when she talked, with a slight blurring of the sharp consonants, and certainly her eyes were not steady. They darted here and there, restlessly, and suddenly she rose.

"Do you mind if I look over the dear old house, Mrs. Asher?"

"Not at all," Elinor said.

The child started to follow her but she said sharply, "No, no, Monica, you mustn't come—"

"She may if she likes," Elinor said.

"No," Jessica cried almost passionately.

"Here, baby, stay with Daddy," Herbert said. The child, an obedient little thing, orphanage-trained, went and sat on his lap, but she did not taste the cookie she still held patiently in her right hand, careful not to soil her dress.

Herbert's eyes brimmed with tears. "I don't know how to say what I have to say, Mr. and Mrs. Asher," he began. The tears spilled and rolled down his cheeks.

"Is something still wrong?" Elinor asked to help him.

"It's my job," Herbert said. "I ought to stay at home. I oughtn't to be way off, maybe on the road goin' to New York, and leavin' her alone at night. I believe that's what set her off before, bein' alone at night, it was always late before I got home, and maybe not gettin' home at all some nights. A chauffeur's life is not his own, so to speak."

"Such a pity she won't have Bertha with her," Elinor observed.

Herbert wiped his face all over with a clean handkerchief and his voice hardened. "I see exactly how she feels about the old woman. Jessica is refined and Bertha is as common as they make 'em. An old German peasant, is what Jessica calls her."

"Do you know what a peasant is, Herbert?" William asked.

Herbert hesitated.

"Never mind," William said. "Only they aren't hateful, as a rule."

"Whatever Jessica feels for the old woman it can't be mended now," Herbert said obstinately. "She can't forget."

"Do you know, Herbert," Elinor said suddenly, "I don't believe that Bertha ever hurt Jessica one bit. Bertha has been with us for forty years and she has never hurt anybody. I have known her all my life and we used to tease her terribly when we were children and she never even got cross. She just used to laugh. She laughed a great deal in those days. Poor soul, she scarcely laughs at all now."

"She hurt Jessica," Herbert said stubbornly.

They did not argue. Elinor spoke to the child persuading her to taste her cookie and William sat silently smoking. Jessica came back after a few minutes, her eyes bemused. "It's all the same," she said softly, "just as I remembered it."

She looked strangely at Herbert. "I wish you'd go in the kitchen a bit. I want to talk privately to Mr. and Mrs. Asher."

Herbert got up, bewildered, letting the child slide to her feet. "What you got to say that's private?"

"Go on—go on!" she cried in quick passion, and stamped her foot.

He went away then humbly, pathetically so, William thought. Well, Herbert had tried beating her and now he was going to try love. It was quite obvious but, he feared, equally hopeless. Was Jessica really well? He watched her intense pretty face. She had seated herself and now she drew her chair close to Elinor.

"Dear Mrs. Asher, you both understand, but perhaps you will understand best. Is there any way that I can get out?"

"Get out?" Elinor repeated.

"Away, away," Jessica said with soft impatience. "It's terrible to live in such a deserted place as the farm. What is the use, Mrs. Asher? The work is all to be done over again every day. I cannot get to a theater, nor even to a movie. If we lived in a town at least I could walk up and down the streets and look in the shop windows. But there is nothing to look at where we live."

"Why don't you ask Herbert to take you into a town?" William asked. This was all ridiculous, the idea of having to spend a Sunday morning upon Jessica!

"He says an apartment of the sort I want costs too much. He says I would be dissatisfied, we couldn't have all our furniture."

"It is your mother's house, I believe?" William said. "That means you pay no rent."

She gave him a strange, cold look, as though she had not understood what he said.

"Jessica," Elinor said kindly, "if you could do exactly what you like best, what would you do?"

The pretty face, so delicately sad, flushed a pale rose. Jessica clasped her hands. "Oh, I would learn painting—it is what I have always wanted, to be an artist."

Elinor considered. She turned to William. "I don't believe that I ever told you Jessica does rather nice water colors. She used to paint her own Christmas cards."

"It has done me no good," Jessica said sadly.

He could see that Elinor was moved but he could not at all believe in Jessica. "If you really want to learn about painting," he said gruffly, "some of the finest artists in the country come to Manchester for the summer. I can easily get you lessons and perhaps for nothing. Why not?"

Her blue eyes flickered away from his face. "It's so hopeless, living where we do."

William was suddenly angry. "Look here, Jessica, stop talking like that. You live in a countryside where plenty of rich people pay money to live. Don't blame the place."

He feared for a moment that he had said too much. Jessica's face lit with anger, she trembled, but only for an instant, and then it was over. She restrained whatever impulse she felt, and her head drooped. "Thank you, Mr. Asher. I believe we ought to be going. I'll just call Herbert."

She disappeared between the open French windows, her slender figure so light that she made not the least noise, and they waited. The lovely child stood looking at them thoughtfully, not afraid, and yet not friendly, a child who had lived among strangers all its life.

The minutes passed. "What can they be doing?" Elinor inquired. But she did not go in to see, and after perhaps five or six minutes Herbert and Jessica came out again.

"Goodbye, Mr. Asher and Mrs. Asher," Jessica said formally. "It has been pleasant to see you. Do come and see us when you can."

"Thank you," Elinor said, bewildered.

"Come, Monica," Jessica said.

Herbert hesitated, and looked as if he must speak. He glanced at Jessica, walking toward the car. Then he leaned toward William. "She says, don't think you can make her take lessons. I don't know what she means but that's what she says."

William was suddenly outraged. "My God, it was her idea, not mine!"

Herbert looked unbelieving. "She says, sir, don't think you can make her do it, that's all."

He stalked away and climbed into the car and they whirled off.

"Did you ever hear of such impudence?" William demanded, glancing at the cloud of dust.

Elinor shook her head. "Let's forget them. They are both incomprehensible. I am glad that Herbert is leaving. Let's not ever see either of them again. The poor little child!"

She stretched herself upon a long chair and turning her face to the sun she closed her eyes. William, gazing upon her gradually relaxing face, felt the impulse to do the same. She had summed up his own conclusions about the human race, wherever one found its peculiar members. They were incomprehensible, in these times, at least. Only history made them seem plain, the classes separate and orderly. Now blessed be the sun shining down upon him and upon Elinor as they accepted what they could not understand.

BERTHA walked stolidly up the gravel walk and they heard her foot-steps and opened their eyes. She was hot and red, and under her toque of crumpled violets which was her Sunday hat they saw at once that something had happened. She paused at the step.

"Jessica and Herbert komm they here?" she demanded.

"They did, Bertha," Elinor said pleasantly. "They brought the little girl."

"I thout it wass so," Bertha muttered. "I did—I did, andt she dondt shpeak to me! She just sees me go by."

She went on around the house and they lay down again and closed their eyes to the sun, determined to forget.

"Amazing," William said, without opening his eyes. "Why do we have to have them? We pay them to do the work and they torture us."

"We are too easily tortured," Elinor said, without opening her eyes. "We ought to be ruthless."

They could not be ruthless, and that was the trouble. They remained human, and upon their tender human feelings, which could not believe that any creature born was purposely cruel or unjust, these ignorant ones trod, not knowing how they wounded nor caring. In a microcosm here was the world within the walls of his own house. They wished to live their pleasant lives, kindly to the suffering but not entangled. It was no longer possible. William felt an outraged anger sweep through his soul and run like heat through his body. He got up with an energy sudden and intense, and Elinor opened her eyes.

"What now?"

"I am going to fire Bertha," he said in deliberate calm.

"Oh no," Elinor cried, "we mustn't—after forty years, William?"

"It should have been done long ago," he declared. "They've clung to the family like leeches, sucking the spirit out of us, feeding on our sympathy, justifying themselves by their impudence. I'll cook the meals."

"Don't be silly," Elinor said.

"I'd rather be silly than go on with this sort of thing."

She watched him in an awe of horror. She was a Winsten, that he could understand, and she had grown up under Bertha. Bertha had her big red hands on every part of the house, it was only Bertha who knew how many linen sheets there were, how many silver spoons, which were the heirlooms and which the wedding presents. Bertha who was supposed to be only the cook was actually the manager, the tyrant, the usurper, and in addition she fed upon their minds and souls, she took their precious time to listen to her woes, she clouded their happiness and destroyed their peace, and they had not had the courage to send her away, because they had been trained in kindness to those weaker than themselves. Well, he was going to put an end to it. It was absurd of course to say that he would do the cooking but there must be other cooks, and he would send them away one after the other instantly if they came out of the kitchen.

He stalked into that room and found Bertha tying a large white apron about her thick waist. Her full purple lips were quivering and the tears were running down her cheeks. She wiped them away with the edge of her apron.

"You vant somedings, Mr. Asher?"

"Yes, Bertha. I want you to go home." He said this in a mild voice that she took as kindness, his wish that she take a day off.

"I haf no home," she wailed, her face wrinkled like an old baby's and the tears welled again.

"Then find a home for old women and go to it," William said in the same steadfast and dreadful voice.

Bertha stopped crying suddenly, her jaw hanging. "You dondt mean you fire me, Mr. Asher!"

"I do," he said. "I mean it exactly."

Her tears dried in the instant. She snatched at the strings of her apron.

"I go, I go now!" she shouted in a high shrill scream.

"No," William said. "I'll drive you to Manchester."

"No, indeed no, you think I drive mit you? No, I von't. I call a taxi, I dondt rite in your *verdammt* car!" She was suddenly beside herself with rage. She clenched her fists and shook them in his face. He had expected a change but this was monstrous. Nevertheless he remained calm, watching her with curiosity. This was what she really was. Perhaps she *had* beaten Jessica. He could believe it now.

"You," she screamed, "you should neffer think you are a family here! You are nottings—a—a—" She spat upon the floor she had scrubbed so many thousands of times. "You a shentlemans! Ha—ha! I tell efferybody how you are. Efferybody will know you different."

"Nobody will believe you," William said inexorably. "Get your things together, Bertha."

"After forty years, you turn me out so," she moaned, collapsing on the wooden chair. "Heinrich allways toldt me, he sayss ofer and ofer, 'Dey turn you oudt, Bertha, ten, tventy, tirty, forty years, any day, dey turn you oudt.'" She snapped her fingers.

"Either you must get out or we must get out," William said gravely. "Since it is our house I suppose we will stay. You will get proper pay."

"Pay," Bertha screamed, "Who pays me back for years I scrub und vash und cook? Going to bed tired effery night?"

"We have paid," William said. "You have been paid in money and in time. You have had a home here and three meals and more a day. You have made your living easily among kind people."

She listened without comprehension. "I go," she said, sobbing. "I go now."

She climbed the stairs to her room above and he heard her moving about. His heart was beating with remorse and sympathy and good impulse and pain. But keep her here he would not. The house must be swept clean of them all. There must be no more Jessica, no more Herbert, no more Bertha, no more even of the piteous Monica. He could bear no more. He must get up in the morning knowing that he would see no stupid face, hear no sullen voice. They would buy machines, many more machines, and when the machines had done the work they would put the machines into the closet and close the door and live in the clean and quiet house where there were no human beings except themselves. The evil and parasitic life of servants would be cleared away, and they would be free forever of voices in the house. He telephoned for a taxi and then sat down on the high kitchen stool, while Bertha pounded to and fro above his head sobbing loudly and crying out to God in heaven, and he waited. Old family servants! They were no part of civilization here. The poison or the health of democracy, put it as one liked, had crept into them all, and they rebelled against themselves while they served others more intelligent than themselves. They could not recognize the truth, that they were doomed by their own stupidity and by that alone, never to rise above the level of their birth. He felt that he was on the verge of discovering things important, though perhaps it was nothing more than the right of those like himself also to be free. The incubus of the stupid and the weak could become a tyranny as intolerable as any others, and should it not, like every other tyranny, be overthrown?

Before he could clarify this discovery Bertha came stumping downstairs with two suitcases and a huge bundle tied in a sheet.

He rose. "Your taxi will soon be here," he said with the same inexorable kindness. "I shall go and write a check that will do you for a couple of months. Within that time I shall compute carefully exactly what you should have as a pension. That money will be sent you every month on the first and the fifteenth, as soon as you send me your address. It will support you amply and in comfort at any old-aged home of middle range."

She made no reply, she sniffed back her tears and again he had to struggle with his impulse to relent. No, he would not relent. To do so would be to make freedom impossible. He walked from the room with dignity and went to the library and there wrote a check for five hundred dollars and blotted it carefully. Then he went back to the kitchen and put it on the table. "The taxi will soon be here. If you wish, please do come and speak to Mrs. Asher. She feels very sorry about this, but we have taken as much as we can."

"You take?" Bertha repeated in a sudden bellow. "It is me—me—" she beat her breast and burst again into angry sobs.

"I am sorry," he said gently. "I don't expect you ever to understand."

He withdrew then silently and went back to the terrace. Elinor was not there. He went indoors and called but there was no answer. He went upstairs to her room and tried to open the door. It was locked.

"Elinor!" he called.

She opened the door at once and looked at him with a queer abasement. "I suddenly felt afraid of Bertha. Isn't that absurd? But when you left me I realized instantly that I've always been afraid of her."

"She has never ill-treated you," he remonstrated.

"No, never, she wouldn't have dared. But though I defended her to Jessica, still I remember I used to feel when I was quite small that she would like to have smacked me, often. I wonder if she didn't smack the older ones? I never heard it said. My mother was very strict with the servants, and then of course when I was married, Bertha was afraid of you."

"Was she, indeed?" he murmured. He stood by the window watching for the taxi.

"Oh, yes," Elinor said, listening. She had locked the door again. "She told me once that you were 'the knowing sort.'"

"Meaning?"

"That you saw more than you told, I suppose. She's afraid of lawyers, anyway."

"Here is the taxi," he said.

She came to his side and they stood there. Bertha was waiting. She came around the side of the house lugging the suitcases, and sent the man for the bundle. They saw her climb into the cab, and then it whirled around the drive and out the gate.

"She did not once look back," Elinor said, half sadly. "The forty years mean nothing to her, I believe. Or perhaps they mean too much. Oh, William, how had you the courage?" They sank on the chaise longue side by side.

"I don't know. It does take courage to violate one's impulse toward kindness. But I was just angry enough. If one can catch the moment, always lasting only a few seconds in people like us, when indignant anger outweighs the habit of careful goodness, one has courage enough for anything. If I had waited five minutes until kindness undid me, I could not have simply ordered her off as I knew I must."

"Poor Bertha," Elinor said.

He refused to allow her to be sad. "Not poor Bertha at all. She has had a good job and a comfortable home for decades, and she will get a pension for the rest of her life. Lucky Bertha!"

Elinor shook her head, not disagreeing, however, he could tell by the softness and even admiration in her eyes as she gazed at him.

"My darling," he said, much moved, for how long had it been since she had so gazed at him? "This is a great day. Put on your hat and we will go out to dinner. A celebration, my love, is in order."

He was charmed with her swift obedience. She waved him away, signifying that a hat was far from enough, that she must change and look her best, and he went into his own room and examined his appearance in the mirror and decided upon a change for himself. He took down from its hanger his best grey suit and clothed himself in it, and chose a blue foulard tie. He saw with modest pride that he was growing handsomer with the years, his grey hair becoming his dark skin and there was no trace of baldness. His father had had a thatch of snow white hair, but he had worn a beard and Elinor did not like beards, a clipped moustache, very close, but no more. Had his upper lip been a trifle shorter, Elinor had once declared, she would have demanded that he shave it.

He presented himself at her door and admired the trimness of her blue suit. "A handsome couple, eh?" he suggested.

She smiled a ravishing youthful smile, indicative, he felt, of her inner rejoicing. Ah, they were going to be happier! He should have rid the house years ago. Might he not have changed the whole course of life had he done so? The cloud would not have come between Edwin and Vera; Winsten, his elder son, would not have looked at him with the hidden doubt so often now in his eyes, kept alive, William felt sure, by the unforgetting silence of Madge. And Susan, ah, Susan might never have married Peter! He was convinced after long pondering in the magnifying small hours of many nights, that Susan had not made up her mind quickly, that it had taken the brutal terrifying moment when the black dog sprang at Pete, to shock her into deciding for him, a perverse atavistic admiration to which modern girls were increasingly prone as the traditional shelter fell. It did not bear thinking of, not now, at any rate. He would take it out again and again in the night when the darkness hid him and ponder upon the monstrous damage that had been done to his family. Then, too, he must reflect upon whether the damage could be mended, and how, their lives changed, they could be restored.

"Where shall we dine?" Elinor was asking.

"Let us set forth and find a place we never saw before," he said. "Let's be made all new, in honor of fair freedom."

Arm in arm they fell into step and marched smartly down the stairs.

SIX WEEKS later on a rainy morning in court he was approached by a clerk who broke in upon his presentation of the witness Arturo Romano, a bookie.

"Excuse me, sir," the clerk whispered. "There is an urgent call for you."

William waved him away with his black-ribboned pince-nez. "I cannot be interrupted."

"Excuse me but somebody's dead—a member of your family, sir," the clerk said.

A member of his family? William appealed to the judge for a brief recess, simply repeating what the man had said, for what else was there to say, and striding through the astonished and staring crowd, he reached a telephone in the adjoining room.

"Mr. Asher—that you?"

He could not recognize the hoarse voice, nor even if it were a woman's voice or a man's.

"Yes, it is," he replied.

"It's me—Bertha."

"Where are you?" he demanded. "What happened?"

"Mr. Asher, sir, Miss Emma—*todt!*"

"I am coming at once."

Cousin Emma! He flung himself from the room, staying only to tell the clerk to report that he would come back when he could. He caught a cab and ordered the man uptown to the apartment.

Cousin Emma had had a bad heart. She was very old, close actually to ninety she must have been. Still nothing excused him for not having been near her for weeks. Elinor had visited her last, actually, and Edwin had talked of going but probably had not. Perhaps Vera was the one who had gone most often to visit her, since she and Edwin had moved into the city to live, so that he need not commute to the office. Edwin was still in the office, delaying his years at the law school, uncertain, it seemed, as to what he wanted to do.

But why was Bertha the one to call him, William asked himself, unless indeed Cousin Emma, with her unfailing kindness, had taken Bertha in? He paid off the taxi and went into the house. Nobody knew, apparently, the doorman was calm, the elevator man was indifferent. He dreaded the entrance, but forced himself sternly to the door. It opened and Bertha stood there, a solid figure in a dingy black suit, her hat awry and her straight grey hair hanging in wisps about her face, a pasty white.

"I komm here," she panted. "I chust come here and she is *todt*—"

He pushed past her down the wide hall to the bedroom. The doors to the living room and dining room stood open, and in a window a canary sang its soaring, trilling song.

"Where is she?" he asked.

"Im bedt," Bertha whispered. "She didn't get up yet. She chust lies—"

He opened the one closed door and saw Cousin Emma. The room was frightfully close, the shades drawn and the heavy long curtains pulled over them. There was some sort of sweet perfume spilled. Everything was in disorder, silly disorder, not like Cousin Emma who was always neat. She lay high on two big pillows in a shape of agony, her knees drawn up, her withered arms bare and distorted, the lace sleeves flung back. Then the light fell on her open eyes. He saw two bright metallic dots glitter suddenly in the very center of her dark pupils. He gave an involuntary groan, and turning on the bed light he stooped and examined her motionless eyes. The two glistening points were indeed metal, the ends of what looked like headless nails, or no—knitting needles! Cousin Emma was always knitting. Someone had thrust deep into each eye a fine thin knitting needle, and blood and fluid had run down her cheeks in two glutinous streams, scarcely dry.

He was sick with horror, his tongue curled in his dry mouth, he could scarcely restrain himself from pulling out the needles, thrust so deep that he saw instantly they must have penetrated the brain.

"Was she like this when you came in?"

"Yes, chust the same," Bertha whispered. She put her black cotton gloves to her lips.

"When did you come?" he demanded.

"Chust before I called you, Mr. Asher. I run right avay qvick to telephone. The girl in the office sayss you are in court and she vants to know vot iss, but I dondt tell it. I sayss I muss myself tell to you. But some mann in court sayss he muss know, before he vill call. So to him I chust sayss some vomans in family iss *todt.*"

No use to feel the heart in that stricken ancient frame, the limbs caught in their astonished writhing. There was no life here now, so little had there been before. He turned to the telephone and called Cousin Emma's doctor, nevertheless, and then hesitating he called Edwin at the office.

"Edwin?"

"Yes, Father."

"Come at once to Cousin Emma's apartment. She has died suddenly."

Edwin was too well trained to ask a single question. "I'll be there at once."

William closed the door and called Bertha into the living room.

"Bertha, listen carefully and answer me. How is it that you are here? I thought you were in Mount Kisco, in that home."

"So vass I," Bertha said.

"Sit down," William commanded. The canary, impelled by their voices, set up his quivering silver-edged music. "Why did you come here, Bertha?" William asked.

Bertha shook her head. Her thick red hands trembled as they clutched her black gloves.

"You must answer me," William said. "Otherwise you will be accused of murder."

The purple lips trembled. "Mr. Asher, sir, *bitte,* help me—"

"I can only help if you tell me the absolute truth," William said sternly.

"Jessica, sir," Bertha whispered, her sobbing breath drew inward. "She vass here."

"Jessica?"

"Ya, she vass—"

"How did you know?"

"She telephoned me she candt shtand Herbert again and so she tells to Miss Emma and Miss Emma says komm here, and so she is here and she says Miss Emma tells me to komm today and she vill to talk mit me. And I thout Miss Emma vants to talk Jessica and me to friendts again, and I vass happy and I komm so qvick."

"Was Jessica here when you came?"

"Ya," Bertha moaned. "She vass."

"And how did this happen?" He glanced toward the closed bedroom door.

"Ya—it chust happens," Bertha moaned. "We fight, Mr. Asher. Jessica fights me. She opens the door und I am in, und she stares, so—"

Bertha widened her eyes frightfully and glared across the room at nothing.

"And then?"

"Und dann she shcreams at me how she hates me, und she vill kill me. I dondt lissen, she didt alvays talk so to me if nobody is mit uns, but I tellt her, 'Be qviet, you make soch a noise for Miss Emma.' So Miss Emma hears us und she kooms outdt the bedt, and opens the door and tellts to Jessica, 'Dondt talk so badt to poor old Bertha.' "

Lies or truth? Lies or truth?

"Und Jessica shpeaks sudden so nize," Bertha went on, sighing in gusts, "she sayss 'Miss Emma dear, get back in bedt, your foots are cold,' and so she goes in mit, und I vait and I vait so long. Und Jessica comes oudt and I am making a liddle coffee and she says, 'I go now to drug store to get some pills Miss Emma iss needing. You vait, please.' So nize she talks! So I vait and I vait, und she dondt komm back, und Miss Emma is so qviet, and so I open the door und I see!"

It was then that he called the nearest police station.

Lies or truth? William examining the fat purplish face could not tell. Forty years had made a mask of flesh. The doorbell rang and Bertha got to her feet by habit at the sound and opened it. Edwin was there.

William rose. "Come in, my son. Come into the other room." He hesitated. Should they leave Bertha, would she try to escape as Jessica had done? But Bertha had sat down again, a heavy almost sodden figure overflowing the straight wooden chair.

"We'll be back in a few minutes, Bertha," he said.

"Dot's all right, Mr. Asher, I vait," she said heartily. She folded her hands, still clutching the black cotton gloves.

William led the way in to the closed bedroom, shielding Edwin, dreading for him the sudden sight of the contorted figure on the bed. Death was dreadful for young eyes and yet all must see it sooner or later. He went directly to the bedside and lit the table light again.

"Do you see her eyes?" This question he put in his normal voice.

Edwin bent to look, his face went white. "Father, how horrible!"

"Jessica was here. But what purpose could there be? That's what we must find out."

"Does she need a purpose if she's mad?"

William did not reply to this. "On the other hand," he went on, "we have only Bertha's word for it that Jessica was here."

"I can't believe Bertha would have the courage for this," Edwin replied. He moved away from the bed, out of sight of the twisted old face.

"We don't know what Bertha is," William said. "I have never told you how violent she was when I sent her away. And Jessica, you know, has always maintained that her mother was cruel."

"Jessica lies and you know it," Edwin cried out.

Ah, William thought, then the wound still remained!

"You don't believe what Jessica says, do you, Father?" Edwin demanded.

"Of course not," William said. He crushed down deep in his mind the knowledge that anything might be true, anything at all. He had seen strange sights in his life as a lawyer and he had heard stranger lies than those Jessica had told even against himself. But Edwin, intuitive beyond either of his other children, felt the reservation.

"You will not grant that absolutely Jessica is a liar," he said bitterly, and then came his revelation of the cloud. "Neither will Vera. She says she is sure that Jessica lied, but she will not say she truly believes that she did. I have to live with that."

"It is very wrong of Vera," William said. "If I hesitate it is merely my lawyer's training which commits me to permanent doubt, even about myself." He decided suddenly to comfort Edwin in the best way that he could, the most self-sacrificing and the most profound. He felt the blood mount to his face, slow and red. "As a matter of fact, Winsten told me that Jessica had made some equally absurd allegations about me."

Instantly he saw that Winsten, or Madge had told Edwin. His face, still so young, could not hide the knowledge, his eyelids fluttered slightly, the look in his eyes grew shy, the very shape of his face changed subtly to signify that he knew.

William tried to speak lightly. "I suppose you boys talked it all over and laughed at the fix the old man was in."

"We did talk about it, sir," Edwin said manfully. "Madge told Vera and me one night when we spent the week end there. I told her that if she ever mentioned the—the matter again I would never speak to her as long as I lived. I told her I was sure it was all lies."

"But you do believe it possible?" William asked quizzically.

The door bell rang loudly again and again before Edwin could answer and they went out together, William closing the door behind him. Suddenly he felt exhausted, almost faint. Bertha was opening the door and down the hall they could see the doctor and with him the police. "Look here," William said urgently to Edwin, "I am going to turn this whole dreadful business over to you. I'll go home and break things to your mother and get in touch with Herbert to find Jessica."

"Very well, Father," Edwin said with assumed composure. There was no time now to answer the question of believing.

William took up his hat and stick and walked down the hall. He shook hands with the doctor and bent his head slightly to the two policemen behind him.

"Now that you are here I shall leave my son in charge," he said gravely. "The deceased is my wife's second cousin, the servant is an old cook in our family, recently retired. She will explain for herself how she happened to be here. If I am wanted my son can reach me. I should go home to be with my wife. My son is in my own law firm and is well qualified to assist you."

He nodded to receive their assent, hurried out of the house and telephoned at the drugstore next door for his car.

The journey home was grateful to him, he needed time to consider what must be done. The new chauffeur, a Vermont farmer's son enamored of the city, drove silently and with a certain *élan* of pleasure in his job. He was still unmarried, and it was enough to have freed himself from the farm. His young enthusiasm filled him with zeal and the desire to please. This, too, would wear away as all else did but it was enjoyable to William while it lasted and today a blessing.

In the vacuum of time moving through space William's legal mind worked quickly and well. He outlined to himself a clear line of action, step by step, which he intended to write down for Edwin's benefit. Bertha, or Jessica, must be defended but the case could not remain with their firm. His mind played over the roster of the city's lawyers and he chose one headed by an old college mate and friend, Barnes, Holt, Mackintosh and Lane.

When the long hours drew to their end and he saw the roof-lines of his home black in the early dark and caught the flow of lighted windows through the trees he felt strong again. He was always strong when he knew what he ought to do.

Elinor met him at the door when he reached home. It was late but she looked so fresh and pleasant that he dreaded to destroy her mood. But it must be done. They kissed, and he put his arm about her.

"My dear, you must prepare to hear a very distressful thing."

Her mind flew at once to the children, the tender grandchildren, the younger ones, as though death always threatened them most nearly. "Is it the children—"

"No, not the children. The oldest person in the family instead—Cousin Emma. My dear, she died very suddenly this morning."

"Oh no, oh William—all alone?"

"Come into the library, Elinor."

There, when she had sat down, very simply he told her what he had found and exactly how he had learned about it.

She was appalled, unable to grasp the full evil of what had happened. It was not death that disturbed her, he could see, for Cousin Emma was so old, but it was the manner of death and the monstrous contrast to Cousin Emma's unfailing goodness.

"She was so good," these were the words she kept repeating. "I cannot imagine why—when she was so good, especially to Jessica, always to Jessica. She always said that we must be kind to Jessica because she was the child of the cook and the butler. She said we must not let Jessica feel any difference. I shall never understand it, Cousin Emma, of all people—do you remember how she thought Jessica should not marry Herbert?"

"We must not be sure that it was Jessica," he warned her. He rose and went to the telephone and called Herbert. The country exchange was slow and he listened lest one of the maids interpose with some household call, but at last he heard Herbert's heavy voice.

"Well?"

"Herbert, this is Mr. Asher."

"Oh, hello, Mr. Asher."

"I am calling from home, Herbert, to inquire how Jessica is."

He waited during a long second or two. Then Herbert said, "Jessica's pretty good, Mr. Asher."

"She's still at home?"

"Yeah, she's here." Herbert turned his head and his voice grew distant but was still clear. "Want to talk to Mr. Asher?" Quite clearly, too, he heard Jessica's peevish reply. "What should I want to talk to that old fox for?"

Herbert's voice was at the mouthpiece again. "She's here busy at something—looks like knitting, I guess."

"You haven't moved to a town after all?"

"No, we ain't goin' to move."

William hesitated. How put the question he needed to have answered? "Someone told me that Jessica was in New York and I wondered if it were true."

Herbert's slow voice repeated the words, "In New York? She ain't been in New York. How'd she get there? I didn't take her."

Herbert's head turned again. "He says you was in New York, Jessica, haw haw!"

"Dirty old beast," Jessica's voice said sharply. "Tell him to mind his own dirty business."

Herbert's voice came back again. "Jessica says tell you no she wasn't in New York. Guess she would like to be, though, but I ain't got the time now with all these chickens on my hands."

"Do I hear your little girl's voice?" William asked pleasantly. He had heard a wail and a slap.

"Yeah, she's just got into something, I guess."

"Well, I won't delay you," William said and hung up. This was very bewildering. Was Jessica lying, was Herbert shielding her? "Herbert says she was not in New York."

"It doesn't matter," Elinor said most sadly. "Poor old Cousin Emma, such a true gentlewoman, if that means anything anymore—I don't know! Only it wasn't fair for her to die like that—so terribly frightened at the end —I can't think of it." She put her hands to her face and hid her eyes.

"Don't think of it," William said. "Only remember how much happiness she got out of being good and kind. She could not have been anything else, whatever the end. She fulfilled her own nature."

"And now Jessica has fulfilled hers," Elinor exclaimed. Her hands dropped to her lap.

"Wait," William reminded her. "We must find out the truth."

The day of the funeral was such a day as Cousin Emma herself might have chosen. Her aged body, distorted by autopsy, was restored again to decency, washed and clothed, her white hair curled skilfully to cover all scars. Her eyelids were drawn like shades over the tragedy they concealed, and she was housed in a handsome casket of mahogany with silvered handles. The family plot was in the Manchester cemetery and the place was crowded with strangers. Few of Cousin Emma's friends had survived to come to her funeral but the dreadful story of her death, flashing through the newspapers, brought scores of cars speeding from all directions.

The family, standing about the open grave, took no notice of the curious crowd except that Elinor, glancing about, said in a low and wretched voice, "How she would have hated this!"

For Cousin Emma did not truly like the common crowd. Scrupulous and delicate in her approach to every human being, she shrank from the many, and lived, it must be said, as a recluse for most of her life, thereby magnifying the value and the meaning of the few persons she knew. But this was her public end, the newspapers screaming the details, and Bertha and Jessica both under arrest.

It could not be prevented. Herbert had come begging to William. "You're a big lawyer, Mr. Asher, you get crooks a trial when everybody knows they're guilty. Here's Jessica locked up when I can swear she was at home. I've had to put the baby in the orphanage again. Bertha ought to be locked up, she was right there, but Jessica wasn't. I can swear—"

"The matter is quite out of my hands," William had said firmly. "It is not possible for me to handle the case."

The minister was dropping the clods, crumbling them to earth, and letting them fall. "Dust unto dust—" his intoning voice went on, and a bird burst into sudden song in the elm tree above his head. What, William wondered senselessly, had become of Cousin Emma's canary? It had been forgotten. Winsten's little girl, the third child, began suddenly to cry. She should not have come, he did not approve of children at funerals but Madge had insisted that it was a family occasion, death as well as birth, and that the children ought to know. They were all there except the baby, the fourth child, the boy.

The funeral was over at last, and local police parted the crowd for the family to walk through to their cars. The family went home alone and closed themselves into the house and the crowd went away again, discussing the guilt of the cook or the maid, betting upon one or the other, while the grave was covered with the displaced earth and then massed with flowers. Not many people remained to give Cousin Emma flowers, and William and Elinor had sent a blanket of white roses and maiden hair fern which made a good show. Edwin's and Vera's pink lilies were at the foot, and Winsten's and Madge's yellow roses at the head. A few people from the crowd had thrown down wild flowers, a homegrown rose, stalks of delphiniums, a handful of daisies.

Cousin Emma was of no importance, William reflected, merely a woman who had lived a kindly, good and somewhat lonely life. But that she had died by violence, that she could be murdered, was significant indeed, and by such a death she became important.

On a certain spring morning, years later when the pattern of life had been pleasant long enough so that William had all but forgotten Jessica, when the Christmas roses Elinor had planted on Cousin Emma's grave were already in bloom, he received a telephone call. It was Saturday morning and he was at home after a late breakfast.

"Who is it?" he demanded.

"It's me, Mr. Asher."

"I don't recognize you."

"It's Herbert Morris, Mr. Asher."

A violent revulsion dashed William's spirits. Why must he hear this voice again?

"Good morning, Herbert," he said with hypocritical calm.

"How are you, Mr. Asher?" Herbert asked.

"Very well, thank you," William replied and was not deceived. He expected the next question.

"Mr. Asher, I wonder could you do something for me?" Herbert was humble indeed.

"I don't know, I am sure," William replied.

"Could you and Mrs. Asher please go to see Jessica, sir, and tell me if you don't think she's well enough now to come home?"

William was stunned at the monstrous request. Was Jessica to rise again from her living grave? Was her voice to be heard again in his house? "I cannot see that it would do any good whatever, Herbert," he replied at his stiffest.

"You see, Mr. Asher, sir," Herbert said with all his old submissive stubbornness, "she looks real well, just like she used to. She talks sensible-like, too. She'd like to come home. She says we ought to be united again. The child is growing up without a mother, sir."

"It is not so simple for Jessica just to come home, Herbert," William said in his gravest voice. "You forget what has happened."

"I'll never believe it was Jessica—who did for Miss Emma, sir," Herbert said earnestly. "If it wasn't Bertha it was some stranger crep' into the house. Jessica couldn't do no such thing as that. She can lose her temper and bite like a kid or sompin like that, but she couldn't murder nobody. Why, I always had to kill the chickens for Sunday dinner. She'd run in the house and shut the door and put her hands to her ears, she'd cover her eyes so she couldn't look out the window and see it floppin'."

"That doesn't change the jury's verdict," William said.

"Well, sir, Mr. Asher, you're a lawyer. You could maybe get the governor to give a pardon—give her another chanct, like. We could maybe even get another trial."

William wavered. His legal mind was touched. He had known prisoners unjustly accused and imprisoned for years. Bertha's exoneration and Jessica's sentence were sound enough, but there were loopholes that no one had been able to explain. Though he had remained determinedly a spectator, except when called upon as a witness, he remembered clearly the weak points of the trial.

"And Jessica hates that asylum somethin' terrible," Herbert pleaded. "She says it turns her stummick to see all those old crazy people, when she ain't crazy herself. And another thing, Mr. Asher, they work her like anything. Soon as they found out she knew waitress work they put her in the dining room where all the doctors eat and she has to wait on 'em and she don't get no pay for it. 'Course they don't want to let her go. It's natural they don't. But is it fair?"

The newspapers in recent months had carried stories about mental institutions, heartrending enough to stir now in William's memory. It was possible that in the huge institution where Jessica was sheltered there were such iniquities, though why, he groaned to himself, need they be his concern, or she, for that matter, a concern he had always unwillingly assumed.

"I will talk to Mrs. Asher," he said, evasively.

"Thank you, Mr. Asher," Herbert said with the quick cheerfulness of the uncomprehending mind. "I sure will appreciate it. You're kind of a big man around here, I guess you know, and they might listen to you while they don't pay no attention to me at all."

The morning was spoiled, William thought gloomily. He had no intention of helping Jessica to get free and yet his wretched sensitive conscience had been stirred again and he knew of old that he would have no rest until he satisfied it. He hung up the receiver and returned to the library where he had been working, but not to his desk. Instead he sat down in the deep window seat facing south where the sun poured in, and saw Elinor in the garden below. He wished he need not tell her of Herbert's call. She looked calmly happy down there in the peony bed, in her old green serge suit. Oh, what a plague could grow within a man's contented home! He recalled, with utmost distaste, the way Bertha had looked at the trial, on just such a sunny morning as this, too, only the sunlight strained through the huge dirty window of the city court room.

She had been called to Miss Emma's apartment, Bertha had declared, by Jessica, her daughter. The matron of the home, summoned as a witness, had confirmed this. Bertha had come downstairs in the morning of the murder dressed to go to town. She said she was going to see a relative of her former employer. She had then taken the bus in front of the home. The matron, a pale exhausted middle-aged woman of a faded genteel appearance, had given the further information that the bus did not use to stop so handy but she had got them to do it, so that her old people would not have to walk in the rain or stand waiting in the cold. "They can come out of the house when they see the bus comin' and get in like it was their own private conveyance," she said, a mild pride brightening her languor.

On the other hand, Jessica had been so entirely herself that William still found it difficult at this moment to face certain questions secret in his own mind. When Jessica had been called upon to rise that day at her trial, she had done so with an air almost sprightly, and with the graceful light step he knew so well she had gone to the stand. Obviously, as he still remembered, she made an appealing impression, her grey suit and lace ruffled blouse, the small grey felt hat on her blonde hair had all the air of a lady, and one still young. As long as she lived, he supposed, Jessica would look young. She had held spotless white kid gloves in her right hand and there was a small pink rose on her lapel. Lifting her head, she had looked about the room, smiling faintly, and the pallor which was habitual to her passed into a sudden delicate flush.

"Is there any reason," the attorney asked very gently, "why you should have disliked Miss Winsten?"

Jessica drew in her breath. "Oh no, sir! On the contrary, she was the kindest member of the family—to me, at least."

"You had known her many years?"

"All my life."

"When is the last time you saw her?"

"I went to see her, sir, after I got out of—one day after I had come home. I had been ill and had been sent away. Miss Emma helped to bring me home again when I was quite well, and then I went to see her."

"How did you get there?"

"I walked to the bus, sir. It's only about a mile from the house. It goes straight to Manchester and there I can always get a train."

Herbert had started up from his chair and had put up his hand like a boy in school but no one heeded him. He sank back, the sweat pouring down his cheeks.

"Do you usually take the bus?" the lawyer asked.

"Oh yes," Jessica said brightly. "I always do, Herbert never takes me anywhere. He's so busy."

"Your Honor," Herbert had shouted at this, getting to his feet.

"Sit down!" the judge thundered. Jessica's head drooped.

"Did you take the train on the morning when your mother says you were at Miss Winsten's apartment?" the lawyer asked Jessica.

She had lifted her head proudly. "I am sure I did not."

"Yet you know, that if what you say is proved true, your mother will be charged with murder?"

"I am saying what's true," Jessica said with frank composure. Then she added with a sad smile, "My mother and I have not spoken in years."

William had stirred and coughed. Now was coming the story of the childhood beatings, the cruelties, all the wicked accusations which might or might not be true—

"My mother," Jessica said touchingly, "was very cruel to me as a child. She locked me in the cellar and when I cried she beat me. I could show—there are still marks on my body of these blows. When I was only seven years old she sent me to a convent in Canada, and I did not see my father except once a year, in the summer. I loved my father and he loved me. Then he died. My mother was cruel to him, too. Miss Emma could never believe it, no matter what I told her."

Sitting in the library window seat now, years later, William suddenly understood that last declaration. He remembered how Jessica's face had changed, had hardened as she spoke these words. She had been opening and shutting the latch of her small handbag nervously and suddenly she snapped it shut with a perceptible click so that he could hear it even where he had been seated far to the side. Of course, of course that was why she had killed poor Cousin Emma! The gentle old lady had sent for her to plead with her once again, for Bertha's sake, to be reconciled. Cousin Emma had never forgiven him for discharging Bertha. He remembered very well when Elinor told him about that. She had gone to see Cousin Emma on one of her usual visits, and had told her where Bertha was and why, and Cousin Emma had been quite distracted about it. She had exclaimed over and over again, "But Elinor, my dear, one has an obligation to an old servant!"

"Bertha is very comfortable, Cousin Emma," Elinor had assured her.

"Oh, but it is the heart that needs comfort," Cousin Emma replied. "I shall send for Jessica, I shall certainly talk to her."

This she had done more than once, William knew, and although he himself told her it would be of no use. But Cousin Emma was incorrigibly softhearted, the more so as she grew older, and so he had not tried to persuade her. He supposed she must have seen Jessica several times, perhaps many times. And doubtless on that final morning she must have persuaded her too much, she might even have accused Jessica of lying, and at that Jessica's mind burst from the cage in which she tried to keep it imprisoned and hidden.

That day at the trial when she declared her mother cruel people had stared at Bertha, but she sat immobile, gazing across the room at the tall windows. The jury had leaned forward to listen to Jessica, always sympathetic, and the questioning went on, until she was finished. Then she sat down and put her white lace handkerchief to her lips.

Bertha had not moved. When her name was called she had started and stared about her as though it was for someone else.

"Come, come," the lawyer said, "get into your place."

She had got to her feet, a thick bewildered figure. She had moved to the stand and taken her oath in a voice so low that it could not be heard. Then clutching the wooden rail, she had waited, gazing humbly at the judge.

"You have heard the accusations of your daughter?" the attorney said.

Bertha gave a massive sigh. "Ya, Jessica talks so—"

"Is it true?"

"I neffer beadt my little childt," Bertha said somberly. "Sometimes I slap her a liddle bit venn she runs in the big haus, ya. There she dondt belong. So muss I teach her, her papa wondt. To beadt—no, neffer!"

She stopped, as though no more could be said.

The questions went on relentlessly. "How did you come to be at Miss Winsten's apartment?"

"Jessica calls me. She tellt to me Miss Emma vants I shouldt come. Miss Emma tellt to me before that sometime when Jessica is home we muss be friends und I say 'Ya, gewiss, vy nott?' So I vish, but Jessica von't. Iss may be because she is sick in the headt she dondt vish, I dondt know."

"Sick in the head?"

"Ya, they sayss so. I dondt know. They take her away and put the baby in a orphanage. Herbert, he vill tell to you. I dondt know."

Herbert had been recalled and questioned. Unwillingly he had given the ugly story of his life with Jessica, her reluctance to grant him his rights, the final struggle, and trying to conceal all he told everything.

William could not bear the memory. He got up and went out into the garden to Elinor. She was on her knees by the peony bed the better to see the pushing young shoots of the peonies.

"They have come through the winter, after all," she said happily when she saw him. She had felt much concern for the peonies, always delicate in the severe Vermont winters, and coaxed through only by the aid of shelter and manure. He came and stood by her side, contemplating the thick rose-red shoots.

Then he told her, grumbling after every sentence, "I do not see why, when things are peaceful, Bertha comfortably senile in Mount Kisco and Jessica locked up safely, we should again stir up everything."

She smiled ruefully, "Except that you know we will, and the more we hate to do it, the more we'll feel we ought. We can't put down the burden. We'll have to go and see for ourselves how Jessica is. Think of the child! Poor Monica—"

They were silent for a few minutes, Elinor on her knees, carefully, with tender fingers, removing the crusts of winter earth from around the shoots, while William watched. He was remembering again, not really watching, recalling unwillingly the last time he had seen Jessica. She had been pronounced insane, and Bertha had been exonerated upon her steadfast and unshakable story. He stooped to touch Elinor's shoulder. "Then you think we had better see Jessica?"

She sat back on her heels and looked up at him and he was startled to see, in the heartless light of the morning sun, that fine wrinkles were now clearly about her eyes and lips.

"Once more," she said gently. "Then perhaps your conscience will rest." He nodded. Ah, she understood him!

The upshot of it was that the next morning, it being Sunday, they decided to make the visit to Jessica instead of going to church, "a good deed instead of a profession," William put it wryly.

The new chauffeur, as they still called him, was accustomed to them, and drove them at a safe and quiet rate the thirty miles to the huge mass of buildings where Doctor Bergstein expected them. William had telephoned the evening before, and the cordial doctor had agreed to be present when they arrived. He was in his office, a bare small room whose walls were lined with file cases and text books, a short kindly looking man, William remembered, whose kindness was nevertheless always cool and businesslike.

"Come in, Mr. Asher, good morning, Mrs. Asher. Please sit down."

They sat down, he took his place behind the desk, and put on a pair of gold spectacles. "I have just been refreshing myself in the case of Jessica Morris." He riffled some papers on the desk. "There is really nothing to report. She was much disturbed when she was placed here three years ago by court order, as you know. She did not respond well to shock treatment, but we gave her hydropathy with good results. At first she refused to work but for the last two years she has worked efficiently and well in the staff dining room and has even taken over the ordering of food supplies. She spends her leisure, I note, in the occupational therapy room and does rather nice water colors and some textile designing for the patients. The occupational therapist reports her intelligent and cooperative."

William's spirits sank. "Does this mean that she is well?"

The doctor shrugged his thick shoulders and spread his hands. "Well? What is well? Here she functions as a well person would. More we do not know."

William exchanged looks with Elinor.

"May we see Jessica for ourselves?" Elinor asked.

"Certainly," the doctor said. "In fact, it is almost time for luncheon.

Why not come to my table and lunch with us? Then you will see Jessica at work."

"An admirable idea," William said.

A few minutes later they followed Dr. Bergstein down bare endless corridors to a rectangular dining room set with many small tables. It was a cheerful room, as it had need to be, William thought. There were flowers on the tables, tastefully arranged.

"The flowers are also Jessica's work," Dr. Bergstein said. "She has a nice taste, very sensitive. Also, obviously, her background has been among cultivated people. She reads books, her English is beautiful. Sit down, please. Let us see if she recognizes you."

He rubbed his hands with sudden enjoyment, his professional curiosity aroused by the new situation.

"There she is," Elinor exclaimed.

Jessica stood against the wall among the other waitresses, easily the most striking among them. Their uniforms were clear blue cotton with white aprons and small white caps. The color was becoming to Jessica, her fair hair was loosely curled, cut short now instead of piled in braids upon her head in the old German fashion. She had lost her extreme thinness, her figure was nicely rounded and yet slender. Her face was alive, her lips red, her bright blue eyes alert.

"I never saw her look so well," William said.

"She is well because she is happy," Dr. Bergstein said. "Yes, here she is happy. She is busy, she tells some others what they should do, she arranges the flowers, she enjoys the library. People like her very much. Sometimes a man likes her too much and then she comes quickly to tell me so, and I must speak to him." He laughed. "Jessica is very moral, very virtuous. She is always reminding everybody that she is a married woman."

"Does she want her husband to visit her regularly?" Elinor asked quietly.

Dr. Bergstein pursed his fleshy lips. "No, I cannot say so. At first she would not see him at all. Then because he has a car and takes her for a drive, with special permission, she began to allow this. Sometimes she will not see him for months. But still," he laughed again, "she is a married woman. It is a protection. She will always want protection while she has her own way. Ah, that is very normal."

Jessica was looking at him and he waved. Suddenly she recognized them. Her face brightened with smiles, she came with her old graceful swiftness across the floor, her step as light as ever.

"Oh Mrs. Asher, dear!" she cried sweetly. She seized Elinor's hand and held it in both her own. "You have come to see me at last, and Mr. Asher, too. Oh, I told Herbert only last week how I wished I could see your faces again! You haven't forgotten me?"

"No, indeed," William said. "How are you, Jessica?"

"Oh, wonderfully well, thank you, Mr. Asher, only longing to get back to my own little house and see my darling child, such a tall girl now, and she needs her mother, I know. How is Mr. Edwin—and Mr. Winsten and Miss Susan?"

"All well, thank you, Jessica," Elinor replied.

They were dazed, she had forgotten everything, or had she really? She was the same warm, young-looking creature, her pretty face pink and white and unlined, her eyes clear.

"You had better bring some food, Jessica," Dr. Bergstein said in good humor. "We are hungry."

"Oh, yes," she exclaimed in her soft eager way. "How shameful of me! I am forgetting my duty." She took their order carefully and tripped away.

"Well," William said, "well, well, well!"

Dr. Bergstein shrugged again. "You see? Who can say?"

"It is very confusing," Elinor said, troubled. "If she is herself again she should not be here."

William could not speak. The prospect of Jessica's future was insupportable, if indeed she was well.

She was back again very soon, and with exquisite service she set before them the dishes they had chosen.

"I remember how you like lamb chops, Mr. Asher," she said playfully. "I had these turned once more for you, knowing you enjoy them well done."

"Thank you," he said.

It was a good meal, simple but well cooked, and William ate it although he was not hungry, replying now and again to some remark of Dr. Bergstein's. Elinor carried the conversation while he caught fragments of it.

"Jessica looks quite different from the others," she was saying.

Dr. Bergstein agreed. "She is different—a very complex case. Very interesting!"

The meal was over at last. "Would you like a little while with Jessica alone?" the doctor asked.

William was about to refuse but Elinor spoke first. "I think I would."

"Then please come into a sitting room for guests. We have one upstairs that is quite private. I will send for Jessica to meet you there."

He led the way and William muttered to Elinor behind his back. "Why on earth must we see her alone? I've had enough."

"Hush," Elinor said.

In a sitting room with livid green upholstery and curtains they sat down and waited in silence. There was much to say to each other, each felt it, but this was not the time. It was not the end of the visit, no conclusions could be made. The room smelled of dust and a peculiar acrid reek that William could not diagnose. He rose and opened a large window, not easily. It had not been opened for a long time.

In ten minutes or so there was a tap on the door. "Come in," Elinor called.

It was Jessica, her uniform changed for a suit of thin navy blue wool with white ruffles at the breast and neck. She looked, as William saw very unwillingly, extremely pretty and she stood hesitating before them, her unchanging smile still on her face.

"Sit down, Jessica," Elinor said.

She sat down then on the straight-backed wooden chair and crossed her narrow feet, encased in black patent leather shoes. William, who seldom noticed women's clothes, noticed these also. It was astonishing that Jessica could have so maintained herself here.

"Well," William said, "Herbert wanted us to come and see you and so we have. We'll tell him you are looking very well."

Jessica dimpled nicely. "Oh, Herbert," she cried, laughing. "He should be ashamed, troubling you! I told him so. But he knew I was longing to see someone from the family." She turned suddenly wistful. "I suppose Mr. Edwin is very happy?"

"He is," Elinor said firmly. "It is a very successful marriage."

The slight cloud was swept from Jessica's face as though by an invisible hand. "And the dear little children, Mr. Winsten's little children, are they well? So big now, I suppose, and I wish I could see them."

"There are five of them now," Elinor said. "I believe Madge wants six."

Jessica shuddered. "Oh no, Mrs. Asher, how can she? It's so dreadful."

William stared at her. "What do you mean by that?"

Jessica laughed again and put up her hand to smooth her hair. "Oh, I don't know, Mr. Asher, I suppose I shouldn't say it. I'm always saying things. Is the house just the same, Mrs. Asher?"

"Quite the same," Elinor said. "We have two very nice young women to help us."

"I wish it were I who was helping you, Mrs. Asher," Jessica said, wistful again. "I should so love it."

"You don't like it here?" William asked.

Jessica shivered and then suddenly covered her face with her hands. "No!" she cried in a small sobbing voice. "I hate it—I'm just a prisoner! They work me—so hard—day and night. I don't get a penny. It's just being —a slave."

William gave a great sigh. He sat back in his chair and looked at Elinor helplessly. Elinor raised her eyebrows. What can be done now, the eyebrows asked.

Jessica was sobbing softly. "I miss my baby so! I've hardly been with her at all—just a few weeks. A child needs her mother. I feel her needing me. But I'm helpless."

William could not endure more. "Look here, Jessica," he said with sudden authority. "If this is the way you truly feel, if you think you can behave yourself and not torture the life out of everyone, for what reason I cannot imagine, because all of us have been kind to you always—"

"Oh, yes, Mr. Asher," Jessica breathed. She lifted her face, rosy with weeping. "You don't need to say that—I never forget anything!"

"Well, then," William went on, "if you want to try again to be a decent reasonable woman, I will see what I can do to get parole for you, at least that. If we can prove that you are well, if you can behave yourself at home, it may be that you might some day be pardoned."

"Pardoned for what, Mr. Asher?" Jessica asked like a child.

"You told me just now that you forget nothing," William said harshly.

"If you mean Miss Emma, sir, I didn't do that," Jessica said in the same eager soft voice. "I was at home with Herbert that very day, all day, or very nearly. It was the day before that I went to see Miss Emma, but that was the day that he was so awful. He tried to—he was like a beast—he—oh, I can't say it! I cannot put it into words! It's—it's indecent. Before the baby, too! I always slept in the baby's room, and he came in anyway, though he had promised—"

He waited, holding his breath, but her fearful sensitive mind felt something dangerous in the silence. She straightened her back with an effort and said in her usual voice, "Such things I try to forget, but kindness I cannot forget. Miss Emma was the kindest person of all—to me, that is, and I loved her. I could not have hurt her. But she never would believe what I said about my mother. It was true, it was true, but Miss Emma wouldn't believe me. Why, even on that last day—"

"What last day?" William demanded.

Jessica's flush faded instantly, "The last day I ever saw her, the day before she died—"

He decided on the final test. "Very well, I am glad to know you want to go home to your husband and child. You seem quite well. I see no reason why you should not go home on parole. I will give my own guarantee that you are well enough and I can, I think, persuade the doctor to release you on parole after the proper permission has been given." He was making a promise impossible to perform, the law could not so easily be set aside, but it was a test which his instinct told him could be risked. He met her eyes fully, concentrated upon his, and allowed her a moment to comprehend what he had said. Then he asked the question, "Would you like to go home at once, today, with us? Herbert would be pleasantly surprised."

"William!" Elinor said. Her voice was a low warning. "You are going too fast," the voice implied, "you are imposing a shock. Besides, suppose she accepts, how would you perform?"

"Now?" Jessica echoed in a high tight voice. She sprang up, her whole body stiffened, even her hair sprang electrically from her head, her eyes dilated, glittered, stared. She screamed. "Oh, you can't make me!" And swinging out her arms as though she were about to fly she ran to the window.

"William!" Elinor cried.

He leaped from his chair and caught Jessica by the waist. The door opened and Dr. Bergstein came in, strode across the small room and seized

Jessica's flailing arms. "Excuse me, I have waited outside. I was afraid of something. So, Jessica, you want to jump out of the window this time." He pulled down the window with a bang. "We never open the windows, Mr. Asher. Now, Jessica, be calm." A nurse in a white uniform came instantly at the touch of his hand on the button set in the wall. Jessica began to cry loudly at the sight of her.

"Jessica," the doctor said. "It is no use. Again, after two years, but it is still no use. Take her to the hydropathic room, Miss Baker."

"Yes, Doctor," the nurse replied.

They heard the dreadful wild sobbing receding down the hall, the frightful screams.

"Is she being hurt?" Elinor said anxiously.

"No, Mrs. Asher," the doctor said. "Do not worry. She is not being hurt. She feels she must scream. We see the other Jessica."

They sat down shaken and for a moment were silent. Then William said with a solemn sadness, "Doctor, I have one more question to ask you."

"So many questions I cannot answer," the doctor said. "I will try this one more." He waited, while the sunny afternoon was wasted.

"Could anything have been done to prevent this?" William asked. "Was some mistake made when she was a child?"

"He means," Elinor interpreted, "could we in the big house have acted somehow differently to Jessica when she was small? Jessica was the daughter of our family cook."

Dr. Bergstein spread his hands and he gave again the heavy shrug. "Who knows? It is a question. But Jessica was born the child of the cook, was she not? She did not wish to remain the cook's child and so she hates the cook, who is nevertheless her mother. She wishes to be a child of the big house, like you, Mrs. Asher, but she is not, and so she hates you. She does not dare to hurt you, because here is Mr. Asher to take care of you, so she hurts a poor old helpless lady, who is also belonging to the big house. She thinks she is in love with a young man in the big house, so that he can bring her into the world she wants to belong to, but unfortunately the young man does not love her. But Jessica does not really love anybody, you know. That is her tragedy. And so all your kindness and goodness—I see you are very kind good people, Mr. and Mrs. Asher— does her no use, for it makes her only to wish that she too was so kind and good, and she knows she is not but she does not know why, and she thinks it is because she is not really one of you, body and soul. She wants to be born again, Mr. and Mrs. Asher, but it is sad we can only be born once. She knows she is a stranger in your house."

They listened to the stout Jewish doctor, speaking from the depths of his own unknown life and hidden experience, and his words fell upon them with the dreadful impact of truth.

"We can never be rid of the burden of Jessica," William said at last, very somberly.

"No," the doctor agreed, "it is true. Being what you are, good people, you cannot be rid of the burdens. You take them and you keep them—but, my dear sir," he leaned forward and put his hand on William's knee, "this is the hope of humanity! If good people can forget, then indeed there is no God."

They rose and the doctor looked at his watch. "Oh, heaven, it is four o'clock nearly. I promised my wife and children—yes, please excuse me. And you are quite satisfied now that Jessica must stay here?"

William hesitated and cleared his throat. "But one more question—do you think Jessica is really insane, Dr. Bergstein? In the technical sense?"

The doctor gave his shrug and spread his hands once more. "Technical? What is that? It is a meaningless word to me. Jessica is not always insane, no, not when she is enjoying her life." He smiled and glanced about. "Here is a big house, too, is it not? A very big house, a very big family. She is more pretty than most of this family, more clever, she is like a sort of princess here, therefore when she is thinking such things she is not insane, not at all. But take her away, put her where she does not wish to be, a big house where she cannot enter except as the child of the cook, and yes, I will say she is insane." He paused and stood, very kindly and solid, fastening upon them the shrewd, assessing, humorous warmth of his gaze. "We may say, my friends, that Jessica is suffering from the effects of democracy. So, if I may say it, are you."

He bowed, smiled, and went away with surprising nimbleness for so large a man.

William stood still for the matter of half a minute, digesting the doctor's last words. He perceived their profundity and did not wish to talk about it. "Come, my dear," he said, turning to Elinor. "Come home. There is nothing more that we can do for Jessica."

They went home in silence almost complete, and when they got out again at their own door, they mounted the steps side by side, somewhat wearily. The house was quiet enough as they stepped into the door. But someone's coat was flung upon the chair by the long oaken table, someone's soft tweed coat and a small round red felt hat with a black pompon of feather caught at one side.

"Susan!" Elinor exclaimed, crossing the hall. "What does this mean? Susan!" she called up the stairs.

Upstairs a door opened, and Susan stood there at the bannisters above them and looked down upon them. Her dark short hair fell on her cheeks, and her large dark eyes made her face pale.

"Where did you come from?" William demanded.

"I've come home," she said.

"Without Peter?"

"Without Peter," Susan said.

Their hearts sank together, his and Elinor's. He could feel the downward plunge in her bosom as clearly as in his own.

"We'll come up," Elinor called, her head tilted back to gaze anxiously at the pale face looking down at them.

"I'll come down," Susan said.

They hung up their wraps soberly, accepting in mutual silence whatever was to be. Then they turned to their daughter, and standing side by side, they regarded her.

They were not prepared for the sudden torrent of Susan's love and pity. She stood before them, quite self-possessed apparently, looking at them, one face and the other, and then suddenly she spread her arms and embraced them both.

"Oh, please don't look like that," she begged. "You make me feel ashamed. You're bracing yourselves, I can see it. You needn't, darlings, nothing awful has happened. It's just that I—well, I had to have time to think and I found I couldn't think unless I came home quite by myself. Where have you been?"

She squeezed herself between them, clinging to an arm of each, and in three they walked toward the east parlor and as three they sat down on the long sofa.

"We went to see Jessica," Elinor said.

"Why on earth—" Susan began.

"Herbert thought she might be well," William broke in. "I am glad we went to see for ourselves. She will never be well, the doctor made it quite clear. She can only be well if she stays where she is, protected, successful, you might say, in her own way. She cannot cope with life as she has found it. She has neither the strength nor the wit for it, but she does not know that."

"What an extraordinary thing!" Susan exclaimed. Her eyes, very thoughtful, did not leave his face. She was thinking, thinking—

"I begin to see the strangest light—a curious twisted sort of light," she said slowly, "but coming somehow from Jessica, here in our house, and shining in the queerest way upon Peter—and me."

She leaned forward between them and buried her face in her hands, but she was not weeping. In an instant she threw back her head and got up, lit a cigarette from the side table and flung herself in a chair by the fireplace opposite them.

"Did you ever see Jessica here in this room, before the mirror?" she demanded.

"Never," Elinor said in surprise.

"I have," William replied.

"Oh, she was often here," Susan declared, "and all alone. We used to watch her when we were kids, Edwin and I. I don't know if Winsten ever saw her. But Edwin and I used to creep down the stairs and watch her when she didn't know. Sometimes we giggled and ran away, and then she cried. We were beasts—all children are. Once when she was here on vacation I went in my room and found her wearing my best party gown. Remember that pink tulle? I gave it to her after that, but she was frightened and wouldn't take it anyway. She said she'd never have a chance to wear it, except like that, here in the house."

"Poor thing," Elinor said, "but all the same it was outrageous."

She was severe, for she was more than tired of Jessica. She could not forget what Dr. Bergstein had said—"if good people can forget—"

"I do declare," she went on suddenly turning to William with a sort of passion, "I wish that we hadn't this big house, or any money, or even any education. I wish, actually, that we were savages of some sort. It's the ignorant and the uncivilized who really own the world today, I do believe, simply by being a burden to the rest of us."

"Oh no, they don't." It was Susan, speaking in the quietest voice. "Not at all, Mother! You are quite wrong." She began to laugh a soft subdued bitter laughter. "Remember," she asked, "remember how I married Peter for shelter, my dears? Remember how I thought him strong because he killed the black dog?" She added mockingly, "With his bare hands, my dears?"

A woman, this Susan, his daughter, William saw suddenly with a thrust of pain at his heart. The child was gone, and gone, too, was the young girl. She was a woman facing her life and seeing it as something entirely different from what she had thought it was.

"And what do you think," she was demanding of them now. "What do you think my Peter is? Not a rock, if you please, not a shelter, but a confused rough child, a boy who is so big he has to shave his beard by day but at night he is afraid of the dark. I don't mean really the dark, not anything as simple as that, but afraid of knowing what he is, ignorant and crude and empty inside." She was smiling, not with mirth but with a fearful sense of the desperate comedy of human life. "Yes, I've found that out now, too. But he comes to me for shelter, if you please. He wants to leave the garage. He hates the house he grew up in, he wants to come here, my darlings, where you could never abide to have him. He thinks we have it easy. That's what he says. He imagines that we know secrets that he doesn't—silly, isn't it? He thinks that if he knew all we do he would be powerful—as he thinks we are—and secure, as he is sure we are and as he isn't. He insists that he has as much right as we have to know enough to win, as he puts it."

To this outpouring William listened, astonished and cautious. What was it, indeed, but that most hateful word, *revolution?* A light illumined his comprehending mind. He saw Peter not alone but one of a vast and piteous company, pushing upward by any means they could into the wider spaces of a world they imagined was above them. So Jessica had tried to do, blindly and stupidly, seeing that world only in the shape of his own house, God help him, from which they had all shut her out, and had to shut her.

Still, they might have understood her dreams, so childish and absurd, since for her dreams she lived and now was all but dead. Beyond her tragic shape he saw the shadowy faces of criminals he had defended and had heard condemned, all struggling and contriving and contending for that upper air.

Dreams! They were the living breath of every human soul and when they died, the soul died with them. What if his own dreams had never come to life? What if there had not been this house and all the love it had contained, or what if his dreams had exceeded the power of his brain to make them true? What if he, as Peter put it, had never had his chance, his right to know enough to win?

The past remained and Jessica herself was buried there. Yet let the past do its work, at least for Peter's sake. How could he explain to these two women whom he loved, who waited for him to tell them what to do? He chose to speak to Susan.

"You should be proud, my dear. You have done something wonderful for Peter, by loving him and marrying him. He is awakened. Of course he belongs to the family. We are all with you—and him."

He turned to Elinor. "We must get behind this boy, my dear. All that business with Jessica—it mustn't happen again, not in this house!"

He was not sure from the look on her face whether she understood, perhaps not altogether, not yet—

But Susan, who never wept, began suddenly to sob. "I know what you mean!" She rolled her handkerchief into a ball and stabbed at her eyes. "I didn't think you could. Oh Dad, thank you!"

He was distressed by her tears and then embarrassed, and he hid himself behind his usual dignity. "Don't cry, Susan. The fact is, I don't doubt I shall enjoy knowing Peter better."

His daughter wiped her eyes at this, she gazed at him with a tenderness he had never seen before, and then inexplicably she laughed, softly, richly.

"I wonder if you realize," she said irrelevantly, "how absolutely precious you are!"

There could be no such thing as a happy ending to a lot of trouble. That, of course, he was too old and seasoned to expect. But the way was clear and he cleared it himself finally by a midnight talk with Elinor. She came into his bed that night as though she were lonely, and suddenly she said, as though she had been thinking about it for hours,

"I love you, William, but I don't really see how we can undertake Peter! He can't be changed now. It's too late. The differences are too deep."

He slipped his right arm about her with accustomed ease, and drew her head to his breast.

"I don't think we should try to change Peter," he said. "That would be a mistake, and, as you say, impossible. I propose simply that as a family we open the house to him."

"I can't imagine Madge—"

The name of Madge recalled his mind to a slowly forming purpose.

"Darling," he said above her head on his breast, "this is a good time to tell you that I have for the past few years been uncomfortable with Madge because she half believed some absurd things that Jessica said about me."

"About you?" Elinor lifted her head, and looked at him in the dimness of the night light.

"Jessica once told Madge and Winsten that I had made love to her." He found the greatest difficulty putting this nonsense into words, not because he any more feared Elinor, indeed, tonight he feared nothing at all, but because his taste, trained to fastidiousness by generations behind him, shrank in disgust. Therefore he spoke the words baldly and quickly, denying himself the familiar luxury of silence.

"How absurd," Elinor said, "and why didn't you tell me long ago? It explains—Madge has been so strange with me sometimes, almost as though she felt sorry for me." She sat up. "It makes me angry, rather!"

"At me?" he asked quietly.

"No, of course not! What do you think?"

"You've said some things to me, you know," he reminded her.

She crept down beside him again. "I know—I can't understand why. There was something wrong in the house."

"Voices," he acknowledged and he stretched his arm about her again. Yes, there had been strange voices, disturbing, corrupting, cutting across the human grain of their common life. Yet Jessica herself had only been some sort of instrument, possessed, people would once have said by a devil, and yet there was no devil in Jessica, no devil perhaps anywhere, except the reverse energy of dreams denied.

"Anyway, you know me now," he said reasonably to Elinor. "You can help to bring Madge back into the family, and Winsten will come back with her."

Elinor opened her eyes. "Winsten never believed you had—"

"Not quite," he agreed, "but somehow as Vera believed Jessica about Edwin, all the time thinking she didn't."

"Now, William, Vera didn't—"

"Not quite, but enough to make Edwin feel that perhaps she did."

He felt something wet upon his bare breast. Elinor's tears! He rubbed her cheek gently with his left palm.

"Now, now," he said, comforting.

"I hope I can keep from hating Jessica," Elinor murmured.

"You can't hate her," he replied. "It doesn't do any good. That's why I want to get the family here under one roof so we can all understand things together."

"Jessica has been a dreadful burden," Elinor insisted.

He considered, remembering the moment when suddenly in the east parlor today he had felt the illumination of his soul. Such light could not last, of course. But he could remember it and he could live in the understanding light of memory.

"Well, yes," he agreed. "Jessica has been a burden. But then we kept trying to bear it as a burden. This was the mistake. We didn't just—let her into the house."

"How could we?" Elinor demanded. "She was a servant—"

He winced and interrupted her. "Hush, don't say that word, my darling. She just happened to be born Bertha's child. Anyway, it's Peter we must think of, now. There's still time for Peter."

And he braced himself for whatever that might mean.

The Long Love

ONE

EDWARD HASLATT was a young man both intelligent and cautious. When he had risen from his bed one fine morning he had not committed himself to a proposal of marriage. That it was possible he admitted. If the day were fair, if he found himself in a happy mood, if Margaret were kind, if they found exactly the spot he wanted for their picnic, then it might very well be that he would ask her to marry him.

He had determined that unless all these details were auspicious, he would wait. He had learned his lesson, he hoped. If she refused him again today it would be for the third time, and he would cease to think of her. That is, he hoped he could cease to think of her. While he dressed himself carefully, with an eye to the wave in his brown hair, and to the color of his tie, which was blue in contrast to his quiet brown eyes, he meditated on his tendency to faithfulness which amounted to stubbornness. Without this trait, he would certainly not have humiliated himself to ask a girl twice to marry him, to have suffered her refusals, and now to contemplate further humiliation.

Prudence and pride combined had often led him to wish that he could stop thinking about Margaret Seaton. His mother had frequently reminded him that she was not the only girl in the world and not even perhaps the prettiest, but such words did not penetrate his heart. There Margaret remained alone, and he had only to consult his heart to remember her in all the detail of her curly black hair, sea-blue eyes, fringed with long black lashes, and her somewhat wide and too mobile mouth. Her profile was to him one of utter beauty. Her forehead was square and smooth, neither high nor low, and without the slight bulge he disliked so much in his own. Between her black brows her nose was low bridged and straight and delicate until the end where it tilted slightly, merely enough to make her upper lip short. He tried to persuade himself that her face had nothing to do with his loving her so painfully, but he knew that without this face, which in every detail was what he liked best in a woman, he would not have found her so inescapable. Without this face, certainly he would not have contemplated asking her for the third time to marry him.

For now, looking out of the window, he knew that there was no excuse to be found in the day. The mists were rolling softly from the round New England hills, and by midmorning even the valleys would be bright. The small clear river was still clouded, but by its own low fog. Once the sun fell upon it this too would be dispelled. The town of Chedbury was northwest of the city of Boston. It lay upon a sloping flank of Granite Mountain, its houses encircling a central green. At the highest point of this green stood the large and ancient church of white-painted wood. Its steeple was noble in design and its roof was high shouldered, as though winged. Chedbury was proud of its church, and its design, pure and spacious, had made it impossible for other denominations to compete among the townsfolk. So wholly did the church dominate that even the town hall, built a hundred years later, dared not stand beside it. Chedbury's town meeting of that date had built the hall behind the church, and had put the firehouse beside it. From down the hill neither could be seen, and on a Sunday, when most of Chedbury sat in the walnut pews of the church, the people felt comfortably that it had been wise of their ancestors to have the fire engines handy in case some secret blaze threatened their prize possession.

Around the green were some twenty houses, a small clean hotel, Mather and Haslatt's Printing Shop, a grocery store, and the post office. Among the twenty houses the Seaton house was the largest, a square compact house, double winged, white shingled with green blinds. Upon the roof was a captain's walk, encircled by a white wooden balustrade, and the same solid balustrade enclosed the porches, both upstairs and down. Margaret, if she were at this moment looking out of the east window of her room, could see the same street upon which Edward gazed from his own window in the small but intensely neat house which was his home. The street looked washed and clean. He and Margaret had grown up on this street, all but neighbors, and he had fallen in love with her in high school. But he had been far from the most handsome or the most brilliant in their class, and she had snubbed him in favor of Harold Ames until their senior year, when, to his family's astonishment and his own, he had suddenly begun to grow tall. This drew Margaret's attention to him, and since Harold had been a year ahead and away at college, he had begun to go with Margaret. But he had not been rash enough to speak of love then, although he was already beginning to fear that he was doomed to love her. His own prudence protected him, and after their graduation he contented himself with asking her to write to him when they separated, he to go to Harvard and she to Vassar, and with seeing her, whenever she was willing, during subsequent summers and winters. This was not enough, for during two summers she was away, one on the Continent, and the other in England, where some of the ancestral Seatons still lived. Her father, Thomas Seaton, was a Tory of British water, in spite of the fact that the first Seaton had fought against the English regulars near Chedbury in 1775.

The Haslatts were English too, but not obtrusively so. Mark Haslatt, Edward's father, was not quite so well placed as Thomas Seaton. The Haslatt family had come to Chedbury a scant fifty years ago, whereas Seatons had always lived here, and as far as anyone knew always in the same old red brick house, to which Thomas Seaton had added the two wings when his children were born. The Haslatts had moved from one house to another, as their fortunes improved. Edward did not know the full history of his father, for his mother kept it wrapped in vagueness. He knew that at one time his father had even been a sheepherder on a Western ranch, and that his mother, the daughter of a homesick New England family, had brought him back to Chedbury. The first years had been desperate ones—that Edward knew, for he could remember them. He had still, in the sore recesses of his early childhood, the memory of ugly houses, poor furniture, a perpetual smell of laundry which grew acute on Monday mornings, when his father rose early to help his mother with the family wash. There was another period when his father was a conductor on the winding little trolley line between Chedbury and Deerbourne, and still another when he was trying to learn to be a contractor, apprenticed to his more successful brother, Henry Baynes. But this, too, had failed. Not until his father found himself in the printers' firm of Loomis and Mather did ease begin to come to the troubled family. There somehow Mark Haslatt fitted, and with security his confidence rose until at last he became a partner. When Loomis, the senior partner, died, the firm became Mather and Haslatt.

By the time Edward was ten years old and his younger brother Baynes was five they were comfortable in this twelve-room house. The white paint, the green blinds, the neat lawn under the elms, his own room in the third story, high enough to look out over the hills, became the setting of his boyhood. His sister Louise knew no other home. But because he could remember the other transient houses, their misery and their smell, he never quite forgot that this home was luxury.

Not that everything had been happy even here. Edward had a deep pride which forced him to frequent suffering. His common sense told him that such suffering was often self-inflicted and unnecessary, and this in turn made him ashamed to speak of it to anyone, and again in turn doubled his suffering. But so it was, and he could do nothing about it. He told himself that if Margaret were ever to marry him and he could be in his own home, free from his mother and her moods and angers, and his father and his efforts to placate and soothe, he could be happy. But he was not sure. He was a creature compound of both parents, and he knew it. He feared sometimes in his darker hours that it was quite possible his moodiness would be too much even for his own marriage.

Nevertheless he refused to face this as knowledge. He steadfastly tried to convince himself that his ups and downs were the result of external circumstances and his need to get away from a home that he had outgrown. Whether his brother and sister felt as he did, he did not know. They were outwardly friendly with him, but they shared no confidences. His parents were determined to send both of the boys to college, and Edward had not the heart to tell his father that no college could possibly provide all that was expected of it. As the eldest, he had been graduated from Harvard this spring with sufficient honor, and Baynes, now at prep school, was to enter in due time. Louise was still in grade school. She was a thin tall girl with nothing remarkable in her face, unless it was her extreme blondness. It was still not decided whether she was to go to college.

Mark Haslatt, so eager for his sons, was dubious about the education of women, and Mrs. Haslatt, who had married at seventeen, had finished only the grade school in the little Kansas town where her father had been the general storekeeper. Edward, in his own pride, had tried recently to rouse ambition in Louise but she had only listened, her pale eyes wary.

"Don't you want to go to college, Louise?" Edward had inquired with sternness.

Louise saw that she was forced to answer. "I don't care if I do," she said in cautious assent. Then immediately she added with more courage, "And I don't care if I don't."

It was a family not unhappy, one tied together with deep and unspoken loyalties, but never quite cheerful. Fear of life, memory of hard times, dread of small slights in the community and the casual forgetfulness of friends, all combined to keep the household temperature low.

For this reason the high and constant gaiety of the Seaton family seemed to Edward fascinating, if not altogether admirable. Self-assured, domineering, careless, old Thomas Seaton loved and quarreled with his handsome, white-haired wife. There was no caution in their tongues, and Edward enjoyed and yet was alarmed by the sharpness of their judgments, the edge of their wit. Without wit himself, he hoped that he might develop it were he in the clear brisk atmosphere that surrounded the Seatons. With them he was quite another man. Quiet and prudent, he was nevertheless courteous and agreeable, and he held his own well enough. He was not cowed by the Seatons, not even by old Thomas. Margaret's first admiring word had come as a consequence. "I must say, Ned, that you do hold up your end very well with Father. He's used to pertness from Sandra and me, and to tempers from Tom, but you're so—impervious. He's not used to that."

Edward had smiled, without betraying the fact that he had smarted under Thomas Seaton's thrust. "A printer, eh? Newspaper?"

"No, sir—books," Edward had answered sturdily.

"You can't get rich on that," Thomas said.

"Getting rich is not my ambition," Edward had replied.

"Ha!" Thomas had snorted. He was a big thick man, white haired and white bearded, and he wore tweed suits in a day when most gentlemen

wore black broadcloth. But that was his English squire affectation, Chedbury thought. Edward had quivered under the portentous grunt, but it was
true that he was not actually afraid of anyone. Doggedly he had overcome
in himself the fears of his family.

"Edward!" Louise's voice now floated up the stairs. "Mama wants to
know if you're ready for breakfast!"

"Coming!" he shouted. He turned from the window, gave himself a final
stare in the mirror and ran downstairs almost content with his appearance.
He had no vanity about his angular face, believing himself far from handsome. But he took some pride in his height and in his good figure, square
shouldered and lean. There were other men worse off than he, was the
way he summed himself up.

Entering the solid comfortable dining room he felt his spirits rise. It
was long before the day of antiques and the furniture was of heavy walnut,
expensive but serviceable. One of the first things his mother had wanted
when money began to accumulate in the bank was a good dining-room set.
The long mirror on the buffet met his eyes as he entered and presented
him with a double vision of the loaded breakfast table, his family seated
about, and himself at the door. Only Baynes was not there and it was of
Baynes that his mother spoke.

"Come in, Edward. I'm telling your father that I thought you cost him
a pretty penny at college but Baynes is going to spare no expense, I see
by the bills we're getting already. Your father has only just got up the
courage to tell me."

"I thought you seemed tired last night, Mary," his father said mildly.
His gray mustache was colored with egg yolk.

"So I was," she retorted, "and I'm tired again now. Do wipe the egg off
yourself!" She looked at her husband while he wiped his mouth and then
she turned to Edward. "Sit down, son. Do you want me to put up some lunch
or will Margaret take the food?"

He sat down and resolutely, although self-consciously, did not bow his
head in silent grace. His father's mumbled "blessing" over these meals had
begun to seem provincial. Yet it took some strength to begin to eat, without
even the gesture. He avoided his mother's eyes, lest catching his she be
emboldened to reprove him again for his godlessness. This made him feel
partially a coward but he was prudent. He poured heavy cream and much
sugar on the bowl of oatmeal that was waiting at his place. "Don't bother,
Mother," he said. "I'll buy something at the store."

"Nonsense," she said incisively. "Store food!"

"Then some of that chocolate cake," he suggested. He was not at all
sure of Margaret's efforts but he would not have revealed this to his family.

His mother looked doubtful. "I'll make some sandwiches, too, out of that
chicken we had last night," she said. "Then you'll be on the safe side."

"Safe side of what?" his father inquired dryly.

Edward smiled and his mother laughed. When she laughed they all forgave her. "Safe side of anything!" she said briskly. "Want more coffee, Mark?"

"No," his father said, "I've got to get down to the shop."

"Don't act like you were sorry to go," his mother rejoined. "You know that the day when you have to quit shop will be the sorriest day of your life."

"Oh, Mama," Louise cried in distress. "Why do you?"

Her mother had risen and was at the kitchen door, but she paused. "Why do I what, miss?" she asked.

"Nothing, nothing," her husband said peaceably. He folded his napkin, stared at the swinging door through which she passed, and then looked at his watch.

"Know what I'm going to do the day I retire?" he asked Louise.

"What, Papa?" she asked with mild interest.

"I'm going to catch the first train west and see where I used to live and maybe stay there," he said.

"Oh, Papa!" she wailed.

"You'll never retire," Edward said comfortably. He was eating buttered muffin with zest and appetite, and since the egg and bacon were exactly as he liked, he added them heartily to the foundation of oatmeal already consumed. He supposed he had stopped growing, but his hunger was huge.

At this moment the telephone rang in the hall, and startled them all. It was a new instrument in the house, and the bell rang harshly and always unexpectedly. Edward hastened out of the room, picked up the heavy receiver and listened to a series of whirrs and rumbles. Out of these came at last Margaret's voice, fresh and impatient. "Is that you, Ned?" she demanded.

"Yes, it is!" he shouted.

"Don't bellow, Ned! It takes off my ear," she called back. "Ned, can you hear me?"

"Yes, I can," he replied in a lower tone.

"You sound so odd," she complained, "as though you were shy."

"I'm not," he said briefly.

"Ned!" she called again.

"Yes?"

"Ned, will you be very disappointed if we put off the picnic?"

His heart fell into the pit of his stomach. Then he grew so angry that he was speechless.

"Ned, did you hear?" she cried.

"Yes, I do hear!" he cried back. "And I shall be very disappointed, Margaret."

There was silence for an instant. Then her voice came back as vigorous as ever.

"It's only that Father has suddenly decided to go to New York and wants me to go with him."

"I've been counting on this day ever since you came home, which is three weeks and more," he replied.

"Oh, Ned!" she cried with new impatience. "You're always here and so am I—as if there weren't millions of days!"

"We may not get such another fine day," he said. Then he went on grimly. "If you don't want to come, then I don't want you to come, but let's not plan another day, Margaret. Let's just say there won't be a picnic—ever again!"

His mother came to the door of the hall, a spoon in her hand, and he saw her make fierce faces at him.

"Edward Haslatt!" she hissed. "If you take this—"

He waved her away, trying to hear Margaret.

"Oh, dear, I knew you'd feel that way," she complained.

"Of course I do," he said stubbornly.

"Ned, if I come, will you promise to behave?"

"Depends on what you mean by that," he said.

He wished his mother would go away, so that he could speak freely. But the telephone was never considered private. His father stood waiting at the front door, and Louise was now in the hall.

"You know what I mean," Margaret insisted.

"I do not," he retorted.

"Edward, you're so—indomitable!" she complained.

"Maybe I am," he agreed.

There was a silence so long that he wondered if she had hung up. Then she said in a resigned voice, "Very well. Do you like ham or beef sandwiches?"

"Mother is putting up some chicken," he said. "Don't you bother."

"Oh, good," Margaret said, without gratitude in her voice. "Then I'll only bring apple pie, shall I?"

"That'll be all right," he said shortly. "I'll come by for you in half an hour."

He hung up the receiver and faced his family. "It's all right," he said shortly.

"Shall I make the sandwiches?" his mother asked.

"Yes, please, Mother," Edward said.

His father kissed his mother and went his way and Louise began to clear the table and his mother returned to the kitchen. He himself went upstairs and to his own room. He felt shaken, and he did not want his mother to see it. The mild hopefulness with which he had begun the morning was now entirely gone. He committed himself to pessimism. Margaret did not love him and would never love him. He wished that he had had the sense to abandon the picnic. Then his deep unalterable stubbornness rose in him. No, he would go, he would do everything exactly as he had planned. He would ask her to marry him and when she refused he would tell her that he would never ask her again.

When he came downstairs with his hard straw hat under his arm, his angular young face was so stern that his mother said not a word when she handed him the neatly wrapped box into which she had packed his lunch. He took it and had already reached the door, when he heard her speak.

He paused.

"What'd you say, Mother?"

Her gray eyes were profoundly tender. "I said, God bless you, my son," she repeated.

He blushed with surprise. "Thank you, Mother," he muttered and was gone.

He had hired a horse and buggy, and from the high seat of the vehicle he saw Margaret waiting for him on the porch of the Seaton house. Any other girl in Chedbury would have waited for him inside the house, and any other girl would have worn hat and coat and possibly gloves. But Margaret sat on the top step, leaning her bare dark head dreamily against the white painted post. She had a paper parcel beside her, undoubtedly the pie, and she wore her old gray tweed suit, the skirt of which he privately considered too short. It was at least six inches above her ankles. She knew how he felt about it, for her too discerning eye had caught his disapproval one rainy day when they had met accidentally on the street.

"What's the matter?" she had demanded. "Do I have a smudge on my face?"

When she had wormed out of him why he had averted his eyes, she had laughed at him. "I tore the edge of my skirt on a barbed wire fence," she said frankly, "and so I had to shorten it all around. Don't be silly, Ned." He had retired into silence and they had parted.

Now as he drew near he felt that had she really cared about him, she would have put on something else. "For two cents I wouldn't ask her to marry me," he thought gloomily, but he knew he would.

She looked up alertly when he reached the gate.

"Slowpoke!" she called. "I've been waiting ages." She jumped up with the lightness that was so pleasant to see, and walked quickly down the path. He knew that at the windows along the streets curtains were drawn back to see them go off, but she would not care.

"It took me considerable time to figure out whether you were coming or not," he said. He made preparations to get out of the buggy, but she swung herself up beside him.

"I see you've got the new horse," she said, paying no heed to his last remark.

"I told Jim I didn't want the balky one," he rejoined. Everyone in Chedbury knew Jim Smiley's horses intimately.

They rode in silence for some time. He was still too ruffled to make talk, and his heart was very low. In spite of the old suit Margaret was looking beautiful. She had put on a blue linen blouse, and he was startled to see that it was collarless. It was almost as strange as if she were décolleté. She caught him looking at her neck.

"If there is anything I hate it is having to wear a high collar on a picnic," she instantly declared. "It's an old blouse and I cut the collar off."

"Looks nice," he said with reserve.

"I don't really care how it looks," she said.

They were silent again for a while. Then being young, she but twenty-one and he twenty-two, the magic of the day stole into their blood. Though they lived to be a hundred, there could not be enough of such days. The mists were gone, and the sun shone down on the changeful autumn colors of the trees. The street of Chedbury, lined with old elms, its white houses set back in green lawns, became soon a country road between low stone walls, and then a wide upward trail into a brilliantly shadowed wood, beside a clear brook.

Edward's mind busied itself with the question of when he should make his proposal of marriage. If he kept it unspoken upon his mind, he could not enjoy his food. On the other hand, he would have no appetite whatever once all hope was gone. He was disgusted with himself to discover that he was so foolish as still to harbor hope in his heart. When she had shown him so plainly this morning!

The trail reached a sudden parting in the trees, and they looked down the beautiful hillside upon which Chedbury lay, now the very picture of a village, the houses glinting white in the sun and the spire of the church lifting itself slender and tall above the surrounding trees. This, he decided suddenly, would be the place, let come what may. He drew up the horse and jumped down.

"Let's stop here, Margaret," he said.

She laughed. "Don't be so grim—unless you are going to murder me, Ned. Heavens!"

But she leaped down in one of her long graceful motions and stood only a little less tall than he, waiting. Her bright blue eyes were knowing and confident, and while he felt all his love rush out toward her it occurred to him that some small amount of shyness in her might have been more natural. There was nothing about her that was like other women, and this was why he loved her so desperately and yet with foreboding. Life with Margaret could not be peaceful, whatever else it was. He did not deceive himself. Had there been any way to save himself, he might have done so, but there was no way. If she would not have him, he supposed in common sense that some day he would marry someone else, but he could not imagine it.

"Sit down on that log, Margaret," he commanded her.

She sat down obediently, and he stood and looked down at her and saw what he expected—that her eyes were full of laughter.

"Put the whip down, Ned," she said gaily. "Suppose old Miss Townsend is using her telescope!"

He turned abruptly without answering, tied the horse, and threw the whip into the buggy. Then he sat down on the log. Sitting thus, they were below the level of the treetops on the hill and therefore invisible. At this hour of a weekday it was not likely that anyone would be on the mountain.

"Margaret," he began firmly, "let's have it out once and for all."

Her hands flew to her face. "Oh, dear!" she said from behind them. "Before lunch?"

"Here and now," he said in the same stubborn voice. "It'll be for the last time, I promise."

"No, Ned, don't promise!" This little voice, coming from behind her hands, threw him off entirely.

"Eh?" he exclaimed. "Why, Margaret!" Mad hope surged up in him. "You don't mean—"

She shook her head, her hands still against her eyes. "I don't mean anything! You're always thinking I mean things!"

He reached over and with both his hands pulled hers away from her face and held them hard. She tried to free herself and could not.

"Say what you do mean," he commanded.

She stopped struggling and looked suddenly sensible and mild. The sun fell full on her vivid face, and it was all he could do to keep from taking her into his arms. "You didn't even bring a hat, and your nose is already freckling," he accused her.

"That wasn't what I thought you were going to say," she said softly.

"It isn't," he retorted, still holding her hands, "but you keep taking my mind off . . . Margaret!"

"Yes?"

"Shall I go on?"

"If you must . . ."

He considered her, the red mouth, the creamy neck, and the little black curls of her hair. "I'll never give up," he muttered.

She lowered her lashes at this and was silent, and he felt the triumph of her yielding.

"Margaret," he spoke her name in a deep and solemn voice, "for the third time, I ask you—will you be my wife?"

Each time he had asked her she had responded differently. The first time she had laughed, had shaken her head, and had run away. He had been fool enough to blurt out his love for her at the senior dance, and almost immediately her next partner had claimed her, a Groton fellow whom he loathed, and not only because he had lost the editorship of the *Harvard Crimson* to him. The second time was well considered. He had walked home with her from church, and artfully taking her the long way around, he had imagined that she would need his help on an icy road. But she had been very independent indeed. When he had again asked her to marry him she had said positively, "No."

"Why not?" he had demanded, instantly hurt.

"I don't feel like it," she had replied.

To that she had not been willing to add one word, and they had walked the rest of the way in silence.

Now he waited trembling. She tugged her hands away suddenly from his, and he was terrified. But he let them go quickly and sat in silence. When she spoke, it was with unexpected thoughtful calm.

"Ned, of course I have been thinking a great deal. I knew you'd ask me again. Goodness, how I know you—much better than you do me! That's the trouble. If I didn't know you so thoroughly I'd probably marry you right off. But—"

She paused, shook her head, and looked sad. He felt his heart fall again, like a stone thrown in a well. "What's the matter with me?" he asked. He was so wounded that he could not summon his pride.

He expected laughter, but he was further confounded when she lifted serious eyes to his. "You're good," she replied with entire honesty. "It's me."

His heart bounced up again. He leaned toward her ardently. "If it's only that, Margaret, darling, darling, leave it to me. I'll take you as you are."

But she moved away from him, out of reach of his hands. "There isn't anything the matter with me, Ned. It's just—I want a very special kind of marriage."

He looked so blank that she gave him a slight push. "There—you see you don't even know what I mean!"

"Why don't you tell me?" he demanded.

She considered this and began again. "I don't want to be married the way other people are. I want it to be splendid—fun, you know, and strong enough for us to fly at each other when we feel like it, and say what we really think, and yet know that nothing can separate us, not even moments of hate. I'm not a careful person, Ned. I don't want to have to stop and think whether something is going to hurt your feelings. I'll get tired of that. Everything's got to be straight and strong and clear."

"I can take that," he said.

"I'm not sure you can," she retorted. Her firm hand busied itself with a bit of crumbling wood on the log. Every time they met he had looked at that hand to see if it wore a ring. The nightmare of his life was that she would engage herself to someone else before he had a chance to make her see she must marry him.

"How can I make you sure?" he asked.

"I don't know," she replied.

He had not imagined such an impasse as this—Margaret willing to marry him if she could be sure he was strong enough! He knew what she meant. With her extraordinary intelligence she had penetrated his weakness, the ease with which he could be wounded—his feelings hurt, as his mother put it.

"You're pretty smart," he said slowly. "Any man takes his life in his hands when he marries a smart woman."

"That's true," she agreed.

"But it's you or none, Margaret. I'm that sort," he said slowly.

"If I marry you," she said gravely, "it will be my life and my career. Will it be yours?"

He looked into the clear and honest depths of her sea-blue eyes, and then he saw dimly a vision of what marriage could mean to a man—a companionship complete, a friendship profound, something as far above the dull mating of the commonplace as man was above the beast. "Yes," he said. "That I can promise—and I do."

"Then will you marry me?" she asked.

The wonder of these words lay in their simplicity. She spoke them quietly, not moving to touch him, not putting out her hand.

"Are you—asking *me?*" he gasped.

"Yes!"

"Oh, Margaret!"

He rose and drew her up to him. "Sure you mean it?"

"If you'll keep your promise."

With his right hand he pressed her head against his breast. "If you know me so well, don't you know I keep my promises?"

She lifted her head and looked at him. "Yes," she said again. It was assent and faith, and he trembled with fear and joy. . . .

Across this sublimity she broke a moment later with a murmur. He bent to hear it.

"I'm hungry," she was saying into his coat, "aren't you?"

He laughed and let her go. "Starved! But we can't eat here on the road."

"Why not? It isn't as private as making marriage proposals."

"No, but it's not my idea." He felt rising amazement. "Matter of fact, none of it's been what I planned this morning."

"You *planned?*"

"Of course. You don't think I would leave the biggest thing in my life to chance, do you?"

"Oh, Ned, do you plan everything?" she cried.

"Of course," he said stoutly.

She flew into a fit of incomprehensible laughter at this and ran to the buggy and he untied the horse and leaped in beside her, and they began to wind slowly up the trail. He put an arm about her and felt the astonishing ineffable joy of her leaning upon him. She said, "I'll always be spoiling your plans, because I only do things when I think of them."

"I'll learn that—and everything," he declared.

"But when you get to the picnic spot—"

"It's not a real spot," he felt it only honest to say.

"Yes, it is, if you dreamed of it!" she insisted.

They found it over the brow of the mountain, beside another stream, that eddied in a small pool. Both of them cried out at the same moment that it was found, he pointing with the whip, she with her forefinger. He unharnessed the horse and tethered it at a little distance and she unpacked the lunch. His mother had put in a small clean tablecloth and inspired by this, Margaret picked red oak leaves and laid them together for plates. Upon them she placed the neat sandwiches, the cake, and the pie. He was about to sit down beside her but she shook her head. "Sit across from me, Ned. I want to see how you'll look every day at breakfast."

He obeyed, and was mortified to feel that he looked foolishly shy. "I'm not much to stare at," he said, trying to be casual.

"I've hated every handsome man I ever saw," she remarked. "Sandwich, Ned!"

He took one and bit into it. "You didn't hate Harold Ames," he reminded her.

"Don't be silly—I did!" she retorted.

"Did he ask you to marry him?"

She bit deeply into her sandwich. "What if he did?" she asked.

"Nothing—only I don't like it." He was ashamed to tell her that jealousy was one of his vices. Instinctively he knew that she would not tolerate jealousy. Then he felt it a necessity to be honest with her. "I'll have to tell you I'm a jealous disposition—at least I think I am."

"I know you are," she said.

He looked at her. "Do you!" he rejoined somewhat feebly. Then his rare humor glinted. "Are you always going to tell me you already know everything I tell you? It'll make for a dull marriage."

"I won't always tell you," she said, dimpling. The two dimples in her cheeks were what he had seen first about her as a little girl at Chedbury birthday parties.

"Know what Lucy Snell used to say about you?" he asked with wicked intent.

"What?"

"She said you laughed on purpose to show your dimples."

She laughed. "Maybe I do."

"Doesn't anything ever make you angry, Margaret?"

"Not if I feel happy, and I nearly always do."

He sighed. "I wish I could say that! I have the devil of a temper."

"I don't mind the temper if you'll bear my not being afraid of it. I shan't take anything from you, Ned."

"I don't want you to." He put down his second sandwich and looked at her earnestly. "Margaret, I want to say something now while I'm calm and happier than I've ever been in my life. And I want you to remember it when I'm in one of my sulks, and pay no mind to me."

"Yes, Ned?" She put down her sandwich that she might listen properly.

"I don't want you to be afraid of me, ever—or ever to yield to me. Stand up to me, Margaret—and help me!"

"I will," she said softly.

"At whatever cost?" he asked sternly.

"Yes!" Again her beautiful full *yes!*

"Even if I should strike you?"

Her eyes flashed. "If you hit me I'll hit you!" she said warmly.

They both laughed. "Free for all, eh?" he said fondly.

By common accord they leaned across the little tablecloth and kissed. Thus passed the glorious day. He would not have dreamed of prolonging it beyond the prudence of Chedbury's watchful eyes. His tenderness for her was bottomless—he would protect her even from himself. So, timing the drive home by the stand of the sun in the sky, soon after four he rose from the spot where he had been lying at her feet while she sat on a low old stump.

"We must be going, Margaret, if we're to get home before sunset."

"Why should we get home before sunset?" she inquired dreamily.

He did not answer at once, busying himself with harnessing the reluctant horse. She knew as well as he did why they should get home and she was teasing him. For a moment he toyed with the idea of accepting the provocation. He might say, "Very well, we won't get home." But he was afraid. There was no telling how far her mischief might carry her. Once when they were children someone had dared her to jump from the barn roof on the Seaton place, and he had stood by, not believing that she would be so foolish. But she had been so foolish and he could never forget the horrible moment when she had jumped into the air and he saw her dark curls flying behind her head and her arms outspread like wings.

"Remember the day you jumped off the barn roof?" he asked now.

"What makes you think of that?" she asked.

"I wonder!" He waited until the horse was ready. "Come, Margaret," he said firmly.

She wavered and then suddenly obeyed. The sight of her thus docile drew the love out of him like lodestone and he took her into his arms and kissed her more ardently than he had yet allowed himself.

"Oh, Ned," she whispered, "we are going to be happy?"

"Of course we are," he agreed.

So they came down the mountain through the late and golden sunshine, and the trail became the country road and the road became again the street of Chedbury, and by the time he reached the gate of her house they were sitting decorously side by side and not too close. He leaped down, opened the gate, and their hands clung for a moment.

"Good night," she said softly and her eyes glowed dark as sapphires.

"Good night, dear love," he said. "I'd call you tonight, but the family is always about. Tomorrow I'll be over to see your father."

"Let me tell him first!"

He paused at this. "No, Margaret—leave it to me to speak for myself."

"But why?"

"I'd feel better to have it so."

"Then I've got to keep it all night? I'll tell Mother at least."

"No, Margaret," he insisted. "Tonight let's just have it all to ourselves."

She opened her mouth to protest, then did not.

"All right, Ned," she said softly, and gave him her quick and brilliant smile.

Upon this he left her and drove the horse and buggy to the livery stable and went home on foot through the golden street.

Now that he was alone he felt solemn, exalted and set apart. He had given his promise to Margaret that their marriage would be his life and his career. What this meant he did not fully know, but he knew that Margaret was his center, and all he did must be built about her. He was capable of devotion as few men were, perhaps, and it did not degrade him to know it. He found a deep fulfillment in self-devotion. But he knew that only Margaret could have called this fulfillment into being. Had he married someone else, he would at this moment have been thinking of himself. Now he was thinking of Margaret.

He lifted his head and breathed in the cool autumn air, sharp and pure. He lifted his eyes to the mountain where so much had taken place. The day was divided as cleanly as if a sword had cut across time. This morning he had been one man and now he was another. His marriage was to be like none he had ever seen.

He opened the heavy walnut door of his father's house and stepped into the hall and listened. The house was silent. Then he heard a murmur of voices from the kitchen, his father's and his mother's. He wanted to tell no one of what had come about this day. Tomorrow when he went to see Mr. Seaton he would have to tell, and then his own family must know. But tonight must be the drawn-out dream which the day had been. He tiptoed upstairs, entered his own room, and stood with his back to the closed door.

The room was impressed upon his memory by childhood and youth, and yet now it looked new to him. No, it looked as old as a shell outgrown, a skin cast aside. His home was here no more.

He moved about silently, washed himself and changed his clothes, and went downstairs. The door of the dining room was open and he saw Louise setting the table.

He paused at the door. "Supper about ready?"

She looked at him vaguely. "I suppose so."

"I'll fetch the milk jug," he said. He went into the kitchen and was immediately aware that he had interrupted talk between his parents. His father looked at him self-consciously, and his mother, continuing to stir the gravy she was making in a saucepan, did not look at him.

"I've come to fetch the milk jug," he said.

"It's there," his mother said.

His father got to his feet from the chair behind the stove. "Have a good day?" he asked, trying to be casual.

"Yes, very good," Edward said, trying to be as casual. He opened the icebox and took out a bottle of milk and poured it and carried the jug into the dining room. Louise had finished the table and was at the window staring into the twilight of the street. He wondered what her thoughts were and could not have asked, knowing full well how he at her age would have refused such a question.

At the same moment his mother pushed open the door and came in, carrying a platter of sliced boiled beef, covered with the gravy. "Come along, now," she said briskly. "Let's eat while the food is hot."

His father came in while she hurried back for potatoes and cabbage, and they sat down. The evening, Edward thought, could be exactly like every other. Only he knew that it was not.

"Edward!"

His mother's ghostly voice woke him that night out of a sound sleep. He saw her standing in the middle of his bedroom, wrapped in her gray flannel dressing gown. Her hair was in curlers and her face was pale in the moonlight that fell through the wide open window.

He sat up in bed, half dazed. "What's wrong, Mother?"

She came near and sat on the bed, then rose and shut the window and sat down in the barrel-backed chair, shivering.

"That's what I don't know," she said in a low tense voice. "I can't sleep for thinking of things."

"What things, Mother?" Instinctively he knew.

"Edward, I know something happened between you and Margaret today."

"What makes you think so, Mother?"

"You were different all evening."

"Was I?" He was flabbergasted at this, having flattered himself that he had been entirely natural.

"Even Louise noticed it," his mother said.

His stubbornness rose up in him and he did not reply. What claim had anybody on his confidence until he chose to give it? He was no longer a child. That he had spoken his love and that Margaret had accepted it made them both free of the past.

"I don't want to seem to inquire into your affairs," his mother said after a decent interval, "but it would hurt me if you got married without telling me, Edward."

"I am not married," he said reluctantly.

"Are you engaged?" She put the question so swiftly that it was like the pounce of a bird. He did not know how to parry it, being too honest. "Well, yes, I am," he said slowly. Then his anger got the better of him.

"I was going to tell you tomorrow, Mother. It did seem to me more decent to speak to Mr. Seaton first, after I'd found out Margaret's mind."

"But I'm your mother," she said.

He recognized the pained sadness in her voice. How often in his childhood had it compelled him to acts which he had hated! In his adolescence it had still compelled him, although he had occasionally protested and with anger. That phase had passed, too, and he had learned to remain silent when he caught the overtones in his mother's voice. Now, sitting up in his bed, he was enraged to feel her forcing him back into his adolescence. All his new manhood resisted her. He set his lips firmly and gazed at a print on the wall above her head. It was one he had chosen himself when he was fifteen, a white ship sailing at full speed over a bright blue sea, under a sky as blue. He knew now that as a print it was not the best, but on so many mornings had he waked to that fresh blue sea and flying ship that he would have missed it, had it been gone. He thought, "I'll want to take that with me."

"You're not going to say a word?" his mother inquired.

"Not till tomorrow, Mother."

"Then I call it heartless of you," she declared. Her square face turned a coppery red and she pulled at her corded belt and tied it more tightly. "And I shall go on and say what I was going to say. We've nothing to be ashamed of. Your father's business is as good as any in Chedbury or around. What I'm saying is for your own good."

"Don't say it, Mother," he broke in.

"I will say it!" Her voice rose. "I'm not to be stopped by my own son, I hope. I warn you, Edward, you'll never be happy with those Seatons. She's a stuck-up proud girl, and she hasn't a proper decency."

He kept his eyes on the flying ship and the blue that was the color of Margaret's eyes.

"A poor housekeeper, too! And, Edward, they don't think a thing of divorce. You know even Thomas Seaton's own sister has been divorced. That's why she has to live in Paris. Decent people won't have her here. And where does old Seaton get his money? He's never worked enough to have it. Somewhere in New York, speculating! Who knows? And they have no religion—he's a freethinker, and she'll have freethinking ways and bring up your children different from all of us, and I'll have no comfort in them."

He glanced nervously at her hands. They were trembling and he knew what would happen. The next moment she began to cry soundlessly, and then she hurried out of the room, leaving the door wide open. He sighed, got up, closed the door and opened the window and turned off the lamp. He'd have to tell Margaret that after all his mother had wormed it out of him. Only by thinking of Margaret, only by going over the whole day, minute by minute, was he able to reinforce his determination and renew his love and so begin again his own life. Then he fell asleep, comforted. His mother did not matter any more.

Under his everyday exterior the next morning Edward concealed from his mother any memory of their conversation in the night. With determination he kept himself from calling Margaret on the telephone, even from his father's office. For his father, after muttering his usual blessing and then in abstraction eating half his breakfast, had suddenly said, "If you have nothing better to do, Edward, I could take a little help in the office this morning."

Edward nodded and nothing more was said between them. His mother was silent, too, beyond the necessary questions about the food, and Louise ate in her usual silence. But Edward knew, as well as though words had told him, that his mother had repeated to his father the midnight scene, and that this morning at the office his father would manage to be alone with him and to say something. He could not imagine what it would be.

But none of it mattered, he told himself. Yesterday was true, and this afternoon he would see Margaret. He did not look forward with pleasure to his interview with Tomas Seaton, but he was not afraid of it. He would be dignified and self-assured, knowing that he had Margaret's promise, and even if the older man objected, the marriage would go on just the same.

The meal was finished, and Edward and his father rose simultaneously. "I'll meet you at the door, Father," he said.

He kissed his mother, as he knew she liked him to do, nodded to Louise, and left the room. Out in the hall he toyed again with the temptation of calling Margaret, and decided against it. He suspected that she slept late and it would be harder to call and not hear her voice than not to call. He put on his brown gabardine topcoat and a few minutes later he and his father were walking down the street together. Chedbury was peculiarly pleasant in the morning, the houses clean, the windows shining, and smoke curling softly from the chimneys. Sooner or later front doors opened and other men came briskly out to go to work. So he and his father proceeded, exchanging few words, but the silence was easy.

At the shop he fell behind to allow his father to go ahead and the men looked up and nodded and he followed his father into the rather large office.

"Sit down there," his father said. "I'll give you some proofs to read."

Edward obeyed, taking off his hat and coat and hanging them on a rack in the corner. The office had not changed during all the years he had known it, and he had often sat here in the odd hours he had helped his father during vacations.

He began to read the proofs, dull pages of a pamphlet being put out by some historical society, and it was the middle of the morning when suddenly his father spoke.

"Edward," he said solemnly, "how do you propose to make your living?"

Edward looked up. He knew that his father had shown extraordinary patience not only on this day, but during the past four years, while he had been pursuing his somewhat leisurely way through college. The very necessity of his father's youth to make an early livelihood had made him take pride in being patient with his son.

"I think it's the first time you have ever asked me the question, Father," he said. He put down proofs and pencil, and wheeled around on his screw-bottomed chair.

"I've never had to ask you," his father said proudly. "But the time has come now when I presume you will want to earn your own way, and certainly the time has come when I'd like to ease your mother's life a little. I want her to have help in the house. She hasn't been willing so long as you were in college and the other two in school. She isn't as strong as she was—it stands to reason a woman can't be. I've told her to hire somebody this week."

"I'm glad of that," Edward said heartily, and paused.

"Well?" his father said.

Edward smiled his slight cool smile. "It would be easy to say I know what I want to do, Father, if I had any special talent. But I haven't—except a general interest in books."

"Books?" his father repeated, astonished.

"Are you surprised?" Edward inquired. "But you've printed books all these years."

"Not just books," his father corrected him. "I've printed anything that came my way—catalogues, pamphlets, bulletins, wedding announcements, Christmas cards, anything."

"I'm thinking you might like me to take the book section of the business and develop it a little," Edward said daringly.

He saw immediately that this was an entirely new and somewhat frightening idea to his father.

"Books are a risk," his father said slowly. "Look at them piled up in the second-hand shops in Boston! It scares me every time I go there. People read them once and then sell them."

"They have to buy them before they can read them," Edward argued.

"All these newfangled public libraries," his father went on. "That fellow Carnegie—the book business will sink to nothing. Who's going to buy a book if he can read it for nothing?"

"Will you take me on for a year?" Edward asked.

His father's opposition crystallized what had been the vaguest wanderings of his own mind. It was true that he did not know what he wanted to do for a livelihood. In college he had lived, by the chance of a roommate, in the midst of a group of young men who had not needed to think of work immediately after graduation, and he had fallen into the way of contemplation rather than activity. Yet he knew that this was an atmosphere entirely alien to him, and that he must indeed work with all his ability as soon as possible. But he had been graduated only last June. Beyond all else, he had felt that until he had settled the matter of his marriage with Margaret, he could not choose a livelihood. Too much depended on the life that she would want and where they might choose to live. He was somewhat perturbed now by his own abruptness in the decision he had made even for a year.

His father meanwhile had been pondering the question. "Maybe for a year," he said slowly. "I'll talk with Mather, provided you don't do anything to call for extra capital."

Edward did not reply for a moment. The business depression, which had terrified his father and had shadowed his last year at college, was perhaps beginning to recede. The banks had been saved by the millionaires, staking their fortunes against the fears of little men with nothing. His father had been almost revoltingly grateful to "the big fellows."

"If I can't convince you by the end of the year to put in some capital, I shall consider myself a failure," Edward said.

He was about to wheel his chair around again when his father raised his hand. "Wait a minute, son—I promised your mother something."

Edward saw him flush and immediately felt at ease. "Mother was cross with me in the night, I know," he said frankly. "But, Father, if you don't mind, I'll just wait until tomorrow and then everything will be clear."

"Your mother is easily hurt, son," his father reminded him.

"I know, because she has passed that same quality on to me," Edward said quietly. "But I think it's wrong to be so quick to be wounded, and it's a trait I mean to get over."

He turned then in good earnest and picking up his pencil he went to work again, and his father said no more. They went home together at noon and only the barest words of business passed between them. They ate in almost entire silence the noon meal of meat and vegetables and an apple pie and then Edward went upstairs to his own room. He knew that Thomas Seaton slept for an hour between one and two. It was his intention to reach the house in time to see Margaret before her father waked and then, as soon as possible afterward, to appear before him.

He washed, examined his somewhat too easily growing beard, and decided to shave again. Then he dressed himself in his good dark blue serge suit, white shirt, and stiff collar. The tie he usually wore was dark blue, too, but today, thinking of Margaret, he chose one she had given him last Christmas of wine-red satin with a stripe of blue. Thus arrayed, with care to his shoes and his nails, he felt that he had done all he could, and he went downstairs and out of doors without seeing his mother or looking for her. But some impulse when he was on his way made him turn his head and he saw her standing at the sitting-room window, looking out after him, her hand over her mouth. He could not see her eyes, but he felt their painful and earnest gaze, and he lifted his arm and waved to her. With no more than an instant's hesitation she waved back to him with her white handkerchief, and at the effort, all his resentment left him.

As well as he knew himself, he knew her and that she had forgiven him and he was the happier for it.

"Softhearted, that's what I am," he thought half sadly, and wondered whether his life would be the harder for his soft heart.

Thus somewhat soberly he approached the big brick house which Chedbury merely called "Seatons'." It stood back from the street in the midst of its traditional elms, and the lawn was thick with falling leaves. No one was to be seen except the small hunched figure of old Bill Core, who tended the garden. He was gathering leaves slowly with a bamboo rake as Edward went up the brick walk.

"Anybody around?" Edward asked.

"Not that I've saw," Bill replied. He leaned on his rake. "Who're you lookin' for?"

"Margaret?" Edward said tentatively.

"Out under the apple tree behind the house last I saw," Bill said. "That was before dinner, though." He chewed slowly and grindingly, and spat a large dark brown blob into the leaves.

But Edward did not go to the apple tree. He felt some formality in the afternoon ahead of him and he went up the five marble steps to the front door of the house. There he rang the bell. Usually the maid opened the door but this time to his pleasure Margaret herself flung it wide.

"I saw you coming," she said softly. "He's just waking up. How beautiful you look! Don't you love that tie? Promise me you'll let me choose all your ties! Shall we stay outside a bit?"

"I'd rather get it over," he said, still on the threshold.

She laughed. "Poor Ned! He's not too bad, really. Though I rather think—" she broke off and shook her head.

He stepped inside the door. "Think what?" he demanded.

"I'd better not tell you."

"Margaret, tell me!" he insisted.

"No, I won't," she declared. "Because it's too silly."

"But you thought it!"

"Well, I think very silly things—often."

Before he could protest again Thomas Seaton's voice shouted suddenly from the library. "Who are you talking to, Margaret?"

She turned her head toward the voice. "To Ned, Father!"

There was a grunt to this and silence.

"He's only just waked," Margaret explained.

"Tell me what you were thinking about?" Edward said stubbornly.

"Oh, my goodness," she said suddenly. "Well, it was this—Father once had the idea that he wanted me to marry somebody—a man in New York."

"He did?" Edward exclaimed. Rage ran in his veins suddenly and he took a step toward the library. Then he turned. She was standing with both hands folded under her chin, looking at him with bright blue eyes, not laughing, and he came back.

"You can't change your mind now," he said gravely.

She shook her head. "No fear," she said.

Thereupon his rage and his pride combined and he walked into the library. The afternoon was warm, and the room was sunlit and silent. Tobacco and leather and old books scented the air with a dry and musky odor. A long window opened to the always neglected gardens and yellow leaves from an elm tree drifted across the panes. Thomas Seaton sat between the arms of a sagging leather armchair and Edward saw his grizzled red head leaning on its back.

"Is that you, Peg?" he said drowsily.

Margaret answered from the door. "Father, I told you Ned was coming to see you."

Edward turned and frowned at her. "Go away, please, Margaret," he said. "I shan't want you here while we're talking."

She made a face at him and vanished, shutting the door with unnecessary noise.

Thomas Seaton laughed. "That's right, my boy," he said in his slow rich voice. "Order her about. It's good for her. Come and sit down."

Without moving even to lift his head, he pursed his thick lips at the chair across the hearth and there Edward sat down. Margaret's father, he thought, was not prepossessing. His stained tweed vest was open and his belt unloosed, and over the brown shirt he wore his big hands were folded. He had taken off his shoes and had put his feet on a faded brown velvet hassock. But his large sleepy face was benign and amused.

"Eh?" he said.

"There's no use my beating about the bush at this late day, Mr. Seaton," Edward said promptly. "I suppose you've noticed that I've been interested in Margaret for years."

"I've noticed," Thomas Seaton said dryly. "But there've been others."

"Well, I'm different from them all, I think," Edward said, allowing himself the smallest of smiles. "I asked her to marry me yesterday and she said she would."

"She's a very changeable miss, and it wouldn't be fair of me to keep that from you," Thomas Seaton retorted.

"She's never said 'yes' to me before, nevertheless, and I shan't let her change her mind," Edward said firmly.

Thomas Seaton laughed again. "Then what have you come to see me about?" he inquired.

"I wanted to tell you myself," Edward said. At the older man's laughter he felt his ready pride ruffle and prick and he was grave.

Thomas Seaton unfolded his hands and pulled out a yellowed silk handkerchief from his pocket and rubbed his face all over. The act seemed to wake him. He opened his eyes wide, sat up in his chair, and began to stuff tobacco into an old meerschaum pipe.

"If I must take this seriously," he said, "then I'd better put my mind to it. Margaret's my favorite child, and I can't just give her away. How are you planning to make a living, young man?"

"I hope you realize I wouldn't ask Margaret to be my wife, without giving some thought as to her support," Edward replied. "My father has the print shop as you know, Mr. Seaton. I shall help him there, and likely take it over some day."

"You aren't the only son," Thomas Seaton said in the same dry voice.

"No, sir, but I'm five years older than Baynes, and there's no competition there. By the time he's ready to work, I'll be well up in the business—maybe its head. Dad owns the business, really. Mr. Mather has turned eighty, you know."

"Don't push your father about," the older man said suddenly.

"I wouldn't think of it," Edward replied hotly.

Thomas Seaton began to puff on his pipe. He leaned back again. "A temper of your own, I see."

"I'm sorry," Edward said instantly.

"How much do you think you'll make—let's say, at your top?"

Edward hesitated. His father made, he supposed, five or six thousand a year. Whether that would seem much or little to a Seaton he had no way of knowing. He looked into Seaton's eyes, blue and bright. "I have no way of knowing," he said frankly. "It all depends on myself. I shall do more than carry on the shop. I've told my father that I want to begin to print books for myself—publish them. That might do very well."

"You like books?" Thomas Seaton inquired.

"There's something about them," Edward admitted reluctantly. He did not wish to reveal to this observing older man the peculiar influence of books upon him. Without any desire to write a book of his own, all his creative mind stirred when he held a good book in his hand. If, after he had read it, he felt it become a part of himself, it was precious to him. He wanted it well bound and more than once he had gone to Boston and had ordered rebound in scraps of leather or mohair some book which he felt had become his own.

"Know anything about book publishing?" Thomas Seaton inquired.

"I have my own feelings about it," Edward replied.

A long silence fell upon them after this. Thomas Seaton's eyes closed and Edward wondered if he were about to fall asleep again. He waited in respectful though impatient silence. But the older man was not asleep. He began to talk, his eyes still closed.

"If you and Margaret have fixed it up, I suppose I'll have to take it. Not that there's any objection to you in my mind! But whether you are the man for her, I don't know, and I don't suppose she knows until she has tried you."

At this Edward remembered the warnings of his mother in the night. Divorce was in this family. He would have none of that, however things went between him and Margaret. "I mean to make a success of my marriage," he said doggedly.

"So do we all," Thomas replied. "But it's more than your marriage, my boy. It's the woman, too, and she can wreck any marriage, if she's a mind to do it. Margaret's a handful, and there's no use in pretending she isn't. She gets it from her mother. I had to beat her mother once—it was with an umbrella, I remember. I'd just come back from London, and she took a fancy to some man or other while I was away. It's in their blood. I'd bought a good strong umbrella at Harridge's and when she told me the first thing that she'd changed her mind about me I said, 'No, you haven't,' and went after her with the umbrella. She cried, but I didn't give an inch. I slept with her that night, and the next day she was all right again. I never even knew the man's name."

He chuckled and Edward listened with horror. What would his mother have said to this sorry tale? Thank God she need never know!

"The moral of that is," Thomas Seaton went on, "you keep a strong hand with Margaret!"

"I'll do my best," Edward said with reserve, "though it could never come to beating—not with me."

"Ah well," Thomas Seaton said. "You'll devise your own weapons. But there's worse than an umbrella." He coughed, sat up and fumbled for his leather slippers, found them, and put them on. Then he stood up. "Peg!" he shouted.

The door opened so quickly that Edward wondered as he rose punctiliously to his feet if Margaret had been listening at the keyhole. He dismissed the thought as unworthy, but her father laughed as he sat down again.

"You've been listening, you scalawag," he said to her.

"No, I haven't," Margaret replied, dimpling. "I would have but I was afraid it might make Ned angry. He isn't used to it. I was only standing ready, on call. Do sit down, Ned."

She sat down on the hassock between the two of them, her long beautiful hands clasped about her knees.

"Well, shall he have me, Father?" she asked.

"He says he will," her father replied.

Great love was between these two, and Edward felt it jealously, as the eyes of father and daughter met and melted and spoke. It was unfair, surely, for the older man to have had the advantage of long years with her, watching her as she grew from birth to womanhood. What other man could hope to have such knowledge of her? Then it occurred to him that there was no such relation between his own father and Louise, and again he knew that there was something in this Seaton family that made them different from his own.

"But will you have him, Peg?" Thomas Seaton asked. "It goes two ways, you know."

Margaret smiled her deep dimpled smile. "It's taken me years to make up my mind," she said frankly.

"Nonsense," Edward said abruptly. "You only made it up yesterday—you know that, Margaret. Why, even yesterday morning, you were wanting to put off the picnic. And twice you—"

He stopped, aware that Thomas Seaton was listening avidly and with laughter bright in his eyes.

"Only twice?" Seaton said. "That's nothing, man! Her mother broke our engagement nine times."

He and Margaret joined in laughter offensively loud to Edward's ear. "At any rate," he said soberly, "she's made up her mind, whether yesterday or not."

Margaret turned on Edward vividly. "I began asking myself the very first day I saw you whether I'd marry you or not."

He could scarcely believe this and yet it stirred him to the bottom of his soul. "But we've always known each other," he said feebly.

"I've always been asking," she said promptly.

"Then why did you turn me down so hard?" he demanded.

"Oh, you took so long to grow up," she said scornfully. "I really thought you'd never be a man—and I hate boys. You're still not really grown up, Ned, but I can see you will be, some day."

Thomas Seaton got to his feet and waved his big hands. "You two are as good as married," he said, swallowing his laughter. "Don't be too sharp with him, Peg. He's a good young man. Don't get wicked with him."

He ambled sidewise toward the door, his hands in his pockets now and his coattails in the air. "And Edward, I advise you—get yourself a good English umbrella. You'll need it."

He went out and left the two of them, taking care to close the door.

Margaret blew a kiss after him and turned to Edward warmly. "Isn't he adorable? He shut the door because he understands us. He understands everybody, I think—me best of all." She pulled the hassock forward and leaned her head upon Edward's knees. "Oh, how blissful I am!"

"Are you really happy?" Edward asked. He had been slightly repelled by her father's forethought as though the old man had coarsely imagined that they would at once want to begin to make love! But he could not resist the sight of Margaret's dark head on his knees. What grace of God that she had her mother's dark curly hair, and her father's blue eyes! With red hair she would have been quite another woman. Besides, he did not like red hair.

"Oh, happy!" she repeated dreamily. "To think I needn't worry any more about getting married! It's all settled at last, and I can put my mind to something else."

He was amazed again, and he said, withdrawing his hand from her head, "Think of what? You needn't have worried about it."

But she took his hand and pillowed her soft cheek in his palm. "Of course I worried," she said frankly. "Every girl does. How did I know you would ask me again, and how did I know whether even if you did I would say yes? And suppose I said no, would you ask me yet again? How did I know? And suppose you didn't, what could I do, that is supposing I wanted you to ask me again?"

He sighed, and then drew her strongly into his arms. "Stop it there, Margaret," he commanded. "Just be still with me for a while, will you? I'm somewhat overcome."

She laughed softly at this, but she yielded, and he sat in the warm golden room, holding her, completely happy, except for the slight gnawing fear that the door might open suddenly to show someone's surprised face. He was chagrined that she divined the fear and rose, walked across the room and locked the door. Then she came back and curled into his arms again, and he sat holding her and feeling his love grow, second by second, until it terrified him with joy. Her right arm crept around him under his coat, and her left hand up to his cheek, and understanding, after a while, the soft steady pressure of that left hand, he yielded, turning his face to hers, and bending to her he joined his lips to hers in a long kiss.

From this kiss it was he who first moved away. He trembled at the power she had over him. Her lips, thus fastened to his, made his blood fire and his limbs were melted. He struggled against such giving up of himself. Somewhere in him, if he was to remain master of his life, there must be a place where he stood alone to survey all that he had, even her.

"Come, my dear," he said resolutely.

She looked at him languidly and he had to harden himself against the roselike face upon his breast.

"I must go home, darling," he said tenderly. "My father and mother must be told, too, you know."

He was utterly unprepared for her again. For she sprang from his arms, her face eager and even excited. "Oh, what fun!" she cried. "Now I'll come with you."

He got to his feet. "But will it be the thing to do?" he muttered.

"Why not?" she asked robustly. "Don't I have to know them? Oughtn't they to know me?"

"I suppose so," he said uncertainly.

She forgot him and looked down at herself. "This old dress!" she exclaimed passionately. "I'll have to change."

He had not noticed what she wore, but now he saw that it was a dress of faded blue linen, crumpled by his crushing her in his arms.

"What'll I wear?" she asked anxiously. Then she put her hand on his lips. "No, don't tell me—I must be myself."

With that she hastened out of the room and he went over to the window and stood looking out into the quiet weedy garden. Some old-fashioned chrysanthemums were blooming under the elms, brilliant spots of red and gold. At the end of the garden the small marble statue of a naked boy looked out mischievously from a pool choked with leaves. A year from now, he supposed, he would be married. He and Margaret would be living somewhere in Chedbury—that was a thing they had to plan, too. He would have no living with their families, neither his nor hers. There was plenty of room in this huge old house, but he would refuse to consider it. If he was to make her happy, he'd have to have her to himself.

She came back in a few minutes, wearing a new autumn suit of a heather blue and a soft felt hat. Nobody in Chedbury wore clothes like hers, so plain and soft, and she was beautiful in them.

"I got it in London," she said. "Do you like it?"

"It suits you," he said. And then overcome with her beauty he was humbled to pain. "Oh, Margaret, can you be patient with me and mine?" he asked. He took her gloved hands. "We're common folk compared to you."

She gave him a smile tender and exquisite. "I'm only marrying you—that's what we've to remember," she said.

He felt her words strong and comforting and he put his arms about her shoulder and gave her a hard squeeze. "That's right," he said heartily. "Remind me of it every morning, will you?"

They walked out into the afternoon sunlight and the sense of the magic of his life crept into Edward's consciousness. It was impossible to imagine that his wife, his house, could be like those of any other man. Whatever the faults of others, he and Margaret were beyond their possibility. They carried happiness within themselves, in their youth and health and humor and in the quality of their love. He strode along at her side, just enough taller than she to be complacent, his step matched to hers, and hidden between them were their clasped hands.

"Ned," she said suddenly, "I'll have to tell you that I did tell Mother last night, after all."

"You did?" he cried.

"I couldn't help it. She came into my room when I was getting ready for bed and saw it all over me, I suppose. So I simply said yes, I was engaged, and she said she was glad of it."

In the agitation of his interview he had forgotten the midnight scene with his own mother. Now he thought of it and was troubled as to whether, in honesty, he should tell Margaret of his mother's doubts. He decided to postpone the telling.

"Is that all your mother said?" he asked.

"Well, she said we'd have to begin talking about when we'd have the wedding, and where we'd live."

"So we shall," he agreed, "and that brings me to the question. What do you want for a ring?"

"A sapphire," she said so promptly that he was surprised.

"Sounds as if you'd had it picked for a long time," he observed.

"I have," she said. "I know exactly where it is—in an old jewelry store in New York."

"Do you mean to say you had the ring picked before you had the man?" he demanded and was vaguely pained.

She laughed and squeezed his arm with both hands. "I began thinking about the ring the night I said I wouldn't marry you—the first time—remember?"

Did he remember! However happy he was he'd never forget that evening.

She had not paused for his answer. "And then I thought, if I ever did marry you, I'd want a sapphire, set in a wide band, and so when I went to New York—"

"Oh, Margaret! And I was suffering so, thinking you'd never have me—"

"Then you were silly. Good sapphires are fearfully hard to find—good ones, that is—and I did find one."

"But suppose it had been sold?"

"Oh, I found it only this spring, and I begged the old man to keep it for me, for I knew I'd be married sometime."

"Even if not to me, I suppose!"

"Don't be jealous, Ned, and he said I surely would, too, but just in case would I put down twenty-five dollars on account."

"Margaret, you didn't!"

"I did, so the ring is safe, and I should think you'd be glad."

He was too confounded by all this to know whether he was glad or sorry, and it took him five full minutes of contemplation. This was only brought to an end by her voice, begging him.

"Ned, please forgive me—it was awfully forward of me. I can see that now."

He was pleased to forgive and he did so fully and magnanimously. "It's odd, Margaret—there's no pretending it isn't. But it's you, and that's all that matters. We'd better go tomorrow to New York and fetch it, I suppose."

"Oh, lovely!" Her rich voice sighed out the rich word, and he knew that he had behaved well. Upon this satisfaction they entered the house and he was pleased to see that his father had just got home and had not time, therefore, to change his respectable office suit of gray cloth for the patched brown smoking jacket in which he spent his evenings, although he was on the stair.

"Father!" he called from the door.

His father turned. "Yes?"

"I've brought Margaret, Father. It's all settled—"

His father came down the two steps he had mounted and held out his hand shyly. "Well, Margaret—we've always known each other, I guess, without much more than speaking—"

"Oh, yes, Mr. Haslatt." Margaret's voice, her outstretched hand were warm and instant.

His mother came to the door of the hall, and slipped off her apron and threw it behind her. Something had been expected, Edward surmised, for she wore her second-best black dress and she had put a fresh white ruching in the high boned collar.

"Edward, am I to congratulate you?" she asked.

Behind the stilted words he saw her as she had been last night and he met her stiffly. "Yes, please, Mother. It's all decided. I had a talk with Mr. Seaton."

"Welcome, Margaret—"

His mother, unrelentingly grave, led them into the sitting room and there Louise sat with a magazine. She got up awkwardly, her face flushing.

"Louise," her mother said formally. "Edward has come to tell us that he and Margaret are engaged."

Louise smiled a little and yielded her hand to Margaret, who clasped it and held it. "Oh, I've known Louise since she was born! I hope you won't mind me! I'm glad to have another sister."

In a moment they were all sitting down, not knowing what to say, and Margaret, her warm eyes seeing everything, began to talk rapidly and gaily.

"Oh, I hope you will all like me—because I do so like all of you. I'm going to try so hard to make Ned a good wife. You'll have to teach me lots, Mrs. Haslatt. Mother's a dreadful housekeeper, in fact. She just doesn't keep house—but I want to be good at it. I don't even want a maid, because if I have one I'll never learn for myself. May I come sometimes on Saturdays and learn, dear Mrs. Haslatt?"

There never was so enchanting a woman, Edward told himself and he saw without surprise that his mother was melting.

"Well, I don't know, I'm sure, that I'm such a wonder," she began.

"Yes, you are, Mother," he said heartily, "and I shall take it as a kindness if you'll tell Margaret everything. I'm sure she's right when she says she doesn't know anything."

He was surprised to hear himself talking in this easy Seaton fashion to his own mother, and she looked at him suspiciously but was silent. Margaret picked up the silver ball of talk where he dropped it.

"Ned, I'll surprise you! I can learn when I want to, and I'm going to buy a little book and put everything into it. 'Mrs. Haslatt's muffins,' 'Mrs. Haslatt's cream tomato soup—'" She broke off. "I can't go on saying Mrs. Haslatt, can I? I'll say Mother Haslatt."

Edward saw his father absorbing all this, drinking in Margaret's warmth and charm and beauty, his eyes yearning and his mouth open under his gray mustache. Louise, too, was gazing at Margaret, forgetting her shyness, leaning forward on her elbows. Only his mother struggled against her own yielding.

"Maybe Edward will like new ways," his father said slowly.

Edward felt as his own the potential hurt to his mother in these words. "There's nothing I like better than the way Mother cooks," he said quickly.

"I didn't mean that," his father replied. "I think it's only right for young people to do differently from the old ones. I'd expect that."

"I'm sure I don't want them to copy my ways," his mother said in the suppressed voice whose misery Edward recognized at once.

"We understand," Margaret said.

Edward got up. "Margaret, I must get you home," he said with authority.

She rose. "All right, Ned." Then she turned impulsively to his mother. "Mrs. Haslatt, will you let us have him tonight for dinner? Is it too selfish of me? But we haven't seen my mother yet—not together. I'll send him home early."

Now his mother was compelled to speak. "I suppose it's all right. Though I have his supper here ready—"

Mark Haslatt spoke suddenly. "Let him go, Ruth. There are not many days like these in any man's life."

The suppressed feeling in all of them was released suddenly with these words and it filled the room. Edward wanted to get away. "I'll be back early, Mother," he muttered. He took Margaret's arm and hurried her away.

The evening was like none he had ever spent in the Seaton house, but then he had never been accepted into the family before. Margaret brought him into the library, pulling him gently with her hand in his. She was the middle child, and her elder brother Tom and her younger sister Sandra were already there, with their parents.

"We always gather in the library for a bit before dinner," she said. It was Seaton to call it dinner, he thought, and he wondered if in his own house his supper would be dinner. He frowned slightly, thinking of how many such things remained ahead of him to decide. For that the decision was chiefly to be his it would not have occurred to him to doubt.

They all looked at him with friendly faces as he came in, but nobody moved. He knew that they had been talking about the engagement, and he felt kindliness in the air, although it was restrained. Tom he knew casually, without intimacy, and Sandra he had noticed chiefly because she was about Louise's age, but so much prettier that he had felt sorry for Louise. She had a bright pert face, and Thomas Seaton had given her his red hair. Margaret's mouth was delicate in its fullness but Sandra's was sulky. Tom did not lift his tall loose-boned body from the deep chair in which he sat, but he grinned. Some shyness made Edward want to draw his fingers from Margaret's, but she held him firmly and marched straight to her mother.

Mrs. Seaton sat in a high-backed red velour-covered chair by the fireplace. The fire had been lit, and since the lamp was shaded the light from the flames flickered over her beautiful and willful face, still so young under the rolls of her white hair. She wore a black velvet gown, old-fashioned in its fullness, and there was a ruffle of white lace about her neck.

"Mother," Margaret said abruptly. "I asked Ned to dinner so that you could get to know him."

Mrs. Seaton put out a hand long and slender like Margaret's, but it was bright with rings. When Edward took it in his hand he knew that although it looked like Margaret's it was soft as hers could never be. There was steel somewhere in Margaret's hand.

"You're so silly, Meg," Mrs. Seaton murmured. "How can I get to know him in one evening?"

"You've got to like him in one evening anyway, Mother, because I'm going to marry him."

"Is there any reason why I should not like you?" Mrs. Seaton inquired, looking at Edward with her direct brown gaze.

"Sit down, my boy," Thomas Seaton intervened. "Don't let yourself be made the center of a sparring match between two women. Tom, why don't you exert yourself?"

Tom did not move. "He may as well know me at my worst, Father," he said in a pleasant deep voice.

"Do sit down, Ned," Margaret said. "Sandra, why are you speechless?"

"Because it seems so odd to think you're going to get married," Sandra retorted. She sat on the leather hassock, bent over so the skirt of her green velvet frock flowed over her feet. "Besides," she said in the drawling voice which was her present affectation, "I can't stand up or he'll see how short this old frock is. Father's too stingy to get me a new one. Edward, that's the kind of family you're marrying into!"

"She's lying, Ned," Margaret said carelessly. "The trouble is she wants one of the new sheath things and Father has only just let me have one."

She went out of the room with her light and springing tread and Edward sat down, feeling more shy and yet excited than he had ever before been in his life. This was the first of many times that he would be in this room with this family. "It won't be so hard after this, though," he thought doggedly and he sat, impervious and silent, under their frank stares. They had all "dressed," as Margaret put it, in some fashion for their evening meal. He had never been here when there was not a party and so he supposed that this was their habit. Even Thomas Seaton had put on an old black velvet coat with his tweed trousers. Tom wore a somewhat old-fashioned tuxedo that did not entirely fit him. Sandra continued her conversation.

"You are so stingy, Papa. You make poor Tom wear your old tux."

"Shut up, Sandra," Tom said amiably.

"It's a good suit of clothes," Thomas Seaton said. "I'd wear it myself if I could get into it."

"But the depression's over and I don't see why—"

"Do be quiet, Sandra," her mother interposed. "I'm sure we're all bored with you."

Silence fell again, and Thomas Seaton leaned over a small table at his side and poured some sherry from a crystal decanter into a small glass. "Take this to your new relative," he commanded his daughter.

Edward sprang to his feet. "I'll get it for myself, thank you." He took the tiny glass with strong feelings of interest and guilt. He had not tasted wine half a dozen times in his life, and his mother worked in the temperance society in Chedbury. Had he believed in it he would have proudly refused the wine, but he disliked intensely the feverishness of women against liquor, even though his reason acknowledged that some of them had undoubtedly endured enough from drunken husbands and empty pay envelopes to justify their fervor. But his father was a teetotaler, and he resented his mother's devotion to a cause so remote from her. He sat down again and sipped his wine.

"I'm glad to see you like a glass of wine," Thomas Seaton said. "Not that what you and I do, and Tom here and a few more like us, will do any good—we're in for a period of morality, my boy. I can feel it coming. The depression scared us to death and we'll be good for a while."

"I'm going to learn to smoke, Papa." Sandra's confident drawl interrupted his slow hesitating rumbling.

"I don't care what you do," Thomas retorted. He was holding his glass against the firelight, squinting one eye through it. "You and your mamma can both smoke if it'll comfort you for getting old."

They pronounced it Papá and Mammá with the accent on the last syllable in a fashion that seemed foreign to Edward and yet that he knew was not affected. They had manners of their own but these were not what had been taught to him as manners. He sat alert and silent, appreciating the ease of this family, valuing without knowing why he did the glint on velvet, the whiteness of Mrs. Seaton's hands folded on her lap, the faded red of the long curtains drawn now across the window. Tom's aquiline profile, sleepy and smiling, was part of it.

"Margaret's taking a long time," Tom said suddenly. He turned to Edward. "You know, I admire your courage. What'll I call you—Ed? She's laid down the law against Ned. That's her own private name. We have to obey her or she has tantrums."

"She doesn't have tantrums," his father said in his slow heavy voice. "You don't know what tantrums are, Tom. You should have seen your mother at Margaret's age. Screaming and shouting when I didn't give you your way, didn't you, my love? But they get over it."

Mrs. Seaton smiled and produced two dimples exactly like Margaret's in the unflawed smoothness of her cheeks. "I wouldn't compete with you, old dear," she said sweetly. "When I shouted you yelled. It got so tiresome. I always lost my voice afterward, I remember."

"You see, Edward," Thomas Seaton said complacently.

"They're lying, both of them," Tom said lazily. "We can't believe a word they say. They make themselves out as hellions when they were our age."

"Anything we do they always pretend they've done worse," Sandra said. "It makes us feel so inferior."

Had they laughed Edward would have joined in their laughter, but they were mischievously grave and he could only smile with discomfort. They would take knowing, he told himself.

At this moment Margaret came into the room, looking, he perceived at once, beautiful beyond anything he had ever seen. She had put on a pale gold sleeveless gown, very long, that fitted her body closely. It was split up the front to a point below her knees and her gold-clad legs were visible. Above the dress her dark head was high and her eyes were sapphire blue and bright. They were all startled and she enjoyed their amazement. Edward knew that she was a vision and he hated the way she looked. She turned around slowly. "I wanted to wear it the first time tonight," she declared. "When it's old I shall keep it and remember."

All of them were looking at her differently. Tom said nothing, but he lit a cigarette and gazed at her, over the curling smoke. Her mother looked critical. "I wonder if women will really take to these tight things," she murmured. "They make such demands on the figure."

"It's sweet!" Sandra cried. "Oh, I can't bear its being so sweet. I want to tear up this old thing of mine!"

"It'll make new men of us all," Thomas declared wickedly.

Tom burst into high laughter and then they all laughed except Edward. He could manage no more than a smile, being rent in two by Margaret's beauty and his own deep distrust of beauty in this shape. When she was his wife he would forbid her wearing such dresses. "The sooner we're married the better," he thought grimly.

He found his eyes caught suddenly by Mrs. Seaton's as though she knew what he was thinking. Then she moved her eyes away quickly. "Come along, we're starving," she declared, and led them behind her toward the dining room. He and Margaret went last of all.

"Don't you like me?" she whispered, her hand warm under his arm.

"I'm not sure I do," he replied.

"Oh, why not?" she asked.

"You're too beautiful," he said and was glad there was time for no more talk.

The evening was over. He was surprised that it had proved so short, in spite of his fears during dinner that it would be long. The family had talked exactly as though he were not present, throwing him a careless handful of words, a reference he could not understand, with smiles always warm and pleasing. They had talked about everything from the grocer's amazing profile to what Thomas Edison had just said about the new flying machines. For the first time in his life he heard the word helicopter, although Tom used it as though it were a household utensil. Thomas Seaton paused for a few minutes in his enjoyment of the stuffed leg of lamb to express his scorn of William Jennings Bryan.

"You've never even seen him," his wife said.

"I've read enough of his sentimental mouthings," he retorted, "and any man who wears his hair long is sure to be unsound."

In the midst of talk that seemed disconnected but was connected, as he perceived, by unseen waves of communication, Edward caught Margaret looking often and thoughtfully at him. He looked back at her, fully aware that some time before they parted this night he would learn what these looks meant. He braced himself somewhat, determined that he would not yield his honest opinion and from that instant began to enjoy the really excellent food.

After dinner everybody had coffee in small cups except Thomas Seaton who parted his short thick beard with his fingers and supped his creamed and sweetened coffee with loud pleasure from a large cup. There was a little desultory talk, then Sandra drifted away and Tom announced that he was going to "see a girl," Mrs. Seaton went gently to sleep, and Thomas picked up the newspaper.

Margaret motioned to Edward. "Come into the garden, Ned."

"I'll fetch your coat."

"It's warm as anything," she objected.

"Where is your coat?" he asked stubbornly when they were in the hall and waited until suddenly she laughed and opened the coat closet and took out her old blue coat.

In the garden, sitting on an iron seat that felt hard and cold through his clothes, she threw the coat back. The moonlight fell on her bare smooth arms and shoulders.

"I shouldn't have worn this dress," she said. "It was silly, perhaps. No, it wasn't—feeling as I do about tonight."

"I shan't like you wearing it before other men," he said.

She turned her startled face toward him. "You think it's not modest?"

"I know it's not," he returned.

She smiled, but not quite enough to bring the dimples. "Now, Ned, how do you know?" she asked warmly. "What makes you feel it's immodest?"

He was shocked by this and made no pretense of hiding his feelings. "I don't think you should even ask."

"You mean I mustn't ask you how you feel when a woman is immodestly dressed?" she asked.

"No," he replied. "It's not fitting."

She considered this. Then suddenly she put the coat on again. "Are you ashamed of the way you feel?" she inquired. Her eyes, wide and curious, were fixed on his face and he could not down his quick flush.

"Margaret, I don't like this talk," he said firmly. He wished that she

would not look at him as she was now doing. There was something provocative, teasing, amused, something almost wicked in her persistent gaze.
He wanted to punish her, to restore her to what he felt was proper decency.
He was afraid of her when she was like this, and he proceeded to choose
his weapons. "It makes me think of what my mother said last night," he
began.

"Ah, you told your mother last night!" she cried.

"I was going to tell you."

"But you didn't tell me, Ned, and I did tell you."

"We got talking about the ring."

"What did she say last night?" she demanded.

He considered. "I won't tell you," he said at last. "You won't forget it."

"Will you tell me if I tell you?"

"Tell me what?"

"What my mother said last night—when I told her."

He considered again. Curiosity overwhelmed him. No, it was more than
curiosity—it was necessity. He ought to know what her mother thought of
him, indeed, he must know in order that he might start fair and square.

"What did she say?" he asked abruptly.

"Will you tell me?"

"I suppose so."

Margaret withdrew a little and composed herself to speak in a clear
distinct voice. "She said, 'How will you manage when he doesn't laugh at
your jokes?'" She looked at him with frank eyes, in which there was a
touch of pity.

"Is that all?" he asked.

She was astonished. "Do you want anything worse?" she demanded.

"I don't think that's so bad," he said.

"Oh, dear." She covered her face with both hands. "Oh, dear, oh, dear,"
she murmured under her breath. She took her hands away again. "Ned, I
can't marry you!"

He was frightened by the gravity of her look and he humbled himself.
"I don't think what either of our mothers says matters," he said stoutly.
"My mother said you'd be a bad housekeeper and even that maybe some-
day you'd talk about divorce. But what does she know?"

"But of course I'm a bad housekeeper," Margaret declared, "and I
don't doubt sometimes I'll want to be divorced."

"Margaret!" he cried wildly.

"All married people do," she went on, "and the only difference is that
the ones who really love each other tell each other everything and the
others don't dare to."

He was stupefied by this, and he was as still as the stone boy in the
fountain behind them.

"Oh!" Margaret cried. "But you mustn't let me go, of course—never—
never—whatever I say."

She flung herself into his arms and he held her hard and all his courage and stubbornness came flooding back into him. His head was whirling but his heart was calm.

"I don't understand you," he said between set teeth. "I never know what to expect. I suppose I never will. But whatever it is you are—I shan't let you go—ever!"

He put his face into the soft curves of her neck, where her hair curled upward, and he was half suffocated with his love.

"Oh!" Margaret sighed, after a long time. "I'm perfectly happy, Ned—even though I know I'll often make you miserable. Please, Ned, forgive me for everything that's going to happen?"

"I'll forgive you everything," he muttered, and was terrified by his weakness.

The prospects of marriage deepened the acquisitive instincts in Edward Haslatt. These were already strong, for he was of a nature that drew to himself what he wanted, and what he had he held. Any impulse to share was secondary and acquired, implanted only by his sense of justice.

Now that Margaret had promised to marry him he became obsessed with the necessity for a home and the means to maintain it. Had his father's business been one that he disliked or thought unsound he would have deserted it in search of something better. But he liked printing. Even as a boy he had enjoyed visiting the shop and after school and in the long vacations, he had besought his father for the lowly positions of errand boy and later of printer's devil. Until his father had become a partner, however, these had been steadily refused, lest Mather or Loomis imagine that he, Mark Haslatt, was trying to get his son into the business. When Loomis died his father had still feared old Robert Mather, and not until Edward's last year of college had he allowed him to come freely into the shop to help with the presses. He had been gratified to discover how much his son already knew about type and was only troubled lest Edward might want new and rare types that could not be used often enough to justify the expense.

"For what we do here now, old-fashioned Scotch type is about all we need," he told Edward. "Of course we have a few special types to please fussy customers, and for wedding announcements and such. You can tie up a lot of money in type that you don't use once in ten years."

Edward had listened respectfully to such advice for as long as he could remember. Now, however, with the promise of being allowed to print a book or two, he pondered it afresh. He genuinely loved books and the prospect of building up, very slowly, of course, what might some day grow into a real publishing house excited him in a measure only second to his marriage. Yet whatever rashness he held in his nature was completely quelled by the necessity of supporting a wife and the children he wanted and expected. His salary concerned him constantly and he urged his father to consult Mr. Mather at the first possible moment, so that he and Margaret would know what they were to live on. His father was pessimistic.

"Bob Mather is so old he doesn't know why anybody needs much to live on," he told Edward one evening. They were in the sitting room and Edward was at home only because Margaret and her mother had gone to New York to buy her trousseau. Secretly Edward had not approved of this. After they were married he would not be able to afford New York clothes and Margaret would have to do with the Chedbury dressmaker. But he did not tell her this, since her father was still paying her bills.

His father, in his shirt sleeves, was sitting in an old Morris chair beside the stove and in other days Edward might also have been without his coat. The permeating influence of Harvard, however, and now of the Seatons compelled him to other ways, even in the home sitting room, and he was encouraged by his mother, who thought it was "nice" of him.

"I'll want two thousand dollars a year," Edward argued.

"Old Mather won't see why," he replied, without lifting his eyes from the newspaper.

"Then I shall look for a job somewhere else," Edward said.

"Well, I'll do what I can," his father replied. He appeared absorbed in his paper.

"When will you, Father?" Edward urged. He was fidgeting over the rack of magazines at the end of the sofa. The slowness of time was intolerable. Margaret had set the wedding for Christmas Eve—a bad time, he thought, for it would be all mixed up with Christmas. But she had persisted, declaring that it would be wonderful to wake up on Christmas morning married. "I've always loved Christmas," she declared, "and now it'll be wonderful." He felt beset with the problems as well as the joys of marriage.

"Hm?" his father asked vaguely. "Well, maybe tomorrow. I have to take some papers up to him anyway."

Robert Mather was too old to come to the office now but every new job had to be laid before him, with full estimates of what it would cost. He examined the figures through his small, sharply focused spectacles and decided whether the job was worth doing. Edward knew his father dreaded these visits to the bedridden old man, but he performed them as his duty, never forgetting that half the business still belonged to Mather.

"Would it be unwise to put the matter of my salary to him at the same time that you are submitting estimates?" he suggested.

His father rubbed his head meditatively. "Well, I'll judge," he said at last. "If Mather's in a good mood, it might be as well to put it to him. If he ain't—I'll see."

He went back to his paper and then a moment later put it down. "Have you thought any of living with one side or the other? I don't know how your mother and Margaret would get along—nor yet how you would do up there. But as far as I'm concerned, if Margaret would do her share in the house—"

"We both feel we must set up our own home," Edward said positively.

"Maybe it's best," his father agreed mildly. This time his attention to his paper was permanent, and the minutes dragged until bedtime.

Chedbury still being empty of Margaret, Edward spent the next morning at the shop, drawing up the estimates on a pamphlet that advertised a life insurance firm. He paused to ponder the matter of life insurance. What if he should die? True, he was young and very healthy, yet completely healthy men could drown or could break their necks in astonishingly simple ways. He made up his mind that old Mather must agree to two thousand dollars or he would leave Chedbury and go to Boston or even to New York.

By evening when his father came home there was no such clear-cut decision offered for him to accept or refuse.

"Well, old Mather said he wouldn't approve more than eighteen hundred the first year, son—but if you worked out good, he'd see about the two hundred extra after that."

"The old skinflint!" Edward spluttered. "I've a good mind to throw it all up."

"I know how you feel," his father said, "but there's a lot of things to consider. Old Mather isn't going to last forever. In fact, he looked bad today. I should be surprised if he lasted out another year."

Edward was silent while prudence worked in him. Chedbury was in a good geographical position, near enough to several big cities to solicit business and yet far enough away to keep overhead costs low. To move elsewhere now would mean extra expense, in addition to uncertainty. Young men fresh from Harvard were no rarity on the market. "Is there any chance of buying Mather out?" he inquired.

His father grinned. "I've been dreaming of that for the last ten years. But I'd need twenty thousand dollars—of which I have five at present."

Then his father sighed and went upstairs with lagging steps, and his mother put her head in the door to announce that she needed more wood for the kitchen stove. Edward rose and went out into the woodshed at the back of the house. It was sunset and the luminous quiet sky spread over the town. His fretfulness faded. Under this sky his beloved was speeding homeward to him. He was meeting her at half past nine, and there was nothing else in the day now except that he would see her. He filled the woodbox with energy, fed his brother's hound dog, and ate a large supper in rising spirits. When he let himself out of the house at nine o'clock his courage was high. The train was fifteen minutes late and at quarter to ten he had Margaret's hands in his and only Mrs. Seaton's imperious cries that there were seven boxes kept him from taking her in his arms. The train stopped three minutes at Chedbury, being bound for larger places, and he dashed into the car to collect the boxes, surprised, in the midst of all his haste, that Margaret had been so extravagant as to take a Pullman, in spite of its being only a day journey to New York.

But tonight he was disposed to criticize her for nothing. They sat side by side in the Seaton carriage, their hands clasped under the robe, while Mrs. Seaton described the unutterable difficulties of shopping in New York. Once at home she declared herself exhausted and went directly upstairs to bed, whither Thomas Seaton had already gone, and Margaret pulled Edward by the hand into the parlor and there behind closed doors they ended their first separation. She flung herself into his arms and he held her to his heart.

"Oh," she breathed at last, "it's terrible being so in love that it makes you miserable!"

She laughed, freed herself from his arms, and shook her skirts. Then she dropped upon the couch. "Did you miss me?" she demanded.

"Every moment," he replied, sitting down beside her.

"I would have missed you if there'd been a second to do it in," she declared frankly. "Oh, Ned, when you see my wedding dress!"

She closed her eyes in ecstasy and clasped her hands behind her head.

"Tell me," he begged, his eyes upon the lovely line of her throat.

"I can't," she answered. "It's to be a cloud of lace. I'm wearing Mother's veil, of course, and she's going to let me have her pearl necklace. I love being married!"

"It's more than the wedding—" he began but she stopped him.

"Don't tell me!" she cried. "I want to enjoy every moment of it as it comes. Just now I'm only thinking of the wedding. When I'm through that I'll think about what comes next and next and next."

She flouted his sober look and then repented and laid her head on his shoulder. "What did you really think about while I was gone?" she demanded.

He put his arm about her, feeling patient and much older than she. "About money mostly," he replied.

"Why money?" she inquired dreamily.

"Because we want our own house to live in, and we want to buy our own bread—"

"And butter," she went on, "and jam."

He broke in on this. "Father asked old Mather how much salary I could have and he said eighteen hundred the first year and two thousand afterward—if everything went right."

"That's plenty," she said still dreamily. "I have a lot of clothes."

"It isn't plenty," he retorted. "I wish to God I could buy the old devil out!"

"Why don't you?" she inquired, and she lifted her forefinger and followed the line of his profile. "You have such a nice nose," she murmured, "and your mouth, sir, is handsome."

He ignored this although he heard it with pleasure. "It would take twenty thousand dollars," he said.

She sat up and stared at him. "Did you know I have twelve thousand dollars of my own? . . . Don't look so shocked—it's true."

"That has nothing to do with me," he said stiffly. In his heart he had often feared that she had money and would not be wholly dependent upon him.

"My grandmamma left it to me, because I was named for her. She left Tom five thousand which he has spent, and Sandra has five thousand which she hasn't spent, because she hasn't got it yet. And I haven't spent mine for the same reason—but I'm to have it the day I marry. That was in Grandmamma's will."

This horrifying information she gave him without the slightest perception of how he would feel when he heard it. He determined instantly that he would never touch any of her money.

"I shall give the money straight to you and you can buy off Mr. Mather, and I'll make my father give you the rest," she went on.

"No!" he exclaimed, stung at last to speech. "I'd never get over the shame."

She sat upright. "What shame?" she demanded.

"I shall support you myself," he announced.

"Why, of course," she agreed, her blue eyes wide and sparkling, "but I want to put my money into our business. And Papa won't mind."

He got to his feet and began to walk up and down the floor, and then he paused before her. "Margaret, if you ask your father for one cent's help for me I'll—I'll—"

"Break the engagement?" she inquired with bright curiosity.

He looked down into the enchanting face. "No," he groaned.

"Then I will do it for you," she declared pretending to pout.

"Please, Margaret," he begged. "Don't tease me."

"Then promise me to take my money," she said.

Cold sweat broke across his forehead. "Don't, darling, please!"

"I was going to buy you something out of the money anyway," she said remorselessly. "Some pearl studs or maybe one of those new motor cars—or a yellow diamond ring for your little finger."

"Now Margaret," he exclaimed, "what would I do with any of those things?"

"So why not take the money and make it work for you—and me, too?" she retorted.

He stood, impressed against his will by this argument, and she pursued ruthlessly her slight advantage. "Don't you see, I'll still be dependent on you," she urged. "If you don't do your work well, we'll be ruined. Doesn't that satisfy you, Ned?"

"You've mixed me all up," he complained.

"Oh, you're so proud!" she cried. "I want you to support me, Ned. I don't want my own money. I'll keep thinking all the time how I could buy a ticket to Europe—when I'm angry with you. Of course I'll often be angry,

Ned, and so will you, and it'll be a mercy if all the money we have is tied up so we can't get it."

The end of all this impetuous talk, this soft pleading, reinforced by her arms around his neck and her clinging body, was to destroy him so completely that he agreed to take the money, which however should be kept in her name, and the stocks it bought held in her name. He would not take money from her father, but he would ask his own father to put in his five thousand, and maybe somewhere they could borrow or scrape together the three thousand more.

Margaret flung herself on the sofa in exhaustion. "Oh, thank God, it's settled!" she sighed. "But if you're always going to be so hard to convince, Ned, I'll not live long."

He ignored this and presented her with the next problem. "Where shall we live, Margaret? Not with your parents or mine, anyway."

To his surprise it appeared that she already knew where they were to live. "I know—we'll rent the old Holcombe house. It's been empty ever since I first saw it and picked it out."

"Margaret, have pity on me," he begged.

She opened her eyes at him. "But it is a lovely house, and all that land around it—"

"It's half a mile from town," he objected.

Everybody in Chedbury knew the Holcombe house and Sunday schools had picnicked for years on the neglected grounds. Old Mrs. Holcombe had been born and had died there when Edward and Margaret were children and her husband had gone away to finish his days in England. Stanley Holcombe had been a don at Oxford when his wife had brought him here to write the many books he had always wanted to write. Strange to say, he had written several of them, and Edward wondered now if his first impulse toward books had not come from the tall delicate-faced Englishman. He had seen him sometimes in the shop, whither Mr. Holcombe came to consult about paper and types and bindings. Twice he had tried to persuade Mr. Loomis to undertake a private printing, but Mr. Loomis had been afraid of it.

"That house will cost much more than we can afford," Edward objected.

"No, it won't," Margaret contradicted him in a fierce whisper. "You'll see!"

When he shook his head and looked doubtful she declared willfully, "Anyway, that is where I am going to live after I am married, and it would be nicer if you'd live with me." Then she sighed. "I'm fearfully tired, Ned. Please go home." She rose and tugged at him until he was on his feet. "Good night, Ned. I do love you."

She kissed him once, a long soft pressure of her lips upon his, and then slipped out of the room and left him there. He stood a moment listening to the clip-clap of her heels on the stairs and realized that she was not coming back and that there was nothing for him except to go home.

Walking along alone through the sharp night air he considered again the matter of her money. He still disliked the thought of it, but his conscience was consoled somewhat by the fact that it would still be hers. When he let himself into the house, through the open door of the sitting room he saw his father at the dining-room table, a paper shade over his eyes, working at sheets of paper. He went in surprised, and his father looked up at him with a faint smile. "Your mother's gone to bed, but I've been figuring all day how I could buy old Mather out. There's no way, unless I mortgage the house, and I've always told your mother I wouldn't do that, come whatever."

What he had not been willing to do for his own sake he was now suddenly happy that he could do for his father's. "I've been talking to Margaret," he said. He sat down and pulled the sheets of figures toward him. "Seems she's going to get twelve thousand dollars the day we're married—by her grandmother's will. I didn't know it until today. She wants to put it in the business."

His father sat back and pushed up the shade. "Well," he breathed, "well, now!"

"I didn't want her to do it at first. You know how I'd feel," Edward went on.

His father's face fell. "Of course not," he said slowly.

"But she insisted. You know how the Seatons are—she's a Seaton, if there ever was one—and so I told her I'd only consent if she kept it in her own name and we'd give her stock in exchange," Edward said.

His father's face lit again. "That we could do," he exclaimed.

"Still it won't be enough," Edward said.

They looked at each other. "I wouldn't mortgage the house," his father said softly, "but I could borrow."

"I don't own a thing," Edward sighed.

"Should I tell your mother?" his father asked. The inquiry was directed to his own conscience, as Edward knew, and he did not answer it. "Funny how women have to be so sure of a roof and a bed," his father mused. "I reckon it's because they feel helpless."

They sat silent again. Suddenly his father shuffled the papers together. "I won't tell. I'll just do it. We'll get it paid back before she knows it."

"All right, Father," Edward said.

He watched his father's absorbed face. Small lines disappeared, and the pursed lips loosened into a smile. His father looked up. "It looks like one of my dreams, anyway, will come true," he said shyly.

He spent the next months waiting for his wedding day and in two frames of mind. There were hours when he was convinced that Christmas Eve would never come, so intolerably did the dawns rise and the twilights fall, and other hours when he felt the day was rushing upon him with something like doom. He was much disturbed by this variance in himself, but it did not occur to him to tell anyone of it. Was there in him somewhere a real reluctance to marriage and if so, could it possibly mean a lack of male vitality? This was a horrifying thought and it made him moody and withdrawn, although he went as usual every evening to see Margaret. As the autumn days had changed to frost and then to cold, their picnics and walks had become hours before the fire in the library, where, after a brief half hour or so of desultory talk with a Seaton or two, they were left alone until eleven o'clock, an hour that Edward had arbitrarily set for going home.

Usually these evenings sped by, for Margaret had samples of carpets and curtains and they discussed the placing of furniture in the rooms of Holcombe's old house, which was now being repaired. The house and its changes were Thomas's wedding present to his daughter and Margaret took passionate delight in every detail. With a wisdom whose depth Edward did not at first divine she had announced that she would not buy a stick of furniture or a yard of carpet, or so much as a sofa pillow without Edward's cooperation and approval.

"Our house is as much your home as mine," she told him.

He was accustomed to his mother's complete power over the house and this new responsibility pleased him and at the same time frightened him. He knew nothing of house furnishing, and his ignorance and Margaret's decisive tastes might very well provide more cause for quarrel than for cooperation.

In one of his darker moods therefore he surveyed one evening samples of stair carpet that she had waiting on the table.

"The real problem is whether we want the blue or the rusty rose," Margaret said.

"Why not this brown?" he inquired gloomily.

He picked a small square of a dun shade that was almost the color of dust.

"You don't feel well tonight, Ned," Margaret said.

"I'm all right," he replied.

Her penetrating blue eyes did not give him up. "Something is wrong," she declared.

He shook his head.

She went on remorselessly. "You get this way every week or so. And I have to guess what it is."

He sat down and lit his new pipe. He had never smoked regularly before, but Thomas had advised him to take up pipe smoking before marriage. "It's a wonderful help," Thomas had said, his eyes laughing under his brushy red brows. "If you have your pipe in your mouth you can't answer right off."

"I know because I feel the same way," Margaret said, her eyes still on his face. He met them and maintained his silence and she continued the one-sided conversation. "Sometimes I just don't want to get married, either."

His heart congealed. The shades of reluctance fled and he cried out, "Margaret, what are you saying?"

"Not that I don't want to marry you, Ned—just that sometimes I feel queer about getting married, now that I really am going to do it."

He took the pipe out of his mouth. "You're sure you will?"

"It's in the abstract, yet—oh, Ned, you mustn't fill your pipe so full, darling!"

A coal of tobacco had fallen upon his coat and she flew to brush it off and examine the damage. A slight brown stain clung to the gray cloth. "Dad fills it only a little over half full."

She took the pipe from his hand and knocked it slightly upon the hearthstone, and he felt silly. But she was unself-conscious as she put it back in his mouth.

"You smoke and let me talk a bit," she said briskly. "That's why Dad smokes, you know—so Mother can talk and he needn't answer."

He spluttered at this. "Now Margaret, how do you know that?" he demanded.

She laughed. "Oh, I know his tricks," she exclaimed. She seated herself on his knee and pulled gently at the lobe of his ear. "Of course I can only guess how you feel, Ned—but here's my guess. We want to get married— we want to marry each other—but when we think about starting off alone in the house, having only each other and being dependent just on each other, well—"

She looked so grave that again he felt frightened. He put down his pipe on the small table beside him and drew her to him. "Don't you dare feel so," he commanded. "Else I'll take you to the justice of the peace and we won't wait for the wedding day."

"Isn't it the way you feel?" she insisted.

"I reckon," he said reluctantly. Where would he ever hide his soul if she could so divine it?

"There's only one cure for feeling afraid of each other," she said and her cheek was against his breast.

"Time," he suggested.

"No, this," she replied.

He held her close then, and they were silent and he felt the rightness of what she had said. To come closer was the answer. He must remember never to yield to remoteness. When he felt far then he must force himself to come near, and in the nearness distance would be no more. It would take an effort of will, even though he loved her so dearly.

"Two must grow used to being one," she murmured upon his breast.

"Yes," he agreed, and then felt the monosyllable too brief. He made an effort. "You'll have to teach me to say things. I live so much in silence."

She replied, "I'll ask you what you are thinking when I want to know, and you must tell me."

She fell silent then, and when he looked down upon her face he saw her gazing into the fire, her eyes steady. She was strongly built, not too thin, but she was so soft, her frame so pliable, that she fitted every curve of his body, and when he held her like this she seemed small and light. His dark mood was gone and he felt only unutterable tenderness. Passion was somewhere waiting but he kept it there. This was only the approach to marriage.

Suddenly, carelessly, the weeks began to gallop, and then he realized that there were no more of them. It became a matter of days, then hours and each hour was no longer than a minute. The two families swung into tense action. Clothes, flowers, food, invitations, the formalities of bridesmaids and best man and parties left him scarcely time to think even of Margaret. Their life together was postponed. At night, when they were alone for a little while they clung together without speaking. "Let me be tired, Ned," Margaret begged. "I have to keep up before everybody else."

"You needn't keep up before me—ever," he said.

"Oh, blessed!" she sighed. "That's why I love you."

He had asked Baynes to be his best man, and then fearful lest a younger brother take such responsibility too lightly, he asked Tom Seaton to keep an eye on him and see that he did his duty. Tom, growing fond of young Baynes, exerted himself unusually and a comradeship sprang up between them. Yet it was Baynes who did duty on the night before the wedding. Tom had let himself get drunk at the bachelors' dinner, and Baynes volunteered to be the one to take him home and put him to bed in the slumbering Seaton house.

"You go to bed," Baynes had muttered to Edward. His gray eyes crinkled. "You need your sleep, old man." So Edward had helped them into a hired cab and let them go.

But Margaret heard the front door open and she came to the stairs, her hair down on her shoulders and a blue kimono wrapped around her. When she saw Tom she ran down the steps, her bare feet noiseless.

"Oh, Tom!" she whispered. "You *would*—you miserable sinner!"

Tom smiled without opening his eyes or making a sound. He swayed back and forth on his feet and Baynes caught him.

"I don't believe he's going to walk up the stairs," Baynes whispered. Without being told he knew that this must be conducted in silence.

"He will, too," Margaret retorted.

With expertness she lifted Tom's hand and bit his thumb and at the same instant clapped her hand over his mouth. Above her head Tom's eyes opened reproachfully.

"Hayfoot-strawfoot," she commanded.

He moved his feet sluggishly and she wound his arm around her shoulder.

"Get under his other arm," she whispered to Baynes.

He obeyed and together they moved up the stairs and into Tom's bedroom. They went to the bed and he dropped upon it. Baynes took off his shoes, and Margaret drew a cover. Tom was already asleep, and they tiptoed from the room.

Outside the door they paused.

"Does he do this very often?" Baynes asked softly.

"Whenever he has the slightest excuse," she said under her breath.

Baynes hesitated, looking down on her with some shyness. He was tall and thin, and in the dim light he looked young and tired. "You go back home as fast as you can," she whispered. "There'll be a lot for you to do tomorrow."

He still hesitated. "What'll I call you?" he inquired.

"Call me?" she repeated.

He went on. "I've always been just a kid to you and Edward—I'll have to call you something now."

"Are you glad?" she asked.

"Yes," he answered. Although he had seldom spoken to her in all the years he had known her, he liked her and felt a strange tingling sense of nearness to her—she was going to be his brother's wife!

"Call me Maggie," she suggested.

"But is that what Edward calls you?" he asked.

"Nobody calls me Maggie. It can be your special name for me," she replied.

He considered this uncertainly. "Will Edward mind?"

"I like him to call me Margaret," she replied. "It seems to suit him."

He had no notion of what she meant by this, but he accepted it. "All right—Maggie."

"And don't tell anybody about Tom," she said.

"I won't," he promised. "But Ed knows, of course."

"Does he?" She paused, then she said, "Sometime I'll tell you why he gets drunk."

"Is there a reason?" he asked in surprise.

"There's always a reason," she said decisively. "Now go home—do!"

He walked home through the cold December air, and let himself into the house. There was neither sound nor light and he stole upstairs to his own room, undressed, and crawled into his cold bed, worrying lest tomorrow Tom could not help him out.

On the other side of the wall Edward lay motionless and awake. What did men think about the night before they were married? It depended, he supposed, upon what sort of men they were. He supposed that for some men it was a night of impatient waiting for physical fulfillment. He had heard of men who could not wait, and who went to a brothel. In the talk of boys together in college there had even been advice that this was a good thing to do, because it kept a man from being too urgent. A woman was always afraid on her wedding night—if she was a virgin, that is. He had heard such talk without seeming to listen, being shy and fastidious. Now he knew that he had listened, for here it all was in his mind. He had thought it filthy talk then and it seemed even more filthy now. He wanted fulfillment, of course—but not at all costs. He wanted the fulfillment of wholeness, but what that was he could not comprehend, except that it was more than physical.

Lying alone in his room for this last night of his solitary life, he was aware of a profound satisfaction that he, too, would go to his marriage a virgin. There would be nothing to tell Margaret tomorrow night—nothing at all. Had there been episodes in his past, he would have been wretched had he not told her. His fearful honesty would have compelled him. He had kissed a few girls—two, to be exact—but the memory of their faces, their lips, were now disgusting to him. He groaned and turned on his side. The folly of the young! Thank God it had carried him no further. That was because he had so early loved Margaret. He sighed, and her face swam out of the darkness. He would take every hour as it came, all the hours ahead, the days, the years. His mind ran down those years and he saw himself and Margaret—children, too, but he could not see their faces. There would be plenty of room in that big house. He supposed that he'd get as used to the Holcombe house as he was to this room. It would cease to be the Holcombe house, it would become his. The spigot of the bathroom leaked—but they were lucky to have a bathroom—most old houses didn't. Mr. Holcombe was English and that was why. He must remember to fix the spigot. He fell asleep at last.

His wedding day was sunny—that he made sure of when he sprang out of bed. Sunshine and blue sky above snow! The gray sky had opened and a steady quiet rain at dusk had changed to snow during the night and the clouds had cleared. He stood at the open window for a moment, breathing in the crisp cold air, and his spirits soared. What had he been afraid of yesterday or any other day? This was the day of his heart's desire, the dream day of his life. Religion was the social custom of church going and the stereotyped prayers of his childhood long since left off, but at this moment he fell to his knees beside his bed and prayed speechlessly that God would help him to be a good man and good husband for his beloved. It was only for a moment and he was on his feet again, half ashamed. But the impulse had done him good. He did not often let himself act upon impulse.

Now, feeling unusually free, he prepared himself for his wedding day. There was plenty to do. He had slept later than his habit, and his mother had not called him. When he had eaten his breakfast he must go to the church for rehearsal, and by the time that was over, it would be noon. Margaret was to sleep for two hours this afternoon—that Mrs. Seaton had told him firmly—and he would go to the shop and work out those two hours as the easiest way to rid himself of them. Then it would be time to bathe and dress and see that the last things were packed into his new pigskin bag, which had been his wedding gift from his father and mother. "It's not your Christmas gift, mind," his mother had taken care to say.

So engrossed was he in his own day that he had not thought of what it would mean to his family, and he was surprised to see them all in the dining room waiting for breakfast with him. He saw when he opened the door that they were even in their second-best clothes. His father was reading the paper, his mother was watering the plants on the window sill, Baynes was whistling the canary into a frenzy, and Louise stood watching. She was always happier when Baynes was at home. Seeing that plain somewhat patient young face, Edward felt a stab of remorse that he so often forgot his sister.

"Well, young man," his father said mildly. He looked over his spectacles.

"I didn't expect to see everybody," Edward said. He felt shy and awkward, hating to be the center of attention.

"It's the last morning," his mother said gently.

The last morning? This, which was all but the first morning for him, was for her the last. For one brief instant he had a dim perception of what time meant to a human life, and he could not answer her. His father answered for him. "Come now, Mother—don't gloom, my dear. We want him to be as happy as we've been, don't we?" He rose, snapped his newspaper together, and took his place at the head of the table.

"Great day in the morning," Baynes murmured.

They sat down and the family breakfast began in silence. Edward looked up and found Louise's eyes fixed on him. She looked away when his eyes met hers.

"Your dress all ready, Louzey?" he asked. The affectionate name of their childhood came unexpectedly from his tongue. She flushed and nodded.

"I didn't think she'd look well in that rose-colored taffeta but she does," his mother said.

"Good," he said heartily. He glanced at his brother. "I gave the ring to Tom, Baynes, but when the moment comes I want you to hand it to me. I'll show you this morning."

"I'll be there," Baynes said. Whether Tom could be was another matter.

The comfortable hearty breakfast went on. The canary fluttered its wings and sang furiously and sunshine fell across the table. The big baseburner in the hall warmed the room. His mother had made muffins and opened a jar of strawberry jam, and Edward ate with appetite. The coffee was good, the cream thick, and the dish of scrambled eggs and bacon was what he liked best, upon a foundation of oatmeal.

"Well, my boy," his father said after a long silence. "I suppose you won't get down to the shop."

"I thought I'd come down for a while this afternoon," Edward replied.

"Don't have to! Let's see—you'll be away two weeks," his father went on.

"It'll be queer to think of you at the seashore," his mother said.

"Can you really go in swimming?" Louise asked in a dreamy voice.

"How queer—when we'll be having Christmas!"

"Hey," Edward cried out. "What about the Christmas tree?" He had forgotten it altogether.

"We'll decorate it tonight, after you've gone," his mother answered. "It'll give us something to do."

She had planned it all, he saw. He was touched that they would miss him, and wondered if it were disloyal to Margaret that he should feel now a pang of vague homesickness because he would not be here tonight to help decorate the tree. Lest his mother discern his heart he answered only Louise.

"Margaret says it'll be that warm." They were going south to New Orleans. It was Margaret's choice and he had been staggered by the distance and the cost.

"I'd like New Orleans well enough," he had replied to this, "but I'd rather go somewhere near enough so that my money will carry us there and back."

"Oh, hush," she had retorted to this. "It's my honeymoon as much as it's yours. I'll pay my half."

But he had refused such compromise. They were going, but only as he could pay for it. That is, they were going by day coach and they had rooms at a boarding house instead of a big hotel.

"I like little clean boarding houses," Margaret had said quickly. "Big hotels are always stuffy."

She had no foolish pride.

"Margaret, behave yourself!" Mrs. Seaton implored. They were rehearsing in the church, decorated for Christmas, and Margaret was willful and teasing and so beautiful that none of them could keep their eyes off her. Edward was bemused with her. He wanted to shake her for her naughtiness and with difficulty he kept from kissing her. He caught Baynes looking at her with infatuation and that sobered him.

"Come," he said with sudden sternness. "Let's get it right."

She quieted at the sound of his voice and went through the ceremony, obeying Dr. Hart, the minister, with an airy demureness. Sandra was patient, Tom was nowhere to be seen, and Baynes had got the ring from him somehow and managed without dropping it.

"Whom God hath brought together let no man . . . et cetera," Dr. Hart finished hastily. "I think that is about all. The rest is familiar. Just pause a moment, Edward, before slipping on the ring. Give me two seconds to round off my phrases."

Baynes put out his hand for the ring.

"I'll keep it now," Edward said.

"Don't forget to give it to me, then," Baynes replied, slightly hurt that he was not trusted.

Dr. Hart listened to this, his eyes amused. He had christened these young people, had later received them into the church, and now they were taking their own part in the eternal pattern of birth and life and death. He bowed his head and walked softly away. Since the manse adjoined the church, he had kept on his carpet slippers and no one noticed his going.

If Edward had hoped for a moment with Margaret alone he did not get it. She squeezed his hand and gave him a long look from under her black lashes. Then she shook her head. "I have to obey Mamma this last day," she said sweetly and followed her mother and Sandra out of the vestry door. He was left alone in the quiet church with Baynes.

"Seem queer?" Baynes asked.

"A bit," he said briefly. He looked at his watch. He wasn't going to talk over anything with a kid like Baynes. "Guess I'll go home and finish packing so that I can go along to the shop after dinner." Then he relented. "I daresay you'd better take the ring after all." He handed it to Baynes and was rewarded by the pleasure in his brother's young face.

"Thanks," Baynes said. "I'll see how Tom is. He was properly stewed last night. He get that way often?"

"I've only seen it a couple of times," Edward said.

They parted, glad to separate. They were still too young to show their fondness for each other or even to know how close they were as brothers. Baynes went along kicking pebbles out of his path and Edward walked home soberly. He wished that Margaret would not get such laughing fits. They were not pure merriment, of that he was sure. Some day he would tell her he did not like them.

When he reached home he went upstairs and found his mother bending over his suitcase.

"Now, Mother," he began warmly.

"I was only putting in a new toothbrush," she said defensively. "Your old one wasn't fit."

He had not thought of so small a thing, but he knew she was right. Would there be other things he had or ways of doing things that would not seem nice?

His mother sat down on the window seat. "I know your father hasn't said a thing to you, Edward. It's queer how men can't talk to each other. I do want to say this—it's so important to a woman that a man is—nice."

He could not answer, nor look at her face. He kept looking at her hands, thin and dry and strong, folded in her lap.

"I'll try to remember," he mumbled.

"Maybe you don't even know what I mean," she said.

"I think I do, Mother."

She sighed and suddenly the tears came to her eyes. "I do hope she'll make a good wife," she said.

"Good or not, I don't want any other," he replied gently.

"Well—" She rose, and going to him she kissed his cheek and he put his arm around her. "Thank you for everything—and I wish I'd been better here at home."

"You've always been a good boy," she replied. "I put your Christmas present in the bottom of your bag—and something for Margaret, too."

She held the embrace a moment too long and then withdrew. "Well, I guess, then—" She broke off, smiled through more tears, and went away.

He sat down where she had been sitting and stared out into the street. Nice? But Margaret might not think niceness was what she wanted. That he would have to find out. Nevertheless, vaguely alarmed by what his mother had said, he looked over his things and rejected a pair of pajamas that were patched and put his best ones on top. He cleaned his razor and washed his comb and brush and took out a new tie for tomorrow morning. New socks, new handkerchiefs, a clean shirt for every day.

The Chinese bells chimed through the house and he went downstairs to dinner, and without desire to eat. His excitement he masked carefully under an air of indifference and he was grateful that no one seemed to notice him. His mother was urging Louise to let her use the curling tongs on her hair and Baynes was abstracted. His father was silent.

"Coming down to the shop with me?" his father asked when the meal was over.

"Yes," he replied.

They put on their coats and hats and walked down the street together. "About that loan," his father began, "I don't suppose you could borrow a thousand yourself?"

Edward considered. "I'd have to talk it over with Margaret."

His father threw him a sharp look. "I'm not telling your mother about our house."

"Margaret and I have made a sort of bargain to be frank with each other," Edward replied.

"We all do at first," his father retorted. They walked for a block in silence, then his father straightened his shoulders. "Well, it's too much to ask on your wedding day," he said abruptly. They entered the shop and parted, his father to the office and he to the pressroom to examine a page of type for a temperance folder ordered by a woman's society in Boston. He studied the proof. "Strong drink destroys a man's soul," the headline announced. He reduced the size of the type and lessened the space between the lines. In one hour and forty minutes he would be standing before the minister, with Margaret at his side. In two hours they would be man and wife.

Edward was completely composed, this to his own astonishment. He went through the ceremony with tender gravity, thinking of Margaret and not himself. The church was full of the people they had both known all their lives, elderly men and women whom they had badgered in one way or another as children, who had been their teachers in school and Sunday school, who had sold them food and clothes and Christmas toys, who had invited them to parties and picnics. And there were the young married, watching with wise bright eyes, confident and approving. Children stared, awed by the mysticism of the ceremony, and girls and boys, too old to be children, watched with hearts beating for themselves when their time came. It was the accomplishment of his one dream, this hour set apart and perfect, the church warm and bright with holly and pine and the lighted lamps of evening streaming out through the windows to lie upon the snow. Organ music filled the shallow arches of the roof and Mrs. Sulley, the old doctor's wife, short and squat and grotesque with fat, poured out a voice powerful and pure. Dr. Sulley had brought both of them into the world, but he was not here. Over in the next valley a farmer's wife was giving birth to a child.

"The voice that breathed o'er Eden," the strong sweet voice was gentle with tenderness.

And Margaret, who this morning had been willful with mischief, was grave and tall. She carried a little ivory prayerbook and no flowers, and her hair was a dark cloud under her lace veil. Sandra and Louise stood behind her like twin roses, and he was surprised to see that Louise was almost pretty. Her mother had curled her hair under the wide velvet hat, and her lips looked red.

He felt Margaret's shoulder against his, her arm touching his, the soft fullness of her white form against his thigh and knees. Her low voice was composed and sure and when he answered his own was unfaltering. Baynes was sweating but when the time came for the ring he handed it to Edward, hooked slightly over the tip of his little finger so that it would not drop.

"With this ring I thee wed."

His voice followed old Dr. Hart's slow steady tone, deep with tenderness. Margaret was looking at him, her blue eyes fathomless. His head swam a little and he held her hand tightly. Their voices repeating, answering, came in perfect rhythm. "Man and wife!" Out of the swirl of joy these words came as clear as bells. It was over. He turned and held his head high and with her hand inside his elbow, they walked down the holly-wreathed aisle. "What God hath joined, let no man put asunder—" No man, not even himself!

"There!" Margaret said.

She took off her hat and put it on the seat opposite.

"It wasn't too bad, was it?" he asked.

The train swerved around a hill and panted steadily on.

"Not for once," she said.

"Not for once only," he retorted.

She smiled at that and she put out her feet. "My shoes, too."

He knelt and took the shoes from her narrow silkshod feet. He held her right foot in his hand. "What a little foot," he murmured foolishly. His restrained blood began to beat. "But it's cold—right through your stocking!" He nursed her foot in both hands. Her instep was high and arched and her heel firm.

She curled her toes into his palm. "You couldn't do this if we were in the day coach, Ned."

He looked up. She was smiling down at him with such a look of tenderness and shyness that he felt half faint, and he managed to keep his head only enough to salvage his pride. At the very moment when they had stepped on the train, the platform crowded with people coming home for Christmas and shouting at the wedding party, Thomas Seaton had thrust an envelope into his coat pocket.

"This is my private wedding gift to you—as man to man," he had muttered.

The train had started immediately after they got on, and he saw a porter taking their bags.

"Wait!" he called.

"Look in your pocket, Ned," Margaret said.

He had looked in the envelope and had found tickets for the drawing room in the sleeping car. "Margaret, you've gone ahead of me again," he had said most reproachfully.

"Ned, I didn't," she answered. "He did it without my knowing it—until five minutes before we got on the train."

He could not be angry with her then and he could not be angry now. It would have been hard indeed to have sat under the staring eyes of a coach full of strangers. Still, there was something deep, somewhere, that would have to be settled between them. His wife must be content with what he could give her—she must forget her father and mother and turn to her husband—but this was not the time for argument between them. He pulled the pillow from the seat and put her feet upon it and covered them with the steamer rug his mother had given them. Then he sat down beside her and drew her into his arms and kissed her.

All these months he had guarded himself, wary of his own heart. Now he held her long—his lips upon hers, and one by one the guards went down. His arms tightened about her and she yielded for a moment. Then he felt her struggle against him. First her hands pushed his shoulders, and then she tore her lips away, and he saw a look of strange inquiry in her eyes.

He released her. "I am too much for you," he said abruptly.

She busied herself with the flowers she wore on her breast. "I don't know yet," she said after a moment. "You see, it's not only you I don't know—it's myself, too."

He had begun to be hurt but with these words she healed.

"We won't rush," he said.

She considered this. "Still, we'll do what we like, shall we?"

Now it was he who considered. "What if one likes and the other doesn't?"

She laughed. "You don't know anything more than I do—I can see that."

"You don't mind?" His pride lifted his head again, on guard, ready to be struck down.

She flung her arms about him. "I think it's lovely. We're starting out absolutely equal. Ned, tell me the truth, have you ever been in love before?"

"No—no," he whispered, and leaning over her, he kissed her temple. He could feel a beating vein there, straight from her heart.

"Nor I!" she sighed with joy.

"Sure?" He lifted his head to look into her eyes.

"Nothing like this."

"But something?" he persisted.

"Just—searchings," she answered.

The quick darkness of December had fallen, and putting off the lights as long as the lines of hills could be seen, they watched the landscape darken. He sat in a dream of delight, his arm around her, her head on his shoulder, until he heard her voice murmuring against his neck.

"Ned!"

"Yes?"

"Could you eat very much at the reception?"

"No—could you?"

"No—and I'm starved."

He reached for the light. The flying landscape disappeared and their room became a cozy cell.

"We'll eat here," he said.

"Oh, yes."

He pressed the button and when the porter had brought the menu, he gave himself to the frowning consideration of the best food for happiness. They studied the dishes together while the porter waited grinning, and then gave their order. Not until Edward was consuming duckling instead of the lamb chops he had ordered and ice cream instead of apple pie, did he realize that he was not eating his favorite foods and finding it all delicious.

"Only what you want," he murmured.

"How do I know what I want?" she asked.

"Then promise to stop me as soon as you know!"

"What if I want more?"

"Promise to tell me!"

"I don't know—if I can."

This interchange in the middle of the night made him sit up in bed and turn on the light. She lay against the pillow, the soft lace of her night-dress open on her bosom. It pleased him that she did not put up her hand to draw the lace together. Her eyes were shy but honest, and she did not hide them from him.

"You aren't afraid of me, Margaret?"

"Are you afraid of me?"

"A little."

"Why?"

"I don't want to offend you."

She lay thinking for a moment, her eyes still on his. "I might offend you," she said at last.

"Only by making me think—I'd done something you didn't like," he replied after a moment, and put out the light again.

They lay side by side, feeling their way toward one another, while the train swayed its way southward through the darkness. Nothing he had known of her in the past helped him now. He had first seen her as a little girl when he was twelve years old. She had been in school with him since they were in first grade and doubtless he had seen her before then. But when he was twelve and she eleven he had seen her one day with a sense of shock and individuality. Her black hair, curling about her face in small feathers, was in two braids tied with scarlet ribbons. Her cheeks were pink and her lips were red, and she had just won a Fourth of July race on the school grounds. He had been holding one end of the string when she flung herself against it. "Peggy's first!" her schoolmates had yelled.

After that he had always seen her first, in the schoolroom in the morning, out in the yard at recess, in church on Sundays. With what pains he had maneuvered his place at the end of the pew so that he might see the back of her head and the occasional turn of her profile, two seats ahead! Yet he had not spoken to her alone for nearly three years after that, when he was fifteen.

Yet all the times they had talked together and walked together, had quarreled and parted to make up shyly again, none of it helped him now. She was new, a stranger, yet the one he loved with his whole being. He was torn between selfishness and love. All the healthy hunger of his young manhood, his unsatisfied, carefully hidden curiosities, the banked passions, the honest animal in him, rose up now. He had no aids to self-control except what he could muster for himself. Church and society had withdrawn. They had given their sanction. Within holy wedlock whatever he wanted was his.

Now it was only love that took command. He loved her so much that he wanted above all to please her. In his total ignorance he had the instinct from somewhere in his intelligence to know that union depended upon two, not one. There was so much about her that he did not know—nay, what did he know? He had no guide to the delicate mechanism of her body and her spirit. Even she could not help him. And he did not want her help, except in response and communication. Had she taken the lead in love, he would have been repelled. The way was his to make. She was the sleeping princess whom he must rouse, not to horror and shame, but to pure delight, so that they might live forever after in happiness.

He was frightened by the responsibility, and fear made him tender and slow. Fear and love mingled together, sharpened every sense and perception, and he was rewarded by her stillness and then by her yielding.

"It hurts me—but I love you."

"You are perfect."

"Ned, did anybody tell you anything?"

"No—did you know anything?"

"Nothing."

"Then we'll find the way ourselves."

"Yes."

They slept, lulled by the rhythm of the train, woke and slept again, until the day broke. He heard her voice at his ear, "Merry Christmas, Ned— Merry Christmas, Merry Christmas—let's open our presents, sleepy head."

He opened his eyes under the curtain of her hair over his face.

Christmas? He pulled her head down to his shoulder. "I'd forgotten."

Reticence being his nature, Edward had conceded the wisdom of a honeymoon as far as possible from home, as different as possible from the accustomed air. The soft warm atmosphere of New Orleans, the sunshine, the mists drifting in from the Gulf and melting away again, the laziness, the sense of holiday, the colors on the streets and houses, the glimpses of flowered inner courts and gardens, everything was new. Their boarding house was small but good. Their room was large and cool, and a balcony hung from the big window. Ironwork as delicate as lace shielded them and revealed to them the patio below, where bamboo and ferns surrounded a pool of clear water, still as the square of sky above them.

They lived as remote from daily life as though they were in a trance. He ate food that he had never tasted before, hotly seasoned, sour and sweet and peppered, fried shrimps and fish and ballooned potato chips, spiced soups and flowered ices. He had always been a sparing eater of plain foods but now he ate heartily, although with more prudence than Margaret did. Indeed he saw to his secret surprise that she could be something of a glutton, for the taste of something that she loved. He ate experimentally, knowing that he would always choose for his daily food the brown bread, the baked beans, the lean meat, of his habitual fare. But Margaret, her cheeks glowing and her eyes sapphire, cried that she could eat of such food forever.

"Why do we eat boiled potatoes and cabbage at home?" she inquired of him.

"I guess we like plain things," he replied.

"I don't!" she declared. "I like things that taste."

Her slender firm body was as hard as his own, defying fat, and she ate as she pleased, slept hours on end when the mood for sleep fell on her or stayed up half the night. All his careful habits were upset and put aside, and he let it be so, knowing that it could not last. He encouraged curiosities that he did not possess and followed her into old shops and churches smelling of mold and he bought for her strange flowers and an old French chair and an ancient prayerbook with a clasp studded with seed pearls and they sat in a square and ate oranges and watched children of every color playing together.

"I didn't think you'd be like this, Ned," she exclaimed one day.

"Like what?" he asked.

"Fun!"

"Why did you marry me then?" he asked.

"Because—"

She walked beside him, both hands clasped over his arm, her head just below the level of his eyes, and he did not press her. He was secretly astonished at his own capacity for enjoyment. Here where they were unknown he felt no embarrassment at her love openly expressed before strangers. They were in a solitude of strangers, one among many couples in love. While the rest of the world worked and went to bed early and rose to work again, they lived the life of royal beings. Their room became a sort of home, and the sight of her clothes hanging beside his grew natural and was no longer a sight for wonder. When she had hung her frocks beside his sober gray second suit, he had made occasion to open the closet door during the day, that he might see again the intimacy. When she asked him what he did, he was ashamed of his softness.

"You must tell me," she insisted.

"I'm a fool, that's all," he had said.

"Ah, don't be ashamed of anything, Ned!"

"Well then," he opened the closet door. "Your frock there—against my things—"

She ran to the closet and nestled her cheek against his coat. "I'll tell you something."

"What?" His heart melted with love and went running through his veins like fire.

"When I told my mother I wasn't sure I wanted to marry you, she said, 'How do you feel when you see his coat hanging in the hall?' So one day when you were there talking to Father—remember?—I went into the hall, and I put my arms around your coat—like this, and I knew."

He was speechless with the wonder of this and he took her in his arms.

In the midst of love and satisfaction he was ashamed to discover in himself, one day, small vague thoughts of business. He stifled these intruders and hid them from Margaret as though they were thoughts of other women. What then was his surprise when after another day of unalloyed joy and idleness she said suddenly, "Don't hate me, Ned, but I have a hankering to get at our house!"

She was lying across the bed on her stomach, clad only in a chemise made of white clouds, and her hair was hanging over her shoulders. He still felt shy about staring at her. "I couldn't hate you, Margaret. I wish you wouldn't say such things."

He was astonished that her courage was more than his. While he had hidden his thought from her, she had dared to speak out. This was intolerable and so he spoke out, too. "Matter of fact, I've been having an idea or two myself about the office."

"Ned, you haven't!"

It was an exclamation and accusation, and he was wounded. "Is that worse than your thinking about the house?"

"No but, Ned—you're thinking wrong things now. I don't mind your wanting to get back to the office, but aren't you interested in the house?"

"Of course I am."

"But you said office!"

He grew dogged. "The office is my job."

"So is the house. We're to do it together."

"I doubt I'll be much good at it."

She shook her head until her hair flared. "If you aren't interested in our home, I'll live in a boarding house."

Some sort of absurd quarrel was brewing between them and he stopped it firmly. "Margaret, let's go home."

She did not answer this. Thinking it over, idly, she wound her dark hair about her throat and tucked in the ends. "How do I look in a high collar, Ned? Everybody will think we didn't have a good honeymoon if we come home early."

"I like your throat bare. What do we care what people think? We know what sort of a honeymoon we've had."

"Have you really liked it?" Her voice was foolishly wistful.

He sat down beside her. "What do you think?"

"I think you have, a little—about as I have. It's been perfect."

He lifted her into his arms. "You'd better think so. It's the only honeymoon you'll ever have."

She sighed. "Oh, Ned, I didn't really think you could be so heavenly nice!"

"I knew how nice you'd be—and you are."

He rocked her back and forth, his face in her neck, and she clung to him with both arms. Then she began to laugh silently.

"Ned!"

"Yes?"

"Know why I'm laughing?"

"Do you?"

"I've thought of something."

"Again?"

"Let's go home secretly and not tell anybody!"

He sat still, contemplating this thought. It would be entirely possible to live for a few days at least in the Holcombe house—in their house, he was trying to call it now—without anyone knowing it. They were not expected back for a week and the house was ready for them except for the last dusting and the hot meal. Mrs. Seaton had hired a maid for them, she had written them, Hattie, an Irish girl. It would be nice to have the house their own by right of possession before she came.

"I am greedy," Margaret said. "I want to begin living now—this minute."

"Isn't this living?" he asked.

"Holiday," she retorted. She lay in his arms, looking at him, and he felt his head whirl. Her complete abandon was entrancing and at the same time it made him uneasy. What was the source of her childlike naturalness and what did it mean? He knew that there was no such relationship between his own father and mother. He knew that to this day his mother undressed in the dark, after his father was in bed. His father was irritated by it because she stumbled over furniture and Edward had heard him grumbling.

Margaret herself had made a quick end to any shyness. She had laughed when he wrapped himself in his brown bathrobe their first evening in the hotel. "Why do you want to put that heavy thing on?" she inquired.

"I'm a hairy sort of a beast," he had replied in an effort to appear casual. "Not beautiful—"

She had come over to him at this and had taken off the robe and looked at him from head to foot. "You have a good figure. Why hide it?" This she had said so dispassionately that he was immediately set at ease. Then her sapphire eyes had sparkled wickedly. "Especially from me!"

They had laughed upon that and he had hung the robe in the closet.

And yet, although he knew well enough that it was not lack of proper modesty, there was danger in her naturalness. What would he do if ever she displayed it to anyone except him? It was a delightful private trait, but could it be kept private? He reviewed in his memory possible occasions when she might have been tainted with what was called "being too free." He could remember nothing of the sort, but he had not been much in the Seaton house. He caught her looking at him curiously now and suddenly he felt ashamed of himself and buried his face in her hair. He doubted that he was good enough for her, even at his best. This doubt at least he determined to keep to himself.

The landscape was deep in snow when they drew up to their own door. They had left the train at Rockford, the station above Chedbury, and then had spent an hour shopping for food. Margaret had bought a huge basket and into this their parcels were piled, while he went to find some sort of conveyance. When he came back he saw that she needed deliverance.

"You strangers around here?" the inquisitive grocer inquired.

"We're moving nearby," Margaret answered.

"Rockford?" the grocer persisted.

"Out in the country," Margaret said calmly.

Edward broke in. "There's a farmer going out our way. I was lucky enough to catch him at the livery stable."

They escaped the grocer and lugging their basket they climbed into the sleigh pulled by a couple of heavy farm horses. The farmer was taciturn and drove them speechlessly to the house. For his silence they were so grateful that Edward added a quarter to the two dollars of the agreed price, but the farmer shook his head, and still silent, he picked out the extra coin and returned it and drove on.

"How wonderful he is!" Margaret cried. "Oh, if everybody in the world were like that—except you and me!"

Edward reached for the key behind the shutter of a window, and fitted it into a frozen lock. It would not turn.

"Breathe into it," Margaret advised.

But his breath was not warm enough, and so she stooped and blew out a frosty gust of sweet warmth. Her breath was always sweet. It was one of his blessings. Together, laughing and blowing, they warmed the lock and the key turned and they stepped into the clean ice-cold house. A look of horror went over her face and she stopped on the threshold without closing the door.

"You didn't lift me over the doorstep!" she cried.

He seized her in his arms, carried her out, and brought her in again, setting her down before the hearth in the living room. He had learned to call it that from her, for in his father's house there was no such room. A parlor, a sitting room, neither was a living room.

"Sit down while I get our fire started," he commanded her.

"Do order me about, Ned, just for sentiment's sake," she replied and sat down.

He knelt on the hearth and put a match to the fire already laid. "As soon as this starts I shall go down cellar and get the furnace going," he said. "But you'll warm your little feet here."

"Light the kitchen range first," she urged. "I can't wait."

She could not keep from singing. Song was impossible to him, but it bubbled out of her. She could not sit still and forgetting his command, as she always did when she wished, she ran about the house. He lit the kitchen stove and downstairs in the cellar he could hear her feet, flying over the floor above his head. They paused at the stair and she called down, "I shan't go upstairs until you come with me!"

"Good girl!" he shouted back.

The furnace was laid ready, too, and he poured a little kerosene on the kindling and heard the roar of fire. This was the warmth of his house and for the first time he felt the house was his own. Then he frowned. There was no sieve for the ashes and there would be waste of coal. The thought of buying a sieve and even of using it gave him pleasure although it was a task that he had detested whenever he had been compelled to do it in his

father's house. He washed his hands at the kitchen sink, saw that the fire
was blazing in the living room, and then went into the hall where Margaret
waited, her foot on the stair. She flung her arm about him and he put
his about her and thus arm in arm they went up the broad stairs. Mr.
Holcombe had not liked the narrow stairs of New England and he had
built his hall spaciously and the stairs wide, as they had been in his home
in England.

"Bless him," Margaret said.

"Are you thinking about Mr. Holcombe, too?" Edward asked amazed.

"Weren't you?" she replied.

They walked the length of the upstairs hall to the room that was to be
their own. This was the room where he was to live his intimate life with
her! His children would be conceived and born here. He would grow old
here, and here, please God, he would die.

Death he had not thought of once since his marriage, and now it sprang
at him monstrously. One of them must die first! It had not occurred to
him that it would be so. But which? Could he live if it were she? And yet
she must not be left alone. Then he put the thought away. Certainly he
must not tell her what he was thinking. He tried quickly to think of something else, lest with her uncanny intuition she discern the cloud of death in
his mind.

"The sun pours in," he murmured. Two wide windows opened to the
south and beyond them the snow-laden hill rose round to the blue sky.

She turned suddenly and hid her face in his breast. "Don't leave me!"
she whispered.

"But of course I shan't leave you," he protested.

"Let me die first," she begged.

"I promise," he said quietly.

He held her and then as suddenly she drew away from him.

"I must cook dinner!" she exclaimed and ran down the stair like thistledown, her skirts floating about her.

They were alone for three days, and during the whole time Edward
worked in almost silent zeal and entire absorption. He went over the entire
house from attic to cellar. While Margaret dusted and arranged closets
and bureau drawers, and put wedding presents into their new places, he
put up hooks, tightened hinges, adjusted doors, painted worn spots on floors
and window sills, and hammered picture hooks. Beyond the windows the
snow remained immovably deep, and he took his exercise in shoveling
paths fiercely and thoroughly. He enjoyed this far more than New Orleans
and faced the truth about himself that however much he longed to enjoy
what might be called pleasure he found his real delight in work. He
tramped around the outside of the house, examining every shutter and
frame and lock. There was a large porch on the back of the house and
there were boards in the floor that had rotted and must be replaced. Hour

by hour he made the house his own and his home and when the fourth night came he had forgotten that Mr. Holcombe had ever lived here. He built the fire in the living room as he had done each evening, and it was his fire and his hearth.

As though Margaret felt his possession she went upstairs after supper was ready and she put on a long-sleeved, long-skirted frock of dark blue velvet. He went to meet her and stood at the foot of the stairs, gazing at her as she came down. She did not evade his adoration and it did not make her shy, and this was another of her traits that he loved. His mother met praise with uneasy laughter and denial but Margaret smiled at him with full acceptance.

"I put this on to celebrate our finishing the house," she said. She stood on the last step and leaned upon his shoulders, and he put his hands about her slender waist and lifted her in his arms and carried her to the big leather chair by the hearth which had been in his room at Harvard, a gift from his father and mother one Christmas. Then he stood and looked around the rooms. Margaret had lit candles and lamps everywhere before she went upstairs, and room opened into room in a glow of light.

"We can live here always," Margaret said. "There's room to grow."

The measure of what he was to have depended now altogether upon himself and he was sure of himself, too. So far in his life, so good.

"Now I know you are really my wife," he said to her.

She smiled up at him, her hands clasped behind her head. "And haven't you known it until now?"

"Not to the bottom of me." He fell on his knees before her.

"I haven't forgotten my promise—to make our marriage my life. I'll not forget that as long as I live."

She took his face in her hands. "I hope I'm good enough for you," she cried softly and when he protested she closed his lips with her kiss.

They ate their supper; they spent the evening in happy wandering through their house; they sat by the fire until it died to coals. Then they locked the house and went to bed. He had not overcome the shyness of his body. He could not put into words the act of his passion. He did not want words. He wanted silence and feeling. But she wanted words and she made talk, laughing, half play, half teasing, as though she evaded the depths of his feeling. He had allowed this playfulness until now but suddenly tonight he made her keep silent.

"Don't talk, don't talk."

"But, Ned, you're so serious, darling! And this is joyful, isn't it?"

He did not answer her and she fell into silence, too, and gravely she accepted his love. When it was over he was astounded and then terrified because she began to cry, silently.

"I hurt you!" he exclaimed.

"No, you didn't," she sobbed.

"Then—why?"

"I don't know—I don't know—I feel different." She whose words came always so easily could tell him no more than that and he held her until she slept, distressed and yet exultant.

He was awakened the next morning by a voice in the lower hall and he got up and put on his bathrobe and went to the stairs. There he looked into the red and frightened face of Hattie, the maid.

"Oh, my soul and body!" she screamed. "I didn't know you was here!"

"We got home early," he explained.

"I didn't bring anything to eat with me," she cried.

"There's food in the storeroom," he told her. "I like oatmeal and scrambled eggs and my wife likes just eggs. Toast, of course, and coffee. We'll be down in half an hour."

Hattie changed everything in the house unconsciously but subtly. He and Margaret were now master and mistress as well as man and wife and they came downstairs decorously to sit down to a meal they had not prepared. Their talk must be fit for a servant to hear and he found himself making plans for the day in so dry a manner that Margaret's eyes grew wide. When Hattie had left the room she looked at him with reproach.

"Is that the way you are going to talk from now on?" she asked.

He pretended not to know what she meant. "Don't you think I ought to get to work and earn our living?"

"But you sound so stuffy," she complained.

"Perhaps work is stuffy," he rejoined.

She made a direct attack. "You know you were talking for Hattie!"

"I was trying to talk in spite of her," he retorted.

"The only way to be happy with servants is to forget they exist," she declared.

He ate in silence for a few minutes. Hattie had made the scrambled eggs today too hard. That would have to be changed sooner or later. Could anyone forget she existed? It would take practice.

Margaret talked on, oblivious of Hattie's comings and goings. "I don't like those curtains in the guest room, after all. What if I change them with the ones in the dressing room? Do you object to large cabbage roses, Ned? I love them—so hearty! Hattie, I don't like my toast so brown—make me another slice, there's a good girl! Or I wouldn't mind having them in my own boudoir, if you think they're too feminine for you—yes, that's better. I'll put them in my boudoir."

She had insisted on a dressing room for him and a boudoir for herself, their bedroom being the big room between, and although he had thought it pretentious, yet he found he had liked dressing in privacy and much as he loved her, he did not mind missing the brief interval between her tumbling out of bed with her curls all flaring and then her appearance again, clothed and the curls smoothed. He disliked disorder, and he knew her well enough to know now that order was not the rhythm of her being as it was of his.

The meal drew to a close and with some sentiment he prepared to leave the house and go to work. But she was preoccupied with the changing of curtains and he thought her casual. When he put his arms about her, in the hall after carefully closing the dining-room door against Hattie, he inquired, "You won't mind being left alone all day?"

"I thought I'd just run home for a bit this morning," she told him.

"Why didn't you tell me before?" he asked a little hurt.

She opened her eyes at him again. "You aren't going to expect me to tell you every time I run home?"

"But this is home now," he reminded her.

"Yes, but you know what I mean. Don't tease!"

He would not allow himself to be jealous of her family. "Call me up at the office?"

"I might even come and see you at the office."

"Do, my darling!"

"We might have luncheon in Chedbury and come home together," she suggested.

"Can you eat that food?" he asked.

"Oh, once in a while," she said.

So their day shaped itself as they stood in each other's arms. He opened the door and looked at her and closed it again to kiss her once more and then ran resolutely out, stopping to wave from the gate, and seeing her face pressed against the window, he forced himself to walk on. Luckily there had been no more snow during the night and the half mile to Chedbury would not be too difficult by means of walking in the ruts of farm wagons. Soon he would have to have a vehicle of some sort.

When three quarters of an hour later he sat at his desk, he knew his man's life had begun, at last.

TWO

EDWARD HASLATT was not one of those who rejoice to see the spring. There was something about winter that he liked. The contrast between the roughness of frozen snow and bitter cold and cruel winds sharpened his sense of combat and deepened the comfort of his house when he opened the front door and stepped into his warm wide hall. During the eleven years since he and Margaret had first begun to live in the house he had improved it until today it was as fine a home as could be found about Chedbury.

Chedbury was, outwardly, as it had always been, except that its ancient beauty had been made more perfect. The church had been recently painted, and since the war, every house about the green had been repaired and freshened with paint.

Actually Chedbury was engaged in a private war of its own. During the World War a manufacturer of steel products, lured by the promise of cheap labor, had tried to buy land at the southern end of the town for a factory. Thomas Seaton had risen from the pleasant lethargy of his life, had led an embattled township with such success that Jim Figaro, the ambitious young industrialist, had not been able to buy land nearer than two miles away. Even this was too near for Chedbury, which complained that the factory smoke spoiled the paint on the church when the wind blew from the wrong direction.

Meanwhile South Chedbury began to grow. Italians, Portuguese, and Canadians had begun to make a town of their own, compounded of small flimsy bungalows. From these the townfolk of Chedbury separated themselves severely and old separations among themselves were forgotten as they banded together against the new. Haslatt now was as good as Seaton, for both alike were against South Chedbury.

Edward smiled wryly when his mother and Mrs. Seaton met at the Village Improvement Society, and yet why not? Margaret was a Seaton and he had built a small, respectable book business about the printing shop, which was now his own. The question today was whether he should not open a New York office. The center of the publishing business was there, as Baynes was always telling him. Writers, it seemed, one found only in the city. Well, he did not want to publish too many books, and he was cautious in the presence of writers.

He stepped out of his house on an early spring morning with his mind full of these problems. Margaret followed him out of the door, and he lingered beside her on the front porch. Two years ago they had torn down the long narrow porch and had put up this wide square one with thick white pillars. It had added dignity to the house and he liked it.

"It's still cold," Margaret said, shivering in her dark woolen frock. "Though it looked as warm as May from the living-room window! I do believe that's a daffodil."

She ran down the steps ahead of him, as lithe and swift as ever and stooping over a flowerbed, now a mass of short green leaves, she plucked a daffodil bud, tipped with yellow.

"It'll bloom quickly enough in the house," he said. "Next week this time they'll all be out."

He kissed her again, first glancing toward the gate. Margaret laughed. "You're still shy about kissing me, aren't you, poor darling!"

He denied this stoutly. "Not shy—it's just that I feel private about it."

Smiling, she thrust the daffodil bud into her fichu, reached up and pulled him by the ears and kissed the underside of his chin. "Good-by, Ned! Don't be late."

"Not tonight. Tomorrow night that fellow's bringing his book."

"Oh, dear," she murmured.

"He's coming on the late train, and if the book seems good, it might be sensible to be friendly, eh, Margaret?"

"Only if his fingernails are clean," she said firmly. "The last one was fearfully grimy and the book wasn't any good after all."

Edward laughed. "I'll ask him to hold out his hands."

He was suddenly grave. The words made him think of something. She caught his look and turned away, a shadow on her face.

"Don't be hard on Mary any more," he said in a low voice. "After all, she's only a little thing yet."

Margaret's full underlip tightened. "I can't bear bitten nails. It's disgusting. Besides, if she doesn't stop now she'll go on all her life."

"You'll turn the child against you, Margaret, and that'll be worse than bitten nails."

Her eyes filled with tears. "I don't care about myself."

"Yes, you do," he urged, "or if you don't, then I care about you. I can't bear the children to think you're scolding them."

"But I must scold them when they're naughty," she insisted. "Else who will teach them anything, Ned? You're away all day and when you come home you just want to pet them. It's I who have to be with them."

"If you are just your own self, dear, they'll learn," he urged.

"Ah, but they don't," she retorted.

He saw the tears glistening on her lashes and forbore. "Well, we won't start arguing on this beautiful day, my love. Go back into the house and get warm. If Mary frets you too much, we'll pack her off to boarding school. It's you I think of first."

She pulled a handkerchief from her white lace cuff, wiped her eyes, and smiled. "I'm not as wicked as you think. I read stories to Mary and I made little cakes yesterday that she likes."

"I know," he said fondly. "You're the best of mothers, at heart."

They had been walking slowly down the clean-swept path and now they were at the gate. He did not kiss her again. Instead he smiled and tipped his hat.

She leaned over the gate after he had closed it. "What time will you be home, Ned?"

"About six, I think," he called back. He waved as she turned, and hastened for the trolley. His eyes were tender when he caught it and found an empty seat.

She'd go back into the house and get Mary into her coat and hood and then, putting on the heather-brown coat that he'd bought for her when they were in England last year, she would walk with the child part way to the new grade-school building. Probably she would take the boy with her. It was strange to think that he was the father of three children, and that little Tom would start school next year. The baby, a girl, Sandy, was a year old. Three children were enough, he had decided. He had been careful that Margaret did not have children too quickly. Each time she had been in good health, rested and ready, and the children had been born strong and handsome. His eyes clouded again at the thought of Mary. What was wrong between Mary and Margaret? There might have been no drop of common blood in them. The child adored her mother and could not please her.

"She's a bit slow," Edward mused, "and Margaret is so flashing quick."

Yes, he had been careful of his wife. He tried always to think first of her and what she wanted instead of his own needs. He sighed, thinking of the years just ahead when Mary must grow and her mother must let her grow. Then he stopped thinking. Habit warned him that the next stop was his. He rose and marched down the aisle, tall, slender, swaying as the car curved and stopped.

"So long, Mr. Haslatt," the conductor said.

"So long, Bob," Edward answered and swung down the step, crossed the street, and went into his own shop. He still called it the shop, as his father had always done, although in the years since he had taken the responsibility for the business, he had steadily enlarged the plant, always with caution, and always against his father's will. Someday he would take over the whole building. He wanted even now to erase old Mather's name and make it Haslatt Sons, Printers and Publishers. Mather had died the year after he had started the publishing.

That first year of probation had been a heartbreaking one. Edward had dreamed of a successful book and a handsome profit. Instead he had only squeaked by. The book that had so fascinated him had made very little money, and he had defended it doggedly before old Mather as he lay on what was to be his deathbed.

"It isn't this one book that I bank on, Mr. Mather," he had said. "It's a first novel and a very good one, considering. The man who wrote this book can write a better one. Why, talking with some publishers in Boston they tell me it's always more than likely that you lose on the first book of any writer. And we've made a hundred and seventy-five dollars."

"Overhead, overhead," old Mather had growled.

"I counted in overhead," Edward had retorted.

Well, he had squeaked by, and the next year Tennant had given him the big book, the one that had made it known all over the world, he liked to think, that Mather and Haslatt were publishers as well as printers. On the strength of real profits he had ventured on eight more books, all of which were failures, so that his second year actually ended with a loss. Old Mather had died during the year, however, and although his father was terrified enough, he had agreed to go on with Edward for another year, and the printing business had held up. The next year he'd got the rights for two British books, and they had sold well, and by the third year Tennant had another big book, and he had insisted on larger offices. The fourth year he had lost Tennant to a New York firm which had wiled him away with a huge advance. That had staggered them a bit until he had found Wellaby, who wrote New England historical romances, and these had carried them ever since. He was somewhat ashamed of the romances but the profits from them enabled him to publish books he could not possibly dare to accept otherwise.

He entered the combination freight and passenger elevator, nodded to the boy who ran it and stood silent while it carried him to the third floor. He arrived half an hour later than the employees and so he went up alone. The elevator came to a too sudden stop and he remonstrated mildly, "Now, Sam, I told you to have your mind on what you are doing."

"Yes sir, Mr. Haslatt," the boy said quickly.

He stepped out, knowing that he had said enough. They were all a little afraid of him and he considered this a good thing. He nodded to the telephone girl and passed his father's office. Then he went back and opened the door. His father was already at his desk, poring over a ledger.

"You're early, aren't you?" Edward asked.

"You're late," his father retorted, without looking up.

Edward smiled. "Some time I'm going to spend the night here. It's the only way I can get ahead of you."

"I can't sleep the way you do," his father replied. "Say, Edward, look at this."

He held a figure firmly with his finger and Edward looked over his shoulder. "You've overadvertised five hundred dollars on Wellaby!"

"Figures aren't all in yet," Edward said sharply. "There was a good sale at Christmas and scarcely any books came back in January."

"Hm, hmm," his father mumbled. "I can't see how it's fair business to take back books just because a bookshop can't sell 'em. You don't send back to Wellaby the books you can't sell."

Edward did not reply. He nodded to his father and went into his own office and closed the door. Jane Hobbs, the secretary he shared with his father, had opened his morning's mail and on top of the letters he saw one from his brother Baynes, whom he had allowed reluctantly to go to New York for a week to bring back estimates of what an office there would cost. Baynes had taken Sandra with him. The New York office, Edward suspected, was more than half her idea.

He took up the letter and read it carefully. Sandra, Baynes said, was proving a great help with the office. Lewis Harrow, the young fellow he was sending to Edward to look over, was bringing a couple of manuscripts with him. They had located an inexpensive place, very small, really only a suite of three rooms, in a building in midtown, occupied by three other publishing firms. The address was a good one. That was Sandra, Edward thought grimly. He put down the letter. He would not be quick about taking on the extra overhead. If he took it on, it would be for only a year, and Baynes would have to bring in enough money to cover the costs. He had not dared to tell his father anything about it yet. He frowned slightly and read the rest of his letters, his mind still busy with Baynes.

This younger brother had complicated life by following in his elder brother's footsteps. Among all the many livelihoods that Baynes might have chosen, he would have only publishing. In printing he had not the slightest interest. He wanted only to make books, perhaps even to write them some day. And he had married Margaret's younger sister. Edward had been not a little disgusted when soon after his own marriage Baynes had confessed that he was in love with Sandra.

"You can't be seriously in love when you are only a freshman in college," he had said sternly, and then being too honest for his own comfort, he had admitted to himself that he had been in love with Margaret long before college.

"Sandra is somewhat frivolous," he had then said to Baynes.

Baynes had grinned and said nothing. He was still growing and Edward saw with displeasure, which he recognized as unreasonable, that his younger brother would eventually be some inches taller than himself.

There had been no more conversation about Sandra, and Baynes had persisted in a desultory courtship that ended in betrothal in his senior year in college. Neither Edward nor Margaret put confidence in the marriage, for Sandra said quite frankly that she did not know whether she would like Baynes when he had finished growing up although now she thought him amusing. Yet in less than a year it had taken place. The young couple had moved at once to New York, where Baynes had worked in lowly positions in several publishing houses, and Sandra's luxuries had continued to be supplied by her father. When war was declared, Baynes, egged on by Sandra, had volunteered for a British regiment, and Sandra followed him to England. Four years of fighting on one front after another had left Baynes still unscathed, and apparently unchanged, except for an even taller frame and broadened shoulders, both of which Sandra approved. When Baynes came back a captain, he got out of uniform as quickly as possible and applied to Edward for a job, declaring that he and Sandra would live at the Seaton house. Neither of them wanted a house of their own and there was still no talk of children. In the last year, however, there had been a great deal of talk about New York. Edward had felt that Baynes coming into the business as a younger brother should learn the printing business from the bottom up, but Baynes persisted in remaining ignorant, declaring that he did not know one type from another. He took no interest in Edward's slowly growing typographical library. To Edward's horror he did not know Scotch type from Garamond and already he spent half his time in New York—hunting writers, he insisted.

"I don't know what to do with Baynes," Edward had confided gloomily to Margaret one winter's night after the children were in bed. He had that day received a letter from Baynes, in which this younger brother swore he had found a genius, whose name was Lewis Harrow, and that upon the strength of this find the city office must be opened immediately and that Sandra was, therefore, looking for an apartment.

"What's the matter with Baynes?" Margaret had inquired sleepily. She had been sledding with the children in the afternoon and her cheeks were scarlet and her lashes drooping.

"He won't learn anything about printing, and still he wants to go into the business," Edward complained.

"Why don't you find out what he already knows?" Margaret asked. "Sandra says he's full of flair."

"Flair for what?" Edward demanded.

"Smelling out people who have books in them."

Edward had not replied to this. "You had better go to bed," he said to Margaret after a few minutes. "It's no good your pretending you aren't asleep."

She rose at that, smiling drowsily, her hair all wisps of curls, and then she had trailed out of the room, her long velvet skirt behind her.

Nevertheless it was on the strength of this possible flair that he had consented soon after that to take Baynes into the shop, and it was still in the hope of this flair that he was considering a New York office. Sooner or later his father would have to be told. Prudent and conservative, Edward was wise enough to know that these two qualities, though essential, were not enough. The publishing business demanded a stretch of the imagination that he was not sure he had. Baynes alone of course would be a menace to the business. Out of a possible hundred ideas that he produced, he would be lucky if five were practical. This Lewis Harrow might be a genius—and might not. Edward sighed, wondered if he ought to refuse his younger brother as assuredly he would have refused any other young man he had hired, and then decided he would risk his faith in the imponderable flair. He had recognized in himself this faith in a quality he saw but did not possess. It was what had made him want to marry Margaret, and it had kept him married to her irrevocably all these years. He was in love with her immortal quality. But where had the immortal dust dropped upon the soul of Baynes, born of the same parents as himself? And assuredly Louise had none of it. Louise, still unmarried, was teaching school in Chedbury. She was one of the stones that he gave his children instead of bread, he sometimes thought grimly. Mary would have her next year in fifth grade, and he did not relish the idea. What did his pallid sister have to give his shy, easily agonized little daughter?

He pressed his clean-shaven lips together firmly, touched a bell, and without looking up when his secretary, Jane Hobbs, came in, he began to dictate.

"Dear Baynes: Yours of the eleventh inst. received. You can go ahead on the office provided the total outlay is not beyond the figures I gave you, including office equipment, etc. As to the author, please make no promises until I have sized him up. Also I must see completed ms. as usual. No advance, of course, until I have made up my mind. The time has come to tell Father about plans and I will do so today. I expect strong objections and I look to you to prove him wrong.

Your aff. Bro.,
Ed."

He dictated steadily for an hour, letters filled with figures, estimates, rejections, complaints, and then fingering the lobe of his ear and pursing his lips, he considered a plunge. Jane Hobbs waited. She was a thin-faced middle-aged woman and she waited, pencil poised. His weakness, as she knew for she was the custodian of his typographical library, was in buying new type.

"What's on your mind?" she now inquired.

He looked at her half slyly, the corners of his mouth twitching. "You know those Fell types?"

"I was looking at 'em yestiddy," she replied.

"We ought to have the Janson, to go with them."

"What's that?" she asked.

"Dutch seventeenth century." He hurried on under her disapproving look. "It's like the Garamond—easy to read, sharp, beautiful type. Yes, I'll have it—"

He dictated the letter brusquely. It had taken five years to make Jane realize he could do as he liked in the business. Five years he had endured her secret returns to his father to report what he was doing. Then one day he had locked the door of the office and standing against it he had told her that he would fire her if ever again she told his father anything. He would talk with his father when it was necessary—not she! And Jane, weeping hideously, had accepted his coming of age.

"You'll have to buy more cases," she said grimly, rising to leave the room.

"Order them," he commanded. "I've decided to bring the fonts for initials and small types out of the shop—have everything together so that I can pick what I want. The men leave things around."

When she was gone he got up and as usual made the rounds of the shop. He liked to be what he called a manufacturing printer. He was proud of his new power presses and his machine-made paper. Above anything he feared the accusation of being artistic. He wanted to be sound. And yet he knew his own weakness. He could not resist fine type and richly made paper. In the six months that he and Margaret had once spent in England and on the Continent, he had visited every old foundry he could find and he had brought back old type faces and handmade papers. The shop now was separated from the offices and the library and reception room by a thick double wall and double doors. He did not want the noise of the machines racking the air where he planned and wrote. But once through the double doors the noise was pleasant to him. He liked the smell of ink and the look of the grimed men watching so intently the pages they set and printed. It was a hobby of his that every man in the shop had to know something of what all other men did, so that each had a feeling for the whole and for himself as a part of the works. He sternly rejected any notion of indispensability. If some man were ill or on vacation, he would not hire another to take his place. Someone in the shop had to know how to take up and he himself was not above spending a morning at type setting.

But what he loved best to see were the sheets of a book rolling off the press, then to be folded, gathered, stitched, and trimmed ready for the casing. The bindery was the newest and most modern part of the shop. He brought Margaret there sometimes to show her samples of cloth and to discuss color and design. He did not expect from her much interest in the business, but sometimes she showed deep and continuing interest in a manuscript and then she wanted to meet the writer and from then until she held the finished book in her hand, she wanted to follow every step. He enjoyed her presence, although it was sometimes troublesome, for she did not realize, or would not, that however exciting a book, it could only be one of many things that he must think about.

He paused beside a press this morning and watched the letters stamp themselves upon a heavy cream-colored paper. He had ordered Caslon type for this particular book, a little book it was, memoirs written by an old gentleman in Boston, and privately printed. Baynes was scornful about private printing. "You only get what other publishers turn down."

But Edward would not agree. "I don't look at it that way," he had replied in the steady somewhat monotonous voice that had become habitual to him these years. "There are books that people don't want put into the trade. They write them for friends or family. It's natural they want a hand in choosing the paper and the type and the binding. I don't see why they shouldn't."

So he had gone on printing small private books of poems and essays and memoirs, and sometimes he had printed sermons and plans for peace and he had never expressed to anyone, not even to Margaret, his secret pleasure in satisfying these individuals who longed to make permanent something of their lives. He motioned to the elderly man who was running the press and the machine stayed.

"Is that ink a true black?" he asked. "I don't want it on the brownish side. I'd rather it had a touch of violet."

"That's what you said," the man replied, "and that's how I mixed it."

"It's all right," Edward said after a moment. "It dries blacker."

"It does," the man agreed.

The machine started again and the creamy paper ran its course. The old gentleman had written about his boyhood in Boston. He could just remember the sailing ships that went to China, and he had taken an hour of Edward's time to explain why he wanted his memories kept for his grandchildren and his great-grandchildren. "It gives meaning to one's life," he had said half diffidently, pulling at his white whiskers.

"It does indeed, Mr. Stallings," Edward had agreed. He wanted meaning in his own life, too.

They had decided on no color in the ornamentation, but there were to be fine initials at the head of each chapter, and black and white fleurons.

He moved on down the aisle. At the next press, in complete contrast, he was doing a banker's biography, set in Bodoni, with wide margins and on hard paper. He paused, admiring in silence the presswork. This press was run by a young man from South Chedbury, John Carosi, whom he had hired only the year before, a brilliant workman, uncertain of temper, and he had a suspicion that the fellow was secretly interested in setting up a union. Well, if he had such ideas he would have to go. A union shop, Edward had said firmly, he would not have.

He decided not to speak to the young pressman and he walked slowly down the central aisle and back to the offices. He had better talk with his father now, before they were both tired with the day's work. He did not like to lose his temper with his parents. Indeed he would not. They were both getting childish and needed care and yet they resented any loss of authority. His father drew the same salary he always had, and this, too, was something that Edward would not think about. Now that Louise was off their hands and Baynes earning his own living Edward could not repress the dogged thought that surely he and Margaret and the growing children needed more than they had. Yet the business could not stand an increase in what he paid himself unless his father took less.

"I'll never suggest it, though," he had said to Margaret only last night.

"Of course not," she had agreed almost indifferently.

To money she was always indifferent. Where it came from, how much they had, whether they were secure, were questions which she never asked. She bought little for herself and wore her old clothes because she liked them, and yet she could commit an extravagance that left him breathless, as when she came home from New York one day wearing an old wrought-gold necklace.

"I'll need a couple of hundred dollars, Ned," she had told him cheerfully.

He had felt the crimson blood fly to his face. "I don't have it, Margaret," he had said simply.

The look of wonder on her face was like a blow. "Oh, I'm sorry." That was all she said. She took the necklace off at once.

His pride had risen at that and he had taken it from her and put it on again. "Keep it," he said. "I'll call it your birthday present."

He had borrowed the money next day from the bank, giving his note for three months. That had been eight years ago. Now, of course, he could easily have paid for the necklace.

He tapped on his father's door and walked in. The old man was leaning back in his chair, drowsing a little, his pencil still in his fingers. He opened his eyes and fumbled at his lips. "I was just adding up sales," he mumbled.

"Good," Edward said cheerfully. He sat down at the chair on the other side of the desk. His father and Baynes shared a desk. "There's something I want to talk over with you, Father. It's been on my mind a good bit. You know I don't like talking until I see through a problem." With this he plunged into the heart of the matter. Better to get it over with!

"I won't say Baynes has influenced me," he concluded. "Yet in a way he has, too. Baynes has something to contribute to the business, Father—something that neither you nor I have—some sort of flair, I suppose! I know a good book when it's brought to me, and I can make a nice thing of type and binding and all that, but I can't nose out books and Baynes can. From asking about, I find that publishers need someone like that. It's lucky, maybe, that we have him in the family. He seems to have found someone already—fellow named Harrow."

He made his tone light to counteract the gathering heaviness of his father's ash-white brows. "Maybe you trust Baynes in New York," his father said, "but I don't—not with that wife of his. She's not like the one you got. Sandra's another piece of goods." He shook his head and his eyes were dark. "Ducks and drakes," he muttered. "Carryings on! Cocktail parties—that's the latest thing, I hear. All charged to expenses—"

"I'll see to that," Edward said firmly. He did not tell his father that he was beginning to understand that a small amount of getting about was perhaps a good thing in the book business. He called it getting about, and he was more than willing that Baynes should undertake it. He had attended a few such gatherings on his rare visits to New York and he had disliked them intensely. Yet it troubled him that he saw there the heads of firms much larger and more important than his own. They were solid men and he could not imagine they enjoyed any more than he did the strange drinks and fancy bits of bread and filling. Especially did he dislike the women writers. Thank God that his only woman author at present was an old lady of sixty, who wrote youthful little stories for children. He considered them trivial and yet they sold well and they made up into pretty books. She had paid for the first one herself as a present to her grandchildren and when it went into the fourth edition, he offered to put the next one into the trade. But he liked to have it said that Haslatt's was a man's publishing house.

His father had sat frowning and ruminating. Now he suddenly banged the ledger shut. "I know very well you and Baynes run things to suit yourselves," he said bitterly. "I ought to be dead, too, like old Mather. The country belongs to the young these days. There's no respect left for the old, whatever sense they've got. It's a queer thing that a man spends his life getting a little wisdom together somehow and then it's not wanted. Young folk think they're born with all the wisdom."

Edward did not at once answer these too familiar remarks. He sat silent for a moment and suddenly he had his inspiration. "That's a nice thing for you to say, just when I was about to suggest something to see how you like it."

His father looked at him sidewise, his eyes frosty under his brows. "Well?" he drawled. "What's the next big idea?"

"What do you say to changing the name of the firm to Haslatt and Sons?" Edward asked.

His father stared at him. "Leave old Mather out?"

"He is out, isn't he?" Edward replied. "Every bit as much as Loomis—"

"Hm," his father said, "I'll have to think a bit."

"But why, Father?" Edward urged. "After all, it was only a printing shop when Mather was here. It's you and I who have built the book business, and now Baynes has come in."

"It's true that Mather didn't like the books," his father conceded.

"We are really making a little on them, Father," Edward went on. "Everybody says you can't make millions on books, but it's a steady respectable business—something more, too, I think, than just business."

"Business is all I want out of it," his father growled with a return to hostility.

"Well, it's not all I want out of anything," Edward said stoutly. "I don't want to be just a businessman. I want some of the good things of life, too—some of the arts and some of the thoughts and some of the friends that making books brings me. I can't write books myself, I know, but I like to take what others write, if it's good, and give it a life of its own. That's important—a business if you like, but still it's something more. A writer would be helpless if he couldn't get his manuscript made into a book. Shakespeare would have been forgotten by now, if it hadn't been for some printer-publisher like us."

His father stared at him. "What's come over you?" he inquired. "I never heard you talk so fancy."

"Trying to convince you," Edward said, and grinned. "But it's what I think and feel, nevertheless."

They sat silent for a moment, as they often did. The sunshine from the narrow window fell across Mark Haslatt's head and turned his thick stiff white hair to snow. He had grown thin and dry in the years that had passed and something dour in his nature had become plain upon his wrinkled face. He hated to grow old and yet he had to grow old. There was no compensation for him in age. Sometimes he looked at his wife across the breakfast table, the children all gone and only the two of them left, and she looked so old that he was frightened. Ten years ago she had been heavy and sound, a kindly woman with a scolding tongue, which he had continually resented, and now she had grown into a thin mild silent old woman. Sometimes he thought her mind was not what it had been and this frightened him more than anything. Maybe his own mind wasn't what it had been. Nobody would tell him, of course. His two sons would go on, as smooth as cream, managing everything and telling him nothing. But he'd kept his hands on the accounts just the same. He wasn't too old yet to know when the figures were in the red.

"Then shall it be Haslatt and Sons, Father?" Edward asked.

He saw his father start, as though he had been dreaming. "Oh, I suppose it might as well be," he said half grumbling. "After all, it is Haslatt and Sons, you might say."

"Exactly," Edward said briskly and he got up. "It's time for your lunch, isn't it? I'll go home with you, if you don't think it'll upset Mother."

"It won't," his father said. He lifted himself up by the arms of his chair, found his hat and Edward held his coat. A few minutes later they were going down the elevator together. "Your mother don't look so good," his father was saying. "I wish you'd take the chance to see what you think."

"I will, Father," Edward promised.

They fell into silence again. A few acquaintances passed them and neither of them talked before outsiders. But silence was easy. Edward was realizing again, as he had begun to do in the last few years, that his father was an old man. There was something very pathetic about age. It fell upon a man like a disease, and it was incurable. He imagined his father's secret dismay as he found himself less able each year than he had been the year before, his strength fading, his mind less alive. And there was nothing to do! How cruel was God—if there was a God! Edward still went to church every Sunday with his family and they all sat together in the Haslatt pew. He continued to do this even though a profound doubt was invading his soul, a doubt that he steadily refused to face. He put it aside now and considered what practical means there might be of comforting his parents for the loneliness of old age. Consideration, of course, and the sparing of every hurt, but this was not enough. There ought to be pleasures in old age. Surely every period of life had its compensations, if one could find them.

People had to be taught how to find pleasure. Perhaps that was the true purpose of education—to help the individual discover the pleasure of being his age. So Edward mused, allowing his mind the liberty it naturally took, unless compelled to labor. And then he thought of his daughter Mary. Louise could never teach her anything about pleasure! A crime this, that his sister should be allowed teaching! Thank God that Margaret still laughed easily.

The noon sun was warm, and along the street children were snatching a few minutes' play between school and their meal. The front door of the house was open and in the hall there was the smell of roast beef from the open kitchen door.

"Mother!" Mark Haslatt shouted. "Ed's here for dinner!" He turned to his son. "I'll bet she's in the kitchen, doing the work while the hired girl looks on. I can't get her to rest."

His mother came to the kitchen door untying her apron. Her wrinkled face cheered as she saw her son. "Why, this is real nice, Edward. Wait till I hang up my apron. What's the matter you've come home?"

He bent to kiss her dry cheek. "Nothing. Just thought I'd see how you are."

"Fine and dandy," she replied. "I do hope the beef's not too done. The girl likes it like leather. Want to wash up?"

"I'll go upstairs," Edward said.

He mounted the stairs to his old room. Everything was exactly as it always had been. Even the bed was made up, as though he were to sleep there tonight. It was like coming back into a warm outgrown shell, and something of his boyhood fell upon him again. He washed his hands at the old-fashioned stand, pouring the water from the ewer into the basin. The house had a bathroom, but his mother had kept the washstands in the bedrooms.

He went downstairs in a few minutes and his parents were waiting for him in their chairs and the girl was putting the roast on the table.

"Hello, Gladys," he said.

"Howdy, Mr. Haslatt," the girl answered. She was a farmer's daughter, pallid and freckled, and her sandy hair was in an elaborate braid. Ten years ago she would have sat at the table with the family but now she did not. The Haslatts had moved up in the town, and Mrs. Haslatt knew better.

She was still president of the Women's Christian Temperance Union, and they met regularly here at the house once a month, important in the knowledge that their work had been successful. Edward never discussed Prohibition with his mother. Old Thomas Seaton had made him feel the folly of forbidding people what they seem determined to do, and the atmosphere of that house was wholly opposed to this one. Thomas Seaton drank as much as ever and fumed at the trouble of getting his liquor, and Tom Seaton had gone into the bootlegging business in a gentlemanly way. That is, he arranged for imports of Scotch whisky. Edward imagined that his mother knew all this, but she, too, did not mention it.

She watched the carving of the roast with anxious gravity. His father was not an expert carver, and she could not rest until she had made sure that the grain of the meat ran opposite to his knife. He had sharpened his knife carefully and he began to cut big thin slices and the red juice ran out. She sighed, relieved. "It's a lovely roast—I'm glad you came today, Edward. How's Margaret and the children?"

"All well," Edward said mildly. "Margaret picked her first daffodil bud today."

"Did she?" Mrs. Haslatt replied. Her mind was occupied now with the baked potatoes that Gladys was handing around. "Take the big one, Edward—you're looking thin."

"You're never satisfied with the way I look," he grumbled amiably. But he took the big potato, dripping with butter.

"Did you put that dressing on the greens like I told you?" Mrs. Haslatt inquired of Gladys.

"Oh, my soul and body," the girl groaned and setting the potatoes on the table she fled toward the kitchen.

"Her memory is no longer than her nose," Mrs. Haslatt remarked.

"Her nose is long enough," Mr. Haslatt said. "It's like her father's. I always say that old Babcock's nose is as long as from here to Jerusalem."

"I'm sure Gladys tells her family every single thing we do," Mrs. Haslatt said, sighing.

Edward smiled. "Well, you don't do anything very bad."

"Has little Tom lost that eye tooth yet?" Mrs. Haslatt demanded after they had eaten for a few minutes.

"He has, and I know it only because he expected a dime under his pillow and I forgot it," Edward confessed.

His father laughed. "I'll bet he didn't let up on you until he got it."

"He didn't," Edward said.

"That little Tom is a real smart boy," his mother exclaimed. "I know you don't like greens, Edward, but these are something new—broccoli, it's called. We get so tired of spinach, now that your father can't digest cabbage."

It was the desultory talk of the old days but it was easy and comfortable. The dining room was warm and the smell of the food whetted his appetite. He took two small feathery rolls and buttered them heavily. He liked being here alone sometimes with his father and mother. They had been kind parents to him and he had forgotten the ways that had irritated him when he was growing up. Now he simply felt that they were good and that they loved him, and that the walls of home were solid here. He wanted his children to feel the same way about his own house.

"Baynes wants to live in New York," his father said suddenly.

Mrs. Haslatt dropped her fork. "For goodness sake—what for?"

"He thinks we need a New York office—get new authors and so on," Edward said, taking another roll from the plate of hot ones that Gladys was passing.

Mrs. Haslatt waited until the girl had left the room. "Seems to me you've got as many books as you can manage a'ready. I couldn't read that last one, *The Singed Flower*—wasn't it?"

"It's beginning to sell, though," Edward said. *The Singed Flower* was a book from a writer he'd found in England, a man named Peter Pitt. He had not understood the book, either, but he had caught a vague feeling from it, as of music in the distance. Margaret had read it three times.

"I don't dare think of Baynes and Sandra in New York," his mother was saying. "Why, they'll spend money like water—the two of them hand in glove! I wish Baynes had a little more character with his wife. He's just putty. Sometimes it's real disgusting."

"I guess we're all putty when it comes to our women," Mark Haslatt said and smiled faintly.

Mrs. Haslatt took mild offense. "Now, Father, I don't know what call you have to say that. I've taken good care to keep my place in the house."

"Oh, well—it's only a joke."

"A mighty poor one!"

"Don't fight, you two," Edward said amiably. "It's a bad example to your children."

"There now, Mother," Mr. Haslatt exclaimed with feeble mischief. "Don't I tell you?"

"Oh, shut up, you—" Mrs. Haslatt said with heavy humor. "Is Tom Seaton acting as bad as ever?"

"I haven't seen him in a month," Edward replied. His wife's brother carried, in this house, the burden of his mother's disapproval. In spite of the double marriages, the two families had remained apart, meeting only at formal occasions. Edward had grown at home in the Seaton house, but Margaret would never be quite at home here. The reason for this, Edward was well aware, was that his mother had always to approve before she could welcome and she could not approve either of her sons' wives. She knew, although she would not acknowledge even to herself, that the Seaton family was higher socially in Chedbury than the Haslatts, but she maintained in her own mind the belief that the Haslatt family had a virtue in its soundness that could not be matched by any Seaton. There had never been a drunkard among the Haslatts and never a divorce. Moreover, the Haslatts were churchgoing and the Seatons were not—or at least only irregularly.

"I've told Baynes that we'll only try it for a year," Edward was saying. "If he can bring in enough business to cover his own salary and the extra overhead, then I'll consider it further."

His father noticed the "I," instead of "we," and did not speak. It was only a sign, unconscious, that Edward thought of himself as the head of the whole business, but it thrust one more thorn into the older man's heart.

"Well, I can't take responsibility for it," he said under his breath. "What's the dessert, Mother?"

"Apple pie," she said promptly, "and I made it myself, for Gladys makes a crust an inch thick and like a piece of rubber. It's sinful to waste good food like that."

The pie came on, still hot, and when Mrs. Haslatt cut it the fragrance of sugar and cinnamon mingled with that of the apples.

"What a dinner!" Edward murmured. "I shan't be able to work for an hour."

"No more you shouldn't," his mother said robustly. Her dry cheeks had grown faintly red and she cut large slices of the pie and passed them proudly. "There's the cream in that luster jug—or would you rather have cheese?"

"I'll take cheese," Edward said, and helped himself to the square of yellow sharp cheese.

He was beginning to feel well fed and relaxed. Of course it would be folly to eat like this every day. His own luncheons were frugal affairs, and he dined at night. But he liked good food and knew that he did and he was rigorous with himself about his waistline. Only when he came home, as now, did he let himself eat as he had when he was a boy.

"I believe we're going to have a little boom in business," he said to his father. "Things look good. That's one reason why we can let Baynes have some head."

"The Republicans'll be in for a change," his father agreed.

"Poor old Wilson," Edward said.

"I don't feel sorry for him one bit," his mother protested. "He was getting us mixed up in everything—he's mixed himself, I'm sure. They say he's kind of lost his mind."

"I don't believe that," Edward replied. He did not tell his parents that he had voted steadfastly for Wilson each four years. The man was decades ahead of the nation, a man who saw over the mountains into the future. Old Thomas Seaton had finally convinced him of that. But it could never be explained to his parents. What change in him his marriage to Margaret had wrought! He smiled at his mother. "I can't eat another bite."

"You've eaten real good," she said fondly. "Now you don't have to go right away, do you? Father always takes a little snooze."

"So he should, but I mustn't—yet," Edward said. "Jane Hobbs will be counting the minutes that I'm late."

"Oh, that old maid," his mother said tolerantly. She regarded all unmarried women as freaks. Then she frowned slightly. "Edward, I wish Louise would get married."

"No one in the offing?" he inquired, folding his napkin and slipping it into his old silver ring.

"She's so closemouthed," his mother complained.

"I think she'll marry late," Edward said to comfort her. "Maybe someone older than herself."

"She ought to get married before she's thirty."

"Well, she has a few years to go."

He rose and leaned over her. "Thanks for a grand dinner. I shan't be able to eat tonight."

"I hope Margaret won't blame me for that," his mother said, bristling slightly.

"She never blames anybody for anything," he said carelessly. "Except Mary, maybe."

"She is hard on that child," his mother exclaimed. "I've noticed it, too —though to me Mary's the best child you have."

"Mothers and daughters," his father murmured. He had risen and was stretched out now on the old leather couch under the window.

"Oh, hush up," Mrs. Haslatt cried. "I was always nice to Louise, I'm sure."

"You never paid her the mind that you did the boys," Mr. Haslatt returned.

"What's the matter with you two?" Edward demanded. "I don't remember your arguing so much when I was young."

"We've got more time for it now," his father said. His eyes were closed but his lips twitched with secret laughter.

"Old men get so independent," his mother complained.

"It's our last chance," his father retorted.

"Oh, you old bum," his mother said with affection.

Edward laughed. "Well, if you're having a good time! See you later, Father."

He went into the hall and put on his hat and coat and glancing back into the dining room he saw his mother sipping her coffee. His father was beginning to snore softly. There was an air of warm content in the room, and he realized how much he loved his old parents. He went back to his office, his heart wrapped in tenderness, and wondered if some day his children would look at him when he was old and love him in the same deep amused fashion. So one generation held the other by the heart.

He went to his own home at the end of the day and the sense of permanence clung to him still. He in his time, and in his approaching prime, was fulfilling his place. The early spring evening was cold and he held the collar of his gray topcoat about his throat. He had left his muffler at home this morning, deceived by the soft spring sky, but now the large white clouds had been blown over the hills on the wings of a north wind. There might still be frost tonight if the wind went down. He walked against the wind toward his house and saw it looming solidly against its background of trees. It was square and the roof was low and the railed porches were white in the evening light. Ten years had deepened the shadows of the woods, and trees that he and Margaret had planted in their first spring together were saplings no longer. The elms leading to the house were beginning to make a noble column. He walked between them up the brick-laid walk and one by one he saw the lights of his home begin to shine. That was Margaret. He knew her trick of going from room to room as soon as the sun had set, and turning on the lights. She did not like the twilight, and the children had learned from her to want the lights as soon as the land turned gray.

Eleven years and the house had grown to be as much a part of him as his own body. The thought of himself and Margaret living there together with their children sent his ambition soaring. He wanted everything for them. Other men could want amusement and travel and fame and money, but whatever he wanted was for them—for Margaret first, and then for the children. Comfort and beauty and richness he would work for that he might bestow all upon them.

He opened the door of the wide deep hall and let himself in and there was Margaret, lighting the last lamp.

"Giver of light," he murmured. Then his heart quickened. He caught a wild sweet gleam in her eye.

"Know why I love you?" she inquired in a matter-of-fact voice that did not deceive him.

"Anything new?" he asked, hanging up his coat in the closet under the stairs.

"Maybe I've never told you," she replied.

"Still hiding things from me, are you?" he retorted.

He put his right arm around her shoulders and tipped her head back with his left hand. "Well, why do you love me?" he inquired.

"Because never once in all these eleven years have you reminded me of electricity bills when I turn on the lights at night!"

"Is that all?" He pretended to be disappointed.

"But that's wonderful!" she exclaimed.

He kissed her lips again gently, tasting their warmth. They were soft and full. Strange how he could tell from the first touch of her lips!

He let her go, knowing now that she did not like to be held too long. He had learned to let her go before she freed herself from him. Ah, what a deal he had learned about loving her! He had been hurt in the old days when they were first married because she twisted herself free so soon. He wanted everything to last forever. Now he knew that anything could become her cage, even his love. He turned to the stair and began to mount slowly to his room and she stood watching him.

"Want another reason why I love you?" she asked.

He paused and she came and laid her hands against the paneling of the stair and he looked down into her blue eyes. "Another reason?"

"One more. It's this—you never turn out the lights that I put on."

"Why should I?" he parried. Only some intuition he had not understood had taught him never to put out a light she had lit. He had often wanted to do it—longed to, in fact, within his prudent soul. It was folly to burn a dozen lights. Then his ceaseless determination to hide nothing from her forced him to tell her this. He leaned over the banisters, and looking down at her he said with half-shamed honesty, "Margaret—look here, I ought to tell you—I've always wanted to turn out the lights. It seemed extravagant to have the whole house lit."

She flung her laughter up at him like a bright bubble. "I know you've wanted to turn them out. But you never have! Sometimes I thought, really he will do it tonight—sometimes when you've been cross or we've had one of our fights. But you never did."

Her intensity warned him. He must not rush down to her and make love to her. These were her approaches. He must withdraw a little, let her pursue until she had committed herself. Oh, he had learned!

"Silly!" he said.

He went on up the stairs and she stood looking after him and he, knowing she was watching, went calmly on his way, his heart hammering against his breastbone.

In his room he washed and changed his clothes and then carefully chose a tie of wine red for his white shirt. She had put on her blue velvet and he had seen it when he came into the house. At first he had been stupid about noticing the small signs but now he had learned. Long ago when he had sworn to have no other love beside her, it had come to him that the variety all men craved could be found in Margaret, if he had the patience and the wit to woo her manifold self.

And yet the evening routine went on as usual. He heard his baby daughter's murmuring voice and going into the small room across the hall he found her in her crib, bathed and fed and ready for sleep. She was pulling the ears of a worn pink teddy bear and its nose was wet with her chewing. When she saw him the teddy bear dropped and she smiled widely, enchanted with him.

"Daddee," she murmured, in ecstasy. He picked her up gently and held her to him and kissed the softness of her fragrant fat neck.

"Ow," she said loudly and giggled. He understood that he needed a shave.

"Thanks for reminding me," he said conversationally and still holding her he pranced about the room noiselessly and was rewarded by ripples of laughter. So free was her laughter indeed that it ended in an attack of hiccoughs which she enjoyed with fresh amazement, and to quiet her he had to give her a drink of water which she then spat out on his clean shirt bosom.

"Here, young woman," he said with decision. He put her back in bed, kissed her on both cheeks, restored her teddy bear and pulled the blond curl on the top of her head. Then he went to his room and shaved and changed his shirt again.

By the time he was ready to go downstairs his son Tom was coming to look for him. And Mary opened the front door. He heard her first inquiry, "Is Daddy home yet, Mother?" Bless her for always making this her first question! She came running up the stairs and burst into his room. Tom was behind her. He looked like old Thomas, a square-set red-headed fellow. Mary was dark. Edward had unknowingly bestowed upon her his own brown eyes and she had Margaret's curly dark hair. But she had none of the brave freedom of Margaret's carriage. She walked timidly, always a little unsure of welcome. It must be part of his job as father, he told himself, to take the shadow from her, so that she moved as one who walked in light. Strange that Margaret could not see what he meant when he tried to tell her!

He put out his arms first to his daughter, and then felt his son seize his arm and pull it away. "Here—ladies first," he said.

"Mary isn't a lady," Tom said scornfully. "She's on'y a girl."

"Lady to you, young man!"

Tom clung to his arm. "Daddy, kin I have a two wheeler? My tricycle's broken. And I'm too big. I could give it to Sandy when she's high enough."

"Oh, gosh, old man. I can't just promise without talking with Mother."

Mary had said not a word. He felt her clinging to him tightly, her arms about his waist, head against his breast.

"How are you, sweetheart?" he said. "Have a nice day?"

"Yes," she whispered.

"Let's go down to dinner—"

He had won a point with Margaret about that. At the Seaton house the children never had dinner with the family. Supper came first for them and then there had been dinner for the parents and their guests.

"All very well for the English," Edward had said. "They don't want their children about, but I do." They had compromised and after their fifth birthdays the children came to dinner.

He took his place tonight at the head of the table and smiled across a pot of spring flowers at his wife. Hattie brought in small bowls of soup and set them down and went out again. The family meal had begun and it went on as usual and as he hoped it always would, as long as he lived. He listened to what the children had to say and he made replies to please them and to correct them, and Margaret joined in with her usual vigor. She had heeded his words of the morning and she was tender of Mary,

refraining, he saw, from correcting her for small mistakes in table manners. It was like any other evening and yet he was perfectly aware that it
was one of their rare evenings, and that in spite of the presence of the
children he and Margaret were alone with each other.

"I had dinner today with Father and Mother," he told her. "Roast beef
and all that—I shan't be able to eat much tonight."

"Roast beef and what?" Tom asked with interest.

"Apple pie," he replied.

"We have chicken and stewed peaches," Margaret said.

Foolish little words and all the time he was aware of a slumberous softness in her eyes. Did the children feel something magic in the air? Had
he ever as a child felt this glinting silvery cobweb being woven across the
table between his parents? He had not been aware of it, but then perhaps
in that house there had been no such weaving. A profound reticence lay
between the generations in any decent house, and his was a decent house
and so had been his father's. Here was something he had discovered;
when Margaret was witty and her laughter sharp, then, though he laughed,
he withdrew, aware of her declaration of solitude. But when she laid aside
wit and did not make laughter, he could come near her and she would not
repulse him. Oh, the misery of her repulse! He still was wary of it, even
after years. For she, the woman, was essentially solitary and he was not,
and this was what astonished him. She had welcomed their children, one by
one, and she was a tender and physical mother, suckling them at her breast.
And yet when the time came to wean them she was ruthless and eager to
be cut off from them. He had not understood this when it had first happened with Mary and he had accused her of coldness to her child. Then
before Tom was born he had occasion to observe a little dog, a female
spaniel he had reared. She had given birth to pups and had nursed them
day and night, never leaving them until suddenly one day when they ran
to suckle her, she had turned on them and had bitten them and they had
gone yelping off, heartbroken. She was through with them and her breast
was dry and she had to force them from her and recover herself.

He had not told Margaret of the parable, but he had pondered it, remembering always his vow that he would make his marriage the main-
stream of his life. How large that promise had been he had not realized
when he gave it, but he could not take it back. And he was aware, too, of
her promise which she had given. He never heard her speak a wish to
separate herself from him. Yet he knew at last that there were times when
she could not bear him near her, even as she had not wanted the child at
her breast any more.

At first he had been wounded to the very core of his being and in
those early days so foolish as to accuse her at times of not loving him.
She declared the accusation was folly and yet she could not explain why
she did not want him near her. "Leave me alone," she had repeated. "Just
leave me alone, will you, Ned?"

"But why, Margaret?"

"How do I know? Only don't touch me."

He had wished, once or twice, that he could confess his troubles to other men with wives, but his stubborn delicacy forbade it. Had he loved her less he might have spoken but he could not reveal her to another's eyes, either in the spirit or in the flesh. So he held back his anger, and once when she had shut the door against him he accepted his humiliation and determined to wait until she came to him. But her pride was equal to his. She did not come, and angry now at himself, he had approached her again, although only with words.

Indeed that it might be no more than words, he had chosen the living room one night after dinner. It was before their trip to England. Mary was then a baby and she had been put early to bed. He had been reading Tennant's second manuscript, he remembered, and Margaret was playing the piano quietly, all her music subdued. He had sat watching her straight and graceful back, her cheek half turned toward him. Then he had spoken. "Margaret!"

At the sound of his voice, though he had made it gentle, she had started violently and her hands crashed the chord.

"Yes?" Her voice was cheerful enough.

"Shall we talk a little while?"

He was not prepared for the joy with which she turned to him at once. "Oh, Ned, will you?"

He had laid his manuscript on the table and she came and sat in the chair opposite him. "Margaret, if you wanted talk why haven't you said so?"

"But you've been a stone!" she cried softly.

He was aghast. "I? You've been miles away from me!"

She shook her head and gazed at him speechlessly, and drew her upper lip down between her teeth.

"You've changed since we've been married," he had accused her. "You used to say anything to me."

Still she did not speak.

"See?" he said, angry in spite of his determination against anger. "You don't help me now. What *is* the matter between us?"

The delicacy of her skin, white against her black hair, was one of her beauties and she had flushed deeply. "I can never get away from you," she had said, and to his horror he saw her begin to tremble, her hands quivering so that she clasped them tightly in her lap and her lips trembling.

She wanted to get away from him! He had waited for a moment until the first surge of hurt died down. Then he had said as quietly as he could, "But you should have told me if you wanted to go away. Would you like to go home for a visit? Hattie can do for me. Or would you like to go to Boston or New York—even England, for that matter?"

"We've always said we'd go to England together," she said.

The absurdity of their position, face to face, and yet struggling to find each other made him ashamed. "It would be easier if we could forget that we're married," he said with sudden inspiration. "Let's imagine that we are as we were before."

She smiled, and he saw her whole body relax. She stopped trembling and then she laughed. "Ned, that's clever of you. Let's do more—let's pretend we're talking about two other people—not you and me—just a he and a she, somewhere, anywhere, anybody, just married and with a small quite nice baby, everything really wonderful, a lovely house, their bills paid —well, very nearly paid. There's my new suit, of course, and I know it was far too expensive but I had to have it for some reason or other—at the moment. I don't care about it now, and I wish I hadn't had it altered."

"It'll be paid for this month," he said, "and so let's call it paid for. All right. He and she—"

He entered into the fiction somewhat stiffly, feeling downright silly. It would have been easier just to speak straight, but perhaps it would not. Anyway, let it be as she wanted. "What about this woman, She?" he inquired. "Does she still love her husband or doesn't she? That's what he keeps asking himself. Maybe he overpersuaded her. After all, he is a stubborn fellow, this He, and he remembers that he insisted—somewhat—upon marrying her."

"Oh, but how can he think she doesn't love him?" Margaret cried. "She feels she is just beginning to know how to love him. That is—sometimes she feels that way."

"Not all the time?"

"She adores him a good deal of the time, she's getting proud of him because she sees he has a lot of brains, really—more than she thought. Her father said to her only the other day—'You've got something in that chap.' But there are times when she wants to be by herself."

"Because she hates him?" he asked.

"No," she replied gravely. "That's what she's beginning to see—not because she hates him but because she just wants sometimes to be alone and whole, complete in herself. She doesn't want to share herself all the time. Most of the time she does want to, though."

He was looking at her who was his wife, his own, and he felt the rending of flesh. "He never wants to be alone, away from her," he told her.

She was trembling again a very little. "Oh, but that's because he's different."

"He's only human—too human, perhaps."

"It's not that—they're both human beings, Ned, and there they are the same."

"Then she's not afraid of him?"

"Oh, no—really she finds him even charming—as a human being!"

Now they were looking at each other steadily. He put the next question. "Does she feel there's a part of him that is not human?"

"She—she doesn't like to say it's not human—"

"But it isn't?"

"Perhaps it's just—natural."

"Nature being different from human?"

"Yes."

Again the long pause and again his question first. "And she hasn't this nature?"

"Yes—yes—she has."

"Then—why does she draw away from him?"

She was thinking intensely and her dark narrow brows were drawn together over her honest eyes. "She doesn't know—but perhaps it's this. In him she feels the nature is something separate from him—always there, waiting."

"Waiting?"

"For a chance."

"A chance?"

She had ignored the question in his voice and hurried on as though she might not hold the words she wanted if she did not keep her thought running in them. "In her, the nature is all mingled with everything. It's not separate—it doesn't wait—in fact, most of the time she doesn't know it's there. It is only when something she sees in him seems especially endearing—oh, sometimes when she sees his profile is really good, or that his shoulders are broad—or maybe when he is simply thinking and she sees his face in a new way—oh, I don't know—but anyway, then she feels—nature in her, too. But it doesn't separate itself from everything else in her and it isn't physical, at first. And it doesn't wait, you know, Ned. It has to be called to."

He had leaned toward her, and would not go near to touch her.

"My dear, but how am I to know?"

She had shaken her head again, and he had been puzzled by that new and shy Margaret. They had talked about everything in the world except this He and this She, who were their secret selves.

"Could you make some small slight sign to me, darling? If you could—"

She shook her head.

"I'd promise not to hurry you," he said quietly. "You'd be the one to make the sign."

"I might be ashamed to."

"Ashamed—with me? Oh, no, Margaret!"

She had not moved her eyes from his face. Still leaning toward her and still careful not to touch her or go near her, as though a butterfly poised upon her knees that must not be frightened away, he had made his voice tender and grave. "Let's not talk any more. I think I understand what you've said. And I'll wait."

She moved quickly and the butterfly seemed to fly away, a thing of gold and blue. "But I don't want to feel you waiting all the time for me to—that's what puts me off, Ned!"

How clumsy he had been—the one wrong word! He shrugged his shoulders. "Then I shan't wait, my dear. After all, you forget I'm a busy man and there's plenty on my mind, beyond sleeping with my beautiful wife, pleasant as that is. I'll keep my mind on other things, and I'll be grateful to you for what you freely give."

He had picked up his manuscript again and had begun to read it, trying to quell the beating of his heart. He was angered and hurt and proud and yet he knew that he loved her exactly the same. So they had sat for some fifteen minutes and then she had come to him and kissed the top of his head delicately.

"Good night, Ned—and thank you."

"Good night, dear. I'll be a little late tonight. I have this to finish."

She had gone away and he had put down the manuscript and had sat long, pondering deeply upon the mystery of marriage. It would have been easy to have his own will, as men did, but then she would escape him altogether. He could not live with her shell. He must have her whole, and that meant that he must have her willing. She could escape him, even when she lay in his arms. He had felt her spirit leave him, and there was only her body beside him and then though it was warm and fragrant, it was dead. Ah, that was where she had him—it was where woman always had man, if he truly loved her. And then there was no pleasure in her for him, not unless he was a clod, which he, Edward Haslatt, was not. There was some strange inner morality in this act of sex. It was moral only when he felt it right and good and he felt it right and good only when her spirit did not escape him. The sin was in the flesh—no, the sin was when flesh was without the spirit. If he were content with her flesh, then it was insult to her who was his love, and whom he loved wholly.

He began dimly to understand the meaning of love. Put to selfish use, it did not function. It had to be unselfish in order to satisfy even selfishly. Had he been of coarser fiber, he might have put woman aside, as a puzzle not to be seriously understood. But then had he been of coarser fiber, he would not now be married to Margaret. He was what he was, and they were inseparably married, unless he drove her spirit from her body. Then wandering and alone, it might never return to him or to his house. The thought of this had put him into a cold terror, and he had sworn to himself a vow that he was never to break, a vow as solemn as his marriage vows, and indeed comprehended in them, as he had come at last to perceive. He would possess her whole or not at all.

He had kept his vow all these years since it was made and he kept it tonight. He had learned, however, that there was always a moment, which if he did not seize, he lost. The delicate manifestations that she made of her mood enchanted him, and his enchantment he had at first allowed to continue too long for her modesty. For if she perceived that she was leading, she instantly withdrew, and then he had lost her again. He could not woo her after she had withdrawn—it was too late. She evaded him. She gave that final swift shake of her head that he dreaded. She began to talk of other things or she took up a book. Positively he must meet her at some point. This point, he had discovered after a year or two of fumbling mistakes, was as soon as she knew that he had understood her manifestation. From the moment she saw that she had made clear to him her mood, then he must take the lead and she must follow. Nor must he postpone too long the consummation. His lead must follow her mood.

How many years it had taken him to learn these things! He had learned them slowly and stupidly, he often told himself. Yet he was compelled to learn them even for his own sake, for he was not a beast. He was above simple lust. Then, having learned, he was tender with her and attuned to her, and he was rewarded. In her content was his own fulfillment. The process had refined his soul while it had sharpened his senses. He and Margaret were so profoundly married, now at the end of eleven years, that he felt, with triumph, that he had made a success of his marriage. Had he been a different kind of man, a man without patience, without the wit to perceive that a man could not be satisfied with a woman unless she was satisfied with him, what loss to him! For he had not changed his whole character or improved his most common faults. He was still easily wounded and susceptible to jealousy, although he thought he had learned to hide it from her. Jealousy she could not tolerate. Stubborn though he was, she had frightened him half beside himself in the second year of their marriage. One night Tom had come to dinner, bringing with him a young Irishman, a blue-eyed, black-haired fool of a fellow, whose tongue was loose at both ends and laced with wit. Margaret had abandoned herself to laughter during dinner, and after dinner when Hattie brought in the coffee, she had patted the place beside her on the couch.

"Come here!" she had cried to Sean Mallory.

Edward had stood watching while the young Irishman sat down beside Margaret. And then she would not look at him, after he had glared at her, after her eyelashes had flickered at him. She had been gay and wild and Tom had encouraged her, and Sean Mallory, quick to perceive the young husband's silence, had yet found it impossible to resist the gay girl's voice, her sparkling provocative talk, her laughter.

When the two guests had gone silence fell as the door closed. Margaret sat on the couch where she had been sitting all evening, and she looked at him with hostility in her blue eyes. He had been confounded by the change in her. It was like seeing a landscape upon a sunny day gone suddenly gray under a cloud. The shock broke his control.

"I can stand anything," he had said to her between his teeth, "anything except what's physical."

She had looked at him honestly bewildered. "Physical?"

"That you asked him to come and sit down beside you, where I was going to sit—you motioned him with your hand—"

She rose, electric with anger. Her eyes gleamed, her hair quivered, her cheeks flamed. "Now that is enough," she said in a quiet and terrible voice. "You will make me despise you if you go on."

She had walked with dignity to the door and there she had turned. "What you say is an insult to me," she declared. "I will not endure it, do you hear me, Ned? If ever again you accuse me of being—physical—with a man I don't love, that day I will leave you."

She went upstairs and he heard her door close. He followed, after a miserable half hour in which he ostentatiously wound the clock and locked the doors and fed the cat and put out all the lights downstairs. When he tried the handle of her door it was locked. He spent a sleepless night, telling himself that he was right to have spoken and that innocent though she was, how was the Irishman to know that she was innocent? How could any man think her innocent when she was so beautiful?

He rose the next morning still angry and cold and she did not come down to breakfast. When he went in to her room to kiss her, her lips were lifeless and her eyes dark. She was unrepentant and he knew her well enough already to know that she would never repent of anything she had said or done and that she did not repent now. Very well, neither would he repent. He had gone away to the day's business, cold and hurt, and when he came home he was very tired. He found her quiet and usual and they had never spoken again of the matter.

But she had not forgotten it. He knew because years later, only last year, indeed, when Sean Mallory having become a poet of almost first water, he had mentioned casually that Haslatt and Mather had a chance to bid for his new book, Margaret had said nothing. She was arranging roses in a bowl on a small table under the wide living-room window and she had continued to choose one flower and then another. He had let the bid go by and Livingstone Hall had published *Fire in the Night*. He had brought home a copy of the book and had put it on the library table. When she saw it she had taken it and thrown it into the wastepaper basket. He had reproved her.

"Margaret, what folly—a new book, with good reviews!" He stooped to pick it out of the basket again.

"Don't put it on the table," she had cried at him.

He had refused to yield to her. "I'll take it back to the office and put it on my own shelves," he had said with dignity.

Afterward he remembered that long ago she had told him she liked to speak out what she felt. "I don't want to have to stop and think whether something is going to hurt your feelings—" That was what she had once said. He had a vague sense that nevertheless she had learned to stop and think about his feelings, and that she no longer spoke out. But he, too, had learned if not to stop feeling yet to stop showing what he felt. In spite of their dreams, their marriage had shaped itself out of what they were. Their faults had made it, as well as their virtues. Well, it was good. He still could not imagine himself loving any woman except Margaret.

A telegram from Baynes the next morning announced the certainty of Lewis Harrow's arrival, and in the late afternoon Edward went to meet the train that was bringing, he hoped, the new author. This morning it seemed settled that the firm was to be Haslatt and Sons and he had called up a sign painter. In the afternoon he and his father had chosen the lettering Haslatt and Sons, Publishers and Printers. His father had actually been excited and Edward was calm, in consequence, though in spite of new pride. Now he wished the sign could be ready for tomorrow morning when Lewis Harrow could see it. He smiled, half ashamed at his impatience.

The train slowed to a stop at the Chedbury station. It was a local running out from Boston, and since Chedbury was next to the last station, few people were aboard. It was easy to discover a thickset young man who wore no hat and a shabby topcoat. He stood looking left and right, and Edward drew near. "Mr. Harrow?"

"Lewis Harrow," the young man said.

His intense eyes did not light under half-lowered lids nor did he smile. He wore a young dark mustache and he carried a worn bag.

"I am Edward Haslatt."

They shook hands and the young man began to speak in an uneven staccato. "Good of you to come and meet me—yourself, I mean."

"Chedbury is a small place and I can walk here to this station quite easily," Edward replied. "I am glad you can spend the night. The trolley is only just around the corner."

They walked away together, the young man with a slight limp, and at the car Edward involuntarily lifted him slightly by the arm.

"Thanks," the young man said. "I got a potshot in the leg in the war."

"Sorry to hear that," Edward said.

"It's nothing—now."

They sat in silence for a moment and then Edward began to talk, diffidently. He was still shy before his authors, still, he feared, more printer than publisher. Then he perceived that Lewis Harrow was even more diffident than himself, and he laid hold of his pride and began to speak with determination. "I hope you won't be impatient with me if I take several days, or more, in reading your manuscript. I read slowly—and perhaps make up my mind slowly, too."

"I don't mind," Lewis Harrow said indifferently. He was gazing out the window. "It's still beautiful country. I was afraid it had changed."

"It's nice," Edward admitted. "Have you been here before?"

"Yes," Harrow said. "But long ago."

Edward looked out on the familiar landscape with complacent pleasure.

Most of the time he forgot it, but when someone approved it, he remembered that it was fine and his own. When he and Margaret were first married he had honestly made great effort to see as quickly as she did the beauty in land and sky, but to his confusion she had soon detected his effort and one day she had said plainly, though with good nature, "Don't pretend, will you, Ned! You needn't care about the sunset."

"Well, I do," he had retorted. "I can see it's beautiful as well as you, but I can't cry out over it."

"How does it make you feel?" she had asked curiously.

"I'm pleased my world contains it," he had answered after some reflection.

"That's well put," she had said as though surprised. "Perhaps it says more than you know."

"Perhaps it does," he had agreed.

Afterward it occurred to him that she lived in every moment entire as it came, but he lived each moment as it was related to the past and the future. Thus he did not see the sunset as only a splendid sight, but he saw it in its place in the landscape of his home.

"You have a family?" Lewis Harrow was asking.

"A son and two daughters," Edward replied, "all small, yet—the youngest a baby."

"I like children," Harrow went on. "I hope yours will like me."

"You'll find Mary shy," Edward replied. As always his heart flew to protect this eldest child. "The others are ordinary enough—though their mother would reproach me for putting it that way. One can't say yet, as a matter of fact, what the baby is. I'm fond enough of my son, but I can't see signs that he'll set the world afire."

Harrow laughed. "A practical man, though a father!"

Edward narrowed his eyes in a small smile. "I hope so," he said dryly. "Here's our stop."

They got out at the corner road and walked the brief distance to the house. Edward said nothing, wanting to catch undiluted by irrelevant talk the stranger's first glimpse of the house. He paused cunningly just before the road turned. "Just around the bend you'll see where we live," he said carelessly. They made the turn and Harrow stopped to exclaim in honest admiration, "What a house!"

"It was built by an Englishman, years ago," Edward explained, taking care to be casual. "His wife died and he went back to England just about the time we were married. It was too big for us then, of course, but—well, we wanted it. My wife was used to space and I wanted to give her what she'd had."

"Is that she?" Harrow asked. They were walking on again.

"Yes." They could see Margaret quite plainly now. She was cutting a few daffodils.

"She looks young," Harrow said.

"A year younger than I," Edward said.

"You're not old," Harrow said, smiling.

"Only older than you," Edward said, returning the smile.

They became aware that they were talking trivially and fell silent. A moment later they were at the gate and there stood Margaret in her blue wool dress, her hands full of the yellow daffodils. Her black hair curled about her face and her eyes in the light of the sunset were a startling blue. Edward felt the old sting of physical jealousy and his palms tingled. Why did she have to stand there looking as though she had suddenly come to life?

"This is Lewis Harrow," he said abruptly. "Harrow, this is my wife."

Margaret put out her hand and the young man took it. "I hope you don't mind my saying you're beautiful."

Edward, surprised by this boldness, stared with displeasure at his guest, and saw for the first time how strange was the color of his eyes, a yellowish hazel. But before he could speak, Margaret said frankly, "I don't mind a bit. Do come in, both of you. Sandy's calling for you, Ned."

The door of the house flew open and Mary darted out. "Oh, Dad!" she cried. "I thought you'd never come." She flung her arms about his waist, a brown-skinned, brown-eyed child whose hair was too long and dark for the small anxious face.

"I told you I had to meet Mr. Harrow," Edward said, hugging her.

"I told her, too," Margaret said, "but she frets about everything."

"Does she!" Harrow said half playfully. "How well I understand that! I always fret."

"Do you?" Mary breathed. "It's awful, isn't it?"

"Really awful!" Harrow agreed.

He seemed to have forgotten Margaret and Edward forgave him on the instant. So seldom did anybody see his plain little daughter.

"What do you fret about?" Mary asked.

"Well, whether your father will like my book," Harrow said mischievously.

"Father!" Mary cried. "You will like his book, won't you?"

"Mary, please go in and have your supper," Margaret said suddenly.

"Isn't she eating with us?" Edward asked.

His eyes met Margaret's. "She and Tom are having their supper early tonight," Margaret said.

The evening passed. At each stage Edward watched Harrow not only with his own eyes but through Margaret's delaying, fluctuating feeling toward the young man. Thus he knew that she was first horrified at Harrow's table manners. He buttered his bread slice whole and ate it so. He gnawed the meat from his lamb chop and wiped his greasy hands shamelessly on his napkin. Whatever he did was unconscious. Obviously he had never been taught manners, nor had he observed them. This physical coarseness was balanced by a delicacy in feeling and perception strange and quick. He lounged on the couch after dinner and shook his head at coffee. "Keeps me awake," he declared, "and sleep is important to me. I want my brain crystal in the morning." But an hour later he divined restlessness in Margaret and he smiled at her boldly.

"You feel you've seen me before, don't you?"

"I do," she replied, "how did you know?"

"I feel you wondering."

"Nonsense!"

"Of course I do," he insisted. "It's my business to feel what people are thinking. Well, you have seen me before."

His confident smile was not attractive but it was compelling.

"Where?" Edward asked with caution.

Harrow gave a loud laugh. "Right here in Chedbury!"

"Wait," Margaret said. "Let me think—"

They waited, their eyes on her vivid thinking face.

"The only thing I can see is our old laundress. There's something about you—"

"There is. I'm her son."

"But her name was Hinkle."

Lewis Harrow interrupted her. "Impossible name for a novelist! As soon as Mother died I changed it. I'm Harrow now, legally."

"You weren't the boy who used to lug in the baskets for her?" she asked.

"I was and am," Harrow said without embarrassment.

"Your face was always dirty."

"Still is, a good deal of the time."

"But how old are you?"

"Twenty-eight."

Edward sat silent. The bright demand in Margaret's voice, the directness of her curiosity, had drawn a fearless response from the young man. He had seen this happen again and again between Margaret and some other human being. She was irresistible when she wanted to be—and when the other person was strong enough for it.

Lewis Harrow was strong and he felt no need for self-defense. He turned now to Edward. "The novel I've got for you tonight is about war. I was in it, of course. I have to get it out of my system. But I've already begun another."

"That's good news," Edward said quietly. "It's what a publisher wants to hear—that there's always another."

It was his turn now, and he took it, and Margaret sat by, listening, her eyes intense and her cheeks flushed, while they talked of the writing of books.

"What do you think of him?" This Edward asked her when long past midnight they were getting ready for bed.

"It depends on what he's doing," she replied. She took off the wrought-gold necklace and the earrings which a few years ago he had bought to match it. "When he's eating he's an animal. Maybe he's an animal anyway. But when he talks he makes me think of Beethoven."

"The two aren't incompatible," Edward murmured. He felt exhausted. There was some force in Harrow that burned the oxygen out of the air. A consuming sort of fellow—he didn't want to be with him too much! There was that manuscript lying on the table in the small study that adjoined the bedroom. He did not intend to go near it tonight. He lay down in his bed a few minutes later, and felt the sheets cool and grateful to his outstretched legs. Margaret was already in her bed, and before he put out the light he took his final look at her through the open door between their rooms. Five years ago they had decided on separate rooms. She lay as always high on two pillows, her soft black hair outspread. She wore a long-sleeved nightgown and there were frills of lace over her clasped hands. Their eyes met and smiled.

"I'd hate to be married to anybody except you," she said sweetly.

"Thank you, my dear," he replied.

They had already kissed and so he put out the light. He heard the small sigh she gave before she slept and then there was silence. She was exhausted, too.

He lay for perhaps an hour, waiting for sleep. He was not a sound sleeper even at the end of his usual days, and tonight he felt his awareness in every nerve and vein. Thus though his heart beat steadily and slowly he could count the pulsation of his blood as it flowed through his body. His hearing sharpened and magnified the cracks of beams above his head, the scrape of a shutter loosened against the outside wall of the house, the slow rise of the night wind. Margaret's breathing, soft and not quite steady, disturbed the rhythm of his own, and involuntarily he tried to keep in tune with her. So for two hours he lay tortured by his wakefulness, troubled by nothing clearly enough to absorb his mind, and yet all the minor troubles of his days flitted darkly across his brain—Margaret's injustice to his dear little Mary, the young man in his printing shop, the labor union that threatened the peace of his work, his father's increasing weakness, his own need for more money and the impossibility of speaking of it, Baynes and the New York office, Baynes and Sandra, this fellow Harrow. He doubted his own ability to handle Harrow. Suppose the fellow turned out to be something stupendous, a really great writer, had he, Edward Haslatt, the skill, the knowledge to shape the notable career of a genius?

Upon this he thought of the manuscript lying on his table and he rose noiselessly and put on the woolen bathrobe and the slippers that were at the foot of his bed. Margaret slept on, and still silent he stole across the room and opened the door into his study.

When he had finished reading the manuscript the dawn was glimmering in the sky. He was shivering cold and his eyelids burned and he felt sick

with weariness. His hands as he turned the last page into its place were
trembling. It was more than fatigue. It was wonder and disgust and admiration and terror. He had found at last a man who could write and was
not afraid of God or man.

"I've got to be strong enough for him." So thinking, Edward crawled
into his cold bed and fell asleep.

Six months later on an evening in late spring, he was still not sure that
he was strong enough. The whole town of Chedbury had gathered in the
courthouse to hear Lewis Harrow talk. His fame had overwhelmed them
irresistibly. The swift and staggering success of his book had astonished
and irritated them. The motive of his novel had been to make a vast joke
of war. His hero was a young officer who early had seen the monstrosity of
urging his men to sacrifice life, their best and most essential possession,
for any cause whatever. In the end he had himself to choose between
sensible escape to save his own life, or death on the battlefield to maintain
illusion for men dependent upon him. Chedbury would have forgiven Lewis
Harrow had his hero chosen death. Instead the heady young officer had
chosen to surrender to his own men, with apology, a swaggering smile,
court-martial and guns facing him as he stood back to a wall.

So unorthodox a bravery had confounded the sober people of Chedbury.
Harrow had brought them fame but its cause was questionable. Reluctantly,
after months of debate, they had decided to give him belated acknowledgment by inviting him to speak to them, and pride had struggled with
curiosity in coming to hear him.

Mrs. Seaton said what many others felt. "It's a pity that it had to be
only Mrs. Hinkle's boy who got us famous."

Old Thomas Seaton had opened his sleepy eyes after dinner when he
heard this. "Yes, why couldn't it have been you, Tom? Or even Meg or
Sandra? Any child of your mother's would have done better than Lew
Hinkle."

Tom had grinned without speaking. He talked less and less and looked
brighter, smarter, and more sleek as he grew older. Still unmarried, he
lived at home, but since he did not now ask for money, his father let
sleeping dogs lie, though well aware that the cause for his son's solitary
content, or resignation, lived in South Chedbury, in the form of a plump
and pretty Italian girl. The cause for Tom's early drunkenness, Margaret
had confided to Edward, was that he had fallen in love with a fair-haired
English girl, whose father was an earl. The Seaton family, so notable in
Chedbury, was less considerable in Great Bairnbourne Castle. Mrs. Seaton
in wounded pride had demanded that Tom came back to Chedbury at once,
and Tom had obeyed, to forget rather easily, it seemed, his first love. He
had recalled it uneasily, however, upon reading Harrow's book, when the
rebellious hero had loved just such a young English girl as he still remembered, when alone sometimes at night. The likeness had not escaped Mrs.

AMERICAN TRIPTYCH

Seaton's sharpness, and between mother and son there had arisen an irritability increased by their determined silence upon the subject of their thoughts.

Even between Edward and Margaret, Lewis Harrow's book had brought a small discord. Physical cowardice she hated and she smelled something foul in the idea of a soldier, an officer, choosing death at the hands of his clan rather than his enemy.

"Maybe they were his real enemies," Edward had suggested.

She had given him a quick look. "It's not like you to be subtle, Ned."

"I don't do it easily," he conceded.

"Explain yourself," she demanded.

But he could never do that and he had tried less and less as the years passed. Words had been essential to her in the early years of their marriage and he had made earnest attempt to use them freely to her then. The fluency that was natural to her made him sweat with effort and he gave it up as unnatural to him.

"I can't explain myself," he now said.

"Try!" So she urged him. When he hesitated she said, biting her red underlip, "How strange it is that men don't mind stripping their bodies naked before women, but ask them to uncover their thoughts and they grow as shy as virgins!"

She had settled herself on the couch to read the evening this went on, and half exasperated, half baffled, he had stopped on his way upstairs to tell the children good night and had taken her head between his two hands, had kissed her and gone on his way. He no longer quarreled with her for any reason.

Meanwhile talk had continued in Chedbury. There had been a good deal of discussion at a meeting two weeks before as to whether they would use the church or the courthouse. The new minister had decided the matter by rising to his feet, very tall and dry. "I've read Harrow's book," he had said. "I feel it would not be safe to allow him the use of the church. Profanity seems natural to him. We'd better compromise on the courthouse."

People had laughed. The salt of their minister's tongue was their everyday blessing. His sermons were plain and sometimes they made a man angry, but at least one knew what they were about. Joseph Barclay had been to sea in his youth and had been converted in Liverpool by an English Methodist preacher making the rounds of the red-light district to rescue the men from the ships. This preacher had rescued the young officer by mighty words and a loud quarrel with the woman who had him in tow. With his two hands he had laid hold on the boy and forced him out into the rainy darkness of an English night. He had taken him home and lectured him and prayed with him and held him God's prisoner until he promised to repent.

So Joseph Barclay had repented and had one day returned to America to keep his word with God. He was fifty years old now, and Chedbury had called him when Dr. Hart had said they must. At seventy Dr. Hart had gone out and searched for the man who must take his place in Chedbury. He had found him in a little church in the city of Lowell, a church so blackened by factory smoke outside and the grimy hands of the congregation inside that anyone else would have passed it by. But Francis Hart had heard of the man who spoke so plainly that people always knew what he was saying, and there he had found him. It had not been too easy to persuade the plain-speaking man to come to Chedbury. "I belong here among the factory folk," he had told old Dr. Hart. "I don't like dressing up. And when I preach I'm liable to take the skin off."

"Factory folk get their skin taken off in other ways," Dr. Hart had retorted. "Nobody dares to skin my folk in Chedbury except me, and after I'm dead they'll grow soft."

He had lived to hear the new minister preach a couple of fine searing sermons and then he had died of pneumonia caught on a zero morning when he insisted on shoveling the snow a blizzard had thrown on his front walk. People did not always like Joseph Barclay but nobody dared rebel because old Dr. Hart had brought him there. And the fellow told the truth so consistently that no one wanted to be the first to speak against him. There was, moreover, a certain excitement in going to church each Sunday. Joseph Barclay never said the same thing twice. He lived alone in the parsonage, was unmarried, and half the time he cooked his own meals because no woman in Chedbury would make fish chowder the way he liked it.

In the courthouse, then, the people of Chedbury sat on a late spring evening, waiting to hear what the son of old Abe Hinkle had to say. The older people could remember the family well, and when Abe died in his final drunken fit, they had helped Mrs. Hinkle by giving her monumental heaps of laundry. Many of the younger people could remember Lew Hinkle, the spindle-shanked boy who went to school with them. They distrusted the change of his name, though he made no pretense of concealing either his father's name or his reason for changing it. "No use keeping a name that's a commercial handicap," Lewis Harrow had said publicly to newspaper reporters, even in New York.

Tonight he stood, too much at ease, some thought, before his audience. He was soberly dressed in a new gray suit, his rough black hair was smooth, and the only exception that the reluctant people of Chedbury could take as they gazed at him was the color of his tie which was red. Edward himself regretted the tie. He disliked bright hues especially when worn by men, and Margaret had learned never to give him anything except a tie of a solid blue or gray. He did possess one tie of wine red that he wore usually on Christmas day with his good dark suit.

The courthouse was of an unusual and somewhat theatrical design. A hundred years ago an ambitious politican had conceived the idea of a central platform where he could hold forth upon occasions. Around this platform set against the north wall five tiers of seats rose toward the door. Since the courthouse stood upon a hill, the effect was dramatic. It had never been more so than tonight, when all of Chedbury had come out to hear this humble and almost unknown son. The Seatons sat together at the left, and with them were Baynes and Sandra, come from New York today. Edward had toyed with the notion of inviting them to the brief dinner that he and Margaret had eaten with Lewis Harrow, and then had decided against it. Sandra had a way of stimulating men to talk and he did not want Harrow exhausted before his speech. There was no use in wasting on Sandra witticisms that might amaze an audience. Sandra had put on a brilliant green dress without sleeves, and she had combed her red hair high, like the crest of a bird. Edward looked away from her impatiently. New York was bringing out the worst in her. Old Tom Seaton was drowsing in his seat and Mrs. Seaton nudged him with her elbow. That was the difference between them. Old Tom slept into his age and she grew more wakeful as death drew near. Edward's own parents sat side by side just in front of himself and Margaret, and with them was Louise. So seldom did he see his sister that he looked at her now with the detached, half-critical mind of a stranger. She looked rather pretty in her quiet unadorned fashion, hair parted and put back into some sort of knot at her neck and a blue dress that made her skin pale and white. Her profile was better than it had been when she was a girl. A certain thickness she had then was worn away and she looked delicate.

He stopped looking at Louise after he perceived these general improvements and settled himself to listen to Lewis Harrow. He had taken Harrow down to the platform a few minutes before and had made a brief introduction. He knew that he was a poor speaker, and being uneasy on his feet, he said a few terse words in a dogged monotone, bare and without congratulation, either to Harrow or to himself as the publisher of a spectacularly successful first novel. But Chedbury was used to Edward Haslatt and they did not judge him. To brisk short applause, he had walked to his seat beside Margaret. She looked up at him softly, laughter hidden in her eyes, and he felt her hand steal into his and cling.

He pondered for a moment the meaning of this inexplicable handclasp as the people settled themselves to listen to Harrow. Nothing Margaret did was without significance. She did not give him one idle caress. Why, then, he asked silently, did she now press her soft palm into his, under the careful cover of her fur cape? Distracted for a moment, he scarcely heard what Harrow was saying.

Lewis Harrow spoke quickly, his deep voice penetrating into the farthest reach of the great round hall. Edward had never seen him discomfited, even when attacked by a galaxy of newspaper men, but tonight he perceived a slight belligerence in Harrow's manner, as though he felt himself on trial before the people of Chedbury. They were haunted perhaps by the memory of a hundred years of other trials in this very place, judgments upon men who had stolen what was not theirs, who had taken lives of other men, women who had wept, clutching the hands of bewildered children. The courthouse was a haunted place.

Lewis Harrow seemed to feel it. He lifted his head and stared about him at them all. The hard central light poured down light and heat upon him and he saw the faces of the people gleaming at him out of the surrounding shadows. Then his diffidence left him and clasping his hands behind him he began to speak with sudden ease.

"What I have done proves nothing, to you or to myself. You have done me an honor in coming to hear me tonight, but I shall not have deserved that honor until I write my second book, and my third. After the third then you may judge me and I will accept your judgment. I can write about war—yes, I grant you that I made you feel something of what men suffer in a war. But anybody can write about such melodrama. The story is ready made. The stage of war is small, the pattern set. The common words are ready—patriotism, bravery, death.

"But can I write about life? That you must decide for me, ten years from now. Take our town! If I were to write a novel about Chedbury where would I begin? Where would you begin, if you were I? I grew up here, among you. You knew my parents. With my mother I came in and out of your houses. Our door was the back door, but for my purposes that was the best one. I saw your kitchens. I heard the underside of your lives. Destined to be what I am, I had even then the mind of a writer. That is, I never forgot anything I saw or heard, I still do not. More than that, I understand far more than a word, I hear infinitely beyond a whisper.

"Where shall I begin my next book? Shall I begin with young Dr. Walters? You remember Bertram Walters, how brilliant he was, how handsome. Why he left Boston and came to settle in our little town we never knew. It took me a long time to find out. Until I knew I could not understand any more than you did, why, at the height of his youth and strength, he should kill himself one hot July day. I can remember the day and the hour. I had been swimming with some of you down at the old hole in the river. You left me at Bolster's Alley where I lived. We in Bolster's Alley heard things before you did, and we already knew that he had shot himself in exactly the correct spot in his heart. He was a perfectionist, you'll remember. I loped up to the Walters' house and saw him dead—just for a minute before they put me out. Something in his face made me hang around the undertaker's place the next day. Jake Bentley and I were friends in a queer sort of way and he let me come in sometimes and look at the dead people. I looked a long time at Dr. Walters. Jake and I talked and wondered why he did it. Something Jake said helped me to find out, later—half accidentally. It would be telling my story too soon if I told you now.

"Or should I begin with Bolster's Alley itself? There was an alley! You have cleaned it up since I lived there. Our town officers are more efficient than they used to be. Maybe it's just that we have more conscience than we used to have. The old Hinkle shack is gone. When I lived there with my mother, you'd be surprised at the good citizens I used to see sometimes, on a dark night, walking along the Alley. My mother was a good woman, too old and fat, maybe, for sin, but there were some beautiful women in the Alley.

"Maybe I ought to begin my story with Henry Croft, that matchless teacher, who beat me half to death when I was a rebellious schoolboy. That was only a decade and a half ago—seems strange that things have changed so much that if anybody beat a child now in the public school of Chedbury, he'd be arrested. But there was war then between Henry Croft and me and he always won. He won, too, in another way. I'm no fool and I began to see that the reason he couldn't keep from beating me was that he knew I had something in me and he was furious because I didn't see it for myself. I guessed it one day, when I was around thirteen. He grew angry with me because I hadn't written a composition. He said to me, 'Down with your bags,' and I got ready. He stared at me and began to cry. The whip dropped from his hand to the floor. For the first time in my life I was scared of him. Then he began to shout at me through his tears. 'Aren't you going to make something of yourself?' That was what he bellowed at me. I pulled up my pants, and I knew he would never beat me again. Then I could talk to him. Then he could talk to me. In the next four years he was the most wonderful teacher a boy ever had. He set my feet upon the path."

Margaret had drawn her hand away and now she sat leaning forward on her elbows. The tears were running down her cheeks. Edward had forgotten her, but he turned and saw the glistening of her eyes. The people of Chedbury were motionless in silence. Mrs. Croft sat in her widow's weeds, tall and gaunt, her face like staring stone. Little old Mrs. Walters bent her head. Thomas Seaton was wide awake and Mrs. Seaton was waving her small sandalwood fan swiftly to and fro.

Edward leaned toward Margaret. "Can we let this go on?"

She shook her head without reply, her eyes fixed on Harrow.

"Where shall I begin my book of life?" he was asking. "Shall I begin it in one of our big houses? It is a house full of life, as you well know. Long ago a strong man married a beautiful woman and they produced beautiful children. What becomes of beautiful children? They begin so full of promise. What happens to them? Shall I tell that story?

"I might choose another house and a plain honest sort of family, the family that lives in every other house in Chedbury. They don't struggle with poverty but they struggle with life. The man started out with modest dreams of himself, of love. The woman had a little dream, too, nothing very big, of course. We are cautious folk here. No use dreaming about what we can't have! But the dreams of this man and this woman were all cautious, possible ones. They could be more than dreams. But they weren't. Why? The man and woman were faithful to each other, of course. We never saw him in the Alley. He always went to church on Sunday with his wife and his children, and he wasn't afraid of anything—except life itself. Ask him if he wanted something, from a helping of chicken pot pie at a church supper to a million dollars and he would have said the same thing, 'I don't care if I do.' The phrase expresses him. Perhaps it expresses Chedbury. And yet, in spite of his dreams, which never came true because he never dared to make them big enough, or bold enough, he's had a life. In a way, he's even had a love, and so has the woman. Yes, perhaps theirs is the true story of Chedbury."

Against his own will, Edward glanced at his father and mother but he could not see their faces. Dangerous, indeed, this fellow Harrow! He had taken Chedbury into the hollow of his hand, and he was looking at them all, like a great Gulliver. They'd be angry tomorrow, and he'd hear from it. Then suddenly he had a grim sort of pleasure in it. Whatever happened, he had his big man. Harrow would make Haslatt and Sons known everywhere in the world. But first it was his job to make Harrow known everywhere in the world, a job he'd dreamed of doing somehow, if he could find the man. He could feel in his hands already the big new book. While Harrow talked, Edward, in his mind, turned fine paper, studied the perfect type, considered the width of margins and the design of a jacket. What color for the binding? Wine red, perhaps, and gold stamping? Tomorrow he'd finger his way through his typebook. He was in the grip of his own private frenzy of creation.

He did not notice that night, when they went home and to bed, that Margaret was silent and thoughtful. She went about the house in her usual way, pouring a last saucer of milk for Mary's kitten, peeling an orange and eating it by the dying coals of the living-room fire, and watching him, her blue eyes thoughtful, as he tested doors, pulled down shades and wound the clock in the hall. He went upstairs before her, because it was he, rather than she, who looked at the two older children. They had been moved out of the nursery into rooms of their own when each was seven, and he tiptoed to one bedside and then the other. Tom he always visited first, because he liked to linger by Mary. The boy was lying outstretched and strong, one leg outside the covers. The windows were wide open and a cool breeze, smelling of the not too distant sea, filled the room. He covered Tom and remembered that his son had lost a tooth that day. He took a nickel from his pocket, and feeling under the pillow he found the tooth and left the nickel. Then he went into the hall and opened the next door.

The night wind was cool here, too, but Mary was curled under a thin silk quilt and when he touched her forehead he found it damp with heat. This child had always the impulse to hide herself, to burrow deep into shelter. He rolled back the quilt cautiously from her neck and she woke at once and stared at him with strange eyes. He saw that she did not recognize him.

"It's me, dearie," he whispered, bending over her.

She flung up her arms and locked them behind his head. "You scared me."

"You mustn't get scared so easily."

"Because I thought it was somebody else!"

"It's always I who come here at night to see if you're all right."

"It mightn't always be you."

Some far truth in this confounded him. He kissed her and drew her arms gently from his neck. "Go to sleep, Mary."

She curled down again and he tiptoed out of the room and met Margaret coming from the nursery.

"Sandy all right?" he inquired.

"Robust and lovely," Margaret said.

The phrase fitted their third child. Sandy, not beautiful except as pink cheeks, blond hair, and innocent blue eyes always carry the implication of beauty, was rich in health and simple charm. She was a child upon whom Edward did not waste an instant's worry.

Later, before he got into his bed, he lingered by Margaret's bed, and remembering the clasp of her hand he stooped and gave her a tentative kiss. She received it without enthusiasm, though kindly, and mindful of the lesson that the years had taught him, he smoothed her hair for a moment and then left her. The exhilaration of his spirit prevented him from perceiving her unusual silence and he slept.

"A nice nest of hornets," Mr. Haslatt said the next morning. He was waiting at the door of the elevator when his son stepped out of it rather more briskly than usual.

A collected stubbornness had gathered in Edward as he proceeded on his usual way to the office. The greetings that he received from meetings in the morning on the trolley were always curt. Chedbury was not at its best before noon. But this morning mumbled words were only nods and men read their morning papers without raising their heads as he passed.

All this was introduction to his father's gritty remark, and Edward, inwardly disturbed, refused to acknowledge it.

"What's the matter?" he asked with involuntary deceit.

"Looks like you'll have to take a choice between that fellow and the rest of the town," his father said.

Edward did not reply. He passed between the desks in the main office without speaking and certainly without allowing himself to notice the suppressed and curious looks that the girls sent him. He went into his office and shut the door after his father.

"Sit down," he said.

He sat down himself behind the square old desk that had once belonged to Mr. Mather and his father took the chair opposite. He was never comfortable thus facing his father, but today he did not allow his feelings to move him. If it were to be necessary to fight all Chedbury for Lewis Harrow, let it begin here. He waited for his father.

"I don't see as Lew Hinkle had any reason to talk the way he did last night," Mr. Haslatt said. He wore an old pepper-and-salt suit upon which the thread had worn down to gray, which made more dun the grayness of his skin and hair. He had grown thin with age and his long nose was pink at the tip. In cold or excitement a drop quivered at his nostril and Edward repressed his old youthful impulse to mention it. If he had to contend with his father on the large matter of Lewis Harrow, he would not indulge himself in small personal repulsions. He looked toward the window. Chedbury was most beautiful now, but man could be as vile here as anywhere.

"You have to let a writer talk anyway he wants," he said. Then without giving his father opportunity to answer he went on. "Baynes will be in soon, I suppose."

"I've lived my life in this town," his father replied.

"I intend to live mine here, too," Edward said doggedly.

"Your mother says Mrs. Walters is terribly upset."

Edward wheeled in his chair. "The real question is whether we are going to go to the top with Harrow or whether we're going to stay right here in Chedbury along with Mrs. Walters and her kind."

"You can't please God and Mammon," Mr. Haslatt said solemnly.

"Mrs. Walters isn't either of them," Edward retorted.

Upon this foolish conversation Baynes burst into the office like a soaring rocket, scattering good humor and optimism. He had on a new suit, a striped thing, and the shoulders had a silly sloped effect.

"Thought I'd find you two here! Wasn't that a swell performance last night? Skinned half the town, didn't he? All as neat as you please! Took 'em out of cold storage. We've been fighting at the Seatons or I'd have been here sooner."

"Mr. Seaton sore?" Mr. Haslatt inquired.

"You can't make that tough old hide sore," Baynes said. "Mrs. Seaton is all upset over bad taste, of course. Curious, young Tom is on her side. Nobody is going to have any peace in the town if Harrow really writes that book. If it's half the book he says it's going to be, we're all set for a fortune."

"That how Sandra looks at it?" Edward asked.

"Sandra's out helping him to pick the site for his house." Baynes sat on the window sill and swung his leg.

"He ain't going to live here!" Mr. Haslatt exclaimed.

"He is," Baynes replied. "He doesn't want to live in any of the old houses he could buy. That's Chedbury for you. Yelling about him and still they'd sell him the house from under their feet if he paid enough. He's going to build his house—wants to make his own ghosts, he says."

Edward considered this with the silence usual to him. Certainly it would have been easier if Lewis Harrow had chosen to live at the safe distance of New York, where Chedbury thought writers belonged. But he would do nothing to jeopardize his precious possession. Once in a lifetime a really great writer fell into a publisher's lap. He saw other publishers, big-city fellows, swarming like sharks about the frail bark of Haslatt and Sons. He would indulge Harrow to the last degree, mindful of the genius that the man contained—a gem in a casket of clay.

"He wants to live where he can look down on Chedbury," Baynes was saying. "Sandra's taking him to the top of Granite."

"Who's goin' to build the road up there?" Mr. Haslatt demanded.

"He will," Baynes said joyously, "out of the money he makes from us."

Mr. Haslatt's eyes grew glassy. "We're gettin' in too deep."

Edward turned to his desk. "We'll swim."

At the brusqueness in his voice, Mr. Haslatt rose. "I'd better get to work and leave you two to do the same," he declared, and closed the door sharply behind him.

Edward looked at his younger brother. Baynes was taking on a curious half-dissipated air. He had grown a strong dark mustache which he trimmed to show his still youthful mouth, and as he stared out of the window he twisted one end of the mustache thoughtfully. His dark eyes narrowed. "We ought to get Harrow nicely married to some high-born Chedbury female. Then he could rip us all up without damage. I don't know the girls any more, though, and you never did. Pity I got Sandra—that would have been so beautiful. A Seaton wed to the washerwoman's son!" Baynes laughed silently.

Edward was repelled by both words and laughter. Baynes had grown coarse from living in New York. Maybe it was only because of Sandra. She was coarse, he had always imagined secretly. There was none of Margaret's delicacy in her, and New York had polished away any semblance of youthful reserve. Sandra, neither young nor old, had taken on all the gloss of a silver statue.

"I'm surprised you talk of your own wife in that way," Edward said. "I hope you two aren't growing apart." He was aware of something stiff and old-fashioned in what he said, but he did not know how to put the words differently.

Baynes was blithe. He swung his leg from the desk and sat down in the chair which his father had left. "Sandra's all right—has to have her head, of course. All women do since the war. Notice how different females are since we came marching home?"

"Since I didn't march, I don't notice it," Edward said dryly. He was sorting his morning's mail carefully into piles, ready for dictation, and he observed with pleasure a statement from a paper mill that the cost of paper had gone down again. It had been ruinously high during the war because the government had used so much to print stuff nobody read, anyhow.

"You and Meg are growing old graciously."

The voice of his younger brother, teasing and impudent, roused Edward.

He folded the morning newspaper and leaning over his desk in a gesture unwontedly youthful, he clapped Baynes on the head.

Baynes pretended alarm. "Hey—there's life in the old dog yet."

Upon this playfulness Jane, the secretary, opened the door. She stared at the two brothers with gravity, decided to ignore what she had seen and came forward.

"About that new type," she began.

Edward sat back, and determined against shame before this elderly creature whom he had inherited from Haslatt and Mather, he answered mildly, "Come in, Jane. I've decided on the Oxford. This new book is going to be twice as long, I can see."

Baynes interrupted, "Want me to wait?"

"Yes. I want to hear every damn city trick we can turn."

So seldom did he swear that Baynes looked surprised and Jane turned a muddy red. Both yielded at once to Edward the place of master of the firm. Jane, respectful for the moment, murmured assent and withdrew, and Baynes settled down to business.

For two hours the brothers sat in close conference, more deeply akin in their common reverence for the good fortune that had fallen into their hands than even they were in blood. Baynes talked in his new impetuous fashion, his sentences city clipped, and Edward listened, weighing, assessing, deciding. They laid plans for advance advertising, for a New York dinner, for some of the new cocktail parties that were becoming the fashion. With growing generosity Edward acknowledged that Baynes and Sandra were becoming essential to Haslatt and Sons. He himself could never have planned so dashing a program, and he would not have allowed Margaret to participate in something that in his heart he considered undignified. But the war, he conceded, had changed everything except Chedbury.

On Granite Mountain Lewis Harrow was roaming. He had mounted one hillock after another upon that massive bosom, looking down at Chedbury with critical eyes. Now as the circle of choice narrowed he climbed a broad smooth height for the fourth time. "This is still the best one," he announced to Sandra.

She, looking a little paler even than usual, was trying not to pant. She sank to a gray rock. "Thank God."

He looked down on her with familiar and cynical eyes. She was the new modern woman whom he had seen in the capitals of Europe and in New York. With all her efforts she did not compare to her older sister. Mrs. Haslatt was a beauty, the sort one saw in the paintings in the Louvre. Queer how he had so loved the monstrosity of a museum that he spent all his leaves in it! There wasn't a girl on the streets of Paris to compare to the lovely women he saw in the Louvre—those women whom he could never conquer.

"You're not as tough as you look," he told Sandra with intentional rudeness. He always wanted to be rude to women like her. He longed to hurt them.

"But the way you've climbed," Sandra complained.

"You didn't have to come."

"Indeed I did. It's all business."

"What—this?"

"Certainly, you're our Great Author—didn't you know?"

"Hell, I know well enough."

"Ask and you shall have anything!" She rose dramatically, holding out her hands.

He turned away from her. "Thanks—I want very little. A house on top of this hill—a low house made of granite, with big windows."

"Where you'll live alone?"

"I've always lived alone."

"Need you?" The red head under a little green hat was gracefully inclined.

"No, I don't need to—I want to."

He began walking down the mountain at great speed, the loose stones rushing under his feet, and she followed.

"With such a temper," she said sweetly, "how wise to live alone!"

He did not answer this, and seeing the broadness of his back she called, "Chalk that off—I didn't say it."

He laughed then and turning he put his arm through hers and they ran down the mountain at dangerous speed. She liked it. Glancing at her rather bold profile he saw that the danger had lit her green eyes and reddened her cheeks. It was a familiar sight. He was quite aware of his power over women and he had used it so often that now he knew he was ready for someone quite different—someone wholly different from this starved slenderness, this sharply pallid face, these chilly thin hands. Plenty of catlike female passion here, of course, but that was all. And passion was cheap— the price was low in any market. It had ceased to be fun. He wanted it with decorations—or perhaps foundations. He wanted something to worship.

They got into his little roadster at the bottom of the hill and wound their way down into Chedbury. At the Seaton house he stopped and she, laying her hand upon his coat, persuaded him. "Come in for a little while."

"You dare me to?"

"Why?"

"I saw your mother looking at me last night through a lorgnette."

"Maybe she'd like you better close."

"All right. If the fur flies it won't be mine."

He climbed out and followed her with stolid footsteps into the great front door. "Handsome house," he murmured, "the wings are wonderful. It took genius to dare to put those balustrades around all the roofs."

"My father did that."

He braced his shoulders and prepared for a handsome old lady with lorgnette and a somnolent old man in a shapeless tweed suit. Old Tom Seaton was not in the big living room but he did not notice it. For Margaret was there—Mrs. Haslatt, he corrected himself. He had kept thinking about her through half the night as she had looked in her own house, as she moved about, so content that it made him angry. Out of this anger he had conceived the things he had later said to Chedbury. She was a queen, possessing a realm and yet, somehow, seeming careless of it. Did she love that dull fellow Haslatt? How could she? Yet she looked impregnable—passionately pure, perhaps. He postponed the thought of passion. He wanted to respect her—perhaps worship her a bit. Life was really fearfully empty.

He went forward gladly, seeing in the light of day that beautiful warm woman whom he had seen last night at her own dinner table. "Mrs. Haslatt!" he exclaimed. "How lucky! Indeed, I didn't expect to see you so soon again."

He clasped her hand in both his own and old Mrs. Seaton sitting by the window observed him with lifted eyebrows. She had withered without growing more gentle, and now her cool gray eyes observed this coarse young man who was holding Margaret's hand. A genius, Margaret had called him. She was too worldly wise not to distrust genius while she valued it. There was nothing more dangerous. And Edward, poor fellow, had none of it. Margaret had married a good man, an excellent man, who was even making her comfortably and quietly rich, but he had no genius. Fortunately this fellow came from impossibly low antecedents. The Haslatts were not aristocrats, but it was a respectable New England family—not quite local gentry, perhaps, but not merchants.

"How do you do, Mr. Harrow," she said, lisping frostily.

"How do you do, Madame Seaton," he replied grandly. He bowed over the narrow old hand she extended.

Only a lowborn person could be so exaggerated, she felt. She was shaken, nevertheless, by the tigerlike eyes so near her own. They were not dark, as she had supposed. They were greenish yellow—an unpleasant color. She withdrew her hand.

Sandra had flung herself into a chair. "He's going to build on the Spur," she announced. She pulled off her hat and shook out her short hair.

"First I must find out who owns it," Harrow said. He sat down by Margaret upon the couch with such assurance that she moved away from him involuntarily. He exuded some sort of faint animal odor, not unpleasant and yet which she disliked.

"I imagine anybody would be glad to sell a piece of Granite," she said.

"I will tempt and beguile and bewitch anybody into doing it," he said turning his tiger-colored eyes upon her. "I will make it impossible for anybody to refuse me."

Mrs. Seaton was suddenly overcome with total dislike for this presence. After all, she had never sat in the same room with the son of a laundress.

She rose and walked slowly to the open French window. "Your father has been asleep quite long enough," she observed to her daughters. "I can see him lying out there under the elm tree with his handkerchief over his face. I shall wake him and tell him he must amuse me."

"Wonderful that he can still amuse," Lewis declared. "What a marriage, madame!"

She inclined her head without answering this ribaldry, and they watched her trailing gray skirts move slowly down the steps.

Now the animal presence became very strong indeed, and the summer air was suddenly stifling. Seated close to Lewis Harrow, it was too near, and Margaret rose. "I must be going home—the children will be waiting for luncheon."

"Invite me," Harrow said shamelessly. "I want to see that beautiful child, Mary. Somewhere she will be entwined in the pages of my book, a little delicate vine, green and tender."

"We have only the lightest of noon meals."

Margaret's unwilling voice protested and he refused to accept it. "It is Mary I want to see."

He followed her from the room with strong footsteps and Sandra, peering out of the window, saw with some astonishment her elder sister seated in the roadster and whirled away. Tom lounged into the room at this moment. He was beginning to grow gray early, and this gave him a look of false distinction.

"Damn quiet house," he remarked. "Where's everybody?"

"Gone," Sandra said, and continued to stare out of the window in a peculiar fashion.

When Edward let himself into his home that night there was nothing to intimate that there had been an animal presence there in his absence. The wide hall was calm and since he was late, he knew that Margaret was upstairs putting their youngest child to bed, and that Mary and Tommy were in the process of cleaning and changing upon which Margaret insisted before dinner. The second maid, Nora, whom he had engaged some weeks before because he thought Margaret looked tired, now stole out of the back-hall door and took his hat and stick.

"Put a little sherry in the living room," he ordered and then slowly he mounted the stairs.

It had been an exhausting, exciting, dangerous sort of day. He had plunged deeply into something new and he was at once frightened and exhilarated. If Harrow's next book failed Haslatt and Sons would fail with it, for he had mortgaged all his profits from the war book. It would be close sailing until he had the finished manuscript in his hands and could decide for himself whether Harrow had more than one book in him. That was the test, true always, of a writer. One book did not prove anyone. What Haslatt and Sons wanted—that is, what Edward himself wanted—

was a man who was a fountain of books, throwing them off with every new facet and stage in his development.

At the top of the stairs the half-opened door revealed to him Margaret with Sandy in her arms beside the crib. She wore the long blue peignoir which he especially liked and his heart throbbed once or twice at the sight of her beauty. Marriage had become her, he flattered himself. She had bloomed gently, like a rose in mild sunshine. He, being a fancier of roses in a small way, liked in his secret musings to liken his wife to a rose. Such was his inner shyness that he had only once or twice been able to tell her of this likeness. Why he had not been able to keep open the doors of communication between himself and Margaret he did not know and he often pondered. Perhaps he loved her too well, and his old defensive pride rose against complete self-revelation. So large was her nature, so comprehensive her understanding, her ancestry so superior to his, he sometimes feared, that all his old sensitivity remained alert in him, the more wary because he could not tell her that it was there. He was ashamed of this and yet helpless to change it. He wanted her to believe that he was no ordinary man and yet there were times when he knew he was only that. The uncertainty of his inner atmosphere was the result of his own inability to judge himself. Whether he was better than other men he did not know. He suspected that his inordinate pride was a sort of vanity. He believed that he was better than the average but he was not sure. Had he been sure, he was coming to think, he could have spoken freely to his wife at any moment.

As it was, though his heart quickened, though he went into the nursery and took her in his arms, child and all, he could only murmur, "I ought not to touch you—I haven't washed." These words his lips said while his silent heart adored.

He imagined, all his sharp senses aware, that there was something reserved in the kiss she gave him. This possibility rendered him completely dumb. With alarm fluttering in his breast he kissed his daughter and leaned on the side of the crib while Margaret covered the child for sleep.

They left the room hand in hand and again he imagined or perceived the less than usual warmth in her hand, although it clasped his with resolution. But there was a difference between clinging and determination.

"Everything all right?" he asked.

"Yes," she answered promptly. "Except—I don't like your Lewis Harrow."

"My Lewis Harrow?" he repeated, smiling slightly.

"Yes, yours," she said, "you've captured him, haven't you?"

"I hope so—for the sake of business."

"There it is," she exclaimed. "I don't like to think he's paying for our bread and butter—"

"And his own cake," Edward put in.

She threw him a strange look, which he could not comprehend. "Do you know why I don't like him? Because he invited himself to luncheon today alone with the children and me!"

"Why didn't you telephone me?"

She looked at him in astonishment. "Honestly, Ned, I didn't think of it." Her amazement at herself was so real that he smiled again.

"You must always think of me, you know," he said mildly. "Was he nice to the children?"

"He didn't notice Tommy or Sandy, but he was foolish to Mary. If she were anything but a child I'd say he—made love to her."

"That's impossible, Margaret."

"Ned, it was disgusting, really!"

He saw that her cheeks were flaming and in the same instant, her eyes were so brightly blue, her hair so black and flying, that he felt her beauty burned into the very flesh of his heart. Had she thus appeared to Harrow? Feeling with dismay the rush of old jealousy he had thought long since disciplined from him, he went into the next room, which was his own, that she might not discern his pitiable condition and grow angry. She had not for years been greatly angry with him, for he had not for those same years allowed his young green jealousy to show itself in words or pique. Now he knew it was there in him still, and must at all costs be hidden from her for the sake of his own self-respect in her eyes.

He felt suddenly very tired and he sank into his old leather chair and covered his eyes with his hands. Why should Harrow shower his attentions upon the child Mary? Why Mary and not Tommy or Sandy? Why except that with his cursed novelist's perception and imagination he had already understood that Margaret did not love her eldest child too well? And with this he had forged a cunning cruel weapon to draw Margaret's eyes to himself. Not for one moment did Edward believe that Lewis Harrow cared for any child.

The monstrosity of this behavior in a man, that he used a child for such a purpose, mingled in Edward's thoughts with jealousy lest that Margaret had indeed noticed Harrow because of this wile and with anger that his favorite child should have been made a tool. He sat motionless in the chair, longing furiously to find Harrow and tell him to get out of his sight and forever. This fury he dealt with in continued silence and by means of reason. Harrow was less than a man. He was a thing of emotions and imaginations, fluid with creation, irresponsible, untrustworthy, a creature to be watched and controlled—yes, and used. It was folly to be jealous of him—as well be jealous of a drunkard or a fool. The man had no being except in imagination. Whatever he had done was no more real than the drama in a play—the fellow was probably acting out a scene in the novel he was about to write. It would be giving him undue importance to think of it as something a real man had done. Genius was as valuable and as unpredictable, perhaps as ungovernable, as the waves of the sea.

Upon this slow rationalizing he heard his door open softly and his daughter Mary come stealing in. It troubled him sometimes that she moved so stilly, as though her vitality were not enough for the speed and noise of childhood. Yet she looked healthy enough as she stood there in the door in her little white muslin frock. She was smiling and he saw the dimples in her cheeks, the gift her mother had given her. Margaret's dimples, born again!

"Shall I come in, Papa?"

"Please do, darling—though I haven't washed yet."

"I won't stay."

She walked softly across the floor, almost tiptoe, and leaned against him. When he put his arm around her she rested her head upon his shoulder and he smelled the clean freshness of her dark hair.

"Had a good day, dear?"

"Yes—almost."

"Why only almost?"

"Papa, do you like Mr. Harrow?"

He evaded this. "Mamma says he was here to lunch."

"Yes. He likes me very much."

"Did he say so?"

"Yes."

He was furious again with Lewis Harrow. This daughter of his! He held her close. "We all like you—love you, you know."

"I know." She sighed and he forbore to ask the cause for it. It was so much easier not to ask. He felt her lips at his ear. "Papa."

"Yes?"

"But he likes me better than he does anybody else."

"Did he say that?"

"Yes."

"Then he told a lie!" These words escaped him forcibly.

She actually drooped. "Did he, Papa?"

"Yes! And it was very wrong for him to talk like that to you, Mary. Mamma didn't like it. She told me about it. And you must forget what he said. Little girls get all the love they need from their parents. You must think about school now, you know, and your friends—Millicent Bascom and Josephine Hill. They're very nice girls. And in two years or so you may have dancing lessons and then you will have other friends, too—boys of your own age."

He was taking it far too seriously, he told himself. He was making everything worse, deepening the very impressions which he hoped to erase. He rose. "Now run along, Mary. I must get ready for dinner."

She went out of the room then, her step lingering, and he went into the bathroom and scrubbed his hands with unnecessary vigor.

That, he might have thought, was the end of it. The dinner passed as usual. He could always be sure of a good meal at night, a dish or two that Margaret had planned and to which she had given some touch of her own. Tonight it was veal, baked in French fashion with wine and herbs, and for dessert a blueberry pie. He was growing to be something of a connoisseur in food, for his appetite was variable and he ate better if he considered flavor and texture. Tonight his awareness of everything was sharp. He saw himself at the head of his own table and unconsciously he straightened his spare tall frame as he looked at Margaret. She had put on a gown of some thin silver-gray stuff, so old he had almost forgotten—or else it was new.

"Is that a new dress?" he asked.

"You should be ashamed, Ned," she replied. "It was part of my trousseau. I wore it in New Orleans, don't you remember? Years ago!"

"I remember only a glorious haze," he said smiling.

"I tried it on for fun—just to see if I could wear it. I believe I'm actually a little thinner than I was then."

He kept looking at her after that, knowing that the girl Margaret had no beauty to compare to this, his wife's.

And from them had come these children. They sat one on either side of the table, quiet at the end of the day. Even Tommy ate in phlegmatic silence. He was a hearty eater, and some day he would be a big ungainly man like old Thomas. But Mary was delicate, and in spite of her prettiness there was something about her which reminded him of his sister.

"Seen Louise lately?" he asked Margaret.

Mary lifted her head. "She was cross with me today, Papa—a little—because I was late in the afternoon for school."

"Did you tell her why?" he asked.

"Yes, I said Mr. Harrow was here with us for lunch and then she got cross—only a little. She said it was no excuse."

"It wasn't, I suppose."

"He kept talking," Margaret said vaguely.

"We ought to have Louise over," he said. "Maybe we could have her sometime with Harrow. It would give her something special. We never do anything for Louise."

Margaret replied, "Of course. Let's remember. Only why must we have him again?"

She made her query with raised and quivering eyebrows, as though laughter waited, and he gave her a steady look. "Think of it as business."

Tommy shifted his attention from a second piece of pie. "I don't like Mr. Harrow," he said in his large deep voice. "When he grabs me he holds too hard. It hurts."

"Hit him in the snoot," Edward said suddenly.

His children looked at him in amazement and then broke into joyful laughter. So seldom was their father funny! Their laughter restored wholesomeness to the evening and Edward in the secrecy of his inner being ridiculed his jealousy.

The small house of Haslatt and Sons was shaken to its roots. A tornado had seized it, bringing life, giving growth, forcing heat and light and a spasm of wind. Again and again Edward Haslatt wished that he had never met Lewis Harrow, that the fellow had stayed in France after the war, that he had been lost in New York, almost that he had strayed into the portals of some other publishing house rather than have come to the quiet town of Chedbury to lay hold upon his own budding business. The swelling advance sales of Harrow's new book marched across the country like a triumphant beast. A vanguard of rumor preceded the three young salesmen whom Edward hired and put into the charge of Baynes with every caution against extravagance. Caution was forgotten. The eagerness of booksellers infected Baynes and spread to the salesmen and they ran hither and thither, praising a book none of them had yet read, that no one had seen except Harrow, and he carelessly writing against time declared that it might or might not be finished by late winter.

"It must be finished," Edward said sternly. "I've gambled everything I have on that book, Lewis," and knew as he spoke that there was no promise to be had out of him.

Harrow had been engrossed in the building of a squat stormproof house on Granite. The walls stood under a wide overhanging roof, and from a distance looked like a bird that had paused to brood upon the mountain. Harrow was amused by the likeness and enhanced it by adding feathery trellises to the wings and a thick short tower to the gate. He called his house The Eagle and on Sundays young people from Chedbury climbed up to see it. He had begun to live in it long before it was finished, and it pleased him to look from the windows and see persons approaching. He rushed out and brought them in, showed them through the low rooms, few in number but huge in size, the windows enormous and set so that he could see for miles when he chose to look out of them. The house stood solidly clawing the ground with its deep foundations, and though the winds roared, it was impervious. Harrow had insisted on walls eighteen inches thick, as he had seen them in the fortresses of Europe. There was neither cellar nor second floor and one room led into another in a semicircle curving toward the mountain.

To Edward the house was astonishing and hideous and he told Margaret what he thought.

"Certainly it is not the house for a family," she replied, "but then I don't think Lewis wants a family. I'm not sure he even wants a wife."

By now Harrow was so much his property that Edward did not inquire how it was that she knew this about him. Women had instinct, of course, and of instinct Margaret had her full share. His jealousy of the spring had passed or perhaps had only been submerged in the rush of increasing business. The revenge that he had feared from Chedbury after the evening in the courthouse had never been taken. Chedbury had bristled, there had been some quiet weeping by Mrs. Walters, and Mrs. Croft was permanently angry. Henry Croft had died ten years ago, and she had been happier without him, as everybody knew, and yet she had not been able to keep from thinking of him for weeks after Lewis Harrow had brought him to life again, bringing back to her the memory of a temper vicious and yet somehow only the dark side of a glittering shield.

Chedbury had grown quiet again, and people watched Harrow come and go up Granite Mountain. However they felt about him, he had his right to be among them, because he had been a child there, a queer cross-grained hungry monolith of a boy whom they had seen without notice when he had lugged baskets in and out of their kitchens; whom now, though they found him repulsive, they respected reluctantly. The weekly paper gave him no notice, and Chuck Williams, the editor, took pride in reading his name in gossip columns of city papers and literary essays in magazines and then in continuing to take no notice. Even when the new book came out, he might take no notice.

In the midst of all this Edward was wakened at two o'clock one morning by the clangor of the telephone in the hall. He rose at once and lifted the receiver and heard his mother's distracted voice.

"Edward, your father's been taken very sick."

"What is it, Mother?"

"He can't speak to me—" Her voice cracked into a sob.

"Have you called the doctor?"

"No. I didn't know what to do."

"I'll call him and then be right up."

He put up the telephone and went softly into Margaret's room. She lay high on her pillows, her long hair braided over her shoulder, her eyes closed in sleep. Tired as he was every night, it had been a long time since he had seen her asleep, and shielding her face from the flashlight he used at night, he was struck with the thinness of her cheeks. He was so close to her and yet somehow they had made no true communication for a long time. He was too busy—so busy that he had neglected to keep his promise to her, made when she said she would marry him. He had let their marriage become secondary to him. That was the problem of a man's life —how to excel in his work and still keep the woman close. Yet how he loved her!

These thoughts, scarcely more than feelings, came in the instant to the surface of his mind and he pushed them down again. He would have to do something about it, but it could not be now. He decided not to wake her, and still treading softly he went out and closed the door.

A few minutes later, having called Dr. Wynne and dressed himself, he was in his car on his way to his father. He had persuaded himself into buying the car a few weeks earlier, on the excuse that he needed it for business.

"Why don't you just say you want it?" Margaret had asked.

He had looked at her half sheepishly. "Seems extravagant, doesn't it?"

"I don't see why," she had replied. "Nothing is extravagant if you can pay for it."

Actually he had finally decided to buy it when he saw Tom Seaton running around in a small roadster on God knew what business. If Tom could buy a car, surely he with his sound progress could do so. He had spent his spare time for a week learning to run it and now it submitted to him pleasantly and increased his sense of power. An occasion such as this, he argued, when his father was taken suddenly ill, justified a car.

He spent the last few minutes thinking about his father. With remorse he reminded himself that he had had no time for months to think about him. The old man had grown increasingly quiet in the office and for days past Edward scarcely remembered seeing him beyond a hasty greeting in the morning. Baynes had run up from New York once or twice every week to confer, and while at first their father had come in to sit with them, in the last fortnight he had not, and they had not noticed, or at least had not spoken of it. Strange how a man's parents, who had been the center of his existence, the spoke upon which the wheel of his life turned, moved out of the center into the periphery and so, he supposed, away forever.

With a sense of impending and inescapable loss, he hastened out of his car and into the house. No one met him and he went straight upstairs to his father's room and opened the door. His father lay on his back in the big double bed where his parents had slept together all these years and his mother sat beside the bed in a small rocking chair tilted forward so that she leaned upon the covers, holding the pale stiff hand. The sound of his father's hard quick breathing filled the room with an angry pulse of sound. The doctor had not yet come.

"Oh, Edward," his mother moaned.

He went near the bed. "When did this happen, Mother?"

"I don't know. I was asleep and then I woke up and felt him in the middle of the bed—he always has taken the middle of the bed—and I told him to move over, just as I do every night. He always does, but tonight he didn't. I gave him a push—just a little one—and felt him so queer and heavy that I put on the light and this is the way he was. He can't even speak to me. Oh, Edward, you don't think—"

"Of course not." He sat down on the bed and looked at his father. Some sort of dreadful subterranean force was moving in that patient lean frame. The left side of his father's face was dragged down, and a drool of saliva crept over his chin.

Edward took his own handkerchief and wiped it away. "The doctor will be here in a minute."

"He's been worrying too much," his mother moaned. "Every night he came home scared to death of what you boys are doing at the office. You shouldn't have borrowed money on the printing shop, Edward. That really belongs to him."

He had a glimpse in his mother's haggard face, made strange by the gray hair that hung loose against her cheeks, of what it meant to grow old. The old ceased to create. They grew afraid of all change, knowing the monstrous change ahead. They wanted no more to build, but only to shelter themselves. Then his own youth asserted itself. "I'm responsible, Mother," he said with an impatience which shamed him but which he could not help. "I wish Father would stop worrying."

The doorbell rang and without waiting for his mother to reply he hastened downstairs to meet the doctor.

"Hello, Ed," the young doctor said. He was still too young to show sleepless nights and long hours. His predecessor, Dr. Sulley, who had been young with Dr. Hart, the old minister, had died the year before in Florida, that land of rest and joy to which he had sent so many patients, and to which he had never found time to go until he was ready to die. Wynne had taken up the practice and was now engaged in a struggle to make his patients come to his office instead of demanding that he got to see them.

"Who does he think he is?" Chedbury growled, forgetting that its people had killed the old doctor.

"What's happened?" the new doctor asked, following Edward up the stairs.

"I'm afraid to guess," Edward said.

They went into the room together and within a minute the doctor had made his quick examination.

"Your mother had better go out and rest while I finish," he told Edward. Without a word she rose, and left the room. The old man she had loved and tended for so many years had now become a male patient and she was a stranger to him. They heard her begin to sob in the hall. The doctor was a kind man. "Better go with her," he said to Edward. "But come back in a minute."

He went out then and putting his arm about his mother's shoulders he patted her, not knowing how to comfort her. Her shoulder felt unfamiliar. Not since he was a child had he touched her and then he had lain his head upon her breast. She had been closer to him than any living creature and now she was an old woman, separated from himself by distances, unspoken and unspeakable. But he had the wisdom to know that she must do something for relief.

"If it isn't asking too much, Mother, I wish you would make us all some coffee. I'm sure Wynne would be glad of it and so would I."

She turned obediently to the stairs and he went back into the bedroom.

"Obviously a stroke," Wynne said. "A pretty bad one, I'm afraid. I'd better send a nurse. It's too much for your mother to manage. I wish Chedbury had a hospital. He can't stand the trip to Boston."

"I was afraid of a stroke," Edward murmured. His father's thin face was congested with purple blood and now his left side was very much drawn.

"I've given him something," Wynne said. "Where's the telephone?"

"In the hall," Edward replied.

He sat down in the chair where his mother had been and gazed at his father. Strange and terrifying to think that he might never hear his father speak again! Now that it was possible he wished that he had taken time in these last months to listen to his father's voice. Yet he could not have acted otherwise than he had done. His opportunity had come to him, as in another time his father's had come, and he had been compelled to seize it. Had he yielded to his father's fears, had he let Harrow go elsewhere, he might have subsided into a mere printer again, running a small local business. As it was, he had begun to have tentacles over the whole world. Only yesterday Ben Ashton, the postman, had with some pride tossed upon his desk letters from England and France. "Looks like you're gettin' to be a somebuddy, Ed," he had cackled. It was true. Harrow had ceased to be a human being; he had become a most valuable property.

This was the inescapable tragedy of life, then, that the generations withdrew from each other, and as he felt the strange pain of separation somewhere deep in his vitals, he loved his father with sudden anguish. He put out his hands and enclosed within them his father's stiff cool hand.

A week later, after days made hideous by the demands of the engine he had set in motion to sell Harrow's new book, a machine which he could neither stop nor deny in its exorbitant demand upon his time, a week during which he worked day and night, rushing between the office and his father's bedside, in which he did not try to go home, in which he saw Margaret only in passing and then at his parents' house with his mother, he and Louise and Baynes gathered hastily at what was to be a deathbed.

His mother was in the rocking chair again, where she had sat almost continuously during the week. She had got up to wash, to put on a clean dress, to eat something when Margaret called. But she would not go unless Louise took her place. Louise had found a substitute teacher and had not left the house for three days. Baynes had come from New York, leaving Sandra to fill his engagements. When the nurse came out of the silent room to call them in, Edward had paused for a moment with Margaret. They were in his old bedroom, she resting upon his bed and he in the green rep armchair that had been his Christmas present the year he was fifteen.

He had risen at the sight of the nurse and when she had gone away quickly, he had turned to Margaret, his heart beating with strange and terrible fear. She had looked at him from the pillow, and he saw that she did not want to come with him.

"I have never seen anybody die," she said in a tight frightened voice.

"Neither have I," he replied.

"Ned—I don't want to be there."

He left her without a word and had not reached the hall before he felt her hands clasping his arm.

"Ned, don't hate me."

"Of course not—only you mustn't delay me now."

Her hands dropped from his arm and he hastened into his father's room, his heart still beating hard with the strange new fear, an animal fear, he thought, as he took his place beside the bed. The presence of the nurse made them all feel strange. They were not alone together. He moved to his mother and knelt down and put his arm about her shoulder, but she did not heed him. All her being was concentrated on the dying man whom she had loved and scolded and cared for and resented and still loved in the cycle of their married life. Baynes looked pale and grave and Louise was crying and the nurse waited quietly for familiar death. It came in a moment, without struggle but with a raucous rattle and choking. Mark Haslatt was dead.

Edward bowed his head on the bed and felt his mother's arms go round his shoulder. He could not think or feel. Then with sudden clarity something occurred to him—"It'll have to be only Haslatt Brothers now," and with these unspoken words he was able to perceive his loss.

Yet life resumed its sway. Within a pitifully few days he had consigned to earth the body of his father and he knew himself the master of his own existence. Though he had not for years taken with sense of obligation anything that his father said, yet that gray shape pervading his days had asserted its claim. Now all claim was gone and memory alone could go to work, unhampered by the living presence, to reconstruct the harassed, silent, and yet kindly man who had been his father. To his father he owed the sound foundation of his business and the principles of industry and caution to which with all his present preoccupation he still held. Prudence he had inherited from his father, and with it he wielded power over Baynes and Sandra, who had none. With prudence, too, he dealt with Lewis Harrow, compelling him to finish his book before the day when he planned formally to open his house by a great party that was to include everybody in Chedbury. "Open house for three days," Harrow declared lavishly, "day and night," he added. "Anybody can come any time."

Harrow had been repulsively pleased at the death of Mark Haslatt. "The sere and yellow leaf," he had called him with scant concealment from Edward and none at all from Baynes. Now that he was dead, Harrow was decent enough not to mention the old man, and he renewed his demands upon Haslatt Brothers, asking for outrageous advances and guarantees of advertisements. Now that his father was gone, Edward found himself renewing his prudence, so that actually the voice of his father was stronger in him than it had been in life.

Hearing this voice he met Harrow firmly one day the next winter. "The Eagle has cost me some odd thousands more than I expected," Harrow came in to announce. Arrogant with his own value he had taken on the habit of entering Edward's office unannounced. This Jane had at first forbidden, but doing battle twice or thrice with Harrow's unchecked tongue, which could return at any hint of enmity to his boyhood rudeness, she now paid him no heed. Some time or other, she reasoned, Edward would have enough of the fellow. At night kneeling by her bed in her old-fashioned cotton nightgown, her feet cold upon the bare floor of her virginal room, she prayed for the time to come soon.

Edward looked up from his desk, his dark eyes cold. "Well?"

"I'd like a couple of thousand advance, Ed."

"You've had a couple of thousand," Edward replied, busy with papers.

Harrow sat down. "Come now, Ed—"

"I'm here."

"You know you stand to get rich off me."

"If I ever get your book."

"It's nearly done, I tell you."

"I haven't seen a page of it."

"God, what's the matter with you? I thought there'd be some life in this firm when the old man went."

"Plenty of life," Edward said. He did not look at Harrow.

"Well," Harrow cried with high impatience, "what you want me to do?"

"Finish your book."

There was a long pause in which Edward read carefully a proposed contract for Spanish rights in the book he had not seen.

"Is that final?" Harrow demanded.

"Wholly," Edward replied.

Harrow bounced from his chair and tore from the room. Two weeks later, during which time no one saw him, he came down Granite Mountain carrying a great bundle wrapped in brown paper. He threw it upon Edward's desk. "Here it is," he shouted. "Now cough up, will you?"

"You've upset the ink," Edward said. He touched a bell and Jane came to the door, looking grim. "Bring a cloth, Jane," he said.

She returned with the same grim look and mopped up the ink. Only when she had gone did Edward allow himself to turn to Harrow.

"Complete?" he asked.

"Not a page missing," Harrow declared. "Where's my two thousand dollars?"

Edward rejected prudence and to get rid of the man that he might devour the book, he drew a checkbook from the drawer of his desk and knowing it madness he made it out for two thousand dollars. His balance was dangerously low, and if that for which he had gambled escaped him, he would have to mortgage his very home. For the first time he was glad that his father was dead.

All afternoon, the great heap of brown paper stood on the end of his desk. He did not dare to begin to read it here. He would not read it until tonight when the children were in bed and he and Margaret were alone. The dread of disappointment dried his very blood. He drank again and again from the water jug on the window and in half an hour was thirsty again. There was no one to keep him from glancing at the first pages and yet he would not have done so for any amount of money. How absurd, he told himself, to be in the power of one man and such a man as Harrow! He had no idea when he thought of publishing books that it would be a business so racking, so dangerous, so devastating. He prayed only that the book might be clearly good or bad. Then he could make his decision. If it were mildly good and not too bad the agony of the present would stretch into months and even years. Let it be good or bad! He was ashamed as a decent Christian to address God with so personal a plea, surely petty in view of the enormous problems now in the world after the war, and yet in his heart he did murmur these words. Immediately they became ridiculous since in fact the book was already finished, it was what it would be, and not even God could do anything about it. He set himself to work doggedly until six o'clock as usual, pausing only to call Baynes in New York by telephone.

"Baynes, that you? I just wanted to say that Harrow has handed in the manuscript. I'm reading it tonight."

Baynes gave a cry of anguish. "Call me at dawn, will you?"

"No, I won't. But I ought to have some sort of notion tomorrow morning when I come to the office."

"I shan't sleep a wink," Baynes declared.

"Maybe I won't, either," Edward replied and hung up.

It had taken all his self-control not to hurry the evening for the children. With rigorous discipline he had compelled himself to conversation through dinner, to ten minutes of nursery rhymes for Sandy and to the reading aloud of *The Swiss Family Robinson,* which he had undertaken as part of the winter's reading for Mary and Tommy. He had said to Margaret in what he hoped was his usual voice, "I shall be up late tonight—Harrow brought me his complete manuscript today."

Interminably the evening wore on, the children were prepared for bed, and he went up to hear their prayers. A vague sense of hypocrisy always troubled him when he saw their innocent faith. He no longer prayed in exact words, and yet he felt that religion was decent and right, an essential in an honest man's life, however expressed. Prayer was a part of religion, he reasoned, and children should be taught its use, without being promised definite returns. Tonight he tried gently to persuade Mary not to pray for a bicycle, since he had no idea of buying it for her. He did not like to see women cycle. It thickened their legs and destroyed their delicacy. When Tommy prayed for an air rifle for his birthday, however, he considered whether the boy was big enough for it and decided that he was. Some discrepancy between his decisions for his daughter and for his son disturbed him, until it struck him that perhaps God Himself was thus compelled to decide between His asking children. For some the gift was unwise; for others, it was possible. This might be the Reason behind the Inscrutable Wisdom.

The children were in bed at last, and with the pleasant comfort of knowing that he was a good father Edward went into his room and changed to his old blue dressing robe. When he went downstairs Margaret was already sitting by the fire in her favorite red velvet chair. She was making lace on a small frame, a task which she learned as a young girl one summer in France and which she declared was soothing to the nerves. He appreciated invariably the picture that she made, and he smiled at her as he drew up a side table and prepared for the hours ahead.

"Don't you want to read Lew's manuscript, too?" he inquired.

Margaret did not look up. "No, thank you, Ned. I'll wait until the book is printed." This she said with lack of interest which, in his eagerness, he did not notice.

He went into the hall and brought back the enormous parcel, and putting it on the floor at his feet he began to unwrap it, as he sat in his own chair opposite her. Between them the wood fire burned pleasantly under the marble mantelpiece. Looking up to meet Margaret's eyes, he found she had not lifted them from her lace.

"Next to various moments with you, my dear," he said, trying not to seem excited, "I suppose this is the most exciting moment of my life."

"Perhaps it is even the most exciting," she answered.

There was something of an edge in her voice which at another time he might have explored, but tonight he could not bear to be diverted.

"You know better than that," he retorted, and immediately he lifted the first chapters from the stack between his feet and began to read.

The scene was Chedbury. Harrow had used the very name. A scrawled note at the top of the first page said, "Call the town anything you like, in printing, but I had to write it what it is."

The book began with a small wretched boy in a meager house on the fringe of the prosperous little town, a boy whose father was a drunkard and whose mother was a laundress. Harrow had determined to write his life out, not only as it was, but in all its ramifications in a society that did not care how he lived and not too much whether he died, except that the townsfolk were reluctant to pay for too many paupers' funerals. Edward plunged into a Chedbury he had never known.

At eleven o'clock Margaret put her lace frame away into a rosewood sewing cabinet.

He looked up reluctantly. "Going to bed?"

"Yes, Ned."

She came over to him and bending she kissed his forehead. His hands were full of pages, and he could only throw back his head. "Kiss me properly, Margaret," he demanded.

She stooped again and kissed him on the lips. "When are you coming up, Ned?"

"I don't know, dear. I think I'll stay by this as long as I can."

"Why must you?"

"I've gambled too much and I must know if I'll win."

She looked down at him half wistfully, and he looked up at her, aware again of something not said between them, and yet again he could not bear to be drawn from the urgency of what he wanted to do.

"Good night, my love," he said.

"Good night, Ned," she replied.

For a moment he heard her step slowly mounting the stairs, and then he forgot her. He was back in Lewis Harrow's world again, a world which in strange subterranean fashion was also his own.

Hours later he put down the last page silently. He had finished the book. He had no doubts and yet he was full of doubt. He had gambled and he had won. Lewis Harrow had written a great book. Haslatt Brothers could build upon a foundation as solid as Granite Mountain itself. Money would continue to flow from the book for Harrow as long as he lived, and for Edward and his family as well. Upon the profits of this treasure Edward foresaw the delight of publishing other books which he might like but which could not possibly pay—a book, for example, upon the varieties of printing types, their history, and their use, a book for the makers of books and not for the writers.

This was his first thought when he had laid down that last page. The fire on his hearth was a heap of ashes, and every voice in his house was stilled in sleep. He alone was awake and knowing, his exhausted mind alive with unnatural awareness. He leaned back in his chair and closed his eyes. The book was cruel, of course. It spared nothing and no one—not even the lean ferocious boy who had grown up, in Harrow's imagination, to be a man greatly rich through the making of steel. Why had he chosen steel? The man loved steel for its purity and its hardness. Harrow had put some love of his own into the symbol. But there were pages of human love, and these were the pages that frightened Edward. The variety was exciting and shameful, and then in the end came one so tender and so exquisite that it did not seem Harrow could know such love. He began to be afraid of the man. Ribaldry and physical lust he took for granted in him, but where had he got this power for tender worship of a woman remote to him?

Now deep doubt came flooding darkly into Edward's solitary mind. There was no possibility of concealment. He recognized the truth too well. The woman who had called forth this sweetness out of a man powerful and crude was one fashioned into an image he well knew, and it was the image of his own wife.

Some time later, having fumbled the pages together and tied the brown paper parcel as it had been, he got up and put out the lights and went upstairs. On all other nights he was used to stealing into Margaret's room and at least looking at her before he slept. But tonight he did not go in. The door between was ajar as she had left it, and he closed it noiselessly and prepared for bed. He saw from the small clock on his table that it was nearly five o'clock, and his blood was beating in his veins with weariness. He would not be able to sleep, he told himself. Yet his mind was unable to think. He lay numb under the covers and felt the night wind blow upon him from the open window. Then the numbness penetrated him like a drug, and postponing his fears, he slept in spite of himself.

He woke late in the morning. The sun shone whitely into his south window and he saw a rim of snow. In the night then it had snowed. There was a heap of snow upon the window sill. He started up and looked at his watch—nine o'clock. The house was silent about him. The children were already at school, and Margaret must have breakfasted. He heard Sandy's voice now upon the stairs and Margaret's hush.

Then he remembered. He lay back, quite still. Harrow had had the audacity to use the very woman Margaret was, her soft dark hair, her sea-blue eyes, her slenderness and height, even the shape of her hands and her high-arched feet. He had dared to imagine the shape of her breasts, her waist, her thighs.

Intolerable doubt! Edward rose from his bed and stirred with unusual noisiness about his room.

"Papa got up!" he heard his little daughter's voice cry out, and a moment later Margaret tapped upon the door and came in. He was shaving and he kissed her lightly.

"You should have waked me," he grumbled.

"I wouldn't have done it for money," she retorted. "You look a ghost, Ned."

"I'm all right."

He continued to scrape his rather long chin while she stood waiting. When he did not speak she could refrain no more.

"How was the book?"

"Absolutely first rate."

"Was it?"

"Yes."

"Then, Ned—"

"Yes?"

"What's the matter with you?"

"Nothing. Well, maybe—I guess he's taken the hide off some of us Chedbury folk, and I'm worried—a little."

"Oh, he's stupid!"

"No, he isn't—he's too smart. Anybody stupid would have changed things so no one would know. He's so smart he's dared say all he wanted to say."

"I don't think I'm going to read it."

"You'll have to someday, Margaret."

She looked at him curiously, and he fancied a reflection of his own doubt in her watching eyes. When their eyes met and clung it was she who looked away. "Don't worry, Ned. And come down—your breakfast is waiting."

She went away with her brisk wifely step, so much the woman he had known since the day of his marriage that he felt assuaged. Then the damnable quality of Harrow's book occurred to him again. There the woman's husband, who had possessed her so long, did not know her at all. The man did not know, dull fellow, that worship was his wife's due, and that in such worship he would have found his own delight. Edward longed upon a strange and sudden impulse to rush downstairs and find Margaret wherever she was and cry out to her, crushed in his arms, "There is no one who could possibly love you as I do!" His natural shyness moved to restrain such monstrous revelation. She would look surprised, she would open her eyes wide. She might even laugh.

He went on with his dressing, more than a little angry at his predicament. Here on a morning when he should be filled only with relief and satisfaction at his own good fortune, when he should have been distracted by nothing that could check his energy, he felt depressed and doubtful. He distrusted his imagination, disturbed by the workings of something so insubstantial as Lewis Harrow's own. What matter if the fellow was attracted to Margaret? Men could be thus attracted to a delicately bred woman, especially lawless lowbred fellows, and it did not mean that the woman even knew it. He was insulting her by his doubts. It would be only decent to keep them to himself, certainly for the present.

Comforted by the righteousness of delay, he chose a somber gray tie that did not lighten in the least his dark suit, and feeling arrayed to fit his mood he went downstairs and ate his morning meal. Margaret sat in her place, and though she had eaten, she poured his coffee and supervised the prattle and play of Sandy, who had built some blocks into a structure in the corner. The uniformity of his outward surroundings was deeply comforting. The day was like any other day, and that was what he wanted. He looked at Margaret and she smiled. Certainly she did not know what Harrow had done, and he would not tell her.

An hour later he was further comforted by the everyday appearance of his office. Jane was accustomedly cross when he came in late. "I don't know when you're going to get your letters done," she remarked when he had sat down in his swivel desk chair. The snow was melting and dripping down the windowpanes, and he could hear the whir of machinery as he opened the door.

"I want to talk to Baynes first," he said. "The letters will have to wait."

The telephone operator was in a good mood, the hour fortunate, and in a very few moments he was calling through to New York.

"That you, Baynes?"

"Yes."

"Well, aren't you going to ask me?"

"No. Aren't you going to tell me?"

Edward laughed. He had not the heart to continue the cruelty of teasing his younger brother. "Well, all we wanted it to be—it is."

"You mean—"

"Yes, I do. He's done something even bigger than the first one."

"Oh, holy cats!"

"It's too long, but I don't know how to shorten it by a word. There is a scene or two, an episode, I could take out altogether."

His smoldering doubt suddenly leaped into suggestion. Why should he not complain of the length to Harrow and insist that the pages—he could remember them even now—the pages between four hundred and twenty-five and five hundred be eliminated? After all, the woman had come in at the very end of the book unheralded except for the desire that had sought her around the world. He spoke to Baynes again.

"Yes, I think I may insist on a few cuts—only one of any importance. But there's nothing to hold us up. I'll want to see the artist myself for the jacket drawing. It ought to be a scene—something like the one I am looking at this very minute out of my office window, the green sloping up to the church and the Seaton house in the foreground, the firehouse, of course, and the store, maybe a snow scene. By the way, we had snow last night—very soft. We'll have to work hard and fast now, Baynes."

"Sandra thinks we ought to have a big dinner on the day of publication. Get all the critics together and so on."

"Whatever you like."

"You mean that?" Baynes demanded with excitement.

"For once, yes."

He hung up the receiver and sat for a moment staring upon the scene he was planning for the jacket. He ought to call Harrow, but there was no telephone to The Eagle. Harrow did not want one. There was nothing to do but wait until the fellow came down the mountain.

In a mood of arrested doubt and of genuine enjoyment he went into the printing shop. The presses rolling off the sheets of the books he had chosen for his firm gave him a pleasant sense of power. He, Edward Haslatt, here in his quiet, purposely old-fashioned office in a small town in an unimportant region of his country, could entice to himself living, thinking people from anywhere in the world, whose minds flamed and exploded into creation.

He had been proud to receive some weeks ago a thin manuscript of poems from a young man in a valley of the Cotswolds. A year ago he would not have dared to publish so risky a venture, but thanks to Lewis Harrow, he had accepted the poems as soon as he had read them and perceived their elements of emotion and pride. He paused beside the press, which was being run by John Carosi, and watched the wide margins, the thick cream paper imprinted in short black lines. He had chosen his latest text type, Poliphus, thick and warm, carrying the illusion of an ancient art. Was it, he pondered, suitable for the young poet? But like so many young, the lines of this poet, in spite of their originality, had echoed. Edward had decided upon the book, not so much for what it was as for the implications of feeling and imagination which gave promise of future richness in the talent.

"Do you ever read any of the sheets you print?" he asked.

Carosi looked at him, surprised. Edward Haslatt did not often speak to the men he employed.

"I don't," he said curtly. "If I did, I couldn't tend the machine. Like as not the ink would be runny."

He bent his head, and Edward went on, pleased enough. He was printing books that were simple, too simple, perhaps, to be called fine. Yet there was elegance in their simplicity, and with elegance came good style. He pondered as he went back to his desk the answer that had been given him. For machines he himself cared nothing. He did not understand them. Cogs and wheels, he called them, and they were blind slaves formed only to give shape and permanence to the thoughts of men. He had grown far beyond his father, who had, he remembered, an actual tenderness for the machines he had bought with such careful economy. What was printed by them Mark Haslatt scarcely cared—advertisements, announcements of marriage and death, bills of sale, posters, and notices. Edward had inherited something from him, but it was fulfilled by a quality entirely his own. Machines were no more than means.

So ruminating, at ease because he had won, Edward circumvented the core of his inner unease. But when he opened the door to his office he felt a shock. Lewis Harrow sat in the swivel chair, his feet on the desk, and he was roaring with laughter into the telephone. He shouted as Edward came in, "I'll be there—to celebrate either my victory or my defeat. Here comes God! . . . Well," he said, and shambled to his feet.

"Don't get up," Edward said with acid courtesy.

"I had pins in my seat while I sat there," Harrow retorted. He dropped into the chair across the desk. "Out with it, Ed. Do you like my book?"

"How can I help it?" Edward asked. "You know as well as I do what you have done. It is wonderful and terrible. But it's too long."

"Now if you start meddling," Harrow began violently.

Edward held up his hand. "I want it seventy-five pages shorter."

Harrow leaped to his feet. "Give me the manuscript!"

"What for?"

"I'll take it to New York."

"Sit down, you fool," Edward said with patience. "I want you to take out the part about that last woman."

Harrow sat down, snarling. "You publish it as it is or you shan't have it."

"She doesn't add anything," Edward said stubbornly. "You had the book all written without her, and then you dragged her in."

Harrow groaned aloud. "If you'd just forget you aren't the author—" He leaned forward, his square blocked face red with swift anger. "Look here, Ed. Can't you see that it's implied—"

"What's implied?" Edward asked grimly.

"That she's changed his life by being inaccessible."

"Oh, she's inaccessible, is she?"

"Sure she is."

Against his better judgment, goaded by his living jealousy, Edward said, "How does he know what her body looks like?"

Harrow refused to accept the knowledge of what was going on in Edward's mind. "Don't you see that my man knows what women are? Out of the dozen and more women he's lived with, slept with, bought, loved—hasn't he learned something? Given a height, a shape, a narrow hand, flying black hair, blue eyes, a high-arched foot—can't he imagine?"

"It's obscene," Edward blurted.

There was a tight silence, then Harrow spoke. "You're obscene."

The silence fell again. Edward stared down at a little white elephant upon his desk, a desk toy Thomas Seaton had given him one Christmas, ivory weighted with lead.

"What's more," Harrow said suddenly, "you don't deserve her. Someday I shall tell her so."

He rose, flung on his shapeless hat, and strode out of the room.

And with him went all the joy of the great day. Edward sat motionless, leaning upon his desk, his hand shading his eyes. He could not endure the torment of his jealousy. It boiled up in him and he leaped to his feet and strode after Harrow and catching him in the outer hall he held him by the shoulder.

"Come back here and tell me what you mean! If it's what I think, you can take your filthy book with you."

He would have welcomed anger in return, so intolerable was his fury. Instead Harrow's strange tawny eyes were remote and calm.

"Sure I'll come back," he said. His voice showed only mild interest.

In the office again, however, the door closed, he looked at Edward with greedy curiosity. "I've never seen you angry before, Ed—it's quite a sight. A quiet man can really put on a show."

"It's not show." A chill came over him as he answered Harrow. He always shivered with cold when his anger drained away. He tried to moisten his lips but his mouth was dry.

"No, I see it isn't." Harrow's voice was musing. He sighed. "How I hate real life!"

Edward did not answer this. He found his pipe in his pocket and lit it, and looking up, saw that Harrow perceived that his hands were trembling.

"Men like you, Ed," Harrow said, "live only in real life. Men like me only use you, and your wives and your children, to write about real life."

"You'd better leave us alone."

"I might be of use to you, though, if you'll accept that of me." Harrow was stubbornly casual.

"Your usefulness is limited to business," Edward retorted and then winced at the pedantry of his words. Why could he not invest his voice with that silver-edged carelessness which sharpened the dullest words? He could not. He was solid, plodding maybe, but without veneer.

Harrow laughed and slapped the desk with his palms. "Ed, will you hear something from me?"

"Maybe."

"Maybe is must, then! You're a fool—that's first."

Edward, sitting now behind the desk, pulled hard on his pipe in lieu of answer. Harrow leaned on his elbows. "Second, if you'll let me go on, your wife, though beautiful, is impregnable. You don't deserve such luck."

"I'd rather you didn't speak of her."

"Don't be such a fool, Ed! I will speak of her, do you hear?"

Harrow's face, so near his across the desk, grew harsh. It was an ugly face, heavy featured, dark, lit only by light eyes and white teeth and changing expression. Eyes and teeth gleamed at him now.

"Of course I'd have been glad to win her away from you. What have you done to deserve her? Can you even appreciate what she is? I doubt it!"

"Stop!" His voice roared at Harrow, strange in his own ears. "You haven't the least idea of the—the relationship between my—my wife and myself. You—you—it takes years to build what we have—and a sort of devotion that you have no notion of."

He was on his feet, shouting at Harrow. His pipe dropped to the floor and a coal of tobacco fell on the carpet and began to burn a hole. He stamped on it and looking down for the moment he heard Harrow laugh softly.

"Don't I know it, man?" Harrow's voice came softly over the desk. "That's why she's impregnable. With all your manifold faults, every one of which you may be sure she sees, she knows what she has and she'll never let herself escape from it. She's accepted the prison of your love."

"It's not a prison."

"Sometimes it is," Harrow insisted. "But most of the time it's a walled garden, and every day she throws away the key to the gate, so she'll never yield to temptations."

"Is she ever—" He could not bring out the word.

"Tempted?" Harrow's voice was delicately cheerful. "Of course she is. Who isn't?"

"I'm not."

"That's the wall around the garden. She knows you, Ed. Take heart from that. It isn't every man who can be known through and through and have his wife value him the more."

A strange reverence crept into Harrow's bantering. "Why, Ed, you're a fool not to live your life in joy. You do possess your wife. Do you know how few men can say that and know it's true? You're cursed with humility."

"Only because she's too good for me, of course." Edward ground out these words from the tightness of his heart cursing Harrow for his searching shrewdness.

"She's not too good for you," Harrow retorted. "No woman can be too good for what you give your wife."

His eyes fell on his wrist watch and he leaped to his feet. "I have to catch a train in ten minutes—promised I'd be in New York."

He caught up his hat and ran out, banging the door. Alone Edward sat without moving. He felt spent, not being used, he supposed, to release of emotions. For a moment he could not collect himself. Then there came creeping into his veins a warmth of transfusion. He remembered again what Harrow had said. Margaret, his wife, was impregnable. His love kept her inviolate. Then she knew how he loved her. He had never been able to tell her entirely, but she knew.

His comfort was short. For how did Harrow know even this about her unless he had had most intimate talk with Margaret? What had they said? How much had Margaret revealed and why? Harrow would henceforward be an unwanted third in their most secret life.

He heard the door open but he did not look up.

"You ready to answer your letters?" Jane's voice inquired.

"No."

She shut the door, and he continued to sit. The clock in the outer office struck twelve, and there was a stir of clerks getting ready to go to lunch. Jane must have told them he did not want to be disturbed, for no one came in his door. He sat another hour, breaking his despair and doubt occasionally to fumble with papers, to read a letter or two, to realize that he did not understand anything except the growing demand of his own heart to know the truth from Margaret herself. While he had been engrossed in these offices, intent upon the making of books and selling them, where had Harrow been? What had he been doing when for weeks he had delayed finishing his book, and why, when he finished it so swiftly, had it been to bring into those pages—Margaret?

There was no truth to be had whole out of Lewis Harrow. That man who so impudently comprehended what went on inside human creatures really could understand nothing. What could he know, and how could he know, what it meant to a man to be as he, Edward Haslatt, was a man, firm in integrity, a faithful husband, a good father, a leading citizen whom all respected? Lewis Harrow, knowing everything, his fertile imagination a ferret running into the secret places of lives with which he could have nothing to do, had crept sniffing and sucking into the precious privacy of a house whose doors he was not fit to enter.

But the truth could be had from Margaret. This dawned upon Edward at last with fainting hope. Margaret had never lied to him. She would not lie to him now. He got to his feet, reached for his hat and coat, and left his office. Seeing his grim face, no one spoke to him as he passed, not even Jane.

His house was silent as he let himself in the front door. The children were not yet home from school and Sandy was deep in her afternoon nap. He hung up his hat and coat and looked into the living room. Margaret was not there. For a moment his jealousy leaped to the possibility that she was out, even now, perhaps, with Harrow. The fellow might have run to tell her about the talk interchanged at the office. She might be meeting him somewhere, even perhaps in New York. More than once Margaret had gone abruptly to the city, leaving only a note.

He checked firmly the rush of quivering fears. In common sense he must not go to her trembling and distraught. Profoundly feeling as she was, she shrank with physical distaste from emotionalism. Surface display she could not accept. He went into the library for a moment to collect himself, and found himself remembering instead the times, now long past, when his instinctive jealousy had first been roused. How long she had delayed in her decision to marry him! If she had loved him as he had loved her since he was seventeen years old, she could not so have delayed. She had said once that her father wanted her to marry someone in New York, a needless thing to tell him, surely, when the man was nothing to her, and there was the evening when he had first come to the Seaton house and she had worn a gown so low in the bosom that it had made him uncomfortable and they had quarreled. Then his unholy jealousy reached into the sacred hours of his honeymoon and his startled, half-guilty delight in the freedom with which she had dressed and undressed in his presence, a lack of modesty, beautiful and dangerous.

Actually she had grown more modest with the years. Without words they had come to behave with graceful courtesy that, he had imagined until now, did not separate them in the least. He did not open her door without knocking—he had not done so since Sandra was born. And she did not come in when he was bathing. It had been their joy to have no walls of privacy when they were first married, but they had built them again, bit by bit, walls no stronger than mist, transparent and yet shielding. Had those walls provided her with secrecy?

For she had changed. The old frank abruptness with which she had once spoken her thoughts, asserting her right to wound him if she must because in love there must be truth—this frankness she no longer had. A silvery gentleness now enclosed her, and he was startled to realize how long it had been since they had really spoken with communication.

At this moment he heard a door open and close, and with an impetuousness entirely foreign to him he leaped to his feet and ran upstairs and knocked at the door of her room.

She was there. He did not know, as he stood staring at her, that in his relief his face began to work as if with tears. She had just taken from her closet a garment of some sort. Evidently she had been resting, for the bed was tumbled and she wore a negligee.

"You aren't sick?" he gasped.

"No—only tired. I thought I'd rest while Sandy slept. Why, Ned, what's the matter?"

"Nothing." He sank down into her velvet armchair.

"Don't be silly, Ned. You look dreadful."

He was speechless. Now that he saw her standing there in her rose dressing gown, looking exactly as she did every morning, her dark hair curling about her face, her eyes calm as the sea under sunshine, he felt his heart swell and his breath grow short. He tried to smile and looked so ghastly that she dropped the garment she held and fell on her knees at his side.

"Ned, speak to me, do you hear? Tell me what it is."

His heart kept swelling until he could not get his breath, and to his horror he heard a loud sob. It was his own.

At this she, who had never seen him weep, began suddenly to weep herself. "Oh, darling, what is it? Don't keep it to yourself, dear. Is it the business? Has something dreadful happened? It isn't Tommy—or Mary?"

Her terror gave him strength, and he lifted her into his lap. "No, no—it's too foolish. You won't forgive me."

"But I'd forgive you anything." Her head was upon his shoulder and he felt her cheek wet.

"Would you, Margaret—will you?"

"Of course—I promise. No, I don't have to promise—you know. Oh, Ned, you frighten me."

"Well, then, listen."

And then, holding her head with his cheek upon her hair so that she could not see his face, he told her of his doubt and his jealousy, and she listened. But he would not tell her of what Harrow had said.

If she had grown angry with him, if her body had stiffened as she lay silent in his arms, he would have been reassured. If she had flown at him with some of the impetuous heat of her girlhood, which now so seldom she did, he would have been reassured. But she lay soft and yielding in his arms. She kept her eyes shut—he felt the lashes curling motionless under his chin. Her hand lay in his, and he imagined only a quickening in the beating of her heart as she lay against him. So there was no way for him to know the truth except to ask for it, and having revealed himself naked to the soul in all his folly of love, he did ask.

"I don't want you to be afraid of me, Margaret. I don't want my love to be a prison. Tell me the truth. If Harrow has made love to you—"

Her voice when she spoke was soft and tired. "Is that it? But it doesn't matter if men make love."

"Then he has?"

"He's the sort that will always keep on trying."

"But you don't—"

"Let him, you mean? Of course not, Ned." She sighed when she had said these words, and still she lay in his arms, soft and inert. "It doesn't mean anything to me what he does, Ned. Only—"

"Only what, dear heart?"

"Are you angry with me?"

"No—but terribly afraid."

"Are you satisfied with me?"

"Absolutely."

Upon this she sat up and faced him, her blue eyes sparkling with sudden anger. "How can you be satisfied with me, Ned, when you don't have anything to say to me, when you aren't with me, when you don't bother to find out anything about me, when you can even suspect me of—of listening to Lew Harrow?" She burst into fresh weeping.

He was so comforted by her anger, so reassured by her fury, so assuaged by her tears, that he could have laughed. He hugged her to him by force, and when she pushed him with her hands against his breast he would not let her loose herself from him.

"Are you satisfied with me?" he demanded.

"No," she sobbed. "No, no, no!"

"Now," he said firmly, "now we have something to talk about. Stop crying and tell me what's wrong. Stop, I say!"

He forced her to look at him, her face still streaming with tears, and he shook her as if she were a child. "I haven't kept my promise to you—isn't that what you're thinking?"

She nodded.

"I've forgotten—or I've been too busy, it's the same thing—to make our marriage the most important thing in my life—isn't that what you're thinking?"

"Yes," she whispered. "It's true. That's exactly what you've done."

"And what you've done," he retorted, "is to let me go on, year after year—"

"Because I thought you wanted to."

"Understanding me so little," he accused her sternly.

"Understanding you very well," she retorted, "but not knowing how to change you—unless you wanted yourself to change. How did I know you weren't tired of me? Men do outgrow their wives. But I'm so used to you now, I can't live except with you."

He groaned. "Oh, Margaret, Margaret, what folly for us!"

"Is it really, Ned?" Her voice and eyes were wistful.

"Why are you humble?" he demanded. "You used never to be humble."

"I think marriage makes women humble," she said, half sadly, "just as it makes men arrogant."

"Nonsense. Your father and mother never were either."

"Ah, but they've never been really married—as we are."

"Take my parents, then."

"They were both humble," she said wisely. "Marriage wasn't good for them—not their marriage."

They fell silent for a moment, each thinking separate thoughts. Marriage, which had made them one, had begun to build a wall between them, had separated them, too, so Edward mused. The necessity to earn a living for them all, the necessity to be father, and she perhaps, with the necessity to be mother—and yet surely somehow this was the proper course of marriage?

"It looks to me as if we'd have to begin over," he said at last. "Maybe it's only second wind we need. Or maybe we need to design our marriage again to what we are now—the man and woman we've become."

Her tears had dried and she smiled. "I do love you." She murmured the words against his lips.

He received them far more solemnly indeed than the first time she had uttered them so long ago, and doubt and jealousy left him suddenly and forever.

"Do you, dear?" If there was less passion in his voice than there had been in his youth, there was tenderness that reached from the bottom of the sea to heaven. "I love you, too, and I want to promise you again, Margaret—"

She laughed with astonishing joy, as though ten minutes ago she had not wept her heart half broken. "Oh, promises," she cried richly, "as if we needed them any more!"

She got up out of his lap and pushed back her tumbled hair.

"What on earth have we been talking about?" she demanded.

"Something important," he retorted.

"Maybe," she said in a practical voice, and began to brush her hair.

He did not reply to this, but sat watching her, a half smile on his lips. It had been something very important indeed. For the rest of his life he would be a different man.

THREE

CHRISTMAS EVE, of the forty-fifth year of Edward Haslatt's life, was a fine one. He had risen in the morning to see Chedbury deep under snow. Over the edge of the hill behind the spire of the church a crimson sun shone in a clear sky. He had a feeling of profound pleasure. Christmas was beginning just as it should. By night his children would be gathered under his roof and his house would be full. His mother and his sister Louise were coming for dinner, and later in the evening their usual Christmas dance would take place. This was also a celebration of his own wedding anniversary. He and Margaret had long ago given up trying to make a private affair out of it, and there were times when his marriage seemed a family rather than a personal matter.

Dallying over his dressing for breakfast, Edward reviewed the recent years. His wedding anniversary always induced reminiscence. The difficult quarrel which he and Margaret had carried through over Harrow's novel remained firm in his memory. Harrow had been damnably right, of course; nevertheless Edward did not like to be indebted for understanding his own wife. Yet he was indebted. In the privacy of his own room and the gloomier hours of night he had read many times Harrow's novel, dwelling always upon the pages where the blue-eyed black-haired woman entered suddenly upon the scene. With each reading he lashed his always ready conscience. Margaret had never blamed him again for neglect.

The novel had been one of the miracles of publishing but he had no wish to repeat it. After his conversation with Harrow about the unwanted episode, which Harrow firmly refused to take out, Edward had referred to it no more. He had even succeeded in removing it from his own thoughts. With grimness he proceeded to make the book a masterful success, maintaining a cold face toward an angry Chedbury when it recognized some of its weaknesses skillfully painted upon the characters in Harrow's novel. "If I can lump it they can," Edward told himself in the deep and secret places of his own being.

He sat in his office, the control room of an enterprise that grew so vast that there were times when he himself was terrified at what he, by the grace of Harrow, had achieved. His presses rolled off the editions, and he was compelled to dangerous postponement of all other business. Even so he could not print enough copies of the book which critics, generous and loud in their praise of new genius, insisted was to be read by every thinking American. People rushed to join the ranks of the thoughtful, and Harrow's book was on every living-room table, when any book was, and upon the surge of popular demand Edward made his first motion picture sale.

His life had been upset and his digestion weakened by the constant demand from Baynes and Sandra that he be present at cocktail parties and dinners in big cities, until the press of work increased the necessity that he stay at his desk. All the furor Harrow enjoyed without apparent damage. He ate at all hours, drank prodigiously, and slept, he declared, on his feet.

Edward watched the bank deposits of his firm rise to comforting figures, and felt for once no pricks from his tender conscience, for Harrow's profits were even greater. In these days, though Edward came and went with his accustomed modesty, Chedbury observed a new confidence in him. He was now a soundly successful man.

He had been staggered, however, one Monday morning when little Mrs. Walters killed herself. No one expected it. She had read the book bravely, ignoring to her closest friends the clearly drawn portrait of her husband, dead so many years ago. She had even come to Edward after church the Sunday before and among Chedbury folk, standing about in the sunshine of the green she had chirped, "I think *Town Square* is simply wonderful!"

"It is a great book, though a harsh one," Edward had replied. "Perhaps Harrow will mellow with years," he had added, after looking down into Mrs. Walters' white wrinkled little face.

"Oh, of course he will!" she had trilled.

That night she had taken the shocking overdose of sleeping pills, and Edward had understood with grateful pity that her courage of the day before had perhaps been in preparation and apology.

He had weathered with outward calm the bitter and even angry surmises of Chedbury, and prudently he had sent only a modest offering of flowers to the bier. Anything more would have been construed by Chedbury as the expression of a guilty conscience. To Harrow, however, he spoke privately and forcibly.

"You see what happens when you tamper with real life."

Harrow had shrugged his heavy shoulders. "How little you understand people, Ed! If she hadn't wanted to die she wouldn't have killed herself. I gave her the excuse, that's all. I'm sure she was grateful."

He stared across the room with eyes so remote and all-seeing that Edward had said no more. That night, however, he told Margaret what Harrow had said to him. They had sat late after the children went to bed, and then before going upstairs themselves they had taken a turn or two in the garden, arm in arm.

"A queer thing to say, wasn't it?" he had remarked.

"Yes," Margaret had replied, "and yet like so many things Lew says, it can't be denied because perhaps it's true."

He digested this remark in silence, admitting its accuracy. The wind had blown cool as they reached the far end of the garden, and so they had gone in.

As though the death of old Mrs. Walters had been relief enough for anger, Chedbury relapsed into its usual somnolence after the funeral, and Harrow went on with energy to finish his monstrous house on Granite Mountain and to plunge into his next novel.

Edward conceded in his more melancholy moods that while Haslatt Brothers were highly respectable publishers they were not spectacular, except for Lewis Harrow's books. Two or three lesser successes, produced by discoveries of Baynes and Sandra, had barely enabled him to maintain his independence before Harrow. There had been nothing further between them of personal matter, and Edward subdued his continuing annoyance at the easy way in which Harrow came and went in this house. Except for the weeks and months of fierce concentration, when Harrow lived aloof and alone on Granite Mountain, there was nothing sacred. For the last week Harrow had been incessantly present and busy about the Christmas party.

To this party all the young people of Chedbury came, together with out-of-town friends the children had made at their various schools, and such business connections as Baynes and Sandra felt were inevitable.

Whether old Thomas Seaton could get here tonight was questionable, if the snow held under this sun. He had grown very shaky in his seventy-seventh year. Mrs. Seaton was as hard as a nut. The fragility that had once been her charm had become sinewy and sinister.

Edward pondered the determination of women to outlast men. Would his own Margaret one day linger long after he was underground? To this melancholy question he found no answer as he continued to dress, listening meanwhile for the voice of Mark, his youngest, born to his astonishment and Margaret's laughter, three years ago. He would never forget his alarm when Margaret came to him and told him she was pregnant, after so many years.

"We should never have gone to Italy," he had said solemnly.

"Why do you blame Italy?" Margaret had demanded.

"You know very well what I mean," he had retorted.

For that year Sandy had been put into boarding school, and he and Margaret had gone to Europe once more. In a manner of speaking, it was a second honeymoon, although neither of them had put the idea into words. He had rejoiced that again he had her to himself, her thoughts to be directed to him alone as they had been in the days when they were newly married. This had not quite come about. The children existed for them both, and even at times when they were most intimately close, as they had been, for example, that night in Venice, he saw a faraway look stealing into her eyes, which meant that she was wondering about the children. Once having given birth to a child, a woman seemed to be forever divided. It had taken him a long time to learn this, and still longer to accept its inevitability.

That night in Venice he remembered in absurdly idyllic circumstances —that is, a moon had risen over St. Mark's and the water in the canal upon which they were riding in a gondola, though actually filthy, was changed into liquid gold. The Italian fellow who was rowing them began to sing a soft shaking melody and his tenor voice, though untrained, had a surprising quality of sweetness. Margaret sitting beside him on the narrow benchlike seat looked like a girl. She had put chiffon or something over her head, and her face was absolutely beautiful. Edward had wanted to make love to her immediately, and in an hour or two he had suggested that they go back to the hotel. She had not wished to go, and this had irritated him. Surely she understood his state of mind, and surely she might have responded to it. He earnestly longed to abandon himself to romantic love. It was not often that he felt he could. That night, far from Chedbury, with no business problems pressing and the children cared for, he had felt entitled to what might be called relaxation. A man of more common clay would have found it in various repulsive ways, but he had turned to his wife.

"Oh, let's enjoy the night as long as we can," Margaret had said, rebelliously.

"You don't enjoy being with me, I suppose," he had retorted. Of course she knew very well what he was feeling.

"We may never see Venice again as long as we live." This was her reply. It was made to remind him of a quarrel they had had once in Kansas. It had been her first journey westward, and her excitement, as tonight, had made her more than usually beautiful. She had gazed at the rising plains over which they were motoring. "It's more lovely than the sea," she had murmured, "because it doesn't change." So beautiful had she been that day, her cheeks sunburned red and her black hair flying, that he had wanted love from her. She had yielded unwillingly, as he had found out only long afterward, because she did not want to hurt him. Nor had this wish to spare him been an unselfish one. She admitted, when he pressed her, that she did not want to have the trouble of a quarrel. Upon this they had quarreled indeed. He had not forgotten the tortuous admissions he had wrung from her.

"You, who insisted that you would marry me only if we could be frank," he had reminded her again. "I am frank enough, but what about you?"

She had been cool and patient. "You make it impossible for me to be frank," she had declared. "If I don't feel just as you do, and when you do, you feel it is my fault. I lie to save myself trouble."

He had refused to acknowledge the possibility of truth in this nonsense, but he knew there was truth in it, though only a wisp, and knew, too, that she was aware of having said something telling. He had made honest efforts, ever afterward, to examine her mood, before indulging his own.

But she had held the Kansas afternoon against him, as he came to know, because while she wanted to be free to enjoy the world through which she passed, he had forced her, because she did not want to hurt him, to center her attention on him. She had never quite forgiven him, nor in a sense had he forgiven her, while he had learned to accept rationally the difference between them, which was that when he was moved by extraordinary experience or pleasure, his impulse was to find release and expression in his love for her. She, he now knew, wanted at such times to be free of him and of love, in order that she might lose herself—and perhaps, him.

For long this difference between them had wounded him deeply, but with the years he had come to believe that it was the difference not only between himself and Margaret, but also between man and woman, and therefore to be accepted.

That night in Venice, with the memory of Kansas alive in him, he had controlled his desire, had sat only holding her hand lightly, had allowed her to wander into dreams she did not share with him, until suddenly long after midnight she had turned to him, her eyes dark.

"Now," she had whispered, "now I am ready."

The outcome of that rewarding night, he was firmly convinced, had been his unexpected son, Mark.

What they would have done without him it was of course impossible now to imagine. A child who upset all their accustomed ways, no less inconvenient to the older children than to himself and Margaret, spoiled as he had become in his irrepressible youth and gaiety, he was a darling headache, as Sandy put it, wherever they took him. Edward adored him privately above all his other children. Some day, he secretly believed, Mark would be the joy of his old age and the mainstay of the business. Baynes had no children and was not likely to have any. Tommy, although now a gangling youth, still showed no interest in anything except football and the curious moaning noises which passed for singing these days. But Mark, even at three, was trying to learn to read. Further than this, Edward tried not to be proud of the fact that, of all his children, only Mark looked like him. So real was the resemblance that there were times when Edward had the illusion that he was looking into his own childish face as he used to remember it, somewhat older than Mark's, in the mirror in his old bedroom. His mother made no pretense that Mark was not her favorite grandchild.

Edward was dressing very slowly, feeling no hurry this morning before Christmas. During the holiday week he tried not to work, if possible, at his usual tasks. He had put on scarcely more than six pounds as he grew older, but Dr. Wynne had warned him of a blood pressure some ten years too old for him. Nothing dangerous, but still it was a barometer. Now he heard a tap on his door.

"Come in," he called, knowing that light metallic sound. Margaret came in, dressed in a new crimson wool dress which struck his eye at once.

"Not too red, is it?" he asked cautiously.

"Is it?" she demanded.

"The skirt's short," he suggested.

"Oh, you!" she said with affectionate humor. "You wouldn't be satisfied unless I went around in some sort of purdah. For heaven's sake, Ned, be your age!"

"I wish you'd be yours," he retorted with good spirit.

Whether it was her slightly graying hair, which made her skin look as fresh as ever, or whether it was the undying blue of her eyes, he did not know, but she had grown more handsome with years. What had been angular and impetuous in her young face had grown smooth and tempered. She had not quite fulfilled his secret longing for moments of high romance, but he did not blame her entirely for that, knowing that to the ordinary eye he was not wholly a romantic figure. His face, as he now looked at it in the mirror while he knotted his brown satin tie, was long and dark. His hair was growing heavily gray and his rather large mouth had taken on a dry and saturnine look, which he did not understand, for he was at heart a shy and still too sensitive man. The last thing Jane Hobbs had said to him one day, now five years ago, when she made ready to walk out of the office for the last time, was, "Now that I'm to be gone for at least a month, do for mercy's sake watch yourself, Ed, and don't give money to any-buddy you don't know."

Poor Jane—none of them had thought she would not be back. She had gone to the hospital for some female operation into whose details he did not inquire, the sort of thing he understood that the wombs of old virgins were liable to develop, and she had not survived the operation that was to make her life better. Perhaps it was better anyway. Who knew? Joseph Barclay with all his sermons had never been able to convince him that there was any sort of real life after the grave. He would not speak this doubt as long as his mother lived, for she had at best too short a time left to her in which to hope to see her husband again. With each year since his father's death, the silence growing deeper as the very memory of his voice was forgotten, his mother was able to remember only his virtues, those good qualities that had appeared so scanty in life. Perhaps the physical awkwardness, the small repulsive habits that his father had never tried to overcome, had died with him, leaving his true image clear. Death had performed a service.

"Well," Margaret said restlessly. "I suppose you'll be down to breakfast when you're ready."

"Aren't you going to kiss me this morning?" he demanded.

She moved to him and their lips met with the ease of long habit. She had taken to wearing lipstick, to his private annoyance, but he had given up protest. She wore it very well, of course, just the slightest tinge and not the solid scarlet that Sandra plastered on her mouth, already somewhat too coarse. But still it was enough so that he had to bother to wipe it off, lest one of his children jeer at him.

"At it again, you two!" Sandy had cried the last time she was home from school, when she saw the stain of red on his chin. Young people these days were purposely ribald.

And yet, he thought, as Margaret's lips met his, this kiss was better than ever. Some of the old sting and novelty perhaps were gone, but the present satisfaction was deeper than he could possibly have felt in his youth. He had still not plumbed all her womanhood. She changed all the time, and he had to keep up with the change. Take, for example, her willfulness about working for these foreign peoples—what on earth did they have to do with Chedbury? Except that he did not like the look of things in the world at that! Even when they had been in Europe there was already some sort of shadow creeping over Denmark and Holland. He didn't see it in Italy or in Germany. Everything there was buoyant and the people were full of hope.

"Germany is about to rise to the height of her nationhood," Heinrich Mundt, the German publisher, had declared.

"What on earth are you thinking about?" Margaret now demanded.

"Not about me."

"It comes of my not having to rush to the office," he confessed.

"What's the use of kissing me if you don't keep your mind on it?" she said and shook him a little and went away.

A rumble at the front door, a slam, and then a loud shouting voice roaring through the house announced the arrival of Lewis Harrow. A moment later the fellow was bellowing up the stairs.

"Ain't you up yet, Ed?"

Lewis affected these days a return to the speech of lower Chedbury, declaring that it was the sort of English he had learned as a child and anything later acquired was pretense. He had never married, and for all these years had continued to live alone at The Eagle, except for long journeys into various parts of the world, in no one knew what company.

Edward opened his door. "Just coming," he said crisply and closed it again. A hoarse growling, as of bears, mingled with shrieks, told him that Mark had rushed out of the kitchen to find his beloved. Strange that nowadays because of the child's joy he should be slightly jealous again of Lewis Harrow! Old roots yielded reluctantly.

He went downstairs wearing, as symbol of holiday, the red velvet jacket that Margaret had given him last Christmas. Lewis Harrow, in shabby tweeds, one elbow ragged, gazed at him as at an apparition. "My God, how handsome you are!" he cried and pretended rude amazement.

Edward smiled. "Thank you," he said with composure. "Have you had breakfast?"

He was pleased to see his small son, wearing a blue sailor suit and his breakfast bib, desert Lewis and come flying with outstretched arms. He picked Mark up and carried him into the dining room and put him into the highchair before he took his own seat.

"I had breakfast before dawn," Lewis shouted, following him into the dining room.

"Foolish of you," Edward remarked. "What have you come here so early for—money?"

Their friendship now was past the possibility of breaking, although twice Lewis had quarreled with him and had gone to other publishers and twice Edward had let him go, knowing grimly that no man could bring him the fortune that Lewis did yearly. Twice Lewis Harrow had come back, complaining and angry. "You're all a lot of thieves, you publishers," he had cried. "I've a good mind to start printing my own books."

"Perhaps you had better," Edward agreed, "then you'll see where the profits go. If you have a thousand dollars left I'll be surprised."

"Shut up and draw a contract for the best book I've written yet," Lewis had ordered. " 'Member that mulatto fellow I told you about last year? I've written a book about him."

"People don't want to read about mulattoes," Edward had complained.

People had, however, read *Pedro and the Public*. It had not been one of Harrow's big books. The critics had been narrow-minded, but plenty of people had read it with joy. It was Harrow's strength that people read him whatever the critics said.

"I don't want any of your filthy money," Lewis now retorted and then corrected himself. "My filthy money, rather. Of course your little shop would go out of business if it weren't for me."

"I did very well when you were fooling around with city men," Edward replied mildly, and fell with appetite to scrambled eggs and bacon.

Lewis stared at him. "My God, look at him eat! It's these rails of men who lay away the grub."

"What did you come for?" Edward asked. "I know you don't climb down Granite on a snowy morning just to watch me eat."

Lifting a forkful of egg at this moment, Edward observed a strange suffused look upon Harrow's face. It had never been a handsome face, and rugged and unaffected, it had changed little with years. Now it was blushing red.

"I came to find out what time Mary's train arrives," Lewis said.

"Why should you bother to meet Mary's train?" Edward inquired. Shades of old jealousy made him look away from Harrow.

"Bacon," Mark said succinctly.

Edward put a rasher on the child's plate.

"Maybe I want to talk about a Christmas present for you," Lewis said.

"Queer you get so red over a Christmas present for me," Edward retorted.

"More bacon," Mark said.

"Don't eat so fast," Edward told his son. "This is the last piece."

"Ain't you going to tell me the train?" Lewis inquired.

"What train?" Margaret asked coming at this moment into the room to find Mark. "Edward, he's already eaten his breakfast and had quantities of bacon."

"I told him this was the last piece," Edward replied.

"Mary's train," Lewis reminded them.

"It gets in just before noon—eleven fifty, isn't it, Ned?" In innocence Margaret spoke.

"Yes," Edward said unwillingly.

"Why didn't you say so?" Lewis shouted. He rose and lumbered from the room, pulling a fur cap out of his pocket as he went.

Margaret sat down at the table and poured herself a cup of coffee. Then deliberately she lit a cigarette, her eyes, as Edward knew, daring him to object. Well, he wasn't going to object. Whatever she did, she could do. She knew that he deplored the habit that women were taking up of smoking cigarettes, but so long as she did it only in her own home, he would not say anything.

"Has it occurred to you that Harrow is behaving a little foolishly about Mary?" he inquired.

The corners of her mouth quivered. "Has it occurred to you that you are growing rather handsome in your old age?"

Edward was embarrassed rather than diverted. "I am scarcely in my old age," he returned. He continued with his coffee which he was trying to learn to drink without cream, because of a slight though increasing tendency to nervous indigestion. With some effort of will he did not look at Margaret, because he knew she was looking at him and daring him to look at her. Suddenly he yielded and their eyes met, hers amused and his shy.

"What makes you say things that make me blush?" he complained. He could scarcely keep from laughter, and he was too honest to deny, at least to himself, that it was pleasant to have one's wife, after years of marriage, mention his increasing good looks.

"You're wearing better than I am," Margaret said. "You looked old for your age when you were young and now you look young for your age. It's monstrously unfair that a wrinkle shows up so on a woman."

"You haven't a wrinkle," he declared loyally. She did have a few, very fine ones, about her eyes, and one, rather deep, between her brows, because she did not want to wear glasses.

"Now about Lewis," she went on. "Yes, I think he is a little silly about

Mary and, yes, it does worry me, for while I know she won't fall in love with a boy of her own age, it doesn't stand to reason that Lewis is the only man possible for her. He wants to worship her and she loves to be worshiped. There's the danger."

He ignored what he believed was an edge of malice in her words. Margaret was behaving well to Mary now as the child grew up. The adolescence that he had dreaded had not been what he had feared. Mary did not conceal the fact that she loved him better than she did her mother, but on the other hand both Tommy and Sandy loved Margaret better. Things evened up in a family, he supposed. Young Mark had learned early to be equal in his demands upon both parents. At any rate, Margaret accepted Mary's partiality for her father.

"I know you don't like me to say this, Ned, but you have spoiled Mary, you know. You've done a little worshiping yourself."

"Nonsense!" He put down his coffee cup.

"Not nonsense, and I don't mind. I wouldn't like worship, for myself."

"Did you once tell Harrow that?"

There was no more than the old shadow of jealousy now. He enjoyed his security as a husband.

"I laughed! There's nothing kills worship so thoroughly as laughter. He was furious with me."

"Can't you tell Mary that?" His eyes upon her were humorous but he was glad he had not known this ten years ago.

"Oh, she's at the serious age. Love with a capital L!" She lifted Mark from his chair, wiped his mouth, and waved her hands at him. "Shoo with you, young man! Go outside and play. Tell Hattie to put on your snow suit and your galoshes."

Left alone with her in the warm and pleasant dining room he felt strangely sentimental. He wanted to convey this to her, and while he was choosing his words, she said, "The real danger is, of course, that Lew has reached the age where he worships youth." A mild cynicism gleamed in her eyes that were still sea blue. "Queer how young men worship old women and old men the girls!"

He disliked hearing this platitude from her lips. Putting down his empty cup he wiped his short mustache carefully. "I was just thinking how much more I love you now than even I did when we were young." Words of love he usually spoke in the night, under the protection of darkness, and he was pleased that here in the bright snow-lit sunshine they did not sound absurd.

"Do you really, Ned?" She leaned on her elbows on the table and inquired this of him with a charming intensity.

The canary in the big bay window, inspired by the musical quality in her voice, burst into sudden song. They listened, gazing at each other with such communication that his answer scarcely seemed necessary. He rose from his chair, impelled to take her in his arms, and she, divining his necessity, rose too and met him in long embrace, which was the more passionate because each expected a door to open upon them. For once none did, and at last he drew away and looked at her. "I wish I could tell you all that I feel, I wish I knew how to put it into words. There are still times—don't laugh—when I really want to write poetry."

"I wouldn't dream of laughing," she said gently. "I think it's dear of you and wonderful—something not to be expected by a woman after she's twenty. I am blessed."

"Sure?" He wanted to penetrate deeply into her. Did he satisfy her every need at last? None of the surface mattered if he could be sure that in her fundamental self she was content with him. But he dared not make further demand. Some profound modesty in him inquired even at this moment why he should imagine that she could find a world within the limitations of his being. His conception of love's function now was that of a guarding if overwhelming tenderness, not so much demanding as providing. Did what he provided, then, complete her dreams?

"I'm sure," she said heartily.

At this moment the interruption came. Tommy strolled in for late breakfast. It did not occur to him that he could be unwelcome anywhere and he entered with all the brightness of unimpeded youth. The only real regret that Edward felt concerning his son was that he had named him after old Thomas Seaton and therefore after Tom. These two had not hidden their peculiar affection for Tommy, and this had provided an escape thereby for Tommy from the somewhat austere attitude of Edward as a father. Tom Seaton had weathered into an elder bachelor who still continued to live with his parents. Long tours around the world, immersions in India and South Africa, and more recently a sudden interest in Italian music had given Tom Seaton an excuse for living. Edward considered him a bad influence on all the young men in Chedbury and especially upon Tommy, who was inclined, as his school career developed, to put on the airs of a man of the world, a world about which he really knew nothing except at second hand through his uncle.

Thus Edward saw his fresh-faced young son, who had recently grown so tall that he looked as though he walked upon stilts, enter the dining room with an air that was all too cheerful.

"Happy returns, you two," he said negligently. "Many more of 'em, et cetera."

Margaret, with pleasant composure, sat down at the table to pour coffee for her son. Edward continued to stand as he lit his pipe.

"Anything I can do for the party tonight?" he inquired.

"Nothing, dear," Margaret replied. It would have been impossible for anyone to have believed that a moment ago she had been a young and flushed woman in her husband's arms. She was now the matron, the mother of a grown son. Edward, looking at her from under his eyelids, felt the private excitement of a clandestine love affair. Nobody knew this woman except himself. Especially did young Tommy know nothing about her. It occurred to him also that they had really settled nothing about Harrow going to meet Mary. He did not want to speak of it before Tommy who had all the surface cynicism of youth about love. He pulled out the gold watch that had Mark Haslatt's name on it. "I shall go to meet Mary," he announced.

"Do, dear," Margaret said smoothly. "I was thinking of going myself but if you're going, I'll meet Sandra. She gets in an hour later. I do wish the girls could synchronize."

"Mary always manages to come alone, for reasons she alone, alone can tell!" Tommy sang in a falsetto.

Both parents looked at him with stern eyes but his smooth pink face was innocent. Edward left the room abruptly. He heartily disliked the constant flippancy of his children's generation but it was incurable. Restrain it anywhere and it burst out somewhere else. He put on his hat and coat with a preoccupied gravity and searched for his cane. It was not to be found. He pressed a button and a new maid, whose name he could not remember, came from the kitchen.

"Where's my cane?" he demanded.

"I'll ask Master Tommy," she said at once.

He waited until she returned. "He says he was using it yestiddy," she murmured.

He waited again until she had returned with the cane, grunted when she handed it to him and went out the door. Surely Tommy was old enough to leave his father's canes alone.

"I'll buy him a cane next year for a Christmas present," Edward growled to himself.

But it was impossible on this morning to remain angry even with callous youth. The sunshine sparkled on the snow in the most obvious Christmas fashion. The merchants of Chedbury, having had a slightly better year than they expected, had gone to the extravagance of a large Christmas tree in the square and festooned lights around the lamp posts. He was pleased to see a sleigh pulled by a horse coming stolidly down the road between the passing automobiles, and then was taken aback by seeing that it was driven by Tom Seaton. There were even sleigh bells around the horse's neck and Tom had found somewhere in the Seaton attic a tall white stovepipe hat. People were laughing at him, moved by Christmas tolerance.

"Tommy up yet?" Tom shouted at Edward, waving a scarlet whip as he passed.

Edward nodded and went on. Though it was a holiday and he had no intention of going to his office he could not forbear passing that way, since he was still early for the train, and then having arrived at the door he went in. He had during the recent years taken over the entire building for his printing shop and his book business. Although he had not allowed the books to absorb the shop, he would not print advertisements of cosmetics, of which he disapproved, but he still printed private cards, wedding and funeral announcements, and the programs for the Sunday services. Occasionally he quarreled with the minister's wording, for Joseph Barclay had grown more rather than less extreme in his middle age, and felt that the world was becoming so comfortable that people had to be scared to God. More than once Edward had returned the sacred copy with a firm note that unless it were modified to some sort of dignity he would not print it. Twice Barclay had refused compromise and twice there had been no printed programs in the church for that week.

The offices were decorated in the best of taste. Aided by Margaret, Edward had contrived just the right atmosphere in his own private office, enlarged by throwing together what had once been his father's office and Mather's. He had paneled the room in oak, and a portrait of his father hung opposite the door and over his own desk. The desk was solid but not large. His infrequent visits to New York offices had confirmed in him a dislike for large light-colored circular desks, confronting anyone who came in. The man behind such a desk designed himself to terrify and for this Edward suspected him of inner weakness.

The shop was of course idle today. It was still an open shop. Edward's blood pressure was points higher than it might have been had he not faced grimly across his desk, some half dozen times, a group of men who came to insist that he operate a closed shop. John Carosi brought them, as he well knew, and time and again he had been on the point of firing the fellow except that in all fairness he had been compelled to promote him for excellence of work until now Carosi was his head foreman. The man was a convinced labor man, and yet so just and truthful that he allowed Edward to argue against unions. And Edward, in decency, was compelled to hear Carosi in reply.

Against Baynes, too, and as heartily, Edward had argued. As Harrow's success had brought the modest spate of novelists to Haslatt Brothers, Baynes, abetted by Sandra, had declared that the offices ought to be moved to New York, leaving only the shop in Chedbury. Edward would not hear of it. Offices in the city and workrooms in Chedbury would have meant, he believed, nothing but confusion.

"You want to keep your hand on everything," Baynes had accused with the irritability that had become natural to him these days.

"I do," Edward agreed. "I've told John he can't even hire a new man without my meeting him and having a talk, and he can't fire anybody unless I see the man myself and know what's gone wrong. It isn't just that I want everything in my own hands, either. I believe that people are reasonable if I take the trouble to explain things to them. I don't want labor and management against each other in our business."

Secretly he wondered whether the deviousness of Sandra had imagined Baynes the real head if the offices were in New York, Edward remaining merely the boss of the printing end. Once he would have spoken his doubt to Margaret, but he had learned as he grew older to withhold judgment, even of his sister-in-law.

Edward regularly went to New York once a fortnight, though Baynes had grown sufficiently steady, after Sandra's escapade with Peter Pitt, to be relied upon.

Three years before this year, now so near its end, the two families of Haslatt and Seaton, as well as the firm of Haslatt Brothers, then at the very height of its first real and permanent prosperity, had been shaken to their combined depths by Sandra's affair. It was all mixed up with business, in the way that only Sandra could mix such incompatibles as love and shop. More and more she had become responsible for publicity and promotion, showing indeed real talent for these unpleasant but essential aspects of publishing. Thus had she arranged for the arrival of Peter Pitt in the United States, for his successful lecture tour, and for the sale of his books, including *The Singed Flower,* as motion pictures.

Not even Edward himself had suspected her of anything more than business acumen. Baynes, later, in the midst of real agony, gave a ghastly grin as he confessed his misery.

"It's beyond me, Ed. She's been driving a hard bargain with Peter Pitt, even while she's been carrying on. Our percentage is higher than ever. I don't know whether to love her or despise her for it."

That midnight now three years gone, when Baynes had rushed from New York to burst into the house, could not be forgotten. Fortunately Edward had not yet gone to bed. As he grew older he needed less sleep, while Margaret needed more, and he had been sitting in the library, his feet to the fire, reading one of the pile of manuscripts with which he never finished. The house was silent, the family asleep. From the distance of a fantastic novel about mountain climbing he had heard a cry and had looked up to see Baynes at the door, as gaunt as a ghost.

Even so Baynes had made a pretense of nonchalance. "There you are, Ed—I was hoping you hadn't gone to bed. Got a cigarette on you? I've consumed all mine."

Cigarette between his trembling lips, Baynes had dropped into a chair and had said in a squeaky voice, "Sandra's left me."

The fantasy slid from Edward's hands. "Where's she gone?"

Baynes held out a note and Edward had read it, his nose in the air as though he smelled something foul. "Dear Bub—" such was Sandra's absurd name for her husband. "Don't hate me, will you! At least not permanently? Pete and I are taking a trip—maybe only a little one. I just had to get some sort of radical change. I don't know why, either. Not your fault! Sandra."

He handed the note again to Baynes. "There's something queer in the Seaton blood," he had said solemnly.

"Have you—is it in Maggie, too?" Baynes had asked with clutching hope.

"No," Edward had said firmly, "not at all."

Baynes had shrugged his shoulders and Edward saw that he was trying not to weep and so he had gone on talking. "You had better go upstairs to the east guest room and get to bed." He was deeply moved by his brother's plight and very angry with Sandra, and so his voice was dry. "Have you eaten anything?"

"Couldn't," Baynes muttered.

"Come with me," Edward ordered, and docile as he had once been in his boyhood, Baynes followed his older brother into the pantry. Edward opened the icebox and took out a ham and some lettuce and a slice of cheese and a roll of butter. He went to the bread box and fetched a loaf and put the kettle on and measured coffee.

"I didn't know you were such a cook," Baynes said. His voice was trembling.

"I get myself a snack sometimes when I've been reading late," Edward replied.

He sliced bread and made a sandwich for Baynes and one for himself, and when the coffee was ready he poured out large cups full and found cream and sugar. Baynes looked at the food as though it sickened him, and then suddenly began to eat and drink and Edward saw the ordinary comfort of hot food seeping from body to soul.

"Of course I saw them running around," Baynes said after his second cup of coffee. "I didn't think anything of it—everybody does that sort of thing now."

"You doing it, too?" Edward inquired.

"Only by way of business."

"Haslatt Brothers doesn't make any such requirements of you," Edward said.

"You don't understand," Baynes retorted with impatience. "You live up here in this pure little town."

"I don't know anything about the purity of the town. All I care about is my own home."

Baynes had looked at him with strange eyes but Edward had not inquired into their meaning.

"More coffee?" he had asked.

"No. I'm going to sleep," Baynes said heavily.

The brothers had separated without more talk.

Sandra had stayed away for nearly four months. She had gone to England and she wrote letters to them all with the most frightful effrontery, exactly as though she were merely visiting the land of her forefathers. She had the further impudence to discover and recommend to Edward a man who she believed could write novels, given sufficient encouragement. Baynes told no one that his wife had left him, and Edward told no one but Margaret. Whether she told the Seatons he did not know. The pretense was kept up in the family that Sandra was merely vacationing. Even Baynes as the weeks went on persuaded himself to the pretense and mentioned to Edward one day in the office, as though he were only mentioning it, that Sandra was returning on the eleventh of July.

Edward, beginning that year to struggle with increasing taxes, had not looked up from his accounts. "She's coming back, is she?"

"She's had her fling," Baynes said.

The affair had dried and hardened him. Ebullience had left him, perhaps forever, and his native New England toughness emerged to take its place. Baynes was no longer young.

"You want her back?" Edward inquired.

"She's still my wife," Baynes replied.

"You're being very decent."

"No—only doing what I want."

So Sandra had come back, and Mrs. Seaton gave her a little dinner party to which Edward found himself too busy to go, but at which, he heard from Margaret, the talk had been all of England. "Mother kept saying, 'Dear old England,' every five minutes," Margaret said and wrinkled her nose.

"Does your mother know?" Edward had demanded. He had got out of bed and gone to Margaret's room when he heard her come in and was lying in her bed when she opened the door.

"Of course Mother knows and so does Dad and so does Tom, but nobody is going to say anything outside, now that Sandra's home again."

"Are you going to say anything to Sandra?" he inquired.

She gave him a quick look, while she unfastened her necklace. "Probably Sandra will tell me everything."

So Sandra had done one day when the two sisters were sitting on the beach alone, the children in the water and the men fishing. Edward had bought a house on the seashore in order that he might not have to decide each year where the family would go for their summers.

There was nothing much to the story, as Margaret told it to him that night. He had allowed himself to get too heavily sunburned and it was difficult to fix his attention on the somewhat dull story of Sandra and Pete, bicycling about England, and apparently doing very little. In the end Sandra had been bored. Nothing, she declared to Margaret, was more boring than trying to live with a writer. Pete, she felt sure, was continually planning to put everything she said and did into some future book. It was a relief to get back to her good old Baynes.

"She'll probably go off again—with a banker or something," Edward had said, trying to find a safe place upon which to rest his sore frame.

"I doubt it," Margaret said. "Sandra isn't really a passionate woman. That end of it bored her no end with Pete."

Edward was startled into forgetting his pains. "Why in God's name then did she—"

"Don't swear, Ned—she just wanted to make sure that there wasn't any more to it than she had with Baynes. Sandra's always been like that—wanting to be sure that she was getting all there was."

"What indecency!" he had cried.

"Isn't it!" Margaret had agreed.

He had not quite liked her placidity, in which he could not discern any of his own disapproval, but he had not pursued the subject further. He had remained cool to Sandra for some time, indeed to some degree ever since, but she seemed not to notice it. The Seaton family held its head as high as ever in Chedbury, and Tom if anything admired his younger sister more than before.

What had gone on between the mother and the daughters after Sandra came home Margaret told Edward only partially, in unwilling fragments. "Mother told Sandra how foolish Aunt Dorothea looked when she was separated from Uncle Harold. A woman alone is so silly. I mean—nobody knows what to do with her." At this moment Margaret had laughed. "Incidentally, Mother was rather nice about you, Ned! She said you had made a really sound and respectable business and Sandra would have been stupid to cut herself off from it—especially for somebody with such a name as Peter Pitt!"

"Thanks," Edward had said with some reserve.

Mrs. Seaton had prevailed and the old New England blood in Baynes had resumed its control. Sandra was thinner than ever and with humor renewed and toughened.

In his own heart Edward asked himself, as he sat in the privacy of his empty offices, how it was that Margaret had grown so well content with him. He believed that she was content. All the impetuous restlessness of her girlhood had left her and she had bloomed into a quiet half-indolent calm, her dark hair graying softly about cheeks still pink. He had never fathomed her altogether, and now he had no wish to do so. If she enjoyed the unfailing stability of his love then he was fortunate.

The sunlight of the cold December shone as bright as polished steel upon the floor and he remembered with a start that he was to meet Mary's train. He rose and went into the shop to see that all was well. No one was here, either—or so he thought, the machines standing in silence, seeming to sleep in their unaccustomed stillness. Then at the end of the long room he saw John Carosi, in his good clothes, bending over a press, a small oil can in his hand.

"Hello, John," he called.

"Hello," Carosi replied. He had never called his employer sir.

"You can't keep away from here, either," Edward said smiling.

"I remembered there was something that didn't work right in this here press," Carosi replied, not acknowledging the smile.

"Well, merry Christmas—I've got to meet the train. My older daughter is coming."

"Mary?" John Carosi spoke her name while he continued to find small holes into which to thrust the pinpoint nozzle of the oil can.

"Yes," Edward said. In Chedbury the first name was the only one, but in his marriage he had absorbed from the Seaton family a sense of class distinction. None of his children shared this, and Mary would have answered joyously to John's use of her name.

He left the pressroom and putting on his hat and coat again and grasping his cane firmly against possibly slippery snow, he decided to walk to the station. From here the distance was short and the exercise would do him good. He mused as he trod firmly on the now hard-packed snow. He had a genuine liking for Carosi. What he disliked in the man was no individual attribute, perhaps, and yet on the other hand it might be just that. Carosi limited his world to his labor union. The small group of working men, dominated by a fiery boss, who was in turn at the command of a central human machine, was the universe within which John Carosi lived. All the multiple affairs of mankind, hunger in Asia, a possible war looming in Europe, the mounting cost of living here at home—all these he saw simply from the point of advantage or disadvantage for his union. Edward had had an argument with him one day on the question of whether the increasing cost of printing, which was nothing but the union pressing for higher wages, might not some day stifle the book business, even as, Baynes had declared, the unions in the city had hamstrung the theater and at the very moment when it had to meet the frightful competition of motion pictures.

"Our welfare can't be independent of union labor," he had urged, "but you in turn depend upon the general welfare."

"I've had enough of that," Carosi had replied with obstinate tranquillity. "We're lookin' after ourselves first, down at the union."

It had been a secret mitigation of the alarming depression still lingering in its aftereffects, that the hordes of the unemployed had thoroughly weakened all labor unions. Yet this slight good could scarcely compensate for the repercussions of the American depression on Europe.

He pondered this gloomily as he trod the sparkling snow this Christmas Eve, absently touching his hat to acquaintances he passed. Carosi's insistence upon the group advantage was more than the symbol of the danger of control of business by labor unions. He, Edward told himself, was entirely willing to grant that owners had been operating for years entirely within their own world, too, but he trusted owners more than labor unions if for no other reason than that owners were on the whole better educated. He was more afraid of ignorance combined with power than of any other element in the world of man, and the more frightened because he saw, though at a distance, labor unions bringing to power a very ignorant fellow in Germany. No man, and no group of men, could live for self alone and be safe or make the world safe for others. Human life was a matter of proportion and balance, which he feared were both to be lost in the approaching future. Even Sandra, careless of the welfare of mankind, had seen from the vantage of England some sort of sinister shadow rising in Germany.

From such dark thoughts he was diverted by the whistle of the train flying into the station while he was still two blocks away, and making haste he arrived as the train was pulling out and in time to see his beloved daughter buried in the depths of the rough fur coat which Lewis Harrow began to wear after Thanksgiving and did not take off until just before Easter.

The train Mary had chosen was a slow one, and there were few people on the platform. For this Edward was thankful as he hastened forward. He did not care for the talkative tongues of Chedbury, after this spectacle. He was further dismayed when his presence did not immediately separate Lew from his daughter. Instead the fellow gave Mary an instant longer in his arms and then she sprang forth laughing, her dimples rampant.

"Dad, darling!" she cried in the fresh voice he was never sure was spontaneous or cultivated. Whichever it was, his heart melted at its music and he allowed Mary to kiss his cheek. She was the center of his heart and he considered her more beautiful even than Margaret had been at her age. This might be, however, merely that he felt in her some quality of his own and himself, an understanding of her that was natural, whereas he had been compelled to achieve such understanding of Margaret through the force of love. However he scolded Mary, and he intended to scold her now as soon as he got her to himself, he felt the bond between them held.

"Well, now," he said dryly. "Come along home. Your mother wants to see you before she has to leave to meet the next train. She wonders that you and Sandy can't synchronize."

"Oh, we never do," Mary exclaimed.

Her charming face was less regular than her mother's, and its whole look was softer, perhaps because her eyes were brown instead of that clear sea blue. Her skin, too, was softly brunette, and her voice low rather than clear. Examining anxiously this lovely young face among flying black curls, under a small dark fur hat, Edward was alarmed to see how womanly it was, how firm were the red lips, how set the rounded chin. How far had Harrow gone into her untried heart? For surely she was as yet only a child.

Tucking her hand under his arm and giving but the smallest of nods to his most important author, Edward walked down the platform. His eyes fell on Mary's shoes. "There now—I wanted to walk home with you but in those shoes we can't. Of course there are your bags. I suppose you are loaded up with luggage as usual. Where is it?"

"Bill took it," Mary said in her composed little voice. "And I'd love to walk."

Bill was the porter. Inside the station he was waiting beside the assortment a young woman brings home for the holidays.

"You'll catch your death," Edward grumbled. "Though I suppose Bill can send the bags up and the sidewalks have been shoveled."

"I'll change as soon as I get home. Come along and don't fuss, darling."

He enjoyed being persuaded by his glowing young daughter, and they set forth upon streets emptied by Chedbury's early lunch hour.

"Oh, isn't it going to be a perfect Christmas?" Mary's feet dancing upon the hard snow caused her to bob upon his arm.

"It's begun," he replied.

Her bright upward look reminded him that he was going to scold her and that he had better begin before they reached home. He never allowed himself to reproach his beloved child in Margaret's presence.

"Except," he said gravely, "I don't like it when Lew embraces you publicly like that. Maybe he's so old that it doesn't really matter."

He cast a sidewise glance down at her to see how this notion of Lew's age would move her. She repudiated it at once.

"Lew isn't old," she said with complete calm. "Besides, I like my men old."

"Lew is one of your men, is he?"

"Always has been," she said dreamily. "Ever since the first day he came to our house to lunch—always has been, always will be—"

He felt sure she was daring him to go on, and reluctantly he took the dare. "Your mother ought to tell you—" he began and paused.

"Tell me what?" she demanded, squeezing his arms. "Not the facts of life—please don't say that, Dad! I don't want to laugh—not at you."

He mustered his dignity. "What I was going to say is that young girls always fall in love with men too old for them. It's not real love."

"Did Mother?" The question was sharp with a sort of jealousy which he was quick to discern. Had this child also inherited his fatality?

"No, your mother is the exception to all rules about women."

"Maybe she didn't tell you."

He paused again on this. "I think she would have told me. She's entirely honest."

He looked down and met her dark eyes. There was something so quizzical, so mature, in this glance, so quickly veiled that he was frightened. The child was a woman!

He wanted to say no more but he loved her too much. "All I want to say now is that I hope you know how dear you are to me. Lew is all very well as an author—one of the great ones, of course—but as a man, he's not fit to tie your shoestrings."

"How do you know, Dad?"

"Because I publish his books, that's how I know! He gets his stuff somewhere and not out of other people's books, either."

Then from her exquisite lips there came these words, blasting his soul and withering his spirit. "I don't care for the old ideas, Dad—I mean about purity and all that. I want a man to be a man, that's all."

"Mary—" he was holding her arm so tightly beneath his own that he was lifting her.

"Let me go, please, Dad."

"I'm sorry—but what I want to say is—there's a lot of men besides Lew—better men."

"Better?" She repudiated the word.

He set his teeth and looked grimly ahead. "See here, Mary—before we get home, let's have this out. You aren't going to marry Lewis Harrow. My son-in-law? It makes me sick. I'll quit publishing his books—damned if I won't!"

He felt her hand tighten on his sleeve. "He hasn't asked me, Dad."

"If he dares to—"

"I will."

They had reached the door of home and before he could utter the groan that welled up in him the door was flung open and Margaret ran down the steps, clad in her furs, a sprig of holly on her lapel, to embrace her daughter. Mary was small in comparison and her cheek sank into the softness of her mother's breast.

"Dear child," Margaret said lightly, "why, you're looking very pretty!"

Mary patted her mother's cheek. "You're looking rather wonderful yourself. Where'd you get that brooch?"

"Your father gave it to me last night for being married to him so long. Now do wash quickly and eat your lunch, you two. It's being kept for you. Tommy was to have been here, but he's staying to luncheon with Mother and Father at the house. Now I must be off, or Sandy will feel nobody's bothered to meet her."

A touch on his arm and she was gone. Edward mounted the steps of his house, feeling as he always did, that when she was not there the house was empty. Mary had run ahead through the hall and up the stairs, and he heard her footsteps in the upper hall. She wanted to avoid him, for the first time in her life, and no wonder, with that avowal upon her lips. What was the use of having children when they broke one's heart? He remembered involuntarily the nights long ago when he had got up with her, wakened by her tiny wail and he fumbling to get the bottle hot. He had taken over the two-o'clock feedings because so often he worked late that it was not worth while to wake Margaret. That image was with him still, the wisp of agony he had held in his arms, the impatience, the despair of a human creature deprived of food, the greedy satisfaction when the seeking mouth found the milk, and then the rosebud child, replete and assured again, filled with warm food. He had not got up with the other children, and perhaps it had been those early-morning hours shared with his first child that had made her so precious to him now. He was far more terrified of her budding spirit today than even he had been of her fragile small body in those first weeks and months of her life. Then it had been a matter of newborn flesh and tender bones. Now it was something else, the birth of a quivering spirit, a heart newborn, a self no longer dependent upon him and seeking its sustenance elsewhere. When he thought of Lewis Harrow as the source to which she turned, his gorge rose.

He went upstairs to his room to be alone for a few minutes before he faced her again at lunch. He felt tired and he took off his shoes, and though it was midday, put on his leather slippers. Mark was asleep doubtless at this hour. With much rebellion, Mark still had to submit to his mother's firm decision for daytime sleep. Since Tommy was away, it meant that today inevitably Edward and Mary must be alone for the meal. He felt dispirited and unequal to the necessity. Was he inadequate as a father? Pride rose to deny it, and he braced his shoulders and after a second's meditation decided to change his tie. He went to the mirror and adjusted the deep crimson tie that he chose, and then brushed his hair carefully. So habitual did the tending of one's body become as years passed, that with something like shyness he peered again at his long, rather sallow face, made more brown by his graying hair. Whatever had been young and fresh in his eyes was gone. They had grown piercing and his mouth was set in lines. Not a face to make a young girl want to confide in him! And confidence could never be forced. He could no more compel his child to open her lips now to speak her heart than he could have forced her baby lips to receive food when she was beyond the want of it. There it was—she was beyond the want of him. Nothing that he could provide did she now need.

With this discovery he knew that it was to Lewis Harrow he must appeal with the mustered force of his fatherhood. All that he could do in his daughter's presence was to be as nearly as he could the father whom she would consider ideal. He went downstairs, determined upon courtesy and even courtliness, the tender consideration of an elderly gentleman who happened to be her father, yielding to her grace and beauty.

She was there waiting for him in the dining room, the table set for two. Now that her fur coat was off she emerged as a small figure in scarlet wool, her curly hair cut to her shoulders in the fashion set by some motion-picture star whose name he could not remember. He disliked motion pictures, although they were becoming an important part of the revenue of his business. He had, however, gone to the filming of Harrow's last book, *The Shrew*. The leading part had been played by the star whose name he could not remember. She had been blond, and he was relieved that Mary could not look like her.

He pulled out her chair and smiled and was rewarded by the thanks he saw in her eyes. Had it been no more he might have been hardened, but he detected a mixture of timidity, her old childish yearning to be loved, and by him. He was melted at once and he gave himself up to being the ideal father that she wanted, as nearly as he could.

The day wore on to evening. He had tried to read some manuscripts, aware of the increasing noise and merriment in his house, and had been glad to give up all pretense when Margaret put her head into the open door of the library.

"Ned, do take Mark somewhere! He is everywhere he's not wanted and I have so much to attend to before the guests come."

"I thought the caterer was supposed to do it all," he grumbled, in spite of gratitude for the interruption.

"Oh, they always forget from year to year where the silver and glass are."

"Tommy home yet?"

"No. I think Tom took him to Boston."

"Did he tell you?"

"No, but Sandra called and said they might be late."

"I don't like Tommy going with Tom like that—he's too young and Tom's too old."

"Oh, well—it's Christmas, and Tom hasn't anybody special. Do hurry, dear, I hear Mark yelling in the butler's pantry."

"Get somebody to put on his outdoor things, will you?"

"I'll have him at the door." She hurried away and he gathered his papers together.

Half an hour later he was walking around the square with his son Mark skipping beside him, very handsome in a woolly brown coat and gaiters and a red knitted cap. The tree was alight and the festoons glittering. Mark was asking questions about Santa Claus and Edward answered them as honestly as he was able, in view of the fact that Margaret had encouraged Mark to believe in the saint's myth.

"Have you seen Santa Claus?" Mark pressed.

"Well, in a way," Edward countered.

"Bringing me things?"

He had never allowed anyone to use baby talk to this intelligent son, and Mark's enunciation of words was pure and precocious.

"Well, bringing things, certainly."

"Which chimney will he come down tonight?"

"I'm not sure."

He diverted the conversation from mythology, which he had never approved on the grounds that it was foolish to build up a faith which had later only to be destroyed, and called Mark's attention to the electric lights on the tree.

"When I was a little boy, we didn't have any electric lights in Chedbury."

"Where did they come from?"

"All the people paid money and put up poles and we got it in from Boston."

Mark was not interested in electricity and having pronounced the name of Boston, Edward fell to musing about the city which he disliked and admired. In the frightful aftermath of the depression, Boston had practically gone bankrupt. It had not been surprising that New York had been in a like fix, and less interesting that Philadelphia, Detroit, and Chicago were all financially unsound at the same period. The swollen rolls of those millions of persons on relief had been maintained at starvation level only by the largesse, actually, of rich men, who had not been willing to lend their money, however, for anything much above starvation. He himself, as one of the leading businessmen of the Boston area, had been invited to go with a committee to wait upon a Boston multimillionaire, who declared that while he did not want to be responsible for people dying in the streets, yet because he had worked for his money, he was sure that others could do so, and therefore he had to have a guarantee that the weekly dole would be a minimum.

Somehow, largely thanks to Harrow, Haslatt Brothers had continued prosperous enough so that in Edward's own house there had been little sign of the shortages which afflicted even houses once well to do. He had insisted that Margaret not serve champagne at their Christmas party last year, when things had been at their worst because trade had fallen off with Europe after American loans had ceased. This year things were better, however, and he had not mentioned the champagne. It would be served tonight, he supposed, in the great cut-glass punch bowl which the old Seatons had given them ten years ago as an anniversary present. Still, he didn't like the looks of things. Huey Long, for instance, was setting himself up in a very peculiar fashion there in the South. It was too much like what was going on in Germany with that fellow Hitler. He was beginning to imagine that Chedbury was nearer both Louisiana and Germany than was comfortable.

The discomfort of his thoughts turned his instincts toward the warm shelter of his house.

"We'd better go home," he said to Mark.

The child had been silent for a while, clinging to his father's hand. His Christmas exuberance was suddenly over.

Edward bent to his beloved son. "Are you cold?" he demanded. He laid his lean cheek against Mark's round and rosy one.

Mark whimpered. "It's getting dark."

Remembering that the child had always been unaccountably afraid of the night, Edward was reassured. "We'll go home right away."

"Can't you see the dark?" Mark asked in a small voice.

"I was thinking of things."

"What things, Daddy?"

"Faraway things—like Germany."

"What's Germany?"

"A place."

"Is it a good place?"

"Not very, I'm afraid—not just now. Come along, trot!"

Together they trotted down the street which had once been a road to the country, and in a half hour or so the house loomed up a mass of light and cheer. Sandy and Tommy had last year devised a system of indirect lighting upon the snow-covered trees which was far more effective than the usual string of small electric bulbs. Tonight Sandy had turned the lights on early, being an extravagant miss. He had not yet seen her, for she had left her Christmas shopping to do in Chedbury, her finishing school being in a remote spot on the Hudson, and she had used all her available afternoons for theater matinees, to which she was addicted.

When he and Mark entered the house she was whirling in a solitary dance of her own under the mistletoe in the hall, and not another soul was in sight. She fell upon him ardently and with kisses when he came in, and she knelt to hug Mark. She was still satisfyingly a girl, with none of the disturbing signs of womanhood. Her short hair, just escaping red, her honestly freckled short nose, and gray-green eyes did not as yet spell beauty.

"I hope you've got my Christmas present," he said by way of a mild preliminary joke.

"I did, you selfish thing," she said laughing. "I've got everybody's presents and I like all I got and I hope people will give me the same things. Dad, I bought Mother a tiny bottle of real perfume—rose! It cost so much that I'm strapped."

"How much do you need?" He put his hand to his pocket, accustomed to this situation.

"Oh, Dad, not tonight—I can't shop tomorrow anyway—but before I go back to school. Mother said I was to take Mark and give him his supper and put him straight to bed."

"I'm going to stay up for the party," Mark shouted, preparing tears.

"When you're six," Edward reminded.

"I'll be going on six soon, next year maybe," Mark retorted.

"Not this year," Edward said with firmness. He did not want this child's fine body destroyed by unwisdom, and he hardened his heart to Mark's loud cries as his sister led him away.

The rooms were warm and beautiful, decked with holly as they were, the chandeliers lighted, the satin sofas gleaming softly. The fires were laid but not lit. It was a home of which any man could be proud. Piece by piece he and Margaret had replaced the cheap things of their first years and now there was not a table, not a chair, of which to be ashamed. He liked only a few pictures on his walls, and when they had been in Italy they had brought back four fine small paintings, not old masterpieces, but good enough to draw the admiration of those who knew such art. The heavy curtains were drawn over the windows and there was a smell of spice in the air, a dash of rum with it. At this hour Margaret would be superintending the eggnog, and he would not disturb her. At the far end of the library, now that the rooms were thrown together, the Christmas tree shone tall and green, decorated in silver. He liked a big tree, remembering the meager trees of his own boyhood.

Then in some haste he pulled out the heavy gold watch his father had left him. He must dress early, for he had to go and fetch his mother and Louise.

The year after his father's death it had become evident that his mother must not live alone, and he had not suggested that she live with him, divining that his house would not be the more peaceful for bringing his mother and Margaret under one roof. Instead he had sought out his sister, living then with another teacher in a small apartment, and with difficulty he had persuaded her to go home and live with their mother.

He had been surprised at the stubbornness with which Louise had met his idea. "It isn't as if you had a real home of your own," he had said.

She had looked at him with strange pale eyes. "That's the very reason I don't want to go," she had replied.

In the end she had gone, however, and he had tried to make it up to her by putting some new comforts into the house, an oil burner, and a new refrigerator instead of the old icebox. Louise had received the benefits in silence. But silence was natural to her. He had no idea what she thought about anything, though he acknowledged that in her tall narrow way she had grown rather distinguished looking, and two years ago she had been appointed assistant to the principal of the Chedbury school. He was sure she was better at administration than at teaching.

He went upstairs and dressed carefully in the new evening things that he had bought just before the depression, at Margaret's insistence. He had resisted her because, not having put on weight, he had thought his college clothes would last him the rest of his life. But as usual, when she appealed to his vanity for her own sake, he had yielded. She had chosen the material, a violet black over which he had demurred because of the price.

"This suit you really may wear the rest of your life," she had argued.

So he had yielded again, and then had been secretly glad to have done so, because the garments were cut to fit his tall bony frame and with a pleasure which he would have been ashamed to acknowledge, he enjoyed the softness of the satin linings.

He looked into the pantry on his way out. Its old-fashioned size was never at better advantage than upon such an occasion, and presiding over the caterer and his minions was Margaret, her hair curling about her face, her cheeks scarlet with heat and excitement. She looked at him.

"Oh, Ned, you're dressed already! Is it so late? What did you do to Mark? He's so excited. I must get dressed at once if you're going for Louise and Mother. Do taste this—it's champagne cup. I made it because so many people secretly don't like eggnog and are ashamed to say so on Christmas." She poured half a glass of the mixture and he drank it, after the first taste, with appreciation.

"Really good!" he exclaimed.

She flushed with his praise, and he would like to have kissed her but could not, under the covertly staring eyes of the minions.

"Don't hurry," he told her. "I shall take my time getting home. Mother's always too early."

He went away, having backed his car out of the garage with unusual skill, for he was not a good driver, far less skillful than any of his older children, and they were apt to blame him for small scratches and scrapes on the fenders. The car was a good one and he was proud of it. He would not for any reason have possessed the showy affair the Seatons had bought some five years ago, which had a glass pane between themselves and poor old Job Brummel, who, though their chauffeur, was still and always would be little more than a handyman. Thomas Seaton had hired Job the year after Bill Core died of old age, because of his strangely English profile, inherited from some faraway ancestor who came to America from London. "Makes me feel as though I was sitting in a 'ackney coach," Thomas said with exaggerated cockneyism.

Edward drove carefully, mindful of ice freezing now on top of the snow, and aware of unsteadiness under the wheels. He wondered if he should have put on chains, which he did not know how to do in any case. In his secret heart he wondered, too, if he ought not to hire a driver when the children went back to school. He could not be sure whether in Chedbury it would be thought pretentious. Though again, he reflected, it might be considered only some of Margaret's Seaton blood, but no, damn it, he would not take refuge behind that. If he wanted a hired man to drive his car, he would have him. But overhead could creep up, and the depression was still far from over. He fell to ruminating again on the painful state of the world, put awry by the war and not yet straight, while clouds of war loomed again over human horizons.

Then resolutely he put away his haunting fears and reaching his mother's house he parked the car fairly well, and went in. His mother was dressed and waiting in the living room, her coat and gloves laid together. Louise was reading a magazine, that new digest, he noticed, which he had declared was ruining the book trade. Who would buy a book for two dollars and a half when he could get such a bulk of reading material for a quarter? Louise was wearing a new dress, a dull blue taffeta that was rather becoming. Her blond hair had not grayed and she put aside her glasses as he came in.

"I'm early," he announced. He bent to kiss his mother's dried cheek. Her middle-aged fleshiness had dropped away and she was withered and old. Her scanty white hair was not curled, but she had put into the knot on top of her head her one treasure, a jeweled comb that his father's grandmother had once owned—how, he had never thought to inquire.

"You look quite handsome, Mother," he said, sitting down. "I never saw the comb look better. It becomes your hair since you've grown white."

"I'm going to give it to Margaret one of these days," she declared. Her voice was as piercing as ever and her eyes were undimmed.

He caught a creeping hostile look on his sister's face but she did not speak. "You must give it to Louise," he said.

"No, for she isn't going to get married, so far as I can see," his mother complained. "I want Mary should have it, really, but I suppose it ought to go to Margaret first, in order."

"I don't see why," he said. "Margaret has her own things to inherit."

"Maybe I will give it to Mary, then," his mother went on. "Did I tell you it came from Spain once?"

"No, did it?" He was interested now. Spain, that country of angels and devils, that past heaven and hotbed of present evil! Only last Sunday he had seen a picture in the Sunday newspaper of the plump portentous little man who was rising to power there. How could people worship such gods? At least let them be beautiful.

"There's a mystery about this comb," his mother said with some reserve. "Your great grandfather gave it to his wife honestly enough but his mother had it from somebuddy—nobuddy knows who. Anyway, it's said that's how the Haslatts come by their dark skins."

He was amused at this possibility in past ages and he laughed soundlessly.

"Oh, Mother," Louise said with impatience. "Everybody is always talking about Spanish ancestors."

"Well, we have the comb, haven't we?" his mother's voice was triumphant.

"What if it's only Portuguese?" Edward inquired with mischief.

His mother rose. "You two are just as contrary as ever you were. Let's go. If we're early maybe I can help Margaret."

He knew Margaret's dismay at this possibility and he made haste to put his mother off. "She's got the caterers there tonight—everything's ready, I believe, but we might as well go."

His mother and Louise both put on their day coats, and he made a mental note that next Christmas he would placate Louise still further by a fur evening cape, and then they were all in the car and he was driving his careful way homeward. His mother, sitting beside him, clutched the arm of the seat in a fashion disheartening to him, but he did not mention it to her, aware that for one who had grown up with horses and buggies, a motor car would always be a hazard.

Once in the house he ensconced his mother in a large armchair and leaving Louise to her own devices he hastened upstairs to find his little son and bid him good night.

Mark was in his bed, his arms under his head, the covers drawn to his neck and his face unusually thoughtful.

"I was waiting for you," he said at the sight of his father.

"I thought you would be," Edward replied and bent to kiss him.

That cheek, so soft, so fragrant under his lips, nearly broke his heart with love. Lest he betray his extravagant tenderness he said in his driest voice, "You'd better go to sleep before the noise begins."

"I like Christmas," Mark said dreamily, "but I don't like the night before, because here I must lie, alone in the dark, while people are alive and laughing everywhere."

"You're alive, too," Edward said sharply.

"Not like in the day," Mark said simply.

The child was really too precocious, Edward told himself. He must talk with Margaret about it after the holidays were over. They must take care of this son, this treasure.

"I shall be coming back to see you every now and then," he said, "and I will light the candles on the mantel, so that you will not be in the dark."

He lit the candles one and the other, and turned to catch his son's smile. "Thank you, Daddy," Mark said, and closed his eyes to sleep.

Christmas Eve proceeded according to a pattern long established and well enjoyed. Chedbury, out of deference to one whom it recognized as a leading citizen, though of a sort they did not wholly comprehend, had years ago decided against any other event on the twenty-fourth of December. Edward Haslatt's party was paramount. It was a heterogeneous affair. To its earlier hours came those citizens who, though entirely welcome to stay out the evening, knew instinctively that eleven o'clock was the hour at which they should appear before host and hostess to say good-by, to give their polite thanks for a "nice time," and to wish a merry Christmas.

The party remained somewhat staid and decorous, a family affair, for those earlier hours. Only near midnight did its loose strands knit themselves into something homogeneous and close. Conversation was no longer labored, and laughter rippled through the rooms. The band, which Edward each year brought from Boston, put aside waltzes and fox trots and set up the catching intoxicating rhythms that had taken such hold upon the youth during the depression. Since there was neither hope nor freedom in the world of reason, they found it in their bodies.

Edward did not like it. He was slightly fatigued by the task of being host to people he had known all his life, to whom he was Ed Haslatt, the son of old Mark, and yet from whom he was now separated because he had built up a business that published books many of which Chedbury could not read. Never quite sure of where Ed left off and Mr. Edward Haslatt began, their old ease was gone, except as Edward himself determinedly kept it. But this, too, was tiring, and as he grew older and his business forced him to become aware of a world of which Chedbury could know nothing, and yet of which it was nonetheless a part in these strange times, he found himself increasingly solitary.

Now, the rooms half emptied, he sat down in an easy chair in a corner of the library to take a few minutes' rest. The champagne cup had gone well. The eggnog would please those who were left. He could see old Thomas Seaton sipping his foaming glass with dreamy pleasure. The old man had given himself up to the joys of the flesh. Everybody was worried

about him and Dr. Wynne warned him every time he saw him. Even tonight he was looking at him, while he sat beside Mrs. Seaton. They were
talking about old Thomas, and Mrs. Seaton assuredly was saying the same
thing she always said: "Thomas says he may as well die an enjoyable
death. He says he doesn't want to die hungry and thirsty, and go empty
and dry into eternity."

The young people were forming themselves together into that new thing,
that rhumba, a savage performance. He saw Lewis Harrow go up to
Margaret and propose himself as her partner. Thank God she was shaking
her head. Harrow looked all too well in evening clothes. His dark hair had
not silvered properly. Instead it had stayed coal black, and grown white
only at the sides, as though it were dyed. Yet in justice he had to acknowledge that Lew would not stoop to such folly as hair dyeing.

Now, as though having invited and been refused by his hostess excused
him for willfully doing what might make his host angry, Harrow went
straight to Mary. She had avoided all other invitations, flitting here and
there in her gown of cloudy white, making a pretense of seeing that her
grandmothers were tended. Now as Edward watched her he saw a pretty
tableau, too distant for him to hear the conversation. The child bent over
her Grandmother Haslatt with all her conscious grace, and he saw his
mother melt under the loving deference that Mary showed her, and that
he was none too sure was not entirely a knowing process of charm. His
mother was saying something. Then she took the high Spanish comb from
her hair and gave it to Mary. The child's hair was short and how could she
wear it? Ah, she was kneeling, and he saw his mother with a sort of tender
triumph gather the dark curls together and catch them on top of Mary's
head and hold them with the jeweled comb. Mary rose to her feet just as
Harrow came near and she looked up at him with that dewy shyness, which
again might be only a process of her conscious charm. Whatever it was,
what man could resist it? He did not believe that Harrow said a word. The
fellow simply held out his arms, and Mary went into them and then the
band, as if the performers saw and understood, began to quicken the subtle
rhythm, to sharpen its passionate accents, and Harrow and Mary were
dancing away as one, and all eyes were on them.

Edward hid his own eyes behind his hand. The fellow danced supremely
well, and he was wooing Mary with all the skills of the flesh, and she, at the
very age when in spite of her delicacies, it was the flesh she craved, could
not but respond. He had not the heart to blame her, remembering himself
and Margaret at that age. But they had not such freedom as this thing, this
rhumba, with all its license, could and did allow.

He rose, intolerably stung, and went toward the dancers. Margaret,
watching him, met him, and slipped her hand under his arm.

"Everything is going well, I think," she said with calm.

"It seems so," Edward replied.

"How do you like my gown?" she demanded.

He looked down at her. It was a violet velvet, very pale and soft. "It's new, isn't it?"

She laughed. "Oh, Ned, you never quite know, do you? Well, yes, it is. Do you think the color is a little old for me?"

"If you mean do you look old in it, the answer is no. Certainly not. Who's that girl Tommy is dancing with?"

"Somebody he brought back from Boston with him, on the spur of the moment."

"I don't like her looks."

"She's very pretty."

"Too obvious."

The girl, wrapped in a sort of sheath of gold, was as thin as a stick and her straight yellow hair floated in ribbons behind her violently moving head.

"What's her name?"

"I don't know—Dinny something."

"Queer times," he commented.

With such camouflage did he conceal the approach to the one thing about which he was thinking. Now he came to it. "Margaret, we've got to do something about Harrow and Mary. I simply won't have it. Why, she might want to marry him!"

"I know, dear. But we can't, you know, any more than I can do anything about my father's fourth cup of eggnog which I see him taking this very minute."

But she would try, nevertheless. Overcome by anxiety she left him swiftly and crossed the floor to the long table in the dining room where old Thomas, already shaky, was holding his cup toward a laughing woman who was filling it.

Thus deserted, Edward felt the blood rise to his brain and intoxicated with his own anger, he walked firmly among the dancers and approached Lewis Harrow and touched him on the arm.

"Come with me a moment, please," he said distinctly.

Harrow, surprised, came out of his trance. "Can't business wait?" he demanded.

"No," Edward said. He met Mary's hot eyes with a cold stare and with Harrow beside him he led the way to his own small study which of all the downstairs rooms had not been thrown open. The sudden quiet behind the shut door only hardened his resolve. "You needn't sit down, Harrow," he said with the same cold distinctiveness of enunciation. "I simply want to say that you are to leave my daughter alone. She's a child."

Harrow blinked. He had been well aware of Edward's anger at the station this morning, but he had been determined to ignore it. He would ignore it now. "She's not quite a child," he said mildly.

"In comparison to you she is," Edward said. "I don't forget all between us that is good and useful to us both, but I'd throw it all away rather than see her—"

"What?" Harrow asked with malicious mischief.

"Commit her heart to you," Edward said gravely.

Harrow flung himself into one of the leather armchairs. "You're so damned serious," he complained.

"About Mary I am," Edward agreed.

Harrow gave him a strange look. He smoothed back the white wings of his hair with his open palms, and lit a cigarette. "Very well, then, I'll be serious. I consider it rather a privilege for a young girl to fall in love for the first time with an older man—especially me."

Edward gazed at him with actual hate. Underneath it his old jealousy burned, transferred now to this young and tender creature who was his daughter and yet somehow compound, too, of Margaret.

"And how do you feel toward her?" he asked in a thick voice. "When you've made her—love you—then what will you do?"

Harrow looked away. "I don't know," he said at last. "I really don't know."

"It's wicked of you," Edward said.

Harrow glanced at him and away. "These things grow."

At this moment the door was flung open. Mary of course he had been expecting, but Mary angry and unreasonable. This was not she. Mary was weeping and she seized his hand.

"Oh, Dad," she gasped. "Oh, Dad—"

"What, dear?"

"Grandfather—he's—he's— Mother says you must come—oh quickly, please, Dad!"

He had no time to decide. Margaret needed him. He left Mary, catching in his distraction one last glimpse of her. Harrow had risen and put out his arms, and she had gone into them. He heard her crying. "Oh, Lew, he's dead—he's dead—I can't bear to see him—"

But he did not pause. Margaret needed him.

Beside the Christmas tree lay Thomas Seaton. He had gone to toast the tree, making a joke of it as he had made a joke of everything in his life.

"Evergreen forever!" he had been declaiming, before the laughing guests. "I who am about to depart—salute thee, the eternal—"

By some strange coincidence of life and death he had fallen at the very moment he lifted the cup to his lips, and the blazing lights of the tree shone down on him as his knees crumpled. Margaret had run to him, but Tom had already caught him. Mrs. Seaton had turned away her head, and Tommy had found Dr. Wynne, napping behind a tubbed palm tree.

Edward hurried to the gathering crowd and parted them with his hands. Margaret sat with her father's head in her lap. She was tearless, and her face was ashen as she lifted it to her husband.

"Come, dear," he said. "Tommy, take your mother's place. Where's Sandy?"

"She ran upstairs—s-sir," Tommy stammered. He looked sick and pale.

"Nothing we can do," the doctor was murmuring. "It came as I feared it would."

"The way he wanted it," Mrs. Seaton said. "Margaret, take me away, please."

Between them they led the quivering old lady upstairs, and into the gray and rose guest room. She was almost entirely calm, and the blow for which she had prepared herself so long had fallen at last and yet she could not quite bear it as she had imagined she could.

"I shall lie down for a bit. Leave me, please, Margaret. I must be alone. Edward, you'll see to everything. Tom's not reliable enough."

"Of course," he said.

"Mother, let me stay—" Margaret began, but Mrs. Seaton would not have it. With a sort of subdued wildness she shook her head. "I must be quite alone—really, I must, just for a bit."

So they left her on the bed under the rose satin quilt, her eyes closed and dry, her lips trembling.

Outside the door Edward took his wife into his arms. "I think of you," he muttered, "only of you."

He put out of his mind the image of Mary alone with Harrow. Doubtless the fellow had told her what had passed. Never mind now—nothing mattered but this straight silent woman in his arms, his beloved, his own. She had buried her face in his shoulder and he thought she would weep but she did not. She held him hard, her hands under his arms and clutching his shoulders, for a long moment. Then she lifted her face and began to cry. "It's strange," she sobbed. "Somehow I clung to Dad in my heart— maybe all daughters do."

Did they? Then what about his own daughter? Who knew what was happening in that small closed room behind the shut door? Old Thomas had not really wanted Margaret to marry him, either, and she had been as willful as Mary was today. Ah, Margaret was his first love, his only love. He put the thought of his child away from him. No child should come between them now. He pressed her head close upon his shoulder and began his comfort. "You were always the best daughter in the world to him. He loved you better than any of his children."

"Do you think so, Ned? Really?" She was trying to control herself, tightening her throat, stopping her tears. She looked up at him and he saw her wet lashes and her eyes blue beneath them and his heart was wrenched with the old painful love, infinitely increased by the years and all that had been and had not been between them.

"I wish I could comfort you," he said with tender wistfulness. "I wish I knew how. I love you so terribly."

He saw her face, so schooled by life, by wifehood and motherhood, soften and quiver and break into a trembling smile, molten with sorrow. "Oh, Ned—oh, Ned—I wish I had been a better wife to you, darling."

"But you have been—you've been perfect."

"No, I haven't. I haven't been half I wanted to be—that day we were first married."

"Then I haven't known it," he said. With astonishment he considered what she had just said, his arms still hard about her. Had she indeed been suffering some private remorse? But for what? He could not imagine.

Then holding her thus, before they returned to the things that had to be done, it came to him that even as he had reproached himself now and again for allowing his worries and cares, even his success, to separate him from her, so she too might have like causes for reproach. They still had a great deal to learn about one another.

"We've only begun to be married," he declared suddenly. "It's taken us all these years to get going—earning a living, raising children—now let's just be married, will you, sweetheart?"

The old name that he had not used for so long, scarcely since she had been a mother to his children, was new again and infinitely exciting. She lifted her lips and he kissed her, the most profound, the most passionate kiss that they had ever shared. All that had been was only the approach to what was yet to be. What was that she had said? That she had clung secretly, as daughters do, to her father! Well, that was over. He had no longer to compete with Thomas Seaton's charm and humor and gaiety. He had Margaret now to himself, forever. Reproaching himself in the midst of sorrow, he pressed her head to his shoulder and she yielded. They stole yet another moment to be alone together and the years slipped away.

Yet underneath the steadfast duty with which he supported his beloved, he suffered an agony of uneasiness. What had taken place between Mary and Lewis Harrow in his study when he was so suddenly called away? He had left them alone together and what more natural than that Harrow had undertaken to comfort his Mary? In the girl's shaken state, weeping for the grandfather she had loved, what more natural than that she would have accepted such comfort?

Edward hastened downstairs, having put Margaret to bed with promises of his swift return to her. But Harrow was gone, as were all the guests. His children were behaving beautifully. Tom had taken his father's body home, and Harrow, Sandy explained, had gone with him to help him.

Edward paused a moment for this younger daughter, perceiving in her manner a humility new and overeager.

"Were you afraid of Grandfather, dear?" he inquired, remembering that Tommy had reported her flight.

Her freckles were submerged in sudden color. "I'm fearfully ashamed —especially when I'm thinking of being a doctor."

"It is hard the first time," he agreed. A doctor? He was not sure women should be doctors, and he forbore discussion of it now. In the distance he saw Mary. "You two girls had better straighten things up," he told Sandy.

"Yes, Dad," she said obediently.

His mother and Louise were still there. In the suddenly quiet house all of them began now to straighten the rooms, putting the chairs in their places, picking up the paper streamers and toy hats, the empty cups and glasses and restoring the house to decency again. Only the Christmas tree had been left blazing and Edward, unable to bear its garishness, touched the button that put out the lights. Thus abruptly, too, had the light of life gone from the shining and vigorous old man.

His daughters were subdued and they moved from room to room and when all was done they bade him good night quietly. He called Mary back.

"Mary!"

"Yes, Father?"

"Wait a minute, please."

"I was going up to Grandmother."

"I think she'd rather be alone."

"But I want to be with her."

Their eyes met, their wills crossed and clashed and he yielded.

"Very well."

"Good night, Father."

"Good night, my dear."

She ran upstairs swiftly, her cloudy skirts held high, the Spanish comb gleaming in her hair, and he sat down exhausted. Yet he must now take his mother and sister home. They were waiting.

"I can drive, unless you think you need the car," Louise suggested.

"I had better have the car tonight," Edward said, considering.

"I never thought old Mr. Seaton would go this way," his mother mourned.

"It was a good way to go," Edward replied. He shrank from his mother's interest in the dying and the dead.

"I suppose you will have to plan the funeral," she went on.

"Joe Barclay will do that," Edward said.

"Oughtn't you go over to the house tonight?" she suggested.

"I suppose so," Edward said unwillingly, "unless Margaret needs me."

"We'd better go home since we're no more use here."

So saying his mother rose and a moment later they were riding through the cold and snowy night. Lights shone from the windows of houses where belated parents were still filling Christmas stockings and decorating trees and the silence broke when the bells of the church began to ring softly the notes of a Christmas hymn. Children half waking would know that Christmas Day had come, would smile and sleep again. Only an old man would never wake.

The solemnity of the ending of Thomas Seaton's life filled Edward's mind. He had never loved his father-in-law, aware, while refusing to acknowledge it, that there had been some secret rivalry between them. Margaret had belonged to them both. She had clung to her father—that was what she had said tonight—but how much? Perhaps the withdrawal of which he had been so often conscious was because the core of her heart had clung to another, not him. It was not the common rivalry between father and husband but between two different men, the one gay and careless, rich in living, humorous, articulate, his words flowing easily, and the other—himself. He remembered absurdly, after these many years, that Thomas Seaton had once wanted Margaret to marry Harold Ames, who was now the president of a great bank in New York. Edward saw his picture sometimes in the Sunday newspapers, opening a campaign for the Republican party, heading a drive for the Red Cross, giving a check to the mayor for city relief. The handsome smooth face might have been Thomas Seaton's own, a quarter of a century younger. Margaret had not, so far as he knew, ever seen Harold Ames again. But his memory perhaps had survived in her love for her father and her father had forever conditioned her heart. The old doubt that he, Edward Haslatt, could ever wholly possess her, added despair to his dejection.

"Here you are, Mother," he said and drew up at the doorway of his father's house.

"Don't get out," she said, preparing the difficult descent.

"Of course I shall," he retorted.

He got out and saw her to the door, unlocking it and turning on the light in the hall before he stooped to kiss her good night. Louise had come in and closed the door, as he found when he turned to go out. The house had seemed strange since his father's death, a house lived in only by women, who in their unconscious fashion had removed from it bit by bit all his father's ways and possessions.

"Good night, Louise," he said, and opened the door.

To his surprise she followed him to the porch and closed the door on the old woman toiling up the stairs.

"Ed, I don't know as I ought to add trouble to this night," Louise said.

He looked down at her pale still face, wrapped around by a knitted woolen scarf that she called a fascinator.

"What do you mean?" he demanded.

She hesitated. "Maybe I oughtn't to say."

"For God's sake, Louise," he exclaimed, "why can you never speak out?"

"You've no call to swear at me, Ed. I only want to do what's right."

Her trembling lips infuriated him. All the anger he never showed to Margaret and Mary sprang out at this dull and pallid sister of his. "I hate hemming and hawing. If you have something to say, then say it."

"All right, and don't blame me—but I saw Mary and that—that—"

"Well?" His voice stabbed her.

"Lew Harrow was hugging her."

"That doesn't mean anything nowadays," he mumbled.

"After you went upstairs," she continued doggedly. "And I heard her say, I will—I will, two times, like that."

"Will what?"

"How could I know?"

"Just how did it happen that you heard anything at all?"

"I went—I went—"

Her voice faltered, her head dropped, and she untied the woolen ends about her neck. A monstrous idea occurred to him. She had gone to see what Harrow was doing!

"Why did it interest you to know what Harrow was doing?"

His own injustice occurred to him with these words. Why did it interest him to know the secrets of his sister?

"I didn't think you'd want Mary—to—to—"

"I have never known you to take so much interest in Mary."

In the light of the circle of electric lights, which made the meager Christmas decoration of the doorway, he saw his sister fling up her head in one of her rare fits of anger. He knew these outbursts, coming perhaps once a year after months of creeping silence, and he braced himself.

"You think you're so wonderful, don't you, Ed? You think you're much better than the rest of your family. Yes, you do. And that's what Uncle Henry thinks, too. You never go to see poor old Uncle Henry, though now he's in the county home."

"What in heaven's name has that old skinflint to do with what you were talking about?"

It was true that he had paid no attention to this old relative who had bullied his father in days when the family was poor. Louise could not remember, nor could Baynes, those early years when he had heard his parents worrying lest Henry might be offended and withdraw the pitiful wages he paid his younger brother Mark.

"Because you think you're so fine," Louise raged. "You think Mary is better than any of the other girls. Well, I taught her in school and I tell you she isn't. She's run after Lew Harrow for years—simply years. She's like any of the other silly girls."

"Stop!" He held his hands to keep from striking this foolish old maid who was his sister.

"I won't stop. I'll tell you the truth if nobody else will. Do you think a man like Lew Harrow could really care for a child, a schoolgirl like Mary? Why, he's famous, he's had lots of women, I guess—anyway, he could."

Her voice broke and as always happened her anger could not sustain itself. She began to cry and turning to the door she fumbled for the knob, the fascinator falling over her face.

He understood suddenly what had made the rage and he was embarrassed, ashamed. They had never been close, he and this sister, and he did not want to know her secrets. He would not tell her what he saw, that she hated his Mary because she herself had, in her feeble way, felt the strength of Harrow's charm—even she! And in her poor way she had fallen in love with him. He pitied her. Impatience changed in him to pity, but shame was still stronger. He would be ashamed before Harrow, lest that man, so acute in the knowledge of the human heart, might already know what he had not known until this moment.

"Let me open the door for you, Louise," he said. His voice was husky. In the space of a minute the curtain between them had been thrown back and he saw her as she had been, a pale little girl hostile to boys and, it seemed to him, including him somehow among boys. She had never learned to come out of herself, and she had never let anyone come in to her heart or mind until now. The monstrous fantasy of her imagination, in dreaming that Harrow could think of her—but perhaps she had not so dreamed. Perhaps it had been enough that she thought of him, that he filled her secret heart, so long as he was not married. She had not minded, perhaps, that he had loved other women unknown to her, but it was intolerable that he might love Mary.

He was fumbling at the door knob, too, while she tried not to sob. He found it and they went in and he stood, not knowing what to say or do. "I am sorry, Louise," he kept saying.

"There's nothing to be sorry for," she gasped. She did not look at him.

He took her hand to press it, but it lay lifeless in his palm and he let it go again. "This has been a trying evening on us all," he stumbled. "You'd better go to bed. I suppose I ought to stop at the Seaton house on my way home, so that I can tell Margaret just what's happened."

She turned from him and went upstairs, trying not to cry.

The cold air was comforting when he was outside again, the cold air and being alone. He would have liked to drive off into the night to have time to disentangle this strange web of affairs in his own house, but he knew he must not. He would stop by and see whether Tommy had gone home, and see what needed to be done for Thomas Seaton yet tonight, if anything could be done. At least it might comfort Margaret more than his presence if he came in saying that all was well there.

Christmas lights had been put out, the streets were still, when he turned in at the circular driveway of the big white house. No one had turned off the two flaming Christmas trees at either side of the door and they blazed on. The lights downstairs were still lit, and upstairs there was one light, in Thomas Seaton's own room.

He rang and no one answered, and trying the latch he found the door open and he walked in.

"Hello," Tom's voice called, his drunken voice, as Edward instantly recognized.

"It is I," Edward replied. He went to the door of the living room and saw Tom there, unsteady upon his feet, pacing back and forth, declaiming to Lewis Harrow, who sat sprawled but sober in a big chair, and to Tommy, his own son, who held a wineglass in his hands from which he drank in small gulps, trying not to show his distaste before his uncle.

"No one understood me except my father," Tom was mourning. "He knew how I felt when Daintree turned me down. Ever know I was in love with Lady Daintree of Montrose Hall? She loved me, too, but her papa wouldn't see it and my mamma told me to come home. I came then, though if it had been now, I wouldn't. I went to my father. He said, 'Never mind, Tom, my son, there's lots of women in the world.' That's where he was wrong—women of course, but not one like my Dainty. A man doesn't live alone, of course—not by bread alone and all that. Fioretta Carosi knows, too. Ever see my Fioretta?"

"I've taken a look at her," Harrow said, with interest.

Upon this Edward came into the room. "Tommy, it is time for you to go home," he said coldly to his son. "Your mother will be worrying about you. Go now, this minute."

Tommy set down his glass. "I only came to help Uncle Tom."

"I will help him now," Edward said in the same cold voice, the voice that Tommy had recognized long ago as the voice of one almighty. "Tell your mother that I shall be home soon."

"But how am I to go?"

"I'll take you," Harrow said. He rose as he spoke. "The minister's upstairs, Ed—and so are Baynes and Sandra. I thought I'd better stay with Tom, who's in his cups, as you see."

Tom had let himself sink into his father's chair and was beginning to weep.

"I'll put him to bed," Edward said.

He stood while Harrow and Tommy left the room, and then he lifted Tom by the armpits and pulled him to his feet. "Come, Tom, you're going to bed."

"The kindest man," Tom was muttering. "The best Goddamned father—always understand—"

Edward guided him firmly toward the stairs.

"Even said I could marry little Fioretta if I wanted to—know Fioretta Carosi, Ed? No, 'course you wouldn't know—I don't want to marry her—that's what I told him—it's a comedown."

Tom was clinging to the balustrade, trying to lift his foot for the stair. A door opened, and at the top of the stairs Baynes stood looking down. "Leave him to me, Ed," he called down softly. "I've done this before—the night before your wedding, for the first time, but plenty of times since."

"Who's this Fioretta he talks about?" Edward demanded.

"John's sister—didn't you know?"

"Good God, no!"

"I didn't tell you. I thought it would mess things up in the shop—but I thought maybe Margaret had told you."

"Does she know?"

"Sandra told her."

Supporting a now somnolent form, they took Tom upstairs, his head lying on Baynes's shoulder. The two brothers looked at each other.

"Queer family we've married into," Baynes said with a ghastly smile. "Leave him to me, now. I don't undress him. I just pitch him on the bed. Sandra is in there with the old man. She might like it if you went in."

He nodded toward Thomas Seaton's room, and leaving him Edward tiptoed toward the half-open door.

Thomas Seaton lay on his great bed, dressed as he had been at the party, a triumphant smile upon his bearded lips. He had smiled as he died, and the smile held. Joseph Barclay knelt beside the bed, and Sandra stood, her face pale as stone and as immobile, looking down at her father. The minister did not move as Edward came in. He was praying and he finished his prayer.

"And if it be thy will, O Almighty God, receive unto thyself this soul. We who know nothing of that path which extends beyond our little world cannot see this soul struggling on its way. But Thou seest, and Thou dost forgive. In Thy name, Amen."

Edward stood silent, until the prayer ended and Joseph Barclay rose to his feet. They shook hands silently. Then the minister said, "I have made all arrangements, I think, Haslatt. The men will be here in the morning to see to things. Mrs. Baynes here has told me what her father wanted. It seems he foresaw something like this."

"I've never seen anybody dead before," Sandra said suddenly. "It's strange when it is my own father."

"Death is not strange," Joseph Barclay said. "Nothing is as strange as life."

"He looks alive," Edward mused.

"He is alive!" Sandra cried. "I'll never believe he is dead. I won't let him be dead. I'll keep him alive thinking about him—forever."

Neither man answered this. Then the words smote Edward with meaning. So might Margaret too keep her father alive, thinking of him, forever.

"I can't do anything here," he murmured. "Baynes is with you, Sandra, and I had better go home to Margaret."

He went away forgetting to say good night, and carried with him the picture of that huge and heavy frame, that mammoth man, that tender father beloved by all his children, whose ghost they would not lay.

His house, when he stepped in the front door, seemed unnaturally still. The hall light burned, but the other rooms were dark. Even Margaret's room, he had noticed as he came up the drive, was unlighted, and the guest room where Mrs. Seaton had gone had been dark ever since they left her there, although Margaret, he supposed, must surely have been to see her mother before she slept. He hung his coat in the closet under the stair, and put his hat upon its shelf. Then he paused, halted by some instinct that he did not understand. Surely the house was too silent! He was not a man of intuition except where the few, the very few, he loved were concerned, but he was aware now of that intuition. Something was wrong.

He mounted the stairs, agitated in spite of his exhaustion, his heart beating wildly, about what he did not know, and hastening toward his own room, he put on the light. The door to Margaret's room was open slightly and now he went to it and threw it wide. She was there. The light fell on her sleeping form. He went near to her and reaching into the pocket where he kept his pipe and matches, he lit a match. The flame shone upon her face. She had been weeping. Her lids were swollen, and the lashes were still wet. Now under the light she opened her eyes heavily.

"Ned—I waited so long."

"Is everything all right?" he cried.

She turned over and pushed back her loosened hair. "What do you mean?"

"The house feels queer."

"I haven't been out of my room except to go and see Mother. But she still didn't want me."

"Didn't you go to see Mark?"

She shook her head. "I thought of course he was asleep."

His first thought now for his son, he turned and went out of the room and across the hall. At the door of Mark's room he touched the light again and it came on softly under a shaded lamp. His eyes were already on the child's bed, and he tiptoed to it. Mark was safe, asleep and tranquil. In this night of death and sorrow he had remained in peace, unknowing. Leaning on the foot of the bed, Edward felt something under his hand and looking down he saw Mark's stocking. Some time after he had been put to bed the child had got up and hung his small stocking at the end of the crib. It dangled there, empty.

Edward's heart smote him. They had given up the habit of hanging stockings when the other children outgrew their babyhood, and had allowed the tree to be their Christmas symbol. But Mark must have heard about a stocking and feeling lonely, he had climbed out of bed and found his own and hung it, a sign of wanting something that he did not have. Oh, these children of his! So did Edward's heart cry out within his breast. How had he failed them? With all his love constantly awake and trembling over them, they were always going beyond him.

He tiptoed back to the door, intent upon returning to tell Margaret that the stocking must be filled somehow from the store accumulated for Mark tomorrow, when in the hall his eyes fell upon the door of Mary's room. It stood partly open and he paused. She had taken during the last year to locking her door at night and when he had remonstrated at this, half hurt because she wanted to receive his good-night kiss downstairs, she had remained sweetly firm. "I'm really grown up now," she had replied.

"But you're at home," he had reminded her.

"I like my door locked," she had replied simply.

Now his instinct was roused again. Not Mark—then Mary? He prowled toward the door, half afraid lest she cry out against him. Yet she might have merely forgotten it in her weariness. He pushed it open and stood, listening for the sound of her breathing. He heard nothing. The room was still, the air warm. She had not opened the window.

He turned on the light. The room was empty, the bed not slept in.

"Margaret!" he called in a low voice.

She heard him instantly and came running in her nightgown, her hair flying over her shoulders. She saw the empty room, the smooth bed, and began to hasten here and there, while he stood staring and bewildered.

"Oh, the silly child!" she muttered.

She was opening drawers, the closet, a hatbox, a jewelry case.

"Oh, what has she done now!" she muttered.

Then she turned to him and flung her arms about him. "Ned, don't look like that."

"Where has she gone?" he asked.

"I don't know—I don't know! Oh, Ned, don't please look so!"

He flung her away from him. "I'm going up to The Eagle."

"No, don't—let's telephone first."

She ran downstairs, barefoot, and he heard her voice demanding over and over again Harrow's telephone number. He stood there, unmoving in the middle of his daughter's empty room. There was no answer from The Eagle. Harrow was not there. He had known the fellow would not be.

She came upstairs again. "Ned, if it's happened—"

"I must go and get the car," he said stupidly.

"No, you will not!" she cried. They were still keeping their voices low, mindful of the other children, mindful of her mother and of Mark. "You will not go! We'll hear. Maybe she's left a note."

She was searching the room again, and he tried to help her, but he felt dull and weary enough to die. His instinct was gone, and he did not know what to do next. There was no note to be found. Mary had never done what she was supposed to.

"I don't know where to turn," he said helplessly. "Where can I go to find her?"

"You shall not go," Margaret declared. "You shall stay here in our house. Come, Ned, come—you will drop." She pulled him by the hand into his room.

But he would not yield to her. "I cannot just accept this—as if it were nothing. Let us think together—where would they go? It is not too late."

"It is too late," she insisted. "Look at the sky!"

It was dawn, and the sky was breaking crimson at the horizon.

"You don't care," he muttered. "You've never cared about her."

"I do care," she answered and began to weep. "I care as much as you do, but I know her better than you ever can. She has got to leave you, Ned —that's what you cannot and will not understand."

"I can bear her leaving me," he insisted, "but not like this and with him!"

"But you must see that it is only like this—and with him—that she can really leave you." They were sitting on the edge of his bed now and her arms were around him.

"You can't understand her," he said. "You can't understand her because you never have loved her as well as the others."

"I understand her because she is the one most like me," she retorted. "She has gone through what I did. She's loved you too much, Ned—as I loved my own father. She hasn't been able to find someone just like you to marry."

"Don't talk like that."

"Oh, Ned, it's true—and she has chosen somebody utterly different from you—so that she can be free of you. Oh, she doesn't know what she's done —she doesn't understand."

"How is it that you understand?" he demanded.

"Because I was like that, Ned." She flung out her arms, imploring him.

"You mean you loved your father—better than me?"

"I always loved the kind of man he was."

"Which I could never be!"

"And that is why I wanted to marry you, to be free of him—can you see that, Ned? Try to see it—for Mary's sake!"

"Then you haven't really loved me all these years!"

"I have—I have! Ned, don't look at me like that, darling! Because I'm going to love you now as I've never known how to love you. My heart has let go. There's only you."

She folded her arms about him again but he did not reply to her words of love. Yet somehow she had healed him. Mary had so loved him, her father, that she had needed to cut the bond between them. How slow, how blind he was, that he had not seen before that what she must have was the freedom of her own heart!

"I hope she will want to come back," he said humbly.

"If you let her go, of course she will," Margaret comforted him.

"It will take time for me to stick having Lew Harrow here—my son-in-law, good God!"

"Don't think about him."

They sat a long while in silence while the room slowly brightened to dawn. The sun came over the horizon a globe of melted fire and the snow grew pink. Not a merry Christmas, he thought heavily, and then he remembered.

"Margaret, Mark's gone and hung his stocking all by himself."

She rose swiftly. "Oh, the poor babe—where is it?"

"At the foot of his bed. He mustn't find it empty."

"Of course not. I'll rob some of the things I was going to put on the tree for him."

She opened a closet and chose half a dozen small wrapped packages and a jumping jack. Together they stole out of the room and across the hall and standing side by side at the foot of his bed they stuffed the stocking full, and out of the top the jumping jack peered, laughing.

In his bed Mark did not wake. He lay high on his single pillow, his arms outspread, the lashes dark upon his red cheeks.

"How he sleeps!" Edward whispered.

"As if he never meant to wake," Margaret whispered back.

"Don't say that," he said sharply under his breath.

"Oh, Ned—you're overwrought—I didn't mean—"

"I know—forgive me."

He crawled into his bed a few minutes later, agreeing with her that they must try to sleep a little while, with the day ahead. Sleep, he told himself, was impossible, until he heard from Mary where they were—and when they were coming back. But he slept at last, and was tortured by dreams of losing Mary somewhere, a small girl who had never grown up, and of searching for her and not being able to find her. Then somehow the little girl she had once been turned to Mark as he was now and it was his son for whom he searched and whom he could not find.

FOUR

THE STILLNESS of Granite Mountain was rent by the war whoops of two shrill voices. Edward Haslatt looked up mildly from a magazine he was reading, while he waited for his wife and daughter to return from their inspection of some new garments in another room. His twin grandsons, in full Indian regalia, tore around one of the stone buttresses of this fantastic house and raced out of sight. He sighed and returned to the magazine. It was a popular one, full of pictures that he disliked because he thought them meaningless exposures. He had never allowed himself to be interested in the physical aspects of women other than his wife, and now he was well past the age for that sort of thing. For this he was grateful. The struggle of the flesh was over. This was not to say that he did not have proper relations with Margaret. He could and did, as often as he felt inclined, which was decently less often as the years went, and she met his inclination gracefully, if not eagerly. Indeed so smoothly were they attuned now, as they stood upon the brink of old age together, that he occasionally felt that he would like to write a book on marriage from the man's point of view. There was something original in the idea, as he toyed with it. It would have to be done anonymously, of course. He knew he would never do it. Self-revelation, even namelessly, was impossible for him.

Though his life as a modestly successful publisher of books had been spent among writers of all varieties, he continued to be amazed, amused and sometimes repelled by their willingness to strip the covers from their most secret parts. Yet sometimes he envied them the relief of complete revelation, even while he knew he could never achieve it. For one thing, Margaret would certainly know about it, and he shrank from such exposure, even to her. She knew him through and through, of that he was well aware, and yet they had never put each other into words, as once she said they must. He had never learned her trick of ready speech. Perhaps she, however, had learned to read through silence.

He put down the magazine restlessly and getting up he went to the stupendous window of paneless glass which Lewis had built so many years ago. Such windows were uncommon then, and visitors from Chedbury had told each other privately that they would not like to live in all outdoors. What was a house for if not to hide those inside from those outside? Chedbury had not changed much in all these years. Even the Second World War had not changed the people much. Young men had gone away and some had not come back, and Chedbury was still wrangling over the sort of monument they should put up to the dead. Tom Seaton wanted a white marble shaft in the middle of the green, but Edward had violently opposed such a monstrosity.

"That's because Mark wasn't killed," Tom had said rudely.

Edward had gazed at him over his glasses. "I believe you, too, did not suffer a personal loss."

"At least I went over and saw our men dying," Tom had retorted, "and Fioretta's nephew was killed."

It was true. John Carosi had lost his son in the Battle of the Bulge. Edward, who had been quarreling with him only the day before over the fourth strike at the shop, had put on his hat and coat and for the first time in his life had gone to South Chedbury. It was the week after Christmas and there was the usual snow on the ground and the driving had been bad, even though he no longer drove himself. His frequent trips to New York demanded a chauffeur, now that he was no longer young.

He had found John sitting in his shirt sleeves in a tiny parlor, his fists clenched on his knees as he stared at a picture of Jack in his uniform. John had grown heavy in his middle age and he was sweating with agony, the tears running down his cheeks. Upstairs his wife was wailing among his daughters.

"John, I'm very sorry to hear this," Edward had said at once.

He had found it difficult to meet John's dark and suffering eyes.

"Sit down, Mr. Haslatt," he said without getting up.

Edward had sat down, his hat and stick between his knees. He felt his skin prickling with pain.

"Jack was a fine boy," he said.

"A great boy," Carosi agreed.

"I wish there was something I could do," Edward went on. "I know there isn't, but for my own sake I just had to come and tell you that I—that I would really have done anything to prevent this."

"It's good of you," Carosi said. "I just have to sweat it through."

Silence had fallen between them. He wished that he could assure Carosi that it was a good way for a boy to die—sweet and right to die for one's country, and all that—but he had not been able to say the words. Death was neither sweet nor right for young men like Jack, full of life and mischief, and he could not bring himself to say a thing he did not believe. He sat with his heart aching in his bosom and thinking of Mark, who unless the vile war ended, would have to get into it.

But the war ended abruptly. Two years later to Edward's dismay Mark decided to enlist anyway, in the air force, "to get his share over with," he said.

Edward told John Carosi in the shop. "I hope he doesn't get ground into the mud, the way mine did," Carosi had answered. "That's what keeps my wife cryin'. There wasn't nothing to bring home to bury."

Edward had not been able to answer this, and before he could conquer the sickness in the pit of his stomach Carosi had turned away and had said brusquely, "I may as well tell you that the union's goin' to push for an increase again."

For once Edward had welcomed the quarrel. "I shall have to stop publishing books at this rate, and you know it. People won't buy novels that cost three and four dollars apiece."

"They still buy Harrow's," Carosi retorted.

"You know I've always liked to publish new writers, young ones," Edward said. "This way I don't dare take the risk."

"That's not my business," Carosi replied.

"It would be your business if Haslatt Brothers failed."

"Personally I'd be sorry, but the union would take care of me," Carosi had said firmly.

. . . He lost his fight with the union and wages went up again. What he had said was true. In any struggle the new and the young went down and sorrowfully he rejected manuscripts of young and awkward writers. He was safe enough only so long as the half dozen or so of his best-selling older authors kept alive. Their books were not as good as they had been— even Harrow's were not. Writers were, he supposed, confounded by the times.

So, for that matter, was he. Mark was still in the air force and he wished he would come home. What was the use of risking one's life every day to carry food into Berlin? He had never wanted the boy to be a pilot. But a son paid no heed nowadays to what his father wanted. His mind harked back, upon this, to his own father. Remembering that kind gray figure, now so long dust save for the spirit of this memory, he took pride in thinking that he had never really defied his own father. Then his sense of justice reminded him that neither had he, as a young man, been confronted with the issues of life and death that faced Mark now.

His imagination, always slow, was nevertheless strong when it was lit by love, and he thought of Mark waking in the morning, day after day, to consider, however swiftly, whether night would see him still alive. The lift was as safe as it could be made, Edward supposed, and yet he had made it his duty to know how many young men actually were killed in this cold combat with a country monstrous in its silent power. He was not for a moment confused by any illusions. It was not to feed hungry people that Mark continually risked his life. Power was being matched against power, even in this trivial way, and his son—oh, agony to think of it—was merely expendable.

He heard footsteps outside the door and he turned from the window, glad to be distracted from his constant and secret worry over Mark. Margaret came in ready to go home. She had put on her hat and the jacket to her new spring suit. It was a matter of course nowadays that she bought her clothes in New York, and this suit was the result of her going with him last week. She and Sandra had gone to some fancy place and picked it out, and at the same time she had bought some things for Mary. He took enormous pride in Margaret's good looks. It was an achievement when a woman kept as slim, or almost as slim, as she had been and without wrinkles. Tom's wife, Fioretta, had run to fat, in the way of Italian women.

Strange marriage that! Thomas Seaton was only cold in his grave when Tom had suddenly decided to marry the pretty Italian girl who was John Carosi's youngest sister, twenty-six years younger than he, and almost as many years younger than Tom. There had been no wedding. Tom had informed the family one day that he and Fioretta would be married and sail at once for Italy, where he might stay a year. He had stayed four months, and meantime Mrs. Seaton, restless in the big empty house, had gone to live in Paris with Dorothea, her divorced sister. Tom had come back suddenly because Fioretta was pregnant and he wanted his child born an American. He had declared that he wanted no children, but that Fioretta, incurably maternal, had cheated him. She had continued to cheat him amiably, and the Seaton house was noisy with three rather spoiled but extremely beautiful little girls.

Edward was secretly fond of his Italian sister-in-law, while realizing that it was a comedown for the Seaton family. But the new times were very queer. Nothing was as it had once been. His own mother, though it had been no business of hers, had made a fuss over the marriage. "I never thought we'd be connected with South Chedbury through the Seatons," she had said acidly.

She never knew either, he supposed, how nearly Baynes and Sandra had come to a divorce five years ago. Sandra had even gone to Reno. As he had surmised, this time it was money, and no other than Harold Ames, still president of a New York bank. It had not come off, however. The directors had met and after violent argument had informed Harold that it would make people lose confidence in the bank if he divorced his old wife to marry a woman who though not young, perhaps, at least looked sinfully young, and if he persisted, another president would be chosen. Harold, confronted with loss of prestige and mindful of his bald head, at which Sandra had unwisely already poked some fun, withdrew prudently before anything was made public.

Sandra had come home at once, pretending that she had only been on a trip. She brought back, with her infallible instinct, a novel about New Mexico written by a young veteran who, dying with tuberculosis, had gone to end his days in the sun, and she had been frank to forestall scolding.

"I see now that Hal only loved me as a sort of shadow sister of yours," she had told Margaret. "I was a fool," she added honestly, "and I shan't be one again. Baynes is an archangel and too good for me."

Baynes was, in a dry way, a saint, Edward admitted. After their mother had died of double pneumonia the winter of unprecedented snows, when Chedbury was without light or fuel for nearly a week, and the whole of New England was winterbound, Baynes had taken Louise to the New York office, where she had become a perfectionist with the adding machine and had risen to be treasurer of the company. Never again had she or Edward referred to the single dreadful night when she had revealed herself of a heart. He continued mildly affectionate toward her, as his sister, and she grew less and less affectionate toward anybody. She maintained a two-room apartment in New York, furnished with her mother's things, and developed a zeal for museums, and had become, to Edward's astonishment, something of an expert in Japanese art. She had a few friends, equally absorbed, and he supposed she was happy. At any rate, he had never been able to do anything about Louise.

Margaret was drawing on her pearl-gray gloves. The gray suit, light enough almost to match her white hair, was, as she well knew, singularly good with her pink cheeks and blue eyes. Her little vanities pleased him and made him love her the more fondly. Beside her Mary looked like a warm dark little dove—a darling dove at that, very pleasant in her swirling brown skirts. Edward liked the new long skirts, after the years of tight and narrow ones, from whose knees he had so often averted his eyes.

"Shall I tell him?" Margaret asked of her daughter.

"Tell me what?" Edward demanded. "Of course I'm to be told."

"Mary is going to have another baby," Margaret announced.

Mary smiled at her father. The marriage, contrary to all his expectations and even wishes, had been a very happy one. Enveloped in her husband's worship, Mary had grown softly dependent and willfully clinging as she left her girlhood behind.

"Lew is going to be surprised," she said sweetly.

"When's he coming back?"

"Next week."

Harrow had flown to London to quarrel with his English publishers over a cut in royalties. The internal troubles of a socialist Britain were none of his affair, he had declared loudly over the transatlantic telephone, and he did not intend to be impoverished by Englishmen. It was not as if he were a Socialist or a Communist or any of these new kinds of persons. As the son of a drunkard and a laundry woman he knew enough about people to believe that they would always sponge on others who had regular jobs, and he considered socialism a delusion, devised by the sons of the rich out of guilty conscience and idleness. Anybody else, he often said, would know better. People would take all they could get, just as he did.

"I thought you weren't going to risk this business again," Edward grumbled. "When the twins were born I certainly remember hearing Lewis say he wouldn't let you have any more children."

"He did say that," Mary replied. Her dark eyes, full of soft mischief, looked into his with deep and worldly wisdom.

"You didn't embark on this purposely, did you?" Edward inquired.

"Not really," she said, ambiguous in his presence. Her soft red lips folded with some of her old stubbornness.

Ah, well, she had grown very far away from him. The days when he had felt her very flesh was his were long gone. She had become a pretty, rather distant woman, who stirred in him only now and then the memories of a small oversensitive girl. If he had lost her there seemed nevertheless to be some sort of increasing friendship between her and her mother, though less a mother-daughter relationship, perhaps, than that of two women who were able at last to like one another. He did not pretend to understand it, especially when he remembered past antagonism and how often he had tried to console his child.

"Well, good-by," he said, sighing. "You'll have to make your own peace with your husband. At least the doctors will be better now than they were ten years ago. I suggest, however, that you don't make it twins again."

Both women laughed, which was what he had intended them to do. He stooped to kiss his daughter, his dry lips frosty and not touching the rich red of her full mouth. He had a horror of lipstick staining his clipped white mustache.

"Good-by, darling," Mary said comfortably. "If you see the Indians on the way down the mountain, please tell them to come and get ready for lunch. I wish you'd stay but Mother says you won't."

"No, no. I like my meals in peace," he declared.

From the comfortable sedan car he looked at his daughter as she stood on the stone threshold of her home. The wind was blowing her short brown curls and except for the content and the wisdom in her eyes she might have been a girl. Certainly she still looked young enough to be Harrow's daughter. He waved and then spoke to the chauffeur as the car moved away.

"Be careful how you go around the bends. My grandsons are probably hiding behind a rock somewhere."

Under the robe his hand sought Margaret's, as usual. He liked to sit beside her, hand in hand, and watch the familiar landscape of Chedbury rise nearer as they descended.

"I wondered why Mary wanted all those negligees," Margaret said, smiling.

"Is it safe to have a Caesarean after thirty-five?" he inquired anxiously. It had been apparent ten years ago when the twins were ready to make their dual appearance that Mary's frame was too delicate for normal functions—too delicate, he did not doubt, to be married at all to the grossness of a man like Lewis Harrow, but on that dark picture he would not allow himself to dwell. He had not been able to sleep the night after Mary's wedding. What was the fellow doing to his little child? It had been almost better not to know where she was, the night she ran away. But the next morning had brought them news in her own voice over the telephone. They were in some little town in Maine, having driven all night, and they were at that moment going to be married before a justice of the peace.

"Stop!" he had commanded that soft determined voice ringing in his ear. "You mustn't do this, Mary! I forbid it—absolutely!"

"I will do it," she had replied and had hung up the receiver. He heard the click which cut her off again and he had turned to Margaret, who was standing beside him, her hands clasped tightly at her throat.

"She's getting married now!" he had gasped.

"Where?" Margaret had cried.

He had stared at her blankly. "I don't know!" Only then had he realized that Mary had not even spoken the name of the town. Ah, purposely she had not told him the name of the town!

She and Lewis Harrow had not come home for nearly two years. They had gone to England and to France. When they did come home to The Eagle it was to rest and to prepare for the birth of the children. He had not been able to believe that the swollen little figure was that of his Mary, his child. For a brief while, when she lay at death's door before the doctor had decided to operate, he had reclaimed her again.

"You shouldn't have married her!" he had exclaimed in utmost agitation to Harrow. "This is your—your—excessive vitality."

In the midst of his own terror Harrow had paused to stare at him and then to burst into loud and unexplained laughter.

When Mary was saved, however, and he went in to see his grandsons, he felt no return of his brief recognition. There she lay, pale and placidly triumphant in her bed, a robust if small infant in either arm. He had been compelled to readjust himself quickly.

"Well, well," he had said with something more than his usual vigor.

"Nice, aren't they?" she had asked.

"They look healthy," he had replied with reserve.

They were healthy. He believed that his grandsons were overstuffed with vitamins. It was difficult, moreover, to talk to two boys, and one could never get them separately. One boy, he sometimes thought, he could have interested in something, say in stamps, or even in some of the types at the printing shop, but two were disconcerting. They began to romp at any moment—rough-housing, they called it. And a grandparent had no chance nowadays in competition with radio programs and comic books. These preoccupations of the immature he deeply disapproved, and yet such was the softness of his heart that he could not forbear picking up a handful of the wretchedly printed books from the newsstands where he bought the morning papers on his days in New York. Two or three times, troubled by the effect of the lurid pictures on his descendants, he had tried to read some of the pages and had not the least notion of what they were about. He was appalled at the taste of his grandsons. There must be, he told himself, something in these comics that he did not see, just as he could not see what Mark had enjoyed in his endless evenings about town, aimlessly, or so he feared, pursuing pleasure. But at the thought of Mark, his heart forbade judgment.

A yell surpassing any he had ever heard before broke off his thoughts. The car came to a violent stop, and two painted heathen jabbered at the window.

"What are they saying?" he demanded of Margaret.

"Give them each a dime," she said, smiling. "They are pretending to hold us up."

"But isn't it very bad for them to think they can succeed?" he asked, anxious as always for their morals.

"It doesn't mean anything," she said comfortably and felt for her own purse.

"Oh, I'll do it," he said with some irritation, "if it has to be done, that is."

He took out his wallet and opening the window he gazed into two round and ruddy faces, so charming in smiles that his heart softened again and trying not to let Margaret see, he took out two quarters instead of dimes and pressed them into the filthiest hands he had touched for years.

"Mind you, this is all against my principles," he said earnestly in the slightly didactic voice of which he was almost entirely unconscious, except when, as now, it grated surprisingly on his own ears. "You shouldn't hold up anybody—most of all your own poor old grandfather. I need my money for my old age. What if I have to go to the poorhouse?"

Compunction appeared in the two pairs of dark eyes.

"You can come and live with us," Peter suggested.

"We'll come and bring you home," Paul added.

"You still want the quarters, I notice," he said dryly, although his heart was further softened to the point, he told himself, of folly.

"Just for the present we need them," Paul said sweetly, clutching his booty.

They let out their war whoops and seeing them dash into the underbrush, he remembered their mother's message and shouted after them, "Go home to luncheon!" He sank back panting. "I doubt they can hear anyone, they're making so much noise."

"Their stomachs will lead them homeward," Margaret replied. She felt for his hand again and leaning toward him she kissed his ear while the car started forward. He glanced involuntarily at the little mirror. The chauffeur's eyes were set coldly ahead, thank God.

"Now what's that for?" he demanded in a guarded voice.

"Because you gave them quarters, Ned," she replied. They looked at each other for a long minute, her eyes were soft and still so blue, and then he was abashed.

"Oh, well," he grumbled, "it's only once—though of course they are utterly without discipline."

He held her hand firmly and was conscious of deep inner happiness.

This welling inner happiness was something that had grown only as he approached what was commonly called old age. In years he knew that indeed he was an aging if not an old man. Mark, his youngest son, was twenty his next birthday and Mark had been a belated child. A child almost perfect, he often reflected with something like fatuousness. He had spent much time upon Mark's education. The other children had grown up in the usual round of schools and college, but Mark had, so to speak, been hand grown.

It had been a disappointment he did not acknowledge even to himself that this dearest son had not shown the slightest sign, as yet, of interest in the firm of Haslatt Brothers. Instead, by some astonishing twist of inheritance Tommy, after deciding not to marry Dinny and then sowing an agitating number of wild oats in that unhappy period between wars, had settled down into the family firm with a gaiety combined with a cynical prudence that forced Edward to realize that perhaps he had produced a publisher superior to himself by nature. By a process of inheritance far beyond the understanding of man, Tommy combined in himself his father's love of books and his uncle Baynes's instinct, or flair. Sandra loudly proclaimed Tommy's virtues and claimed him as the son she herself should have had, if she had only had the sense to know it earlier. After years of refusing to have any children Sandra now at a lean and chic middle age wished that she had let nature take its course with her, although she added, "Nature on the loose would probably have produced something that looked neither like Baynes or me." She remembered the grimness of the remote Uncle Henry Haslatt, now long dead, and declared finally that his visage alone made her content to be childless. Nevertheless she adored her Tommy, and was far more proud than Margaret had been when he chose as his wife the prettiest debutante of her year in New York.

After this marriage Sandra had tried to force Tom and Fioretta out of the old Seaton house, because she maintained that Fioretta made it look like something in South Chedbury whereas Diantha would have made it what it had been designed to be, a family seat.

Edward had taken the side of Tom and Fioretta, however. He was grateful to her for marrying Tom and removing him as a bad influence upon his elder son, and therefore even remotely, perhaps, from Mark. At any rate it was only after Tom's marriage that the great change had appeared in Tommy.

Thinking of Fioretta now he drew his old gold watch from his pocket.

"We have time to stop by Tom's, if you like. I don't suppose Mary would mind if we mention her condition. Fioretta is always so pleased at the prospect of a new child in the family."

"Very well," Margaret replied, her voice pleasant.

Some moments later Edward leaned toward the chauffeur and directed his stop at the white painted gate which Tom had set between the stone posts in order to keep his offspring within the bounds of Fioretta's hearty cries. Fioretta sensibly had not wanted the house changed and it looked as it always had, a little less spotless than of old, perhaps, as to white paint. The flowers, too, had degenerated from lilies and English tree roses to a general effect of zinnias and marigolds, and he disapproved the row of tall sunflowers against the dignified background of the house itself. Fioretta kept chickens in the back yard, and considered sunflower seeds conducive to eggs.

As usual she saw them through the window and came running out to greet them warmly. She had been plump when Tom married her, a darkly rosy creature with huge black eyes and a red mouth. Now she was frankly more than plump. She still loved the bright deep orange hues and crimsons of her girlhood and they somehow became her in spite of spread.

"Uncle Ed—Auntie Margaret!" she cried in her fresh voice. The one sign of her insecurity in this family was that she had never brought herself to call them by their first names. Only when the children grew old enough to talk had she solved the problem by calling them what she taught the children to say.

"Come in, do! I've just got lunch on the table—special ravioli Tom does love. Ah, now, sit down! For what else should you come just when I tell the girl to dish up?"

"We can't, dear," Margaret said gently. "Ned doesn't digest starches, and luncheon is waiting for us, I'm sure. And you know how it puts the cook out if we don't come home. We just wanted to see you and the children and Tom, if he's home, to tell you the latest family news."

"The children are coming home from school this minute and Tom is mending the grape arbor. I tell him every year we should have more grapes so I can make all our wine at home. It is better for Tom than the boughten stuff. My poppa taught me how to make it so good, like they do at home in Italy."

"It is delicious," Margaret said.

"Now," Fioretta said in her cozy busy voice, "what's the news?"

"We've just come from The Eagle and Mary told us today that she is going to have a baby." Margaret spoke simply as though to a child.

"My God, how nice!" Fioretta's great eyes rolled and she threw up her hands. "So she's goin' to get ahead of me? She's goin' to have the next baby. I'm goin' to tell Tom. He won't let me have any more little babies. What you think of that? And me with my arms empty! My children are all too big. You know what? That Viola of mine she's kissing a boy already. Can you imagine!"

Fioretta flung back her head and laughter rolled from her rich red mouth.

Edward as usual was silent. He basked in this generous presence of Fioretta. Actually they had very little to say to each other. Fioretta had never, so far as he knew, read a book. John Carosi, now, was a reader. In later years he had often quarreled with his employer over the books published by Haslatt Brothers. Last year, when Edward had chosen to publish *The Rights of Employers in a Democracy,* written by the head of a great utility firm, John had thrown his gray cap on the floor one morning when Edward came into the shop.

"Mr. Haslatt, I don't work the press on that book!"

"Very well, John," Edward had replied. "I'll give it to one of the other men."

"I don't work in this shop," John had declared next.

"I don't want you to stop with me any longer than you wish," Edward had replied with dignity. "But I do reserve the right to publish two sides of any question. Don't forget I was entirely willing to publish *The Union and the Worker* last year."

"There can't be two sides to the right," John said.

"There are two sides to everything," Edward had retorted. He had proceeded through the shop, examining, with eyes grown quick and shrewd through the years, the presses pounding out the books he had chosen to present to the world. He had steadfastly resisted both Baynes and Tommy on the matter of enlarging the works.

"I do not intend to publish more books," he said at least several times a month. "Better ones, yes, every year—but no more."

"Come next Sunday then, please," Fioretta was urging. "I will make something special for you, Uncle Ed, not starch, a beef stew like something in Italy. Please, please!"

The children had reached home and came swarming out in a dark brood, all of them more Italian than English in their looks. Their eyes were lively, their voices piercing, and their health apparent in every move and word. They surrounded their mother and hugged her ardently while she laughed. "Look, now, at my monkeys. Children, you should beg Uncle Ed to come to Sunday dinner!"

"Uncle Ed, please."

"Auntie Margaret, make him."

He was inevitably pleased at their loud desire to have his company, though why he did not know, for he found very little to say to children at any time.

"Now why do you want me to come?" he demanded, mildly jocular. "I can't run around with you and I don't play any games."

Dark eyes met dark eyes and silence fell.

"Speak, children," Fioretta commanded with the warm imperiousness born of absolute love. "Say what is in your hearts. Don't be afraid."

Viola threw back her heavy curls. "I'll tell you why, Uncle Ed—we all feel you like us."

"There!" Fioretta cried admiringly. "Isn't that the truth! Nice the way she said it!"

"Very nice!" he admitted, and putting out his hand he touched the child's warm olive cheek.

"Lovely," Margaret said tenderly, "and we will come. Now you must all go and have your luncheon."

The ardent children left their mother and pressed around them, and upon this picture in the warm spring sunshine Tom appeared, the father of this family, to be sure, and yet always seeming somewhat puzzled and even astonished by what he had brought almost unwittingly into existence.

Lean and sandy hued as ever, he wore an overall of khaki color and in his hand he held a pruning knife. "They'll strangle you," he said. "I know what it's like. They try to choke me every day of their lives."

He waved the knife, pretending to stay them as they swarmed now toward him at the sound of his voice. He elbowed the older ones aside ruthlessly and opened his arms to his youngest daughter. "Come here, Baby," he said. "You're the only one that can kiss me. Here on the cheek, please!"

She planted a noisy kiss at the spot he indicated and Margaret laughed. "Tom, Tom, I wonder that our father doesn't rise from his grave!"

Fioretta turned solemn. "You think the old man wouldn't like it?"

"He'd love it, bless him," Margaret said. "He'd love you, Fioretta. Bless you, too."

She kissed Fioretta's round and rosy cheek. "We all do, darling. Don't mind me. And if I say anything you don't understand just forget it. Tom knows what I mean and he'll tell you."

"Aren't you going to stop for lunch?" Tom demanded.

"No, dear. We're coming Sunday."

Fioretta suddenly bethought herself of the news. "Tom, what you think? Mary is going to have a baby! Now, Tom, I ask you, why can she have a baby and not me?"

"Shut up, Fioretta," he answered with affection. "We've got more than we need now and there'll be an accident or two. I know you."

"Aw, Poppa, we'd like a new baby!" Viola pleaded.

"You just wait, my girl," Tom told his daughter. "You'll have your own all too soon."

He turned to his sister. "Meg, do you think Mary ought, when you consider the twins?"

"It's too late now," Margaret said with the tranquillity that was the chief sign of her years. "We'll just have to keep prodding Lew to take care of her. He means to, but he forgets when he's writing, as usual, his greatest novel."

Tom's thin and handsome lip lifted in something like a sneer. "Count upon it, Ed, there'll be a childbirth in the book, a husband, like as not, hanging over his dying wife's bed, and moaning that he'd rather have lost the child."

"Don't joke, Tom," Margaret said sharply.

Fioretta, listening, was suddenly angry. "Ain't he wicked? My God, sometimes I think I got the worst man in the world! Mary won't die—what the devil!"

When she was angry and in the bosom of the family Fioretta returned wholeheartedly to South Chedbury. Indignation burned in the hot gaze she now bestowed upon her husband.

"Shut up, Fioretta," Tom said, from habit. "Well, we'll be looking for you Sunday, Ed."

They turned away, knowing that until they left Tom's brood would delay in the sunshine, and sitting in the car again, hand in hand, they rode in silence, each aware of warmth in the other's heart.

"Do you really think your father would have approved South Chedbury in his house?" Edward asked.

"Of course it couldn't have been in his day," she replied. "Things were so defined then, somehow. Mother would have made it impossible for Fioretta. But if it had been Mother who died instead of Father, I think he could have lived there quite happily with Fioretta, growing drowsy in the grape arbor, drinking her wine and spotting his waistcoat more and more— and the little girls would have loved him extravagantly."

"They love everything extravagantly," he murmured.

He was surprised at her reply.

"Do you know, Ned, I've come to believe in extravagant love—it's the only thing that makes life in this world possible. Maybe Fioretta's children will teach us all."

He knew the deep distress in her mind these days. She had given up much that she had once done. After the war she had even given up Red Cross work. "It all seems useless," she had said to him one night. "It's just patchwork. There has to be something different in the world, a new approach to the whole of life."

They talked together now more than they ever had. He looked back on his earlier years with a sort of wonder. He had been so busy when his children were young that he had very little time for talk, or indeed for anything except the anxieties of a livelihood for those whom he loved and had too little time to enjoy. It was he alone, or so he had felt, who stood between them and the overwhelming world.

One of his most successful books had been written by an explorer in the jungles of Sumatra, an adventuring sort of fellow whom he had heartily disliked when he met him at a dinner Baynes and Sandra had given for him in New York when the book was published. The jungle, however, Edward had never forgotten. It had crept up on him in the night for years until he had been able to identify it with the overwhelming world he feared. Stoutly conservative, even to the extent of present distress over the socialism now rampant in England, he would have declared himself at all times unafraid of the insecurities of extreme individualism. Yet the nightmare of the encroaching jungle had beset him until one night in his wakefulness he had confided to Margaret the recurrence of the dream.

"I seem to be walking along a narrow path, enclosed in walls of the most livid green trees and vines. They aren't ordinary greenery—nothing like what we have here in New England. They're horrible, they keep growing new branches and tentacles. The roots of the trees are not even decent. They're like great sucking mouths, clutching the earth and draining it dry. The further I go—and I must go on—I can't help myself, it seems—the tighter the green walls press around me, and I can't see ahead. You are following behind me—sometimes just you and Mark, sometimes all of you —sometimes lately only Mark. I keep fighting off the horrible green tendrils reaching out. But they get me at last and I wake, strangling."

Margaret, waked from sleep, had listened, her eyes startled. "You're worrying about something," she declared. "You haven't told me everything."

"I've told you all I know," he had protested in honesty.

For the next few months she had persuaded him toward going to a psychiatrist, which he had resisted with profound conviction that such stuff was all charlatanry. In the end he had gone, however, commanded by Wynne, his doctor these many years.

"Your blood pressure is far too high, and yet you're as lean as a hound dog," Wynne had told him. "It isn't overeating that's doing it. It's whatever is gnawing at your mind. You're a born worrier like your New England ancestors. Go and have a talk with some professional—unless you can confess to a Catholic priest."

Confession was impossible to Edward's Protestant mind, and he had in the end made a carefully noncommittal appointment with an unknown though highly recommended name in New York. There he had gone soon after the inevitability of the war had burst upon his dismayed and terrified consciousness. Dr. Hastings had proved a tall, spare, pleasantly cold-looking gentleman who had listened respectfully to Edward's halting account of his nightmare. A succession of detached though acute questions had led after two hours or so to a conclusion that had been immensely helpful.

"There is nothing wrong with you, Mr. Haslatt," Hastings had said. "You seem an exceptionally well-balanced and disciplined person. What you are suffering from is a disease called modern times. You, like all of us, have no security. Our American way of life so far does not provide it. Whether this is good or bad is beside the point. I am no moralist. But you have to recognize that though you are by nature and choice an individualist of the strongest dye, yet the fact is you are unconsciously frightened of the present hazards of extreme individualism, even while you reject anything else. You must learn to accept insecurity. As long as you live our society will not provide it for you. Say to yourself, 'I have an ample income and a satisfying wife'—you are sure you are telling me the truth there?"

"Completely," Edward replied. "I am what is called a one-woman man —that is, in my wife I have found all women. She is beautiful and intelligent."

"Very unusual," Dr. Hastings had said in a dry voice. "Such being the case, I am sure you can deal with your own fears of insecurity. Consider it part of the world state of mind, the atmosphere of our generation."

He had left the doctor's office strangely lighthearted. It was true that in the midst of the hazards of business he had always made a good and on the whole increasingly ample income, though he was sound rather than rich. He had never lost anyone he loved, his parents he supposed scarcely coming under the category of real love. Margaret had passed through her middle years without the neuroticism to which he had heard women were susceptible, and she did not find him unpleasing in their intimate relations, even as she grew older. He tried, of course, to be considerate. He had even bought a book on menopause in women, which she had snatched away from him, laughing at him as she did so.

"Don't read up on me, Ned!" she had exclaimed. "I'm as normal as possible, thank God, and I still love you."

She had been a perfect wife, or as nearly so as a mortal man could expect. Her few faults were negligible—a tendency to be careless about the house as she grew older, dust and so on seeming less important to her while it became more important to him, and his clothes were not always sent to be pressed when he wished them to be. He felt, sometimes, too, that she thought about a good many things of which she did not tell him, though when he questioned her, asking, for example, so direct a demand as, "What are you thinking about when you look like that?" she answered only vaguely. Once she had almost lost her temper.

"I do wish," she had said with some of her old girlish vigor, "that you would not ask me what I am thinking. My thoughts are ungovernable and always were. I let them lead me by the nose and I'd be ashamed sometimes to tell where I am."

"You needn't be ashamed before me," he had reminded her.

"Oh, I wouldn't be exactly ashamed," she had said carelessly. "It's just that it would be too bothersome to explain how I got to thinking whatever I'm thinking."

"Do you remember," he had reminded her, "how, when we were about to be engaged, you demanded complete and perfect truth between us?"

This she had answered inconsequentially, he thought. She had said, "I knew nothing whatever then about being married. If I had always told you the truth, you'd have divorced me by now."

"Never!" he exclaimed, much alarmed.

"Besides," she had gone on, "what I didn't know is that when two people live together long and closely they tell each other less and less in words. They know everything anyway—everything, that is, except what they don't want to know."

"Has there been something about me that you haven't wanted to know?" he had asked after some thought.

"Nothing important," she had said in the same half-careless fashion. "When you've fretted—and you do fret, Ned, though I wish you wouldn't —it doesn't always seem worth while to bother about what little thing is fretting you."

He had been a good deal hurt when she said this and had retired into silence. Then after reflecting upon it he had been compelled to acknowledge that she was right. Had she been torn by every worry that had tortured him, she would have lost her calm, that blessed atmosphere in which he found such strength and refuge. All the same, it had been his fretting, as she called it, that had made his business a success when other publishers were failing. Not even Harrow could have saved him had he been incautious.

Now on this perfect day in May all struggles were in the past. He had got rid of the jungle, by will power and by reading philosophy again. In his day at Harvard William James had been a professor of philosophy and remembering that vivid life-loving figure, he had returned to books he had not read since he left the presence of his teacher. He had been too shy to tell James what he felt about him in those college years, and had passed through his classes merely a name on a roll call.

Reading and rereading these books, Edward in his approaching old age felt a new vigor of the soul return to him. William James had been an American, he told himself, a philosopher, a thinking active man, who gloried in the pragmatism that was a part of America's very soul. He read aloud sometimes to Margaret in the evening the striding powerful words, the abhorrence of violence and war which today, in spite of the mildness of the May sunshine, overshadowed the sky of every intelligent mind.

What had happened to make Americans now think the cruelties of violence signified strength? Strength was to be found only in "the moral equivalent of war," a powerful wisdom, a discipline stronger than any military force could develop, because it was discipline of the self by the self.

He dared not voice such thoughts. Chedbury would never have understood them and he would have been smeared with red. Yet did the young men never think such thoughts, as they marched on alien roads in half the countries of the world?

He remembered a night, soon after Pearl Harbor, when Mark was a boy of thirteen. He had gone upstairs to Mark's room to tell him good night —a discarded habit, for the growing boy did not like to be babied. But he had not been able to restrain his fears. Surely the war would be over before Mark grew up. He had bent over his son and had kissed his windburned cheek. Mark had been skating all day on the first thick ice of the season.

"You've had a good day," Edward had said. "I can tell it from your face."

"I've had a swell day," Mark had replied. He had gazed into his father's face for a long moment, his eyes dark with what he could not know. Then, inexplicably, he had spoken those words that were graven upon Edward's heart.

"I hope I can live," Mark had said.

Edward had restrained the first impulse of his life to weep wildly. "Of course you will live," he had said. Then unable to bear the pain in his throat he had gone into the hall and shut the door and let the silent tears flow down his cheeks. He had not been able to repeat the scene to Margaret, for shame lest he weep again, and it remained locked within him.

Neither of his sons had been interested in philosophy. Tommy had majored harmlessly in English literature and Mark had cared for nothing but science, and especially physics. Sandy had actually gone in for medicine. He did not approve women doctors but he felt it only decent not to say so while his younger daughter plowed her difficult way through to successful practice. She had put up her shingle now in Boston, and every quarter he paid such bills as she had not been able to manage and prayed that she would marry some decent man and give up the struggle. Sandy, the grimmest and the gayest of his children, was not likely to give up. She was handsome rather than pretty, her Grandfather Haslatt having left her his somewhat too long nose, but she was the favorite of her Grandmother Seaton and likely, Margaret had said one day, to come into something substantial when old Mrs. Seaton died.

"That is nothing to me," he had said stiffly.

"It's something to me, you old poker back," Margaret had retorted laughing at him. "Sandy will never get married to that nice boy who is in love with her unless she can pay her share of the expenses."

"You aren't wishing for your mother's death, I hope," he had replied.

"Of course not," Margaret had said in her most cheerful voice. "At the same time, Mother cannot live forever, and I am glad she likes Sandy and I hope she persuades Aunt Dorothea, who seems perennial, to give what she has to Sandy, too. Mary doesn't need it, and the boys can manage."

"Who's this fellow in love with Sandy?" he had then demanded.

"Don't you remember the young man she brought down last Christmas Eve?"

"Not particularly," he had been compelled to say, scraping his memory.

"The big one who broke the footstool when he sat on it?"

"That fellow! I remember thinking I wouldn't like him messing around inside me—a surgeon, wasn't he?"

"He is," Margaret said. "He has curiously delicate hands. In debt up to his neck, too, for his education—it'll be years before they can make ends meet."

This had troubled him a good deal, and he had pondered ways of making marriage possible for this daughter upon whom he had never until now spent much thought. Sandy had been so healthy, so normal, whatever that meant, that she had grown up almost without his noticing her, except to see, with an irritation which made him ashamed, that she got better grades at school than either of her brothers. Ought not parents to make it possible, he asked himself, for young people to marry at the reasonable hour of the highest biological urge? He and Margaret had been young, and the costs of living then were low. Now it was practically impossible, unless one were a war veteran, to synchronize marriage and biological needs. He had a horror of the easy sexual intercourse that seemed acceptable today even among his friends, and though he could see nothing he could do about it, he did not like the numbers of illegitimate children being born. Such polygamous children were the problems of a monogamous society. Surely there had been far fewer in his youth. Tom's daughter Viola, he feared, was not the premature infant she had been tactfully declared. Very robust, for prematurity! But nothing had been said in Chedbury, of course—not openly. Nobody had dared to say anything to him, naturally.

He preferred not to think it possible that Sandy might be sleeping with her young man, fortified by the astounding amount of protective information that she might have. Agitated, however, by this possibility, he had been casting about in his mind how he could offer her an income without offending her pride, when Mrs. Seaton died suddenly a year ago this May. He refused to think it opportune but the truth was there. He and Margaret had gone over to Paris and had brought the narrow and ancient body back with them in a metal casket. Margaret had not wept. Prepared for her tears he had been nevertheless relieved when they did not flow.

"You aren't hiding your feelings from me?" he had inquired anxiously. Her hand on his cheek had comforted him. "No, darling. It was time."

This was all she had said. They had left an even more desiccated old woman behind them in the overdecorated French apartment, a frame so ancient, a visage so withered that it was impossible to believe that for her sake a young and ardent man had once fled both fame and fortune to live with her in happy sin for nearly twoscore years.

"Good-by, children," Aunt Dorothea had said, presenting both her leathery cheeks. To her they were children, though with graying hair and grandchildren of their own.

"It is frightening to live so long," Margaret had said.

Sitting beside her as they drove into the wide gate of their comfortable home, he had wondered rather soberly if what she had said was true. It did not seem possible, this May morning, that anything could be worse than death.

The pleasant weather held through the week with increasing and unseasonable heat. In the garden after breakfast on Sunday morning Margaret exclaimed over flowers forcing themselves to premature blooming.

The roses, she told Edward, were pushing out buds that could not come to maturity.

"I wonder if that wretched atom bomb has set up some sort of heat inside the earth," she mused.

He had been tempted by the ardent sunshine to leave his pile of manuscripts, his constant week-end task, and come out into the garden just as he was, bareheaded and without putting on his topcoat. He saw her, bareheaded too, busy with a trowel, her sleeves rolled high on her still shapely arms. Sunday was her day of gardening, the aged, vociferous, and agitating Italian, Tony Antonelli, who considered the garden his possession, being that day safely at home in South Chedbury. On Mondays Margaret did not go near the garden, allowing Tony time to get over his wrath at what she had done. By Tuesday they were able to quarrel again without rancor.

"I suppose Mark could tell you," Edward now said in answer to her question. They had discussed the atom bomb through many mealtimes together. She was positive of its entire evil, and railed at him when he could not utterly agree. It was, he said, only one evil thing in an evil business. How devastating it really was he could not find out and he had made up his mind that when Mark came back he would go into the science of this most devilish of weapons. What troubled him most was not the bomb itself so much as the lack of moral principle in the scientists who had allowed themselves to make it. Surely scientists, he had told himself, ought to be the new leaders of morality, all else having failed. When Joseph Barclay had preached a violent sermon against the use of the atomic bomb, a sermon during which Margaret had sat tense, her hands clasped tightly together, Edward had wondered at such resentment. Was not the bomb merely the logical means of an inhuman process?

This he dared not say to Margaret. Instead he remarked now with a mildness to suit the day, "I suppose we should be getting ready for church —unless the sunshine can tempt you to stay home."

"I don't want to go to church," she said, "and yet somehow these days I feel we must."

"Why?" he asked with his undying curiosity concerning all she felt and thought.

"Because we are so helpless," she answered.

He did not ask, helpless against what? He knew that in spite of all he could do she was somehow, underneath her tranquillity, allowing her personal content, even her happiness, to become involved in the incomprehensible events taking place in the world. Both of them had been vaguely cheered at the stolid way in which their own people had taken hold of the political elections six months ago. Voting Republican from long habit, he had been amazed to find that Margaret had voted against him. She had not at first wanted to vote at all, maintaining that she despised equally all the presidential candidates. She would not, she declared, even go to the polls. She would stay home and crochet a doily in her new luncheon set.

This he flouted as a gesture. She crocheted beautifully as she did all things well, and there were times when he liked to see the ivory needle in her long narrow hands flashing in and out of the daffodil yellow thread. But he had learned that when she picked up such handiwork it was in the nature of a retreat from life.

"You must go," he had exclaimed. "If you do not the whole of Chedbury will know, and after your preachments, my dear, in recent years, concerning the responsibilities of women, it would not do. You may cast a blank ballot, if you like, but you must go into the booth."

Her stupefaction the next morning had aroused his immediate question.

"I thought I was making a strong protest vote," she told him, more confounded than he had ever seen her. "Instead I'm on the winning side."

"What did you do there alone in that booth?" he demanded.

She looked at him with merry eyes. "I voted the straight Democratic ticket—that's what I did—as the strongest protest I could think of against everything I didn't like."

"Do you think you'll like what you got?" he inquired with grimness.

"How do I know what I've got?" she countered. "Maybe if I'd known I was going to get it, I wouldn't have voted for it."

He had snorted at this. "That's democracy for you!"

Afterward in his office he had thought of it again and had laughed silently and alone. All over the country, he supposed, other stupefied people were discovering that they, too, had voted on the winning side. He had written an unusually cheerful letter to Mark, describing his mother's surprise, and remarking that for his own part he was glad to see people get up a little spunk.

Now, in spite of the warmth of the sunshine on this day, he was aware that the momentary optimism over such spunk was dying down. He did not at all like the look of certain signs on the horizon. At his age he did not care to face what he had gone through before in the depression. He wished Mark would come home. He could talk to Mark. A misery of longing for his son swept over him and for a moment he saw him so vividly that he all but cried out, while Margaret bent over the hyacinth bed.

"The white hyacinths are the most beautiful," she was saying. "I believe I'll cut a few spikes and put them on the church altar."

He did not answer. Lifting his eyes he could imagine he saw Mark's face, the strong lines of jaw and high cheekbones, his eyes, dark and filled with some sort of surprise, gay or not, happy or not, he could not tell. He was leaning out of the cockpit, as he had seen him lean, when he leaped up on wings from the earth.

"What did you say, Ned?" Margaret was asking.

"I said nothing," he replied. He went on with difficulty. "Suddenly I saw Mark."

"You saw him?"

"As if he were here."

He looked at her and saw her wondering, half-frightened face.

"You've been thinking too much about him," she said. "Come, let's go to church."

Vague as he was about his religion, and in spite of basic faith being still assailed by the manifold doubt of his times, he felt comfort today in the morning service. The pew he and Margaret used had belonged to his parents, and he had sat here restlessly as a small boy, and then unwillingly in his youth. Here, too, his children had sat between their parents. Once Mark, at three, always unable to be still, had fallen backward through the seat, and he had reached after him and drawn him up and had hushed his sobs against his shoulder until he slept.

The church was sweet with the scent of early lilacs, and Margaret had set the white hyacinths in a silver bowl between two bunches of the feathery flowers. The place was seldom filled nowadays and it fretted Joseph Barclay that his fiery messages found no response in the cool hearts of today's young. Though he loved them and yearned for their souls, they did not hear him. Mark had been the arch rebel.

"I can't and won't go to any more of old Joe's rantings," he had said.

"I see the man behind the words," Edward had replied.

"I can't see the man for the words," Mark had retorted too smartly.

"Shame," his mother had put in. "Think of all the minister used to do for you children—the tree at Christmastime, the parties, the baseball in spring in the square, coaching you at football, getting the money together for the swimming pool."

"All granted," Mark had replied instantly. "But preaching still turns my stomach, Mother."

They had not pressed him and when the minister had asked diffidently why Mark no longer came to church with them, Edward had told the truth. "They can't listen to sermons, nowadays, I'm afraid."

Of Mark's soul, Edward felt, he knew nothing at all. He had come near to a glimpse of it one night a week before Mark's enlistment when, his mother having gone to bed, he and the boy had sat together in the library, he marking a manuscript for the printer the next day, and Mark sunk in the biggest chair, and lost in a book of nuclear physics. He had shut it suddenly with so loud a bang that Edward had started and dropped his spectacles.

"Sorry, Dad," Mark had said.

"You are feeling vigorous," Edward had replied.

"No, only somehow for the first time glad I'm going across instead of staying home."

He had looked at his son and it seemed to him that the boy looked careworn, as though he had been sleepless.

"Can you tell me why?" he asked, delicate always before apparent probing.

Mark had answered after a moment with strange gravity. "It postpones what I really want to do."

"Well?"

"If I stayed at home I'd go straight on with my research work in atomic energy. It's what I want to know about, more than anything else. I've got to know. The whole future of man depends upon our knowing."

"Well?"

Mark had hesitated again. He was rubbing his dark hair slowly with both hands into something more than its usual disorder. "I know a fellow older than me—just got married. He's finished college—took exactly the course I want. He has to have a job, of course. Well, the only job he can get is in one of the new war plants. That's a fix, isn't it? You spend four years of your life learning something and then you've got to use what you know to kill people."

He had often wondered what Mark felt about war. They had never discussed it. That night he perceived that this duty was loathsome, and he longed to spare him, and did not know how. There was no escape for the young nowadays.

"It can't last," he had said, and had heard the words feeble in his own ears.

Mark had got to his feet and yawned. "It doesn't do to think. One day at a time, I guess. And maybe no tomorrow."

"Don't say that, son," Edward had remonstrated. "It sounds cynical."

"Sorry, Dad—only why are you older ones so afraid of sounding cynical?"

He had paused upon Mark's question.

"I suppose we were brought up to believe in the goodness of God," he had said at last.

Mark, kicking the coals into the fireplace, had not answered.

"I fear we have somehow failed you," Edward had continued. "I would like you to believe in the goodness of God and the value of life, but I don't know how to teach you. Things were simpler when I was young."

"Oh, I believe in the value of life, all right," Mark had replied. He had folded his arms on the big oaken mantel and leaning his head upon his arms he gazed down into the dying coals. "Life is wonderful—could be, that is."

"If what?" Edward asked, daring another step.

"If it could last," Mark said.

He shook himself like a big dog, stretched his arms their enormous length and yawned again. "Why am I getting serious at this time of night? Must be talking in my sleep! Good night, Dad."

"Good night, my dear son," he had replied.

Left alone he had sat puzzling for a while over the meaning of what

Mark had said. Did he mean more or less than the words contained? Who knew? So different was this world from that in which he himself had grown up that the heart even of his son was strange to him. Mark was set upon a solitary path and in spite of all the yearning of his elders, he had to tread the way alone.

The minister was proclaiming the closing hymn. What the sermon had been about Edward did not know. He had not heard a word of it. But the familiar words of the hymn fell on his ears and resounded with memory. "Lead, Kindly Light, amid th' encircling gloom." It had been his father's favorite hymn. He stood up, holding one side of the hymnbook with Margaret. He never sang, having no ear for music, but he liked to hear her clear voice singing. She had sung to their babies in the nursery, though when Mark had been born he had been compelled to remind her, so that Mark would not miss the memory of falling to sleep wrapped in the music of his mother's voice. She had been half ashamed and half laughing. "You see how much too old I am to have this baby," she had told him, pretending to pout. But she had been lovely to his eyes all over again, because he had forgotten how she looked, holding a baby in her arms, rocking and singing. Queer how they used to say a mother shouldn't rock a child! Margaret had rocked theirs because she liked to, flouting the books and doctors, and yet the other day from a manuscript that came into his office from some psychologist, he learned that after all it was the right thing to rock little babies and sing to them, to pick them up when they cried. He was glad he had always picked up Mark when he cried, and glad for the nights he had sat with him through thunderstorms until he was a big boy.

The benediction was over and he and Margaret went out of the church, greeting their friends as usual. Fioretta was a Catholic and she took Tom and the children with her to mass, early mass this morning probably, dragging them out of their sleep so that she would have plenty of time in the kitchen to prepare the huge meal that he shrank from even in contemplation. His digestion was healthy but delicate.

The sun was hotter than ever when they came out to the sloping lawn. On the horizon over Chedbury below them evil-looking clouds were looming. There would be a thunderstorm later in the afternoon, and then the night would be cool.

He paused, looking down over the green, and then feeling strangely weary he sat down for a moment on the mass of rock outside the church door. The rock had been the subject of argument and controversy in town meeting more than once. Some of the citizens of Chedbury wanted it dynamited and carried away, but he and others had opposed this stoutly. Gray and lichen covered, the huge mass had been here in the time of Chedbury's first settlers. He preferred it to grass. There was something symbolic about rock in New England. It lent character even to the church.

At the end of the war he had been inspired by an idea. He still felt it was an inspiration. Instead of the pretentious shaft of marble upon the green as a memorial to the twelve Chedbury boys who had been killed in Europe and in Asia, he had suggested a heavy bronze plate sunk into this rock. Chedbury folk had doubted so unconventional an idea, but the minister had pushed it through.

"A wonderful conception," he had declared in town meeting. "There's something eternal about rock."

The grocer had finally cast the deciding vote, won by the fact that a bronze plate cost next to nothing. Edward turned his head to read again the twelve names. John Carosi's son headed the list, "John Brown Carosi, aged nineteen." He remembered Jack as a lively small boy, squeezing his way between the presses to find his father and beg for a nickel.

"Aren't you well?" Margaret asked.

"Quite well," he replied, lying a little. He got up and they walked slowly down the sidewalk that bordered the green, circling it to the white house at the foot.

The sun poured sultry into the yard, but the old trees cast a heavy shade and they walked in silence toward the door. A croquet game was going on in the back yard and they heard the children screaming over the wickets.

"I believe the bees are out," Margaret said.

"They are thought to be fretful when a thunderstorm is coming," he replied.

So heavy was his sense of doom as he mounted the steps slowly that he wondered if he, like old Tom Seaton, was to die by a stroke. The front door was open and the house was strangely quiet. Where was Fioretta and where was Tom?

He stood for a moment looking into the shadows of the wide hall. Then he saw Tom and knew that doom had fallen. Tom stood at the wall telephone, the receiver in his hand, his face white and stiff. He hung the receiver upon the hook, and came toward them slowly.

"That was for you, Ed. A telegram. Brace yourself. It's about Mark."

They stared at him, two aging parents.

"He crashed," Tom said, "coming in from Berlin."

His first feeling, stupid with grief, was one of envy. He wished that he could wail aloud as Fioretta was wailing. She stood in the kitchen door, holding her big white apron to her face, sobbing. It would help him if Margaret could weep aloud. But she, too, could not weep.

She sat down on the carved chest beside the stair. He leaned against the wall. Tom repeated the bare words of official regret, as he could remember them.

"Hank wanted to type it out but there was nobody to send, since it's Sunday. He'll drop it in the mail."

"I'll go around and get it," Edward said quietly. He felt suddenly strong and alert.

"I'll fetch my car," Tom said.

"Let me come," Margaret begged. She turned to Fioretta. "My dear, give the children their dinner. Don't let it be spoiled for them."

"I can't eat a bite," Fioretta sobbed.

But she would eat, he knew. She would eat and cry at the same time. He never wanted to eat again. His stomach felt shriveled and dry. But he held himself straight as usual and Margaret slipped her hand into his elbow while Tom whirled the car out of the garage.

They drove in silence through the humid sunshine toward the small railroad station where Hank Parker, the station master, received telegrams. The station was empty. Hank stood behind the window in his shirt sleeves, his eyes shaded by a piece of green paper held under his cap. He looked at them sorrowfully from behind the thin iron bars.

"I'd ha' given a million not to have got this," he said simply. He pushed the yellow slip of paper between the bars and Edward took it. He held it for Margaret to read with him and Tom waited, his face red and grave.

There was nothing told in the bare words except the monstrous fact. How it had come about he must wait to know. Mark, who had never had an accident, his genius son, was dead. He had an unutterable longing to get home, into his own house.

"Thank you, Hank," he managed to say. "We'll have to learn how to get along somehow, now."

"Folks have had to," Hank said. He scratched his ear with his pencil.

"Yes," Margaret said. "Plenty of folk have had to."

"Let's go home," Edward muttered.

"Please, Tom," Margaret said.

They climbed into the car again and Tom took them to their own gate. "I wish to God there was something I could do," he urged.

"There's nothing, of course," Edward said.

"You might tell a few people," Margaret said. "You'll know the right ones. Ask them not to call us up for a bit."

"I will," he promised.

They watched him drive away and then they walked wearily along the brick path between the two rows of flaming scarlet tulips. They mounted the steps and opened the door and shut it again. The house was empty. Even the servants were gone on a Sunday afternoon. He had never imagined such terrifying stillness. He turned to Margaret and caught her in his arms and together they began to weep.

It was Lewis Harrow, strangely, who gave him his first comfort. The amazing ineptitude of people who sought to assuage his sorrow made him ashamed for their sakes and he found himself coming to their aid with his utmost efforts. "Yes," he said, "I know—God's will is inscrutable. . . . Yes, it is good that we have our other children—and of course our grandchildren.

. . . Of course," he agreed, "life is difficult today for the young. Perhaps Mark is spared a great deal."

He allowed Joseph Barclay to pray with him, first alone and then with Margaret. Margaret bowed her head, her face white and still, her hands clasped on her knees.

She had the wisdom not to try to comfort him, and he did not try to comfort her. For them there was no comfort—not yet. Together they reached the ultimate in pain, and dimly he began to perceive that of all the divisions among people, the deepest and the most universal is that abyss which lies between those who have suffered the ultimate in pain and those who have not. Those who had suffered spoke few words, but the clasp of their hands upon his was strong and warm.

He held his daughter Mary in his arms and let her sob, knowing that she, too, understood nothing yet of sorrow. "Don't cry, my dear," he said almost pleasantly. "You have a responsibility toward life, you know. You mustn't forget that."

The hardest comfort of all was from those who tried to find meaning in Mark's death. He loved Joseph Barclay because he was not one of these. When he prayed, the minister had said, "I could tell you this is God's will but I don't believe it is. I could point out to you that Mark died while he was taking food to those who had been his enemies, but we know they weren't his enemies and never had been, his or ours. He was taking food to the Germans so that they wouldn't turn Communist. Maybe that will prove worth dying for, but I can't promise you that it will."

"Joe, you are a man of God, and now I know it," Edward had replied.

It was Harrow who came flying back across the Atlantic bringing comfort. Upon receiving Mary's cable he had flown straight to Germany, slashing his way through red tape, more arrogant than any officer, inquiring of them all if they knew who he was.

"By God, I'm the most famous writer in the United States," he shouted, furrowing his thick black brows. "What I can write about you and where I can publish it would surprise you!" By such totalitarian methods he had forced his way to the scene of Mark's death.

Once home again, he rushed from the landing field to Chedbury and went straight to the house, where he found Edward and Margaret walking in the garden after the food they had tried to eat at midday.

"I've come as soon as I could," he announced. "I knew you'd want to know exactly what happened. I went to find out and I think I got it all."

"Come inside, Lew," Edward said.

"Dear Lewis," Margaret said and took his hand. "How did you know what we wanted?"

"My damned intuition, I suppose," he retorted. They were in the empty living room. Margaret had made it as pretty as usual with her flowers. Baynes and Sandra had come, of course, and most of Chedbury had streamed quietly through the door. That was over now. Edward had not allowed even Tommy and Sandy to stay. He wanted to be alone with Margaret. They were face to face with the days, one after another.

Harrow sat down. He flung off his topcoat as though it stifled him. The weather had turned cool again, after the frightful thunderstorm on the Sunday they had first heard Mark was dead.

Harrow leaned forward, his big ugly mouth working, his dark hair straight on his forehead.

"I wish to God I could tell you something wonderful," he said. "I wish Mark had died saving somebody or something. But there isn't anything wonderful. He was simply part of the machine. The planes leave every few minutes from the American zone and fly over the border into the Russian zone. It's not easy because of the hours and the Russians' potshots, and sometimes the weather. It's round-the-clock stuff. The planes keep in line— every few minutes. If they can't land at the receiving end for some reason or other they just fly back to where they started from and get in line again and start over. That's what Mark did. Something must have been wrong with his plane and he didn't dare to land and so he just went back to the starting place and tried to come down there. A ground man said he saw one of the wheels roll away, and then Mark crashed nose down into the earth and his plane began to burn."

"Was—his body—destroyed?" He put the question which he saw in Margaret's eyes.

"No—injured, of course. But it's in a coffin. I arranged for that. It'll be over—in due course. You know 'in due course'? Hah!" Lewis snorted and looked away out of the window. He said roughly, "If you have the sense I hope you have, you won't open the coffin. Just have a nice funeral."

He sighed enormously and got to his feet. "I wish I knew how to say things to you, but I don't. There's no sense to anything, I guess."

He lumbered toward the door and Margaret stopped him.

"Lew, my dear."

He turned.

Her face, wet with tears, was shining and tender. "Has Mary told you?"

"Told me what?" he demanded. "I only had the cable about Mark. I've been rushing around too much for letters."

"Then let me tell you," Margaret said. "Mary won't mind—for my comfort. She's going to have a baby. Lew, you're going to have another little child."

He stared at her for a moment and then rushed to her and fell upon his knees before her. "I worship you," he muttered. "Ed, I worship this wife of yours!"

"So do I," Edward said. "So do I."

They sat quietly looking at each other when he had gone. They smiled at each other. Once or twice he thought he might try to put into words how for him their love had passed now into something transcendental, something crystal and clear, like light enfolding them both. Life they knew and now death they knew, and nothing could separate them, not time and not eternity.

He felt unutterably weary, yet not spent. Looking into her face, he understood that she, too, felt as he did. They needed something to renew their bodies, that the spirit which dwelled in them both might live.

"Shall I fetch a little of Fioretta's wine?" he asked.

Fioretta, longing to be of use to them, had sent a jug of her homemade wine.

"That would be nice," Margaret said. She leaned back in her chair and folded her hands on her knees. He went to her and knelt before her and kissed her hands. She leaned forward and took his head between her palms and kissed his forehead and then his lips.

"Dear love," she said, "bring a little bread with the wine."

He went away to bring that for which she had asked. He poured the wine into an old amber glass pitcher that had once been his mother's. She had poured milk from it when he was a boy. Now he filled it with the wine. He took a loaf from the breadbox of yellow painted tin and broke it upon a silver tray and putting two wine glasses too on the tray, he carried everything back to the living room. There he poured the wine and gave it to her, and he poured his own and he passed her the bread and they ate and drank.

When they had finished, Margaret took the cups and set them on the tray.

"Now that we know everything," she said, "now that we know there is no use in trying to understand, shall we go out into the garden, Ned?"

"Yes, let us go," he said. "It looks as though the sunset would be splendid."